CAT PORTER

Wildflower Ink, LLC

Visit my website at www.catporter.eu

Cover Designer
Najla Qamber, Najla Qamber Designs
www.najlaqamberdesigns.com

Cover Models
Travis Cadeau
Memphis Cadeau

Photographer
Mark Wong Photography

Editor
Jennifer Roberts-Hall

Content Editor
Christina Trevaskis
www.bookmatchmaker.com

Formatting & Interior Design
Nada Qamber, Najla Qamber Designs
www.najlaqamberdesigns.com

"Lenore's Lace" logo by Lori Jackson Design
www.lorijacksondesign.com

Proofreading
Penelope Croci

ISBN-13: 978-0-9903085-6-0

for Kandace

Because you happened to ask me about Finger at the very same time that I was becoming madly obsessed with him. He'd intrigued you from the beginning, just as he had me. At the time I was writing another book and had just realized I needed to break it into two, yet on top of all that madness, I couldn't stop thinking about Finger. I contacted you to vent, and you were the first person to whom I confessed my Finger obsession and how I wanted to write his story.
And even though you were in the middle of a meeting at work, you texted me back, saying—
"Gimme Finger"
It made me laugh, it made me cry. And it was exactly what I needed.
And because in this little life of mine,
believers and readers and book sisters and friends and good, strong women with huge hearts like you
are everything.

GUIDE

Author's note: the players on this landscape are numerous, therefore names and organizations are outlined here for the reader

MOTORCYCLE CLUBS
The Flames of Hell - Fuse, Finger, Reich, Kerry, Chaz, Cooper, Siggy, Gyp, Kwik, Drac, Slade, Lenox, Led, Catch, Den, Split, Priest, Deanna, Krystal
The Smoking Guns - Med, Motormouth, Scrib, Dog
The One-Eyed Jacks - Jump, Dig, Boner, Butler, Lock, Judge, Kicker, Alicia, Mary Lynn, Dee, Grace, Jill, Nina
The Broken Blades - Zed, Notch, Pick
The Demon Seeds - Jimmy, Vig

ORGANIZED CRIME SYNDICATES
Guardino - Turo DeMarco
Tantucci
The Calderas Group - Alejandro Calderón

PROLOGUE

I WAS BORN, BUT NOT RAISED.

I erupted.

I am the weed that grew in the distance fed by rainwater whenever the skies deigned to yield it, sharpened by brisk winds, hardened and spiked by icy cold. Hued by occasional kindnesses, the heat of the sun's glare.

No, I was forged the day I met Serena. A blade sharpened, a gun barrel loaded, a fuse lit.

My track was laid over her rocky earth, and it only made my soul darker, my heart denser, my blood fiercer, my purpose raw.

With her I was everything I'd never known before. Not helpless, not exposed. Not powerless.

And even through all these years without her and all that I've achieved in the world, I've been nothing but an open hand grenade, idling, ready to detonate.

Now, having broken into her house, standing here in her bedroom, selfishly stealing the air she breathes as she sleeps, that idling is over.

Her sleep is fitful. She murmurs words, she scowls and twists the sheets in a fist the same way I do.

I still have the dreams, too, baby.

"Touch me. I need you to—" I'd once pleaded with her in the dark.

In my dreams I plead and I wait for that touch to come, like it once had. But it never does. I strain against the iron, but she's not there. I'm alone. That dream used to come more frequently, regular-

1

ly. Each nightmare was a visitation reinforcing my passion for her, my passion to love her, to hate her. Each morning, my resolve would be screwed on tight once more, an unyielding cap on an ancient bottle.

This morning, before the dawn had even broken on this brand new day, that resolve was stronger than ever, but my purpose has changed.

I want her back.

I hope she dreams of me. I hope her dreams are as tangled and snarled as mine. The cut of the blade, the sting of her mouth remain fresh. They've inspired me, demented me.

All the jagged pieces of our hearts, be they sharp, be they blunt, red or black or gray, are indiscernible now. Me and her, we're in pieces, shards, but we aren't broken. She had given up, let go, and so had I. But standing here, inches away from her, I know deep, deep inside I hadn't, not ever.

Not essentially.

I run a thumb over her full, soft lips, and they part under my touch. A slight intake of breath passes between them, warming my skin. Beautiful lips that were once mine. Lips that once shared words and thoughts and hopes with me, the good kind. Lips that shared fears and horrors. Lips that offered a violent heaven.

I want to take those lips now, possess them, but I stop myself. I need her to give them to me willingly.

And she will.

My finger grazes the tip of her nose. Her eyes dance under her lids, blinking open.

Blue green glory.

My heart settles in my chest and kicks to life all at once, and I know nothing has changed.

Soul dark,

Heart dense,

Blood fierce,

Purpose raw.

I'm a quiet man, observant, introverted, not given to dramatic declarations. But here I stand, feeling that agony, that swell of emotion that only she invokes in me, all of it wiping away the ugly I've been clinging to all this time; the remote wilderness where I dwell.

Those eyes hang on mine, and I see her reflection in all the shards of me. She is at the crux. She is the flame. My fever, my fury.

Let it roar.

1

25 YEARS AGO

KID

"Should we keep him or kill him?"

Someone kicked my calves, shoved at my back, and I sprawled on the cold floor. The hood was torn off my head, and I blinked in the bright light. A tall heavy set man stood before me, bulky tattooed arms crossed over his chest. Med, the famed President of the Kansas Smoking Guns, a man I'd heard about almost all my life.

The devil himself.

In the flesh.

"You know where you are?" his deep voice practically growled.

I shook my head, unsure of how to answer. The truth often got me in trouble in the past. Why should now be any different?

Med only sneered, or maybe that was just his way of smiling like Jack Nicholson's Joker. "What do they call you?"

I pushed up on my arms, but my limbs were still numb from being held down in the van on the endless ride here. "I'm-I'm Kid."

Laughter fizzed around me like a can of shaken beer going off. "Aww, ain't that cute?" a voice behind me said.

"Prospect, eh?" Med asked, his eyes wandering over my cut.

"Yeah."

"Perfect." That Joker grin deepened, and the blood backed up in my veins.

"They probably won't give too much of a shit about you." He raised his chin at someone to my side and my cut was ripped off me. "More fun for us."

"Hey!" I choked out.

4

They kicked me and ripped off my boots, socks, jeans. I was naked. Thick metal cuffs were attached to my wrists, my ankles, my neck and linked to heavy chains. My head swam, a cold sweat tracked over my skin, my heart plodded through mud.

"You know why we took you?" Med asked.

"'Cause it's the kinda shit you do?" A slap cracked across my face. A silvery haze shadowed my vision.

"It's because the Flames of Hell think they can do whatever the fuck they want. Time to show your club how pissed off I am at catching them on my territory doing what I'd warned them not to ever do."

My stomach dropped. Reich, our VP, had found a dealer in southern Kansas who used to be supplied by the Smoking Guns, but the Guns had recently iced him, not paying him what he felt they owed. Reich had stepped in and provided Flames of Hell made-product to find new buyers, new addicts along that guy's route, a route we'd never had access to before. Money was money, and we wanted more of it, just like everybody else.

My dad, a club old-timer and former officer, had told him it was a bad idea. For decades now, our club constantly fought with the Guns over territory, over trade routes, over women, over you name it. All I heard growing up was *this shit's gotta stop already!* but it never did. It had become part of our day to day, part of our fun. I didn't think either club knew how not to shit on the other.

In front of everybody, my dad had told Reich his plan was fucking stupid and careless as all hell. Reich's response? He chose me to make the delivery with another club member, and it got approved real quick.

I'd gotten the surprise of my life when I opened the door to the dealer's house and saw him hanging from a hook in his ceiling. Me and Siggy ran straight out, got shot at, chased into the woods. Siggy got shot in the face as he climbed a tree. They'd pinned me down at gunpoint and dragged me here to their clubhouse. I was alive, but not so fucking lucky.

My pulse pounded in my ears, my heart muscle vaulting over never-ending hurdles in my chest.

Med made a hand gesture in the air, and kicks and punches rained down on me. I collapsed and went sailing up in someone's tight hold. Blows and bashes cracked and smashed over my body, pain exploding through me. My head swung to the side, and I gasped for air, choking on my own saliva and blood.

His pinned eyes on me, Med admired my bloodied pulp. "Ah, welcome to the Smoking Guns, Kid."

They let go, and I crumpled to the floor. Chained to hooks in a concrete post in the middle of a big room, I strained to keep my sore eyes open as they partied and argued around me. Men and women stared at me, laughing, talking, and I stared back. I was the new attraction at the zoo. The freak at the circus, their chained cyclops shuddering in a mangled heap, settling in a pool of his own piss, sweat, and blood.

I pressed back against the post, keeping still. I knew how to do that pretty good. All my life I'd been somebody's afterthought, a gray part of the landscape, but that had just changed.

Now I was front and center.

I gotta keep it together. Keep it together.

Would they kill me? Ask for some kind of ransom? I was sure my dad and my club were working to bust me out. Working on some sort of plan, working hard. They had to be.

One figure, a slight one, stood motionless just beyond the men. A girl. Long bright red hair, and her eyes...the most mesmerizing eyes I'd ever seen. An odd combination of blue and green, like pictures of the Caribbean Sea that I'd seen in magazines. Was it 'cause her eyes were so big? I held her serious gaze, and she didn't look away. Her expression was somber, not teasing, not mocking. I wasn't entertaining her. My vision was still fuzzy, and I blinked, but she was gone. She was probably a mirage. A mirage of hope and empathy in this crazy Roman fucking orgy in the middle of Buttfuck, Kansas.

I counted the lines in the cracked flooring, but I got lost. They were only quivering scratches, and I couldn't keep track of them. My joints ached, my bare body cold against the hard floor. I lay in a ball on that floor through hours and hours and hours. Got kicked, got spit on. Finally, they brought me to a prison cell where I got some sleep. The next night they brought me back out to the main room and chained me back to that post again.

"Hey, Kid! Guess what?" shouted somebody. "It's been two days, and your club's playing hard ball. Told ya they wouldn't care so much about some prospect of theirs."

Laughs and whoops filled the room, pounding into my aching skull. A kick jabbed me in the leg. My tired eyes lifted.

Med stared down at me. "You're Fuse's son, huh? Ain't that something. Known him a long time. Well, the bad news is, your daddy's dead, and they're too busy with his funeral to deal with your ass. How 'bout that, huh?"

Dad dead? No, no, it can't be. We'd just started to really hang out. I was a prospect now...not now...not...

Sour bile jerked up my insides and shot up my throat. I retched all over myself. Whatever was left of myself. The music roared again, and I shut my eyes, my body curling into a ball.

My hair got pushed over my arm, away from my face, and I flinched at the contact. A cool towel swept over my skin, scouring my flesh like sandpaper. Those blue green eyes were over me.

"Just cleaning you up," she said.

I stared at her. Who was she? Why was she bothering? Maybe she'd pull a blade and play with me too. My aching muscles stayed tense as her towel, a thick faded red, stroked over me carefully.

"Why?" I asked. "They're just gonna do it again."

Her gaze met mine, and in it I saw a flicker of something, not cold or hard, like indifference or duty, but a split second of warmth that raced over my flesh like the sure strokes of her towel.

"I know," she said quietly. "They will." That deep voice was frank, resigned, and I leaned in closer to hear more of it. She dipped the towel in a small bowl of water and soap.

"Did they kill him?" my voice croaked. "My dad? Do you know?"

"No, they didn't kill him. He was at your club, had a heart attack."

A heart attack. He'd had a heart attack once before when he'd been in jail years ago. A heart attack induced by something else Reich had done. Now Dad was gone, and I wouldn't see him again.

Wouldn't ride with him again. He wouldn't be there when I got patched in.

If I patched in.

If I ever made it out of here alive.

The girl wiped at my leg and down the other. Her attention was some sort of seduction. She was just prepping me for more torture, wasn't she?

"Get the fuck off me," I said through gritted teeth.

She stopped and sat back on her heels, her lips pressed together. She took her towel and bowl and slid back into the crowd. I choked down the tears, the ache. I was nothing but pain.

Nothing but alone.

2

RENA

ONE BLOODIED EYE HUNG ON me.

The white was washed with red, but at the center was the most startling eye I'd ever seen, and certainly the most alive. That molten iron eye held my gaze, gleaming, defying, and I was rooted to the cement floor by its brawn.

In the two days since he'd been here, the prisoner had shut down. He'd been brought to this dark basement cell after the first night, and he'd barely spoken since, except just now to tell Motormouth to go fuck himself. He'd tried strangling Motor with his chains, but he was weak and Motor got him down and punched him out, then he'd shortened the chains. I'd heard the yelling from the top of the stairs, and I'd come running.

"You're gonna feel everything we dish out from here on in." Motormouth's sneering voice made me clench my jaw. "Med wants you wide awake, feeling like misery and wishing for death. You got that?" Motormouth's steel-toed boot kicked at his ribs, and Kid's body shoved over on the floor closer to my feet, his other eye swollen and ugly. Sealed shut.

"Fuck you!" the prisoner spit out along with blood and goop.

Motormouth's hands gripped his neck, throttling him, and the prisoner's legs thrashed, his heels digging into the cement. Wheezing, choking filled the dank space, the clang and ringing of metal chains straining, dragging. I swallowed hard, but I couldn't look away. I wasn't allowed to look away, so I watched everything. It wasn't new, but seeing a man fight for another breath was always inspiring.

9

That was me, fighting for my next breath.

Motormouth released him. "You don't mouth off like that again, you got that, you little shit? See, your fucking club ain't coming' to get you. They're playing us and playing you, prospect." He smacked Kid on the face.

The prisoner gulped for air, his arms wrenching against the chains, then finally dropping. Not giving up or giving in, just taking a much needed break. That one bloodied eye blinked, his head lolling on the cement floor. He didn't moan or beg. He only turned away, his chest heaving for air, the skin of his throat banded with red.

"Damn, it stinks in here. Hose him down." Motormouth belched. "I need a drink." Footsteps. The door slammed closed, shutting out the sounds of carousing, celebrating, madness.

"Motor!" *Shit.* I was locked in here now.

I moved toward the small sphere of dim light over the prisoner. His head turned to me, and the eye only blinked. The jaw remained tightly held, screwed in place by mistrust, by anger, defensiveness. Or that last struggle to fight for his life no matter what I did or said. I couldn't let go of his ferocious gaze. I didn't want to.

Some would have already given up by now. He'd been here in a cell two days already, and his expression had yet to change. He still hadn't opened his mouth to curse me or call me some variation of cunt or whore or bitch like I'd expected. Despite his chains, he hadn't tried to lunge at me or kick me. No, he was motionless, watching me like a snake waiting for the right moment to launch, fangs bared to do their worst. They hadn't yanked too many of his teeth yet. Two only, in the back, but there would probably be more taken out tomorrow.

Still, no reply.

I opened the old yellow hose and the water spurted out, splattering on the spotted cement. "Drink. Come on, drink."

He didn't move.

"Get all that blood and gunk off your face and hands too."

He still didn't move. Only the eye watched me.

"Come on. I won't mess with you."

A large shaky hand reached out toward the thick spray of water, his lips parted just a fraction. He glanced at me with that eye and cupped his hands, rinsing his face. The red water swirled and gurgled around the drain.

I held the hose steady as his mouth opened, and he drank and drank and drank watching me. My face heated under his unrelenting hard gaze. I shut off the water. "You need to pee? Now's the time."

He pushed his naked body up on the cement with his bruised and swollen hands. His dick stirred, and he peed in the direction of the puddle heading for the drain. That defined, sharp jaw finally slackened, his long hair falling over his face.

I hosed down the last of his piss as he sank back onto the floor, his dick dropping over his thigh. His dark hair splayed out behind him. His legs wide open.

I gathered the hose and arranged it in a tight circle, setting it back in its corner and went to him. "They'll be back soon to fuck with you again," I said, my voice low. "There's no more food for you. Only that one piece of Wonder Bread you get every morning. So you better eat it the next time." A shiver crawled over my skin. "I know what that's like."

His eye narrowed at me. Why should he believe anything I said? But I wanted him to, I did. He couldn't be much older than me, but he'd aged overnight, ever since they told him his dad had died. He'd stayed still, quiet. Like I had those first weeks.

A lit bulb from the hallway shot a dim glow through the tiny window in the steel door. I took in his strong features. Muscular and lean, he had thinned out since they'd first brought him here. No, he wasn't the gnarled and beefy type of biker with an attitude that I knew so well. A hard cut to his jaw, a slight indention in his chin, visible cheekbones, and the hollows beneath. His full long lips had a sensual curve to them. He was handsome.

He didn't seem to be the loud, arrogant asshole type, although, hell, I didn't know him, did I? Making assumptions about men was a mistake. I never looked twice at any man, or I'd be in big trouble. Anyhow, that spring of desire had dried up inside, sparks of attraction no longer existed for me. I had shut it down because it only had gotten me into trouble. A magic potion releasing a thick sweet haze that would unfurl around me, blinding me, leading me into a maze of wrong turns and dead ends. And once, a cliff. No, acting on desire only led to being at the mercy of others.

Like me, Kid was just a grunt who did what he was told. He too had been in the wrong place at the wrong time. Something about him had made me stop and notice him from the very beginning. I recognized it. It mirrored how I felt on the inside. A quiet sort of defiance. Contempt with a spine of sorrow. That recognition had rooted me to the spot that first night after they'd chained him to the post. Only an eye glared at me, muscles straining.

Yes, I see you.

Vulnerability, that was it.

I had forgotten that feeling; it had hardened inside me like melted chocolate over cold marble.

I sat down on the floor next to him and that one eye stayed on me, waiting, wondering. My fingers roamed over his hair and face, and he let out a noise. Was it relief or annoyance?

I offered him a small smile. "You okay?" It was a totally stupid question, but I wanted to know.

His tongue lazily licked at his dried and bloodied swollen lower lip. His lips moved once more, but still, no words came out.

"Are y—"

"Who are you?" his voice creaked.

"Just a girl."

"Yeah right. You doing a number on me, being nice?"

"Being nice is no longer a good thing, huh?"

"I don't think so," he breathed, his tone haunted, his eye widening. "I don't know anymore."

My stomach dropped. I didn't know either.

"Why are you here?" he asked.

"I live here."

"Oh yeah?"

"Yeah." I tucked my legs underneath me, my sweaty palms pressing into my thighs.

The quiet and the darkness of the cell crept over me like a thick dirty blanket, and I didn't like it, but I had to wait for them to unlock the door for me. Although, knowing Motormouth, who was pretty drunk and high, he was probably busy with his girlfriend. Who could blame him? I was forgotten about, for the time being at least. There would be hell to pay later, that was for sure.

"What's wrong?" came his voice.

"Nothing."

"You're nervous."

"Do you have bat radar?" I snapped.

"What's wrong?"

My pulse dragged. "I don't like the dark much."

"You must be kidding."

"No, I'm not kidding."

"There a reason?"

"I used to get locked in a closet."

"When you were a kid?"

"No. Here."

"Oh."

"You ever been locked in a closet before?" I asked.

"No, but I've been locked in my own room."

"By your parents?"

"Didn't really have parents."

"What do you mean 'didn't really'?"

"My mom was never around much. I don't think I'd even recognize her anymore if I saw her again. My dad took me with him to his club and stashed me there."

"Stashed you?"

"Yeah. He had his own family. I stayed at the MC clubhouse, grew up there. You grow up here?"

"No, no, no. With my grandmother. She looked out for me while my mom worked. My dad joined the Marines and didn't come back."

"Sorry."

"No, I mean he came back alive, but not to us. He found himself a new family he liked better."

He let out a grunt. "Yeah, gotcha."

Silence. The chains scraped the floor.

13

"See that?"

My back stiffened. "What? A rat?"

"No. You weren't so nervous once you got to talking."

I settled back on my legs and let out a tiny breath, wiping my damp hair back from my face. "I guess."

"How'd you get here from Grandmaland?"

"I went to a club party one night. I was dating this guy, Jimmy, who wanted to prospect for the Demon Seeds."

"The Seeds in Montana?"

"Yep, I'm from Montana. There was a party at their clubhouse, and I went with him."

"Shouldn't have gone."

I snorted. "I didn't know that then. Neither did he. Jimmy thought I was the bomb. He thought bringing me on his arm would score him some points with his brothers-to-be."

Kid didn't say anything. He just stared at me, his eyes hard. He knew what was coming.

"I got noticed by a member of a visiting club. I didn't know who he was. He'd covered up his colors, his patch. I was having a good ol' time, laughing, talking. He kept getting me drinks and flirting with me. I got up to find Jimmy, to leave. I thanked him for the drinks and everything, and suddenly he got all serious. People were looking at me funny. He grabbed my arm and said, 'This is how it's gonna go down, baby.'"

I hadn't thought about these details, the details that got me here, in a long time. I'd quit stretching and snapping them like rubber bands in my brain after the second month. Now, an odd relief washed through me as I released the words and Kid listened.

"I tried to explain that I was with another man from the Demon Seeds. All he said was 'You come willingly or little Jimmy gets a beat down.'"

"He'd targeted you, huh?"

"Yeah."

"And good ol' Jimmy?"

"Jimmy said nothing. Did nothing. Only slunk into the crowd. I'll never forget that look on his face. A mix of fear and powerlessness. Giving in."

My shoulders bunched together. Jimmy had slunk into the crowd that night the same way my dad had slunk away and never returned. The same way my mom would slink out the door every afternoon after sleeping all day, preferring to be at the bar she owned than at home in the grind of real life. Maybe that's why it hadn't shocked me that much when Jimmy had left me in the frying pan. I'd been upset, but not so surprised.

"Fuck," said Kid.

"Even though Jimmy and I both gave in, he got beat down by the other club anyway. They made me watch while I got groped, then we took off. We did a lot of traveling those first few months. I'd either be locked up in a motel room or locked in a closet, always being told it was to protect me from the other men."

"Probably true, but...shit."

"We finally settled here. He kept me like his doll, I guess is the best way to describe it. He'd show me off. Do me the way he wanted whenever he wanted. Once, a couple of his pals thought I was the club toy and tried to play with me. One got his eye gouged out for touching me."

"Ouch."

I let out a dry laugh. "Yeah, I got to watch that too."

"He gets off on it, huh?"

I wiped my hands up and down my legs. "Hmm."

"Sorry."

"Thanks."

"What the hell for?" he asked.

I shrugged, my skin tightening. Was it stupid to want things from him? Things like understanding, compassion. Kindness. I thought I'd shut that off, dammit. If I exposed myself in the tiniest degree, let anything through the cracks, I was fucking doomed in here. I had trained myself to cut that off. Now what was I doing? Suddenly, I couldn't stop talking.

I licked my lips, biting down on the edges. "Thanks for getting me, I mean."

He propped his head up on his hand. "You stay cool to survive, don't you?"

"Yeah. I felt I'd have better luck getting free one day if I stuck it out with him than if I got tangled up with some other asshole. So I got to know his buttons, his habits. He hates the word no, so I avoid it. He wants dedication, enthusiasm. I do my best to provide it. For now at least."

"I do a lot of that myself. Doing what I'm told."

"I don't like it much."

"Me neither," he said on a sigh.

"You're a prospect, right? Doing what you're told is what it's all about."

"Hey, I've been around this shit almost all my life. My dad was a member, and so was his dad. My grandad was an original founding member of the Flames of Hell, in fact." He was proud, but his voice seemed distant, far off.

"Wow. Do they know that?" I gestured toward the cell door. "They must. Shit, they scored big with you."

"Yeah. Real big." His tone was flat, ironic even.

Our eyes held each other's in the dim streak of light. We held on, all right. There was nothing else in this room, in this world right now. Nothing but me and him.

"I hope you make it out of here alive," I said.

"You do?" He wasn't convinced.

"Yeah, I do."

"Hope you make it out, too. If that's what you want."

"That's what I want."

"Yeah? How bad?"

"Real bad," I whispered roughly.

His leg pressed against me. "You feeling better now, about being in here in the dark?"

I took in a tight breath. "A little."

"I'm edgy. What the fuck did they shoot me up with? I can't relax. I can't—"

"One of their special brews." My hand touched the hard, smooth planes of his chest, and we both sucked in air at the contact.

A ripple of tension spread through my insides as I stroked his

pecs. Back and forth. Down his middle, his abs shuddering under my fingertips, his body flinching slightly and easing. My heart
picked up speed, thudding in my chest, as my hand slid over his
thigh and around his length. His breath caught, his eyes gleamed at
me. His long fingers clamped around my wrist, a noise escaping the
back of his throat.

Or was it from me?

"Let me give you something." I stroked over his cock, and his
hips jerked. "Relax. I don't have any weapons on me. I'm not going
to cut your dick off or anything."

His brows jammed up his forehead.

"Check for yourself." I presented myself as close as possible for
his inspection. My pulse pounded as his hand shuffled over my
chest, quickly around each breast, my middle, around my waist, the
small of my back, in and around my boots.

"Okay? It's just me." I stroked him again. He stiffened in my
hand, and my insides tightened. For the first time in a long time I
wanted to touch someone else. For the first time in a long time, I
really liked it—the feel of his skin, his muscles tensing, his uneven
breaths.

That eye pierced mine. "Why are you here?" his voice was husky,
scratched, damaged from Motormouth's assault.

"I'm not supposed to be here."

His grip on my wrist tightened. He didn't like my answer. I
only kept stroking. He still didn't let go of my wrist. My eyes held
his fierce one as I stroked harder, firmer, faster. His jaw loosened,
his breathing grew loud and choppy, his hips flexed a few degrees,
rocking toward my hand.

The drawn face of the young warrior became softer. Pleading and
full of need. A need that was savage and deep. My insides pulled and
twined as his grip tightened around my wrist. He held me against
his cock, his face drawn tight.

I knew about that kind of need.

I leaned down closer to him, and his face tilted up toward mine.
He didn't want to lose contact either. He wanted more. Was this crazy, searching for pleasure in hell? All I knew was I felt compelled to

offer him something, some measure of comfort. Just for a moment.

And I wanted some myself.

A groan escaped those bloodied lips, and his one good eye winced shut, his head knocking back. He hadn't groaned or grunted or cried out very much at all as he'd endured the beatings, the slaps, the punches, the slashes the past two days. But here he was, crying out and moaning for me, coming in my hand. There was something thrilling about it, exciting.

Our secret in the dark.

He cried out softly. My heart lurched.

"That's it, yeah," slipped from my mouth, my pulse racing at the throb of him in my hand, the swarming sounds of his pleasure in the throes of all that pain still clutching his body. I swept back his long hair from his sweaty forehead.

What the hell are you doing?

His head stirred under the contact, and he moaned a little louder. My heart lurched under its bolts as he came in my hand, his cock pulsing, cum spurting, his head thrown back. I gently stroked his spent cock, and his tense features finally softened. Those lips wobbled. He wanted to speak, to say something, but words didn't come out.

I released him, and his breathing deepened. I leaned over the puddle of water next to us and swirled my hand in it, rinsing off his spunk.

"Sleep now." I took in a deep breath and ran a hand lightly across his forehead, down the sides of his face, his shoulder. The inside of his arm where his skin was smooth and hairless. Down and up again. His skin cooled under my fingertips, and that eyelid drifted shut and didn't open again.

"You have to go?" he asked, his voice suddenly small, that vulnerability coloring it like a wash of indigo blue over a canvas. Moody, soft, eerie.

"No. I'm stuck here 'til they come get me. They forgot about me."

"Huh. I get forgotten about a lot too," he said. "Lie down next to me."

I laid down next to Kid and curled my body against his. He

smelled of perspiration and blood, and I inhaled it in, focusing on that, the warmth of his skin and the movement of his chest beside me as he breathed in sleep. Yes, he was lost in sleep. I wanted to be too. Badly.

I closed my eyes, my lips brushing his flesh.

At least, this time, I wasn't alone in the dark.

3
KID

THERE WAS ONLY THAT ONE slice of motherfucking Wonder Bread every morning, or at least I assumed it was morning, but I couldn't be sure, here in this dark cell in the bowels of their fort of a clubhouse. My cell.

The first day I spit it out.

The second day I didn't even open my mouth.

The third day I ate it, and I got a reward for my good behavior. I got her mouth on me.

"What are you doing—fuck!"

No. Stop. I'm not giving in to you. You are the fucking devil.

But I didn't want her to stop. I looked forward to her visits. Her voice was slightly deep, and every time she spoke, each word out of her mouth went straight to my dick, making my blood jump in my veins. A turn on and a relief, plain and simple. My flesh began to feel her touch before she even came close. And she came close. I'd eat the bread, and then I'd get her mouth.

I ate the bread the next day and the next.

And the next and the next.

And the next.

All I knew now was the touch of her lips. Their width, their soft thickness, the excruciating pressure they exerted. Her mouth took me all the way in, and I bumped her fucking throat. I wanted as much as I could get. My chained hands tightened into fists as her mouth fucked me, her fingertips digging into my hips, keeping me steady. I had no control over my weakened body any longer. All I knew, all I wanted, was her mouth. I craved that mouth, those sensations only it could give me.

This is what nirvana must feel like. Yeah, this is it.

That bliss was all there was. It was blinding, detonating through me, filling the room.

I barely had the energy to respond to the sliced white bread let alone the peanuts she'd snuck me a couple of times and pushed past my lips and made me chew. But respond I did to that mouth. That mouth owned my body, that tongue offered precious moments of salvation. I was dirty, I smelled foul. But the mouth didn't care. The mouth provided and gave, gave, gave, and did it so fucking good.

I came, I soared.

Thank you, mouth.

Mouth swallowed my cum, and I was clean. For this one, one moment I was clean, unsoiled, free.

Her hands released me.

No more touch, no more strands of her long hair brushing the skin of my legs, no more hot humid breaths steaming over my skin. Just my naked body, alone, twisting on the damp concrete, chained to the floor, wanting more. So much fucking more.

And only from her.

"Let me...let me..."

She leaned over me. "What? What'd you say?"

"Let me suck on you. Let me touch you, something. Come on. Sit on me, something..."

"No."

My legs kicked out, searching for her in the dark. "Let me make you come."

"Why? Why would you want to—"

"I want to. I want to feel you so damn bad. I won't hurt you. Sit on my hand at least." No answer. "Hey, are you there?"

"I'm here. How do I know you won't hurt me?" she asked, that voice was now hushed.

Hurt you? You're my fucking goddess.

"I'd never hurt you. I want you on me. I want to get you off. I want to taste you. I have to. Fuck my face. Do it."

They had shot me up with something the first day, a small dose

21

to keep me swiveling. The high was really just a haze of confusion to keep me compliant.

The aftereffects, though, were intense.

They wanted me wide awake and feeling every inch of misery, and I was. My skin was needling, I was edgy, impatient, hungry for a sensory overload of any fucking kind and pissed as hell that I wasn't getting it. My stomach and head reeled with starvation. Peanuts in her pockets and once, a small cereal bar that was more like cemented sawdust were rare treats. There was no real food for me, but there was this, there was her.

"I want you on me, dammit," I shot back.

I was rabid, foaming at the mouth. A suck and fuck vessel. I could smell her arousal, taste her salty wetness on my tongue already. I knew in the back of my mind, in the tiny rational section that was still functioning, that this was all a game that they had set up, but I didn't give a shit. Every cell in my being craved that one thing. Craved her.

Any way I could get her.

"I should trust you?" she asked.

"Yes."

"But there's no such thing as trust. You still haven't learned that?" Her voice teased but there was an edge of grim soberness to it that I recognized.

"I know."

She slumped down next to me, her eyes tense. She was uncomfortable, unnerved. She took in a deep breath of air like she had to bolster herself. "They forgot about me again."

"Good. You're stuck with me," I pleaded for my life.

No answer, only her heavy breathing, her feet shuffling.

My scalp prickled. "Where are you? What's wrong?"

"I'm getting dizzy. I don't feel too good."

I twisted my torso toward her, the chains clanking and dragging with my sudden movement. "Hold my hand. Take it."

A soft hand grasped mine. Her skin was cool against my sweaty one.

My heart thudded in my chest, and I entwined my fingers with hers. "I've gotten used to the dark since I've been here. I'll be your ray of sunshine, and you can be mine, how's that?"

"Kind of silly." She let out a small laugh, and a ripple of heat prickled through my flesh. That genuine, easy laugh was more than appreciation for a dumb joke. It was a bright instant of carefree in this dark, bleak prison cell.

I'd never take a lighthearted moment for granted again.

I'll start with right now.

This girl was sad way down deep. An overwhelming urge to relieve her of the heavy weight of that sadness engulfed me. I wanted to make her smile again. Make her laugh. Make her forget her hell for just a second more. Show her the sunshine.

"Take my other hand," I said. "Climb on top of me. Do it. Come on."

She straddled my waist and grasped my other hand. I clutched her fingers tight. They were long and thin and cold. Her weight on me kicked up my pulse again.

I flexed my hips up, my every muscle straining for more of her. "Kiss me, sunshine," I whispered roughly.

She leaned over me. *Yes, now, yes. Fuck yes.*

Her lips pressed against mine, and a new soft, warm world erupted over me; something smooth and delicate for just a moment. A flower opening its petals in pinks and blues and creamy yellows. My chest ached. I wanted to see those colors again, to feel cool breezes once more. I wanted to be held. I raised my head off the floor, my mouth open, my tongue ready to claim and conquer, but she moved back.

I groaned, my neck aching, my cock raging. "Please. Please, give me more."

Her hair fell over us, its gentle drape keeping us safe and secret. I inhaled her light and flowery fragrance. That scent lifted me on a magic cloud, and I clung to it.

Lips on mine, unsealing, and soft, not hard, not demanding. Those sweet colors burst behind my lids as her warmth revealed itself to me, growing hotter. She kissed me, her tongue sliding against mine. I was lifted from the dank pit, I floated on the surface of the well, weightless. The two of us.

Her mouth released me. A small moan filled my ears, and her

fingers squeezed mine.

"Did that make the dark better for you?" My voice came out low, thick.

"Yes," came the raw whisper.

"Me too."

She snatched her hands out of my grip.

I braced. Was she going to stab me with a hidden knife? Scream for help? Shit, I was the real prisoner here. I'd crossed the line, gone too far. I needed to wake the fuck up. I needed to—

She rose from my chest. Movement. Material shuffled in the dark.

"Here I am," she rasped.

Her musk filled my nostrils. Her thighs, damp with sweat and her arousal, were on either side of my face. My pulse screamed and pounded. My pelvis flexed on instinct, hoping for friction, hoping for her.

She was grabbing at the light when she could. Just like me. Light was rare.

I raised my chin and my tongue reached out and found glorious wet heat. I swiped and licked and swirled. A choked moan sounded from somewhere above me as she rocked over my eager mouth, and I dragged my tongue over her, sucking hard, giving her a rhythm. She moved faster. She wanted to come bad, and I gave her all the intensity I could offer.

Fuck the char-grilled rib eye I'd been daydreaming about, the soft mattress and clean sheets, icy bottles of pop. Fuck all that. This was...all I wanted was this.

My cock was harder than hard. I grunted, every cell of my being concentrating on making her come, lapping at her, consuming her, pulsating with her body. Not one cry escaped her mouth, and I was positive it was so they wouldn't hear us. Only her hips moved over my face, her silkiness throbbing against my lips, her thighs tensing around me. I suckled her clit and focused everything I had on it.

Come, come, come, come.

A tiny, high-pitched gasp was quickly swallowed, and her body seized over me. Her wet cunt throbbed as I applied broader, tense strokes. She ground over me slowly and melted at my side, her hair touching my arms, the sensation taking me by surprise like the edges of a bird's wing that flits by too close.

I was so fucking high.

She moved her legs, detaching herself from me. Her body bunched up in a ball at my side, her breaths uneven and short.

I needed something more right now in the dark. "Touch me. I need you to—"

Her hand slid around my bicep. "Here. I'm right here." Her voice was so small.

"Closer."

Her damp curves melded to my body, and I closed my eyes. We stayed still and silent. Water dripped at the other end of the cell.

"What is it, Sunshine?" I whispered against her forehead. "I promise I won't tell anyone."

She let out that light laugh again. "Yeah, you better not."

"I won't."

She only let out a jagged sigh. No words.

"Okay, let's forget the chit chat. How about instead, you get back on and fuck me?" I said into her hair, my leg rubbing up against hers.

My mind and body raced, imagining how thrusting inside her would feel. My blood simmered at the idea, my skin flaring with heat. I was an animal. That's all that was left of me. We could just fuck each other for hours and they'd find us wrapped around each other days later. That'd be good.

"Oh, I can't do that." She almost sounded amused.

My heart shrank along with my cock. "Why the hell not?" My wrists strained against the thick metal cuffs, my weak muscles shuddering, the fucking chains scraping along the cement, and my aching body reminding me of reality.

Her legs straightened and pressed together. "I can't."

"That'd be cheating, huh? Fucking the enemy prisoner." A chuckle rolled out of me.

"Stop."

"Why do you stick around anyway? Why haven't you gotten out?"

"I've tried to run away, and I'll try again. The last time I got caught, he said he'd kill me. He realized my dedication to him has tarnished. But I'll deal."

"You'll deal? Why don't you—"

"I like being alive." Her voice was firm, steady. "No matter what, I want to stay alive."

My arms hung at my sides, shame dripping over me like a splatter of paint down a wall. Her confidence in a better day, her desire to live, her bravery, the sheer force of her will humbled me.

Was I like that? I just existed, walked through paces set by everyone around me. She made tough decisions every day. She held it together. She calculated and risked and pushed through.

My mouth dried, my skull pounded. I was coming down again. I needed her on me, her touch, her skin, her mouth, more than fucking food. More than a hit of any chemical. I wanted to feel her tits in my hands. I didn't fucking care that she could be doing this on their orders. Who the fuck knew for sure? She was my banquet and I wanted to feast.

My tongue lashed against the side of her neck. "Blow me again at least?"

"Once was enough for today." She drew a fingertip down the center of my lips, and I let out a low hiss. My lips captured that slim finger and sucked. Fuck yes, I was desperate. A monster of need.

"More tomorrow," she said, her voice low. "When you're really hungry."

She was hungry. I could tell by the way her lips parted as I sucked on her finger, how she lingered over me, rubbed a foot against my calf.

I wanted her to be hungry for me.

I released her finger. "I'm starving here. You don't have to stand on ceremony or keep to some schedule with me. Suck away."

"You're funny."

My pulse skipped at that playful tone in her voice. Was that a yes?

My every muscle tightened as she gently stroked the underside of my balls, murmuring something. I couldn't hear her, I didn't care. I was mesmerized by her warm, sure touch, her sultry voice. That voice was heat blooming over my skin from the inside out. My heart raced in my chest, and a cool sweat broke out along my scalp. I wanted to come now, in her hands. I'd do anything she said just to fucking release this volcano between my legs. I wanted to come for her.

I was at her mercy.

"Tomorrow." Her thumb rubbed at my tip, and she released me.

I grunted. Not happy. "Come on. Wait, wait—what's your name?"

"That doesn't matter, does it?"

"Yes, yes it fucking does matter to me. I want to hear it. All this time, and I don't know your name." I wanted to know it as bad as I always wanted ice cream on a sweaty, dusty summer afternoon. As bad as I now craved a shower, sunlight, my bike underneath me and a cold wind battering my face.

"Tell me. Give me that at least."

She leaned over me. "My real name is Serena."

The syllables cascaded over me like ribbons of silk fabric. *Fucking goddess.* I was right all along.

"Serena. That's pretty. I like that."

A smile flickered over her lips. "You like that?"

Did that give her pleasure? A lift? I fucking hoped so.

"Like serene? At peace?" I asked.

"Yeah. Untroubled and tranquil." A quick smirk passed over her features. Irony. Weariness. "My grandmother was Italian. It was her mother's name. I loved her name, though. Eleonora."

"That's real pretty too." I grinned at her. "Never met a Serena before."

"I'm your first and probably your last." Her words echoed inside me, her fingers brushing over my skin.

First and last. A thick sweet vapor steamed between us.

"Yeah, you will be," I said.

"Here they call me Rena. Bikers like nicknames."

The lock turned, metal ground against metal.

She moved away from me, jerking up to her feet. The door shoved open.

"Rena?" said a deep voice.

She stepped off of our private little fluffy cloud and charged through the door, leaving me alone with my slimy chains on hard, damp, mildewed cement.

4
KID

"GIVE THE KID A DRINK!" Med shouted loudly.

The infamous Scott "Medicine Man" McGuire, so named because he'd been one of the first to create meth factories in the state and provide his clients with all kinds of powdered and tablet style feel-good remedies. Med stood over me, eyeing me like I was the Thanksgiving turkey and he'd been waiting a very long time to carve with style and dig in.

A large unlabeled glass bottle was shoved in my mouth. Another hand dug in my hair, tugging my head back. The sickening fumes of sweat, body odor, and burly booze filled my nostrils. The alcohol flooded my mouth like liquid fire, searing my throat. I gagged and sputtered, spitting out whatever I could.

Laughter and howls ripped through the brightly lit smoke-filled room.

I pushed back and spit again, my eyes tearing. "What the fuck was that?"

"Our moonshine. You don't like it?"

"No." I blinked and scanned the crowded room. The Guns had company tonight. Another chapter of their club from California was here.

"You rejecting our hospitality? We're celebrating tonight. We got our bros here from out west, and we just closed a sweet deal."

Cheers and hoots rose all around me, and I cringed at the noise. Shocking. Nauseating.

"We've all decided that we should move on from our differences with your club. Flames of Hell finally got back to us and we reached an agreement. So the other news of the evening is we're gonna let you go."

Boos and howls filled the room.

My club had negotiated for me? Something inside me went to leap, but I pulled it back.

Med looked me square in the face. Everything about him was square. Square jaw, square mouth, boxy end to his nose. Stocky, not too tall, no real neck, compact. Leather cuffs at his wrists and a full mop of long wavy brown hair.

I swallowed against the lingering burn in my throat. "What kind of agreement?"

"Prospect, you don't worry about the details. You just worry about doing what you're told." He smacked my face once, twice, and settled a thick paw on my shoulder. "This here party is your send off. You're gonna have fun. I know we will."

Sticky laughter bubbled in the giant cauldron of a room. The air was hot, stifling. So many men and women, their eyes gleaming and heavy on me. I searched for Serena, but I didn't see her in the blur of faces and bodies. I searched for those eyes. I wanted to see her. I needed to see her.

They shoved me forward, and my body swerved toward the other side of the room. Two girls were on top of a long table, both of them getting fucked, a group of men around them watching intently, waiting their turn. Two other girls were on top of another smaller table, both of them fingering and licking each other with a circle of men watching. Something for everybody.

My chains were yanked, and I hit a table.

"Lay him out," came Med's voice.

They laid me out on a long wood table and fastened the chains at my hands and legs to big pegs on the surface. Was I part of the entertainment? My heart banged against my ribs. "What the fuck? You just said you were letting me go. You said this shit was done with."

"Yeah, but tonight, you're my glorious main event," he spit out on a huge grin. His ferocious excitement speared my insides.

They partied all around me. For hours they hung over me, putting their cigarettes out on my legs and chest, the sides of my torso.

Even the women came over and teased me. "Aw, look at that sad cock! Poor baby!" They laughed. "Here dicky dicky! Here!"

The music banged off the walls, the vibrations radiating through me. They poured more of their moonshine in my mouth and made me swallow with sweaty hands gripping my chin, sealing my lips shut.

The room hushed, and I turned my head toward that voice. Med was talking to his bros. "This little peace treaty between us and the Flames will go into effect tomorrow. I know a lot of you ain't for it, but it's the best thing. It's been a fun time, but we need to focus on business again. Now we voted on it, but to make it stick I think we need something real memorable. Something sweet to seal this deal, so that I know you all will commit to it. So, I think we need more than that show of hands and that round of "ayes" from before. I have a better idea. Baby? Baby, where are you?"

There was movement and shuffling as people parted. A young woman moved though them toward Med, who eyed her like a lion, satisfied and proud.

It was her.

He cupped her chin and planted a kiss on her lips. "Get up on that table, baby." Another guy hoisted her up onto a small table at her side.

"Y'all know Rena, my old lady. Isn't she the finest thing?"

Med's old lady? Serena was Med's old lady? No. No. No. He was old enough to be her father. He was—

Her eyes found mine. The vibrant eyes I'd been mesmerized by all these days together in the half dark of my cell, were now blank, dull.

"Clothes off, darlin'," Med said.

Rena swallowed and stripped off her cropped T-shirt and shorts without registering any surprise or shock. She was bare naked underneath. She kept her boots on.

"Ain't my baby beautiful?" Med rubbed her ass with one hand, in his other he held a cigar.

Murmurs of approval and coughing rose from the onlookers.

"This treaty with the Flames of Hell has to stick. It's gotta get done and stay done. I want to see your commitment. I want those ayes of yours confirmed."

Some of the men standing up front shifted their weight, their jaws tightening. A lot of Med's men made faces, briefly glancing at each other. They didn't seem to agree with him, weren't sure what to do. Did his men usually do as they were told to keep the peace or out of fear? Med was that evil beast spawned from cleverness and paranoia.

"Tonight I thought I'd share my little treasure for this special occasion. Show me your dedication to our cause by licking my old lady 'till she comes." He squeezed one of her tits, his eyes on his men.

A sudden silence seized the room. Nausea swirled in my gut. A pendulum blade swung past me and back again, taking my breath with it.

Med exhaled a puff of cigar smoke. "'Cause if you break this treaty, you'll have gone against my special, personal gift to you, and I'll be offended."

Smack. He slapped Rena's ass with force, and she stumbled forward, steadying herself. The men standing in the front widened their eyes. Others rubbed hands down their faces.

"Consider my offering of my woman's pussy a real special bond. Y'all are gonna think twice before breaking that, ain't ya?" He laughed hard.

He was fucking insane.

An icy silence descended on the smoke-filled room. Rena lifted her gaze to mine, and a chill swept through my veins.

He smacked her ass again, and she jolted forward, biting down on her lower lip. "Get down and spread those legs, honey." Rena's chin lifted slightly, and she laid down on the table. Med rested a hand on her bent knee, stroking her thigh up and down. "Who says Aye now?"

"Aye!" voices rang out.

The music got louder, and my lungs squeezed tighter. Men from the California chapter gathered around Rena.

Med slapped a heavyset bearded man on the shoulder like he'd done to me earlier. The guy leaned down between her legs, and her whole body twisted on the table.

"Aye!" the guy next to him grunted, his eyes intent on his buddy's moves.

Her eyes were intent on me.

My pulse thudded in my veins. If I could help her somehow, if I could make them stop, if I could make this all go away for her.

Her body stiffened, her eyelids closed. Was she coming?

The man jerked up off her, his hands in the air, his lips shiny. "Fuck yeah! Aye!"

Rena's legs shook slightly and sagged to the side.

The men around him clapped. A bottle of booze was tipped between her legs, and she winced, her body straining. The liquor ran over the table, splatting on the floor. A puddle formed below her.

"Next!"

The eager guy on the side took over, a hand squeezing her tit hard. He rolled his head, made faces, making the men around him laugh and clap. Another man. Another. They were into it now. One by one, they were all putting on their show of allegiance, indulgence.

"Stop it! What the fuck are you doing?" raged out of my mouth loud and clear.

An eyebrow jumped on Med's face. "Pardon me?" he said, his tone sarcastic.

Muttering and moans filled the room along with the *thump thump* of hard rock music against the walls.

"Boy, you got a mouth on you, huh?" Med laughed loudly.

Rena whimpered, and the guy jacked up from her, hands in the air. He grabbed the liquor bottle and poured some over her pussy. He took a swig from the bottle.

Rena's eyes pleaded with me. *No. Don't.*

"What's your fucking problem, Kid? She's coming non-stop. What woman don't love that?"

More laughter.

His eyes narrowed. "Maybe you want in too?"

The laughter fizzled as Med moved toward me, eyes pinned. "Who's next?" Med asked his men, his eyes remaining on me.

The next Smoking Gun pulled Rena's hips down further on the table.

Med approached me. "You still ain't showing me proper humility, Kid, and I don't like that. Tells me you're a hard nut to break. You sure don't tell me what I'm gonna do and how I'm gonna do it with what's mine."

His hands grabbed my neck and squeezed, crushing my throat. I choked, fighting for air, fighting against the blinding pain radiating through me, shutting me off, shutting me down. My arms pulled against my chains, my muscles quivering, shaking to break free. His eyes bulged. "In here, you are mine, you piece of shit! Same as her."

He released me, and I saw stars. I sputtered, gasping for air. My throat burned and ached.

Med gestured with his cigar at Rena. "She does as she's goddamn told. I think you need to learn your place before tonight is done. Tape his mouth up."

Rip. Duct tape stretched across my mouth, motor oil stained fingers pressing down on either sides of my face.

"Watch and see how it's done, boy."

The next guy bent over Rena, grinning up at his buddies as he lapped at the liquor between her legs. Her head twisted and she turned her face, her eyes finding mine again, and I held them.

I'm here, Serena. Fuck him, fuck them all. We'll get through this together. Do not give up. Don't. Stay with me. With me. Me. Me. Me.

Man after man after man after man. Poking, licking, grabbing, sucking, smacking. She only stared at me, and me at her. From that first instant, and the long brutal seconds ticking into minutes, we drowned out the cannibals and their drums of war, and there was only me and her.

Only me and her.

I tucked her inside me, held her in the deepest chamber of my heart, in the dark vault of my soul where I'd never lingered too long before. No one could touch us there. Just us holding onto each other. Shielding each other, breathing together. Coming together.

You and me, I insisted. I grit my teeth, my gums aching.

Serena, I called out to her. *You and me.*

Yes, she replied. *You and me.*

The party played on around us. We were the entertainment, the spectacle in this binge of raunch and insanity.

Med polished off a bottle of rum and smashed it on the floor. Yeah, he was a real fucking pirate king.

He wiped at his mouth, staring at me. "Flame Boy! I figure I can't let you go home without a little something to remember us by, now can I? Otherwise, our time together will have been meaningless and it won't be a lasting lesson for the Flames of Hell, now will it?" His men cheered him on, bottles of alcohol were raised in the air. "You know, they didn't give too much of a shit about you. They played it real cool about getting you back, and that pissed me the fuck off. Your disrespectful attitude before pissed me off all over again."

"Show him what we're made of! Do it, Med!" someone shouted out. "Fucking Flame!"

"You're gonna be set free first thing in the morning." He tapped a thick finger on my forehead. "But tonight you're still mine."

"Yeah! He's ours!" someone shouted.

"I need you to be a living, breathing reminder of this clusterfuck for your club. A reminder of their need to respect me. Like the White House is a reminder of America's power, like the Statue of Liberty is a reminder of liberty or whatever the fuck. Point is, people look at those symbols, and they get these feelings. No words needed, no explanations, no blah blah blah."

My brain couldn't register his pompous babble. A politician enjoying the mob's attention.

His eyes creased as he ran a hand down his chest, slanting his head to a bro next to him. "Get her."

Rena was released from her table and brought over to me. She stumbled, blinked, her gaze glued to Med.

"Climb on him. Do him, baby. I need him happy."

She clambered up on the table, settling between my legs. Up this close, I saw the bite marks over her chest, the welts on her swaying breasts and her thin pale thighs. Her hand cupped my balls firmly, and I hissed in air.

"Get in there, bitch." Med shoved her face down between my legs, and her mouth immediately swallowed my cock, sucking it all the way down her throat.

My breath stuttered.

I wanted to fight it, but I couldn't. I wanted not to respond to their taunts and games. But her mouth was all I knew. Her mouth was everything. I hardened for her immediately, my pelvis bucking. My body electrified and surrendered to her without a second's hesitation.

For it.

For her.

For it.

I didn't fucking know anymore, and my need was one and the same now, all of it Serena.

I lost her mouth and my head shot up.

Med was at her side, trash talking in her ear, his hand at her throat. She was pale as snow, biting down on her lip. He let go of her, and she straddled me and took my cock in her cunt.

Dreams come true when you least expect it.

But this wasn't what I'd wanted.

Our eyes locked on each other's as she moved over me, hips rocking, taking me in deeper and deeper the way I'd been imagining. The air left me in a rush, my chest constricted. Whoops and shouts broke out around us.

Whatever we'd shared before in the darkness of my cell was beautiful compared to this. This ugliness out in the harsh light, so many people watching us, breathing over us. This forced, mechanical—

Med cupped one of her tits. "Yeah, that's it, baby, ride him. Ride him good and hard. And don't fuckin' stop."

Smack.

Her body jerked under his assault, and she rode me faster. Trained and obedient. He gripped her ass, controlling her movement. Her neck stiffened, her jaw tight, but those incredible, fierce blue green eyes held my gaze.

The crowd didn't matter. Nothing mattered. Just her and me. Me in her.

I pulled on my chains, my hips driving into hers. I pumped inside her silken heat with whatever energy I could muster. My arms were being stretched out, my hands were being tugged on. Flattened against the table. *No!* Now I only wanted to touch her, feel her flesh come alive, fill my hands with her.

Fill, give, take, soar.

Her eyes widened. Fear.

The spring and press of metal.

My brain blanked.

My body went numb.

Blood spattered on Serena's bare skin. My blood. Red on her breasts, her stomach.

My flesh caught on fire.

I howled.

Laughter.

A bloody object was held in the air and tossed on my bare chest. My eyes struggled to focus on it. My finger. He chopped off my middle finger.

No, no don't look. She pleaded with me through the storm and rode and rode.

A large nipper tool was held in the air then dove on the other side of me. Grips tightened on my other arm, my wrist, my fingers.

Spring. Press. Crack. Crunch.

My vision blurred, everything whitened. Another nudge on my chest. I blinked. Another finger. My eyes went to my right hand. My middle finger was missing, the ugly wound bled and bled. More blood pooled on my chest and splattered over her hands pressing down on me.

A claw in my hair, rum breath in my face. "Your club said fuck you to us." My bloodied, cut off finger dangled in front of me. "Now we've taken that away so you'll never forget. Respect, for the Smoking Guns. Respect!" Med roared, dropping my finger on my chest.

His crowd roared back, "Respect!"

My two bloody fingers stared at me from my chest. I shuddered, trembled. So cold, so cold.

She rode me. Her eyes glazed, her lips parted, my blood smattered all over her pale skin.

Stay with me, Kid. Stay with me.

"Cauterize that shit! Don't want him to bleed out on us now. I still got more fun planned here."

Searing hot metal burned at my raw flesh. I choked on the stench, twisted at the flare of pain, my back arching off the table.

"Bitch, get off him. Suck on that cock now. I want it up, way the fuck up."

"Wake his cock the fuck up!" came a shout. Hooting and more clapping filled my ears.

Through the blur, the heat released me, and I let out a groan. A different kind of heat enveloped my cock, taking it in, demanding from it. I raised my head a fraction. Through my blurred vision, Serena's head bobbed between my legs. Her slim hand at my base rubbed, another at my balls stroked. My head sank back. Binding and pulling on my hands. Men wrapped up my bleeding wounds where my middle fingers once were.

My fingers.

The pain hammered through me fresh and boiled in my arms, my shoulders. She pulled at me. A whirlpool of nausea and dizziness and madness spun me loose. My head dropped to the side, and the tape was ripped off my mouth. My insides heaved, and I threw up.

"I need creativity. A flare, here." Med spun around, facing his audience. "Anyone?"

"Anything I want?" another voice piped up.

"What do you got?" asked Med.

My strained, cloudy vision found Serena's flushed face, her wide eyes the most supernatural blue green I had ever seen. I clung to them. They were my lush jungle, my flowing river, flowing me out of this fume-filled hell and into her blue green Garden of Eden.

Stay with me, her eyes said.

Yes, yes. With you, I replied.

Hands held down my head to the left, and I lost her. My heart pounded as I got harder in her mouth. Harder and harder. My cock throbbed and I came, I came into my haven, that mouth. Serena's fingertips dug into my legs.

A sharp sting lashed my cheek. A glint of steel flashed over me.

They're cutting me!

Another searing sting.

Hands turned my head to the other side.

The slashes carved on my skin stung and blared with pain. I held back the scream, held it back with every ounce of grit and resolve I had left in me. The coppery taste in my mouth, a thickness on my tongue. My blood. So many eyes loomed over me, grins, bitter hate and bitter fun all swirled into a lunatic kaleidoscope.

"You scribble good with that knife, bro!" Med said. "What pretty, pretty F's, huh?"

"From now on, no more fuck yous from the Flames," replied the scribbler. He let out a rich, rolling laugh that ended in a fit of coughing.

Serena was pulled off me, and I was exposed. Cold. Alone. Decimated.

I gave in.

I screamed.

5
KID

Stinging.

My face.

Numb.

A wall of warmth next to me.

"I'm just changing the bandages. Could've been worse."

My eyes drifted to hers. "You a doctor?" It hurt when I spoke, and I didn't even recognize my own voice now—scratchy, husky, coarse. Another souvenir of my time here.

"No. I'm not anything," she said quietly.

You're wrong. You're everything.

"They're dropping you off today at some meeting point, and your club is going to pick you up and take you home."

Home? A simple word, a simple idea for most. For her and me? My home. Her home. Whatever the fuck.

"They'll get you a doctor, right?" she said. "If you're hungry, I brought soup. It's from a can, but it's good. I like it."

I shook my head slightly. "Everything hurts, I can't."

"I'll help you."

"No."

"I want to. Please."

Her low, emotional voice danced over my skin. My eyes lifted to hers. Had anyone ever said the word please to me before? No. It was always *do this, clean it up, get that done, bring that, fetch, stop. Drink, kill, set it on fire. Now. Go.* Never once a *please*.

"Not chicken noodle. Hate chicken noodle," I mumbled.

A small smile curved her sexy mouth. I'd pleased her. "No, it's

39

tomato. I like tomato. Just open your mouth a tiny bit more so I can get the spoon in there."

I parted my lips as far as they would go, my face screaming. She concentrated on getting the full spoon in my mouth.

Did she take care of all the prisoners like this? Fuck all the prisoners? Tend to their wounds? Was I just another idiot in a long line of prisoners? After I left would someone else fill my spot in her life?

"Soup okay?"

I nodded, and she fed me again. And again.

We didn't have much time left. No time left. I wanted to listen to her speak. Hear her. Anything I could get.

I asked, "Why do you like tomato soup?"

"When I was a kid I used to make this soup from this can every Saturday. I'd heat up the soup, and my grandma would make the grilled cheese sandwiches." Her face flushed.

Imagining her as a little girl, an innocent, laughing child sharing a meal with her daddy, made my chest pinch together.

Look where she ended up.

"When were you going to tell me about you being Med's old lady?"

She didn't answer.

"How old are you?" I asked.

"Twenty-one."

"How long you been here?"

"Almost four years."

"Med's around fifty or so, isn't he?"

"Fifty-two."

"He likes to collect women, huh?"

"He likes to collect a lot of things," she replied. "He wanted to keep you, actually. But he knew he had to give you back otherwise there'd be a huge war." Her thumb lightly brushed the edge of my jaw, and a shiver raced over me. "Now he left his mark on you. Made you his for everyone to see."

"I'm not anybody's. Nobody owns me."

"I'm sorry about what I did."

"What? What did you do?"

"Getting you off while they—"

"He made you do it. He makes you do lots of shit, huh?"

"Yeah, but not like last night."

We stared at each other. She didn't have to explain or go into any other sure to be fucked up details. It was in the dull steadiness of her gaze. Unspeakable things, humiliating things.

"He doesn't own me inside, though, and he knows it. He used to be really possessive of me, but that's changed lately. Before, he never would've suggested I bring you food or have any contact with a prisoner. I haven't done anything wrong. I don't know what it could be."

"He's crazy. It's got nothing to do with you. You can see that, right?"

She swallowed hard, her eyebrows knitting close together. She was struggling with reality. Med had really done a number on her. "Last night was a first, so I don't think—"

"I'll help you."

"Help me?"

"I'll come back for you."

Her face tightened. "Why? What for? So I can be yours? So I can suck your cock whenever you want?"

"No, no, I didn't mean that. I don't want to own you like some slave. I meant so you could be free."

Her face blanked.

I wanted to see her free. Even if she wasn't with me, knowing she was out there with a smile on her face doing her own thing would be great.

"That's nice to hear, but you're just another prospect and from an enemy club. Kid, you and me don't matter. We're the cogs in the wheel. The little people who get stepped on and used. We're just jagged stones in their path. They kick us out of the way as they move along. You realize that, don't you? After last night, after what he made me do, I think my old lady status is done. There are plenty more girls waiting to take my place too."

My pulse kicked up. "I want to get you out of here. You want that don't you?"

She averted her gaze. "I'll bet you'll be a hero when you get back to your club. I'm sure you will be. You survived, you showed bravery. You never ratted them out. But me? Me, I'm just a nothing. An empty bottle they toss after they're finished drinking their fill. And now..."

"You're no empty bottle. You're beautiful, you're—"

"Shh. Please. You've got a fever as it is. You need to rest."

I licked my cracked lips and tasted my own blood. Would they really let me go? Maybe they'd pop a bullet in the back of my head or knife me in front of my bros. Maybe I'd pass out from the pain any minute.

Would I ever see her again?

I wanted her to know my name. A name no one ever used for me. I was desperate for her to think about me and have my name for my face, for the memory of us, for the intense feelings between us, whatever the hell they were. A dull ache clouded my head, and I couldn't catch up with my choppy breaths. Anguish streaked through me along with a strange kind of anticipation, each pulling me in opposite directions.

Our discovery of each other, our stolen orgasms in the dark, had been nicks in the chains holding us both. The conversations, the small laughs and threads of understanding between us, had been moments of warmth and sun in that shithole dungeon. Med making us perform for him had been brutal. Fucking was something that we'd both wanted bad but hadn't done. Having been forced to do it in the spotlit center ring of Med's circus was all sorts of crazy.

But here she was, not a dream, not a phantom who'd visit my cell and disappear. Here she was making sure I got something to eat. Caring about me.

We had to see each other again. We had to. A wall of dark water towered over me, threatening to crush everything to bits.

I said, "My name's Justin."

Her brows knit together. "I've got to go."

"Hey!"

She stopped in her tracks. "I shouldn't be here."

"Please say it. Say my name. No one says it. Not ever. I want to hear you say it. I need to. Say it," I begged. There was nothing more important than this right now. Nothing. "Say it."

Her blue green eyes lifted to mine. They were heavy. "Justin," she whispered.

A thrill spinning in the mud of misery, the vehicle stuck, going nowhere. Hello and goodbye. Whatever was between us was all over before it began, but somehow I felt as if I'd lived a hundred lives in this dungeon and now had to let them all go.

"Again."

"Justin."

My heart squeezed. Her saying my name was a touch, a hug. I didn't remember being held before by anyone. Patted on the back, a clap on the shoulder, a ruffle through my hair, but not ever being held, the life squeezed out of me. Someone really psyched to see me, someone not wanting to let me go.

Now all I wanted was for her to take me in her arms, hold me close and whisper my name, whisper goodbyes in my ear.

Fucking goodbye.

"I'm going to miss you." My voice broke.

She sucked in a tiny breath. "Me too." She grabbed the mug and the spoon. "I hope you can forget all this. Maybe someday you will. Maybe one day everything that happened to you here won't matter. It'll just be a story you tell around the fire over a few beers to impress people. A wild piece of your club history." Her teeth scraped her lips. "You go and have a good life."

"Forgetting this means forgetting you. And I'll never forget you, Serena."

"I'll never forget you either, Justin." She scrambled for the door.

Something bright and sharp slid through me. "When I come back for you, will you come with me?"

She stopped in the doorway and turned. Her lips parted as if she were listening to beautiful music, astounding music.

"Hell yes."

6
KID

I was delivered back to Missouri, dumped on the icy hard ground in a field in the middle of winter like a sack of garbage. Familiar faces filled my vision.

"You're home now, Kid." My heartbeat settled at the sound of my Vice President's deep voice. Chaz held my head in his lap in the back of the van that barreled toward the clubhouse.

Once there and settled on a pool table, needles punctured me, an IV inserted. The doctor scowled as he unwrapped the gauze bandages covering my hands.

"Ah, shit." Chaz groaned. "Oh man, oh man," he muttered over and over again, rubbing a hand down his mouth, staggering back a step.

I succumbed to the dull throb of the tugging, cleaning, wrapping.

Where was she?

I searched for her eyes, her touch, those soft fingers skimming my skin. A slight tickle, soothing, slow. Yeah, that was it. Up my arm. A kiss inside my elbow, her lips lingering there, her breath a soothing mist over me.

Rena.

Wait, no, no.

Serena.

A needle pricked my skin.

I sank and flew with her whispering sweet words into my ear, her hands in my hair, fingertips trailing up and down my arms. I reached for her like I always did.

Touch me. Touch me.

"Get these antibiotics, more of these bandages. Pain meds. He's badly dehydrated too."

My other hand was being tugged. My eyelids stretched and strained toward the dull ache. The doctor was bent over my hand, concentrating. Stitching. My head knocked back against the table. I searched the faces that hovered over me. I was back at the club. Back at the Flames of Hell.

It all came rushing back like a movie at high speed.

Siggy? Dad? Where's Dad?

My chest caved in. Siggy was gone. The old man was dead. I'd forgotten. For a split second I'd fucking forgotten.

The bandages on my face were peeled back. I breathed through my mouth, my heels digging into the table, grunts escaping my lips.

"Jesus."

The medicinal smell of cleaning solutions, careful dabs.

I settled into a dark pool and floated on the murky surface.

Floated into the dark.

I FORCED MY EYES OPEN.

My leather jacket hung on my chair the way I always kept it. "Black Elk", my used paperback about a Sioux mystic, sat on the same corner of the desk where I'd last left it.

My desk. My bed. My room.

"He's awake."

"Finally. It's been a few days."

People visited and smiled at me. A shiny vase with a top on it I'd never seen before caught my eyes on the dresser opposite my bed.

"Chaz?" I gestured at the vase with a lift of my chin.

"It's your old man, Kid. Cremated." Chaz shrugged, gnawing on his lower lip.

I stared at the vase. It stared at me.

The old ladies ran around applying ice packs, aloe vera, and vitamin E gel on my wounds, making sure I took my meds on time, feeding me soups and stews.

Some young girl I didn't know set down a paper plate filled with

45

small sandwich squares. "It's smoked turkey with bacon and Swiss. They told me to make it for you. That it's your favorite." She smiled nervously. "I cut it into small pieces so it would be easy for you to handle." She darted out of my room.

My eyes landed on the sandwich. A dizzying spiral uncoiled in my stomach, looping through my gut, squeezing in my chest.

Sliced white bread. Sliced white bread.

The stench of the cell.

Serena feeding me.

The touch of her hand. A slight smile in the dim light that lit my world.

The cold slime of the concrete under me.

Drip of the hose.

My mouth dried, and I heaved for air. Cold sweat prickled at my hairline.

The vase across the room.

The vase.

Have to get away. Have to make it stop.

I kicked my legs.

The sandwich stared back at me. If I ate it, would she come to me? My Serena? No, no, she wasn't here and we weren't together. There wouldn't be any touching, there would be no—

"Honey, you want me to help you with the sandwich?" Kerry, Chaz's old lady, stood over me. "Kid, you okay? You don't look so good. Is the fever back?" She leaned over me her hand moving toward my face.

Not her touch, not hers… "Don't!" I choked on my breath.

"What is it, baby? What is it?"

My arm wouldn't obey my command. It wouldn't lift, wouldn't point at that fucking white Wonder bread a few inches from me. Block it from my view.

"No!"

Kerry snapped up the dish and handed it to the sandwich girl who appeared behind her, eyes round. "Get it out of here."

I collapsed back on the bed, moaning.

"It's all right, baby, it's gone. Is that what it was, the sandwich?"

I wanted to bury my face in my pillow, but I couldn't do that. My face burned.

"No more sandwiches, okay?" she said.

Sandwich girl brought in a bowl of chili and dashed back out of my room. Kerry helped me eat. When we finished, Kerry brought in Ryan, an occupational therapist friend of hers to look at my hands, at my stumps.

Ryan examined me and said I was going to have to work on "fine and gross motor coordination." He told me we'd be using small balls and hand grips to strengthen my forearms, wrists, and fingers to help compensate for the loss of my middle fingers. Gripping and grasping exercises to accelerate the return of my grip strength and improve my dexterity would become my new everyday habit. As I got stronger, we'd add a variety of dumbbells and weight plates for me to pinch and claw and pull, and different kinds of handles to hold and drag all kinds of weights.

Both Kerry and Ryan waited for some kind of response out of me.

I had to be able to ride, hold a gun, use a knife. I didn't want stiffness to get in my way, hold me back, and I sure didn't want arthritis when I got older. No fucking way.

"I know you're in pain now," Ryan said. "And all this probably sounds overwhelming, but—"

"Bring it on," I said.

He smiled. "I'll set up a schedule for you."

Ryan left my room, and Kerry handed me a tall plastic cup with water and a straw. I wasn't thirsty. I wanted answers.

"Kerry, tell me what happened with my dad."

She set the cup back on the desk by the bed. "They haven't told you?"

"No one's said a thing. I've been asking. But—"

"They don't want to upset you. You've been in and out of consciousness for a few days now, honey."

"Tell me."

"Kid..." She pressed her lips together.

"What the hell's going on?"

"Calm down. You just got over a high fever."

"Tell me the fucking truth!"

Kerry let out a breath. "Fuse had a heart attack. He collapsed on the spot."

What Serena had told me was true.

"He was real upset about you going on that drop," Kerry said. "He'd followed you and Siggy that night. He saw them kill Siggy, he saw them take you."

"I knew it. I thought I'd heard him yelling."

"He came back and flipped out. Then the not knowing what they were doing to you, hearing the threats and what it meant for you, for the club. He wasn't eating right or getting any sleep, constantly wired. He wouldn't let me take him to the doctor. Probably wasn't taking his pills. You know how he got."

"Did you see? Were you there? Was he alone?" My scratched voice choked on itself, I couldn't get the words out, goddammit.

"It was late at night. He was in the office with Reich. Reich said—"

"Just the two of them?"

"Yeah." She let out an exhale. "Why don't you take a nap? I'm gonna get a move on and get home. I'm real sorry, baby. Real sorry. We all miss him." She folded over the napkin she'd used on my mouth, dropped it in the empty chili bowl, and left.

My pulse rattled in my throat, and I took in a deep breath to fight it. My dad never liked Reich. Dad was the veteran, the old codger, the has been, the back seat driver, but a figure to be respected. Around the club, the elders deserved special consideration, and they got it. For the most part. Fuse had made his mark on his club and had been a bro for over thirty years. Reich was the up and coming officer, the Sergeant at Arms with new ideas and a lofty sense of self.

I needed to keep my cool, keep it together, find out more.

My head sank back into the pillow, my eyes landing on the vase again. Urn. Whatever.

A swirl of dizziness overtook my brain, my stomach twisted. I moved my hand, and the numbness and stiffness of that ugly paw only made my chest heavy. That aching, shooting pain was still there where my finger used to be.

I jammed my eyes closed and clung to the fact that my dad had stood up for me to his literal dying breath. I clung to that like it was a piece of scrap metal skimming the surface of the ocean after the plane crash of my life. Whenever he had stood up for me, which wasn't too often, he did it big.

The first time Fuse stood up for me was when he'd got me out from under my mother's crazy. He'd actually given a shit.

I LAID EYES ON MY FATHER for the first time when I was seven years old. He was this giant of a man from where I was playing on the floor in front of the television at the neighbor's house. His dark brown eyes flashed at me, his wide shoulders and massive chest expanded under a worn black leather jacket, and a chill raced up my neck. I dropped the Hot Wheels car in my hand.

He plucked me up from the floor, and we sailed through the living room, past Miss Sally, through her front hall that always smelled of Lysol right to the front door.

"Wait, wait, what's going on now?" Miss Sally said, her voice shrill, her worn house slippers shuffling behind us.

He didn't stop or slow down as he moved us out the door. "This is my kid," he said as he lifted me up onto the saddle of his towering, two-wheeled, metal monster. His voice was sure, firm. He would not be denied. My fingertips curled into the thick leather of his jacket.

Finally. Finally my dad had come for me. I had a dad like I always believed I did. Mom would never talk about him. Never ever. She'd just ignore my questions every time, huffing and puffing, making faces, grabbing another cigarette.

Miss Sally made one last effort. "Yes, but his mother—"

"How long she been gone this time?" He slid big leather gloves on his enormous hands. In fact, his whole outfit was leather. Totally cool.

Miss Sally pressed her lips together, her arms stiff. "'Bout a month this time."

He got on the monster bike and the thing jerked in his hands. With a sudden movement, it blew up and roared, shuddering underneath us. My heart raced and boomed along with that great big engine. I looked down to see the shiny metal rattling. Would I ever see this place again? Miss Sally? Mom? I didn't care, this was too exciting. New adventure. I was going somewhere new, somewhere better. I was gonna get more.

He kicked at something and we took off. Whoa. Sitting on that saddle, we were so high. So very high. He picked up speed real fast.

"Hold on, kid."

And I did. I held on real tight.

I pressed into his huge back, all of me clinging to him, to his motorcycle. He drove so fast, the laugh froze in my throat, my bones vibrating with his engine.

He was taking me home with him. A home where there'd be more than what I'd ever known so far, a more that I knew existed for me.

On the road we stopped for a burger and a milkshake, and he got me my own helmet.

He laid a hand on the top of my head over the helmet. "You like that?"

I loved it. I grinned. "Oh yeah. I like it."

Ohio.

Indiana.

Illinois.

Missouri.

We arrived at a gate that opened as if by magic. The yard was filled with men wearing jackets with blood red flames. Just like my dad's. They were all staring at me.

"What the hell is this? Who's he?" A tall, pretty, dark haired lady stood in front of us as we got off the bike.

"He's my kid," came his reply.

My kid. Heat flared over my face and down my chest.

The woman's face suddenly turned ugly, and she exploded like firecrackers on the Fourth of July. Nasty words erupted from her mouth, the same kind of words that Mommy always used when she complained about men.

She didn't want me.

"Meghan, come on!"

"How the hell do you know he's yours?"

"I just know," he said.

"That's bullshit."

"I couldn't just leave him. She'd dumped him at a neighbor's house and took off. Wasn't right." He glanced at me. "I couldn't just leave him."

I had his dark eyes, thick lashes, dark wavy hair, and a dimple in my chin just like his. He later showed me a photo of himself at my age with his dad. Yep, the three of us looked alike. Same long nose, same moody facial expression. It wasn't science, but it was enough for him. For me too.

"Well, you can do it on your own," said Meghan. "You are not bringing your bastard into my house. Not under my roof with my girls."

"They're my girls too, you know!" he shot back.

"Oh I know. Do you know?" She charged off.

"Aw, come on, Meghan! Come on, baby. What's one more mouth to feed?" He stalked off after her, the two of them yelling and lots more bad words splatting everywhere like muddy rain drops.

I stumbled. My back hurt, my legs and arms ached, my head pounded. A young lady took my hand and led me inside a building that was more warehouse than house. We walked into a kitchen with big old fashioned dingy white appliances.

"You hungry, honey?"

I shook my head. My stomach was cramping something awful. "Bathroom please."

Miss Sally always made sure I said please for everything otherwise I'd get me a dark look along with a *tsk tsk*, a lecture about ungrateful children, and a stinging pinch in my side to drive her point home. I'd learned fast.

The lady took me to a bathroom, turning on the light switch for me. I closed the door. Everything we'd eaten on the road came up and out of me. I cleaned up after myself and scrubbed my hands and face with plenty of soap and cold water.

She knocked. "You okay in there?"

I opened the bathroom door. "Tired."

"How about you lie down for a bit, huh? Take a nap. They might be a while."

"Yes, please."

She opened another door. There was a small room with no window, but a big bed with a bright blue cover, a small wooden table with bad words carved on it, and a crooked lamp. I took off my shoes and socks and fell face down on that bed. The bed cover smelled clean and powdery. Not musty like Miss Sally's or dirty like Mommy's.

I slept.

When I woke up, the room was in darkness, and I was alone. I scrounged around for my socks and shoes, put them on, and pressed down the hallway. Where was Dad? He didn't forget me, did he? No way. He'd brought me all the way here to be with him.

I entered a big, noisy room. Men wore leather vests like my father's. A lot of them had really long hair, beards and mustaches, big jewelry that looked scary and mean. They played cards, pool, drinking from bottles, watching TV.

"Hey, who's the kid?"

"He's Fuse's," answered another voice.

"Oh yeah?"

"Is that why Meghan's in an epic snit?" asked someone else.

A roar of laughter.

"Hey, kid, come sit here if you want." They made room for me on the sofa. I climbed in and sat down with them.

"Wanna slice?" A beer bottle gestured at a half empty pizza box. "Have at it."

I ate. We watched TV shows about bounty hunters, crocodiles, shark attacks. They talked loudly. I fell asleep on that sofa.

I woke up and the TV was off, but heavy breathing and soft crying filled the darkness along with the smells of old beer and smoke. I rubbed at my eyes. A girl and a man kissed and wrestled on another sofa like I used to sometimes watch Mommy do in our house.

My mouth was dry, and I got up to find something to drink. I found a cola in the fridge back in the kitchen where the light was on. Around the corner from the kitchen, feeling down the walls, I found the room where I'd slept before. I was relieved I didn't get lost. I nosedived back into that nice smelling big bed, wrapping the soft blue cover around me.

I woke up the next morning and I was still in my clothes, on that bed, in that room. Dad hadn't come for me. Tears welled up in my eyes and blinded my vision. I couldn't see the room no more. I was alone in a strange place. More than alone. My insides ached in a new, different way than all the other times before when Mom would leave me and Miss Sally would come get me.

I saw my dad two days later.

"Hey kid, how you doing, huh?" He gripped my shoulder. "You having fun?"

My stomach squeezed together like an accordion. *Fun? I guess. Sure. Wait, what?* What if I said the wrong thing?

"Uh, yeah," I replied.

"Cool." He rubbed the toe of his right boot into the ground as he stared at me. He turned and strode off, taking the moment with him.

I didn't realize it then, but that's what I'd get with my dad. A bunch of moments here and there.

I ended up staying on my own in that bedroom at the clubhouse for the next sixteen years. I was the club's kid. One of the old ladies or the girls who'd hang out would take me to school. I got fed three square meals and plenty more each day.

I didn't want to leave, so I figured out how to be useful.

By the time I was eleven, I'd learned how to cook for myself and for the others, making big batches of spaghetti and meat sauce every Thursday night for everyone. I figured out how to do laundry, separating whites, bright colors, and darks. Figured out the dishwasher, too.

At family type dinners, I watched my dad sit with Meghan and their two daughters. He sometimes ran a hand over one of the girl's braids, and the girl would barely notice as she yakked with her sister and played with her Barbie. If it had been me, I would've noticed. I would've.

I didn't live with Dad and Meghan and their two daughters at their house, and Meghan didn't let me and my half-sisters hang out or play together either. The three of them usually eyed me from a distance like I was a dirty curiosity, until eventually they'd lost interest. I barely knew them.

The "old ladies" took turns looking out for me, and Kerry was my favorite. She'd pick me up from school, help me sometimes with my homework, take me to the movies with her two kids, and bring me her homemade brownies and pie. I was older than her kids, so by the time I was thirteen, I'd babysit them once in a while.

The nights when it was just the men partying at the clubhouse without their old ladies, like when they celebrated the membership of a new brother, I'd get locked in my room. A few times they'd forget though, and I'd watch the party from the kitchen. On one of those party nights, I spotted Dad with a girl on his lap I'd never seen around before. He pulled her top off and stuck one of her boobs in his mouth. She was laughing and rubbing herself up against him. All the guys were doing different shit with different girls, drinking, smoking from bongs or just plain cigarettes.

"Oh aren't you a cutie pie?" A blonde girl came up next to me. "Hey, do you know where I can find a lighter or some matches?"

I took a lighter out of my pocket and handed it to her. I was always prepared. Someone always needed something. That was me. Water carrier. Beer bringer. Lighter bearer.

"Yay." She planted a wet kiss on my cheek and took off into the thick of the party.

The girl Dad was with did a little dance for him, and he laughed loudly.

Meghan's outrage at my existence hadn't died down all these years. Years later he'd tell me he'd brought Meghan home the clap after being with my mom. First a disease, then a kid. No wonder she was super pissed with him on a permanent basis.

I'd learned that Dad couldn't help himself where women and booze were concerned, like I couldn't say no to Oreos or chocolate ice cream. But I didn't get it. Seemed like he had stuck himself in one big stupid mess. And he still couldn't be my dad. Not like the other dads were with their kids. Like he was with his daughters.

I remained the one thing he openly denied and rejected to appease Meghan. The booze and the bitches were okay, though. He'd slapped me on the same scale as his raunchy habits, but I was the one who weighed the whole damned thing down.

I made sure I fit in at the club. This was my home now. My more than before. There was no more to be had. This was good enough, and I was good with that.

By the time I turned fifteen, Dad had landed in jail for possession. Meghan got real mad at him and started turning on the charm with Reich. Instead of returning the charm, Reich seduced her sixteen-year old daughter. I'd found them fucking on the kitchen table one night.

My room being just down from the kitchen, I used to hear a lot of shit. That night a girl's high-pitched squeaking noises had woken me up, and I went to investigate, figuring I'd see something I could use as a visual once I got back to my own bed. But what I saw nauseated me. Tracy, my half sister, had this expression on her face that was something in between fear and excitement. Reich had his one hand around her throat, and her face was red.

Reich noticed me, but kept pumping into her fast, glaring at me from the kitchen island where he had her splayed out half-naked. He tilted his head and flashed me a dramatic snarl of his white teeth, like a wolf warding off a competitor to his prey. He grabbed a tight hold of a titty, taking full possession of his meat of the day. She let out a wail.

"You like that, don't you, you little fucking tease!" he'd said through his clenched jaw, and she only moaned in reply.

I'd receded into the dark hallway once more and went back to my room where I finished a half empty bottle of bourbon I'd taken from the bar earlier. I drank and listened to the sounds of their bodies slapping together, her cries, his thick grunts.

The next day Reich threatened me, telling me to keep my mouth shut or he'd tell Meghan that I'd been the one who'd touched her precious daughter. I was sure he'd probably told Tracy to back him up on that, and I was sure she would. I knew better than to get involved in that mess. Meghan would only blame me for something.

But Meghan was no dummy. She figured out the truth real quick, and wasted no time going to the state pen and telling Dad all about it. She left him steaming, and he had his first major heart attack. That night he was taken to the hospital where I got to see him after he had a bypass operation. Meghan didn't bother visiting him. She left the club with her girls to go out east.

Two years later, when Dad got out of prison, first thing he did was go after Reich, but by that time Reich was a big shit around the club, and Dad's quest for revenge wasn't met with too much sympathy by his bros. I don't think he'd ever gotten over the lack of vengeance or the lack of true brotherhood in the face of such an injustice.

Dad didn't hear from Meghan and his girls much or talk about them, at least to me, and I was glad. I didn't give a fuck about them. They were like mosquitoes trapped in your room at night, always present, buzzing around. I was relieved to be rid of them.

As I'd gotten older, Dad had taken more of an interest in me, whenever he was around, that is. Maybe it was easier for him once I hit my late teen years; we were two guys with some shit in common. He helped me pay for my own bike and fix it up. He taught me stuff he knew well: setting bombs, setting fires for insurance fraud, covering your tracks, shooting straight, how to survive long runs, how to drink, how to roll a joint, how to fuck a woman.

I wanted nothing more than to prospect for the club once I got out of high school. He'd told me his father had been a founding member in the years after the Vietnam War. Dad had dropped out of high school and joined up in the heyday of the club in the explosion that was the seventies. Now it was my turn. The day it became official that I was to prospect, he gave me a gift. A small package covered in brown paper.

I tore open the paper.

"It was your grandad's," he said.

A brass compass slightly smaller than my palm. Dented in spots, scratched. Beautiful. Intriguing.

"Said it was his lucky charm," Dad continued. "Got him out of a lot of scrapes with the commies. It's from World War II actually. He always kept it with him, and he used it here riding. Said he needed it to keep him on the straight and narrow. If there was one thing he wasn't, though, it was straight and narrow." He laughed loudly, and I grinned at him, envious of the memories he was reliving. "He gave it to me when I got patched in, and I want you to have it now. I'm real proud of you, Kid. Real proud that you're shooting to be a Flame. He would've been too."

My heart lurched.

I wanted to hug him, needed to hug him. I would've, but I stopped myself. Dad wasn't a hugger or affectionate, even with his old lady and their daughters. If I was lucky, I'd get pats on the back here and there, a hand ruffling through my hair. I'd learned to enjoy the fleeting loaded silences between us.

I'd been a prospect for three months when I'd been taken by the Smoking Guns, taken as payback for us ignoring their warnings to stay off their territory.

Doing business on their territory with one of their contacts had been Reich's great idea, and everyone had been game. *"Show them what we're made of!"* But I remember Dad shaking his head, grumbling the words "stupid show off" as he'd lit another cigarette.

"Justin!" Dad had yelled out in the woods. That's the last thing I remember, him shouting my name. He'd never said my name before. I was hauled off by the enemy like a hunted buck deer, and Dad's deep voice had stretched out toward me in the dark.

"Justin!"

But I was on my own.

7
KID

THE NEXT TWO NIGHTS, LOADS of the guys came in bringing me stuff to eat, movies to watch, booze. Even Sandwich Girl came in and danced for us, stripping off her clothes. I'd forced myself to give everyone a few grins so they felt good about their efforts. I did appreciate it, but it was a lot of fucking noise. The movies were a blur, the girl gyrating was a blur.

Tonight, Chaz checked in on me, bringing me my favorite double cheeseburger from the local burger joint. He cracked open a beer from the six pack he'd brought with him as he watched me peel the bun off the meat. He drank as I got through half the burger and a slimy leaf of lettuce, all of it styrofoam in my mouth, my stomach churning.

He snapped open a third beer. A fourth. He was uncomfortable. "Man, sorry about your dad. He was a one in a million. Kerry told me she told you about it."

"Yeah."

"You know how I felt about him." He glanced at me, then went back to staring at his beer can, rubbing the smooth aluminum. "He was real special to me."

I said nothing. I covered my burger remnants with the greasy paper wrapper.

Chaz sniffed in air. "We had a good funeral for him. Stellar. He woulda loved it, you know. We sang all his favorites. Real good turnout."

"How did it happen? Tell me the truth."

"Heart attack. He was real upset about you—"

"Chaz, come on. It was just him and Reich here late at night?"

"Yeah."

"You gonna believe Reich?"

Chaz shifted his weight in the creaky wooden chair. "You need to watch what you say, Kid. Yeah, they'd been arguing. Your dad wasn't happy with the way negotiations were going with the Smoking Guns to get you free. He wanted definitive blow out, full scale invasion and retrieval of you. Cooper and Reich, they thought it was better—"

"To sacrifice me?"

"They thought it was wiser if we played it cool, see how far the Guns would take it." He glanced at my bandaged hands. "They took it far all right. Thing was, we really didn't think they'd kill you, you know?"

"And what did you think?"

"I wanted to get you out first thing, but all eyes were on us, Kid. They were gonna play with us, play with you, get their licks in, make their point, and in the end give it up. Give you up. Coop thought it was best to wait it out, give them the opportunity to shoot themselves in the foot."

I was collateral damage. A calculated expense in the throes of political maneuvers and battle strategies.

My dad had argued with Reich over how negotiations were going or not going with the Smoking Guns over my release. Had Reich killed him or just got him angry enough to set off a heart attack? Dad had been denying his bad health for a while. Blood pressure, cholesterol, you name it, he had it. Whatever happened that night, my father had stood up for what was right. For me.

"Hey, Fuse fixed your Panhead before he—" Chaz's voice brought my attention back to my gloomy room, the stench of french fries and burger grease still hanging in the air.

"He did?"

"Yeah. It's waiting on you."

At least there was that, my bike, the one he'd help me choose, the one he'd shown me how to ride, keep clean, keep in tune. My sore eyes fell on his urn.

Chaz let out a huff of air. "You gonna get outta this bed and outta this room or what?"

"I will. I have to." I'd also have to learn how to hold a fork, use a pen again, and grip my handlebars. And I would.

"We gotta just put this shit behind us," muttered Chaz. "We gotta move on from this. The FBI and the ATF are breathing down our necks just waiting for us to blow, to get crazy. We've got too much at stake right now, and business has been real tight for too long. We got to play it cool for a while, gain some ground back."

He crushed his empty beer can and stuffed the oily food wrappers in the take out bag. This was him making sure that I didn't get crazy and towed the party line. Laying down the law for me, while expressing empathy for my situation.

Real kind of him.

He lit the cigarette he had stashed behind his ear and leaned back in the chair once more. He needed to confirm that I was on board with the plan, that I wouldn't make trouble for Reich.

Chaz let out a short, loud laugh. "The pain getting any better? We got plenty of shit for that."

Med's frenzied crystal fog-filled eyes flashed before me, and I winced.

"Nah, I'm good. Don't need anything," I lied.

AFTER CHAZ LEFT, TAKING HIS fast food debris and pointed words with him, I leaned over and opened the top desk drawer and got out my compass. The sight of it within my bandaged mutilated hand made my breath catch in my throat and burn there. This was my new reality.

What would my grandad say if he could see me? Dad? My eyes filled with water, and I wiped at them with my other hand. I carefully propped the compass up on the dresser and dropped back against the mattress, staring at the antique. I didn't know what was ahead for me, but I would handle it, just like my grandad and my dad, head on.

The nightmares would be back again tonight, just like every

night. Those hands holding me down. Holding me down while the cuts blazed into me. But at least this time, when I did wake up, I'd have the compass in front of me, to remind me that I was made of sterner stuff, that I too was a survivor. I would probably face even greater hells in time, but for now, for right now, I could handle this, because I had good, strong men behind me who had handled just as much crazy as any man.

I wiped the cold sweat from my face and throat. I gulped in air. No more feeling helpless, no more feeling powerless, weak, vulnerable. Exposed. I would obliterate all that shit, commanding a force from within me any way I could. I had choices. I could change course.

North. South. East. West.

Staring at my compass, my eyes finally drifted shut.

I WAS PATCHED IN THE MOMENT I could stand without wobbling.

I put on the new leather vest Chaz presented to me. Flames colors. My club. I was following in my grandad and my dad's footsteps. Chaz smacked me once on the back. Reich did the same and pushed me toward Lyon, the club secretary, who squeezed my shoulder.

"Congrats, Kid. Your father would be real proud if he could see you now."

Chaz whistled sharply, and we all turned our attention to Coop, the president.

"Fuck 'em," my president's voice rumbled through the meeting room. "They took your fingers, but they didn't take your pride, your will to survive. You're a man. Now, a brother. They took and tortured, but you held on. You wear your scars with pride just like your colors. You battled, and you won. Your soul, your heart, your mind got nothing to do with the scratches on your face and a missing finger or two."

And so I was named.

Finger. Reminding me of what I'd lost. How I'd paid for my club loyalty in flesh and blood and bone. Yet also reminding me of my tenacity, my determination.

I'd gotten what I'd wanted for so long—to be a full-fledged brother of the Flames of Hell. I was in. This was it. And I'd earned it

But my dad wasn't here to congratulate me. To beam a proud smile, to lift that sharp edged and dimpled chin of his at me like he had a few memorable times before.

"A dimple in the chin means the devil within," he'd told me when as a boy I'd first poked my finger into that indentation of his flesh and he'd poked his finger into mine and we'd laughed.

The party to celebrate my membership played like a puppet show on the stage of my whirling emotions. I was the audience of one, sitting alone in the theater, strapped to the seat.

I'd survived, but with Dad gone, I had no one to come home to. My thoughts went to Serena, as they usually did. Hell, I wouldn't be alive if it wasn't for her. Her kindness, understanding with a word, a look, her touch. But she was still there, suffering at the hands of that maniac.

"I like being alive."

Rena wanted to live, and the sheer force of that quiet yet iron will of hers humbled me. I wanted to help her make that dream of a real life come true.

Did she miss me like I missed her? It was more than just missing somebody. A power supply had been cut off, unplugged. Suddenly, I was disconnected from something necessary that I hadn't been aware of ever before. Not like this.

Had things gotten worse for her? Med enjoyed ratcheting up the intensity of his games once he got started. He'd punished her for some unknown sin that last night and maybe he was continuing that punishment. She'd probably lost her old lady status. Maybe he would ditch her. Fuck, we both knew what that meant. I wanted her alive and living a real life, be that with me or without me. Not suffering a prisoner's nightmare.

"Finger." My VP stood in front of me.

I blinked at Chaz.

He slanted his head. "Man, you good?"

"Yeah, sure. Yeah." I shrugged and scanned the crowded room

once again, trying to look interested in the doings. Trying not to feel sick.

"Join the party. It's your party. Got bitches here who want a piece of you." Chaz put an arm around my shoulder, and I stiffened, my throat closed. I unstuck myself from his arm.

"Sorry," he mumbled.

I didn't like anyone touching me. Not anymore. In the short time that I'd been home they'd all figured that out. My sullenness, my unwillingness to talk, kept most of them at a distance anyhow.

"Dude, you pissing on your own party?" Reich asked, swigging a beer from a long neck. "Get out there and blow off that steam, motherfucker."

I ground my jaw and shot him a glare. His face soured, and he turned away, slinging his arm over some girl.

"Come on, brother. Let it go. Time to celebrate," said Chaz, his voice softer than usual. Concern laced with impatience. I'd been crowned tonight. I had a new life now. I needed to play the part.

I did my best to crack a grin. A flash of stinging pain raced over my tight skin, and I swallowed it back down like a balloon of cocaine. "You're right."

I drank, I smoked, I danced. I got high. I got drunk. I threw up the tequila I'd downed at the sight of sliced white bread in the piles of sandwiches the girls had made. I looked for Serena's face in the crowd. Hoping. Hoping.

I threw myself on a sofa, too dizzy to stand. A woman straddled me and kissed my chest, my throat, my face. My scars stung under her lips. My lungs squeezed. I was hard as a rock.

I can't. I can't.

It was her warm skin against mine. The scent of her sweat and perfume in my nostrils. Yeah, I'd be with her, my body flaring to life under her, and then...then...

The flickers shivered through me, the torment simmered. I focused on the face inches from mine. Not Serena's mouth, not Serena's eyes.

"Get off me!" I grabbed the girl's arms and shoved her away.

She slid down on the floor between my legs on a laugh, tugged down the zipper of my jeans and swallowed my dick.

I twisted away from her. "I said fucking stop!"

"Yeah, that's what he needs, give it to him!" Reich's voice jumped out at me. He shoved the girl back on me, keeping her head down over me, and she took me in deeper.

Images of *her* eyes, the feel of *her* mouth, *her* body against mine assaulted me. I chased them all.

Serena.

I raised my hips, jamming my dick in her throat, and it scraped past her teeth. Something behind my eyes exploded, and I grunted at the flash of pain. Yes, the pain. That was real, that was familiar.

That was me and Serena.

My blood rushed into my skull as the orgasm crushed my insides. I moaned out loud, but not in pleasure. That phantom pain raced like electricity over my hands to where my middle fingers once were, across the skin of my face. My heart twisted tight as I waited for the knives...the roar of pain...that fuck's laughter. Serena's mouth was on me, wasn't it? Her hands gripped my shattered body. The ghost of her caresses prickled over my skin.

I waited, but she wasn't there, she wasn't there. Not the lazy flick of her tongue, the nuzzling of her soft lips, the deep press of her fingertips in my flesh signaling *I'm here for you, we got this, we can.*

I'd never associated coming with a specific girl. Getting off was getting off. But not now. Now I needed Serena. She was inside my orgasms. I wanted *her*. I needed *her*.

Where the fuck are you, Serena?

The girl released me and, pushing down on my thighs, lifted up from the floor. She strolled off in her high-heeled boots.

I had to get out of here.

Staggering toward my room, my forehead slammed against the wall. This wasn't what I wanted. This wasn't enough.

Not anymore.

I'd never known what expectations felt like, never known any way better than the way I'd grown up. Never put a label on my situation, my feelings. My shoulders slumped, my insides ached. I wasn't the club's kid anymore.

All those years I'd burned for something I'd never known, and now I knew what that was. It was stronger than me. It was grinding and crushing and exhilarating, and I was nothing but dust before it. My throat thickened, my vision got hazy. I allowed that dark shadowy sensation to seep through and sink me to the bottom of my murky ocean. For the first time ever in my scrap of a fucking life I could name it, and I had to face it.

Loneliness.

So much goddamn loneliness.

I slid to the floor. Good enough was no longer enough.

Nothing is enough.

Still, deep, deep in the pit of my soul, a sad but clear pair of blue green eyes smoldered through the blur. Her long fingers beckoned me, her deep, steady voice promised me, her touch embraced me, and the pressure lifted off my chest. No, there was no escaping her. There would never be any escape.

I took in a long, deep breath and exhaled slowly. I had to make her escape happen.

For the first time in what felt like forever, that dead weight in my chest lifted.

And I smiled.

8
FINGER

Dᴀʏs ʀᴏʟʟᴇᴅ ʙʏ.

One week connected to the next.

I got assignments, and I got them done. I spoke when spoken to. I hung out with the bros as often I could bear it. I hated calling attention to myself anymore than I had to, I was already enough of a freak with my fucked up hands and facial scars. Not to mention those looks of pity.

Spring was finally sticking around, and we were on a run to Austin, Texas. It felt so damned good to be back on my bike and riding for a long stretch on the open road. No ice, no snow, no rain. All of us in our tight formation, Flames before and behind me on the highway, Flames as far as the eye could see. We had stopped at a big bar on the outskirts of town. My eyes followed Reich, who as usual was the center of attention, the life of the party. He had a new girlfriend he'd brought with him, and was parading her around the crowded parking lot, shaking hands with men from another friendly club, not a care in the world.

I still couldn't shake the bitterness inside me over the part Reich had played in my dad's demise. I fanned those flames inside me every chance I got. It was my addiction.

"Man, you okay?"

I tore my focus away from Reich and steadied my gaze on Gyp, who'd been a fellow prospect and was now a junior member like me.

"Yeah, yeah, I'm great."

"Have another beer."

I was wasted already, but I took the icy bottle from him and drank deep.

"You two oversee the prospects guarding our bikes," said a familiar cutting voice.

"Us?" blurted out Gyp.

You didn't talk back like that to an order. I raised my head. Reich stood in front of us, his bitch on his arm. "You want to rethink your question, fuckhead? You gotta show 'em how it's done, Gyp. Lotta clubs out here from all over. Ain't taking any chances."

"Yeah, 'course. We'll make sure everything's good out here," Gyp replied, his teeth dragging along his thick lip, his left leg shaking. His nervous tic. He had to cut that shit out.

Reich laughed, his attention shifting to me. "Yeah. How about you, cowboy? You been keeping mighty quiet these days. You got anything to say?"

"Nope."

"Huh," his eyes narrowed at me. He strode off.

Gyp and I stayed outside with the two prospects and made sure no one touched or breathed on our brothers' bikes. There were plenty of people out here, everyone talking shit, sharing weed, buying and selling almost everything else, checking out each other's rides. After a few hours the party inside had emptied out to the parking lot and the open area was banging with music and liquor and food service.

Reich was talking with Demon Seeds from Montana and One-Eyed Jacks from Colorado. Making cocktail party talk, slapping hands on shoulders, laughing at stupid jokes, flirting with different women, while he flirted with someone else.

A fight broke out just past where our last bike was parked.

"Stay here!" I shouted at Gyp over the roar of the crowd in the lot. I loved a good fight and was sick of standing around playing classroom monitor. Anyhow, Gyp was messing around with some girl he'd met, and he wasn't about to go nowhere. He already had his tongue down her throat and his hand up her skirt.

One of our guys was involved in the fight, and I dove in to take his back. I got shoved and shoved back. People slammed into me, and I slammed right back. The booze, the wild jungle vibe, the driving metal music of the band playing only took me higher and deeper into the crush. I punched, I slugged, I bashed.

A hand grabbed me by the jacket collar and pulled. Reich.

"Get the fuck off me!" I yelled, twisting in his grip.

He sneered. "You nuts or something? You got five guys on you!"

That ages old hatred and resentment blistered inside me. I didn't care about the five or five hundred men hitting me, I only cared that Reich was in my face. "Get off me, asshole!"

"Such a shit! Just like your ol' man."

"Fuck you! He'd still be here if it wasn't for you. You—You killed him! You killed my dad, I know you did!"

He grabbed me by the throat and pulled me out of the throng like a school principal dragging a misbehaving boy out of the playground. He shoved me up against the high fence. "Listen and listen good. Your old man was a pain in my ass. Wouldn't shut the fuck up, always arguing, butting in, contradicting just to hear himself blow air in the room."

"My dad lived and breathed this club. It was literally in his fucking blood. He stood up for what he thought was right." I ground my heels into the asphalt, my head twisting.

Reich's eyebrows arched high and tight. "What he thought was wrong. You gonna tell me different now?"

"My dad was fighting for me. For the dignity of the Flames."

"Dignity?" He let out a dry laugh, his eyes piercing mine. "There's a fine word. Bet you don't even know the meaning of it."

I knew what Reich thought of me. I was the club puppy, the junkyard mutt. I was there to do his bidding only, not be a true brother, not to have a voice.

"You got to learn your place." His tone seethed.

"My place? All my life I've been tucked into a place and stayed there, head down, out of people's way, convenient for everybody else. Not anymore!" I pushed against him, and he head-butted me.

I reeled backwards, pain exploding through my skull.

"There's plenty more if you don't watch your mouth. You have no idea what it takes to run a club, make tough decisions."

I steadied myself on my feet. "Yeah, you're really impressing me now."

His hands flew in my face, his arms snapping my head flat against the ground. He pushed himself on me, his beer breath filling my nostrils. "Don't you ever fucking open your mouth to me again. I swear I'm gonna finish what the Smoking Guns started by slicing off that tongue and feeding it to my dog. You're here to obey orders and do as you're told. Not to question, not to make waves."

He released me, pushing me forward and kicking me in the back. I skidded to the pavement, the side of my face scraping on the gravelly cement, the pain excruciating. Brand new, pointy, dark brown boots appeared in my sightline.

Reich kicked me in the side. "You feeling me now, kid?"

I choked on the dust and dirt, blood on the back of my hand where I'd wiped my face.

He spit on the ground and walked off.

My head throbbed, and pain radiated through my body. I pushed myself over onto my back and gulped in fresh air, but the air wasn't fresh. The thick humidity of the night was ripe with pot and cigarettes, beer on cement, scorched rubber on asphalt.

Reich was going to pay. One day I would make him pay.

T WO WEEKS LATER, OUR CHAPTER got back from Texas. We had a meeting to go over old business and new.

"One more thing," Coop announced, his hands spread open on the table. "Finger, you're being sent to the northern Nebraska chapter of the Flames of Hell. Membership has been dwindling down there and they need good people."

My back stiffened. Northern Nebraska? One of the shittiest chapters on the map.

Chaz's face was set in a scowl as he busied himself collecting a bunch of maps and papers into a pile. The other members muttered and sighed, shifting in their seats, sharing glances.

"Nebraska?" I repeated.

"What the fuck?" Gyp mumbled next to me, a hand tugging through his spiky black hair.

Down the long meeting table, Reich studied me, his muscular

arms folded tightly across his chest, a toothpick shifting between his lips.

He couldn't just take me out, or keep making my life miserable. Nah, he wouldn't dare. I was a symbol for the Flames now. With my pedigree, POW status, and scars, I was a huge asset, a living testimonial to standing up to the brutality of the enemy, and also of the new treaty between our historically hostile clubs.

Nebraska. Change.

I needed a change. I was chased by ghosts here, wasn't I? Ghosts of my past and an uncertain present, not to mention a future that seemed distant, unclear. I was still living in that same small dorm room I grew up in at the club, for shit's sake, surrounding myself with bits and scraps I'd scavenged.

Somewhere else, I could make something of myself without all this drama if I put in the effort. Yes, even in Nebraska.

Something for me.

What do I have? My colors.

In Nebraska I wouldn't be Reich's bitch waiting for him to drop kick me whenever he felt like it, however it entertained him. Things in Nebraska were crap, bottom rung on the ladder, but I could work with that. That was an opportunity.

It was time for me to invest in me.

I could finally plan on getting Serena out and bringing her with me, keeping her safe.

I had to plan.

When I was fourteen, I'd gone out one night with my dad to set a bomb at this rich guy's house who owed money to someone the club owed a favor to. My dad had set up this intricate wiring in his basement workroom, then at three in the morning we'd laid it out at the target location, setting up the bells and whistles.

"Why don't you just set up a thingamajig with a remote control and let that be the end of it?" I'd whined in the icy cold air, slipping on a patch of mud for the tenth time.

He'd grabbed onto my arm and pulled me close to him. "I don't just blow shit up, Kid. I design an experience. It's a thing of wonder for them and for me. You know those cartoons and old western movies with the long cord connected to the pack of dynamite? And it sparks along, traveling up the cord until kaboom, it blows?"

"Yeah, yeah, of course."

"There may not be cords and dynamite packs anymore, but I still set the distance, the time interval of the kaboom—it's a dance. I don't just blow shit up like some moron. You got to consider the timing, the spectacle, and the afterwards. Each one has its own requirements and rewards. It's up to you to set the time for yourself to move to a safe distance, 'cause you still want to be part of the experience. At least, I do. It demands patience, planning, precise calculating. And many times you need to improvise at the last minute. You gotta be ready for anything at any time." His eyes actually gleamed. "Any jackass can mouth off, pick a fight, shoot his gun. What I'm talking about takes creativity. Know your opponent, be conscious of the blow back, where the particles will fall. And leave no clues behind. It's always tempting to go the big immediate route, but trust me. It ain't worth it. Most assholes don't get that, but I'm telling you, it's worth the work you put into it."

My father, the Fuse, was a fucking smart man.

A smile broadened my lips, my gaze remaining on Reich.

Yeah, Nebraska.

I leaned forward on the great wood table, folding my hands together. "Nebraska, huh? Cool."

Chaz glanced at me, sitting up in his chair. Reich's eyes narrowed at me, his brow a tense ridge. His highly anticipated explosive device had malfunctioned.

"They need good people there. You'll be an asset, Finger." Coop knocked his gavel against wood, and my pulse thudded.

Fuck you, Reich.

I pushed back from the table and strode out the door. I packed my extra pair of boots, my two other jackets, the few clothes I had, the compass, and headed for my bike.

I never wanted to be reminded of that room again. That room being the only home I'd ever known since I was seven years old. All the shit in it—the small TV, the clock radio, the posters, the worn out blankets, the whatever the fuck, weren't mine, but theirs, and I wanted no part of any of it no more. I was going to shake all of it and all of them off me like dust.

Dust.

I grabbed the urn filled with my dad's remains.

"Finger, wait up!" Gyp came running after me as I loaded the back of my bike. "Oh man, this sucks."

"Nah, it's fine. It's better this way. I'm good with it." I pulled tight on the bungee straps over my duffle bag and clipped them over the back.

"You left a lot of shit behind. You want me to pack it up and send it to you?"

"No. You take whatever you want. Dump the rest."

"You sure?"

"I'm sure."

"Shit, I'm gonna miss you." Gyp hugged me and let me go real quick. "Sorry."

I shrugged. "Come for a visit."

He shoved his hands in his pockets. "Yeah."

I got on my Panhead and started her up. Her roar warmed my blood in the cold morning air. I swung out of the property and took off.

Three and a half hours later on Highway 136, I finally got to the border of Nebraska at Brownville. The iron suspension bridge spanning the Missouri River beckoned me in the distance.

I pulled over at the side of the road, grabbed the urn and headed into a grove of trees. I hurled my father's ashes over the straggly green grasses and short bushes, dumping the urn.

"Goodbye, Fuse."

He belonged here. I didn't. I knew I didn't.

I got back on my bike and started her up, my eyes landing on the old narrow truss bridge over the Missouri. My pulse picked up, I grinned. It was hardly a magnificent gateway to a new life, but it was my gateway, my new world.

I would create my own place in the Elk charter, and I would earn it, make it mine.

Up on the slight incline of the ramp I kicked up my speed and crossed over the great river into Nebraska.

9
FINGER

Reich wanted me out, and he got it. But I wanted Reich to remember me and my fucking dignity. To remember that I knew. That I'd always be watching him. That he hadn't put me down; he had to reckon with me.

A few weeks later I returned to Missouri.

A party raged at the clubhouse. One of those open house occasions to ring in the summer. The type of party where the club's infamous "moon juice" was brewed. A shiny trash can filled with all kinds of booze and gallon jugs of cheap and colorful juice. A whole bottle of liquid LSD would be added to unhinge the ride from the rollercoaster track, and tabs of peace and sunshine acid would be thrown in for extra sparkles. A real Hawaiian Punch bomb.

The club was jammed full of people hunting the ultimate good time, hangers on wanting to prove themselves, chicks wanting to get noticed.

I waited.

I didn't want to be seen or be recognized by anybody, so the waiting was fine by me when the end result would be so fucking sweet and last so fucking long.

Four a.m.

I slid through the gap in the fence at the back that Gyp had once repaired and done a totally shit job on. A few men staggered through the courtyard, a woman's laughter rose in the distance. No music, no bike engines.

He'd be in his room off the left hallway.

I pushed at the half open door, rumbling breathing rose from the bed across the room. Reich was on his back naked. A naked blonde lay at his side, her face by his feet, his hand on the ass of another naked girl sprawled on his other side. Perfect.

Reich loved moon juice. He loved making it. He was the master of ceremonies. The showman of the grand cocktail. The warlock of the juju. He always made a big show of mixing it up with this huge wooden paddle he'd found at a hardware store. Then he'd make girls line up, lick it, and he'd paddle their asses with it—the paddle parade contest or some shit, he'd called it—and the prize was licking his cock. So creative. Sure enough, the paddle lay on the floor by the foot of his big bed. The stale stench of berries and alcohol fumes lingered over it, mingling with the odor of sweat and sex.

I bit down on a smile and slid the door closed. I put on my thin latex gloves, slipped the box cutter from my back pocket and leaned over him. Taking his soft dick in my hand, I slashed at his foreskin. Blood spurted on my fingers, and my pulse pounded at the sight, feeding my lust to take more from him. A beast unfurled inside me demanding more. A beast whose hunger was raw and desperate. I cut him in sure, precise strokes. No hesitation, no fear, only satisfaction buzzed through me.

Keeping up with my hand and grip exercises had really come through for me.

Reich howled, his eyes jerking open, his body flinching, hands searching in the dark. His eyes rolled in the back of his head, body twisting, and he whimpered and fought for air, but he was oblivious, clueless, still tripping.

He settled, and I made two more quick slashes until I was happy with my quasi-circumcision. I wanted him to live with a mark, my mark on his precious tool. Let him feel pain and anxiety whenever he got a hard on, and humiliation at his scarred cock. His "intact" cock was his pride for sure; he'd always bragged about how he wasn't cut and more of a man since there was more of him. Now I'd made his dick ugly. Just enough that he'd always be reminded that he'd been assaulted when he was down. Maybe he'd get some kind of infection, definitely a scar. He would never know how it happened, who did it to him, but it would be there and he would know and so would I. He'd never tell anyone about it, I was sure of it.

I slid my box cutter in my back pocket. "For my dad, you fuck. For me."

Reich's eyes jerked open at the sound of my voice and darted over me. Those rubbery lips warbled, sounds croaked from his mouth. His head knocked back on a groan, eyes closed.

My heart pounded full and hard, the surge of adrenaline through my veins intense. I was glad he opened his eyes and saw me. Once he sobered up, he'd never be sure if he'd really seen me or he'd been hallucinating. The question would always be there in his mind, forever teasing him with my venom.

I prowled out of that clubhouse, savoring the rush. Excitement, satisfaction on a whole other level. I rode hard all the way back to Elk, making the ten hours it normally would have taken, barely eight.

My thirst for revenge on that fucker was sated for now. But I knew it was a thirst for a sweet frothy cocktail that would never end.

Damn, I liked the flavor.

10
FINGER

"YOU'RE GONNA LOVE THIS BLAST, man. Especially since blowing shit up is your favorite hobby." Drac burst into a rich rolling laugh, handing me a fresh beer.

His long, fang-like incisors showed in his wide grin, hence his nickname for the most famous vampire of them all. Plus, he seemed to stay pale as snow all year long.

When I first landed at the Flames clubhouse in Elk, Nebraska—a clubhouse that was a rented crumbling old farmhouse with boarded up windows, a newly installed bar and a pool table with a broken leg—Drac, who was Sergeant-at-Arms, and I had clicked from the moment we met.

He was friendly without being annoying, fair minded and practical, and had a wicked sense of humor without being a clown. Unlike me, he found the positive in most shit. I didn't speak or laugh much, and Drac often tried translating my moods and expressions and usually got it right. He didn't get put off by those moods, and he didn't fill the silences between us with too much talk. I liked him. Other than Drac and the Prez, the handful of other members seemed pretty sluggish and indifferent about life in general.

We were in South Dakota at a night blast at the Crazy Horse Memorial. I was really looking forward to seeing this series of continuous mini-explosions blasting the granite of the mountain. Crazy Horse's face was outlined in rock, a feat which had taken decades. His horse and his pointing arm still had to be fully cut. Holy hell, that was patience, dedication to a cause. Here was a thing of dynamic beauty and dignity wrought from a harsh mountain of unforgiving rock.

I really liked the Great Plains. The land in Nebraska and the Dakotas was different from Missouri. Maybe I'd never paid too much attention to Missouri, but now that I'd chosen to call Nebraska home, the area intrigued me. The riding was amazing from lush grasslands, dense forests and reservoirs, to the endless prairies and the ominous Badlands. Extremes for every mood were to be found in the Dakotas and Nebraska. Of course, you had to deal with brutal cold and snow, but it was worth it. I liked that extreme cycle of seasons. Clear markers of the passing of time. A lot of people consider the flat, open space of the area tedious, monotonous. Not me. I was impressed by the massive scope of the land. I felt bound to the earth as I rode it.

In the short while that I'd been here, I'd spearheaded cleaning up and renovating the old rundown farmhouse the chapter rented for a clubhouse. The Prez, Bill "Kwik" Kwikowski let me run with it, and I did. No more rusted holes, badly repaired fences, mildewed roof, crap plumbing. We got an up to date security system and new, higher fences. The one barn at the front of the property got upgraded into an industrial type warehouse to lessen any kind of curb appeal from passers by. I'd insisted on a real workout room, and we invested in new weights and barbells and a good bench. Continuing to push myself with the exercises and workouts Ryan had given me, I'd gotten stronger than I'd ever been before.

I volunteered for every shit job and for every difficult job. The men in the club were slightly in awe of me at first and kept their distance. Drac was the only one who treated me like a person, a brother, a potential friend, not some anomaly.

The first week I'd landed here, the VP had gotten himself killed running a red light, sliding in a patch of black ice, and crashing into a supermarket truck. The following week, Kwik had me ride shotgun with him and Drac to Montana for negotiations with clubs from out west he was dealing with, the Demon Seeds being one of them. They didn't take our chapter too seriously, considering it an insignificant outpost of the Flames of Hell. I kept silent. My harshly scarred poker face did all the talking for me, inciting tension at that first meeting.

While everyone else did a lot of talking and bullshitting, I observed. I listened to what was being said underneath the words, behind the gestures. A different story emerged, as it usually did. I dug some on my own and found out about an alternate deal the Demon Seeds were trying to keep on the QT, shutting us out. Armed with this information, Kwik was able to make negotiations go his way.

Kwik liked my unassuming initiative. Drac liked my instincts. I got elected VP once we got back to Nebraska.

I knew that every effort I made, every job I completed, put me one step closer to getting Serena in my life. A life where no one would have any control over us.

Here at the Crazy Horse Memorial, I had a quick meeting with Dig Quillen, the Sergeant at Arms of the One-Eyed Jacks in nearby Meager, South Dakota. Dig and I had known each other from a run down to Colorado when I'd first gotten to the club in Nebraska. Whenever we'd seen each other, on the road, at bars, at concert venues, we were carefully friendly. Ordinarily, I kept my distance from members of other clubs, but the Jacks were located nearby, just over two hours away, so it paid to be "friendly." Anyway, him I didn't mind. He wasn't a show off, and he didn't have a chip on his shoulder or a big dick complex that he shoved in your face with every gesture or word that came out of his mouth. He didn't talk shit and had a good sense of humor too, even if I barely let it show that I thought he was funny. He seemed respectful, and I liked that.

I'd tested his waters a couple of weeks ago. I had an emergency, one brother out when his old lady was having a baby, and I'd needed someone to fill in on a moment's notice on a delivery to a contact in southwestern Wyoming and everyone else was in Ohio at a Flames assembly. I took the risk and called Dig.

My Prez was interested in pushing at the Jacks to see where they lay in the bigger picture in the area. They were a small club, only with another chapter in North Dakota and one in Colorado. Were they more useful to us cooperative or crushed? We knew the Demon Seeds had been making life and business difficult for them for years now. We could help them out for a price if they needed a big brother to step in. Always good to have alliances with smaller clubs against the larger ones.

I contacted Dig, and he got my job done. He didn't tell his crew, and I didn't tell mine. When it was done, I was impressed, and he got rewarded, but he refused the money. Instead, he wanted to stay in touch and be available for me in the future.

Today he'd requested two minutes of my time. I met up with him by the bathrooms at the Memorial an hour before the blast. Native American singing and drum beats filled the air from a show given by Native dancers on a small stage across the center as I made my way to the designated spot.

Dig was pleased to see me, and relieved, judging from his grin. He made a pitch—a network, an alliance between the Flames, his club, and the Broken Blades, another small club who were our neighbors in Nebraska.

"The three of us form a velvet network in our region through our territories. A network no outsider is going to want to fuck with and never will."

The Jacks were obviously feeling the heat from the Demon Seeds these days.

I took in a long slow breath. "We don't work with other clubs longterm, Dig. You know that."

"I know. We like our independence, too, and want to keep it that way," he replied. "Our clubs have been coexisting peacefully for years, respecting each other from afar. Why can't our organizations work together if it's mutually beneficial? We could keep it simple. Offer you a specific service at a discount, of course. I've noticed a few glitches here and there between you and the Blades. I could help."

He gave me a few examples. Dig was observant, smart. He wasn't talking out of his ass, making a play to get a backstage pass. He saw the road ahead was paved with Demon Seed intervention and pressure on the smaller clubs in our region.

"I'll talk to my prez," I said, giving Dig my standard response.

His shoulders eased, his odd light brown eyes flared. He was good with it. "Okay. I'll wait to hear from you. You need anything in the meantime, let me know. I'll take care of it myself."

I believed him.

We tagged fists, and I took off, heading into the full crowd that had gathered for the night blast. I found Drac and Slade, another brother we hung with. Couldn't miss his mohawk.

"How'd it go?" Drac asked, draining his can of beer.

"It went." I took a long swig and wiped a hand across my mouth. "The Demon Seeds keep squeezing the Jacks, soon enough they'll be squeezing the Broken Blades at some point, just to get in our face on our turf. Ultimately, Dig's after our protection through an alliance."

"You know Vig, the Seed's VP, has been out in Cali hanging with fucking Russians. Could get messy," said Slade.

"From what I hear, it's already messy. Vig's got some balls, man," Drac said.

"Dig wants no part of messy," I said. "He doesn't want the Jacks to be a sitting duck to anyone's shit, and I don't blame him. The Jacks have got a good thing going and they're good at keeping things low key. They could be an asset. Dig's product gets rave reviews. We could get in on that, make it ours one day."

"We could. You bringing it to Kwik?" asked Slade.

"Definitely."

The sun had set and the night sky was perfectly dark, sparked with a sea of stars. The fireworks started as a prelude to the main event. The blast began and it was nothing short of magic. The series of small fires illuminated Crazy Horse's stern face in the rock. The pounding successive explosions detonated in the big sky on a stunning primitive beat. Drac and Slade were speechless, their lips parted, their faces glowing gold in the reflections of the fires.

My eyes wandered over the crowd near us. Plenty of bikers from different clubs were here tonight. I spotted Dig, his arms wrapped around a young woman. I'd done my homework on Dig Quillen. He had an old lady, Grace or "Sister" as they called her. She was around twenty-two, but looked younger, the girl next door. They'd been together for over a year and both still seemed totally into each other, attached, like they were high on being together. He bent over and whispered in her ear, and they both grinned. All was right in their world. No rough seas, no questions.

Dig kissed Sister, starting off slow and sweet and then it turned hungry. Something coiled tightly in my chest. Those two had a place together. Serena flashed in front of my eyes in the darkness, and my muscles seized as if I'd gotten stung by a wasp. I wanted her here with me, like Quillen had his woman at his side, giving him a look that said she adored him, trusted him, was a part of him, was his and was thrilled to be, come what fucking may.

Yeah, the come what fucking may was easier when you were together.

The eruptions ceased and the crowd cheered and applauded.

Sister gave Dig a warm satisfied smile, wrapping her arm around his waist as their crew left the mountain along with the massive crowd. My insides curled in burning heat like paper in fire.

I wanted what Dig had.

I'd never had a girlfriend. Didn't know what that felt like or was supposed to be like. And I didn't mean just some woman I slept with on a regular basis or hung out with. No, a connection. I knew I wanted to see that satisfied smile of Sister's on Serena's face. I wanted to feel the weight of her relaxed body against mine. I wanted to give her this cloudless star-filled night of fireworks and explosions and music, where the only thing she had to worry about was what outfit to wear, what to pack for a camping trip, what souvenirs she wanted me to buy her. Because she'd want a souvenir. She'd want to preserve these moments of ours together. They'd be new, and to us they'd always be that kind of significant, shiny special.

Not—*would this be the night she'd get killed? Would this be the night they'd drag her back, tear her to shreds? String me up and chop me?*

I'd make it happen, her and me, and I'd give her all the shiny, special she needed.

"Let's go," Slade muttered.

Slade, Drac, and I took off, leaving the crowd at the Crazy Horse Monument behind and headed for the campground just past Mt. Rushmore, where our club waited for us.

We got lost in the party, and the next day, as I finally left the long line at the beer truck, I saw a familiar face.

"Gyp!"

Still the same tall, skinny goof with olive skin and messy jet black hair, every inch the gypsy. I slapped a hand on his shoulder. "What are you doing here, man? Good to see you!"

He slung an arm around my shoulders. "I called Nebraska, and they said you were out here, so I was hoping to catch you. I'm on my way back to Missouri. Had to visit my mom in Utah, she just got married."

"How many does this make?"

He laughed, snorting loudly. "The fifth, I think. She's happy, whatever. I came through this way to see you."

"Glad you did. Real glad. This is Slade and Drac."

"Hey."

The four of us roamed over the campgrounds, drinking and talking. We checked out the games and bike races some of the clubs were having.

"I really miss this, Finger, miss hanging out with you." Gyp drained another watery beer.

"Me too. You doing good out there? Things okay at the club?"

Gyp shrugged. "Yeah sure, I guess. Money's coming in steadier nowadays, so Coop's happy, Chaz is happy. Reich left by the way."

My pulse skipped at the sound of that name. "Oh yeah?"

"Yeah, he took off for Ohio."

"For National?" Our national board was located just outside of Dayton.

"He's been real jumpy and paranoid since you left. Losing his shit over nothing all the time. Shit got crazy." Gyp shook his head. "He got himself transferred to the chapter out there and seems to have settled in real nice. Guess he's in line for the big leagues, eh?"

Reich had taken off. I guess getting his dick assaulted was a real nasty hit for him. He saw enemies everywhere.

"Oh hey, before I left to see my ma, Coop had a big meet and greet with the motherfuckers that took you," said Gyp.

"With the Smoking Guns? With Med?"

"Yeah, bro. He is one fucked up dude. Total dust freak. Coop said he kept babbling on and on, then he'd start making some sense then drift again. Oh, and Coop said he's got a fucking harem going."

"A harem?"

"He's got more than one old lady. Like one of those cults out in Utah." Gyp snorted. "Is that how it was when you were there? Would've like to have seen that. Sounds like a pain in the ass, though. Don't they get fucking jealous? Shit, remember when Tracy tore out that skank's hair over Marty? That was something—"

"No, Med only had one old lady when I was there."

"Coop said he's got three or four now. Passes the older ones around too. What a fucked up fucker."

"Yeah. Fucked up is right," I murmured, my heart thudding in my chest. Serena had been with Med for over four years now. She was definitely the older old lady in his harem. *"After last night...I'm on the shit list now."*

My stomach cramped. The beer suddenly tasted like piss, and I spit it out.

Gyp let out a loud, long burp. "You okay?"

"Yeah, yeah." I wiped a hand across my mouth.

I'd had to be the good soldier in Nebraska, and I had been. Now I had to make my plans. Secret, against-all-the-rules, insane plans. How much time did she have left?

"Hey man, watch it."

I bumped into a long-haired blond guy with the name "Butler" patched on his colors, a One-Eyed Jack from Dig's chapter here in South Dakota. He had his arm hanging around Sister's shoulders, steering her through the crowd, and they were laughing. She caught my eye and sobered up, looking away quickly just like most people.

"Asshole," muttered Gyp.

"Heads up. Something's going on over there." Drac gestured with his beer down the small hill.

Slade gave us a lift of his chin from where he stood at the base of the slope. His eyes lit up, a huge grin splitting his face. "Fight!" You would've thought Muhammed Ali was down there by the way he'd said it. Nothing like a good fight. After all, riding and fighting were who we were.

We made our way over to check it out. The Broken Blades, our frenemies from Nebraska, were arguing with another club. My face fell. The Prez of the Blades was arguing with Dig.

Ah shit. Dig was facing off with the club he'd wanted to make an alliance with? Over what?

Notch, the Blade's VP, had some teenage girl tied to a leash and was pulling her around, making her available to everybody. She didn't seem to mind, she was laughing, and so were the men standing around them.

"Don't you think she's a little young for this shit?" Dig bit out, his face red, veins popping along his neck. His bros shoved him back and held onto him as he argued with Notch and the Blades Prez, Zed.

"You gonna tell us how we gonna be?" Zed yelled. "Fuck no!"

Battle lines drawn, excuses made, attitudes hardened, weapons at the ready.

"He gets in my face one more time, that's gonna be the end of him," declared Notch as he pushed his little underage bitch, sporting a bikini and a bulging fanny pack slung around her waist, toward two other Blades. Most likely Notch has stuffed that fanny pack with all sorts of narcotic goodies. His men latched onto her like hungry puppies being rewarded with bacon for good behavior.

Notch was a known freak, but who the hell wasn't? To overstep the way Dig did just now was not done, especially with an officer of another club. And it wasn't over an old lady, but some random piece of ass. I guess Dig had moral principles.

Dig's troubled eyes snagged on mine, an eyebrow jumped. He knew he'd stepped over the line. I shook my head at him, and a shadow passed over his straining features. He was pulled away like a wild animal having been given a tranquilizer, crumpling in his brothers' hold. His old lady and that Butler guy came running.

I pressed my lips together. I wouldn't be telling Kwik about Dig's offer, Dig's grand idea, even though it sounded useful to us. I couldn't now. This sort of hostility between the Jacks and the Blades was a liability and it could only get worse. So much for a "velvet network." Fuck, on the turn of a dime, on tempers and highs, plans get destroyed like a glass slipping out of your hands, shattering on the floor around you.

End of story before it had even begun.

Shame.

"Fuck, what a mess," muttered Drac.

We kept walking, heading for a concert on the other end of the campsite. The rest of the evening we partied, we had fun. Little did we realize, that night's mess would create a monster pissing bitterness and rage for years to come.

One day I would be the one who'd slash its throat and make it bleed.

11
FINGER

I'D BEEN KEEPING WATCH ON the movement of the Kansas City Smoking Guns for weeks. Of course, we did that in general, but I needed to find the right time and right way to get in and get Serena out.

I couldn't tell Drac or Slade about it, about her. I didn't want nobody to talk me out of it, or freak out on me and get me busted for it.

Only one person.

I pulled up to the laundromat two towns over and headed for the bank of pay phones at the end of the small strip of shops. My office of choice. I popped in the change and dialed. The beeper beeped, and I pushed in the number, hung up the phone, and waited.

Mrs. Macafee from the diner in town came out of the laundromat with a huge blue nylon laundry bag in a cart, tossing me her usual frown, and as usual I ignored it.

The phone rang, and I grabbed it.

"Yeah?" came his voice.

"Dig?"

"That's me."

"It's Finger."

"Hey, man." The husky tone of his voice lightened. "How're you doing?"

"Need help from you."

"You got it."

"This is between us. Has nothing to do with my club or yours. You still interested?"

"Tell me."

"I'm gonna need a safe house in South Dakota. Might have to keep someone there for a week or two, then we'll be out of your hair."

"Not a problem. Got just the place, and it's mine. No one knows about it."

"What do you want for it? I got some money, and I can give you—"

"I don't want your money. I just want you to be open to working with me, grease that channel with your club. I know what happened with me and Notch fucked things up with the Blades, and that doesn't seem to be going away. You calling me to ask, shows that you knew I'd help you."

The Blades and the Jacks were now on totally shit terms, shittiest in their history. That new friction was causing lots of problems for all of us.

"Yeah. That sucked."

He let out a laugh. "That's the word for it."

"I'll do what I can. I promise."

"I appreciate it. When do you need the safe house?"

"Not sure yet. It'll be a last minute kind of thing."

"Try to give me a week's heads up at least, and I'll let you know how to get there."

As I listened to his smooth voice, my insides squeezed with the knowledge that I was one step closer to what I wanted most in the world.

"Dig?"

"Yeah?"

"Thanks, man."

"Means a lot that you'd come to me for this."

"Means a lot that you agreed."

THE HUGE YEARLY MEETING OF the Flames was set to happen in LA, and all the officers and most of the members from our chapter were going. At the same time, the huge yearly meeting of the Smoking Guns was happening not too far away in San Diego.

The two clubs often managed to have these convention like meetings in close proximity and at around the same time. Provoking each other and making the FBI and local police forces freak out were opportunities too good to pass up.

"Finger!" my President's voice called me from down the hallway as I passed.

I went into his office. "Hey, Kwik."

"Listen, I appreciate all the prep you've been putting into this trip."

"Yeah, of course," I replied.

"But I'm going to have to ask you to stay here. Dwyer got taken to the hospital this morning with pneumonia. Idiot never took those antibiotics he was supposed to be taking when he got that bad cold last month after his run up to Canada, and now he's fucked but good. Need you to cover his pick up in Sioux City. You know how big this one is for us. No one I trust more."

My face slackened, my mouth opening to protest.

Hold up.

That Sioux City run wasn't for another four days. Also, Med wouldn't take Serena along to California. Old ladies weren't welcome at these conventions. My muscles tightened. This was my time.

I raised my chin at Kwik. "No problem." If anyone found out what I was planning, I'd be thrown in a cell and locked up for insanity.

I took care of a few last minute errands for the run, then headed back to the laundromat payphone to contact Dig.

No answer.

No answer.

Shit. I'd try again tonight. I had to make this happen tomorrow. Fucking hell. Tomorrow.

12
FINGER

She wasn't at the house she shared with Med. She wasn't anywhere in town. Not at the grocery store, not at the Army & Navy store, the only stores in town. There was no way to contact her, and frankly, I didn't want to give her a heads up, 'cause she just might tell me no. She'd been with him a while now. Maybe she'd gotten used to being a prisoner? Gotten comfortable in her hell? You either got desensitized to constant fear or you were a ball of fear yourself.

I rubbed a hand across my mouth. She'd said yes though, hadn't she? She said she'd come with me if I showed up to get her out.

My skin crawled as I guided my bike through the quiet roads of Emmet, a small town west of Agra, Kansas, just below the Nebraska state line.

Along with watching their clubhouse for over a day, I'd been watching a house a few members frequented, but no sight of her. Did they keep her at the club 24/7? I'd spotted a young girl enter and leave with a backpack, but that was it. Was she part of Med's harem?

I'd managed to find out that this morning at nine thirty a delivery truck from the local grocery store with booze, soda, and food would make a delivery there. I checked my watch. Nine o'clock. I had to get on that truck.

At the store, one middle-aged man loaded crates of beer, sodas, and two large kegs into the back. Another man came out with a wad of papers in his hand and got in the driver's side of the cab. He lit a cigarette and waited.

I stashed my bike in a far corner down the street behind an abandoned store. There were plenty of closed businesses in this area. The recession had torn through here like a tornado. Keeping my gloves on, I put a thin black hoodie over my colors.

I didn't use my own bike. That would've been stupid. This bike was a piece I'd stolen a while back to rebuild, along with a plate that I'd stashed for a project like this. If I had to, I could abandon it without worrying that it would get traced back to my club or to me.

In the parking lot, the truck doors gaped open, and the guy loading turned his back, bending toward another crate. I slid inside the hold, flattening myself against the wall by crates filled with cereal and packages of sliced bread and coffee. My mouth dried as the double doors slammed close and the bolt lock slid across them. Voices, goodbyes. The truck jerked to a start and took off out of the store parking lot.

I was closer.

One step closer with every breath, every chug and pull of the truck.

Over fifteen minutes later, the truck slowed down and lurched to a stop.

A sweat broke out over my lip and my brow, and I swiped it away as I remained crouched down by the fucking sliced bread. I turned my head, taking in a deep breath.

The door pulled open, and light and hot air suddenly flooded the space. I shook my hair in front of my face and snatched the baseball cap from my back pocket. Grabbing a crate of cola cans, I backed down out of the truck.

"Hey! Where'd you come from?" asked the driver.

I slanted my head. "A lot to unload. Gotta get this shit done. You got a problem with that?"

His eyes narrowed, inspecting my torn jeans, tats up my arms, and ringed fingers. Was I Smoking Guns biker material enough for him?

"Nope, sure don't." He got inside the truck and shoved and pushed at crates.

I headed toward the back door of the Smoking Guns clubhouse.

A skinny brunette cleaned a large tabletop with a spray bottle and paper towels. She eyed me as I walked past, raising the crate in my arms.

"Over there." She gestured down a hall with the spray bottle. "Past the kitchen."

I walked into a ratty kitchen with aging appliances. A girl with long red hair was making sandwiches at the counter. She glanced up at me, and my heart stopped.

Serena gripped the knife in her hand tightly. Her gorgeous blue green eyes widened. "What are you—"

My gut seized. Her face was striped with black and blue marks down one side. Purple welts were over her chest peeking out from the V neck of her T-shirt. All I wanted to do was take her in my arms and hug her hard. Kiss over the bruises. Grab her and run. Fly into the sky like fucking Superman. But I was no Superman.

"Where should I put these?" My voice came out lower and scratchier than ever.

She only stared at me, stock still.

"Just answer the question," I said softly.

Light streamed in from the window behind her, a golden aura floating around her head. She looked like some magic fairy from another world.

Yeah, she was magic all right. *My magic.*

She rubbed her hands on a towel, her eyes hardening, never leaving mine. "Over here. Follow me." She tossed the towel to the side.

"What's up, Rena?" asked a deep voice. A Gun strode through the kitchen toward her, and I froze. Young, buzzed head, lots of earrings in one ear. He ripped open a bag of potato chips, chomping as he stared at her.

Serena's eyes darted to him. "Pop and beer delivery."

"Ah yeah, good. We're outta Dew, get me a can."

"Sure. Your sandwich is ready."

"Cool." He tossed the bag of chips onto the counter, slid onto a stool, and stuffed a chunk of sandwich in his mouth.

Serena moved toward me again.

"Hey," he growled through a mouthful of food, turning his head to the side.

She stopped once more, standing perfectly still, and my lungs crushed together.

"Don't forget the cans for recycling out back," he said.

"I won't." She finally left the kitchen, and I breathed again.

My pulse raced as I followed her down a back hallway. A line of vending machines and refrigerators stood against the end wall. Serena walked slowly, stiffly, a slight limp to her gait. My jaw tightened. What the hell had that motherfucking whack done to her?

She opened the door of a large commercial refrigerator. "Load them in here."

I bent over and took the cold soda cans from the crate and lined them up on the shelves. "You all right? What happened?"

"Are you crazy?" she said her voice low, eyes flashing.

"I told you I'd come for you."

"You did, but—"

"You didn't believe me?"

Her eyes searched mine. "I don't believe in anything."

My lips curved up. "That's why I had to come."

Her eyes flared, lips parted. A mental stutter. I'd shocked her. Something in my chest slid into place. Locked and primed.

"They've gone to California for the week."

"I know. Who's here?"

"A couple of prospects at the gate, and three more in here wandering around."

"You got a car?"

"Me? No. But Jan does. The girl inside."

"Can you borrow it and get us out of here?"

She grinned. "No, she hates me, but I'll get her keys."

"You can't take anything with you."

She let out a huff of air. "Nothing I want from here anyhow. I'll be right back."

She took off down another hall and was back within a few minutes carrying a pink handbag.

"It's Jan's," she said and fished out a pink teddy bear key chain. "Car."

I smiled, and she smiled back, and that unique heat shot through my veins adding its special hit of spice to my adrenaline rush. She took out Jan's wallet, grabbed the cash, and tucked it in her front jeans pocket. "All set, let's go."

Serena took my hand in hers, and I gripped her tight. She led me down the other end of the hallway. We got outside, and the hot sun roiled over my skin, shocking my eyeballs into submission. I pulled my cap down lower.

We headed for a small gray Ford Fiesta with Oklahoma plates out in the lot.

"She's from Oklahoma?"

"Yeah."

I opened the trunk, and she whispered, her voice shaky, "You know I trust you."

"Good."

"But I can't get in there. I can't. They had me—"

My eyes flared with the memory of her telling me how Med would lock her in his closet whenever he wanted, which was a lot of the time.

"Back seat." I grabbed what looked like a rolled up workout mat from the trunk and gave it to her and closed the door. She crouched on the floor of the backseat and covered herself with the purple rubber mat.

I got in the driver's seat, the thick plastic of the wheel burning through my thin gloves. I started the car and rolled to the front gate, my redneck baseball cap pulled down low at an angle, my bandana up high to cover my scars. The grocery truck had just taken off and rounded the corner at the end of the street.

"Who the hell are you?" asked a short, stocky, blond guy, a meatball sub hanging from his hand at the gatehouse.

"Jan's ex. Bitch took my shit when she left me in Oklahoma. I'm taking back what's mine."

"That can't happen, man," said the blond, his thick eyebrows rising into peaks. "How the fuck did you get in here?"

"You all can have her whoring ass. I just want my wheels back. Now open the goddam gate."

"Hey, you look—"

"Stop! That's my car! Stop!" Jan came running toward us, arms waving, brown hair flying.

I whipped out my Kimber and fired at the blond guy. His mess of a sandwich fell to the ground in a splatter of blood and tomato sauce, his body crumpling in a pile next to it. I jumped into his booth and pushed at the buttons of the control panel box. The gate slid open.

"Holy shit!" Jan screamed.

"What the fuck?" shouted that guy from the kitchen, running toward us, eyes raging, gun in the air. I shot him in the chest, his buzzed head snapping back, his body twisting, falling to the ground.

Lunging back into the car, I reached out to close the door and a blade ripped into my arm, pain tearing through me. Holding a bloodied knife, Jan dove at me again. I grabbed the bitch's hair with my other hand, pulling her head back. She screeched, and I yanked harder on her. The knife went flying.

Bam.

She dropped to the ground like a puppet whose strings had been cut.

Serena stood over her, a gun in her hand. Her dark eyes met mine. "No one hurts you. Not again. Not ever."

The vision of Avenging Serena burned a hole right through me and made me forget any kind of pain.

"You got a gun on you?" I said.

"I'd be stupid not to."

I let out a laugh. "You ain't stupid."

"They're a couple more men out in the back."

"Baby, get in the car."

Serena tucked the Glock in the back of her jeans, and she folded herself under the mat again as I slammed her door shut. I kicked Jan's body away from the driver side door, got in the car, and tore out of the Smoking Guns property just as two other men came running toward us. I wiped the sweat from my face, and my arm burned, but I ignored it as I gunned the engine.

We finally got into town. I took Serena by the hand and quickly led her to my bike. I lit up the ignition, stealing a glance at her. She grinned at me, her fingers brushing over the scars on my cheek. Her lips landed on mine, and my lungs crushed against my rib cage.

It was true, it was real. We'd made it fucking happen. She was free, and we were together.

"Justin—"

"Get on," I choked out.

She swung on my bike and settled in behind me with a wince and a small groan.

My hand reached back and squeezed her leg. "You okay?"

"I'll be fine." She put her hair up in a knot and adjusted herself on the saddle. "You're the one bleeding."

"Huh?"

"Your arm."

Blood had soaked through my shirt and streamed down my arm. The sting remained steady, but I pushed back the wave of pain.

"You have something I can wrap it with?" Her hands made quick work of the buckles on my saddlebag. She found a bandana and quickly tied it around my bleeding arm.

The roar of pipes screamed in the air. They were onto us. "Fuck it, we gotta move."

She wrapped her arms around me, her hold firm. "Get us out of here."

13
FINGER

WE'D GOTTEN OUT OF TOWN and laid low in a ravine, hiding until I was sure the two men on our tail were circling and couldn't find us. I stopped at three different rest areas to use a pay phone. Each time was a fail.

No Dig.

Once more, I tapped out my number on the metallic keypad. I waited. And waited. No return call. Through the scratched, cloudy glass of the phone booth, I watched Serena arch her back, adjusting herself on the saddle.

We would head north out of Kansas through Nebraska to South Dakota, a trip that would take roughly five hours. I'd feel better about everything once we got out of Nebraska, but shit, Serena wasn't looking so good.

She was pale, her thin form curved over the seat. She wore the extra pair of shades I kept on my bike, and they were plenty big on her face, overtaking her delicate features. She was delicate, yeah, but invincible.

Still nothing. No return call.

Where the hell was Dig, goddammit?

I wanted us off the major highways, to lay low, but I also needed access to a goddamn phone. My nerves scraped through my flesh. The Guns could have scouts everywhere.

I abandoned the phone booth. "You sure you don't want to get up, stretch out?" I asked her.

She only shook her head tightly.

Was she sick? Or maybe they did something to her to match the bruises on her face? I could tell she was uncomfortable with every small move she made, adjusting her ass on the seat, taking in a deep breath as she rolled her shoulders back, flexing her feet, stretching out one leg at a time.

At the next rest stop, I bought us orange juice and a package of small blueberry muffins, which we downed quickly. I made her get up this time, and I wrapped my arm around her, holding her against my body as I again punched the number of the payphone onto the keypad.

No answer.

"Fuck, fuck, fuck!" I slammed the receiver onto the phone.

"Shh, don't attract attention," she said into my neck, her cool lips moving against my skin, a hand stroking my back.

"I can't fucking believe this shit. He promised me. I should've made sure before I left. Damn it!"

"Is there anybody else you can call?"

I released my hold on the payphone and caught a glimpse of vulnerability and fear gliding over her face like a quick moving cloud.

I had to keep it together. Yeah, things were not going as planned, or everything was fucking unplanned on my part—my fault—but I had to let it go and focus. I took in a breath. "Yeah, yeah. I'll try him at another number."

I dialed the number for the One-Eyed Jacks clubhouse. I'd memorized it a long time ago, like I'd memorized a lot of phone numbers out of necessity.

"Yeah?"

"Is Dig there?"

"Who's this?" came an amused male voice on the other end of the line.

"I'm a friend of his."

"Oh yeah? Well, Dig's not here, friend."

"I need to contact him. "

"Who the hell is this?"

My pulse quickened. "This is Finger. Who the hell are you?"

"This is Jump," he replied. Jump was an officer of the Jacks, their Secretary.

"He's not answering his beeper. Where is he?"

"Dig's got a lot of beepers, man."

"Don't we all?" I shot back. "I need to talk to him. It's important."

"Dig's away, out of town. He left all his beepers behind, except for one. And only I've got that number, and it's for 911s. Only."

This asshole.

"He's expecting my call. You call him for me, then. I don't give a shit. I just need to hear from him."

"Ain't that interesting? No can do. Man's on his honeymoon. A honeymoon that got delayed since his flash wedding a few weeks ago."

"Wedding?"

"Sorry, you didn't get the invite. It was a spur of the moment thing. So no, I ain't disturbing him for anything or anybody. Man never gets away, and this was a special deal. You got something you want, you can tell me."

I wasn't about to tell Jump shit, but I needed help. I was counting on Dig's fucking safe house. I needed to get Serena safe.

"Dig promised me access to a safe house in South Dakota."

"Huh. You're shitting me."

"I'm not shitting you, and I need access. Now."

"Oh, now, huh? That ain't gonna happen. Ever. He had no right to promise you shit, and I'll deal with him when I see him. I don't want to know what you got going on, but you aren't involving the Jacks in any of your shit. Crap between you and every other club on the map is hot, and I ain't risking my club for any of you."

"Jump, I need—"

"I don't give a shit what you need. Can't help you."

"Just for a couple of days, then I'll be gone. I need to lay low for a few—"

"And that is your fucking problem. Why should I take a risk for you? No fucking way. Dig's been chasing your skirt for a while now, don't think I haven't noticed. But it ends here and now, with me."

Serena pulled at the blood soaked bandana on my arm, and I sucked in air. Was that why nausea was roiling in my gut, and my vision was getting dazed? Yeah, that must be it. Bleeding at the side of the road.

"Got to keep moving," Serena mouthed silently.

"Fuck you, motherfucker," I spit into the phone. "I ain't ever gonna forget this."

"I already have," Jump replied.

The line went dead.

I slammed the phone into the cradle and stood there, my skin hot, my eyes burning. Serena's hand slid up my back.

I wrapped my good arm around her shoulders and pressed my lips against the side of her face. "We'll keep heading north."

Even though we were now in my club's territory, I couldn't risk being seen by one of my own. I'd get us out of Nebraska and north into South Dakota, into Jacks territory. Jump be damned.

"Just a a few more hours."

"You don't have to make it pretty for me."

"Five hours. Five hours till we cross into South Dakota. Can you hold on till then?"

I hated myself for not having a backup plan. I hated myself for leading her into a black hole of the unknown. I hated myself for not being worthy of her trust.

She nodded, her hand squeezing my bicep tightly. I planted a quick kiss on her forehead, and we got back on my bike.

An hour later, we stopped at a convenience store to get something to munch on, plus I wanted to give her a break. The store was closed, but luckily there were two vending machines to the side. Serena sat on the curb in the sun while I got us cereal bars and sodas.

A guy on a dirty, dented bike with a beanie slouched down over his forehead pulled into the parking lot. Serena stiffened at my side. These small, almost abandoned towns in Nebraska were quiet, but a hotbed of minor criminal activity. She peeked up at him, her face a mask of get-the-fuck-away-from-me.

"Hey, not open?" He gestured at the store, his ratty windbreaker hanging on him.

"No."

"Shame. You got a smoke? Need one bad."

"Don't have any," I said, handing a cold soda can to Serena who remained still behind me.

"Aw c'mon, man." He sidled up next to us at the vending machine. "I'm low on cash, ya know?"

"That's too bad."

"Yeah, sucks." He licked at his bottom lip eyeing his beat up Honda and my Harley. "Nice bike. Haven't seen you two before."

"And you won't be seeing us again."

"Not from around here, huh? If you two need something stronger than cola, I got it."

"Not interested." I said through gritted teeth. "Step back, man." With a hand on her arm, I guided Serena back to my bike.

"You on a long trip, huh? From Kansas maybe?"

Serena's breath caught, a small, choking sound. I launched at him, my fist bashing into his side, his back, his face. A glare flashed in my vision. Serena's yelp punched the hot air.

A blade tore over my chest. "Shit!" The sting leapt through me.

He grunted and slumped in my hold, his body suddenly heavy against mine. I let go, and he crumpled to the ground. Serena stood over us, his knife in her hand.

"Serena—"

"I'm not ever going back. Not ever."

My hand shot out toward her. "Okay, okay."

"This is the farthest I've ever gotten. And I've tried a time or two or three, and paid for it. Not this time. Not now, with you. And I won't have you punished for trying."

Her arm shook as she wiped the blood on the guy's jeans and slid the weapon in her boot. "They've been following us. Maybe they pushed us toward here. And if they don't hear from him—"

A beeper went off as she said the words.

I kicked him over. He wore a dirty faded hoodie under his ratty windbreaker. I unzipped it. No colors. He could be a local contact of theirs, a dealer, a mover.

I crushed the beeper with the heel of my boot and tossed it in the garbage dumpster behind us. I grunted, dragging his body to the dumpster and curling him up into a ball. Just another dealer having a bad day. We took his .380 and two knives. Serena piled cardboard boxes that poked out from the dumpster and put them to the side of

the metal structure, hiding his body from view. I went ove
and pushed it to the back of the store by where he lay.

"Should give us some time."

"They know where we are."

"We don't know that for sure. He could just be some local ass-hole."

"You know that's not true."

"We gotta keep moving."

"They know." Her body shook, her gaze shifting up and down
the quiet road. She was exhausted, ravaged by a potent cocktail of
hope, anxiety, and adrenaline.

"Serena, you hear me? We gotta keep moving. Don't quit on me
now. We're close. We're almost in South Dakota."

"So what? So what?"

"I'm never gonna let them take you back."

"So what?" she repeated.

I gripped her jaw, and her blood shot eyes widened. "Listen to
me," I said. "We're getting back on my bike and leaving."

"I'm always leaving and never getting anywhere. In my dreams
or here, right now, it just doesn't matter, does it? Look at us. We're
both bleeding, both exhausted."

"What did they do to you? You're hurting." I stretched out a
hand to her and she smacked it away, turning her face from me,
wiping at her eyes.

I rubbed my hand across my chest and blood stained my skin. I
swayed under the heat of the sun. Under the specter of them finding us.

Don't give up, Serena. Please, don't give up.

14
FINGER

W E RODE ON, TAKING LOW traffic routes when we could, then I'd switch it up. Being in public might be a good thing. I needed to make up for the time lost with the stops we'd made. Plus, stops made it harder for her to get back on and ride. I grit my teeth every time I saw her squirming on the seat.

Two bikes riding together appeared in my left rear view mirror, and my pulse picked up speed along with my throttle. I was suspicious of everyone and everything. They turned off on an exit after at the next town.

We made it to South Dakota.

I turned off for Route 50 to find a gas station and something to eat.

A crooked sign hanging from a tall rusty pole blazed in the late afternoon sun over the entrance to the small lot. Tipson's Gas Stop. A lone forest green SUV sat in front of the store. I parked in the back and lifted Serena off the bike. She gripped my neck, and I held her in my arms, savoring the feeling of her holding onto me, pressing into me, needing me. Everything would be okay. It fucking had to be.

"Want a big steak dinner?" I laughed, knowing the only thing we'd find inside were chips, cookies, bad muffins, cardboard nachos, and candy if we were lucky.

She only shook her head in the crook of my neck.

I put her down and took her hand. "Let's go inside. Come on."

Bike engines from out front cut through the heat in the air and Rena stopped in her tracks, her eyes widening.

I squeezed her hand. "We don't know who it is. There are plenty of riders out here."

"It's over. It's over. It's over," she chanted. Serena took out her gun, and I ripped it out of her strong grip.

"No. No!" I pushed her against the back wall of the gas station. "Where's the girl who wanted to live no matter what?"

"I'd rather do it myself than give them back the opportunity!" Her voice was a snarl.

"You're scared. I am too. I am." My pelvis pressed into hers. "Baby, come on. We'll get through this. We will. Stay with me here. Just a little longer. Please."

Her muscles eased one by one, and she finally curled herself into me. I let out a heavy breath, holding onto her tight, sliding her gun down my jeans with the other.

I pulled and pushed on the knob of the bathroom door to the left of us but it was locked. I yanked on my wallet chain, grabbed the mini knife I had hanging there and jammed it into the lock, jimmying the old piece of shit. The door opened, and I pushed Rena in there. "You stay here while I go into the store."

"I should go in. You're a little memorable."

"And you're either gonna pull a weapon on the cashier or collapse. You stay here." She lowered herself onto the dirty tiled floor of the bathroom, her head in her hands, the door ajar.

I hid my bike behind a row of tall recycling bins.

I couldn't get back on the road with Serena like this. I had to calm her down. See to my cuts, get her food. Something. Maybe we should get on a fucking bus?

Keep your shit in check.

A woman in her early twenties with shiny black hair, wearing jeans and a tie-dyed blouse stood in the doorway of the bathroom, her body rigid. Large dark eyes swallowing us in.

Fuck.

"Hey. My girlfriend's sick," I muttered, crouching by Serena, my hand on her head, ready to pounce. If I had to kill someone else, I fucking would.

Serena slumped over onto the floor.

"Oh my God! Is she okay?" The girl squatted down next to me.

I scooped Serena up in my arms. "Baby!"

Nothing.

Dark Eyes reached out and touched her face.

"I got her. Don't touch her! Don't you touch her!" ripped out of my throat.

The girl let out a gasp. "Oh my God, the bruises on her face—"

"It wasn't me."

The girl jumped to her feet, stepping back. "I should believe you? What, are you drug addicts or something?"

"No, dammit. I got her away from her ex. He's been beating on her, doing shit..." I hoisted Serena up in my arms and leaned her against the wall. "He's after us now."

Serena's head wobbled up, and her arm slid around my neck.

"Are you okay?" the girl asked her.

"Please. Please, help us," Serena said, her voice small. "Help him."

Footsteps crunched on gravel. The girl glanced at me, and I put my hand over Serena's mouth. Dark Eyes pulled the door closed behind us, but a hand planted on the door stopping her. A ringed, tattooed hand.

"Hey, excuse me?" said Dark Eyes standing in the slit of the doorway, her tone full of vinegar.

"Sorry, uh, thought this was free."

"Obviously not. Think you can wait?"

"You alone in there?"

"Are you fucking kidding me?"

Go, girl.

"Are you, honey?" The man's shadow filled the doorway, his low chuckle rolling through the space.

I pressed Serena's gun against the hand Dark Eyes had on the knob. She took it and released the safety, making a show of it to the guy. "No, honey, I'm not alone. Now back the fuck off so a girl can pee without having to call 9-1-1."

"Yeah, yeah, easy there. All right."

"All right what, exactly?"

"I'm leaving!"

"That's good." Dark Eyes slammed the door shut and locked it. I motioned for her to come get Serena. She handed me the gun back and took Serena in her arms while I stood by the door and listened. Muffled voices. Gravel crunching.

We waited in that grimy bathroom. The seconds ticked by in our drumming heartbeats, our tight breaths, the stifling stench of dried earth and piss.

Was this it? They'd be back, they'd be circling. Two sets of pipes blared, popped, and raged off into the distance.

My head dropped, the gun sticking to my sweaty hand.

I turned back to the women, both of them clinging to each other, faces grim.

"We got to get outta here," I said barely above a scratched whisper.

The girl held my gaze. "I'll help you."

I eyed her. No screams, no freak outs, no crying. Just an offer to help.

Thank fuck.

"What's your name?" I asked her.

"Tania. What's yours?"

"You don't need to know, Tania."

"Since you're the one with the gun, I'll go with that for now. But that's going to have to change once I get you two in my car."

15
FINGER

Tania drove with Serena laying down in her backseat. She had a ton of shit in her car, like she was moving or something. We managed to squash some of it into the front seat and to the side to make room for Serena.

I followed them on my bike.

Three towns down, she pulled up at a motel. "I'll go get us rooms. You stay here."

I got in the back with Serena, her head in my lap. Her tired gaze hung on mine as she slugged down water from a small bottle Tania had given her.

"Why are you helping us?" I asked Tania.

"Isn't it a bit late to be asking that question?" Tania shot me a look as she took her wallet from her backpack.

"I'm curious 'cause you don't seem the type to—"

"That's why, right there." A grin grew on her lips. "By the looks of you I should've run the other way at top speed, but here I am. You obviously really needed help."

"Well, I appreciate it," I replied.

"This is about me as much as it is about you."

"What the hell does that mean?"

"It means I need to take risks, which I tried to do very recently and failed at pretty miserably. And today, what drops down in front of me? The two of you. Literally dropped down in front of me in a crap gas station bathroom outside of Tripp of all places. That's a pretty huge opportunity for a second chance at risk-taking that the Universe just laid at my feet, I'd say."

"I had other plans, but they fucking fell though."

"Believe me, I get it. 'Other plans' usually do fall through," Tania agreed. "I'm going to go in. You guys duck down or whatever. You know."

"You're funny."

"Yeah, that's me." Her gaze lingered on us. She was concerned.

"You go on ahead," I murmured, my hand stroking Serena's cool face.

Her pale lips tipped up into a weak smile.

Tania came back within ten minutes. "There was only one room. Two double beds though. I took it, but I'm sure you guys are going to want your privacy and I—"

"And you're afraid I'm going to assault you, slit your throat in the middle of the night, take your shit and run," I said.

"Maybe."

"Not gonna do that. First, you're helping me out, and I respect that. Second, I'm no rapist. And third, I'm too fuckin' tired for anything but sleep tonight."

"Well, all righty then." Tania grabbed a small duffel bag out of the passenger side front seat. "Let's go."

"Serena, we're going to go inside this motel now. Gonna get cleaned up and into bed. Sounds good, right?"

Serena only let out a small sound, and I slid my arm around her and lifted her out of the car. The three of us moved toward Room 110. Tania slid the key in the door, the *click* giving me a ping of hope for the first time in hours. We moved into the stuffy, dark space.

"You wanna get clean?" I asked Serena as Tania turned on the bathroom light.

"I can help, if you want," said Tania. "If you need me to, that is. Sorry, I don't mean to...Look, I've got some extra clothes that will probably fit her. She's really thin, so they may be big."

"That'd be great."

"Sure. Let's get her in the bathroom."

We both took Serena in the bathroom. I ripped off my gloves and undressed her, my fingers shaking.

Tania glanced at my damaged hands and blinked. "You want me

to do this? I mean, are you okay? You must be stressed out, huh?"

"Yeah."

Tania helped Serena take off her shirt.

"Oh God." Tania's face flared, her voice a rough whisper.

Bruises and scars from cuts and cigarette burns mottled Serena's pale skin.

"That motherfucker," I said on a hiss.

We got her naked, her ribs and pelvic bones peeking through her bruised flesh. I ripped off my clothes and guided her into the shower stall. Tania turned on the water, and Serena shuddered in my arms, clinging to me, moaning.

Tania's face flushed, as if she'd now realized that I was naked too. She stepped out of the small bathroom. "I-I'll be outside if you need anything."

"Don't go anywhere. Wait for us to come out. My gun's in my jacket if you need it."

"Goody." She closed the door.

I held up Serena and washed every inch of her, my fingers smoothing over her white skin, the pink and blue veins visible at every curve. "I got you, baby. You're with me now. I'll send Tania out to get us something to eat. We'll watch some TV and get sleep. Sounds good, right?"

Her head knocked back against the white tile wall, and her lips tipped up in a smile. I kissed her and the world stopped spinning. My soapy hands slid down her back and stopped at her ass. She let out a cry and buried her face in my chest.

If we walked out of this bathroom and that Tania chick blew us to bits, I wouldn't give a fuck. I'd had this. Serena and me. Naked to each other, skin to skin under a stream of clean, hot water. No chains, no audience, no jeering, just us. Us together.

No, there was nothing less and nothing more I wanted.

I GOT SERENA INTO BED AND climbed in after her. She fell asleep right away in the crook of my arm.

"I'm going to get you a T-shirt and some first aid stuff for your arm and chest. And food," whispered Tania.

"I got money in my wallet. Take whatever."

"No, I got this."

"You sure?"

"Yeah, I'm sure."

"Thanks, Tania. Hey, a favor? No sliced white bread for me."

Her eyebrows lifted. "Okay, Mr. F," she said gesturing to the scars on my cheek and the tattoos down my chest of a series of F's in different styles I'd gotten recently. I was owning it.

"You come back with good shit, I'll tell you my name," I said.

"That's a deal." She closed the door gently behind her.

Black darkness had fallen outside and the air was cooler. I heaved a sigh, sinking my head back against the pillow, Serena's sweet body on mine, and let sleep overtake me.

Gnawing hunger woke me, and my eyes unglued. The bathroom light was on. I sat up, pressing Serena's body back into the bed. A form was in the other bed, the deep breathing telling me Tania was asleep.

Plastic bags from a convenience store sat on the dresser, and I opened them. Apples, bananas, wrap sandwiches, crusty whole wheat roll sandwiches. I ripped open the thick roll and bit into it. Peanut butter and jelly. Nothing better. I slumped on the edge of the bed and ate.

Muttering rose up behind me, the sheets were tugged and twisted at my side. Serena was having a nightmare. I tossed the food back on the dresser and leaned over her.

"Hey, hey, Serena. It's okay. Shh."

I slid in beside her in bed and wrapped my arm around her. She gnashed her teeth, her head shaking back and forth, fists curling in the sheet, warding off someone, defensive. Her legs kicked out, her breathing hard and choppy.

I lifted up, smoothing a hand over her taut face. "Serena."

She jacked up from the mattress, gasping for air over the edge of the bed.

I clicked on the bedside lamp. "Hey, it's me, Justin. You okay? You were having a nightmare."

She only nodded, her head turned away from me.

My hand slid up her damp back, arching under my touch. "I won't hurt you, you know that, right?"

Her head slumped down.

"Look at me, baby. Please."

She pulled at the sheets and raised her eyes to mine. So tired.

"Can I touch you?" I asked her. "Can I hold you?"

She nodded, her body shuddering, arms curled against her chest. I moved closer and she fell into my embrace, her cool damp skin against mine. "It's okay. You're here with me now. It's over. It's really over. You want something to drink?"

"Water," she whispered hoarsely.

"Got bottles right here."

I got out of the bed and grabbed a cold bottle from the pack Tania had stashed in the mini fridge and opened it for her. She took it, and I watched her throat move as she gulped.

"Slowly, baby. Slowly."

She pulled the bottle away, her lips shiny and wet, her eyes gleaming. Better.

"You hungry? I was eating a PB and J Tania bought."

"Okay."

I handed her the other half and she ate. We sat on the bed cross-legged, facing each other like two kids staying up late sneaking treats in the dark. Only we were naked and my cock was hard as a rock.

Her eyes danced in the half-light. "That's good."

I slanted my head at her. "The sandwich?"

We laughed.

"You want something else?"

"No more food." Her knees grazed mine. "This is nice."

"Yeah."

"I haven't had much of any nice."

"You got it now."

She leaned over and planted a soft kiss on the side of my face. "Hold me."

I lifted her into my lap, wrapped her legs around me, and held her tightly. "Not letting go."

"Don't."

She burrowed into me. My dick was thrilled to be making contact with her body again.

We fell back on the bed taking in each other's breaths. My hand stroked her sides, and I gently kissed the tops of each soft breast as her fingers slid through my hair. I lay my head on her chest, and we drifted asleep on the erratic rhythm of each other's heartbeats.

THE SWEEP OF SOMETHING COOL whispered up over my naked body, and I forced my eyelids open. Tania. She pulled the sheet up over me and Serena who was asleep on my chest. I let out a grunt as I shifted her bare body to my side under the sheet.

"You okay?" Tania asked.

"Yeah."

"You sure?"

I rubbed my eyes. "Yeah."

"Go back to sleep. I didn't mean to wake you. You two just looked like abandoned puppies for a minute there."

I wiped a hand down my stubbly face and swung out of the bed, feet planting on the floor. "I'm going to take a shower."

She cleared her throat at the sight of my morning wood. "Um, I got us some breakfast." She turned away from me and quickly climbed back into her bed.

"Great."

By the time I got out of the bathroom, Serena and Tania were talking and spreading the food out on Tania's made up bed. Tania had gotten us scrambled eggs with cheese and ham on English muffins. We ate and it was so fucking good. Serena looked at my wound and applied disinfectant and gel and wrapped it firmly with a sterile bandage.

"I got you this too." Tania took out a box from a plastic bag and tossed it on the bed by Serena. Hair dye. Dark brown. "Your red really stands out. I thought you'd want to change it."

Serena only stared at the box.

I crumpled up the foil from the sandwich. "That's good, right?"

"I figured you two wanted to stay out of sight," Tania said. "Or did I get that wrong?" She drained her paper coffee cup.

"You're right," Serena said. "Could you help me?"

"Sure," Tania replied, a grin on her face. The girl liked being useful. "I've done it plenty of times with my friends back home." She cleaned up the food and juice and coffee containers from the bed. "Sorry, I'm blabbing."

"I like your blabbing. Where are you from, Tania?" asked Serena, her voice steady, her eyes bright. Tania's friendliness was a good, unusual vibe for her. I leaned back against the headboard as Tania told us about her hometown. Meager, South Dakota.

Meager. Home of the One-Eyed Jacks.

Tania's eyes skidded over the tattoo of flames that ran down one side of my chest and the other tattoo of a knife over my left hip.

"I went to college in Chicago," Tania said. "I graduated this past May. I don't have a job or anything yet. No specific plans, but I know I wanted out of Meager. My best friend just got married to the man of her dreams. Her dreams, certainly not mine."

I unwrapped the pack of smokes Tania had bought me earlier. "You mind if I smoke in here, Tania?"

"No, go ahead," she said, shifting herself on the bed, uncrossing her legs yet again. "You're a member of the Flames, aren't you? I saw your tattoo."

"Yeah, I am. You know any Flames?"

She shook her head. "No."

"Keep it that way."

Her eyes flashed, her brows lifted. "Huh."

I got the impression, she wanted to say something but swallowed it back down. There was a lull in the conversation, a thick awkwardness hanging between us. I dragged on my smoke, and that tension pulled on my lungs. Shit, I don't know why I smoked tobacco half the time.

I rubbed a hand over my chest. "What are you going to do in Chicago now?"

Tania refolded her legs the other way. "I just want to get back there. I don't want to just get any old job, but I will if I have to."

She rolled her eyes, tilting her head. "I'll figure it out once I get back to the city. Of course, my mother and my sister had a cow over my decision, but I couldn't sit still in Meager. No way. There's more to life than..."

Tania continued on in her condemnation of small town life in Nowheresville, South Dakota while I smoked. Serena opened the box of hair dye, taking out the tube of color, another bottle, and the plastic gloves, unfolding the instructions.

The women went into the bathroom and dyed Serena's hair. I switched channels on the television. Serena came out with a mountain of blackish goo swirled over her head, making faces, and Tania and I laughed. A half an hour later, after a shower, Serena emerged from the bathroom with a brand new look. They'd even cut her hair shorter. She looked sleek. Edgy. Even through the exhaustion and the anxiety she was fucking gorgeous. My dick hardened in my jeans, and I adjusted myself on the bed. Serena stared at me, a sly smile growing on those lips, which only made my cock harder and my pulse race.

"We need to change your bandage," Tania said gesturing at my arm.

"Huh?" I cleared my throat and sat up. "Oh. Yeah."

Tania came over with a small plastic bag from a pharmacy and sat down next to me. A whiff of fancy perfume came up between us. She smelled nice. She had nice clothes and used fancy words. I'd never been this up close to anyone like her before. Her big dark eyes concentrated on dabbing antibiotic ointment over my cut, applying new tiny sticky bandages to keep the wound together.

"You got experience with this shit?" I asked.

"I grew up on a farm. You learn to get the basics of life done on your own."

"What kind of farm? Soy? Wheat?"

"A little bit of those, but mostly sunflowers."

"Nice."

"Yeah, it is nice. It was. Where are you from?"

"Nebraska."

"Not too far away." Her cool fingers smoothed over the edges of the bandage and traced along my skin where my flaming arrow tattoo was, next to my own scars from my time at the Smoking Guns. Her gaze snagged on mine. You could lose yourself in those big dark eyes. I took out another cigarette.

"Those are a hell of a lot of scars. They look recent too," she said.

"They are."

"You get in fights a lot?"

"Yep."

"Serena's got a lot of the same scars on her. Plenty more, though."

I lit another smoke, inhaling deep. "Her ex did a job on both of us."

"And your hands?" She pressed her lips together and took in a tiny breath waiting for my answer.

I only nodded.

Tania turned away from me and packed up the first aid material and shoved it back in the pharmacy bag. She rolled up the waste paper from the bandages in a ball and tossed them in the garbage basket at the side of the dresser.

"Don't leave those there," I said. "Don't want to leave anything behind for anyone to trace us."

"Oh. Right." Tania grabbed the stuff she'd thrown in the basket and shoved it in another plastic bag and then in her duffle. "So what's the plan? How long do you think we should lay low here?"

I glanced at Serena who had curled up on the bed behind Tania and fallen asleep. She looked more like a twelve year old than a full grown woman.

"I want her to gain her strength back. She wasn't eating or sleeping right. For years, I expect. They beat her up bad the night before I went in and got her."

"They?" Tania's face tightened. "I thought you said her ex?"

"Her ex is part of a bike club too."

"Oh shit." Tania's face reddened.

"They abused her." I grabbed another smoke from the pack at my side and clicked my lighter on.

Tania sucked in a breath. "Oh, I forgot, I got you some ibuprofen. I have naproxen sodium too. It's stronger, if you want, if you—"

"Yeah, load me up, Tania." I shot her a smirk as she launched from the bed to her handbag and got out two pill bottles. I took one of each and chased them with the soda I'd been nursing all morning. I laid back down on the bed alongside Serena. "I'd like her to get stronger, then I'll get her out of here."

"They're looking for her, right? Why don't you come with me to Chicago? You two could get lost in the big city or—"

"I can't leave, Tania. I got to stay around here."

She laid down on the other side of me. "Your club?"

"Don't ask me anymore. I ain't gonna tell you anyhow."

"I don't want to know," she whispered. "What I really want to know is what happened to your face. Sorry, but, it's pretty brutal looking."

"I'm ugly, huh?"

She smiled. A gentle smile, a smile that was so unexpected, so relaxed and welcoming, I didn't know what to fucking do with it.

"You're not ugly. The scars are, but you aren't. Not at all." Her face reddened again.

A flash of heat went off in my chest, and the tension there melted at the gentleness of her voice, the sincerity of her tone.

"Thanks. I guess." We both laughed.

"Can I have a cigarette?" she asked.

"Yeah, sure." I lit a cigarette and passed it to her and lit another for me.

"I've only smoked a few times before, but what the hell. I've done plenty of shit I've never done before in the last twenty-four hours."

We talked, and she told me more about her sister and her baby brother. How she felt guilty leaving them, but she had to leave now or she knew she never would. She didn't want to end up married and pregnant before she was twenty-two.

Serena woke up, stretching out on the mattress next to me. "I think we need to drink."

"Let me go out and buy a bottle of whatever you guys want. It'll cost less than opening those tiny bottles in the minibar," said Tania.

"Very practical, Tania. I like that." I tossed a twenty dollar bill on the bed. "Grab us a bottle of Jack."

"Jack it is." Tania took the bill, tucked her feet into her hot pink All-Stars, grabbed her bag, and left the room.

"I like her," said Serena.

"Me too. We got real lucky."

"See? Our luck has changed. The winds of fortune are blowing us on the right course."

"There's a course for good fortune?"

"Destiny always has a course for us."

"You believe in that shit?"

"A part of me has faith in it. The little girl part of me. Like that part of Tania that wants to believe there has to be something more in her life than just a farm and the same faces."

"Somewhere, over the rainbow, huh?"

She grinned. "Yeah. The three of us and Dorothy."

I let out a laugh. "Let's not forget the scruffy dog."

"Toto!" Serena squealed like a kid, hands in the air.

"Yeah, Toto. Pity there ain't no Auntie Em for us to go home to, baby."

"We got each other." She pushed the hair from my face, and my heart squeezed at her words.

"Yeah, we do." I sat up on my elbows. "How you feeling?"

"Better. I keep thinking I have stuff to do, but I don't."

"No, you don't. No more." I took in a breath. "Get closer."

She crawled up alongside me like a cat and hovered over me. The heat rising from her skin was palpable, and I craved it all over me, inside me, on me.

"Hi," she whispered, her breath mingling with mine.

"Hi."

I pulled on her tresses of dark brown hair and tugged her face toward me, brushing her lips with mine. She kissed me long and slow, our tongues stroking, sliding, exploring. A moan escaped my throat, and my hands cradled the back of her head.

"I've been wanting you to kiss me like this so bad," she said.

"I've been wanting you, period, so goddamn bad," I replied.

Our tongues tangled together wildly, and I held her close. She settled on top of me and rubbed herself up and down over my body. My hands gripped her ass, bringing her tight over my cock, holding her there. My fingers slid over the bare skin of her thighs and under her panties, digging into her soft flesh.

Our breathing grew ragged and short, and I flexed my hips against hers. "Fuck, you feel good. So damn good."

The key bolted abruptly in the lock, and our bodies stiffened. My hand shot out toward my gun on the nightstand.

"Hey, it's me." Tania stood in the doorway, her expression freezing. "Oh, geez, sorry."

"I thought—"

"Just me. I-I got the Jack." She held up a paper bag. "But I can go."

"No, Tania. Get in here." Serena slid off me. "I'll get glasses."

Tania locked the door behind her. She took the bottle of booze out of the bag and threw two bags of barbecue potato chips at me.

"Good choice," I said, sitting up and ripping into the chips.

The girls drank out of the two glasses Serena brought over from the dresser, and I chugged straight from the bottle.

A bang on the door made my body stiffen. Tania and Serena froze. I slanted my head at Serena, and she slid soundlessly off the mattress and under the bed. I gestured at the door to Tania, and she nodded, flinging the quilt over the drink glasses. Taking the bottle with me, I went to the other side of the door.

Tania glanced around the room one final time and holding my gaze, put a hand on the doorknob. "Who is it?"

"It's the police, ma'am."

Her gaze jumped to mine. I nodded and stepped back against the wall.

"Oh, okay. Do you have a badge?"

"Sure do," came the reply.

She opened the door a crack. "Hi."

"Sorry to bother you, but I'm looking for—"

"Your badge?"

"Yeah, right here. "

Tania's shoulders grew rigid, an eyebrow followed suit. She

wasn't buying it.

"I'm a detective. Looking for a teenage girl."

"Uh huh. Well, I'm not her, that's for sure."

He laughed. "Not too far off, though."

Tania grinned. A brittle, impatient, get-the-fuck-on-with-it grin.

"Yeah, well, this girl's a runaway." He held up a photograph. "You seen anyone to fit that bill?" He shifted his weight, his feet shuffling in the doorway.

"No, but I haven't been out either. I've been holed up here, waiting for my boyfriend. He's about ten minutes out on his way from Meager. I'm getting ready for our own private party. So, no, I haven't seen any runaway teenagers. This motel room is all I'm interested in tonight, if you get my drift. We're out of here first thing in the morning. So, if you'll excuse me—"

Tania closed the door, but a large hand planted itself on the surface pushing it back. Her face reddened.

"I don't think you understand, ma'am. What did you say your name was?"

"I didn't say. And don't you dare push this door again or I'm going to have to yell for help."

"Sorry. Look, I'm just eager to find this girl. I mean, this is my first case solo."

"Okay. Good luck to you. Like I said, I haven't seen anyone fitting that description."

"Right, okay."

Tania swiftly stepped back and firmly shut the door in one move, bolting the chain lock with a shaky hand, her lips parted. She pressed her palms against the door.

I moved to her. "You did good, Tania. Real good," I whispered, wrapping my arm around her waist. She fell into me, inhaling deeply. I rubbed a hand down her back. "You okay?"

She nodded. "He didn't look like any police detective. He looked like an underground—"

"Bet he's from Med," came Serena's voice.

Tania and I turned around. Serena stood by the bed. "We can't stay here much longer."

Tania grabbed the bottle from my hands and took a swig. "Hold on." She picked up the room phone and dialed. "Hi, I'm in room 110, and a man was just here, saying he was a police detective looking for a—" Her eyebrows lifted. "Oh, he is a local officer?" She glanced at me as she gnawed on her lip. "Oh, okay, I wasn't sure. Good to hear. I'm glad I called you then. Thanks."

Tania put the phone back on the receiver. "He really is a cop. Front desk lady said he's one of the local boys. She's known him since he was in diapers."

Serena let out a deep breath and dropped herself on the edge of the bed.

I took the bottle from Tania and drank. "We got to get a plan together."

"Aren't you taking Serena with you to wherever in Nebraska?" Tania asked, taking the bottle from me and passing it to Serena.

"No, I can't. She's got to lay low for a while. I was hoping this guy I know here in South Dakota was going to help, but it didn't work out that way. Can't trust nobody."

"You can trust me," said Tania.

"You've been great, Tania. Don't know what we would've done without you. But I can't get you more involved than you already are."

She sat up on the bed, leaning on one arm. "Serena could come with me to Chicago. I'm staying with a friend there for a few days, but I've got money saved up and have a lead on an apartment, and I'm planning on moving in real soon. Serena could stay with me until things cool down."

Serena blinked. "Tania, that's—"

"That's a real good idea and a real generous offer," I said. "Tania's got a point. No one knows we know each other. But you can't ever tell anybody about us, Tania. Not your ma or your sister or your brother or a boyfriend. Not even your best friend. Nobody. You get that?"

"I can keep a secret. I want you two to be safe. That's what's important. Safe and alive."

Serena put a hand on her arm. "Thank you."

"Of course."

"All right then. Chicago it is. You good with that?" I asked Serena. The thought of her so far away from me twisted my insides, but it was the best solution, and it would be temporary.

Temporary.

"I'm good with that," she replied quietly.

My beeper went off, and I glanced at it where it lay on the small table by the door. Los Angeles area code. Fuck, Kwik was checking in, and I was supposed to be on my way to that pickup in Sioux City. Luckily, it wasn't too far from where we were, but I needed to contact Kwik, claim bike problems and get to Sioux City as soon as possible.

I turned the beeper over. "Don't worry about money, I'll send you whatever you need. I'll find ways to keep in touch. You just need to expect it."

Serena's lips tipped up. "Sounds like a plan."

"I got to go make some phone calls," I said. "So Tania, how's all this risk-taking feel now?"

A slow smile broke over her mouth. "Like the best fucking rush ever."

16
FINGER

"THEY CALL YOU FINGER NOW?" Serena asked, her voice just above a whisper.

I turned on the motel bed and took her in. The lamplight created a golden glow over her. Her eyes were full and round. "Yeah. I earned my patch in a big way."

A serious look passed over her face as her hand stroked over my chest, lingering there, sending shivers skittering over my flesh, my pulse charging like a generator kicking in under storm conditions. She planted light kisses on my pecs, gentle, revering, almost timid. She bit her lip, the side of her face sinking into my arm.

This was our first time together, alone, like normal people, a normal couple. But there didn't seem to be much normal about us. Yet here we were together, and here she was, mine, and I was so fucking grateful.

My heartbeat hammered like I was a boy about to kiss his first girl—a girl he really liked and didn't think he'd ever have. A girl whose light touch drove me just as crazy with lust and emotion as her mouth around my cock once had. This was different, though. Right now, these heady looks, light but sizzling touches of hers over my skin were pulling me under. This was more, more in a way that I couldn't explain, but my body knew. I knew.

I kissed the side of her face, my hand at her jaw, my lips trailing to the edge of hers, and her mouth opened to mine. Her warm hand slid around my neck, the caramel taste of the whiskey still on her tongue. She made a soft noise in the back of her throat, her hips rising, and I crushed her body with my own.

Yeah, we both knew.

I pulled back, my thumb rubbing over her full lower lip. "I love being with you, here, like this, free and in the light. I like seeing you when we touch. Seeing your body with my eyes, not just my hands."

"Me too." A slow smile lit her face. She pulled my head down to hers and kissed me, a more insistent kiss, her one leg wrapping over mine, pressing.

Tania was taking a bath. A long, long bath, with her ear plugs in and her Sony Discman on. I could hear faint strains of the music through the closed bathroom door. She was a good kid and smart on the uptake. She was giving us some private time without being asked.

"I'm sorry for what they did to you." Serena's warm breath fanned my skin as her fingers traced over the grooves on my face. "I'm sorry for helping them. For—"

"Stop. You got nothing to be sorry for. Sometimes I forget, you know. But then I pass a mirror or a window and see my reflection. I notice that look people give me. It's a split second of horror, a mental and physical freeze. They look away real fast, they back off."

She took my right hand in hers and brought it to her mouth, and I hissed in a breath as her tongue danced over the nub of where my middle finger used to be.

I grit my teeth at the sensation springing over the stub. "You kissing my claws?"

"These hands aren't claws. They hold me, carry me. They fight for me and make my dreams come true in hell and high water. These hands are beautiful and strong." She ripped off her T-shirt and placed my hands on her breasts. My skin heated at the feel of her tits, at the sight of them covered with my large damaged paws. She raked her nails over them. "And they're mine."

My heartbeat grew louder at her words. That deep, sensual tone of her voice that was just for me, ticked off a time bomb deep inside me that I didn't even know was there.

Her fingers went to my lips, stroked down my chest, my middle. Tucking her hands under the waistband of my boxer briefs, she tugged them down, and I flexed my hips so we could get them off.

My head twisted back, my hips shifted, and both our gazes fell to her hand working my already rock hard cock.

My breath jammed in my lungs. "Serena." I closed my eyes, letting out a grunt. I buried my face in her throat, nuzzling her warm skin. "It ain't the same anymore. It hurts now."

Her hand stopped moving. "Your dick?"

I put my hand over hers and brought it back to my cock. "I start coming and expect the chop, the pain, it just hangs over me. I come jerking off, but I don't get *in there* anymore, just can't. Can't let go."

"It's okay. I understand." Her hand stroked firmly under mine. "Don't I understand?" A knowing smirk passed over her face.

I stopped her hand. "Hey, you're no whore. No whore," I breathed, my lips brushing the side of her throat, nuzzling the warm delicate skin, inhaling her soap fresh scent to push back the demons.

Clean, clean, we're both clean now, aren't we?

"I know exactly what you're talking about. I learned to shut it off," she said, her voice low.

"I don't want you shut off with me," I said. "What they did to you isn't what we do. Different..." I struggled to find the right words.

"I don't want to be shut off anymore, and definitely not with you," she breathed, her warm fingers opening over my cock once more, stroking.

In her hand my need grew ferocious. That familiar pressure cast its net over me, pulling, pulling...

I winced.

"What is it? Did I—"

I swallowed down the knot in my throat. "It starts burning with a hint of fear. The one time I'm supposed to be letting loose, I can't."

"I helped them do that to you," she whispered, pulling back from me.

"No." I grabbed onto her hands. "You're the only one who understands. You were there. You were in all of that hell with me. You know." I kissed her, my throat thick, my breath all fisted up in a knot. "I need you. Only you."

"Justin—"

"You."

"Let me change it for you." She put my hands over her tits again, and my pulse hammered. Her small nipples were as hard as tiny stones against my skin.

"You're so beautiful," my voice quaked, like my rattling insides. Her face softened, a hint of a surprised, shy smile lighting up those incredible eyes.

Wild magic. All of it for me.

I'd never said nice things to a girl before. Never spoke during sex. To say what? *Yeah, like that. Harder. Open more.* But now I wanted to, I wanted to make Serena happy, make her smile with pleasure which made me lighter and warmer inside. I wanted to fill her with my tumbling thoughts, my crazy feelings. I couldn't stop it.

Why should I?

I gently cupped a silky soft breast, and she whimpered and moved under my exploring touch. She leaned back, bringing my head closer to her breasts, offering her body to me.

"You don't have to do anything. I know you think you do, but you don't," I whispered. "If you don't want to, if you don't want me—"

"Oh, Justin..." Her hands dug into my hair. "I feel and I want, and I want you. I want to be with you, make things better for you, and I want you to make things better for me. I want so much, so badly."

"You want to live," I whispered. *I want to live too.*

"Yes, yes..." She planted kisses on my forehead. "And I want you to feel good again."

"We got plenty of time for that."

"Do we? Really? We might only have tonight."

"What are you talking about?"

"What if they find us? What if Tania turns out to be a psycho serial killer and murders us in our sleep with some lethal injections she's got stashed in her bag? What if aliens land in South Dakota tonight and take over the world?"

I laughed, and she stroked my cock again.

"Oh fuck, Serena..." I slid my forehead against hers, my grip on her shoulders real tight. Overwhelmed.

"Let me have you. Please let me have you," she murmured.

She slid down alongside me and took me in her mouth, and I let out a long hiss of air. It'd been so long, so long since I hadn't dreaded being touched by a woman. So long since I'd wanted to come. Since Serena in that hellhole dungeon.

I was fucking coming tonight. I was unraveling.

"Serena..."

She sucked on me, her head moving between my legs. I pulled her new dark hair out of the way, and she moaned as I wound it tightly in my grip.

"Fuck yes, yes." My insides roared, my every muscle was on fire straining with need. I wanted nothing more than to come at her will, to come the way she wanted me to. To spill myself inside her, and feel her take all of me in.

My heart pounded as my hips moved against her on some wild, animal instinct. There was no thinking now, only giving in, giving over. The swell of heat and excitement roared in my veins, only it tore at me, ripping. That familiar panic edged around my heart like a steel cage. The blade was at the ready, the spill of my blood.

A black fog filled my eyes. My skin was covered in a film of sweat, my neck twisted, my eyes jammed shut. "Stop. Stop." I pulled back, and so did she. "I can't. I start and then, there's the knife and the—"

"Shh." Her hand smoothed across my hot face. "Concentrate on my voice, on my body around you. Listen to me and take me. It's just you and me here in this bed. You and me."

She was saying it to herself as much as to me.

I swallowed hard. "Yeah, you and me."

She turned on the bed and spread her legs. "Kiss me."

I didn't need to be convinced. I sank my mouth between her legs and relished the taste of her musky arousal that I knew so well. A narcotic filling my veins. I lapped at her slick flesh, taking in every detail, every throb and shudder and cry of her body. Thread by thread, ounce by ounce, I let go of that red-stained terror, the anxiety unchaining me, the shroud of pain lifting a few degrees more and more, fading.

Yes. Yes. This is better, so much better. Making her fly for me.

She moved underneath me, her hands tugging roughly on my hair, her eyes on me. She spoke to me in a steady stream of urgent words. Words of encouragement, words of lust. I focused on her voice and let it wrap around me and hold me.

I wanted more of her. I wanted her to explode for me, on me. Sliding my index finger inside her, I rubbed at her inner wall. A few years back one of the girls at the club had showed me how. Hitting the G-spot, she'd told me, was worth every ounce of effort and not enough men bothered. I wanted to bother for Serena. I wanted to shower her with gold and silver and diamonds, dazzle her, give her everything she'd never had. Give her a fuck of worship and adoration.

I churned my hand, forgetting I didn't have a middle finger to slide inside her and give her a more intense experience. I gnashed my teeth together, doing battle with those same dark villains that I dueled with every fucking day. Inadequacy, resentment. Anger. Even here, in bed with the woman I craved, they wouldn't leave me the hell alone.

That phantom ache sprinted over my chopped knuckle, reminding me.

Focus.

My muscles relaxed as I settled into a rhythm, my breathing easier with every moan that escaped her mouth. She cried out, once, twice, her back arching, body stiffening. A prickle raced over my scalp. That cry wasn't from pleasure. No, I damn well knew the difference.

That was pain.

My heart clutched, and I stopped, rising up, bringing my face to hers. "Serena? What is it? You okay?"

"Please, please, keep going. Don't stop." She bit at her lip, her face turning away from mine, her arms taut against my shoulders, her jaw stiff like she was holding back being sick.

"Am I doing something wrong? You don't like it? Tell me—"

"No! No, it's not you," she bit out.

My chest constricted. "What the fuck they do to you?"

"Please, please, Justin." Her fingers touched my rigid jaw as if persuading it to ease. "Please..."

"What did those fuckers do to you?" I ground my forehead into hers, her tears wetting my lips.

"Justin—"

"Tell me!"

Her legs pressed together against mine. "He had me do a train the night before they left for San Diego, so I wouldn't forget my place at the club."

My heart flew up my throat and jammed there. "Fuck! Fuck!"

"And Jan—"

"Jan? The girl you shot? Whose car we took?"

"Yeah, she's his new favorite. He had her pick the order of the men."

"Jesus." My grip on her flesh tightened.

"Don't say another word." Her hand swept my hair from my face. "Please."

"How about, I'm real glad you fucking shot her."

A weak smile flickered across her face. "Me too." Her legs pressed around mine. "Keep going, Justin. I want to feel you inside me."

"You're all bruised inside, then you rode all day. I'm not ... I can't...Shit."

"I don't care. I want you, I want you inside me. I want you to make it all go away."

"Baby, you need to heal."

"It's you I need. You—"

"You'll get better. You will. This will all get better. Not right away, but soon."

"Wait. Let me talk. Let me say whatever I want. I haven't been able to do that in years."

I brushed her lips with mine. "You say and do whatever the hell you want, baby. You're out of there. You're free."

"I'm free, but I can't do what I want right now which is have sex with you. I'm free, but I feel trapped and I don't want to be trapped."

"What they did to you was a violent assault, not sex, not any kind of sex. That was a power trip, a form of torture. It has nothing to do with you, with what you want, how you feel, who you are, all right?"

She hiccuped, short breaths heating my shoulder. "I don't want to be broken."

I held her close. "You're not broken, you're not. And from now on, you'll always be free. I promise you." More tears came. Silent at first, then real weeping. She emptied herself. I'd bet good money she hadn't cried in years. I murmured into her hair, losing myself in the warmth of her skin, her body clinging to mine.

The bathroom door slowly opened and the light switched off. Muffled footsteps. "Is everything okay?" Tania whispered. "Am I— Should I—"

"No." I pushed my hair from my face as I sat up. "Her ex fucked with her, and ..."

"Oh shit, I'm sorry. Honey…"

Serena turned in my arms and held out her hand and Tania took it, sinking on the edge of our bed. The fresh scent from the soap Tania had used broke through and lightened the thick murk of misery and unsatisfied craving that was now plastered over me and Serena.

"It's okay, Serena. It's early days yet," said Tania, her voice gentle. "You need to give yourself time. Both of you do." She glanced at me and back to Serena. "Sucks, but that's the truth."

"What's your truth?" Serena asked.

Tania's head jerked back. "My what?"

"What are you running away from? Really running away from? It's not your family or your home town. Not really."

Tania's shoulders fell. "I want to break out of my mold, but I haven't been able to yet."

"Why?" Serena pressed.

"I'm afraid. Uptight," Tania replied quickly, her eyes lifting back to Serena. "I had a chance recently to step out of my homemade box, my tight little comfort zone, but I backed out in the end. And I regret not taking that risk."

"With a man?"

"A hot man. Real hot." She rolled her eyes and tilted her head down, a noise rising in the back of her throat.

Serena sat up straighter. The sheet falling from her bare chest.

"You're taking a huge risk now, with us, aren't you?"

"Yeah. I have to confess, you two scare the living daylights out of me."

Letting out a dry laugh, I reached for a cigarette on the side table. I lit up and sucked in deep, the smoke searing my lungs.

"We won't bite, unless bitten," said Serena. "And anyway, I trust you, Tania."

"I trust you, too. I do," whispered Tania. "You two should be happy, though. You're together now. Isn't that something to be happy about? I'm happy for you."

"You're too sweet," said Serena.

"Yeah, I'm sweet all right." Tania let out a dark laugh.

"What's so funny?" I asked.

"I don't think I've ever been called that before. Lately, it's been bitch or cold, hard bitch or—"

"That isn't you," Serena said. "Not you."

"Not you." I exhaled a thick stream of smoke to the side.

Serena leaned over and planted a soft kiss on Tania's mouth, and Tania's eyes widened. Her fingers went to her mouth as Serena pulled back. My muscles tightened. What the fuck?

"Tania," Serena whispered. "I need you."

"W-What is it?"

"I can't be with Finger the way I want to be."

Tania's head dipped slightly. "You can't what?"

"My ex hurt me the other day, real bad, and I...I can't be with Finger the way I want, in every way. Help me. Please? Help us."

"Serena!" My voice was sharp, and Tania's eyes cut to me.

"Wait, what?" Tania spit out. "I don't understand. How do you want me to..."

Serena stroked Tania's arm. "Together we could help each other feel good."

Tania's face froze. "Uh, I..I've never...I don't know...I mean...I—"

"Serena," I said, my voice low, the cigarette burning down between my thumb and forefinger.

"You don't have to do anything you don't want to do, Tania," Serena continued. "I'll show you. It'll be good for you, I promise."

Tania gripped Serena's wandering hand on her arm. "Serena, Finger's your man, your—"

"I want him to be inside me, but he can't be right now. And it's hard for him too, after what they did to him. We all need this right now, Tania. We need each other."

Her frank words, her emotional, raw voice settled over me like a hot wind when your skin is already on fire.

"We know each other. We like each other, right? I'll make it good for you," Serena said. "We both will."

Tania blinked. "Yeah, yeah, but—"

Serena raised up on the bed, her back straight, her beautiful full tits clearly visible in the television light. "I just want to feel good tonight. Don't you? I don't want to struggle or cry or be afraid. Not tonight. Not now. This might be all we have left together. When we leave tomorrow, this is what I want to remember and take with me. This, us together, us doing something good for ourselves and each other."

My heart thudded in my chest. She was fucking right.

Serena took Tania's hand and placed it on her tit. Tania sucked in a quick breath, her eyes darting to Serena's chest.

"I'm going to kiss you again," Serena whispered, and my painfully hard cock twitched under the sheet.

Tania nodded.

I tossed what was left of my cigarette in the water glass at my side.

Serena leaned forward and planted another kiss on Tania's mouth, gentle, sensual. Tania's eyes fluttered closed. Serena's tongue flicked against Tania's parted lips. Tania opened up and they kissed full on, and I held my fucking breath. Serena's hands lifted Tania's shirt up, and Tania raised her arms. The shirt dropped to the floor and Serena fondled Tania's tits. I licked my lips, my cock aching, my balls seizing.

Serena touched my hand. "Kiss Tania."

My pulse spiked, and I leaned over and kissed Tania. Her lips were warm, and they quivered under mine. A moan escaped her, and I liked that. I liked that Serena had just been there. I could feel the heat of Serena's gaze on us, and it made my blood quicken in my veins.

Serena tugged down Tania's pajama shorts and Tania kicked them off. She was naked on our bed now. Serena guided her to turning slightly and leaning back against me. Her hand went in between Tania's legs and stroked.

Fuck.

Tania gasped, her hips lifting, her back pushing into my chest. She let out a cry, her nails digging into my thighs.

We were doing this, and yeah, I wanted it. If this was the only way to be with Serena, why the hell not?

I cupped Tania's breasts, squeezing them hard and kissed her again, my tongue sliding against hers. Tania's hands rose up around my neck.

I caught Serena's pleased gaze. She lowered her head in between Tania's legs, her eyes hanging on mine.

"Shit!" Tania yelped, seizing in my hold.

Tania turned her head against my chest. "Holy shit, she's—"

"Yeah, she is." I grinned at Serena, tugging on Tania's nipple, my other hand going to her clit, a finger flicking against Serena's mouth. Serena's tongue swirled over my pulsing fingers, and we both worked Tania. I rubbed my cock against Tania's ass. Our shared lust rose up like vines around our limbs, tightening over my flesh, burning through me.

I backed up on the bed until my feet hit the floor. Tania's eyes fluttered as I pulled her back, her head falling off the side of the mattress. I tapped her lips with my stiff cock. "Take it."

Her eyes widened as my hand cuffed her neck, supporting her, applying pressure. I slid my hard length past her parted lips and fucked her mouth. Her chest heaved as Serena sucked on her pussy. Within moments Tania's body shuddered in our grip, her hips jerking. Her mouth released my cock, and she let out a wild cry. Serena slithered up Tania's body and kissed her, their tongues dancing in a frenzy.

I fell onto the bed at their side, my cock throbbing. I needed Serena. Suddenly her lips were on mine, and I tasted Tania on her.

My simmering blood rushed through my veins making me dizzy, my vision blurry. "So fucking good," I breathed.

"Oh hey, I've got a pack of condoms in my bag." Tania's lazy laughter filled the room.

We were high.

I wanted Serena so fucking bad. I wanted Tania so fucking bad. I wanted them both on me. But that fear danced in my insides, skittered over my skin.

Serena's eyes hung on mine in the semi-darkness. She knew.

I'm at your mercy, baby. Deliver me.

With a firm hand at the base of my cock, she said, "Get a condom, Tania."

Tania scrambled from the bed and went to her handbag. She came back, flinging a thick pack of rubbers on the bed.

"Take his cock in your mouth," Serena said. "Blow him slow."

Tania's eyebrows jumped and she crouched on the bed, ass in the air and took my dick in her mouth. I let out a grunt, my hand sliding down her ass as she moved. She pulled on me once, twice, her hands clamping around my thighs. Her moans rose between me and Serena as Serena brought my free hand to her mouth and licked at the nub of where my one middle finger once was.

"Baby," I groaned, my throat aching.

She flicked at the scarred area slowly with her tongue, nuzzling it, sucking on it with her lips.

"Serena..." I whispered hoarsely, my chest burning, my cock throbbing in Tania's mouth. I dug a hand into Tania's hair, holding her head against me.

Serena stroked Tania's back. "Put a rubber on him."

Tania released my protesting cock and tore open a packet. She fit the rubber on my dick, and I helped her pull it in place.

Serena pressed me down on the bed. She guided Tania to straddling me and kissed the side of her face. "Make him feel good for me. For us."

Serena held the base of my cock in her hands as she guided her on me. Tania's eyes closed as she sank down over me, a hand on my middle. "Ohhhhh."

"That's it," Serena's husky voice licked over me. She slid her fingers down between Tania's legs, rubbing at her clit in circles as Tania rocked over me, taking me in deeper. "You like that?"

Tania let out a long moan in response, her head falling back. I'd bet the girl had never had it so good. I moved inside Tania, my eyes on both women who were side by side over me, taking them in. We found a rhythm to our fucking, and Serena's strokes on Tania and over my cock got faster, tenser. She kissed Tania on the lips. Kissed the side of her face, sucked on her earlobe, squeezed a breast, murmuring encouragements to Tania.

"Oh yeah. Yeah..." Tania rode me harder.

Serena bent over and kissed me, her fingernails cutting a fierce path down my taut chest. Goosebumps rose on Tania's skin. I gripped her damp thighs tighter and we fucked faster. That rush of adrenaline came at me like a steel wall, preparing me for the chop, preparing me for the blood, warning me about the burn. I couldn't stop it.

Serena kissed my throat up to my ear. "You want me?" she whispered and my chest squeezed.

"Fuck yes!" My neck strained up.

Serena turned, facing Tania, and straddling my face, lowered her hips over my mouth.

Yes. Yes. Yes.

I sucked on Serena, lapped at her. I'd never been so greedy, so hungry, so high, even in that dungeon. Serena leaned forward and kissed Tania. Murmurs, and moans, tongues reveling, flesh slapping. There was no thinking, only flying, only bursting. I thrust harder into Tania, and she cried out loudly. Serena came on me, and I came in Tania, and we were a glorious fucking hot mess.

No chopping, no cutting, no pain, no terror. Only the glory of breaking through, coming pure and simple with Serena.

She climbed off me and laid down on the pillows around my head. I kissed her.

"You're amazing," I breathed.

Sounded so stupid, but it was the truth. I was fucking tongue tied. Incapable of thoughts, speech, anything. Serena only stroked my chest, and I took her hand in mine.

Sputtering, Tania collapsed on the other side of me.

Serena slid a hand in her hair. "Did you like that?"

"Yeah, I did." Tania caught her breath. "I've never done a three-some or even kissed another girl before. I've never even come during sex, how about that?

Serena propped her head on her hand. "Never?"

"No. I did now, though." She let out a lazy laugh. "Twice, in fact. Can you believe that? That was—I don't know what that was. Are you okay? How was it for you?"

Serena's face bloomed into a grin. "That was really good for me too." She took Tania's hand in hers and kissed it.

I pulled the full condom off my dick, and the rubber snapped. Tania's eyes darted to my cock, to my hands at work tying up the rubber.

She bit her lip and sat up. "I'll go back to my bed so you two can..."

"No," said Serena. "We just got started."

Tania's lips parted. "Oh?"

"Don't you want to do more?" Serena asked, a finger coiling in a lock of Tania's hair. "It's a long night."

The women glanced at me.

"I'm not going to say no," I said.

"Neither am I," replied Tania.

"Good," Serena said.

Tania's large eyes darted to mine, and I leaned back on the bed again and stroked my cock up and down, up and down.

Serena's face blazed and she nestled in between my legs and went down on me, sucking on my balls as I continued to work myself staring at Tania who blushed bright red.

"How do you like it, Finger?" Tania asked, sliding a hand up and down Serena's bare back, stroking her.

"I like it hard," I said through gritted teeth, and Serena pushed my hand away and pressed her tongue down the side of my cock and back up, flicking at my wet tip. I fisted a hand in her hair as she took me in, swallowed me whole. "Yeah, oh yeah—"

Totally at her fucking mercy, and I loved it. She was my portal to hell and to heaven. She was making a kind of heaven come true for me right now, for both of us, and for Tania too.

Tania's cool hand cupped my balls making my breath catch. She stroked and massaged me as Serena sucked and swallowed. The two of them working me blew my mind and every cell in my body. My vision blurred, my lungs crushed together. The steel wall still built over me blade by blade.

"We're right here, baby," Serena reminded me, and I breathed in again.

She released me and guided Tania to lay stomach-down on the bed. She quickly put another condom on my stiff cock. "Fuck her from behind."

I got out of the bed, and, planting my feet on the floor, I gripped Tania's hips and rubbed my cock in between her ass cheeks, dipping in her wetness. Tania gasped, shuddering in my tight hold.

"I don't know about...I mean, I've never..."

"I like playing with you, Tania." I thrust easily into her wet cunt and she moaned loudly.

Serena positioned herself at Tania's head, spreading her legs, a hand at Tania's face. "I want to come for you, Tania," she whispered. "Make me crazy, the way Finger is making you crazy."

Tania's face sank over Serena's bare pussy, and Serena sucked in a breath. I pounded into Tania as I watched them, licking my lips. I could still taste Serena on my mouth as Tania's tight heat drove me insane. She groaned loudly and pushed back against my every thrust. Serena squirmed on the bed, her hands curling in the twisted sheets, in the mattress, her tits swaying under the thorough invasion of Tania's mouth and the relentless pounding I gave Tania.

Our ragged breaths, the sliding of our wet flesh, the jerking of the bed scraping against the wall filled the room. My eyes held Serena's but the burn, the burn unfurled inside me, clouding everything.

"Finger—you're here with me and Tania." Serena's voice sliced through the dark and into my soul. "We've got you inside us. You're fucking us so good. So good. Don't stop. Give us more. Right here, right now. Listen to me, honey. Look at me. Feel Tania all around

135

you. Watch me. I'm loving this. Loving it."

I groaned at her words, pushing the stinging flames in my hands back. I gripped Tania's ass harder, and she jolted forward on a grunt. The raw slapping of our bodies together grew even more urgent. I thrust in her faster. I thrust in Serena.

Serena.

Serena.

Serena.

"Fuck yes." Her one hand cupped Tania's head. "Feels so good. So fucking good."

Tania only moaned as I pumped inside her viciously. Serena's back arched and she cried out, her hips rocking faster against Tania's face. The heat bunched in my lower back and shot through my legs, my hips driving into both of these magnificent women.

There were no knives, no chains, no acid laughter, not now. Now there was only these beautiful women giving to me, all of us giving to each other, moving together, creating a wave of raw heat together. My pulse roared in my neck, my heart exploded in my chest.

"Fuck!"

I came, I came, I came.

Tania collapsed on Serena's torso, shuddering under my final grinding assault. Her hands landed on Serena's tits, stroking them, her mouth nuzzling them, a search for gentleness. I pulled out of Tania and climbed on the bed with them. They wrapped themselves around me, and I held them close. I needed their touch, their smell, their skin against mine.

Tania practically purred against my chest, and Serena laughed softly. I didn't think I'd ever heard her laugh before. Pure joy, ease, and delight which wrapped around my torn up soul and squeezed, mending it, sending me higher, sending me somewhere good, full, rich.

"I want to live."

Yeah, I'd never heard anything like that laugh before in my life.

LIGHT FILTERED THROUGH THE MOTEL room shade,

prickling my eyes.

Desperate whimpers penetrated my brain, and I forced my eyes open. I held Tania from behind, and in front of her on the bed was Serena, her back to Tania. The whimpers and moans grew louder. Serena was coming.

Tania's one leg was thrown over Serena's hip, her hand over her waist, stroking in between her legs, the two of them rocking together in a rhythm, moaning together.

Shit, what a sight to wake up to.

I want in.

I dipped my fingers through Tania's ass crack and found her wet slit. She gasped and threw her head back against my shoulder. I played with her, my rhythm steady, and she mumbled something incoherent. I raised my finger back up her ass and toyed with her tight hole and she let out a hiss. I retreated, laying kisses across her damp neck, around her throat, and she finally relaxed in my hold once more. Again, I nudged my finger past her tight ring, and she gasped.

"Let me in, Tania," I whispered. Gently, I slid in further and further. "Yeah, yeah, that's it."

Serena came, her moans ringing out, and my chest contracted at the sound. She turned around immediately and kissed Tania's mouth, kissed and licked her tits as I worked Tania's ass.

"Let him in, Tania, it's all right," Serena said against Tania's skin. She slid up her body and kissed her mouth again. "He wants us both coming all over him now."

Tania let out another low moan.

These two were killing me.

Serena pushed down the bed and buried her face in Tania's pussy, a hand curling around her ass, meeting my busy fingers. Tania squirmed, moaning loudly as Serena slid two of her fingers inside her pussy, working her as I worked Tania's ass with steady, careful strokes. I'd never been with a virgin before, ass or otherwise. I liked it, I liked giving Tania something new, something only the three of us shared.

"Oh fuck! Oh fuck!" Tania jolted in my hold, her skin wet,

her body stiff. I bit her neck, and she came hard, her groans and cries somewhere between shock and ecstasy, her body trembling yet bound between me and Serena. She clung to us, we clung to her.

Serena kissed her mouth gently until she relaxed. I released Tania's ass, and my palm squeezed down over her wet pussy. Serena kissed me while Tania's hand reached back and found my stiff cock.

"Shit, you're incredible," Tania muttered pulling on my cock. My last drop of self-control evaporated.

"If we had lube, I'd be in your ass right now," I muttered.

Letting out a grunt, I sat up on my haunches taking in a breath, wiping the sweat from my eyes, down my chest. Serena took my cock in her mouth, her eyes on me.

"Baby—"

Tania curled behind me, her tongue laying a wet trail up my spine to the base of my skull. Her nails skimmed down my shoulders and arms, her fingers traveled to my nipples, scraping around them and down my middle as she rubbed her body against my back. Shivers streaked over my flesh.

Hands, tongues, lips, sucks.

Tania's tongue clashed with Serena's as they both ravaged my cock and my balls with their greedy mouths. I slid my fingers between Tania's thighs, in her ass again and she squirmed and writhed against my touch. My other hand kneaded Serena's tit.

They were my women, mine for right now, mine in this goddamn bed.

My hands dug in their hair as I pumped my hips. The burn whipped around us, hot and thick. This burn was good, galvanizing. The three of us rode that fever, they rode it with me as they gave to me, taking me higher, giving me this insane pleasure. The pressure built in my cock and nothing stopped me, nothing ripped at me. I stayed inside it and rode its wave. I focused on their hands on my flesh, their wet tongues. They kept me close, the heat of their bodies blending with mine. I let myself into this vortex the three of us created and I didn't get scorched. I fucking flew.

Specfuckingtacular.

I came, grunting loudly, making a mess on both of them. I collapsed on the bed in between them, our limbs tangling, our breaths making short, savage noises. The three of us kissed and groped and sucked, our bodies wet, our skin burning.

We spent the whole day on that bed fucking any way we could until we had to leave.

Until I had to leave them at the mercy of the rotten world outside that precious room.

T HE SHOWER WATER RAN, THE sound cutting through the fog of my sleep. I jacked up in bed. Tania was curled up, clutching a pillow on the other side of the mattress. Serena was missing. I tripped out of the bed on the twisted sheet and darted into the steam-filled bathroom. She stood at the sink, her body dripping wet from the shower. Her head was bent over her arm.

Red blood splattered onto the white porcelain.

"What the hell are you doing? Are you okay?"

Her head lifted to mine, her eyes heavy. In one hand she held my knife, blood dribbling from her abdomen, her other arm.

"What the fuck?" I grabbed the knife from her.

I wiped a hand across the blood just above her pussy. She had cut over the tattoo of the Smoking Gun skeleton. I gripped her bleeding arm. Another small red line rose up in blood there, about two inches below her wrist.

"Baby—"

"Finish them both for me." Our eyes met in the steamy mirror.

"What the hell are you talking about? Jesus."

"I want to obliterate their brand and put your mark on me. And one over my wrist. Just like yours on your face. I want it on me."

"That's crazy."

"You finish it for me."

"No. You don't want that."

"I do. I do. Today we say goodbye for however long, maybe forever."

"That's not true. We'll have another day and another and another. We're gonna make it happen."

"Until then...please."

I scanned all the ugly bruises and scars over her beautiful body. "Baby..."

She gave me a watery smile. "This is my choice. This mark I want, and I want it from you." Her voice was thick and determined. "Why should I only have scars of what they did to me? Of my stupidity in ending up with them? Why? Why can't I have a good memory on my body? So that every time I see it, touch it, I'm filled with the good that is us, the good that these two days brought us. Knowing it matches yours. Last night was fantastic. It made me feel good, feel free, powerful even. I want to remember that victory every day, I don't want to forget. It's going to be a rough road without you. I need this, Justin. I need it from you."

I took the knife from the sink and pressing my lips together, I sliced the two dashes along the line she'd made over the tattoo. The letter "F" rose up in red on her pale flesh.

"Finish my wrist now."

I slashed quickly on the delicate skin of her wrist. Dropping the knife in the sink, I licked over the wound, and she let out a cry. We were both marked with each other, for fucking ever. Not just skin and blood, but soul deep, that shadowy place where twisted secrets are spun and hidden from even ourselves.

Lifting her up on the edge of the bathroom counter, I spread her legs wide with a shove of my hips.

She dug her hands in my hair, a line of blood skating down her arm, another down into her cunt. "Yes, yes. One last time."

"Stop talking like that." I dropped to my knees on the damp tile floor and kissed her pussy, licking at her blood, her wet heat.

She clung to me, crying out, her blood smearing my face.

Making every moment count, every moment between us last. Wherever and whenever. Even here in a motel bathroom in Who Knows Where, South Dakota at four twenty in the morning.

"This is just the beginning," I said against her skin. "Just the fucking beginning."

17
SERENA

"YOU SURE?" FINGER ASKED, AGAIN, buckling the saddlebag on his bike.

"Positive," Tania replied.

"This is the best idea. It is." I shifted my weight, ignoring my sudden inability to breathe properly. Ignoring the early morning heat bouncing up off the asphalt of the motel parking lot making me even more lightheaded, even more dizzy.

Finger stared at me and Tania, calculating, regretting.

"You go. You've got to go," I said. And he did, he had some club business to take care of in Nebraska today.

"Go," Tania added.

My watery eyes hung on his. Something pinched inside my chest and twisted and twisted. This was the first time I'd be alone. On my own, without the framework of the Smoking Guns, without a specific place in a horrible hierarchy which was, of course, liberating, but also oddly terrifying. Now, I would be without Justin.

When I'd first met him a spark had gone off inside me and unspooled everything I'd had rolled up tight. All the long weeks afterward, I'd kept that sparkling thread under my heart muscle and would take it out before I'd go to sleep, right before I'd close my eyes. I'd wind that delicate, vibrant twine around me tightly and burrow my face into my pillow and wish and dream. And the dream had come true. He'd done as he'd said. He'd come back for me. He'd broken me out and given me a new chance at a new life. I wanted that new life with him in it.

But now we had to separate, say goodbye.

We'd had two nights. They'd been priceless. Now they too would become memories to spool and unspool in the dark of my night.

Something dislodged inside me and threatened to slide out from under me. My stomach hardened against it. If I lost it now, got emotional and crazy, all of me would let go and go tumbling into a pit that there would be no climbing out from. I needed to choke it down and carry on without him holding my hand, without him whispering my name against my skin, and laughing softly in my ear.

Tania stepped back from us, and turned to her car, busied herself pushing shit around in the crowded trunk. Finger kissed me, cradling my face in his hands. I pressed into him, my arms wrapping around his waist, and squeezed him hard. My fingertips dug into the taut muscles of his back, memorizing their feel, their curves, how they stretched and tightened against me. How it felt, the two of us together in the world.

Would there ever be a place for us in this world?

"I'll get you a driver's license with a new name and date of birth. We got people in DMVs all over, won't be a problem."

"Goodbye, Serena," I quipped.

"Yeah." His eyes clouded at the sound of that terrible word. Goodbye. He fisted my hair, keeping me close. "I'll be in touch real soon. You know that, right?" His voice was even more hoarse than usual, that odd, scratchy, husky quality more pronounced now.

"I know," I said into his chest, breathing in the fresh soapy scent we shared from a shower the two of us had hastily taken together only half an hour ago.

Remember this. Remember how this feels.

He released me and pressed a round hard object covered in a worn suede pouch into my palm. "I want you to have this." I glanced up at him as I opened the pouch and pulled out an old pocket watch.

He flipped the top. No, it wasn't a watch.

"A compass?"

"My dad gave it to me. His dad had given it to him. It's the compass he used in the army in Vietnam. Take it."

"I can't. It's precious to you, it's—"

He took my face in his hands, his fierce eyes drilling into mine. "You're precious to me. You mean everything to me." He swallowed hard. "I can't explain it, but I have this mess of feelings for you. Actually, it's not a mess, it's real clear how important you are to me." He took in a breath, his brows knitting. "Knowing you have the compass is a solid promise. My promise that I will always find you. I will always come for you, that you and me, we're connected like the laws of gravity and magnetics and physics that govern this earth. You and me, we're inevitable."

My heart pounded in my chest as I held his iron gaze. Urgent faith, sturdy strength for the both of us.

A commitment.

"We're going to be together one day, Serena. One day real soon."

"One day," I breathed, knowing in my gut what that meant.

Things were shit now. Med would be on the warpath, out for blood. He just might figure out that it was Finger who had helped me—or he wouldn't. Either way, it meant that Finger and I couldn't be together in plain sight. We would have to lay low for a long time yet.

How long?

"No one's going to keep us apart." Finger closed the antique brass compass and put his palm over it, pressing it in my hand. "We will be together, we'll find a way. We can't not find a way."

"One day."

"One day." He kissed me hard, and a noise escaped the back of his throat. He pulled me into his chest, kissing the top of my head, burying his face in my hair.

I hung on. This was too hard, too awful. Too everything.

"We should get moving," came Tania's soft voice from somewhere behind me.

He let me go and hugged Tania. "Thank you. For everything."

"You're welcome." Tania hugged him back. "This will all work out. You'll see. She'll be fine." She pulled back from him and put her arm through mine.

"You take care of her for me," he said to her.

"I will. We'll take care of each other. Now go."

Finger got on his bike and started her up. That blast ripped the air, making my heart beat even faster. I'd considered it an ugly sound for so long, yet right this second it was a symphony bursting with promise and possibility and glory. He put his gloves on, looking away, on purpose, I was sure of it, as he adjusted himself in his saddle. It had only been a couple of days since he'd been on a bike, but I could tell it had felt like forever for him.

He sucked in a deep breath, his back straightening, and stared at me and Tania. His dark eyes were now shielded by his goggles, but I knew they burned, burned same as mine. One day soon I would be on a bike with him, and we would ride together without hiding, without fear. That longing, that emotion, that determination radiated between us, and I sucked in its heady fragrance through every pore and let it fill me, fill me with courage to face the very next moment without him, and then the next, and the next.

My eyes blinked from behind my sunglasses, and something in my stomach dropped and unspooled, but I pulled it in. Yes, one day soon. I had to believe. I had to be patient.

I had to be careful.

His chest heaved. "Tell me to go. I don't think I can—"

"Go, baby," I breathed. "You have to go."

I clasped the compass tightly. It was the one thing I owned now, the one thing that was mine in all this world. He'd lain his heart and soul in my hands, and I would keep them safe. I would never let them go.

Ever.

WE MADE IT TO CHICAGO.

Tania and I got that apartment she'd had a lead on, a tiny walk-up in a crap building in Pilsen. The neighborhood's charming decrepit buildings were slowly starting to turn into lofts, but it was still affordable, plus the area had a lot of ethnic diversity which we both liked.

Within a few weeks of landing in Chicago, Tania got her old job back at a restaurant as a waitress and substitute bartender a few nights out of the week, and an additional job at an art gallery during the day with Neil, a good friend of hers from college. I found work at a vintage clothing store taking in stock and keeping it organized which I was very good at. I dressed the way I wanted to, bought clothes at a big discount for myself and Tania. It was fun.

Finger had gotten me a new name, Social Security number, and driver's license as promised, but I was nervous about using the number so I managed to get paid under the table. I'd told my boss I'd just gotten a nasty divorce and wanted to stay under the radar for a while, and he was cool about it. I was now "Ashley Wyeth" to the world.

Hello world, hello shiny normal life.

Well. Kind of normal.

Tania and I settled into being roommates very easily. She took the one small bedroom, and I slept on a futon sofa in a corner of the living room. I'd separated my corner from the rest of the room with a broken Asian screen we'd found on the street which we cleaned up, patched, and repainted. I didn't mind the living room. In fact, I preferred being in the much larger open space instead of that tiny, tiny bedroom. I couldn't breathe in there.

Tania loved flea markets and rummage sales, and I discovered I did too. We spent our weekends scouring Maxwell Street Market, which was gritty but had loads of character. We always found something we had to have. Tania often brought home odd pieces she'd find on the sidewalks that other people had thrown away. She saw something in each piece, and I loved getting my hands on whatever it was and giving it new life. We made a good design team.

We worked hard on making our living space special. I would scrub a trashed piece of wood furniture clean, stripping it, varnishing, painting it an odd color, then scrub it again to make it seem antiqued. I'd find quirky hardware pieces and use them for handles or as eccentric details. We decorated the apartment with inexpensive tapestries. I made a mini chandelier of sorts out of rusty bicycle chains and the prettiest small bulbs. Tania bought old pillows, and I patched up any holes or tears with contrasting fabric. Each time I opened the front door, the colors, the textures, the lines all sang to me in a bright rich chorus of YES.

On the weekends, Tania and Neil would drag me with them to funky art parties at galleries or artists' studios or performance spaces. I met people my age, I made friends. Well, sort of. I made acquaintances. I wasn't ready to let people in, I wasn't sure when I would be. I stuck to Tania and Neil. They were enough for me for now.

What I really wanted, needed, was out of my reach.

AFTER TOO MANY WEEKS, FINGER was finally able to come to Chicago for a visit.

He didn't come to the apartment. In fact, I didn't think he ever would. We'd agreed it was best that when he was able to come to Chicago, he and I would meet on neutral ground in case he was being watched or followed.

I headed to the low budget motel in the northern outskirts of town. I knocked on room 103, my stomach churning, my mouth dry. Three sets of two knocks as he'd told me to do.

The door opened, and I held my breath. A threshold to a new life, one with him in it. Would the emotional and physical intensity between us be the same? I didn't want the heady chemistry between us to change, but maybe it would be different now. Would we still want and need each other the way we had in that motel, or was all that only us being swept up in a life-threatening drama? We still were in a life-threatening drama, but without the immediate fear of death and destruction hanging over us like the last time.

I stepped through the doorway, thrumming somewhere between anxiety and excitement. My skin tingled, my pulse pounded. The motel room was dark, and the door thudded and clicked shut behind me. A deep, ragged exhale released next to me.

I reached out. "Finger?"

Strong arms embraced me. "Baby."

I held onto him, squeezed him, smelled his skin, sweat, soap, and cedar. I turned and buried my face in his throat, took in his breath, reveled in the press of his body. His lips found mine and we kissed. My heart thundered in my chest, I couldn't breathe right.

He lifted me up in his arms. The need to touch his bare skin

146

overwhelmed me. I didn't want to think. Need and desire flung us all around the room like a bottle rocket.

I pulled on his T-shirt underneath his hoodie. I only wanted to consume him, us, before anyone could take it away again. Before I was told to stop, to leave, to not look back. Would this be the last time for a long time? Would it be a disaster and then he'd never contact me again? Would he still want me?

Would I be able to handle all this?

I squirmed away from him and tore off my jacket, my shirt, my bra. He hit a switch, and a dim light further in the room by the bed popped on. He stood there, watching me like a hungry creature of the night, his jaw tense, eyes shining, his built chest rising and falling quickly. Those once ugly scars on his face had become a part of his skin. A short beard now covered his chin and the sides of his face, his hair was still long. He was gorgeous. I lunged at him, pushing him back onto the bed which creaked and squeaked under our weight. I kissed and tasted, I dug my hands in his loose, long hair. He was beautiful, so beautiful.

All mine, all for me.

I sucked on an earlobe, tugging on it while I moved over his body, finding his erection and rubbing a hand over it.

"Baby, wait."

No, no waiting.

Hands gripped my hips, stopping me. "Serena—"

What?

"Babe, wait! Hang on." His hands cradled my face, his legs anchored mine on the bed, holding me still.

My breath was tight. My chest hurt. I blinked at the haze. "What? What is it? What's wrong?"

"Just slow down, honey. Slow down."

"Why? What are you—"

"Listen to me." His voice was firm, yet tender. His eyes searched mine. "Are you listening?"

My shoulders tensed, my grip on his flesh tightening. "Yeah?"

He smoothed a hand down the side of my face, my neck, and a small moan escaped my lips at the sudden gentleness.

"There's nothing to worry about," he said. "I want you bad, too."

Heat unfurled inside me at his words, at the care in his touch. "Okay."

"I want you to know that you don't have to convince me or rush anything," he said. "I don't want to rush. I want us to feel everything. We can stay in this room all day and all night and just fuck if you want, but I don't want to rush. I want you, not someone you think you have to be for me. I wanted you to know that."

My chest caved in, a cool shiver raced over my bare flesh.

"You came in through the door just now and suddenly it felt like a first time, a new time," he said, his voice a rough whisper. "We've been through a hell of a lot to get to this very second, and from now on, I want it to be good for you. I need it to be good for you. And after what you've been through—"

"And you."

"Yeah, and me. I know it's gonna take time, and I want you to know that I'll listen. I'm going to do everything I can so that this won't get taken away from us, if that's what you still want. An 'us,' I mean."

I held onto him tighter. "Justin—"

"You don't need to prove anything to me," he continued. "And you don't owe me anything, I need you to know that. I get you being nervous and wanting to get it over with right off the bat. Is that what this is?"

I swallowed. "Maybe. A part of me was worried about freaking out on you."

He let out a small laugh. "Look who you're talking to, baby. I'm the freak."

"No, no you aren't." I pushed up on his chest. "Are you nervous?"

His Adam's apple plunged up and down in his throat. "I guess, yeah. A little."

"Justin—"

"You mean a lot to me, Serena. I want—so much. But mostly I want to help you get to a better place, no matter what you choose."

"There is no choice to make. I want you."

He lifted his head on a slant, his eyes watery, his lips tipping up in a slight smile, and my heart squeezed. He was relieved. Happy.

I kissed his lips slowly and curled up on his chest. "I missed you so much." I gave the words to the darkness, to his skin.

"I missed you too."

We lay there in silence, him stroking my bare back, his heartbeat a steady rhythm beneath me. He ran his hands through my hair and a few moments later sat up, taking me with him, keeping me steady against his body. "Tell me how much you missed me."

I met his gaze. "It's an ache in the pit of my stomach. A thud in my chest."

"Me too. Exactly." A hand cupped a breast. "Tell me more."

His lips took in a nipple gently, and my body sang a delicate melody.

My head fell back. "I think of you every night in my bed, and every morning when I wake up."

"You touch yourself when you think of me?" He nipped at my flesh.

"Yes, and it feels good, but then I wonder who you're talking to. If you're laughing or smiling, if you're mad, how your scars are feeling, if you're screwing someone else."

"I haven't touched nobody else. Don't want to. Only you, Serena." His breath heated my skin, his arms wrapping around me. "You and Tania? Have you two…"

"No. No." My legs rubbed against his. "No."

He stroked my thigh. "I don't want there to be any distance between us during sex. The last time we were real good there, amazing, but we had Tania as a buffer."

"A buffer?" I asked.

"That night in the motel, the three of us said fuck it to everything. Getting Tania off, getting each other off, was this mutual goal we shared, and it morphed into a whole lot more. It was a perfect ice breaker and an awesome distraction." His thumb rubbed the corner of my mouth.

"It was." I flicked my tongue over his thumb.

"But now you and me alone is gonna be intense on a whole other level. I know I've built it up in my head." He cleared his throat.

"You know, it's cool if you're not ready. We can do other stuff, go slow."

"I don't want to go slow."

"I can tell." He rubbed my back, a dirty smile enlivened his face. "Whichever way you want it. You call it."

I'd rarely felt lucky in my life, but I felt lucky now. This wonderful man wanted to give to me, help me reclaim myself, my sense of worth.

His thumb tugged at my lower lip. "You been sleeping through the night? Because I haven't been."

"Not really." I sucked on his thumb and released it, and he let out a hiss of air. "It's getting better, though. I can't wait to sleep with you again tonight, after we exhaust each other first, of course."

His hands pressed over my ass, squeezing. "You feel so good."

"So good." My body moved against his again, needing more. I bit his upper lip. "Now fuck me."

He let out a groan. "You want to stop, you stop. Don't worry about me, you hear?"

My eyes held his. "I want it to be good for you too."

He pushed my hair back from my face and whispered, "Right now, I want to make you come."

Laughing, I raised myself up and brushed a breast across his mouth. "Make me come, baby."

He licked and nuzzled my nipple, scraping it carefully with his teeth, making my limbs weaken, my insides melt.

"Take my clothes off," he said, his voice gruff.

My pulse kicked up at the urgency in his command. I moved into action, unzipping his pants, yanking them down his long legs, tugging off his shirt. My hands ran up and down his beautiful, sculpted chest. He found my clit and stroked hard over it as I ground myself against his hand, holding onto his shoulders. The wave built and built inside me.

I wanted to come.

I wanted to come for him.

I wanted to come out the other side and still be me, not some wounded, stiff creature.

He pushed me back on the bed and licked a trail down my body, his eyes on me. "Going down on you."

"Yes, yes…"

I raised my hips, and his face sank between my legs. He explored me with his tongue, a tight grip on my hips. His hands slid to my inner thighs, pressing them apart, the flat pad of his tongue stroking hard over my clit. The intensity set my every nerve ablaze. There was no escaping his gifts.

My hands clenched into fists at my sides. I held my breath. I fought with memories, shrill laughs, the sound of liquor dripping to the floor from between my legs, a cold, hard table underneath my bare body.

Finger sat up and, taking his dick in hand, rubbed his thick length over my slick pussy. Up and down. Up and down.

"We're both so wet, baby. Wet as fuck."

That insane pressure built over my sensitive flesh, electrifying me. My heart went into overdrive. It couldn't keep up. I couldn't keep up. I was coming, coming hard.

He clutched at my leg, his hard length continuing its steady and slow pace along my slit.

"Ahh!" My head twisted back. A thumb passed over my mouth, and I tasted myself on him.

He leaned over me, his voice deep, rough. "Say it, say, 'I'm wet as fuck for you.'"

I raised my head off the mattress meeting his harsh, gleaming eyes. "I'm wet as fuck for you. For you, Justin."

His eyes gleamed, his mouth curled into a grin. Satisfaction. Utter lasciviousness. The sensations overtook me, and my head fell back again.

The crinkle of plastic. *Rip.*

My eyes blinked open, and I grinned. Finger fitted himself with a rubber. He yanked me down to the edge of the mattress and spread my legs wide.

"Hold my hands down," I said, raising my arms over my head.

His eyes narrowed as he bent over me and did it. I brought my legs up high the way I'd always done with Med. That was his favorite first position of any session. Open to him and his assault. Holding my arms down, he'd enter me on one fierce thrust, and jackhammer away at different angles, then take me from the side, then squash my face into the mattress and take me from behind. Always commenting about my jiggling tits, always asking me questions. A constant stream of chatter.

"You feeling it, Reen? You feeling my cock? Take it deep, Reen, Take it. Take it."

I wanted Finger to blow that all to bits.

Finger entered me slowly, smoothly, his eyes closing. "Oh damn, baby." He pulsed long and slow, going deeper with each thrust. "You feel so good. So beautiful. Your cunt is smooth as silk."

Gilded torture.

Again and again.

"Faster," I said through gritted teeth, fighting that voice, that body from my mind and soul.

He moved faster. My one leg arched over his hips, clinging to him. We were linked together, the bed shuddering underneath us. Sweat glistened on his chest above me. His thrusts became harsher, his kneading my tits more aggressive. Full possession. This perfect combination of rough and pleasure kept me focused on him, on us.

"Shit." His face twisted in a dark scowl, the curve of his shoulders tense. He grabbed one of my hands and brought it to his chest. "Need you…" he breathed.

He needs me.

I moved my hands over his slick damp skin, down his smooth back to his clenching ass, bringing him closer to me. I held onto him, climbing on him, meeting his every thrust with my own, rubbing my chest against his.

"Fuck me, Serena. You fuck me the way you want," he said on a grunt, his lips tense.

I pushed him over on the bed, and he slid out of me, his eyes flaring. I straddled him and quickly tucked him back in, my hands planted on his chest, my nails digging into his flesh. I rocked over him, and his hold on me tightened. The pleasure built around us, my head spun, my insides swirling.

I listened, but there was no audience, no hooting, no snickering, no—

"Look at me, Sunshine," he muttered through short breaths, a hand pinching my ass cheek.

My eyes snapped open at the sting, snagging on his fierce gaze.

"This is you and me, baby. Me and you."

Yes, yes, you.

His hips rolled into mine, their rhythm quick and steady. "Say it."

"Me and you."

His hand went between my legs, the smooth nub of his cut off finger pressing on my sensitive flesh.

Everything shimmered and shattered inside me.

You. You. You.

18
FINGER

WE WERE ON THE WAY home from a charity run in Pennsylvania and had landed in Ohio for the night. At Reich's chapter.

I wasn't eager to spend any more time with him than I had to, but what the hell, there were five chapters of the Flames of Hell on this run together. I could continue to get lost in the crowd if I wanted to. We hadn't spoken two words to each other in PA, just acknowledged each other's presence with a lift of chins, a nod.

Eager for booze and loud music after hours on the road, we strode into the Peghorn Saloon, the local Flames hangout. It was after two in the morning, and there were still plenty of bikes and cars in the parking lot. The Smoking Guns logo screamed at me from the gas tank of a number of bikes. A sharp ache needled through the joints in my fingers and raced up my arms, my muscles stiffening.

Reich pushed open the old metal doors.

No music's playing.

"Been trying to call ya, Reich. Couldn't get through." His glassy eyes wide, his voice shaky, Garrett, the owner of the Peghorn, stood in a bar that was barely recognizable.

Pool tables flipped over, broken cues and balls littering the floor. Shattered bottles and glass everywhere. Men and women were glued to the walls, a din of mumbling, crying, and shifting chairs zipping around the large bar.

Smoking Guns everywhere.

"It's about fucking time." Med slammed a hand down on the bar, a bottle of liquor in his hands.

My heart stopped. His snarl. That voice. Those eyes. A cold sting washed over me and settled in my bones. My fingers curled into tight fists, even my middle fingers that were no longer there.

"Holy fucking shit," Drac muttered next to me.

It'd been four months since I'd been released from Med's hell-hole, but the sight of him, the sound of his voice, generated a tidal wave of nausea and fear, my pulse pounding, my blood jamming in my veins—as if I was still there, still his prisoner. Even now, surrounded by my brothers. Even now.

I hated him. I feared him. I hated him.

I wanted him dead.

He and his crew had been in Pennsylvania, too, but we'd all steered clear. Things were cool, I'd thought. I'd been relieved. There hadn't been no skirmishes, no fights, only the usual long brooding looks and caustic threats between two rival clubs.

"Where's the kid?" he asked.

"What kid?" spit out Reich.

"The one I made a man. The one I created for you."

A laugh rolled through the room, one distinct ringing laugh above all the others.

Scrib.

My breathing got shallow, a cold sweat suddenly swamped my body. The smoke and the heat in the room was stifling, and I tried swallowing, but my mouth and throat wouldn't cooperate. My body wavered, and Drac pressed his side into mine.

"What for?" Kwik stepped forward. "What the fuck is this?"

"Saw you all in Pennsylvania. Saw him. Got me thinking." Med took a long swig from a bottle of expensive rum.

"Oh yeah?"

"Bet he's the one who took something of mine."

"Like what? A popsicle stick?" Reich said on a sneer. "You dumped him all bloodied, chopped and cut with barely his clothes on. What the fuck you talking about?"

Med's satanic gaze found mine and drilled a sizzling hole through me. "My girl."

My girl.

Serena's blue green eyes formed a haze between me and Med. A blue green haze. Desire. Justice. Hate. Passion.

Reich's head tilted at Med. A challenge. "The fuck you say."

My brothers from five different chapters crowded around me. Shielding me. Taking my back. Not one looked at me, questioned me. There was no question.

"Got no other explanation for it." Med's voice thundered. "I gave him hospitality."

"Hospitality, huh? Chained like an animal in a prison cell?" said Kwik, his voice raised.

"I let him live, motherfucker." Med jabbed a finger in the air. "I let him live."

"Get out," said Reich. "Get out of our territory and don't come through here again. I'm willing to overlook this mess you made at my favorite watering hole, chalk it up to a misunderstanding. But it's the first and last time, you got that?"

"I want my girl back!" howled Med, smashing the bottle against the side of the bar top without even flinching.

Kwik raised his chin at Scrib. "Leave. We're through with this bullshit, and you're outnumbered, asshole." He turned to Med. "Your girlfriend ran off? Cry me a river. Find yourself a new one."

Med's eyes stayed on mine all through Kwik's rush of words. His eyelids lowered and he licked at his full lower lip, a creepy smile breaking out on his face. "I'm still looking for her, and when I find her…"

"Get out!" Reich said.

Med's hand went to the front of his jacket, patting the zippered pocket at his chest. "Want your fingers back, Kid? Got 'em right here. Favorite trophy of all time."

A wave of acid went off in my mouth, lit up my eyes, burned my veins, scorched my heart with its liquid fire. My bros latched onto me.

But I didn't lunge forward for a fight.

"You keep 'em," I replied, my voice loud and coarse. "Don't want you to ever forget me. Not ever. The name is Finger."

Med's eyes narrowed. He hadn't gotten the response he'd been hoping for. Muttering, he kicked at the remnants of his rum bottle, sending them spinning, smashing, splattering across the floor. A woman screeched. Med stumbled forward on an odd limping saunter to the exit, greasy, sweaty hair in his face. Scrib eyed me as he and the rest of his men followed Med outside.

We all stood in silence in the bar. Outside, the roar of pipes rumbled and screamed, finally fading. Me and my bros picked up chairs and tables, swept the broken glass and dishes in a corner. A couple of women cried and some of the men talked to them, easing their fears. Garrett and his bartender and waitresses ran around pouring and serving drinks. The music played at a lower volume than usual.

Reich snapped his head at me, the look on his face searing. "What the hell did you do? You take his property? You actually fool enough to go back there?"

I eyed him.

He believed the worst of me. He believed the best of me.

Everyone stopped what they were doing and waited for my answer. There was awe in that silence. There was dread. My brothers had defended me and they would to the death because they were my brothers and that always came first against the enemy, but the question hung in the air.

"Lay off my VP, Reich." Kwik's sharp voice sliced between us. "From day one, Finger's been a solid member, working side by side with me."

"VP," muttered Reich, as if he had to spit the word out before it choked him.

"Enough." Kwik's voice was firm.

Reich headed to the bar, but the weight of everyone's stares remained on me. Kwik squeezed my shoulder and shot me a look as I let go of a heavy breath. He wasn't sure either. "You good?"

"Yeah."

"Get things done in here and then we all need sleep, not more booze."

"You bet," I replied.

I would get things done all right. I would have to be more careful than I'd previously planned on. I had no doubt if Med ever caught me and Serena, he'd tear us limb from limb. Seeing her in Chicago was going to be a bitch and a half, but I would do it every chance I got. I would find a way. I would take the risk. Risk showed you what you were made of. And I had it in me to risk everything over and over again for her.

The only thing I didn't realize was how deep risks could cut and make you bleed.

19

SERENA

"ARE YOU SHANE?"

"That's me," replied the guy at the counter in the tattoo shop.

"I need a fix."

"What kind?"

"I have a tat I don't want anymore, and I wanted you to—"

"Laser it off? Black it out?"

"No. I want you to make it something different, beautiful."

"Uh huh." He shuffled a small pile of papers at the reception desk. "Why don't you show it to me, and tell me what you're thinking of?" He gestured to a lounger behind an elaborately painted screen with lightening bolts and flowers. I hopped up on the padded chair and stretched out, unzipped my jeans and lowered them.

Shane's eyes followed my movements as I pulled down the top of my panty. He leaned over me, studying the design on my lower abs. A skeleton holding two smoking guns in his bony hands. No words, just the symbol. And even though Finger had cut his F over it that last night at the motel in South Dakota, that fucking ink remained.

Their brand. Med's brand.

I wanted it changed forever. Now.

"Turo told me you do good work," I said.

Translation: You keep quiet when you have to.

Shane's eyes darted to mine and hung there. "Yeah, yeah I do."

"Good."

Turo was a mafia hitman. Turo's girlfriend was Ciara, who shopped at my store regularly, always on the hunt for gently used vintage designer pieces. I would let her know when we'd get Pra-

159

da and Chloe handbags on consignment, and she would be crazy grateful.

We'd fallen into an easy friendship since we'd first met, a couple of weeks into my job. We started going out frequently for drinks or food. The other day she took me shopping with her to the high end stores on Michigan Ave, Barneys New York, being her favorite. I put together outfits for her and the shoes to go with them, and she bought them all with a chunk of cash Turo had given her. Then with whatever money was left, we made a beeline to the store's makeup department and did major damage together. Ciara had a couple of cute tattoos of hearts on her wrist and daisies around her ankle, so I'd asked her for a recommendation for a good, reliable tattoo artist. Someone who could be discreet if necessary. She'd sent me to Shane.

"Hey, Shane. You taking care of my girl?" came a high, sultry, female voice.

Ciara.

Shane's head swung to the side of the divider, and I sat up.

Ciara leaned on the counter, her dark red fingernails flicking at her carefully highlighted golden hair which cascaded past her shoulders. She was stunningly beautiful, and worked hard at it every day.

"Ciara, hey," he said. "Uh, yeah. Yeah, just checking out what I've got to work with." He swallowed, his eyes going back to my tat.

"Hi," I said, smiling at her as Shane bent over my lower body once more.

"Sorry I'm late, babe. Had a busy morning." She winked at me.

"No problem. I just introduced myself to Shane here."

"I can see that," she replied.

Shane rose, his shoulders straightening. "So, you got any ideas for what you want?"

"Yes." I pushed up on my elbows and pointed to what was left of the skeleton and his guns. "I want to hide the last traces of it with a mass of flowers. Roses, peonies. I want it to be elegant and beautiful."

"Elegant and beautiful?" repeated Shane, eyebrows lifting.

My grandmother Eleonora had taught me about elegance and beauty. One day she'd taken a piece of lace and held it up over my skin under the sunlight.

"You see, Serena? You see the shapes?"

The shadows of the lace danced on my skin. "So pretty, Gran."

"You can make pretty things, and you can make the things around you pretty, no matter what they are. All it takes is imagination and willpower to transform anything. Your imagination is very powerful and very special. Just like you. Never forget that. Come, I'll show you how to make your own lace."

I was going to make my own lace.

"That's right, elegant and beautiful," I said. "And pretty. Can you do that?"

Shane's gaze darted at Ciara for a moment. "I can do whatever you want," he replied. "How about a ribbon to go around your hips while we're down there, tying the flowers around you?"

"I like that. But not a ribbon. A thorny vine."

A tight grin appeared on Shane's face. "You got it. That scar looks a little new though. I'll work around it today, and you can come back in a couple weeks and I'll finish over it."

"Great," I replied.

He grabbed a sketchpad and a pencil and began drawing.

Shane did a beautiful job on the flowers and the vine. I became a regular client of his, and Shane and I became great friends. I had him color my body with another thorny vine from the spray of flowers up around my torso and along my back. Whenever I could afford it, he'd add on new flowers and stars and moons, flying mermaids, soaring fairies, a dragon. A chain of tiny linked letter J's up the back of my right leg for Justin, entwined with baby rosebuds. In between tattoos, I had him pierce my nose and my nipples, too.

"Why the hell did you do that?" Tania winced, sucking in a breath as I used the aftercare spray on my piercings.

"Because I'm the one doing it to my body. Me." I carefully tugged on my sports bra.

"Didn't it hurt? Shit." She crossed her arms over her chest, and I let out a laugh.

"It stung for a second, but it was fine. Shane's experienced at this." I slid my favorite T-shirt over my head.

"Ugh, my boobs hurt now. You're a whack." Tania headed for

the kitchen. "I need a drink."

T ANIA LET ME STYLE HER outfits on big nights out.

Her eyes met mine in the full length mirror on her bedroom door. "I never would've thought to wear the long beaded necklace with this dress and the hanging sash belt."

"I'm glad you like it." I adjusted the belt on her hips. "Plus, it will take Whatshisface a long, slow time to get you naked."

"I'm not sleeping with Brian, Serena."

I stepped back and looked at her reflection. "Maybe tonight's the night, Tan."

She only shrugged. "I like him, but not that much."

"You're so picky. He's cute, he's funny, and he's totally in to you. Take advantage and have some fun." I flopped back on her bed.

"He's an actor in my acting class, and super ambitious, so it could be a big mistake to take our flirting any further. Plus, he talks about himself and all his plans and auditions and agent contacts way too much. He's all, *me, me, me.* The last thing I need is—"

"I didn't say marry him or be his girlfriend. I said sleeeeeep with him. You haven't been with anyone since that Lewis guy. No sex makes Tania cranky."

"Cranky is part of my charm." Tania dabbed gloss over her wine-colored lips. "I liked Lewis, too."

"Kiss Brian tonight. Maybe he has a magic tongue that can make all your sex dreams come true."

"Truth be told, I would be damn grateful if he knew how to use his tongue. Lewis didn't, that's for sure."

"You should find out then. See, I'm offering practical advice. I'm learning from you."

Tania fluffed her layered hair with her fingers. "Yeah, that's me. Practical."

"Not!" We both laughed.

She sat on the edge of the bed and slipped her high-heeled boots on. "I don't even know if he's coming by the gallery tonight. He said he would, but I'm not counting on it. You're still meeting Finger tonight, right? It's still on?"

"Yep." That tight sensation gripped my insides, sprinting around every nerve ending. "He should be in town in about two hours."

"I'll bet you've been counting the minutes since you woke up this morning."

"No, since yesterday morning." I let out a laugh, stretching out on her bed. "It really sucked that he couldn't make it the last time. I hope nothing else comes up at the last minute and he has to cancel."

"I know."

I took in a deep breath. I could practically smell him, feel him on me. "I can't wait to see him."

Tania stuck out her tongue and wagged it. "You can't wait to have sex with him."

I laughed. "I miss him."

"I know you do. So things going okay? I mean, after what you went through."

"It's good. Very good. I still get a little anxious, but I'm more relaxed and Finger is amazing. He takes his time with me, he listens. He doesn't push, even when I want him too. Sometimes I wish I didn't have all this shit clouding my head, knotting my muscles, but it's a process, and it's my process."

Tania grinned. "I love you, you know."

"I know. I love you too."

She got up from the bed, smoothing down her jersey knit dress. "Okay, I'm off. Give him a hug for me." She didn't see Finger whenever he came up. We'd all agreed it was safer that way.

"I will."

Tania grabbed her small black handbag. "Have fun. Be careful. And I'll see you when I see you. Could you call me, though, at some point, let me know you're okay?" She hugged me. Tania was a mother type, and I kind of liked it.

"Will do. You, however, be not so careful tonight," I said.

Tania only rolled her eyes at me as she walked out our front door, into the dark hallway of our third floor walkup.

"Have fun!" I shouted after her.

The telephone rang, and I quickly locked the door and picked up the phone.

"Baby?"

That deep tickle unfurled in my chest and bloomed in all my lady parts at the sound of his throaty voice.

"Hey!"

"You ready for me?"

"Yes, yes, oh yes."

He chuckled, and I closed my eyes, taking in the hearty sound. Sexy as hell. *Can't wait.*

"321 45 87. And fast, Sunshine."

We had a secret code just in case anyone was listening. Even though he used a number of different pay phones, we never took chances. We'd even come up with a hand sign in case one of us needed to signal the other to back off because of danger lurking.

"I'll be there."

"I'm hard already just knowing I'm twenty minutes out from fucking you."

My hand tightened over the phone handle. "I think I just came. A mini-pop."

"Save them for me." A low growl unfurled under his words. "Get moving."

I hung up and grabbed my vintage carpetbag that I'd packed and stashed at the side of my futon for two days, and charged outside, a huge grin on my face.

THE SECOND WE GOT TO the room, Finger kicked the door shut, locking it. We yanked at each other's clothes and humped on the floor like desperate animals in heat. We were desperate, desperate for each other, desperate for our closeness, for that joy that only being together brought us. The moment he'd first entered me, a flash of blue light had flared behind my lids. I was ecstatic, there was no getting enough of him.

We made it to the bed for the next round.

We slid back to the floor for the next.

"Holy shit, are those J's?" His index finger traced a line down the back of my thigh to my calf.

"Hmm, a chain of Justins just for me."

"Fuck." He dove between my legs again.

A few hours later we forced ourselves to stand upright and shower and get dressed again. If we didn't, we'd stay on that floor all night, which would be great, but we wanted to do things together. We wanted to do normal things like any other couple.

Life had taught us to make every moment count, to not take anything for granted, so we would make memories and have experiences we could wrap ourselves in and hold onto until the next time we'd be together. Whenever that would be. But we wouldn't dwell on that shit now.

He had his colors covered in a hoodie, a baseball cap pulled down low, and the hood of his jacket over that and up around the sides of his face. The scars on his cheeks made recognizing him easy. I had a lot of heavy eyeliner on, brown contact lenses, fake glasses, and a short blonde wig.

We had a burrito dinner at a store front walk-in named Mi Ranchito, strolled around Navy Pier people gawking, then headed toward a big movie theater complex on Chestnut St. After the sci-fi movie finished, we walked up swanky Michigan Avenue joined at the hip, our arms wrapped around each other's waists. Finger was patient with every stop I made to ooh and ahh at the designer clothes in the windows of fancy department stores.

We stopped in front of an Azzedine Alaia window at Barneys. "I was here last week with this woman I met at my store, Ciara. I helped her find a dress for this fancy dinner party she was going to with her boyfriend. She dropped a huge wad of his cash without blinking. He's some mafia guy."

Finger's head snapped at me. "What? Who?"

"Turo DeMarco. He's with the Guardino family," I whispered.

"Baby—"

"I haven't met him, and I would never tell Ciara anything about me, about us."

His face was eerily pale under the bright disco type lighting from the Alaia window display. "I know, but—"

"I realize the Guns have connections to organized crime and gangs all over the Midwest. Med was always pissed off at somebody and used to tell me shit he didn't trust to anyone else, a lot of stuff he probably shouldn't have. I think he considered me a deaf mute most of the time."

Finger leaned into me, his eyes hard. "Baby, you got to be real careful here. Real careful. If this Turo ever finds out who you are, you just don't know how he'll react or what his boss's relationship is with Med—or was. Fuck, nobody knows that shit for sure."

"I know. You're right."

"Maybe you shouldn't be such good pals with this…"

"Ciara."

"Yeah, Ciara."

"I'm careful."

His lips pressed together, the scars on his face tightened. We left the dazzle of Barneys behind us and walked in a tense silence for several blocks, his hand squeezing mine.

We got ice cream cones at Ghirardelli's new ice cream shop, and he swallowed his in four bites. I laughed, and in response, he took a bite of my fudge chocolate and coffee ice cream wrapped in a homemade cone. I took a bite after him, the ice cream smudging my cheek. He leaned over and swiped at my face with his tongue then kissed me. Sweet cream, cool chocolate. These were the flavors, the sensations of happiness, weren't they? I kissed him back, wanting more, always more, and he bit my lips.

"Ah!" I pulled back, and he chomped on my vulnerable cone, devouring the last bit.

"Hey!"

"It's so good." Finger laughed, a hand wiping at his mouth.

I punched at his massive, solid shoulder. "The last bite is always the best."

"I know," he said, eyeing me. He brushed my cheek with his cold, wet lips. "I'll make it up to you, baby. I promise I'll lick you better than I did that ice cream cone." He bit my earlobe. "And bite you."

"Hmm." I licked my fingers, my insides as gooey as the melted ice cream.

But I couldn't wait.

I tugged on his hand, leading him around the corner. A narrow side street. A tower of fire escapes gleamed at us overhead. I stepped in a puddle as I pulled him against me, leaning against the slimy graffitied wall. We kissed hard, and I lifted a leg around his hips, pressing into his erection.

"Fuck me."

He chuckled under his breath as I unsnapped the buttons on my bodysuit between my legs, under my skirt. He fumbled with his jeans and hoisted me up. I slid my hand over his smooth, hard length and guided it to where I needed it to be. I tightened my insides around him, holding onto his cock.

"Baby, shit." He throbbed, his body stiffening against mine. "Jesus."

The world moved around us in the shadowy dark as we took our bite of bright heaven.

We ended up at Dave & Busters, a new large arcade on North Clark Street and played pin ball and race car games. Finger played a shooting game, a huge plastic rifle in his hands, his shoulders rigid with focus. He landed every bullseye. He was good.

Of course he was good. This was a game played for tokens with imaginary digital targets, but out there on the street, on the road it was the life he lived. I'd lived it too.

We exited the arcade, and I spotted a photo booth at the entrance.

"Come here!" I tugged him inside and pushed him down on the stool. I sat in his lap, and he pulled me in close. Popping change in the slot, we posed making faces, crossing our eyes, another with our tongues sticking out and touching, the last with our faces pressed together, serious.

We waited, and finally, the strip landed in my eager hand. "Oh, look. I love them."

He kissed the side of my face. "You're going to have to get rid of it, though. Promise me. Tomorrow, rip it up, throw it away. Leave no clues behind."

"I know," I said, my fingers clinging to the edge of the damp strip of photos. "I know."

We went by the art gallery where Tania worked on Wells Street in River North. Tonight they were having an opening for a new contemporary painter who had been getting lots of buzz. Finger studied the huge canvas of abstract purple and mustard strokes in the front window of the gallery.

"What the hell is that supposed to be?" he asked.

"Whatever you want it to be," I replied.

Tania noticed us from inside the gallery. She only raised an eyebrow and shot us a grin. She knew how to keep things discreet at all times. I smiled back at her.

"You want to go in?" Finger tugged on my hand.

"No."

"You sure?" His eyes creased. He hated keeping me from doing things or going places I wanted to go to because of us having to keep our anonymity.

"I'm very sure. I go to these all the time with Tania. Not being a painter or a sculptor or some kind of artist or gallery person, I'm not invested in having to go to all these parties and be seen, hang out, and make contacts and all that like she is. I enjoy them, but not all the time. And anyway, this is our time together."

He kissed the side of my face, his arm circling my shoulders pulling me in close. "Yeah, it is."

Two women exited the gallery, strutting down the sidewalk past us, and my eyes zeroed in on their Japanese-style asymmetrical coats and oversized scarves.

"You like clothes a lot don't you?" he asked, tucking my hand inside his large gloved one.

"No, I LOVE clothes." I laughed.

"All you girls do, don't you?"

"My grandmother and I were really close. She pretty much raised me, and she had lots of hobbies she shared with me—knitting, crocheting, sewing. She'd taught me all those things by the time I was ten. I'd pick out patterns for a dress or a blouse, choose a great fabric, and then we'd rush home and pin the pattern on the

168

material, cut it out, and then she'd sit at her sewing machine and bam—new dress, new blouse, new skirt. The whole process was very satisfying. Fashion for me is about how colors and textures and lines sing together and create a particular magic for each individual.

"Oh man—particular magic."

"Yes. Unique possibilities. Fashion isn't some static work of art that you stare at like those paintings on the wall at the gallery. It's more." My face heated. "For me, anyway. Sounds silly?"

"No, I like it. I get it. You got all excited there. Your eyes lit up."

"Oh yeah?" I stood on my toes and pressed my lips against his warm ones. "I only light up for you."

His eyes closed, his tongue swiping at my lips. He took in a deep breath. "We need to get back to the hotel because I'm dying here."

"Do me here."

"No fucking way. As much as I love your demanding side, this park is a wide open space. Any weirdo could come along and try to get in on our action. Then I'd have to kill him, then the police would come after us. Just a shitty idea all around."

"Then I'll make good use of this blondie getup and hail us a cab to get us to the hotel as quickly as possible."

"Good call."

I turned on the sidewalk and stepped to the edge, facing the steady stream of traffic as I raised my hand. A cab screeched to a halt before us within moments.

"Maybe you should consider the blonde thing permanently, baby," Finger whispered as we slid into the backseat.

I gave the driver the address, and as soon as I got the street name past my lips, Finger's hand went under my skirt, pushed past the elastic of my bodysuit, and slid down my pussy. His fingers stroked and dazzled me the whole ride, teasing me, keeping me just on the edge of coming. I clutched onto his leather jacket.

"Is this because of the blonde hair?"

He breathed heavily in my ear. "No, it's because of your lush cunt."

"Did you really just say lush?" I let out a laugh.

"That's what it is." His index finger thrust in my pussy and stroked against my inner wall, holding me prisoner. I let out a hiss.

"I can't wait to suck on this lush. Eat it up, fuck it with my tongue. I want to make your sugar sweet bod wet over and over just for me."

I groaned. "Then what?"

"Then my cock is going to pound it." He stroked quicker, his finger churning. "And this pussy's gonna come on my cock. Come so hard, you're gonna be shouting."

His thumb pressed over my clit roughly, and I stumbled on a breath.

"Don't shout now though, Sunshine. You stay real quiet for me, and I'm gonna give it to you so fucking good the second we get through the door. Then that sweet ass will be crying out for me, won't it?"

"Oh yeah," I breathed against his throat, my lips nuzzling his damp skin for dear life.

I bit down hard on my lip refusing to moan and groan in front of the taxi driver. But that was proving to be really difficult as Finger spoke non-stop in hushed tones against my ear, my hips rocking against his hand more desperately with his every filthy remark. I glanced up at the rear view mirror. The driver shot us a curious glare.

Within moments the taxi braked at the corner. "Here you go."

"You better pay, baby, 'cause..." Finger broke out into a dark laugh. His fingers squeezed my clit one exquisitely painful last time, snapping at the elastic as they left me. He leaned back in the seat and sucked on his finger and thumb, shiny with my wet in the car light the driver had switched on.

I handed the driver a ten dollar bill as Finger adjusted his jeans. I got my change and pushed Finger out the door.

Holding hands, laughing, we raced up the creaky stairs of that grim hotel to our room. And in that room, we reveled in our own magnificent, beautiful world.

20
SERENA

Almost two months later, Finger called me. Password given, and I headed downtown to a really cheap dive of a hotel that doubled as a rooming house for the homeless. We were in a tiny, shabby room that belonged to a friend of a friend of a friend of Finger's who let us have it for the night. Coughing, arguing, the occasional curse echoed in the hallway along with the constant blare of the Cubs game on TV. We added to the cacophony with the screeching of the old metal springs on the twin bed we were fucking on.

I always counted the days, the weeks between Finger's visits. Keeping track kept me steady, and the anticipation made my insides hum. I looked forward to his visits, planning things to do and see. Being with him wasn't only the hot times together in bed. Being with him was home to me, be it making love in a mildewy room at a flophouse in a bad neighborhood, sharing a deep dish pizza in a crowded restaurant, walking all over town arm in arm in the icy cold rain.

His groans in my ear, his body crushing mine, a small smile just for me when he hardly ever smiled. My special, secret place was me and him. I danced there. Sang out loud and off key, hands in the air, his wind in my hair.

I didn't think I had much emotion to give anymore. Med had squashed that for me with his cruelty. But Finger, oh Finger, he was cruel and loving all at once. Brutal in his intensity, in the ferocity of his need, but delicate in his mercy, and that awakened the greedy, hungry woman in me.

His tongue flicked and tugged at my nipple piercings. "Fuck, I love these. Fuck." The arousal built again, zig zagging through my flesh, the kind of pleasure you think you won't survive. Explosive. Furious.

"Finger," I whispered, my legs wrapping around his hips. "Need you so bad. Want your cock inside me."

He only made a grunting sound. He loved it when I talked during sex. Being with Med—well, you just did what you were told and only spoke when spoken to, and even then, you needed to agree with whatever he said. I hadn't realized how I'd gotten used to that.

With Finger, sex was a whole other level of freedom. Freedom to touch him, explore, to give to him, to play and know that the playfulness, that joy of discovery was appreciated and mutual. There would be no punishments, no retributions, no report card at the end.

I roughly stroked his cock until it was hard and ready to do damage. That's what I wanted. His fierceness taking me over. I scooted down and pushed him over on his back. Climbing on him, I sank on his cock and rode him. He held onto my tits in his tight grip and flexed his hips up into mine. The sight of his maimed hands on my body made my adrenaline spike, my blood rush to my head. My nipples stung and burned deliciously, and I grit my teeth and rode him faster, my fingernails digging into his wrists.

"I love you," I murmured. "Love you. Love you."

"I love you too." One hand slid down my hip and held it, the other went between our slick bodies and rubbed my clit hard and fast. "I'm all yours, baby. You're all mine, aren't you?"

"Only yours. Yours."

We reassured each other of this fact frequently during sex. Being apart for long stretches of time, often going without communicating because he was usually on the road on secret missions and not wanting our connection to be traced in any way. So when we were together, every word, every touch took on a mad significance.

"All yours." I came once more, tears and sweat blurring my vision.

He flipped me face down on the bed and holding me there, thrust into me fast from behind, my hair in his fist. I ground back into him, tightening my insides around his hard length.

Finger always went fast when he needed to come. He wasn't only chasing his orgasm, but escaping the pain his body and his mind still associated with coming inside of me. His grip on my hair and back tightened, and I bit down on my lip as he tugged my head higher. My fingers curled in the nubby sheet, and my eyes found his.

His jaw set tightly, his eyes were ablaze, his breathing heavy and harsh. Was he still fighting the memories? I thought so. Those memories were still alive in his hands, on his face.

I tightened around his length again, and he groaned. "You and me," I stuttered.

Another groan.

"Yes, yes, feels so good," I murmured. Every time I felt I had to assure him, encourage him. Otherwise, we'd always be in Med's grip, and there was no way. I was peeling it off for the both of us, layer by layer every time.

His fingers dug into my middle, and he collapsed on top of me.

Holding each other, we rolled over and stared at the peeling paint on the ceiling, the mold in the corners. He took my hand in his, and I closed my eyes, the sound of our choppy breathing lulling me into a sweet haze, the tremors of my flesh vibrating through me. I brought his hand to my lips and kissed it. Sitting up, I slid the condom from his relaxed cock and took his damp cock in my mouth. I wanted to taste him and commit that taste to memory through the many days and nights ahead on my own.

"Bitch, stop," he groaned, laughing.

Releasing his slick velvety smoothness, I giggled, resting my head on his middle. "I have good news for you, baby."

His scarred hand went to the side of my face. "Oh yeah? Tell me."

"I got into a design school, part time. I start in a few weeks."

"Huh?" Blinking, he wiped a hand across his eyes.

I sat up and straddled his lap, facing him. "An art school here in Chicago. I got in."

"What do you mean?"

"I applied to the night program at a school for fashion design and tailoring, and I got in."

He didn't reply.

My back tensed under his suddenly firmer grip. "I thought you'd be proud of me. Happy for me."

He let out a ragged breath. "I am. I mean, yeah, that's great. Really great. I'm proud of you, baby, I am."

"Then?"

"That means that you'll be staying here, though. You see?"

"Right."

"I want you closer to me. I thought that's what you wanted too."

"I do want that, more than anything. But things haven't really changed. I can't just walk into your clubhouse, the two of us hand in hand, can I?"

His eyes tightened, his jaw hardening. He was angry, frustrated.

"What is it? Did something happen? Tell me."

"It's Med. I saw him. He's still looking for you. He's real pissed. He made accusations about me taking you, and my prez defended me. All my bros did."

An icy chill stole through me. "Shit."

"We got to keep things real tight for a little while longer. So, yeah, actually, you staying put here is probably for the best. Little while longer."

A dull weight rolled over me like a heavy boulder, but I shoved it back. I wasn't going to dwell on Med, not now. No way. "I have more good news, too."

"Oh yeah?"

"I qualified for a work/study plan at this school, a paid internship. And I'm going to keep working a few days a week plus weekends at the store."

"Cool. You still liking your job?"

"I love my job, and I'm loving my new name, too. There's something clean about it—Ashley Wyeth."

He let out a huff of air. "Hey, Ashley. You give amazing head and fuck like a demon."

I squeezed his balls.

His hand slapped around my wrist. "Why don't you do that a little nicer, while you tell me about your school?"

"Turn over. I want to see my name on you again."

A smirk full of heat etched his face. He loved that I loved his surprise for me, a new tattoo on his skin. He turned over, and my fingers ran up the long gothic S, for Serena, now inked on his upper spine. The letter was hidden in the long plume of flames that rose from his lower back, fanned out across his shoulder blades and blew all the way up his neck. I kissed and nipped his spine then turned him over on the mattress, my hand slowly stroking his thick length. His body relaxed as I blathered on about the kinds of classes I'd be taking.

"What do you think?" I asked.

"You're happy. You're excited about something you really like, and I'm glad." He planted a light kiss on my mouth, letting out a soft moan.

"I get excited by you." I squeezed his firm dick.

"I know, but I mean, you're excited about something new in your life, an objective, a passion you want to explore."

"A passion, yeah, that's what it is."

"I'll give you money to pay for it."

"You don't have to."

"I want to." His index finger lazed down my middle and slid between my legs. "Let me share in your excitement."

His finger wound and circled its way to my core. My breath hitched as he gently, gently stroked, and I lost myself in the sensations he knew so well how to conjure in me. I came quickly, crying out.

"This is all because of you, you know." I kissed him. "I wouldn't be here in Chicago pursuing dreams I didn't know I had if it wasn't for you." My trembling body curled into his.

"What's going on?" he asked, his voice low, a hand around my neck. "Are you crying? Those are good tears, right?"

I only nodded, unable to find my voice.

His finger traced the vine up my side to my breast. "Your ink is wild, and keeps getting wilder. I feel like I'm missing out on something with you, and I hate that. It makes me realize how far apart we are every time I see you."

I met his gaze. "Every piece is about me, me and you. Us. Like spring blooming. Our spring. We're different than we were before the Smoking Guns. They damaged us, but it made us stronger. We have color. Great big splashes of bright color, great big bursts of it, all outside the lines, and I want to celebrate that."

"Celebrate." He uttered the word like it was a new flavor and he liked how it tasted.

"Yes, celebrate. So every time you discover a new tat on me, know it's our celebration, a new song I've written calling out to you." My face heated. "They may have used me for a few years there, but my body is mine and I want to make it beautiful again—"

"You are beautiful."

"But on my own terms, my choice."

He raised my chin in his hand and kissed me. A hungry kiss. A sweet kiss. I sat up and slid into his lap, straddling him. He held me close, the two of us breathing against each other's skin.

I slid my forehead against his. "I bet most of your bros have old ladies now, right? I'm sure they're expecting you to bring one home too."

His hand went to a breast, his thumb stroking a nipple barbell. "I don't give a shit what anyone expects."

"You give a shit about your president, though. And you should."

"I do." He pressed his lips together.

"I wish I could get on the back of your bike and go to Nebraska and stroll into your clubhouse with you, but I can't. I'm sure they're suspicious already. It's been months of you not bringing anyone around or screwing around. You disappearing whenever you can."

"They know that's me. That I keep mostly to myself. That's how shit's been for me since I got out from under the Guns. They get it."

"They may get it, Finger, but I guarantee they don't trust it. You've got them curious. And now with Med accusing you in front of everybody? Maybe that curiosity will change to outright suspicion. It's only a matter of time until they dig a little deeper and find us together. They'll find something."

His one hand fisted in my hair and pulled. He glared at me. Confusion. Irritation. "What the hell are you trying to say? What are we supposed to do? Give up?"

"Not give up, but maybe—"

"No."

"No?"

"NO!" he exploded. "No fucking way. I'm not giving you up for anyone or anything." His voice thundered. "Not even for you!" His dark eyes were fierce. "Why are you talking like this? You giving in?"

"I'm not giving in. I'm being smart." I gulped in air. "It's just... not good."

"What? The situation?" He released his hold on my hair. "Of course it's not good."

"It's just so damned difficult."

"Difficult? Is that what's climbed up your ass? Difficult? Everything is difficult in this life. Every fucking thing."

I touched the hard edge of his jaw. "I feel like we have some sort of expiration date hanging over us. And we keep managing to push it back a little here and a little bit there, but how long can that last?"

"Serena—"

My fingertips brushed his lips. "We've killed people to be together," I whispered.

He snatched at my hand, crushing it in his. "We're surviving."

My fingers throbbed in his steel grip. Surviving. Agony was entwined in that word, and a desperation that I knew so well. I'd been surviving for a long, long time. But now, with Justin, it was another kind of pact, a better, richer promise. And suddenly, there was more at stake.

"How many more victims will have to pay the price for our survival?" My fingers curled around his. "There will be more, you know there will be. I'm always looking over my shoulder."

"You'll always have to. Unless maybe you move to some shack in Greenland. Is that what you want to do?"

"Why not?"

He released my hand. The skin was red.

"But you couldn't go," I said. "You're a Flame. A Flame through and through."

"Is that a bad thing?"

"No, it's not. But what we're doing to survive is at odds with your life as a Flame. One day, things will get out of hand, and then what? How much more brotherhood are you going to have to sacrifice in the name of us? You're heading for a crucifixion by your own hand."

"I was already crucified," spilled from his lips. "With you I got my resurrection."

I wrapped my arms around him, pulling him close, my heart galloping in my chest.

He whispered roughly, "Don't talk like this. I don't know who I am without you."

"Maybe you should find out."

The side of his scarred face stroked my cheek. He planted a kiss on my neck. "I love you, baby. I need to love you."

Those three words. Simple, complicated, glorious, insane. I breathed them in. They'd never been given to me before. Not like this, not ever. I kissed him. A delicate, gentle kiss, sealing the vow between us.

"What I feel for you is bigger and deeper than some tagline I've always heard thrown around," he said. "I can't define it, and I don't need to. These feelings I got for you aren't just a part of me or one piece I got stashed inside. They are me."

My heart squeezed in my chest, my mouth dried. *Yes. Yes. Yes. It's the same for me.* "I love you too."

He swallowed hard, his gaze focusing on my mouth, his hands rubbing the back of my neck. I pressed a hand over his chest where his heart beat hard and strong. I was safe there. I was on a beautiful adventure there.

His eyes brightened. "I liked hearing you say that."

"Good."

"I told my bros that I got a woman out of state, and they're good with that," he said, his voice lower. "And in case you're wondering, the whores know it too."

I ground my hips against his thigh, a small smile tugging on my lips. "I trust you."

He slid a hand down my ass and pulled me against his erection, and I let out a gasp at the precise friction. "You're going to be meeting college boys now, artsy-fartsy pretentious fuckers who are gonna try to get inside your panties."

"So not interested. I've got the finest man ever, and he gives me everything I need. Everything I've ever wanted."

He licked at my lips and they parted for him. He took my mouth, and I took his, our tongues greedy for one another. His thumb swept the side of my face. "I don't want you worrying about this shit. I told the guys my woman's got family problems, a sick dad with terminal cancer and she's taking care of him and can't leave home right now."

Funny. I'd never pretended about having my dad in my life. Once he'd left, I'd shut him out. Was he still alive? Was he healthy, enjoying the good life with his new family, playing golf on the week-ends in some fancy suburb and taking them on vacations? I'd never know, and I'd trained myself long ago not to care.

I swept the hair back from Finger's face. He always kept it in his face, like he was hiding. I wanted to see him. My fingertips traced around those hard, dark eyes, the long, lean nose, rigid jaw, scarred, hollowed cheeks, dimpled chin.

"So many lies," I said. "Always lies. You think we'll ever be able to tell the truth?"

"As long as we never lie to each other, that's all that matters. That's what keeps this sweet," he whispered hoarsely as his thumb swirled over my center. I rocked my hips to meet his steady, slick rhythm. "Yeah, so fucking sweet."

He held my gaze, his eyes shining as the pleasure washed over me, sweeping me away with him into that spiraling current.

"You want a house one day? A kid?" he whispered. "Tell me what you want."

"Yes, our house. Our baby." I grinned. "Me baking brownies and you teaching him—"

"Or her."

"Or her how to ride a bicycle in the yard." I let out a laugh at my all-American cliché dream. But it was true.

"What a nice dream." He stroked faster, his hips thrusting against mine. "I love you, Serena. That's no dream. It's real. You're keeping that safe for me, aren't you?" he breathed. "You have to. I need to know you are. That's what keeps me sane."

Being on the pill was the best. I pushed his hand away and guided his bare cock inside me. His loud gasp made my insides flutter.

I rocked into him. "Me too, baby. Every day."

21
FINGER

I PARKED MY BIKE AND HUNTED for a pay phone.

Over three months had gone by since I'd seen her, touched her. We both had cell phones now, frequently switching out numbers and cards. I used burners as well, but again, couldn't take chances, so I used pay phones when I could. Since we'd last seen each other, she'd started school and loved it.

Today would be another visit to the flophouse. I called Serena and gave her the code for the time and place.

She'd only laughed.

My heart lurched at the sound of that laugh. Any other woman might have complained, bitched, and moaned. Not my woman. She was grateful for anything we managed to get.

"I'm bringing my own clean sheets this time," she said.

Taking precautions got old, but we were used to it now. The risk still hung over us, clawed at us. You never knew what the fuck might find you around the corner. Med and his crew were on the move, and he was as unpredictable as ever, instigating aggression and negativity with the Flames, truce or no truce.

I was in Chicago on business this time, a scouting mission on the Smoking Guns' relationship with a crime family. We knew they had ties, but National decided they wanted more specific intel. I had volunteered for the job, figuring I could slip in some time with my woman, plus I had a contact in Chicago who I'd put on the case. I couldn't do much inconspicuous legwork with my scars.

The Smoking Guns had first raised their level of notoriety and cash flow in the eighties by being the errand boys for the Tantucci family. Once they made a name for themselves, they separated themselves from obvious ties with Italian mafia and worked hard to make their reputation seem more "road outlaw." They weren't the purebred motorcycle club they pretended to be. Not like us.

My buddy Rhys, one of my few friends from high school in Missouri, was acting as my scout. I'd found him by chance on my last visit to Chicago, spotting him in a park strung out on drugs the VA had shoved in his hand before kicking his ass out. Rhys was former Special Forces, three tours of duty. After his years of service, he'd been living in his car and on the streets.

I'd given Rhys a chance by offering him a small job, a delivery. He'd come through on his first go round, and I'd paid him all the money I'd gotten for it. With me, he got straight and got busy, and I trusted him. I'd offered him a job as a freelancer and kept his existence a secret.

We were going to meet late tonight so he could tell me what he found out. He'd been following the Sergeant at Arms of the local Guns chapter the past month as well as two Tantucci foot soldiers.

Since I'd gotten into Chicago early and got my shit done, I had time to check out a man from another Chicago family before I met up with Serena. She still hung out with Ciara, but I'd insisted she didn't get too comfy with her and definitely kept away from Turo. She promised she'd avoid him and not spend so much time with Ciara anymore.

I wanted to see him for myself.

I found Turo by finding Ciara. The two of them had lunch at a French restaurant, then they strolled up Oak Street where he waited for her outside a shoe store, smoking some fancy short, thin cigar. He was average height, sported wavy reddish-blond hair he put effort into slicking back with shiny gel, a smooth shaved face, and light colored eyes. He wore an overcoat that hung on his wide shoulders, a slim-fitting suit and a perfectly tied tie, a small knot smack at the base of his long throat, and a starched collar so stiff any momma would approve of. I'd bet his fingernails were professionally manicured.

He put a gloved hand on Ciara's chin and dropped a quick kiss on her lips then opened a taxi door for her. She pouted, he ignored it and shut the car door and walked off on his own.

Trashing the remaining Italian beef sandwich with sweet peppers I'd gotten a few streets back, I brushed my hands together to be rid of the crumbs and grease and headed uptown to the shit neighborhood where I was meeting Serena.

I finally got to the hotel with ten minutes to spare. We'd meet in the lobby, in a phone booth at the back. I jumped the stairs two at a time, heat flaring through me. What would she be wearing? What color would her hair be? Would she have any new tattoos I could lick?

"Dude! Finger, that you?"

My heart froze mid-beat. I swiveled on the stairs. Skid. A Flame from Ohio. A skinhead disciple of Reich's white supremacist ways.

"What's up, man?" Skid jogged up the stairs and slapped my shoulder with his hand. "What are you doing out here from the boonies?"

"On an assignment."

He cast a look at the entrance to the small hotel where three backpackers stood looking at a map. "What the hell you doing here?" He nudged me with an elbow. "Gay boys come here, man."

"Oh yeah?"

"Fuck yeah. Ain't you staying at the club over on—"

"I just got in, been working most of the afternoon. I needed to take a leak, figured I'd find a john I could use in here."

"Better watch your back while you're taking a piss, man." He let out a loud, obnoxious laugh.

I forced my mouth to curl up into a tight grin.

"But you know Chicago real well, don't you?" he asked, his eyes hanging on mine.

"What do you mean?" I tugged on my jacket collar.

"I heard you come out this way a lot."

"You heard?"

"Yeah, Reich mentioned it. You know, I got a brother-in-law here at the Chicago chapter. He hasn't seen you around any, though."

A prickle tracked up my spine. I didn't usually poke my head in to the local chapters whenever I was in town, but Reich was keeping tabs on me? Of course he was.

I shrugged. "I'm in, I'm out, off and on."

"Right."

I held his gaze straight on. "What are you doing out this way?"

"Organizing a rally here," Skid said. "We're coming this way just before winter hits hard. Last run of the season for us." He rubbed a hand over his buzzed head.

"Cool."

"Gonna be a real good time. I'm heading over there now for some drinks and food."

"Oh yeah?"

"Come with me."

How was I going to get out of this now? I wasn't. I fucking wasn't. I couldn't. Skid would be reporting back to Reich, and I couldn't take any chances.

I shifted my weight and out of the corner of my eye I saw her. Striding up to the hotel, walking fast, holding a purple jacket close together against the cold wind. Large cat-eyed sunglasses over her face, a short red wig, or was it her own hair, I didn't fucking know. That old corduroy carpet bag on her shoulder. She took me in and smoothly slowed down her pace. She took out her cell phone from her bag and stared at it, hitting buttons. But there would be no message from me.

I had to give her the signal now. We'd never had to do it before, but there was a first time for everything. Hers was changing the rings on her fingers.

"Sounds like a good time," I said to Skid. I raised my hands and swept my long hair back into a ponytail.

I never put my hair up, but always had a hair band ready on my wrist for the signal. I stretched the band and twisted my hair into it, pulled my long hair through, and tugged it out.

No, don't approach me.

No, don't talk to me.

No, we can't meet.

You don't know me.

You don't even notice me.

Get out of the area fast.

Keep moving.

Get lost.

Do not contact me until I contact you.

No.

No.

Fuck, fuck, NO.

She stepped forward, tucking her phone back in her bag. An eyebrow raised from behind the sunglasses. She kept walking straight ahead. That's good. To have turned around suddenly and walk back from where she came from would have been obvious.

She walked toward me,

toward us,

past me,

past us,

past what would've been now,

right now,

tonight.

Jasmine and coriander wafted by me for a moment. Her latest perfume. I closed my eyes and held it in.

Gone.

An ache stabbed at my insides. Too brief, too quick.

I had to deny myself. Again. Denied like I'd been as a kid. That *kid*. What should have been mine was taken away over and over again. And now that I had something, someone wonderful, in order to preserve it I had to deny it. Reject it.

My stomach twisted, my jaw clenching against the ugly tide of emotion and anger. I wasn't sure when I'd be able to get back out here to see her. Reich was on my ass and obviously more suspicious of me than usual since Med's accusations. I had to be even more careful. I wouldn't put Serena in a vulnerable position.

If Reich ever found out, if he ever found her, he'd deliver her back to Med with a smile on his face and come up with a great way to punish me. I'd probably be applauded for my balls, but at the end of the day, it'd be deemed a crazy bad move.

Fuck, none of that mattered now. All that mattered was that she was gone. It took all the strength I had not to look after her as she walked past.

Skid let out a low whistle. "Fuuuuuck. I've seen more hot women around today. Shit."

My muscles tightened. "Huh?"

He gestured to two blondes on the other side of us who both grinned at his blatant attention. Attention they liked. I released the breath I'd been holding.

Skid shook his head. "So fucking hot. Come on, man, let's go. I suddenly need to get laid. You're gonna need me to put in a good word for you with the girls, 'cause that face of yours..." Another raw, loud laugh.

I pulled tight on the goddamn ponytail again, and the cold wind raced over my exposed neck and slid inside me. The world slowed down around me, and I was at its center, stuck, standing still.

I jammed my hands in my pockets and forced my legs to move. "I could use a drink."

We left the hotel behind us. I left my woman behind us, my heart and soul. Everything inside me shuttered down like a house under a sudden hurricane warning.

Windows taped and boarded.

Evacuate.

Abandon.

When the hell would I see her again?

22
SERENA

Finger and I managed to continue seeing each other—irregularly, very irregularly—but we managed it. Three years had passed, and I'd moved out of Tania's apartment and gotten my own place in the same neighborhood. A teeny tiny studio, but it was all mine. I set up a second-hand sewing machine I'd bought on a long table in the center of the space. At any time of day or night I'd sketch and pin patterns and cut and make a mess while Etta James sang for me on my portable CD player, and I loved it.

I decorated with Tania's help and made pretty things out of the simple, sometimes broken objects around me, just like my grandmother had done for me. I missed Grandma.

My own mother never had the time or the inclination for such creativity. She'd glance at me and Grandma, our heads bent over a piece of embroidery, as she'd be getting dressed to head back to the bar. "That's nice for some," she'd mutter, slipping on her high heels, that eternally pissed-off look etched on her face, a cigarette hanging from her lips. "But the rest of us have to live in the real world." My grandmother would ignore those swipes, only taking in a tiny tight breath as she continued showing me her needlework. On her way out the door, Mom would always mumble a "Later" to us, as if it were some kind of promise of better things, but it was a later that would never come.

Once things got busy for me with school, I wasn't able to hang out with Ciara as much as before, which was just as well as far as Finger was concerned. At school I met photographers and models through my various internships, and I volunteered to style their shoots which eventually turned into paying jobs. I kept my job at the store and was now the weekend manager. There, I learned about the business of running a business, about marketing and the art of designing a great storefront window, cultivating clients and keeping them.

Plenty of attractive guys buzzed around at school, at work, at the parties I went to, but none of them were My Man. Every sexy come on smile, every gym-trained body, clever twist of phrase, and suggestive look had a certain appeal, but none had any power over me. Only he did. Only Finger could unwind me with a look, destroy me with a touch, tangle me with a hoarse whisper against my skin.

Being true to him wasn't a hardship. It was the way it was.

Finger got me a cell phone when he got himself one, and he either called me a lot or not at all for stretches of time. I would offer to meet him somewhere halfway between wherever he was and Chicago, but he'd always refuse to let me take the chance to travel alone. He was traveling a lot, rising the ranks of his club, proving his dependability, his resourcefulness. And ruthlessness, I had no doubt.

We'd had a close call that one time when he'd used his signal to tell me to stay away, that our rendezvous was cancelled and to not contact him until he did. He'd put his long hair up in a ponytail, something he rarely did. That spooked me. A reminder that neither of us could ignore. Being happy was dangerous for us. Happy together meant letting our guard down. It meant fucked up consequences for us. We would never ever be safe to live freely. We couldn't ever get comfortable, we had to stay vigilant.

I would never forget that afternoon. I'd walked past Finger and the biker he was with in front of that hotel and tracked down Tania and Neil at a restaurant. I spent the night club hopping with them, forcing myself to appear to be having fun, not a care in the fucking world. I got drunk on purpose and crashed at Tania's apartment for the whole weekend. It took me days to get over the anxiety and the disappointment of having been so close to him, of seeing him again, and yet having to walk away as if he were invisible. I felt invisible. My heart hollow.

Up until that aborted meeting, I'd been feeling almost normal, content even. Afterwards, I'd eventually managed to settle into a routine again. Three years had gone by since then, the best three years of my life, and I'd almost forgotten to keep looking over my shoulder.

Almost.

"Do you have any maxi skirts with high slits?" came the loud, nasally voice from the center of the store.

A voice I knew.

My pulse sprang in my neck as I lifted my eyes from my computer screen at the front where our two cash registers were lined up on a high platform. From my perch I had a great view of the entire store.

A short blonde woman on high heels, in her late thirties, waved a long skirt on a hanger at Beth, my best salesgirl. Beth led the blonde to a set of racks further down the aisle.

Luckily, today I wore my brown contact lenses, but I took the oversized aviator sunglasses that rested on my head and slipped them down over my face. Why take any unnecessary chances? My long black hair was now streaked with green and blue and shaved on the sides. New tats swirled around my upper arms. Would she recognize me?

She'd barely spoken to me my last year at the club, but I knew her. Anne Marie, the old lady to one of Med's men. She was friendly, she was smug, she was arrogant. She was everything I'd never wanted to be. And here she was shopping in my corner of Chicago, Illinois.

Was Ann Marie here on purpose or was this simply a coincidence of fate? Had they found me and sent her in as a preamble to the slaughter or to make me some sort of deal? Did she have friends or relatives in Chicago? I couldn't remember. Was her old man, Scrib, in town too?

Scrib. Scrib had carved up Finger's face.

My breath shorted as Anne Marie swept out of the dressing room wearing a tight cheetah print maxi skirt Beth had found for her. She smoothed the material down her thigh as Beth adjusted the cropped top at her swollen middle. The outfit wasn't right for her body type, and I was sure she knew it, too, but Anne Marie always got what Anne Marie wanted.

I steadied myself and scanned the store window. People passed by on the busy sidewalk. Cars and buses cruised up the street. No men in leather stood on the street from the sweeping view I had of the outside. I shifted my weight and returned to my work at the computer. I wasn't going to run and hide. And anyway, there were a number of customers in the store. I couldn't just take off and leave Beth on her own. I took in a quick breath and focused on the computer screen, returning to the emails detailing upcoming deliveries.

"Ashley will take your purchases. Thanks again." Beth's sweet voice snapped me to attention as the cheetah print skirt and the striped crop top slid on the counter in front of me. Beth left me with Ann Marie.

I shot her a quick smile and rang up the two items. "That will be sixty-seven twenty-three."

She snapped a credit card on the counter, her long, glossy, French manicured fingernails glinting in the overhead lamp. I slid her card through the machine, handed her the receipt the register spit out, and she signed, her dangling earrings swinging.

"You finished or what? Let's go already."

My blood froze in my veins. My throat constricted at the sound of that deep voice. A heavy set biker stood in the entryway of the store, a little boy at his side. Scrib was here with his son, Logan.

I used to babysit Logan. Feed him, read to him, give him baths. I'd give him popsicles when he had a fever and sing to him. Once he even insisted on my spending the night at their house. Logan had to be eight or nine years old now.

Anne Marie rolled her eyes as she tossed the pen on the counter toward me and grabbed at her receipt from my hand. "Don't ever get married. Husbands are always trying to tell you what to do." She turned to her old man. "I'm done! Geez, would you relax?"

My lips curled into a small grin as I handed her the shopping bag. I opened my mouth to thank her, but shut it quickly. I'd been lucky my appearance had thrown her off, but maybe my voice would spark a memory.

She snatched the bag from my hand and sauntered over to her husband. Logan stared at me.

"You got what you wanted?" Scrib asked his old lady, throwing a glance at me.

I paid no attention, pretending something I didn't understand had just appeared on the screen.

"Yeah, I did," Anne Marie said as he pushed back the door for her.

"Logan, let's go!" Scrib bellowed in that demanding voice, and my stomach cramped. But it wasn't just the voice of a stressed out parent. The last time I'd heard it, he'd been jamming his cock into me, holding my wrists over my head. *"Come on, come on, yeah, bitch. This is how it's done."*

"Look at that lady!" Logan's clear voice rang out.

"What lady?" asked his father.

"Her!" Logan pointed straight at me, and my eyes darted to him like arrows, my heart hammering in my chest, the hairs on the back of my neck standing on end.

Scrib shot me an impatient look, but this time his eyes lingered. Ann Marie glanced back at me, flipping her hair from her face. Scrib's head suddenly slanted as he took me in, and my breath burned in my throat.

"She's got the same green and blue hair like the magic witch in my comic book!" said Logan.

"Yeah, yeah, she does," his father muttered, guiding his son out the door by the shoulder. The three of them stalked off down the sidewalk.

"Twenty, nineteen, eighteen..." I counted as much to keep my breathing steady as to time when I should look up from my screen once again, in case they or anyone else was watching me. "...two, one, zero."

My knees gave way, and I slid down to the floor, shuddering, taking in great big gulps of air. I wrapped my trembling arms around my chest and bit down on my tongue to stop the moans from escaping.

The next time we spoke, I told Finger what had happened.

"Oh fuck. Baby…" His breath hissed sharply over the phone. "Goddammit."

"They didn't recognized me," I assured him. "It was okay. I'm okay."

But silently, I asked myself how long could that "okay" possibly last?

23
SERENA

"ARE YOU SURE ABOUT QUITTING the gallery?" I asked Tania.

She handed me a mug of hot chocolate as I folded my legs underneath me on her sofa. We were catching up on each other's news, not having been able to see each other for weeks because of our hectic schedules.

"I'm sure and terrified, but I know I need to do it. I'd rather be an independent dealer working for collectors and representing artists. I've learned a lot about the art business and the art world, met a lot of personalities, understood how things work, but at the end of the day, I don't want to own my own gallery or run someone else's. The job's been feeling dead-end for a while now."

"Just a job."

"Exactly. And I don't want just a job. I want something more."

"How did Neil take it?" I asked.

"He tried to talk me out of it, but he gets it. We'd talked about opening our own gallery together one day, but my heart's just not in it."

"Good for you for realizing that," I said. "That would be awful if you made a commitment to Neil and then you weren't really into it."

"That's how I feel. Better to explore now, and if I want, I can go back, right?"

"Sure, why not? I'm excited for you, my adventurer."

"Thank you."

"It's wonderful. It's the right move."

My gaze fell on a framed photo of Tania and her best friend Grace from high school back in South Dakota. Grace had just got-

193

ten married when I'd first met Tania four years ago, and she had married a biker, Dig, an officer of the One-Eyed Jacks, their local club. Recently, Dig had gotten killed in some sort of assassination by a rival club. Tania had told me how her mother had called her to tell her the horrible news. Grace had survived a bullet wound, and the death of her unborn child, and she'd killed the fucker who'd gunned down her man.

Good for you, Grace. Good for you.

"How's Grace doing?" I asked.

"I don't know."

"What do you mean, you don't know?"

"I went home for Dig's funeral."

"Right."

"The night before she tried to kill herself in the hospital."

"No!"

"Yes. It was horrible. They pumped her stomach, though. None of us could see her after, and then I had to leave the next day to get back here for work. After I left, Grace's sister, Ruby, let my mom see her, which was good. Mom said she was far gone, very depressed." Tania wiped at her watery eyes. "Grace was the one who always looked at the positive in any situation. I was always Ms. Worst Case Scenario. She really wanted that baby. Their baby. Now no baby, and—oh yeah—no more babies for her ever again after her injuries and the surgery she had to have. I have no idea how to help her."

"Maybe now she just needs to focus on herself, and soon enough she'll be ready for friends and be open to you reaching out. All you can do is be patient and understanding and be there for her whenever she's ready."

"Grace got out of the hospital, but she hasn't returned my calls. I called Ruby last week, and she was pretty tight-lipped with me, which pissed me off. I'm trying to be understanding, but it's harder than I expected."

"Tough."

"I know."

A pounding at the door. Our heads jerked toward the booming noise. "Who the hell is that this time of night?" Tania shot up from her sofa.

I grabbed her arm. "I'm going in your bedroom."

"Go."

I gathered my mug and sweater, jacket and backpack, and went into Tania's small bedroom. I stashed everything under the bed, closed the door behind me and waited, every cell in my body listening.

Was it finally happening? Did they find me?

"Boner? What the hell are you doing here?" Tania's shriek was somewhere between shock and delight.

Boner was a member of the One-Eyed Jacks from her hometown. Tania had told me he was Dig's best friend and a close friend of Grace's.

"Where is she?" His voice was tortured, loud, almost off key.

I went to the door and peeked through the opening I'd left. Boner was tall and thin, with long dark wavy hair and green eyes that gleamed in the lamp light. He was emotional, distraught. Something was very wrong.

"Who?" asked Tania.

"Who? Are you kidding me? I've been riding straight to get to you so I could look you in the eye myself 'cause I can tell when I'm being lied to. Don't you fucking lie to me!"

"Calm the hell down and talk some sense, would you?" Tania shot back. "You want a drink? Let me pour you a drink."

Glasses clinked, a liquid poured from beyond my sightline. Heavy breathing and the sofa creaked. "What's going on?" Tania's even voice rose.

"She's missing. Sister's missing."

Sister was the club's nickname for Grace.

"What the hell are you talking about missing? Someone kidnap her or—" Tania's voice was high pitched, making the hairs on the back of my neck stand on end. My stomach dove and twisted like the innards of a washing machine with a double load on full power mode.

"No, not that," said Boner. "She picked up and left. Not a word to anybody."

"And Ruby?"

"Went with her. But that was weeks ago. Ruby's back now and ain't talking. She put Dig and Grace's shit in storage, sold their house real quick. Now she's left town too and got a job in Rapid. I went to see her, but she ain't talking. You know Ruby."

"Hard as nails."

"Yeah."

A glass slammed on the table.

"You were her best friend, Tania. You gotta tell me where she is. I gotta see her, make sure she's okay. I can't not know where she is. I just can't!"

My heart twisted in my chest at the anguish in his voice.

"I wish I knew, but I don't."

"Don't say you don't know, Tan! Don't say that! How is that possible? You two—"

"Since the funeral I've been calling her, but she never answers. Now you're telling me she up and left town? Her home? Her friends?"

"Yeah. Gone. How could she do this? She needs us! I need her."

"Yes, but she's lost now, right? Oh shit, Boner..." Tania dissolved into tears.

Mumbling and muffled voices. Heated words.

I slid down to the floor. Grace, who'd had everything to live for, a husband she loved, a baby on the way, a good club as her family to protect her and keep her safe. But Grace was now destroyed. All of it gone, her whole world shattered, ripped from her. The two most important people in her life taken from her—her old man and their unborn baby. Taken by another club's wrath, for real reasons or shits and giggles, who knew. Anything was possible on the turn of a dime.

Anything.

I knew that better than most, didn't I?

My heart careened in my chest at the thought of losing Finger. Losing him now when we had gained so much. So much.

"Do you think she went into hiding for a reason? Are the Demon Seeds after her now?" Tania asked, her tone urgent.

"That's what I'm trying to figure out here. I need to find her.

Help her. She's in the pit now. I know what that's like, and I gotta pull her out. She contacts you, you let me know. Promise me."

"I promise. You too. You find her, you call me. Please."

"I will," said Boner.

"If she can't even talk to me or you right now," said Tania, "then maybe she's just getting out to start fresh. Maybe she needs to put all of it and all of us behind her for a little while. We're all different, Boner. Maybe that's what she needs and we have to give it to her."

"No."

"Maybe it's too hard for her to stay and be surrounded by the Jacks, by everything that was Dig. Even you. She needs to get clean if she's going to stay alive." Tania let out a heavy sigh.

Boner and Tania continued their conversation, resignation and sadness clinging to every word. I leaned my head against the wall, the agony and frustration in their voices scouring through me. No one was sure if Dig's death was a random kill or club rooted. The Jacks were on alert, on the defensive, ready for anything; a dangerous, treacherous place to be.

Did all that matter to Grace? I doubted it. Either way, for whatever reason, her family was destroyed, and she'd chosen to leave her home to stay sane.

"I'm outta here," Boner said.

"You sure you're okay?"

"I gotta get my shit together." He sniffed in air. "You call me."

"I will. You too."

Pats on backs, murmuring, the door opened and shut. The chain drawn.

Tania opened the bedroom door and fell into my embrace. "Oh my God. Oh my God."

I squeezed her tightly. "You okay?"

"I don't know. Shit, I don't know."

"I think you're right. I think Grace is just doing what she needs to do. Fresh start and all."

"I hope so."

I whispered, "I know so."

24
SERENA

I HAD FOUR HOURS UNTIL MY next class. I planned on hitting the gym for a Tae Bo session, a quick shower after, and then back to school to get some research done in the library on post-WWI design, a revolutionary era in women's fashion. I threw my handbag on the table and headed back to the front door to twist the lock shut.

Sipping on the last of my raspberry iced tea, I reached out toward the lock, but the door burst open, and I went flying, falling on my back in the middle of my apartment. Ice exploded from my cup, pitching on the wood floor, clattering, sliding.

"Knew it was you! I knew it!" a man's voice hurled at me.

My eyes blinked and focused on a heavy set, leather-clothed man. Knobby nose, thin lips. His skeleton patch. Motormouth from Med's club.

"What the hell?" I sputtered, crawling backward like a spider who'd been newly uncovered, scooting back from the rising tide of evil before me. My back slammed into a leg of my dining table.

"I saw you on the street. My sister lives up here so I come up when I can to hang out with her and her kids. We were at this hippy coffeeshop in Bucktown yesterday and I saw you. Something about the way you walk, swishing that tiny ass, your smirk. You were with some black haired bitch who wouldn't shut up. I followed you here. Today, I went to that coffeeshop again, thinking maybe I'd spot you. Just to be sure it was you. And yeah, you showed up, but this time you took off your sunglasses. This time I was sure." He lunged on top of me, his smoky breath heaving on my face.

"Get off me!"

"No, no, no. That's not how this is going to go, Reen."

"Motormouth! We started out together. You were just a grunt when I showed up. We put up with their shit together."

He laughed. A dry laugh. A you-know-better-than-that laugh. My heart shriveled at the sound, my stomach curdled.

When Med had first brought me to his club, Motormouth had been a prospect, wide-eyed and eager to please. We'd struck up an easy going friendship, a friendship that Med picked up on and was suspicious of. He had forbidden us from any form of contact.

Motor released me and sat up. "Yeah, we started out together all right. You, me, and Rosie. Remember Rosie? Maybe you forgot her here in your new life."

Rosie was Motormouth's girlfriend. She was a pretty Asian American girl who danced for a living and enjoyed partying with the club. She was also a single mom to a young boy. Motor adored her. She was a sweetheart and we'd become good friends, my one bright spot in those years with Med.

My right hand flexed over my thigh, and the large white-blue moonstone ring I wore stared back at me. Rosie had lent it to me to wear one night out when we'd gotten all dressed up, then insisted I keep it.

"No, Motor. I haven't forgotten Rosie. "

His eyes hung on mine. Cloudy grey blue, pinched and worn. "She's gone, Reen. And you did that. What do you care, huh? Now you got yourself a new friend to take her place."

"What are you talking about?"

"You took off, and Med blamed Rosie. Said she'd helped you out seeing as how the two of you were buds."

"She didn't help me. I hadn't even planned on running off. It just happened."

"Just happened, huh? Well, that didn't matter none to Med. Rosie was connected to you." He nodded his head, a faraway look in those murky eyes. He was reliving it, and it was stinging him all over again. "There was a party, and he gave her away."

"Gave her away?"

"Yeah. When we were in California, we met these bros from a new chapter up in northern New York. They ended up coming back with us to Kansas and stayed to party before heading home. Med was furious that you'd taken off. That night we were all playing a crazy game of poker, and he used her as a chip. He lost her."

"Lost her?"

"Yeah." His voice was seeped in misery. "With that fucking grin on his face. You know the one."

"I know the one," I breathed.

"He gave them my Rosie." He brushed a hand across his mouth. "She wasn't my old lady. Kept insisting we were good as we were 'cause she was still planning on leaving Kansas and going to Vegas to find work. That night she didn't get what was going on. She was high and just didn't get it, laughing out in the parking lot as they took her with 'em."

"Motor—"

He gnawed on his lips. "Went out of my mind—"

"And Ricky?" Rosie's son was five years old now.

Motor's eyes closed for a moment. "I don't know."

My hand flew to my mouth. I reached out and touched his arm, and in a flash of movement he grabbed my hand, twisting hard. A streak of pain exploded in my wrist, my elbow. I gasped loudly, my body wrenching to the side, my shoulder screaming.

He hoisted me up against him, and pressed his stubbly face against the side of my cheek, sniffing deeply. "But I found you. I did."

"Motor—"

"Baby, I can't let you go." He shook his thick, curly brown hair back from his sweaty face.

"Don't do this. Don't be like him."

He shoved me, and I went flying against the dining table. "You left a fat mess behind you. Nit and Jan dead. You got to answer for that. I mean, shit, what the fuck did you expect, huh?" His voice got higher, drilling into me.

He planted his hands on his waist, his jacket hanging open, his gun visible on his side. I was sure he also had two knives at his back, as always. Motor had a knife collection. He was always sharpening them, choosing different blades to carry according to his mood for the day. He'd once introduced them all to me and Rosie. He'd named one Sadie, the other Heidi, one Jesse, another Mo. I'd pretended to be interested.

"Reen, baby, if I bring you in, that's gonna mean big rewards for me. Things have been really shitty for me lately."

Such a gentle, sad voice paired with such cold, lethal words. I gritted my teeth to remain still against the shivering that was taking over my body.

"Look, chicky." Motor's favorite nickname for women brought me back to reality. "You got out, you had your wild ride, your good time, okay, but now you gotta go back where you belong."

Back where I belong?

I didn't belong there, and I didn't belong to them, to Med.

No way in hell.

When I was little, I dreamed of having a Barbie Townhouse I'd seen on a television commercial. That dollhouse was really expensive, and I knew I'd never ever get it, but I still liked daydreaming about having it, where I'd put it in my room, what it would be like to play with. Now, my adult wish for freedom and a life on my own terms had actually come true. It was no overpriced plastic tower that I constantly daydreamed about. The dream had become real, and I was living it. It was mine.

And no one was going to take that away.

Especially now.

Motor eyed me. He needed me in line to score points. Like my mother had needed me in line to get on with her life and make herself happy. Like Med had needed me in line so he could have his way. Again, I would be a pawn in someone else's game? And what I wanted, what I craved, would be meaningless, unimportant, a joke?

No. Not again. Not me. Not now. Everything was different. I was different. Forever different.

Motormouth shoved past me, heading for the table behind me. He went through my purse, tossing the contents onto the polished wood surface into a messy heap. The strip of black and white photos of me and Finger hovered at the edge of the table. Motor made a face as he opened my wallet and took out what little cash I had in there.

I held my breath, my mouth dried, my heart banging in my chest. My eyes darted to the strip of photos. *Fuck.*

I hadn't gotten rid of the photographs like I knew I should. I loved them too much. We were kissing, laughing, making faces at each other, having fun. In one we were pressed cheek to cheek, eyes closed. They were beautiful. I'd only wanted to save something tangible of us a little bit longer. I missed him all the time. Why couldn't I keep just one thing? Just *one?*

Motormouth tossed the wallet, and it banged on the table. The strip of photos hopped up, catching his attention. He plucked it up off the table, his shoulders lifting. He spun around and faced me, my photos in his hand. "What the fuck? This is him, ain't it? That kid from the Flames? The one that we—He's the one who got you out?" He stared at me, standing taller. "Scrib had asked around town, and the delivery guy told him about seeing a guy with scars. We figured it coulda been him, but we didn't tell Med nothing. Didn't want to start a war with him freaking out the way he was. So we agreed to keep that shit quiet for the time being. But Scrib was right." Motormouth's bloodshot eyes blazed like one hundred watt lightbulbs glaring at me in the dark. "He comes and sees you? You with him now?"

I said nothing, remaining still.

"Just you wait, you goddamn whore." He turned to the shelves on the wall at the side of the table and dug his hands into my books and papers, sweeping my color-coded folders into the air. Patterns and designs wafted between us. Glass candle holders went flying. Papers floated, books thudded to the floor, small painted bowls I'd made in a pottery class smashed into bits and pieces.

Crash. Crash. Crash.

"Stop it!" I screamed.

He shot me a hard look, his eyes shimmering.

"Please, Motor. Please!"

"Please, what?" He kicked through the mess he'd created on the floor, barreling over to my dresser, touching every object, every perfume bottle there, tossing whatever was in front of him that didn't hold any appeal or worth. A wild bull in my crystal house.

Smash.

"Come on, Reen. Someone's gotta pay for killing Nit and for stealing from us. You want your lover boy to pay?" He waved the photo strip in the air. "'Cause I can make that happen real easy." He shoved the pictures in his pocket. "Yeah, Med's gonna love these."

"No. You can't tell him."

"Then come with me."

My throat tightened. I couldn't get words out.

His chest rose on a breath, his face was ruddy, his nostrils flaring. He grabbed the hand painted porcelain box from my night table, flipping it open. My heart stopped.

Justin's brass compass was in his grubby fist. "What's this, an antique watch or some shit? This has gotta be worth a few."

I launched at him, reaching for the compass. "Don't take that! Take whatever else you want. Not that."

He shoved me off him, and the porcelain box went flying, smashing into pieces on the floor.

"No! That's all I have left of—"

"Of what?" his voice raged, a fierce rage. Bitter and heartbreaking. "Of what, Reen, huh?" A sour smile contorted his lips, and he threw the compass down and bashed it with his heel.

I slumped to the floor, pressing my fists to the side of my head.

"Now you got nothing left," he muttered. "Just like me."

But he was wrong. So wrong.

"Don't do this." My chin trembled. "Med doesn't want me anymore. I'm just another girl. One of hundreds. I was trash around there at the end, you know that. There are always new ones to take your place. He has new ones now, doesn't he?"

"You weren't nothing special, you know. Just another hole, another set of tits and ass. But he had this crazy thing for you, and that's what counts. You're the one who got away." He let out a short chuckle.

"He doesn't need—"

He lunged at me, his fingers digging into the sides of my face.

"I need this, bitch. I need it." A chuckle escaped his mouth as his hands spanned my hips and slid down to my ass and my stomach flew up to my throat. He pulled me in against his body and rocked me against his erection. "And I sure as fuck need some of that. Oh, I'm finally but finally gonna get me some of that. Everyone else did, but me. He wouldn't let me at you that night, would he? That fuck. Holds a grudge like nobody's business."

He undid my belt, my pulse thudding in my neck. The leather slid and snapped from the buckle. The familiar clink of the metal. A knell of doom.

I pulled in my stomach muscles, steadying myself.

Never again. Not ever.

Not now.

I'd gone to see a doctor the other day. With my hectic schedule, I hadn't noticed that I'd skipped periods and felt off. I thought it was anxiety and fatigue, not eating right. And now, here I was, almost three months pregnant. I was in awe, I was in shock. I was elated, I was terrified. And I wasn't going to let Motormouth take my precious family away from me or destroy it. Everything was down to me, right this very now.

"You know what I need?" I whispered into his sweaty throat, my hands sliding around his thick belly.

He laughed. "Oh, fuckbunny, I got an idea or two or ten." His mouth nuzzled my neck, his teeth sinking into my skin.

Yes.

I relished the pain, that pain that signaled assault. Annihilation. That I knew.

Bring it the hell on.

He shoved my jeans down my hips, untucking my shirt as he went. "Now shut the fuck up, get on your knees and open that mouth."

I pressed my chest against his, my hands rubbing his lower back. "You sure that's what you want?"

One hand squeezed my ass, the other, a breast. "Yeah, that's what I fucking want, and that's just for starters. Now get down, dammit!"

Lifting the edges of his jacket, I closed my hand over a thick handle at his back. In one quick move I slid one of his knives from its holster and jammed the blade deep between his ribs.

He didn't have a return remark this time. Only his eyes bulged, the whites showing, a strangled hiss of air. He staggered and dropped to the floor at my feet. A choking cry.

The blood, the blood seeped everywhere.

Everywhere blood.

MY THROAT BURNED THE MOMENT I saw him sitting at the bar.

He noticed me immediately, his light colored eyes flaring then narrowing as I approached him. Recognition. Suspicion. In a graceful yet tight movement, his head slanted and he brought the thin dark cigarette that burned between his fingers to his mouth and inhaled deeply, his piercing eyes on me. The Mercenary Prince of the Night.

"Turo."

Those eyes glinted with a dark sort of amusement. He exhaled the fragrant smoke and sat up straighter. "Ashley."

My heart banged in my chest, my stomach churning with acid. I ignored the discomfort. "Could I talk to you?"

"Please do." He pulled out the chair next to him. I sat down.

"Aaron—" He gestured at the bartender who immediately set a bulbous wine glass before me and filled it halfway with an amethyst liquid.

My eyes met Turo's and my insides knotted. He was waiting, he was fascinated. I was making my debut on the stage. "I need to ask you for help."

He said nothing. Only brought his wine glass to his lips and drank. My words hung in the air between us, fading quickly like mist.

Turo placed his glass carefully on the bar top. "You're coming to me for a favor?"

I needed help from a professional. I couldn't go to Tania. Absolutely not. I'd love to run to her and burrow myself in one of her tight hugs and snuggle on her sofa with a cup of tea and a blanket and pretend none of this had happened.

But it had happened. And I was a realist.

I couldn't contact Finger. He hadn't called me or texted or anything since he'd given the signal that day. And anyway, wherever he was, odds were he was too far away to be able to dash over to Chicago and deal with a dead body for his secret girlfriend. Furthermore, I didn't want him to have his hands dirtied with Smoking Gun blood. I didn't want him implicated in anything that would ruin his career, his life.

I'd never met Turo before, but I'd seen him from afar once or twice when he'd picked up Ciara at the store, waiting for her across the street, a solemn statue of a man. Tonight I'd found him at his favorite restaurant in Bucktown. A trendy Mediterranean-French type bistro with low lighting and lots of candles in small wooden lanterns. Ciara had mentioned to me that they met here every Thursday night for a drink and *meze* before going out for the evening. Thursday night was their night. It was early and I knew Ciara worked late on Thursdays, so I took a chance and went to the restaurant. He was notoriously punctual and Ciara was always racing to meet him on time at their various rendezvous. She usually failed miserably. I desperately needed her to fail tonight.

"Try the wine," he said.

Taking in a tight breath, I raised the delicate glass and sipped. His heavy gaze remained on me as he exhaled a long, long stream of smoke, immediately crushing his cigarette in an ashtray. He peeled the glass out of my shaky, damp hand and set it back on the bar.

"This is between you and me. I don't want Ciara to know," I said, savoring the smooth wine in my mouth. Its silky warmth was civilized, soothing, and loosened the knot pinching my insides.

He leaned into me, his expensive citrusy Italian cologne filling the air between us. Ciara showed me the bottle once at Barney's. I'd been impressed. "Ciara doesn't know a lot of things," he said. "Let's hear it."

"I was being followed."

"Past tense? Do you know him?"

I would avoid that question for now. "He broke into my apartment today."

Turo's face stiffened. "Did he rob you? Do damage?"

"He tried. He tried to do damage to me," my voice broke.

"Ash—" A warm hand gently cradled my chin, an arm went around the back of my chair. "Ash, look at me."

My body shook, and he took me in his embrace, but it only made me colder. "Tell me now. Whisper it in my ear," he said against my hair, his breath warm against my neck.

"I killed him," I whispered, making my nightmare real.

"You killed him?" His lips brushed my earlobe, and a shiver raced over my skin.

"Yes."

He pulled back from me and laughed.

My shoulders stiffened. "What's so funny?"

"Ciara gets upset by a fucking spider, forget the roaches." He drank more wine.

"Good thing Ciara wasn't at my place today then."

He stared at me, a glimmer in his eyes, his tongue slowly swiping at his generous bottom lip. He handed me the glass of wine again. "Why did you call me?" he asked.

I took a small sip. A fleeting hint of chocolate and berries perfumed my strained senses, warmth raced through my chest.

"Say it, gorgeous. I want to hear you say it."

I set the wine glass down, pushing it away. "I need you to clean it up."

"You need me to clean it up," he repeated, his very keen gaze sending a sharp jolt through my veins. He was thrilled to hear those words come out of my mouth.

"Yes." I was crossing a line, and we both knew it. Brazen acknowledgement, tacit understanding.

"Why didn't you call 911?"

"Plenty of reasons," I replied.

He leaned his head down to mine, and I inhaled his warm breath. Wine and a fragrant tobacco, the sophisticated side of corruption.

"Then you've come to the right man," he said, his voice a smooth baritone.

"I wouldn't have asked otherwise."

"You appreciate my professional talents?"

"I admire them from afar."

A smile broke out over his lips. He gestured for me to come closer, but I only lifted an eyebrow in response. "How did you do it?" he asked.

"He had knives on him. I grabbed one and stabbed him in the side with it."

"Good girl."

"So, can you take care of this for me, or are we just chatting over vino while my flooring gets soaked in the other red stuff?"

He let out a chuckle. "Of course I can." He poured more wine for himself. "I won't ask what you're hiding. That wouldn't be professional of me. And I am a professional. After all, that's why you came to me, isn't it?"

"Yes."

He tucked his hand inside his jacket breast pocket and took out his cell phone. It was one of those newer ones, a really small model and thinner than any cell I'd seen before. Must have cost him a mint. He tapped a button.

"Hey," he said into his phone, his voice curt. "Meet me in Pilsen with your toolbox. Now." He gave him an address, a block over from my apartment.

Turo snapped his slim phone shut, the dull clap making me flinch.

"You know my address."

"Of course I do."

I let out a breath, but the dizziness still swirled in my head.

"Give me your keys."

I handed him my keys.

He flipped them over in his palm and tucked them in his jacket pocket. "I'll call you when it's done. You stay here. Have dinner. Dessert. This might take a while."

"Isn't Ciara meeting you here?" I asked.

"I'm going to call her now to cancel."

"I ruined your evening. I'm sorry—"

"Oh, no," he said. "You just made it infinitely more interesting."

He turned and gestured at the bartender, a very handsome model-type dressed in a tight black T-shirt outlining his perfect body. He was almost too pretty. "Aaron, my friend is staying for dinner. Whatever she wants—the works—on my tab."

"Absolutely, Mr. DeMarco." Aaron nodded at Turo and placed a long card of a menu on the bar top in front of me.

I glanced down at the beautifully designed menu edged in bronze trim, but it might as well have been written in Chinese.

"I don't think I can eat," I said.

"When was the last time you did?"

"I don't remember."

"Aaron, get the lady the arugula and mesclun salad with feta and the steak frites. Medium rare. And whatever else she'd like."

"Coming right up." Aaron vanished, taking the menu with him.

"Turo—"

"You like the wine? It's a very fine Cabernet from Argentina." His voice was relaxed. Just another night out with a woman. I tensed, expecting his hands to settle on a shoulder, my back, my arm. Thankfully, the touch never came; the weight of his gaze was heavy enough.

I said what I knew he wanted to hear, "The wine is very nice." I wouldn't be drinking anymore though.

"Stay here, eat, and relax." He leaned in even closer. "I'll call you, let you know when you can come home," he whispered in my ear, that icy shiver racing over the back of my neck once more.

"You have my number?" I asked.

He slid on a dark overcoat. "Oh, I've had it from the beginning, Ash."

Sweeping past me, Turo was gone.

25
SERENA

TWO O'CLOCK IN THE MORNING. A bleach-y, chemical odor stung my nostrils.

"All done," came Turo's voice behind me as I entered my apartment.

"All done," I murmured.

The apartment was immaculate, undefiled. All signs of death and destruction were now absent. But no fairy godmother had swooped in and performed this magical cleanup.

The door clicked shut behind me, and I flinched despite the weariness from the food, the hour, the adrenaline. Turo studied my reaction, but I kept it in check. He was always trying to read me. It was subtle but unsettling.

"You didn't have to wait for me downstairs," I said.

"Of course I did. You had a dead body in your apartment. You think I'm not going to make sure you're okay when you get yourself back in here? What kind of man do you think I am?"

"I don't think about you, Turo." I threw my handbag on the chair by the door. I swallowed down the tension that crept up my legs, my middle, my throat.

"You thought about me for this, though, didn't you?"

My eyes scanned the apartment. Everything in place. "I knew you could get the job done."

"You don't know anything about me."

"You're right, I don't. I made assumptions. See how that turned out, though?"

"You've got good instincts, Ash. I got that about you from day one."

210

Good instincts. Hmm. Instinct to kill, instinct to go to an underworld crime figure for help. My instinct to survive was a good one, that I knew. The pounding at the base of my skull thrummed. I was relieved, relieved I'd "handled" a murder and its messy aftermath all in the course of an evening.

He smoothed a hand down his crumpled striped dress shirt. "You okay to be here by yourself tonight?"

"Yeah. I'm good."

"She's good," he muttered.

"I'm not tired, I'll just stay up and work anyhow. I do most nights."

"Very ambitious."

"Determined."

A faint smile whisked across his lips. "I like that." He moved toward the door.

"Turo, thank you. Everything looks...." Oh hell, how do you thank someone for cleaning a dead body from your apartment and leaving your place spotless? "You'd never know. What do I owe you for this?"

He eyed me, and my stomach tightened waiting for his answer. Payment would be heavy.

"Tell me who he was."

I shrugged. "A one night stand from years ago."

His eyes narrowed, his lips curved up at the edges. "That's funny. Don't lie to me. We just went through a very intimate event together. Come on, gorgeous. Who was he?"

Before I'd left Motor's corpse in my apartment, I'd taken his club colors off his heavy body, cut them up with my shearing scissors, and put the pieces in separate trash bags and dumped them all along the walk to the bistro to find Turo. The tattoos on Motor's body would betray his club membership, but there was nothing I could do about that now. At least there was no evidence that he was from Med's chapter. The Smoking Guns were a huge organization. Motor could be an ex-member. He could have come from Australia for all anyone knew.

I'd taken the photos of me and Finger from his pocket and lit them on fire in my kitchen sink.

"Goodbye," I'd whispered to the carefree images of us, soaking in them one last time as the blue orange flames licked at them, consumed them, charring them into delicate curls of singed paper and ash. I'd turned on the faucet full blast, sending the remains down the drain.

Leave no clues behind.

I hadn't forgotten our rule, but that happy girl inside me, the one in the throes of first love, bursting with rainbows and lollipops, had wanted to keep those pics so badly. She'd pushed Rena aside and jammed her own bright pink flag in the brittle earth, declaring herself. She believed that everything would work out the way she wanted. She believed that she could hold onto souvenirs of a special night like any other girl in love would.

She was wrong.

Holding on could get you killed.

My heart hurt as I'd gathered up the pieces of the broken compass into a small plastic bag and shoved it in my handbag. I'd promised Finger I'd keep it safe, but I hadn't been able to. I'd failed.

I cleared my throat and prepared a response to Turo's question. "I didn't know him. He said he'd been following me for a while now, like I told you."

"No, you didn't tell me. You just didn't answer that question when I'd asked it."

"He followed me on the street, to my favorite coffeeshop, not once, but twice. Then he broke in here before I got a chance to lock the door behind me and he attacked me."

Turo rubbed a thumb at the corner of his mouth. "Should I leave one of my boys on the street?"

He was dropping it for now.

I swallowed hard, averting my gaze. "No, I'll be fine."

"I insist. You need anything else, you call me. I'll check in with you tomorrow."

"Okay. Thank you."

He leaned over me and planted a kiss on my mouth. Not quick, not slow. No tongue. But a kiss that was more than a goodbye peck.

He pulled back and let out a long breath as if he'd just taken a drag on a quality cigar and he was appraising the flavor. "You're welcome."

He brushed past me. My door jerked open, and Turo DeMarco's well-soled footsteps passed into the night.

26
SERENA

I OPENED MY DOOR A CRACK. The security chain stretched taut across my narrow view of Turo's face.

"What is it?"

"Good evening to you too, baby."

"Don't call me that."

"Let me in."

"No."

"I have something I need to discuss with you."

"Like what? The weather? The stock market crashing? Clinton's latest affair?"

He let out a laugh, his face relaxing. "No." His eyes traveled down my short kimono, lingering on my bare legs.

I pushed the door shut, but he quickly jammed his hand against the edge of the door, catching it. "This is business." One of his eyebrows lifted as he slanted his head against the door jamb, his eyes piercing mine. "Let me in."

Clenching my jaw, I unlocked the chain, opening the door for him. He entered, the shoulders of his expensive black trench coat brushing against me. His reddish blond hair was slicked back, his face freshly shaved, and with him wafted in the brisk scent of citrus cut with a dose of anise, almond, and musk. He stood in my living room, glancing at my work table which was strewn with drawings torn from my sketchbook. Drawings I hated. Drawings that were uninspired and bland. I hadn't been able to work. I'd been distracted and moody. And anxious, very anxious. In the handful of days that had passed, I'd been avoiding Tania and friends from school. I still hadn't heard from Finger.

Turo turned to me, his polished leather shoes catching the light from my work lamp. "I did some homework," he said. "Took me a while. Had to go through a lot of different channels, but I've been doing this a long time."

"What are you talking about?"

"You fascinate me."

I raised my eyes level with his. "Why?"

"I've always liked you. You have a certain something. I can't put my finger on it, but it's interesting. You keep to yourself. You don't play games. You're sexy as fuck."

"I'm your girlfriend's friend."

"Yes, you are. From the beginning I needed to make sure Ciara wasn't hanging out with some lowlife or someone who was using her to get to me. It's happened before, and I had to deal with both of them. Can't be too careful."

"No, I agree, you can't."

"I checked you out and didn't come up with much. Then you came to me for help, because you knifed a man to death. Well, that set off a mellifluous kind of music in my ears."

"Did it?"

"Yes."

"Again, your point?"

He leaned in close to me, his lips at my ear, his pricey manly scent attractive, asphyxiating. "Your secret is safe with me, Rena."

My pulse jammed in my veins, jamming my ability to breathe, speak, move.

"Serena Barnstone, gone missing at the age of seventeen. A high school teacher reports her disappearance, but Serena's mother chalks it up to her rebellious teen daughter running away. The girl re-surfaces a year later as Rena, old lady to one Medicine Man McGuire, President of the Smoking Guns of northern, Kansas. Within four years she falls out of favor and becomes nothing better than a slave to him and his club."

"Not anymore."

"No, not anymore." His eyes roved over me. "How did you

manage to get out? You were bored one rainy day and shot those two by yourself and skipped out of their compound?"

"It was sunny that day. Very sunny."

An eyebrow lifted. "Ah, protecting someone. Someone special to you. Who could that be?"

"Is there more? Are you going to blackmail me now? Threaten me with your little piece of juicy information that will get me imprisoned, tortured, and killed? You want an in with the Smoking Guns, is that it?"

"No, no, no. I don't want an 'in' with those fuckers." He enunciated the word as if it were sour on his tongue. He picked up one of my sketches and studied it, placing it carefully back on the table, smoothing down the edge of the paper. "I'm not here to send you back to them or blow the whistle on you."

I was still, revealing nothing.

"You don't believe me? Why, angel?" he asked.

"Because I know that the Smoking Guns are very friendly with plenty of organized crime families."

"Yes, they are. Not with mine, though. And I wouldn't call it friendly. I'd call it something else."

"What do you want from me, Turo?"

"Cooperation. I want information. Anything you can give me on your ex-old man and your colorful past."

He stared at me, studying my responses, taking in my levels of fear, anxiety. The silence stretched between us, and I waited for it to twang like a guitar string in a hushed concert arena.

"Information about Med?" I finally asked.

"Yes."

"Why would you need information from me? I was just one of the many girls he kept."

"No, you weren't. Not just some girl." He tipped his chin, licking his bottom lip. "What is it? Do you feel loyalty or duty toward the man who kidnapped you, raped you, and kept you for years? I will tell you this. Medicine Man and his glorious club crossed the line one too many times with the organization I work for. And that's something you do not do without pissing off very powerful and very intolerant people."

"That's one of his favorite hobbies, though."

A smile broke over his face. "That's no way to conduct business."

"You think he cares about business ethics?"

Turo took one, two, three steps toward me and stopped. "I want your help to make his life miserable and cut down our competition in the process. Win for me. Plus, I figured you might enjoy the opportunity I'm offering to make him suffer. Win for you."

I didn't answer.

He whispered roughly, "Don't forget, gorgeous, you owe me."

"I'll never forget. I know I do."

"Good. I realize I'm asking you to rat, something that's not done."

"Same applies in your world, doesn't it?"

"Hmm." A grin broke over his carved lips.

"So you understand the position you're putting me in."

"They're still looking for you," he said, an eyebrow raised. "Was that what happened with Mr. Motormouth? He found you?"

"Yes."

His eyes hardened. "I can protect you." "Oh, I've heard that before. Don't sugarcoat this shit. I'll keep owing you and owing you, right? Until my usefulness runs out, and then—"

"I wouldn't feed you to those dogs." His voice was firm. "I like you, *Ashley*, and I'm sympathetic to your situation. I'd like to see you thrive far away from that trash. I really would. You say yes, and I'll plant evidence of Mr. Mouth outside of Chicago. Way outside of Chicago, on the road leading back to Kansas."

Had he saved a tattooed arm or Motor's tattooed torso to plant somewhere? His bike? His knives?

"What would you do with information? Feed it to the feds or the cops?"

The lines on his forehead deepened for just a moment. "No feeding any of it to anybody. This will be all mine. I don't even want anyone to know this information is coming from me. Which means no one will ever know it's coming from you."

I held his steady gaze.

Was I really considering this?

This was crazy. This was a road to perdition. Eventually. But right now, I couldn't see a way out of it. This was everything Finger had warned me about. Getting too close, owing and being obligated. I'd put myself in a position of weakness and vulnerability, hadn't I?

Med had kidnapped me, raped me, kept me locked in dark closets, terrorized me, and petted me like his favorite kitty all at the same time. I'd done everything he'd asked me and made me do, and then in one night all that had changed. And it had been a brutal change. I had no doubt that if Finger hadn't come for me when he had, I'd be nothing but body parts all over Kansas right now.

"Only between you and me," Turo said.

Turo was a player in a powerful crime syndicate. Maybe he really could keep the wild wolves at bay for me once and for all, and there would be no more hiding, no more wondering, no more wandering. At least for a little while. It would be a good jump start.

I swallowed hard, squashing the sour seeping up my throat back down. "Only between you and me. No go betweens or other representatives from your organization. Not even a bodyguard. And definitely no Ciara. No one else can know. Promise me."

"I promise."

I believed him.

He removed his trench coat and swept it over a chair in a precise fold. *Burberry* said the inside lining. He took off his lean suit jacket and folded that over as well. Letting out a sigh, Turo sat down on my small sofa, an incongruous vision in starched lines and immaculate black and white tailoring in contrast to the woven purple and red pillows he leaned against on the turquoise sofa.

"I've got an hour to kill." His eyes dove to my bare legs and his jaw clenched. "Get yourself dressed, make us coffee," he stroked the cushion next to where he sat on the sofa, "and come entertain me with tales of your sordid underworld."

27
SERENA

"I CAN'T WAIT TO SEE YOU. Jesus, it's been so fucking long," Finger's scratched and husky voice leapt at me through the telephone, making my pulse speed.

"I know, baby. I'm so excited." I wouldn't ask him where he was in relation to Chicago. He wouldn't have told me anyhow. He was in the middle of club business, hooking through Chicago for two days to see me before heading back to Nebraska. "I can't wait to kiss you tomorrow."

"Oh, and that's not all, babe." He let out a laugh. "Love you."

My heart squeezed. "Love you too."

Finally.

After not hearing from him for so long, he was finally on his way, and I'd be seeing him in a matter of hours. I would tell him everything then. About Motormouth, about Turo.

About our baby.

I'd taken the day off from work, packed up my new wine-colored satchel bag, baked a small pan of brownies and packed them in a plastic container tied with silver ribbon. I couldn't wait to give him the brownies and see his reaction. See if he remembered my silly dream for our one day together future: *I'm baking brownies, and you're teaching our kid to ride a bicycle out in the yard.* Then I'd tell him about the baby.

I waited in my apartment for his call, dressed and ready to rock and roll from six in the morning.

It was twelve noon now.

Nothing.

Four in the afternoon.

Still nothing.

Nine at night.

Not a word.

I hadn't eaten all day. My head swam.

I stayed glued to my sofa, my phone at my side.

I clicked a lamp on.

Ten thirty-five pm.

I closed my eyes.

The phone rang. I fumbled with it as if I'd never handled a cell phone before. "Yes? Hello?"

"Ash, it's me."

My chest caved. "Oh. Hey, Tania."

"What are you doing? Come meet me at Arena!" she practically shouted over loud music and a noisy crowd. She was at a bar. Her latest boyfriend loved sports bars.

"What?"

"Come out. I need girl power, and I haven't seen you in a long time."

"No."

"Why not?"

"I'm waiting for someone."

"Oh. Oh! Good! Sorry. I'll talk to you whenever. Call me, okay? Have fun!"

Fun. I tugged my hands through my hair, nausea swirled in my gut. Something had to be wrong. Something.

I got up and filled a tall glass with water, gulping in one long swallow. I had to wait. Just sit tight and wait. It wasn't the first time he'd been delayed or a no show, and it wouldn't be the last. I grabbed the last half of a chocolate bar I'd stashed in my small fridge, kicked off my shoes, and nestled into the corner of my sofa, flipping channels on the remote control.

Dumbass high school comedy. News. Beer commercial. "Mad About You" rerun. Car commercial. Toni Braxton music video. Epilator infomercial.

News it is. At least I'd catch the weather for tonight and tomorrow. Be prepared.

I bit into the last piece of chocolate. Tasteless, too sweet.

The cops had arrested a man who'd broken into several apartments in the same neighborhood. The reporter's face morphed into a rigid frown. "In related news, the skeletal remains found earlier this month outside of DeKalb have been formally identified by investigators as those of Rose Shohito."

I froze.

A photograph of a young Rose appeared on the screen stamped with her name in big block letters.

"At the time of her disappearance the victim was an exotic dancer and a groupie of the notorious Smoking Guns Motorcycle Club. Ms. Shohito also had a five year old son. After her disappearance, the boy's care was taken over by the state, his name changed for his protection. The cause of Ms. Shohito's death appears to be repeated blows to the skull..."

Rose, Rose, what did they do to you?

Maybe she'd tried to escape, to get back to her son, to Motor, and they'd caught her and...

The room tilted, and I gripped my knees to steady myself.

An image of Rose flashed before my eyes. Her squealing laughter, her arm around my shoulders as we got beers at that heavy metal concert in Florida on a winter run.

The reporter talked investigation, bone fragments, a ditch.

Motor's haunted voice came back to me. *"He used her as a chip. He lost her."*

Rose had gotten traded like a baseball card between kids, like a fur pelt between an Indian and a frontiersman. And her boy? Abandoned, given away, name changed. His mother erased.

Erased.

A wail escaped my throat. "Rosie..."

Lost forever.

Her boy would never know her or know of her. And there was no one to tell him either. Rose's life had been brutally snuffed out for no reason, and her memory forgotten except by me and Motormouth.

And now I'd snuffed him out.

I buried my face in my lap, my hands over the back of my head. "NO!" I yelled.

She was a good friend, a sweet mom, a happy spirit. But that's not what would remain of Rose. After listening to that news report, people would only think: "She got what she deserved for being so loose, so reckless and irresponsible. What the hell did she expect?"

"...Partly cloudy with a slight possibility of showers late in the afternoon," blared the television. "That'll do it for me. Jane, back to you!"

"Thanks, Kevin. Next up, Roger Emery with tonight's sports scores..."

Yes, forgotten.

Numb, I slid onto the floor.

THUNDER. BANGING.

"Ash? Ash? Open up, it's me."

I popped up from the floor, my neck protesting, my shoulder sore from where I'd fallen asleep on it.

"Ashley!"

I shut off the television. What time was it?

Hard knocking.

My limbs were heavy and not cooperating. I pushed up from the floor, somehow making it to the door. "Tania?"

"Open up already!"

I unlocked the door and swung it open. "What's going on?"

She wore a baseball cap over her dark hair, men's pajama pants stuffed in tall rain boots and a University of Chicago hoodie with an oversized Cubs windbreaker. She closed the door behind me. Her face was pale, she was tired. "Did you hear from Finger last night?"

"No, nothing. Why?"

"He called me this morning."

"What?"

"About half an hour ago. I came right over—"

"What are you talking about. Are you sure? Are you—"

She grabbed my arms tightly, facing me. "Listen to me," her

voice was even, firm. "Finger called me. From jail."

My heart snagged on barbed wire. "What?"

"He got arrested yesterday just outside of town."

My mind blanked.

She threw off the baseball cap and the windbreaker. "Finger got arrested last night and he's in jail. He got a hold of a cell phone from some other inmate and called me to tell me to let you know. It was a thirty-second call at best. He didn't use my name, just started talking at me."

"Why? What did he—"

"They got him for possession of bomb making material related to this explosion in Springfield the day before. Two related felonies, maybe more charges. There's no bail. He's looking at time. Seven years, he said, something like that."

Arrested.

The FBI must be all over Finger right this very moment like a swarm of flies on picnic food, trying to get info out of him. I was sure the Flames of Hell had a lawyer on retainer for situations like this, but who knew if he'd be able to get Finger out? Was there enough evidence to make a conviction stick? And if so, for how long?

I wouldn't be able to visit him. He'd be watched by his club and others, and I wouldn't be able to see him, talk to him. I wouldn't even trust letters. Would he even be safe in jail? Would rival clubs or gangs or whoever be on his tail?

"The last thing he said was, "Remember this—leave no clues behind, Sunshine. I've got my hair up in a ponytail for the ride.'"

My stomach cramped, my chest caved in.

"I'm guessing you know what that means?" Tania asked.

The room swerved out from under me. Tania was a blur.

Goodbye, baby. Goodbye.

I wouldn't be seeing Finger today or any other day. I wouldn't be able to tell him about killing Motormouth, about Scrib suspecting he'd been the one to have gotten me out, about Turo.

About our baby.

Our baby.

"Honey, I'm sorry—" Tania reached out toward me.

I shrank away from her. "No!"

I was on my own. Alone. Arctic winds blew loud and fierce around me and the landscape offered no comforts whatsoever. Bleak, barren.

People like me and Finger had plenty of dreams, but mostly we kept our heads down, out of those pretty clouds, and we lived by the skin of our teeth.

The ache building in my heart cracked wide open and multiplied into a thousand aches like fractures rupturing over an ice covered lake, the noise deafening.

Doom.

Tears choked me. I gave in and swirled in the flood of salty water.

Tears were supposed to be cathartic, cleansing, but not mine. My tears were flammable gasoline.

I would have to light the match and set it all on fire.

TANIA BUSIED HERSELF IN MY tiny strip of a kitchen making us tea. I couldn't listen to her stream of words. I was too busy listening to my own.

One thought overtook me.

If Grace could do it, Grace the widow, Grace the childless mother with the torn body and ripped soul, why couldn't I?

There would be no better solutions, no other choices. I had gotten myself into an impossible situation once again, but this time I had to get myself out. Finger had given me the gift of freedom. He'd made me a promise that he'd come back for me, and he had. Tania had put herself on the line to help us, and she did. I was free to live in that sunshine they both had showed me. I was free to love him and be loved in return.

I just couldn't be with him.

What had Boner said? *"She's in the pit now. I know what that's like, and I gotta pull her out."* I'd been in several pits already, and right now there was no one who could pull me out—no Grandma, not Tania, not Finger. Hell knew where he'd end up to do his time and for how long, and there could be no contact. And Tania needed to stay clean and clear of it all.

This time, I couldn't cling to hopes, waiting for an optimal opportunity. I had to protect our baby which was growing inside me every day, and do it now. I had to protect my man. Being together could get us all killed or worse.

I saw the choice I had to make as clear as a toll booth up ahead on the highway. Payment had to be made in order to pass, and there wasn't much time to scrounge the coins together.

I have to keep my family safe.

That drumbeat of war boomed in my head. Unmistakeable, steady, loud.

I'd gotten comfortable and that had been a mistake. I knew better, but I'd been enjoying myself. I'd enjoyed believing.

I'd had a brush with Scrib. Motormouth had found me. Somewhere down the line, some other Gun would find me, take me back, and I'd be punished in some horrible way for the glory of their honor, their pride, or just for the hell of it.

I had started clinging to hopes this past year, nurturing them, but there could be no more of that. Hopes were like wisps of glittery diaphanous fabric—dreamy, fanciful. Impractical. Nothing good ever lasted for me, that had been proven true over and over.

I had to make a move.

"Tea and Oreos, breakfast of champions." Tania set a tray of steaming mugs and cookies on napkins in front of me on the coffee table.

I would stay away from Tania to keep her safe. I had to. She deserved only the best. I had to leave Chicago, and leave no clues behind.

I would perfect that principle this time. That was now my truth, my religion, my creed.

Steam rose from the surface of the tea, and my mother's words came back to me: *"Some of us have to live in the real world."*

Oh, I did live in the real world. I knew that for me to grab at any happiness, there would always be something to hide, someone to kill, someone to pay off, someone to owe.

And now, I had something precious they could take from me and destroy, but I wouldn't let them.

I would take it away myself first.

28
FINGER

"Out in four if you behave," the club lawyer said. "Maybe even three, but I can't promise anything."

My chained hands curled into tight fists on the table.

I'd gotten caught on my way to Chicago. This job in Springfield, Illinois had come in at the last minute from National. I got it done, and the next day I headed to Chicago. In a little over twenty minutes I would've been in the city limits, and in my woman's arms.

Instead I'd landed in a jail cell.

He leaned in closer to me, his fingers pressing down over his navy blue tie. "Your club needs you in jail. You're agreeing to a deal, and they're going to send you to the state pen. Usually this sort of thing gets tagged for the Feds and they swoop in and send you boys to some facility way across the country just for the hell of it. That won't happen here. So you do your time, and you'll be out in a few years."

"What's the hook?"

Across the table, he passed me two black and white photos of two different men.

"Last year, the President and Vice President of the Silver Crows were incarcerated in northern Illinois..."

The rest was a fucking laundry list of what I needed to do for the greatness of the Flames.

"Who? Tell me who."

"Who?" The lawyer squinted, slanting his head as if he'd had trouble deciphering my use of the English language.

"Whose idea was this, fuckwad?" I said through gritted teeth.

He sat up straight in his chair, his forehead wrinkling. "This came from the top."

"From National?"

"Yes."

"Tell me who."

"It was agreed on by the board."

"Someone made the pitch."

He folded his hands over a manila folder. "Reich Malone. He's new on the board, lots of ideas. Kick ass ideas, I was told. He's been working on some new venture out here in Illinois and needs the Silver Crows on board."

Reich. Pushing me down, shoving me into his fucking holes to fill gaps yet again. Worst fucking timing in the world.

I'd been on my way to see Serena for the first time in three months. I hadn't been able to contact her much lately as things had gotten fucked up with the Smoking Guns again. A small outbreak of tension with Med's crew, and it was better to lay low for a while until things cooled off. Better to lay low now that I knew that Reich had eyes on me.

Had he seen us together? With me out of the way would he now swoop in and grab her? I dropped my head in my hands. At least I'd talked to Tania on the phone and gave her the head's up. She'd go to Serena and tell her. How had she reacted? What was going through her mind?

I banged my fists on the table.

Again, I was a prisoner, but this time with a serial number to match and clean clothes provided by the state. Another prison where I had to not feel, not give in, not give up, and survive. A cog in the wheel, the junkyard dog. Kicked at. Maneuvered.

But this time there would be no Serena to whisper with in the gloomy shadows. No Serena to brighten the wretched darkness. No Serena to touch and be touched by, to hold and be held by.

The lawyer pushed back from the table and stood, adjusting his jacket, grabbing his briefcase. "I'll let you know what the DA says. Remember, you don't talk to anyone but me."

I swung my head back. "Fuck you."

29
SERENA

Tania stood with me at the side of the road where I was meeting Stephanie, a friend from school, who was driving home to Texas. I was hitching a ride with her.

Anywhere out of Chicago.

Tania grabbed my hand. "You don't have to do this."

My throat was dry, and I was too weary to even swallow past the soreness. "Tan, I have to." My heel shoved at my two big duffel bags stuffed with clothes, sketchpads, and my small sewing machine. I'd managed to sell and give everything else away, and even got out of my lease on my apartment.

I looked away, choking on a breath, tears streaming down my face despite my determination to be stoic. I used to be good at stoic.

Tania pulled me close. "Honey, I know this is horrible right now, but he'll be out in a few years."

"We don't know anything for sure."

"It seems like a long time right now, but when he gets out, maybe things will be different and then—"

"Nothing will be different, Tania. Nothing. They'll still be after us, after me. And I won't put you in danger, and I can't—"

"Shh. I know. We've been over it enough times." Tania didn't necessarily agree with my decision, but she supported me like a true sister would.

The bright white headlights of a truck thundering by us on the road flashed over our faces. Here I was again, on the run, anxious. But this time, I was in control.

"I know you'll get your second chance together one day," she said. "You have to."

"I've had my fill of second chances, Tan. Girls like me have a limited number. You wouldn't understand. Thank your God that you never will."

She only squeezed my hand tighter, and I squeezed back.

A small car approached, slowing down. Stephanie's red Honda Accord ground to a halt alongside us, the engine running.

Tania and I hugged. Tears and laughter and promises surged up like frothing bubbles in that embrace. "I love you," she whispered, her voice tight.

"I love you too."

"We're soul sisters, you and me," Tania said. "I'll always be there for you, no matter what. Don't forget that."

"I won't. Same goes for me."

"Let me come visit you. Just once. Just—"

"No, Tania. We agreed."

We let go, both of us wiping at our faces.

"And no more tears," I said.

She sniffed. "Right."

I took one duffel and Tania took the other, and we shoved them in Stephanie's trunk. I got my ass in the front seat and left Chicago behind me.

FOR ABOUT A YEAR I wandered through a few states, then I decided on a new frontier—California. First, I returned to Chicago to ask Turo for a favor. I'd fed him plenty of information before I'd left and stayed in touch and answered any random questions, confirmed names.

"It was by far one of the best ideas I've ever had." Turo sat down at the other end of the same bench as me in Olive Park, pretending to talk on his cell phone. He still wore that same unique fragrance. The crispness of it made my insides stand at attention. Or was it the brittle memories of the time I'd spent with him?

"What's that?" I asked quietly, pretending to read a fashion magazine.

"The information you gave me made a huge difference this past year. I used them little by little, month by month."

"I don't want to know details. Although I may have read about a few deaths in the newspaper."

He let out one of those expressive sighs of his—an audible smirk. "That's just on the surface."

"Well, I'm happy you're happy."

"We should celebrate."

"We don't have to do that."

"I want to." He crossed his finely trousered legs, a dark argyle patterned sock peeking out under the cuff, just over his Italian leather shoes. "I haven't seen you in a long while. Too long."

"I picked up a few jobs out of town," I lied.

"Are you back for good now?"

"No."

"I'll take you out tonight."

"I don't think that's a good idea, do you?" I closed the magazine and lifted my face toward the rays of the sun, my eyes closed.

"Ciara is out of town." He'd read my mind.

"Ciara has friends all over town," I replied.

"True. But I want to enjoy this with you, Ash. I want to offer you a special something."

"I don't want special somethings from you. I want this over."

"It is over, officially."

"Good." I leaned back against the bench, clutching my magazine. Out of the corner of my eye, I spotted his sly smile tinged with genuine excitement.

"As a thank you, I'd like to give you anything you want," he said.

A thank you for an obligation? Hell no. Was he offering money? A shopping spree? Jewelry? A vacation? All the things he would give to Ciara so freely. I'd never accepted things from Turo. He'd tried from the very beginning, and I'd rejected the first, a super expensive new cell phone. Then I'd rejected money for a new sewing machine. He hadn't tried again. I didn't want any of that. I didn't need any of that. What I needed I couldn't have.

"That's why I asked to see you," I said.

"Ah, she does want something." His voice was mellow and sensual, like a mouthful of fine brandy. "Anything but the Baptist's head, my little Salome."

"Oh, I would never ask that."

"I know. That's why I like you so much," he whispered roughly.

I smoothed a hand down the cover of the magazine. "There is one thing."

A slow smile warmed his face. I could feel its rays of heat over the side of my body. "Hmm. Tell me. Tell me what you need, and I'll get it done for you. Personally."

"I want a new identity. Name, social security number, history. All of it," I replied.

He cleared his throat as he removed the cell phone from his ear, and holding it in his hands, flipped it over, rubbing a thumb over its matte black surface once, twice. "Leaving town again?"

"For good this time."

"That's too bad."

"Necessary."

"Understood. Done. What else?"

"Nothing else. There's nothing."

"There has to be something."

Of course there was something. If only I could ask him to get me information on Finger. If only I could ask him...

But I couldn't. I didn't want anyone to know Finger and I had a connection, and I certainly didn't want Turo to know that I was on intimate terms with a Flame of Hell. He'd use that to his advantage at some point. Whether they wore leather and colors or finely tailored suits and high-priced cologne, if men wanted things, they demanded them from you, then they were done.

Except one man. One man.

"Just this—" I slid a business card out from the magazine onto the bench in between us. "I'd like this first name if possible."

I wanted my grandmother's name. If I was to be reborn yet again, this time, I wanted the most beautiful name to me, to honor her, but also to keep a piece of her with me in this new life, a living souvenir. I had nothing of hers, no keepsake, no memento, no nothing, only memories and inspiration.

Turo casually slid the card into his pocket in one swift move, crossing his legs.

"May be difficult. But I'll do my best. When do you need it?"

"How soon can you get it?"

"Two weeks, maybe three."

"Let me know." I tossed my empty coffee cup in the metal waste-basket to my left, tucked the magazine into my tote bag and stood up, adjusting my coat. "I have an appointment to get to."

He stretched his arms out over the back of the bench, his long legs before him. "Good-bye, gorgeous."

TEN DAYS LATER IN THE middle of the night, Turo showed up at where I'd been staying, a friend's small photography studio.

He placed a padded envelope on the metal console table. "New name, social, driver's license."

"Thank you."

"You're welcome."

He scanned the room, an eyebrow lifting at the sight of the light stands and filters. Lightboxes, a drafting table, a backdrop screen, a desktop computer. The futon sofa where I'd been sleeping the past two weeks. His gaze returned to me and grew heavy. I held my breath as we stared at each other in silence.

"Can I have a drink?" he asked.

"There's vodka."

"Vodka, then."

I poured him the liquor in a glass tumbler. He took a drink and handed it to me. I took a sip. He took back the glass and finished it, putting it back on the counter, his oddly colored eyes on me.

"When are you leaving?" he asked.

"In a couple of days."

"Do you need—"

"No." I smiled. "But thank you."

His forehead creased. "Where are you going?"

"Greenland."

His eyes flared, his head rocked back and he laughed, a deep rolling rumble of a laugh. Something in my chest tightened. This was a side of him I'd never seen before. Warm. Human.

"I'm going to miss you," he said.

"We barely know each other. What's there to miss, Turo?"

"This."

In a sudden movement, he yanked on the belt of my kimono and dropped it to the floor. A rush of cool air whispered over my now visible bare skin.

"Oh, this," he repeated, his voice low.

"Turo—"

He took in a deep breath, his jaw tight, his heady gaze burning over my chest. "I'm going to miss you." He took another step closer toward me, his hair in his eyes. He'd let it grow out. Shadows fell over his cheekbones. A knight borne of the darkness, walking in shadows.

"My angel, never wanted anything for herself." His cool hand cupped a breast, and I let out a short gasp. His lips parted, the amber in his intent eyes now molten in the glow from the desk lamp I'd put on when he'd knocked on the door. His thumb stroked over a curve, and his breath caught.

"Turo."

"I can't not touch you anymore," he breathed.

He got on his knees before me, and my insides plunged like a stone under water. He gently swept my silk kimono away from my nakedness, and his breath caught. His cool hands dragged up and down the sides of my hips, my thighs.

"Ciara used to tell me you never had a boyfriend, didn't do hook-ups." He planted a kiss on my left thigh, my right. "I watched you. She was right. No boyfriends, no hookups. Yet you always look so fucking hungry underneath your cool facade." His gleaming eyes hung on mine, his one hand circling my leg. "Let me give you what you need tonight. Just this once. For goodbye."

A large thumb grazed the sensitive flesh between my legs, and my body seized. He licked his lips. "Only if you let me." He bent and feathered kisses over my lower tummy, his eyes closing for a moment. "I can't stop thinking about you."

I shoved at him with my leg. "You're such a shit, Turo. You have Ciara. You have so many women to choose from all the time, and I'm sure you do just that."

He nipped at my inner thigh, and I bit down on my lip. Was he chastising me? His tongue grazed over the bite, and a hot rush of sensation swarmed through me. "None of them are you." He didn't grin smugly or laugh. His face was etched with something else, something somber, something dark.

I hadn't been with anyone since Finger. I just couldn't, and I had no urge to be. I didn't deserve to feel any spark of happiness or relief, not even for the short time it would take to get off. I wanted to keep a clear head. No distractions. No noise. I didn't want any kind of physical intimacy with anyone; it almost seemed trivial in the scheme of things.

I'd been in a kind of limbo this past year, but now I was really moving on. If Finger ever got out of jail, he would probably try to find me. But after what I'd done, he'd never want any part of me.

Why not make it final, that separation? Not just on paper with my new name and identity, but physically as well as in my head? Unglue Finger from me.

Was that even possible?

I should try. Shove myself over that edge and crash.

Turo's mouth laid a dangerous trail up my thigh, and I grit my teeth.

"Let me fuck you, gorgeous," he whispered in the semi-darkness, his light colored eyes gleaming up at me. "Let me give you what you need. You and me. This has got nothing to do with business, or anything or anybody else. I want you. I've wanted you for so long. You know I have."

"I know," I choked out the whisper.

"I've been a gentleman all this time. I've been good to you."

Turo had been good to me. He hadn't been sleazy or pushy. Slightly flirtatious, suggestive here and there, but the man had style. He had gauged me well. He knew better than to push me. There had been knowing looks, but no raunchy comments, or actual physical passes, and he could've tried so easily. Any other man in his position would have. He also could have forced himself on me like I'd expected him to from the very beginning.

But he didn't. He hadn't. Not once. He was a tightly tuned instrument of the highest caliber, its music eerie.

"I've missed you. Really missed you." Another kiss hovered a hot breath away from my core. "Say yes, angel."

My heart thudded in my chest, my every nerve on fire.

"That animal hurt you. What he did to you—" he said on a hiss.

Huh. He thought I was hesitating because I still suffered from post-Med sexual trauma. Maybe I was, but that wasn't the reason my weary claws held onto the edge of my cliff.

"I'll kill him for you," he said. "I will."

I touched the side of his face. His skin was smooth, flawless under my fingertips, and a piece of my heart broke at the velvety sensation. "It's not him, Turo. It's someone else. The man who saved me, who risked everything for me. He's the…"

My eyes filled with water and, like acid, dissolved the images of Finger I had stored there. Turo's grip on my legs tightened, and his warm tongue lashed slowly at my slit. I cried out, my lungs crushing together.

A groan escaped his throat. "Say yes, say yes," he said against my skin, his voice hoarse, insistent.

The great divide was before me: The no going back. The change it all forever. The smash yourself to bits and march over the pieces, sink your own ship as the band plays on.

I nodded.

He pulled me in closer, tighter, deeper, and took me fully in his mouth. I squirmed in his grip, and he reached up and ripped the robe off me, yanking me down to the floor.

He was no gentleman now. He was aggressive, forceful. He was loud.

I'd always imagined that as a trained assassin, Turo must be extremely still, quiet, and patient in the line of duty. He had to be. But not now. Now, he was the ravenous lion finally consuming his long hoped for prey. Vehement. Unstoppable.

On the floor of that studio, Turo tormented my body and punished my soul with his generous violence.

My heart shattered into shards of jagged glass, dripping with my own blood. Everything sped past me in a whirling blur.

I was the blur, circling the rusted drain of me.

30
SERENA

I'D MADE IT TO LOS Angeles and, through a friend from school, I'd found work as a tailor, a seamstress, which led to being a wardrobe person, then an assistant to a celebrity stylist. In the beginning I'd volunteered for a lot of different projects and willingly took low pay on a lot of jobs. All in the name of networking, keeping busy.

After all, I was haunted.

Two years later, I'd found my stride as a stylist for photographers and independent films and music video productions.

"Really? You like this shirt on me?" Eric, the lead guitarist for an up and coming band who were shooting their second video today, shifted his weight for the umpteenth time, wiping his wavy light brown hair behind his ears.

"No, I love this shirt." I tugged at the slanted edge of the ripped shirt I had created for him. "It's hot. You're hot. You in the shirt—way hot. See how that works?"

His hazel eyes lit up, and he let out a nervous laugh. "I guess. I don't know. I'm just used to wearing my jeans, old tees, and flannel shirts. What a cliché, huh?"

"If you tell me you're from Seattle, then yes, that would be a cliché."

"Well, that's a relief. I'm not from Seattle. I'm from South Dakota."

"Oh, really?"

"Don't tell me you've been there?"

"No," I lied.

"Where are you from?"

"Chicago originally," I lied again. "Now I'm here."

"Now you're here." He held my gaze, an index finger flicking at one of my long beaded earrings. "And I'm glad you're here."

"Me too."

He traced a zig zag over my shoulder and down my upper arm where my latest tattoo design sprawled over my skin, and I stiffened, moving away from him.

"What's all this?" he asked.

"A treasure hunt."

I had continued my odyssey with tattoos, getting more and more. Erasing the scars the Smoking Guns had left on me was important to me, but it had quickly transformed into commemorating the beautiful that could arise in the aftermath of hell. I needed to remind myself every moment of every day that I was persevering, that I'd found a way, even though the price I'd paid had been extraordinarily high.

The ultimate price.

Eric chuckled. An eyebrow quirked, a lopsided grin. He was cute. The boy next door who gave good hugs and whose gaze lingered on you when you spoke. "A treasure hunt, huh? I like hunting. What am I looking for?"

I stood up and eyed the results of my Eric Lanier makeover. "Treasure, of course," I replied.

Yes, treasure, but it wasn't for anyone to find. It was for me, buried in flowers and fairies and suns and moons, in stars and sea waves rippling over my skin. A desperate symphony of my endurance.

"Your whole damned body is a treasure," he blurted.

I let out a laugh. "Well, don't you say the nicest things?"

He laughed with me. "You think? Jesus, I've been a jerk lately, just ask my manager. All this promotion and publicity shit makes me nervous. So many details, so many new people involved all of a sudden."

"People like me?"

"Yeah. It's not just me and the boys anymore. Everything's different, and it's all moving and changing so fast."

"You're on the verge. You guys are good, Eric. Everyone's saying this album is a winner. I really like the song for this video."

His shoulders relaxed, his features eased as if I'd pulled a string and made it happen myself. "What's your name again? Sorry, I've just met so many people today, and I don't want to not remember you."

"You don't have to remember me," I replied.

I often wished people didn't.

"I want to," he said, his tone playful, easy. "Aside from the fact that you're incredibly pretty and totally hot, it's so good to have a normal conversation for a change."

I tossed the safety pins onto my worktable and held his gaze. "Yeah, normal is nice, isn't it?"

"Sure is. Let's do some normal together." He stepped closer to me, his lips tipping up. "What's your name, you beautiful, unforgettable girl?"

I let out a tiny breath, my face heating. "My name's Lenore."

31
FINGER

As promised, I'd gotten out of jail early after having delivered all my Silver Crows intel along the way. Over the three years I was inside, I'd created an actual bond with their Prez and VP, which I kept to myself.

I'd learned a lot of things in prison.

Jail was rough, it was shit, but it made me rely on myself more than anything ever had. For three years I'd been stripped not only of any external power and control but also of my own ideas of the power and control I'd always assumed I had over things, over people, situations. Letting go was gut wrenching, but illuminating. Accepting this from early on had only made me realize the bitter truth that the only things we really do have control over in this life are our own selves, our actions. Essentials.

Others dictated when I slept, where I slept, who I lived with, what work I did, what I ate. There was plenty of sliced white bread too, and I had to steel myself in its presence. I did it, considering it another form of daily exercise along with the five hundred push ups I did to keep my hands and arms strong. I'd read books that I'd never otherwise gotten a chance to read, I made new alliances, new enemies. I had brutally honest conversations for the first time in a very long time.

Keeping organized and clean, fit and strong, was my way of exercising the control I did have; my routine, my success. Some read the Bible, others took education courses, some got obsessed with chess or fitness. Whatever I was engaged in, I used my time wisely to expand my consciousness of myself and stay sharp.

You got a lot of time on your hands in prison, time to panic, time to think, to worry, to obsess, to be angry. Time also stands still for the prisoner. Somehow we believe that when we get out, everything—friends, family, work—will be the same way we'd left it. But over these past three years the world kept on moving without me, and at a clip that was almost incomprehensible.

The day I got out, my one thought was getting to Serena. Drac and Slade met me on the outside, bringing me my old Heritage Softail. My hand shook as it stroked over the saddle. I hadn't ridden in three whole years. A lifetime. We went to Chicago, and after one night on the town together, I told them I needed a couple weeks on my own before going home. They returned to Nebraska, and I headed to Tania's. I'd had Rhys keep an eye out for Serena, but after the first few weeks, he'd told me she'd disappeared. I'd told myself she was being cautious now that I was in jail, leaving no clues behind.

I found Tania. She blinked at seeing me in her doorway.

"What?"

She shrugged. "You look different. Bigger, meaner."

"I've been inside for three years, Tania."

"I know. Come in. "

I went in.

Her eyes went to my colors. "You on your way back to Nebraska now, to your club?"

"Yeah, of course, but I wanted to see her first. Got to see her. And I can't find her."

Tania's lips pressed together. "I don't know where she is. She left town after you got arrested. We kept in touch in the beginning, but I haven't heard from her in over three and a half years now."

"Jesus. She's protecting you by keeping away."

I couldn't find any trace of "Ashley Wyeth" anywhere, and neither could Rhys. Had she gotten a new name and ID?

"You remember that friend of hers, Ciara?" I asked Tania.

"I do."

"You got her number?"

"I used to. I'll look." Tania found Ciara's phone number in an old notebook and called her, asking if she'd heard from "Ashley" and if she knew where she was.

Tania listened and made a face at me. "All right, sorry to bother you. Thanks anyway."

"What'd she say?"

"She said she hasn't seen Ashley for years. That Ashley started blowing her off a while before that, and she just gave up on her. She sounded irritated."

I got in touch with Rhys, and we met at his apartment in Chicago, which was more of a shabby garage than a normal living space.

I opened another can of beer. "Anything new with Med?" I'd been keeping tabs on him and his crew from jail through word of mouth, through the internet, through Rhys.

"His club is still having a hard time bouncing back from that series of surprise attacks. He hasn't been on his home ground in maybe two years now."

"You'd told me, but I figured that was temporary."

"He's still keeping himself on the move. No one ever really knows where or when he'll pop up, posse in tow."

"So he's spooked down deep."

"Oh yeah. Couldn't have happened to a nicer guy."

"Don't you think it's odd that suddenly all these fires blew up around him and he's been on the run? Moving around only with a core group of men, keeping his head down low? Is it the eighties all over again, and nobody sent us the memo?"

Rhys shrugged as he lit a cigarette. "From what I hear, the *famiglia* isn't happy with this mess."

"The Tantuccis? The Smoking Guns always worked with the Tantuccis," I said.

"Yeah, them."

"The Tantuccis got any enemies?"

"Doesn't everyone?" Rhys let out a tight laugh.

"I mean a specific rival. Someone who'd benefit from a branch of the Tantucci labor force being shut down."

Rhys took in a breath, leaning back in his ratty vinyl sofa. "Well, I got to say, the hate the Tantuccis got for the Guardinos is legendary around this town. Those two families have been enemies from

Prohibition days. You think maybe Med got himself in the middle of that lasagna, and the Guardinos are using him for target practice to keep the Tantuccis in line?"

"Why not? I followed one of the Guardinos' hit men years back. Remember, when you were helping me out, keeping an eye on—"

"DeMarco, right?"

"Yeah. Turo DeMarco."

"He's top tier now, dude." Rhys shook his brown hair from his dark blue eyes as he played with his lighter, adjusting the flame. "He's risen up in the world since then. His name turns heads, that's for sure. Started low level over a decade ago, but he's a decision maker now. Played his cards right. He's real smooth."

"Oh yeah?"

"Oh yeah."

Real smooth. I grabbed the bottle of bourbon and gulped down a mouthful. "If Med's got Turo DeMarco after him…"

"Boom." A chuckle rumbled deep in Rhys's big chest.

"Huh." I wiped at my mouth, my throat burning in a blaze of bourbon. Med's business targeted and Med on the run. My veins raced with heat, and it wasn't from the booze.

Med had pissed someone off and in a big way. But what intrigued me was that only someone from the inside would know how to pinpoint all these hotspots that had been raided, spots that had been in his territory and notoriously under the grid. Med was a paranoid psycho to begin with, and now he was shaken up, freaking out, and on the run like a cockroach scurrying across a bullet ridden wall in the darkness.

I saw the connection like a map spread out before me. And on that map flashed a route between DeMarco and someone who knew the inside of Med's club.

And that someone could only be, had to be, Serena.

Rhys tamped down on the leaves in his pipe, lit it, and took a couple of stiff inhales. "Ah. You always come through for me, man. Damn. Shit's fine."

He passed the pipe to me, and I took a hit.

"You game for something crazy?" I asked.

"Fuck yeah. It's what I breathe for."

During his third tour of duty, Rhys had been discharged after going overboard on a mission where he'd ended up slaughtering a family of women and children in Iraq. Enthusiastic. Focused. Unpredictable.

"I need to talk to DeMarco."

He stared at me, his head slanting as if he were listening to the undercurrent beneath my words. He never asked me why. Ever.

Maybe Turo had figured out who Serena was. Maybe he'd twisted her arm to get information from her, and she'd complied and took off. I was glad that Med was getting his ass kicked, but what would stop Turo from going after other clubs, manipulating any club in Med's orbit?

Did Turo know where she was? I needed to know and then stop anyone else from finding out. I needed to stamp out any connection there was between them. If I had suspected, maybe a Smoking Gun would too?

I sat up, putting the bottle down. "Do it."

He only nodded, taking another drag on his pipe, his head lifting as he savored the weed.

"After, you can do whatever you want with him."

Rhys's full red eyes met mine.

"You do this for me, man, and you won't be just my go-to guy no more," I said. "I'll share your talents. Set you loose officially with the Flames."

He exhaled a plume of smoke, his head shaking. "I don't think I can do the group bro thing. I'm just not—"

"I know, I know. We'll figure it out." I slid my arm over his shoulders. "A nomad, yeah? It's all good."

"Nomad, huh? Long term benefits included? Health, disability, retirement fund?"

We both laughed.

His eyes remained grim, hanging on mine through the haze of smoke. "I'm with you, brother. You know that. To the end, wherever this takes me."

I let out a heavy breath.

I wasn't sure what I'd find out about Serena—why she'd taken off, cut herself off, any connection she had with Turo—but I had to cover all the possible angles until I got to the end, as Rhys said.

I lifted the bourbon bottle in the air. "To the end."

No matter how bitter.

32
FINGER

Rᴴʏꜱ ꜱᴛᴜᴅɪᴇᴅ Tᴜʀᴏ DᴇMᴀʀᴄᴏ ᴀɴᴅ nabbed him on the tenth day. He had his chest and legs wrapped in plastic to a chair on the roof of a building in Serena's old neighborhood. Turo finally came to from the drugs Rhys had shot him up with earlier in a coat check room at a restaurant.

I stood over him. His hair was mussed, his pretty face unbruised. So far.

DeMarco blinked, his head straining. "What the fuck is this, and who the hell are you?"

Rhys faded into the darkness. I had the floor.

"Ashley," I said.

His cold light-colored eyes betrayed nothing.

"I need to find her."

"I don't know any Ashley."

"I know a Ciara," I said and his jaw tightened ever so slightly. "Shouldn't you be at The Vine right now listening to her sing her cabaret songs? Don't worry, one of my men is there, hanging on every note that comes out of that mouth."

His eyes hardened and went to my patches. "Why should I talk to you? Are you after Ashley to kill her?"

"Did you force her to rat for you?"

"I never forced her to do anything."

My pulse ratcheted up a hundred notches. "I'm sure you laid all sorts of pretty words on her. Threatened her. She isn't stupid, but she's vulnerable."

"She's made of steel," he said, his voice clear, sharp. Did he think

246

he was telling me something new? Something I didn't already know?

I took in a deep breath against the idea of this douche knowing my woman. Knowing her in any way at all.

My hand snaked around his throat and tightened there. "She's disappeared, and I think you helped her get new ID and take off."

Turo's forehead wrinkled, his eyes sheets of tinted glass. "Who the fuck are you?" His tone was cold, it was hard, but it wasn't defensive. It was protective. He was protecting Serena.

I got in his face. "I'm the one who got her out of that shithole. I'm the one who got her to Chicago."

His eyes flared. "You're the one?"

Had I answered a mystery he'd been wanting to solve?

My hand fell from his throat. "I'm the one."

"I've been wondering who was crazy enough to go in there and get her out."

"Someone with nothing left to lose."

He smiled at me, his eyebrows lifting, his features relaxing for the first time. "I don't know where she is. She didn't tell me where she was going."

"Her new name. That's what I want from you. I want her name. You put her in danger by having her rat. If I figured it out, I'm sure her old club isn't too far behind. Were you going to protect her once they came gunning for her? I doubt it. Would've gotten your suit messy. I figure you would've left her hanging in the wind. She took a risk, and it paid off for you big, didn't it? For her? Not so sure."

He gestured at me with his chin. "They did that to you? You were there with her, and they—"

"Yes."

"Hmm." He studied me.

"Believe me, I'm glad you've been making Medicine Man tap dance to your beat. Like it a lot. That sick fuck deserves that and much, much more."

"It's been a long, joy-filled ride. I wanted him to suffer first, have him watch his little paper kingdom rip and burn around him. Now his time is up."

"I need to make sure she isn't your collateral damage," I said.

"I've had eyes and ears on Med's crew for a while. There's been no chatter about Rena. None. She's good. Wherever she is."

"I'm supposed to believe you give a shit."

"I give way more than a shit. Where were you when she needed help?"

My vision went red, and I roared, "I've been in jail the past three years!"

His brow wrinkled again. "They came after her. That's why she came to me, to clean it up. Her wanting new ID came later."

My heartbeat skidded to a halt. "Who came after her? Clean what up?"

"She killed a Smoking Gun. He attacked her in her apartment. She got him with his own knife and didn't want to call the cops."

A cold sea sloshed through me, jagged rocks of ice ripping at my veins. "She went to you?"

"Yes."

He told me.

My insides twisted. Images of her alone, covered in that fuck's blood. Struggling with his corpse, gulping it all down to stand up and keep it together. The fear, the fucking tidal wave of fear at being dragged back to Kansas.

Feeling she had no choice but to go to Turo DeMarco.

He eyed me. "It was a mess, and I handled it for her."

"And what the hell did you want in return, huh?"

"Information on Med."

"That's it?"

"That's it. And that was plenty."

I leaned my head back, facing up at the dark sky. The clouds had smudged the ink of the nigh. There were no visible stars, not with the insistent glare from the city lights either. This wasn't Nebraska. I gulped in the cold air, but the lightheadedness remained.

"She handled it all very well. She'd made up her mind and took care of business."

I stared at the blurry cityscape of lights and dark outlines. "Thank you," I muttered, the words leaving ash in my mouth.

His chin lifted. "They did that to you, didn't they? Your face, your fingers. I remember it. What a fucking story."

"It isn't some story. This is my life."

Holding my gaze, he took in a breath, the sudden silence stretching between us. "Are you and your buddy going to finish me off or what? If not, I need to go. I have an important meeting at midnight, and if I don't show up there's going to be trouble. I detest being late."

"So do I. Give me her new name."

"Lenore Yaeger."

Lenore.

Turo had helped her, watched out for her. We both shared an admiration for her. I wasn't sure if anything had happened between them, but I was fucking positive he'd tried. He wouldn't be a man if he didn't.

No, I wouldn't kill him. I'd wanted to, that had been my rabid intention, but Turo DeMarco would be a useful connection. High level Guardino. A link to the most powerful family in Chicago. No, you didn't kill somebody useful. I swallowed down the bloodlust that had coated the back of my throat, pooled in my mouth.

"You ever heard of Reich Malone?" I asked.

Reich had been looking to break into Chicago organized crime. He kept trying to court different families at different times. He was all for having a big organization at his back, the Flames back. That's what his skinhead underling had been up to when I'd seen him in town that time. How far had that gotten?

"Flames of Hell from Ohio. Tries hard. Pompous pain in the ass," he replied.

I squatted in front of him, so we were eye to eye. "He's the one who put me in jail. I've known him since I was a boy. Ultimately, he's the one responsible for this too." I gestured at my face, with a maimed hand. "We have a healthy disregard for each other."

"I'll bet."

"You ever worked with him?"

"I've met him, heard his pitch one too many times. I don't care for his...style."

"He has no style."

He lifted an eyebrow. "No, he doesn't."

The enemy of my enemy is my friend, goes the old saying.

I slit the plastic and cut the ties on his wrists. "I'm grateful that you helped Rena. She trusted you, and you delivered."

He rubbed his left wrist, his right, his eyes on mine. He was waiting for more. I'd give it. It was worth it.

I slid my knife back in my leathers. "I may have been…zealous in my approach this evening."

He arched an eyebrow, a stiff smile etching his lips. "She's worth it. Now you have something to lose, don't you?"

I didn't answer. Whatever happened between them, whatever they'd shared, I knew that when I found her, once we stood before each other, our eyes locked, the unmistakable, undeniable, unforgettable would boil between us as it always had. Everything that had come before would be rendered unimportant and obliterated.

"I won't lose her," I replied.

Turo rose to his feet, smoothing down his suit jacket. "Don't ever fucking touch me again," he said on a malicious hiss. A reptilian threat.

"I won't," I said. "You ever need anything under your radar, I can be of help."

The muscle along his jaw clenched and unclenched as he adjusted the cuffs of his shirt. "I have a special delivery coming from New Mexico next week. A new shipper an associate brought in is suddenly playing hard ball, and it's pissing my boss off. In fact, that's what tonight's meeting is about. I was asked to get involved to resolve the problem."

I had no doubt he would.

I checked my watch. Eleven o'clock on the dot. "You've got plenty of time, but you'd prefer to walk in there with your own solution, wouldn't you?"

His lips tipped up into an odd crooked grin. I'd figured him out, and he liked it. "Always optimum," he replied.

"I've got my own system from California through Utah. You arrange for pickup in Nebraska, I'll have it ready."

"Your own system?"

"Carefully calibrated. I may have been in jail all this time, but I kept my shit up and running. Improved on it."

"How can I be sure this isn't you being pompous?"

"I gave you your life back just now, didn't I? How many people take the great Turo DeMarco for a little rooftop Q & A? My friend here—" I gestured toward where Rhys stood still in the dark shadows. "—is an independent contractor and local. He can be your go-to man for the operation. Any operation, in fact. No one knows he exists. He's a specialist. Has talents you'd appreciate."

"You got a cigarette?" Turo asked. "I quit last week."

I handed him my pack and lighter. He lit up and took in a deep drag. "It's Reich."

"Reich?"

He handed me back the lighter and my cigarettes. "Tonight. My problematic shipper."

Yes, the enemy of my enemy is my friend.

"Give me the details and I'll have a plan in place within thirty minutes," I said.

He expelled a long stream of smoke, his eyes lighting up. "Impress me." He gave me that crooked grin once more.

In that grin, my father's words washed over me. *"You got to consider the timing, the spectacle, and the afterwards...Know your opponent, be conscious of the blow back, where the particles will fall."*

I grinned back at Turo and flicked my lighter on. Off. On.

Yeah. Couldn't wait to see those flaming particles fall.

33

LENORE

"I LOVE HOW YOU CUT THE dress. It looks so much better now, Lenore," said Kelly, my assistant. We were on the set of a music video for an all-female alternative rock group, Sugar Dip.

"Molly has incredible legs. They need to be shown off."

"And that slouchy boot is sheer genius," Kelly whispered in my ear as filming began. "The corset showing just right underneath? It's perfect. I can't believe you made it yourself. I need one."

I bumped her hip with mine. "I'll make you one," I mouthed, winking at her.

The band performed on a set designed like an old playground where all the rides were broken. Jamming on her guitar, Molly belted out the first line of her new single as she wandered through the broken swing set. The new, improved dress floated perfectly over her knees as she swayed and jerked her hips to the music playing over the speakers.

Kelly took a few notes as we both watched the performances and the choreography carefully, studying how the clothing moved on the women, and how the patterns and colors were working with the set pieces. I smiled to myself. We'd done a good job.

Filming wrapped, and I slipped out the security doors, down the hall back to wardrobe. Kelly would collect the clothing from the band, and then we had outfits to review one last time for tomorrow's shoot with another singer, and more clothes to choose and inventory for three assignments next week.

I pushed open the door as I checked my phone for messages. The door slammed shut behind me on its own. My head snapped up, and I froze before the reflection in the large vanity mirror, my eyes hooking on his.

Finger stood against the wall, a large, tanned hand splayed against the door. He was bigger, his shoulders and arms bulkier, his chest pronounced under a tight tee stretching across his upper body. His hair was shorter, barely touching his shoulders, his beard fuller. A faded red bandana at his neck. Dressed in black leather, coated with dust and dirt, probably from miles of riding, his thick boots splashed in mud.

He flipped the lock. "Hello, Lenore."

My pulse screeched to a halt, my mouth dried.

Three years. Three years of him in jail, me on my own. Three, three, three years...

"Got nothing for me? No hello? No how's it going? No, I missed you, so good to see you?"

I only stared at the vision before me, unable to move, to breathe, to think. But he was no vision. He was a man—rugged, virile, coarse, larger-than-life.

"Huh." He cocked an eyebrow, slanting his head at a slight angle, the grooves on his face prominent. "That's too bad." He was amused.

"How did you find me?" I asked.

"I'll always find you."

My stomach clenched at those words. I had tried to do the right thing, and it was a painful thing, but I'd done it. And instead of leaving a clean cut behind me, I had left a trail of blood, flesh, and bone.

And misery.

That's what I saw in his big metal-brown eyes. Sheer misery repressed and now rising, steaming, mingling with mine.

"Nice new name, I like it," he said.

"It was as close to my grandmother's name as I could get."

"Is that what you ratted out to Turo DeMarco for?" he spit out.

"You here to kill me for going against the bro code?"

"No." His lips curved up slightly at the ends, and my heart squeezed. "No, I'm glad you did it. I'm here to take you home with me."

"No."

His chest rose and fell sharply, his eyes piercing mine.

A chaos of panic and emotion gripped me. Tentacles of wild feeling curled in my chest, pulling and twisting on my heart, bruising it. The tagged clothes hanging on the racks all around us listened, waiting. All the colors and textures in the dressing room faded, and there was only Finger. My Finger.

"I'm here to take you…"

I licked my lips. "I—"

He lunged at me, pulling me in his arms roughly, and crushed my mouth to his, smashing me up against the wall. Our bodies crashed together, and my breath jammed in my lungs. The scents of aged leather, dull metal, and the faded cinnamon of his taste took over, and I sucked them all in, wanting more. My hands dug into his hair, and I opened my mouth to his, knowing I'd be lost.

I was lost. I was damned.

Yet I was set free.

The two of us slid down the wall to the floor. The demand of his tongue, the sound of his hard breathing, the press of his body against mine, a stronger, harder, more developed body, made me greedy, satisfying the need I had put on ice so long ago. My soul cried out for him, for his touch with a sharp urgency that built and built. Memories clashed with sensation, with desperation. I ached.

My dress ripped, my underwear was yanked to the side. Fumbling, tugging, whimpers, groans. His grip tightened on my flesh, and he was inside me.

"Serena…" that husky, scratched voice filled my ear and uncoiled that intense rough desire that only he inspired in me. I clung to him.

His forehead slid to mine. "Baby."

We both gasped, our skin damp. My body trembled.

I miss you.

I miss you.

The dam I had erected with the heavy stones of agony and necessity cracked and burst open with every fiery pulse of his powerful body inside mine, with every rasp of his jumbled words. Desperate words. I embraced them all, wrapped them around me, clutching him to me. I flew, charged on our hungry emotions, our hungry bodies. On the high that was us, on our absolute need to be together.

He throbbed against me, and a piece of me, that piece that was his, whisked away with him to somewhere else, somewhere beautiful and unfettered. Breathless, soaring. My fingers dug into the edges of his leather jacket, brushing over a stitched patch.

And I dropped back down to earth.

My heart filled with lead. My limbs stiffened. "We shouldn't have done this. It's not—"

"It's been a long time. I know it has. But we're so good together. Always will be, no matter what." He nuzzled the side of my throat. "There's never been a goodbye between you and me. Never will be. I love you. I'll always love you."

I pushed my hands against his chest, against those sweet hopes, and pulled back from him. His brow knit together as he slid out of me on a grunt. A chill raced up the base of my spine at the sudden hollowness inside me. At what I'd done.

I'd opened my Pandora's box. How would I ever shut it closed again?

Finger adjusted himself. I sat up straight against the wall, my knees bent and pulled into my chest, pressing my shaking legs together.

Before Finger I'd never believed I was strong, not enough, not enough for the real world. And now he'd torn through any lines of defense I thought I'd built around myself these past three years alone. Crossed the moat, scaled the wall, battered down the gate.

I shoved my tattered armor back on.

He spoke. The sounds muffled in my head.

"Baby, none of that matters," he said. "I get it, I don't get it, I don't give two fucks. I'm out, you're free, you're coming with me and we're gonna be together."

His words clattered to the floor at my feet.

"Finger."

His eyes were full, shiny. "Yeah?"

I braced. "I'm getting married next month."

His jaw stiffened, his eyes flashed. "Married?"

Yes, yes, fling your flaming arrows in our grey sky. I deserve every single one.

"Married?" he repeated.

"Yes."

"To who?" The most ridiculous thing he'd ever heard.

"To someone else," slid out of my mouth.

"Someone normal?"

"He's not in the life. Has no idea."

"Marry me," he said.

"I can't."

His head fell back against the wall, his body sagging. An inhuman, savage wail escaped his lips. "You're my heaven and my hell, you know that?" came his hoarse voice prickling the dull air.

"You're mine too."

The silence between us was thick and thorny.

His broad chest heaved. "You doing this on purpose? To get out from under me?"

"It has nothing to do with you," I lied.

Eric and I had been together for a year now, and he was everything Finger wasn't. He was incredibly easygoing, never had much of a strong opinion about anything except his music. The mood between us was light; he didn't demand deep from me and I didn't offer. The daily cares were dealt with and met with a smile every time. Eric was a ride in a convertible on a Sunday afternoon, top down, sun in your eyes, a song on the radio blaring that you both sing along to.

Finger was a hard ride on a loud motorcycle, a hundred miles an hour through a tunnel of fire. Heart pounding, holding on tight for your life, yet you knew you wouldn't fall off.

You'd never felt more alive.

"What was this just now, then?" Finger snapped at me. "Your last little fling with dirty?"

"No, I just—"

"Thing is, I don't want to get out from under you," he said, his voice low, unsteady. "I've been enduring this all these years because

256

you and me....you and me..."

His mouth, the mouth I knew so well, the mouth I'd retraced over and over on my own lips in the hellish quiet of the night all these years, would still feel on my flesh like the visitation of a ghost, pressed into a firm line. His shimmering dark metallic eyes sunk their fangs in my soul, drawing blood from the artery in my neck. The fierce sting shuddered through me. There would be no healing from this gash. I would bear the mark forever, like so many other marks.

Now so would he.

"I was pregnant," I blurted.

"What?"

"I found out just before you got arrested. I thought I had some virus or it was stress. I got tested, and it was positive."

He stilled, his stony eyes on me, his face pale, hard. "That was years ago. What—did you have an ab—"

"I lost it." I stretched my dress further down my legs.

"A miscarriage?"

"I went to Turo for a reason. It wasn't just for a new identity. Motormouth found me. He broke into my apartment and told me he was bringing me back to Med."

"I know. Turo told me."

"Motormouth saw photos of you and me. He was going to tell Med that you had gotten me out. I couldn't let him take me back or ruin you. I couldn't let them hurt you again."

"Serena—"

"Guess murder affected me more than I expected, now that I live among civilized, normal society."

His eyes shifted over me. Could he see the blood? Could he smell the agony that still clung to me?

"I killed Motormouth to protect myself, you, us, our baby. But I lost the baby a few weeks after. And that's when I thought, is that how we're going to start a life together, by killing? By kicking more of this horrible shit under the rug? It was just the beginning of his tiny life. Probably no bigger than a bean inside me, but—"

"Stop!" His eyes glimmered with water.

"So I left Chicago."

"We can have another kid. Miscarriages happen to people all the time."

"Do they happen because the mother kills over and over again? Because the mother is on the run, hiding from killers?"

"Mothers kill to protect their families!"

"Yes, yes, families. But we—"

"We already are a family. We always will be."

"A family that can't ever be together!" I bit out. "Can't you see that, after everything that's happened? After all this time?"

He winced as if I'd hit him, his eyes narrowing.

"I was going to tell you about Motor, about…" I took in a deep breath, but the knots inside me kept on knotting and twisting. "You didn't come that day, that night. Tania came over and told me about you being in jail, and she gave me your message. I knew then that I couldn't keep clinging to this dream we both had, a dream that would never come true for us. We'd always just have pieces of each other, once in a while fragments. That's all."

He shook his head at me. "You didn't tell Tania?"

"About killing a Smoking Gun in my apartment with his own knife? No, I left that out. I refused to put her in any more danger."

"Jesus." His jaw hardened.

"I can't go back with you." I slid up higher against the wall. "You need to get yourself an old lady who can be by your side in every way."

He stared at me as if I was suddenly speaking in an exotic foreign language.

Incredulity…

Impatience…

Irritation.

His eyes blazed. "I've been in jail for three years, and I just got out a couple of weeks ago. I jerk off, I'm thinking of you. I watch porn, I see a stripper, a pretty girl on the street, I'm thinking of you. There's only you. Only you inside me and out."

My heartbeat kicked up in my chest, and I pulled tighter on the garrote I'd wrapped around it three years ago. "How was jail?"

He let out a huff of air. "Jail turned out to be a set up. They needed me inside."

A hard, bitter laugh escaped me. "Yeah, they needed you."

He dug a hand in his hair. "You're tired now. You've been on your own through all this heavy shit. You were lonely, I get it. Take some time. You..." He gulped for air, for reality to go away and come again another day. "Rethink this. Don't just—"

"I've had nothing but time to think about this, to live with it," I said. "We kept waiting for things to get better, Finger, but they didn't. There is no spectacular holy glimmer of light that's going to appear over the cave we've been burrowed in and announce, "It's all good now! Come out, come out wherever you are!""

"You said you'd keep what we had safe. You said—"

"I did, I did keep it safe." I swallowed hard. "But we're not some fairy tale."

"We're my fairy tale!" his voice broke.

A tear slid down my face, and I quickly wiped it away. "Well, this one doesn't get a happily ever after."

"In jail, I felt you on me, inside me, under my skin, and I kept that fire burning, fed it, fed myself on it. Even though right this very second, right here, I'm hating you, I can't cut you off. I don't know how."

I pressed my back into the hard wall. Finger penetrated deep, over and over again. And it hurt. But you needed that kind of hurt to keep you aware. Keep you fired up. You needed the clawing, the teeth cutting skin. Traces of blood. The sting. That was where he and I knew where we stood. That was our truth. That was how we functioned.

Finger crackled. Everything with him was raw and seething with blood and boiling oil.

He took in a deep breath. "You're all up in your head right now because of losing the baby, being on your own all this time. And I'm real sorry about that. But I know this, what you're doing—getting married to somebody else—is about you being upset, you willing to sacrifice us for something safe, for your idea of normal."

He rose to his feet, adjusting his leathers, fastening his pants, sealing himself up. "I'm going to leave now, because if I don't I'm going to say and do shit I'm going to regret later. You're freaked out, I get that. But being apart doesn't solve anything. Doesn't cure anything. Being apart is nothing but hopeless for us. How can you not fucking see that?"

"Stop it!" I crossed my arms and stepped back from him, from the great swell of emotion raging from him, sucking me into its heaving, hot waves.

"You can't look me in the eyes, can you? Even now that you're gutting me." His hand cuffed my throat as he leaned in closer, forcing my gaze to meet his.

Raw.

My hand clutched his wrist. "Let go of me."

"Don't make me the villain in this story. You are. You took this away from us. *You* did this." His voice seethed like a blade sliding in between my ribs, slow and steady, absolute. A noise rose from the back of his throat as his hand left my neck and trailed along my jaw, the edge of my face, his breath hot on my skin. My veins flooded with sour wine, searing acid.

"I'll let go." Finger's voice was low, lifeless. He released his hold on me.

He threw open the door and stalked out of the dressing room. The door slammed behind him, and I flinched.

My tattered heart, along with any self-respect I'd managed to patch together these three years, shuddered like a wooden house in the line of a rushing raging river.

Overflow. Buckle. Collapse.

A cold sweat raced over my skin. The tagged clothes hanging on the door swung back and forth. The silence was stifling. The air smelled differently without him here. Stale. The colors in the room, dull. I gulped for oxygen, but none came.

My legs gave way. I caught myself, clinging to my worktable. Pens and bobbins of thread, safety pins, Post-its, notepads, phone chargers, empty coffee cups cascaded over the edge.

I wanted to pull on the brakes of the locomotive hurtling down the tracks even though I was the one who'd fed it coal.

Justin. Justin.

I knocked my head against the table. Once. Twice. A low howl ripped from me.

This was the end of the fairy tale, and I'd pushed the hero over the cliff. I'd torn the last page of the story from the binding of the book and shredded it, tossing the pieces in the air. Those pieces of paper scattered around me, and I knew that on that final page, there was no "...and they lived happily ever after."

Smeared in our blood and entrails, there was only, "The Brutal, Ugly, Fucked Up End."

34
FINGER

I GOT THE FUCK OUT OF California on my bike and headed back to Nebraska. I was exhausted, worn out.

How was I supposed to do this? Breathe? Move without the promise of her within my grasp. In the distance on the road, a blurry figure, pink and blue hair flying, arms lifting over her head, reaching toward the sky, showing me the way, welcoming me home.

This way, baby. Right here. Here I am. Here we are.

She was my exit, the next one coming up, the one I was straining to get to, leaning forward in my saddle, throttle high, engine screaming, wind beating on me.

No more.

No exits. Keep rolling, keep going, going, going.

I blinked past the blur and focused on the road.

Cars. Road. Bikes. Trucks. Trucks. Road.

I'd reached Denver, and a wisp of metal scraped under my chin, the wind lifting the helmet up off my head.

Dammit.

The clasp on my skull helmet had snapped.

I changed lanes, got out of the flow of traffic, pulled over, and tied the frayed ends together. This was one of my oldest and most favorite lids. I'd had it since I'd left Missouri, and I never rode without one. I'd seen too many brains splattered on roads all over the country. I needed a new one, fast. I got back onto the highway and veered off onto W. County Line Road in Littleton, where I knew there was a Harley Davidson store.

The summer heat was suffocating, and I hadn't realized how

much until I'd pulled up in the parking lot. I entered the shop, and my every pore sucked in the stunning air conditioning, my muscles relaxing as I stretched out my back, enjoying the blanket of cold. I avoided what seemed like a shiny Harley souvenir shop section and tracked over to the helmets.

I passed a saleswoman with light brown hair pulled back in a ponytail wearing black jeans, black boots, and a black Harley T who was talking to a guy over a new Dyna Glide. He flirted with her more than he listened to her pitch or paid attention to the bike. She was explaining the bike's new features to him and knew what she was talking about, but he kept sinking the conversation with bullshit. *Idiot.*

I grabbed a helmet.

"Can I help you, sir?"

"Yeah." I turned to the middle-aged balding man who stood in front of me. Lucky me. I raised the lid. "I need this."

"Very good. Anything else I can help you with today?"

"I'll take a look," I said to get rid of him. He took the helmet and moved toward the cash registers.

My eyes trailed back to the woman. Something about her was familiar, but I hadn't seen her face yet. I didn't forget a face.

"Thanks for all the info, hon." The dark haired man waved at her as he walked off, a huge smile on his face.

"Sure. You're welcome." She turned, stacking a bunch of brochures into a neat pile, the smile on her face quickly fading.

My pulse thudded in my chest.

It's her.

Sister, Dig's old lady. No. Now she was Dig's widow. I'd heard about his murder just before I'd gotten arrested. What the fuck was she doing here? Why wasn't she home in South Dakota surrounded by friends and family?

A dull look was stamped on her face. Stamped and sealed there. She was going through the motions of the living. Getting by.

What would Dig say if he could see her now? Like this? Dangling? Coasting?

I rubbed a hand across my chest. I wasn't dead, and neither was

Serena.

Lenore. Her name's Lenore now.

Lenore was out in the world breathing in the air, and I was grateful she was safe and alive. I didn't have her with me, but if I really wanted to I could hold her or touch her or hear her voice. She wasn't buried in the cold, hard ground.

What did Dig's widow have? Fading memories, thick shadows. Echoes of pounding heartbeats in the dark night.

I got Serena out of her hell. I got her to a safe place, a place where she bloomed and took her first steps in new shoes. I did that. We'd done it together. In jail, I'd clung to a hope that there would be a one day with us, but she didn't see it that way. Or maybe she just didn't want that anymore. Want me enough. She'd convinced herself.

I had to stay sane now, stay whole, whatever the fuck that was. Somehow I had to figure out how to live without her, without the promise of her inspiring me. That promise had kept me warm all these years like a slow burning fire in a field of snow and ice. I had to pick myself up from the debris we'd left behind. *Somehow…*

I squelched down the urge to walk over to Sister. To look her in the eyes and tell her I was sorry about Dig. To tell her—

Tell her what?

My neck flared with heat, and I turned away. She wouldn't want to see me. I'd bring it all back up for her. Memories of good times, memories of bad times. And every single one of those damned memories had her old man pulsing at its core. Why should I ruin her running away, her jamming the brake on all that pain?

That's what I have to do, isn't it? Stop the pain.

Being with Serena had made me be the man I'd always wanted to be. Daring, determined, brave. Devoted. We'd reveled outside in the sun together. Now, what was I without her?

I went to the cash register and tossed two one hundred dollar bills on the counter. My gaze returned to Dig's old lady who absently smoothed a hand over the leather saddle of a brand new Fat Bob. She strode to the other end of the brightly lit showroom where a young upscale couple were lusting over a new bike.

"Okay, here's your change. Sir?"

"That saleswoman over there? The one in black?"

His gaze darted over at Sister. "Grace?"

"She been with you a while? She seems familiar. I know I've seen her somewhere."

"She just started here. Came up from Texas. Worked at a Harley store in Dallas."

"Must be it," I replied. "I go through Dallas a lot."

"Well, don't bother trying it on with her. She'll only shoot you down."

"Oh yeah? Thanks."

"Sure thing."

Grace had run away. Grace was on the carousel of go round and round and make it all a blur.

Dig was dead and gone; that was absolute. Like my and Serena's baby.

A baby...

We'd had a baby...

My brain couldn't even begin to wrap around that one. Something stung in my chest, wrenching there like a flaming poker.

In jail, my first bunkmate was obsessed with Hinduism and meditation. He'd yelp about reincarnation and karma as I'd be smashing cockroaches in our cell. Had my baby's soul been waiting for its cue to come to us? After the miscarriage did his soul go somewhere else, to another family? Does he belong now to better, more deserving parents?

Stop. Stop. Shut the fuck up.

Serena had suffered all that on her own while Reich had sent me to prison—Motormouth finding her, her killing him, then losing our kid. All of it on her own. I should have been there. I should have found a way for us; a better way than hiding and biding our time. Had we wasted our time? At least she was still alive. Unlike Dig. Unlike the robot that was Grace right now.

Grace let out a long breath, her head nodding as she pretended to listen to her customers' chatter. What if I were dead, and Serena was stuck in grief, shuffling through her life like Grace?

I didn't want that for Serena.

I rubbed an aching hand across my jaw. I needed to let Lenore have her "normal." Let her have a life the way she chose. After everything she'd been through before me, with me, she deserved to have what she wanted, even if it didn't make sense to me.

Even if it killed me.

She was marrying another man, and I was heading back to Nebraska, back to what I knew, back to the life I'd carved out for myself all these years. A life I was born into. One I liked, and one I'd intended to make richer, fuller, complete with her in it. Now that was over, and I had to accept it. I had to accept we might be better off apart, no matter how insane and how painful that felt right now. Maybe she had a point. Maybe there was too much pain, too much sorrow dividing us along with the scars.

I charged out of the store and got on my bike, swinging through the back section of the parking lot where I figured the employees kept their vehicles. There it was. Texas plates. I memorized the number.

I could keep a look out for Grace. No one knew the real reasons Dig had gotten assassinated. On the outside it seemed like a drug deal gone wrong, but you never knew. The rivalry between the Demon Seeds and the One-Eyed Jacks had revived with his murder, and things were shit all across our territories now. Yeah, I would do that for him, check in on his woman. I would. He was dead, and she was smoldering like a full blown bonfire put out too early.

Smoldering, like I was.

35

FINGER

The concert was packed.

I was selling my dope to my usual customers at the May Day Rock Fest just over the border in Colorado. Drac stuck by my side, keeping an eye out for anything or anyone questionable, any potential agents of the law. People had endured a long, cold winter, and they were starving for the sun on their skin, riding, and partying outdoors. The few spring music festivals there were around rocked for business heading into the summer tidal wave. It was low grade action, but steady. The civilians wanted their party supply, from high schoolers to college pricks to upper middle class white collar types. Plus, a number of my Flame brothers and members of other clubs from far and wide ordered up bulk amounts ahead of time.

The sun was dropping in the red sky. The whole night lay ahead of us. The wild ones had been unleashed.

A local band that had made good was the third group up. They were all right. Not my scene. I preferred heavy metal to this grungy whiney shit with too much guitar thrown in for a classic rock effect. Everyone was trying to sing like Eddie Vedder these days, but nope, only in their sorry ass dreams.

"My heart's on fire! My heart's on fire!" the lead singer screeched.

I knew this song. I'd been hearing it from every open car window I'd passed on the road this week.

And that's when I saw her.

My stomach nosedived like an elevator run amok.

Everything suddenly blurred out. Everything was fuzzy except for her. Only yards from me. Could've been five thousand or four, three, two, one. I'd know the curve of that face, those lips, the slim column of that throat. All my senses flared to life again. That ache twisted inside me hard, and it hurt.

Now she had blonde hair, waves of warm honey. Her arms were swirling with tats, her chest dancing with bold designs and colors showing from under the long white sundress she wore. She clapped and cheered for the band.

I was rooted to the spot. It had been over six months since I'd seen her. Half a year. An eternity.

Serena. Serena.

She turned.

Those blue green eyes. Oh God, those eyes.

Those eyes locked on mine, making the blood freeze in my veins and roar to life, rising like whirling storm winds, ripping and un-rooting everything in their path. A sensation unlike any other—a burn, a sizzle, an electric misfire that exploded and combusted instead of simply charging.

That fuse that we'd shorted was lit once again.

She stumbled, her body twisting just a bit, and my eyes widened. That white dress stretched over a high, round middle. Her hand rose, pressing against her full belly as if guarding it from the rays of my vision.

She was pregnant. Pregnant.

Something wrenched in my chest, jamming there. A cold hammer banged at my pulse, zapping the easy lethargy of the beer and weed I'd consumed all afternoon. A fist twisted inside me and yanked whatever there existed inside me, flinging it on the ground, shredding it as it went, pitching it between me and her.

Rings were on that finger on her hand. Did she get married like she said she would? Now she was having that fucker's baby? My eyes snapped to the stage. Of course. The guitarist.

After that time I'd tracked her down in LA, I'd found out she'd been seeing a musician, Eric Lanier.

"I'm getting married."

Congratufuckinglations.

Now she was having a baby. His baby.

She was in someone else's tide. A moon in another solar system. Another hemisphere. She'd dropped the axe, cut the line. Her taste of normal was working out for her.

My head spun. I didn't have to do the math in my head. That could be my baby. Would she really have married someone else if it was? Fuck, I didn't know. I was going to find out, though. My chest was on fire. Somehow my feet remembered how to walk, my knees to bend. I moved forward.

Her eyes widened, her mouth tightening as I stalked toward her. She reached back, grabbing her long blonde hair, pulling a stretchy around the thick handful into a ponytail.

My signal. *Keep moving. You don't know me. Don't contact me.*

I stopped dead in my tracks.

She removed a large ring on her index finger and put it on the index finger of her other hand, and my pulse kicked at my veins.

Her signal. *Keep moving. You don't know me. I'm okay, but you have to go. Don't contact me.*

Double signals. Both of them. Definitive.

I raised my chin, my jaw grinding together.

Her hand remained on her stomach, her back rigid. She turned away, focusing her attention back on the stage. On her new man up there playing his fucking guitar, howling out his douchebag lyrics.

My heart pumped hard, straining against the thick wave of venom filling my veins. My eyes remained glued on her.

Why couldn't it be us, dammit? You and me? I screamed at her across the campground.

I roared.

I pleaded.

My fingers crushed the packets of weed, blow, and assorted pills I had in my pockets. I swallowed hard, my heels digging in the damp ground.

Here I was cutting deals, scoring big, scoring little, but what did it amount to? She was the only person on the planet that I'd ever felt close to, and now she was bearing a living, breathing miracle in her body, where once our miracle had taken root. But I had no part in it. Not me. Her body was not mine to hold and take care of, that body growing inside her not of me. Nothing to do with me.

Nothing.

A bucket of ice water smashed over me.

New life. New world. And I had no clue.

I blinked, willing my vision to clear, my breath to even out, the back of my hand scrubbing across my mouth. I'd never know that kind of life, that level of intimacy. I never would, not if it couldn't be with her.

A heavy hand fell on my back, and I bolted upright.

"Man, I can't listen to this shit," muttered Drac. "Let's head over to the other side of the concert area. Our bros from Oregon are over there."

"Yeah."

What I had now was good. I was an officer. I had brothers who I trusted and who trusted me. I was doing good. I wasn't the "kid" any more.

So why did I feel like I was on the outside looking in again? Tossed back on the dusty shelf, labeled, "just not good enough." That shadow of Meghan's withering looks passed through me again. *"He's not coming to our house."*

Second best. Second rate. Under the table. Unwanted. Dirty little secret.

"Let's go." Drac nudged me with his shoulder.

Women were screaming, singing along with the band. I threw a final look back at the stage. The band's name was "Cruel Fate."

Fuck you.

"Yeah, let's go." Flexing my throbbing fingers, the fingers that weren't there, I forced my lungs to take in air, forced my cold brittle bones to move.

Move forward.

Move.

Move.

And don't look back.

36
FINGER

"I FORGOT HOW GOOD YOUR MARGARITAS are, Jerry."
The girl at the bar licked her lips as she slid her empty glass toward
the bartender.

A prickle tracked up the back of my neck at the sound of that
silky voice.

I was on my way home to bury my head in Nebraska soil and
forget everything I'd seen and felt in Colorado. The four bros I'd
ridden with from Denver were hanging with women at a table by
the dance floor, but I wasn't much in the mood.

Those new scars over my soul still stung.

I leaned my head lower to get a better look at the woman. One
thick lock of shoulder-length dark hair hung over an eye, and she
shook her head to get it out of the way. She straightened her shoulders, letting out a quick breath. "Make me another, pretty please."

"You sure, honey?"

"Extremely sure," came the reply. She was determined. She was
getting hammered.

Three boys down the bar gawked at her as they drank, getting
their engines ready to close in on her finish line. I drained my Bushmills and set the glass back on the counter, wiping at the edge of my
mouth with a flick of my thumb.

Tania looked good.

I hadn't laid eyes on her in years, but I couldn't mistake that
shiny black hair and those huge dark eyes holding court at the long
bar of Dead Ringer's Roadhouse just outside of Meager, South Dakota. I moved down the bar over to Tania as a blond guy strutted

271

toward her. I gave him a searing get-back-into-the-hole-you-just-crawled-out-of look and he stopped short, his buddies grabbing his shirt, reeling him back in.

I bent over her shoulder, catching her gaze in the mirror behind the bar. "Fancy meeting you here."

She jumped, twisting around, her glossy hair flying in my face. "Oh my God! Where the hell did you come from?"

"Colorado."

She punched my shoulder and gripped my tee. "Finger!" she whispered, a grin lighting up her face.

"Actually I came from a couple of barstools down. I stopped for a drink. Been riding all night, needed a break. How about you? What the hell are you doing here? You left Chicago and living here now?"

"No, no. I had business out here, and now I'm on my way home to see my mom." A huge smile broke out over her face as she released my shirt. "It's good to see you."

"Good to see you too." I settled onto the stool next to her. "What business?"

A huge margarita slid towards Tania.

"You good, babe?" the bartender asked, glancing at me, his lips tight.

Tania waved a hand as she leaned over her new glass of booze and slurped from the frosty green top. "Yes, Jerry. I know this guy, don't worry. He won't bite."

Jerry made a face. He didn't look convinced.

"Actually, he does bite." Tania drank more, rolling her eyes.

My head knocked back, and I let out a dry laugh. I could still laugh, and it felt fucking good. "What are you doing here by yourself?"

"Pul-leaze—I've been coming to Dead Ringer's since I was in high school." She batted her thick eyelashes at me as she drank.

"You're here, at a known biker bar, on your own getting sloshed."

"Is that totally unacceptable behavior for me?" She set her glass back on the bar top.

"Yeah, reckless."

She wagged a finger at me. "You hit the nail on the head, dar-lin'."

"Which nail would that be?"

"One of the many." She laughed, her eyes darting over me. "Let me get you a drink."

I shook my head at her as I raised my glass at Jerry. He shot into action, bringing over the bottle of Bushmills and refilling my glass.

"A bottle of brew too," I said.

"Which would you like?" he asked.

"As local as you got."

"Coming right up." Jerry sprang down the bar.

"How are things?" I asked Tania.

"Still in Chicago. I was roaming around here on family business and me business. At least I like to think so."

"What the hell does that mean?"

"The me business was looking at antiques, buying, reselling. Go-ing to garage sales, estate sales, stopping on the road whenever I notice fascinating junk piled in someone's yard."

"Huh. Interesting."

"I like the scavenging, talking with the collectors, the artists. I'm good at it. Actually, I was supposed to be on this trip with this guy I've been seeing, but he decided to do something else. Or I should say, do someone else."

"Asshole."

Her black eyes flared. She was angry. "That's all you have to say?"

"What do you want me to say?"

"I don't know, something more!"

"Fuck him."

"Yeah, fuck him." She held up her glass. "Let's drink."

"We are."

"Keep it coming then." She gulped down her margarita.

"You drink. I'll get you home. Meager's on my way."

"How gallant."

I pushed aside my empty whisky glass as Jerry popped open a large bottle of a local craft brew. "Yeah, that's me, gallant. I'd only do that kind of shit for you."

"I'm touched."

I chuckled. "Chicago still being good to you?"

"Still struggling for bucks, but it's better."

I raised my beer bottle at her. "Drink."

She told me stories about her art dealing business struggles and recent travels through Michigan. I told her stories about my bros and their women.

"You don't have an old lady?"

"Nah."

"Why not? No, wait, don't tell me—"

"Don't you fucking say her name," I said on a hiss, my eyes holding hers.

Her back straightened. "Okay. Well, she probably got herself a new name anyway, right?"

"She did."

We drank in silence.

"My sister's getting married next month."

"Congrats."

"I'm the maid of honor, and that's the family reason I came out here. To try on the dress and help with the planning. I hate the stupid dress. It's yellow. I can't wear a yellow dress with a huge bow over my ass. Ugh, it's so ugly. She's doing this to me on purpose, I know it."

"Simple solution. Wear the dress for the ceremony, the pictures, then don't wear it to the party."

Tania stilled, gesturing at me with her near empty glass. "That's brilliant." Her face dropped, and she swiped at her mouth with the back of her hand.

"You okay?"

"I don't know these days. I'm drifting. My sister's getting married to her first love, most of my friends are in serious relationships and making the big bucks, getting on with their lives like they're supposed to, and—"

"Supposed to? Supposed to what? That's your problem right there. You're hung up on that shit word."

"Finger, I can't even hang onto a boyfriend. I know I'm difficult.

Hard to please, can't admit I'm wrong. I didn't even want anything serious—I thought guys liked that. So it must be me."

I took a swig of my icy beer.

"But when I caught Andrew in bed with Shelly the other day, I freaked. I heard them, I saw them...it was awful." Her voice shook, her head sinking into her hand on the bar. "I didn't think I'd care so much, but I did. I do." She raised her head. Her eyes were wet. "Paying my bills is hard enough, trying to keep a business afloat... there has to be something I'm not doing right. Obviously, my karma is crap, and I'm fucking doomed. I should just give up."

"You never fucking give up."

"Easy for you to say."

"You think?" I shot her a look.

"No, no. I'm sorry." Tania jumped up on her toes and threw her arms around me. She nestled her face into my neck and sighed, her body pressing into mine. "Forgive me."

She smelled good. Of pricey perfume, of clean. Her skin was warm against mine and had my pulse drumming a little faster. Tania's skin, her skin...all three of us in that bed came running back to me, flashing behind my eyes.

I wrapped my arms around her.

"They'll be other chances, other assholes," I murmured.

"Is that what you tell yourself when you look in the mirror every day?" she asked.

"I don't look in the fucking mirror."

A sad smile clung to one side of her mouth. "Well, you know what I see?" She leaned in close to me. "Hurt, pain, anger, resentment. And love. So much fucking love," she whispered in my ear, her lips grazing my skin, her fingers at my neck.

"Shut the fuck up." I tightened my hold on her, liking the feel of her pressed against me, sharing her frustrations with me.

"Tell me it's been easy without her. Tell me you've forgotten her," she said.

"I don't want to forget. I can't cut her out."

Tania slid down my body, releasing me. "You two...you were my idols. My sure thing." Averting her gaze, she grabbed my beer bottle and drained it.

I brushed the hair from her face, my fingers lingering on her neck, her shoulder, catching in her sleeve, pulling it. A shiny black bra strap revealed itself. Tania eyed me. I held her gaze, the question, the idea.

"There's a motel across the highway," I said.

Her eyes narrowed. "I know."

"That Andrew any good in the sack?"

She let out a curt brittle laugh. "He was...fine."

"Let's go," I said.

Her face reddened.

I tugged on the black strap. "You want to fuck? You want me to give it to you?"

Her shoulder jerked under my hand. "Shut up," she whispered roughly, her dark brows twisting.

"What do you want, Tan? You. No past, no future. Just right the hell now. Tell me what you want."

"Stop. It."

"Why? Stop what? Wanting?" I slanted my head. "I want you. Now, you tell me. Come on. I dare you."

Her jaw slackened, her heavy gaze on mine.

"Say it."

"Finger..."

"Say it now."

"Yeah, I want it. I want it from you." She pressed her lips together. "But somehow this feels like cheating."

"On who? Andy and Shelley?"

"Oh, geez, come on—"

"Tania, she's married."

"She what?"

"You heard me."

"Really?"

"Yeah, really. And pregnant."

Her eyes widened. "Oh. Shit. I'm sorry. I—"

"Let's get out of here."

"Finger, wait..."

"What do you want, Tania? You want pretty words and slippery suggestions? You want me to tell you how those cut off shorts you're wearing have been turning me on since the second I saw you? They have. You want me to say I remember how your tits feel in my mouth? I do. You want me to say I want to make you come on my cock all night in that dirt bag motel? Most definitely."

"Slow the hell down—"

I grabbed her upper arm and yanked her in close to me. "Tell me. Now. Right this very second, do you want to feel alive? Do you want to feel something good? Because you know I can make you feel good." I kissed her, and it all came surging back: the grasping in the dark, the moans of satisfaction, tongues and flesh and sweat everywhere. "And you do the same for me."

Her gaze darted to my lips. Her breathing picked up.

"This ain't some trashy anonymous pickup, if that's your hang-up here," I continued. "We've done this before. We know each other."

"Yes, but—"

I grabbed her hand and planted a kiss on one finger after the other, my tongue lashing at her skin. Her eyes narrowed as if she were in pain, and she let out a jagged gasp.

"Where's the fucking but, Tan? Why the fuck not?" Goosebumps rose on the skin of her arm under my grip.

A pact. A goal to forget, live, exist in the now.

"Hey, everything all right here?" Jerry, the bartender's stiff voice sliced between us.

Tania's shoulders dropped and she licked her lips, her eyes remaining on mine. "Everything's good. Real good." She turned to Jerry. "What do we owe you?"

I threw a fifty dollar bill on the bar top. "Keep the change."

Tania and I strode out of Dead Ringer's. We were on a mission.

She got in her car and I got on my bike, and we went to the motel across the way where I got us a room. We shed our clothes and I made her forget any second thoughts, any rights, wrongs, supposed to's that were taking up space in her head. I made her body respond to mine, and got gasps and curses and moans in return.

I made sure we both enjoyed it.

I didn't have to bother with small talk, or waste time being annoyed that she expected more from me afterward like some of the girls I'd been with recently, because Tania didn't. And she knew me, not the Flames officer. This was blunt. Straightforward. And it felt fucking good.

To be with Tania again. To fuck the ghost of Rena, Serena, Ashley, Lenore out from under me. To fuck past the disappointment and that never-ending ache with someone who knew. Yeah, she was with me and Tania on that bed. I searched for her on that bed. And Tania? She shot the finger at her disappointments as they fell to the wayside. A gloom hung in the air of that motel room, but we both worked hard to ignore it.

Tania's body, her scent, her taste, her sounds were a pillow muffling the noise in my head, but I was still pissed as hell that Serena wasn't here with us, with me.

I was looking for her, letting go of her, spitting at her.

All at the same fucking time.

I ripped the third condom wrapper and fitted myself up. Lifting up Tania's hips, I got her up on all fours.

"Whoa, what are you doing—" her fatigued voice came from somewhere over the mattress.

I clenched an ass cheek, and my red imprint appeared on her flesh, my balls twitching at the sight. "Did you let Andy in this ass?"

She let out an exhausted laugh. "He wouldn't have known what to do."

Using my cum and her wetness as lube, I fingered her ass. "Touch your clit." She did it, her ass rocking up.

She relaxed again, and I entered her carefully, pulsing inside her, driving deeper each time.

Her body shuddered at my assault. "Oh my G…"

After, I rolled a joint, and we got high and drifted off to sleep.

And I slept.

No usual round of nightmares: the sting of the knife, those eyes, hands holding me down, those blue green eyes locked on mine across the room, that voice calling me. That sour taste of white mushy bread. That mouth. Scrib's laugh.

I woke up with a start. Was it morning? Still night?

Tania was curled up against my back, her breaths warm on my skin. The hotel room chair and table just beyond the bed came into soft focus, and my pulse slowed.

There was no one here from my club checking on me. Who I was with, who I was talking to, who I was fucking. This was only me and Tania. My neck relaxed back into the pillow, and I turned to my side, letting out a breath.

Tania's lips grazed my back, dragging over the welts that had now hardened into scars. "Is this okay?"

"Yeah," I replied. It was good, which surprised me. I didn't go for affection, for quiet moments.

I'd only had that once before, with one person. And that's where that was going to stay.

"You good?" I asked, turning my head slightly from the pillow. "I'm good."

I squeezed her arm and relaxed my muscles against her, letting her explore me. I wasn't going to pretend it was Serena holding me like I'd done with the women I'd fucked at the concert campgrounds. Serena's sweat on my skin. Serena's mouth on me. No, I was here with Tania, and I liked it. The stinging had eased. No reason to cut and run. Tania was my sugar making the medicine go down.

"If I'm ever around Chicago, I'll call you."

"You don't have to feed me lines, Finger. Not you. Come on. I'm not some star-struck biker groupie chick."

"I'm serious." I turned over, facing her.

Tania's hands fell to my chest. "What are you saying?"

"I'm saying, if I call you, and you're free, meet up with me. I'm not saying dinner and a movie, roses in hand."

She let out a laugh. "Oh, I don't want roses from you. Anyhow, I'm done with the roses and the dating bullshit."

I gripped her ass and her hands slid down to my abs, to my hips, my thighs.

I grinned, pressing against her. "If you want a good fuck without the aforementioned bullshit, you call me, and I'll call you. Either way, we'll meet up."

"I've got plenty of traveling coming up actually, so, we might cross paths more often than not across the country."

"I'm always on the road. I'll make it happen." I was usually on a run, taking jobs others didn't want, because they were dangerous, because they had families. I didn't.

She only grinned. She liked how that sounded. Her eyes darted down my body, and a blush rose on her skin from her face, her throat, all the way down the pale skin of her chest.

I raised her chin. "You don't have to be shy or uncomfortable with me."

"I'm trying not to be." She stroked my hardening cock. Her touch grew tense, rough.

"That's it." My voice came out low. "Yeah, fuck. That's it."

She kept working me. Her touch, the feel of her tits brushing over my flesh were getting me there fast.

"Fuck everything, Tania. Go on, say it," I rasped.

"Fuck everything," came her breathy reply.

My thumb brushed over her lower lip. "Now suck me off."

She slid down my body and licked my tip, that tongue of hers extended, licking some more.

A growl rose in my chest. "What did I say?"

Her mouth finally took me in. All the way in.

My hips rocked up. "Harder."

Only dirty sugar made that medicine go down.

37
LENORE

THE SUN WAS DAZZLING.

The cold air was crisp, but the unexpected sunlight shed its warmth over the crowd gathered in downtown Rapid for the lighting of the Christmas tree. For the zillionth time, I tucked the navy blue fleece blanket around my baby son nestled in his stroller, sucking avidly on his pacifier. Last week snow and subzero temperatures prevailed, but today was almost like spring in comparison, and I couldn't resist bringing him to the Winter Market to get a whiff of Christmas spirit.

A thirty foot blue spruce decorated with hundreds of light bulbs towered over us. The tree lighting ceremony would begin at five followed by the Festival of Lights Parade at six, but we wouldn't be sticking around for that. The sun would be gone by then, and real cold would settle in.

Maybe next year.

I was always taking notes in my head of what to do, where to go with my boy. A long, long list of items was already filed under the "maybe next year" heading.

I'd loved Christmas when my grandmother was alive. She was an enthusiastic baker and decorator. Buttery cinnamon sugar toast was the daily breakfast ritual for the two of us. The radio was always tuned to a holiday station, filling the house with an endless round of the same old carols but performed by every artist under the sun from Bing Crosby to Nat King Cole to Elvis, even elevator music versions. She made sure we watched all the children's holiday television shows together, and she'd take me to our local bookstore where she'd buy me one special illustrated book of my choice. I would help her unwrap her collection of Christmas angels and we'd put them around the house. It was magical.

After she'd passed away, there had been no more bracing anticipation or crisp excitement to those days, no more cinnamon and nutmeg. The magic had evaporated. They'd become ordinary days. Very ordinary just like the ones before and the days that followed. A brightly colored balloon now deflated, thudding along the floor. That's when I realized that Christmas really was about sharing traditions with special people in your life.

I was going to create new traditions for me and my son. I would bake for him and decorate and shop for him, read the right books to him. I glanced at the gingerbread reindeer, sugar cookie stars, and shortbread covered in mounds of confectioners sugar.

Yes, cinnamon and nutmeg.

I steered the stroller through the booths which showcased handcrafted ornaments, jewelry, and home decor. I bought a big three-dimensional snowflake made out of wood, painted white. Vendors sold jars of their homemade jams, jellies, and salsas all dressed up in pretty holiday ribbons, gorgeous sweet yeasty breads, a dizzying selection of old-fashioned lollipops and candies and cookies.

"Thank you!" a girl with a Santa cap on her head said as I tossed a wrapped gift into the Toys for Tots donation box.

"My pleasure," I replied.

"Here you go." She handed me a complimentary cup of hot chocolate.

Santa had made his grand entrance earlier, escorted by a city fire truck. A long line of kids waited to take photos with him, and I pushed the stroller in his direction. I definitely wanted him to see Santa. I didn't want him to miss out on anything. I wanted him to always have these experiences, these memories. Although I was sure Eric would think I was a nut job for taking him out in the cold today, sun or no.

Rapid City was our home, as well as LA, but Rapid had my heart. I took a final sip of the hot chocolate, bringing the stroller to a stop by the rope barrier on the other side of the long winding line.

I grinned. Definitely next year.

I crouched down next to the stroller, my hand over the blanket under which his legs were kicking and popping against the thick fleece. "Look, honey, it's Santa. He's come from the North Pole to meet us. You're excited, huh? Me too! What's he going to bring you for Christmas this year? Your first Christmas." I tickled his tummy, and he scrunched his mouth at me.

It sure felt like my first Christmas. It would be the first of so very many good ones.

I kissed his cheek, pulled down his hat with the bear ears on top, and stood up, pulling the stroller back a little from the extended line of kids and their parents.

"You been naughty or you been nice?" a deep, scratchy voice filled my ear.

My heart stopped. I spun around, my grip tightening on the stroller handles. Finger stood there in his colors, his huge worn leather jacket zipped to the top, a scarf bundled around his neck, a charcoal gray knit cap pulled down over his head. A dark beard covered his jaw.

I blinked. My hands clamped tightly over the curved handles. "Hey."

He said nothing. He studied me, his one eyebrow arched, the line of his jaw set.

I last saw him in May across the field at a music festival in Colorado. I'd been six months pregnant and shocked as hell to spot him that afternoon. The look on his face when he realized I was pregnant. I'll never forget it. Not ever.

My baby was four months old now.

Was he keeping track of me?

A choir of cheery voices swelled in the distance, "...with boughs of holly..."

His guarded eyes went to my baby, then back to me. "Boy?"

My breath shorted. "Yes."

"What's his name?"

"Beck."

"Beck?"

"...Fa la la la la la la la la..."

283

"Beck," he repeated.

My heart thudded in my chest.

"Is Beck mine?"

My skin heated, my stomach cramped. "Finger—"

"Is he mine?"

"No. I was already pregnant when I saw you in LA."

On a hiss of air, he averted his gaze with a sharp movement, his head swinging away from me, his shoulders rigid. Had he been clinging to a sliver of hope about the baby? The what-might-have-been flared between us like the slicing blast of a police siren.

He leaned into me, eyes blazing. "You were pregnant with another man's kid and you let me touch you? Why?" I didn't see disgust in his face nor hear hatred in his voice, only that harsh demand for the truth and an eerie curiosity.

"Excuse me, sorry—could we get through?" A mom holding two twin girls by the hands bumped into me, pushing me closer to Finger. My face brushed his chest. The scent of leather and tobacco, cinnamon gum, and him.

Another life, another world.

Worlds collide.

"Answer me."

"I'm selfish," I replied.

His iron eyes widened, his chin lifted. A sound rumbled in the back of this throat as his lips tipped up. He liked that answer. "So am I." The lick of pleasure in his tone was almost sinister.

He leaned down, studying Beck who kicked at his blanket under Finger's stare. "Goodbye, Beck. Hope Santa brings you everything you want."

He turned and stalked off into the crowd. Away. No final glance at me. No meaningful look. No cold squint.

My eyes flooded with water. I put a mittened hand to my mouth to keep the wail that rose up my throat locked inside. The crowd swirled around me, children laughed, shouted, mothers talked loudly, the choir continued with fucking Jingle Bells.

I wiped at my eyes and maneuvered the stroller away from the Santa display and back up on the sidewalk. My insides twisted as

I scanned the crowd, greedily looking for him, a last taste of the brownie batter on the spatula before tossing it in the sink. One last look. Anything. Something. That tall body, that rigid line of neck and broad shoulders, those fierce dark eyes, those scars, that long and steady gait.

But there was no trace of him.

My head spun, my heart thudded off beat. I was off beat, defeated, small.

Beck fussed, letting out a whiny cry. "Okay, honey. Okay. We're going."

Through blurry vision, I guided the stroller back to my car.

After we first met, Eric and I had started sleeping together right away. We'd been careless once, and I hadn't cared. We were careless a second time, and he'd freaked out. Not me, though. In fact, I'd dared destiny, flipping it the bird to prove my track record of being on the receiving end of lousy trick or treat candy wrong.

And destiny had given me a gift.

I was glad and relieved, because I knew a baby with another man would separate me from Finger and my past forever, a cement barrier on that perilous road that was us. It would force both of us to move forward and move apart. When I'd told Eric I was pregnant, he'd freaked out, lapsing into speechlessness. I told him it was cool, that I wanted to keep the baby on my own. Then he'd taken me in his arms and said, "Marry me."

And I did.

When Finger had surprised me in LA, when he'd touched me, I couldn't stop it, I hadn't wanted to. Hell, I'd wanted him badly the moment I'd heard his voice, saw his reflection in the mirror. Then he'd kissed me. Breathed me in. And something volatile erupted inside me. Would that ever change?

And then I'd seen Finger at that concert and knew what was going on in his head. "Is that my baby?" Pulling the signal on him had upset me, the look on his face shattering. But he had to know. There was no going back, no second chances.

I sniffed in the icy air, gripping the stroller handles tighter. The glitter of the lights, the joy in people's singing in the distance and the red and green decorations had all lost their sparkle and promise. Everything was flat, dull. Artificial.

I unlocked my car, got Beck in his car seat and buckled him in. He tugged on a lock of my hair, his pudgy legs kicking up at me under the blanket I tucked around him. "Going home now, Beck. Okay?"

"Gook." He mashed his lips together, watching me intently.

Yes, home. A home I'd created. A home I was responsible for. Me.

This was for the best.

Then why did it burn so much?

38
FINGER

WINTER FADED, SPRING PASSED THROUGH, summer conquered in all its heat-filled heady glory. I rode every day without fail. I kept busy on jobs, on charity runs, on looking out for the prospects.

I was in Minneapolis for a meeting of the Midwestern chapters, representing our region. I'd called Tania a few days before, and she'd agreed to meet me. I was at my pow wow all day, and she was at some museum. We met at a motel in the afternoon. I had to be back at the local chapter's clubhouse for the big shindig before me and Drac left the next day.

Tania passed me the roach, and I took a deep drag on the last of it. "Did you like that?"

"What exactly?" She raised her head up off the bed. "The weed or your cock gymnastics?"

"The weed. Take some home with you."

"That is damned good happy green."

"It is. You never take any home with you."

"I like doing it with you. I don't want to do it on my own or share it. Then they'd ask me where I got it, and I'd have to admit that I know an outlaw, and that's a well guarded secret by me and my snatch."

I dropped what was left of the roach in the empty beer can by the bed. "You need any cash?"

She raised herself up on her elbows, shooting me a frown.

"Don't give me that look. I want to help you if you need help. I like helping you. I happen to have cash this month, I'd like to use it

287

for a good reason."

She gazed up at the ceiling. "I appreciate that, but it's okay. Really."

"You found a new job yet?"

"I'm hostessing at this fancy restaurant now. I just got a raise as I'm the only one who can function at seven a.m. for the business breakfast crowd. I can remember names and faces, make introductions, be cheery, and keep those tables moving."

"You should work for me."

She let out a laugh and rolled on her side, facing me, her head propped up on her hand. "Hey, what happened with Gloria? Last time we saw each other, you said you were going to—"

I shrugged. "Yeah, I did. Then I got rid of her."

"You already ditched your first old lady? Finger!"

"She was in my shit all the time."

"If you're in a relationship with someone, that's how it is, from what I can remember. They're in your shit, and you're in theirs."

"Don't like it."

She turned over on the bed. "You're impossible." Her tone was quiet this time, not the usual sarcastic.

"Hey." I touched the curve of her lower back, and she immediately looked up at me. I didn't usually touch her much after we'd finish. "What is it?" I whispered.

"I only wish you felt bad," she said.

"About what?"

"About anything!" Tania flopped onto her back. "I wish you felt something. That you felt bad for breaking up with Gloria. That you felt bad for ditching Donna last year and cheating on her with me. That you felt anything, for fuck's sake!" She raised her voice.

My pulse heated. "I'm sick of feeling, Tania. It's nothing but a ripping in my gut, bleeding me dry over and over again."

She jacked up on her knees on the mattress. "You've seen her, haven't you?"

That image of Lenore and her baby—her husband's baby—in the middle of that Christmas wonderland flashed in front of my eyes. Thick bile and vinegar slid down my chest, searing my insides.

I jerked off the bed and slid my leathers up my legs, grabbed my tee from the floor and pulled it over my head.

"Finger!"

"Yes! I saw her." I shoved my feet in my boots, buttoned my leathers.

"Wait—What are you—"

I couldn't. I didn't want to discuss, didn't want to deal. Didn't.

Snapping up my keys on the small table, I threw open the motel room door and stormed outside to my bike.

I didn't want to talk about her. I couldn't talk about her. I was still trying not to think about her. I couldn't even say her name anymore, not even with Tania. I didn't want to. That made the loss of her acute. More acute.

She was good where she was; a memory I'd stuffed into a bottle, corked and sealed and tossed to bob in my sea. Always in view, though.

I needed that view.

I rode off, leaving Tania and the motel behind me in a cloud of dust. I didn't know if I'd hear from her again, but I also knew I didn't have to explain myself. We were good that way. I'd leave it up to her.

Three months later she called me.

"I'm on a vacation in New Mexico with a couple of girlfriends. Are you...around?" she asked, her voice breathy, hesitant.

I happened to be in Arizona on a run to oversee a new meth distribution operation in the area. I could only spare maybe two hours with her at best with the riding time included. I couldn't be under the radar too long, but I'd do it to see Tania again.

"Hell yeah, I'm in Arizona. What are you doing now?"

"I'm in the hot tub by the pool getting picked up by these men my friends like, but I can't say I do."

"I can be there in four hours. Can your hormones wait until then?"

Only her laughter filled the line.

"Give me the hotel information."

Once I got into town, Tania texted me. She was in the bar lounge of a sprawling resort hotel where she was drinking with two other women and two men. I spotted her the moment I entered, my colors covered up by a thin black hoodie. She blushed, that slight smile perked up on her lips as she uncrossed her long legs, and I gestured with a slant of my head toward the bathrooms by the elevators.

She shot up from the small sofa where she sat with one of the guys who tugged her back close to him. She bent over and whispered in his ear, and his face lit up like she'd promised him a lap dance once she returned. He let her go and she moved away from him. She wore a short tight green dress that looked hot on her pale skin paired with high heels.

Rolling her eyes, she strode across the lobby towards the bathrooms, her hips swaying, making my dick come to life in my leathers. She turned the corner, and my arm shot out pulling her into the men's bathroom. I headed for a stall, her heels eagerly clipping the tile floor behind me.

In the stall, she plastered herself against the wall and raised her arms high. She knew my drill. I locked the door and slid my hand down over her ass. My pulse fired. "Fuck, Tania. No panties tonight?"

"That's for you."

I yanked up her dress. "You're totally bare."

"That's for my bikini."

"I like it." I palmed her, my hand sliding over damp, smooth skin. "You don't want to fuck anyone out there tonight?"

"They're jerks. My friends like them, but I'm not into drunken bonkfests. They're really drunk too, so it's only going to be sloppy, and they'll probably whip out their phones and film the whole thing. Nowadays everyone thinks they're doing a spring break video for the Playboy Channel."

Tania talked. A lot. That hadn't changed, and I liked it. My muscles relaxed. She wasn't mad at me for being out of touch for so long. She still wanted it from me, and I definitely still wanted it from her. We were good. I squeezed her tits over the slippery fabric of her dress. No bra either.

Her fingertips curled into my beard, tugging. "Shit, your beard got longer. It really suits you."

"You like it?"

"Yeah—" She stumbled on her high heels.

I suited up in a rubber, and hitching her legs around me, thrust inside her slickness.

She let out a loud cry, clutching my shoulders. "Tomorrow, when they can't remember shit about whatever they do tonight, I'm going to remember this."

I dug my fingers into her ass, nailing her up against the quivering divider. Banging her.

She came, and I pulled out of her, turned her around. She trembled in my grip, and my blood rushed into my head at the feel of her anticipation, her jitteriness, her lust. I thrust into her very wet pussy and pumped fast and hard. My balls screamed, my muscles burned. She moaned loudly, shuddering, and I roared right after.

I ripped the condom off me. "Get on your knees and get me there again." I yanked the top of her dress down and her breasts spilled out. "I want to come on those tits."

She wiped the sweat from her upper lip and got down on her knees in the stall and worked my cock until I started coming in her mouth. I spattered my cum over her tits.

"Rub it in. Let 'em smell me on you."

She made a face at me, but she did it. I helped her up, and she wiped at her skin and dabbed at her dress with a wad of toilet paper.

"I'm not done," I said, pinching a nipple.

She grinned. Neither was she.

Twenty minutes later, with the urinals being used and flushed in the next room, men's knowing chuckles and overly loud coughs having set a soundtrack to our fucking, I sent her back out to her friends, a lazy grin on her rosy face, her legs wobbling on those hot high heels.

"I'll call you."

"You do that," she mumbled as we passed each other in the lobby, her hands smoothing over her hips.

I strode down the grand front staircase of the resort hotel, the parking valet boy shuffling back in my wake.

For years, Tania and I met in towns and cities all over the country, sometimes in motels for a night or only a couple of hours during the day. Anywhere convenient for a quick fuck. It was never regular, once every few months at most, off and on. But it happened, and I liked it.

We never discussed any other women in my life, of which there were many.

And we never discussed *her*. Not ever again.

"Hey."

"Hey."

"I got your text message," said Tania. Wind blew hard in the background from the payphone she was using somewhere in Chicago.

"I'll be there by three. This cold weather sucks, icy rain in the forecast too."

"Finger?"

"Yeah?"

"The thing is, I can't meet up today."

Her voice was unsteady. Ordinarily, if one of us said no, we didn't ask details about why. But something in her tone made me want to know.

"What's going on?"

"I met someone."

I didn't respond.

"It's going well, and just keeps getting better and better, and I want to give it a real shot, so I can't meet up with you anymore."

I breathed out.

Almost ten years had passed since me and Tania had started meeting up. Life was moving on, no matter how I tried to shape and mold it to my will, to keep it still or keep it narrow. I was glad for her. She should be getting on with her life, not slipping me in whenever and wherever as we'd been doing over the years. We'd had our fun. We'd both gotten satisfaction out of it.

I was going to miss it.

"I'm sorry," she said, her voice filling the silence between us.

"You don't have to be sorry."

Lenore had gotten married, had her son. And now Tania was actually committing to a relationship. We were all older now, were we wiser? Stronger?

"You be happy, Tania."

"I will," she replied, her voice steadier. "I want you to be happy too."

I didn't answer. I hung up.

39
LENORE

"I DON'T KNOW WHERE YOU ARE, but I do know where you aren't." Eric made a face, his lips bunching together as he packed his guitar into its traveling case. "And that's here."

I braced for yet another argument. "I'm right here, Eric. With our son—"

"Yeah, yeah, that's your excuse—Beck."

"Beck is not an excuse. You're the one out of town all the time."

Eric glanced quickly at his Blackberry and shoved it into his pocket. "What I'm saying is that when I am home, you've got so much shit going on in your head, it's like you're not even here. You're still having the nightmares, talking in your sleep, but you're not getting any help."

"For shit's sake, I'm not into therapy like you and all your friends are."

"It might help you, but the point is, you're just not willing to go there."

I used to have nightmares regularly—about Med, about Motormouth, Turo. But they had all faded. Eric was wrong. Dreams of Finger haunted me now. Ever since I'd had the baby, Finger's face, his voice, his touch, even had come back to haunt me, as if the vault door had suddenly sprang open inside me. I'd woken up this morning in a sweat at the memory of his words.

You're the villain here. Not me.

Disappointment settled over me like a layer of wet cement hardening quickly.

"What's the matter, Eric? You need more attention from me?" I lashed back.

He propped the guitar case up on the sofa. "It'd be nice for a change, instead of being your goddamn afterthought. I get that you work, I know Beck's a handful. But when we're both in the same location, you don't act like you really want me here. I feel like I'm in your goddamn way."

I chewed on my lips, staring at my bare feet. He had a point. In the beginning of our relationship, I enjoyed spending every minute with him and the other members of Cruel Fate and their crew. But it had gotten tedious real quick, especially when I was in the last months of my pregnancy. Once I had Beck, who we named after Eric's rock hero, Jeff Beck, I'd preferred to stay home with my baby, rather than be a part of Eric's background noise.

Eric ran a hand through his thick mop of blondish brown hair. "I'm a little busy as a working musician here. I wish I could take years off between albums to hang out with you and live in our castle in the south of France drinking Evian or some shit, but those of us who aren't superstars have to actually sweat for a living. If I'm not out there touring, I'm writing and recording. The pressure to produce is harsher than ever, Len. Album sales are tanking, you know this. We haven't had a hit single in years."

"I know. Sales are shit for everyone, Eric. All I'm saying is that we'll never get this time back with Beck. You weren't around when he started to eat solid foods, to speak, to walk, his first day of school."

"I know, but it doesn't mean I'm a shit dad if I can't be around because of work. Fuck, there you go again, turning this into something else—I'm supporting us, I only wish you could support me!" His voice rose.

"I do support you! How can you say that? I stopped working full time so I could be there for you whenever and wherever you needed me. I was always the first to compromise in this relationship, especially now that we have Beck."

"You're the mother!" he shouted.

"Yes, yes, I am. I'm the mother."

No truer words had been spoken. I thrilled at those words, that title. They were a part of me, and I delighted in them; they were written across my soul, just like Beck's name had been tattooed over my heart in bold red letters.

Our little boy had been born healthy and energetic. I adored him, and I adored being his mom. For weeks, every morning I would rush to his crib to watch him sleep, still barely able to believe that I had a child. I had achieved this dream, and the dream was real, and I was happy.

Wasn't I?

We lived in our house in LA most of the time, and spent the odd month here and there at the house in Rapid City. Our lifestyle wasn't red carpets, paparazzi, and private jets, but it was a recording contract, tour dates, video clips, supportive fans, and a manager who believed in the talent.

We had just come off a tour of the southern states, and it had been challenging with Beck in tow. But I figured if Linda McCartney had done it with four kids, I could do it with one. I did, but I was happy to be back at the house in Rapid.

Eric pulled on his jacket. "Look, David is threatening to pull out of the group and that can't happen. I need him to write with. I need him onstage. It won't be the same for me without him. If he leaves, it'll be the beginning of the end for Cruel Fate."

"Yeah, well, David needs cocaine to write with you, and he needs cocaine to perform with you. If he doesn't get help soon—"

"Sure, of course." Eric shrugged. "But he needs the music, Len. He needs us. We're his family. We can help him through this."

"Eric, you haven't been able to help him through this in over fifteen years. Come on!"

"You don't get it."

I waved my hands in the air and picked up Beck's superhero figures from the living room floor. "Right, right, I forgot, I don't get it."

If only he knew.

Eric didn't know anything about my past. I'd only told him that I'd come from Chicago, studied design, and was good with a sewing machine. I'd explained the scars on my body with a detail-less story about an abusive stepfather, and he never pressed me for more.

Eric gnawed on his lower lip. "Look, I have to get to LA. I just need to make sure David's okay and get him to finish this album once and for all. I've got to get him in gear."

"Hmm. Right."

David also had a little sister who'd had a crush on Eric from day one, and Eric was sweet on Pam. They'd had a thing off and on for years before I'd come along. Sara, one of the groupies of the band that I'd befriended from the very beginning, had called me in a drunken haze last month and told me she'd seen Eric and Pam together before and after a show at a small club in San Diego in between concert dates. Pam was a professional cheerleader for an NBA team in California, and hot as hell. Who could say no to adoration from a girl ten years younger than you with pompoms and twerking moves?

The taxi honked its horn outside.

"You go to LA, Eric. Say hi to Pammy for me when you see her."

"What?" Eric, his eyes wide, stood motionless in the middle of our living room in a sea of Beck's metal yellow Tonka trucks. His jaw stiffened, and he snatched a Batman doll from the sofa and tossed it into the toy basket at my side. "Pam's in Houston."

"Is she? That's too bad."

Eric grabbed his guitar case. "I'll call you."

He stalked down the hallway, his footsteps thudding down the glossy hardwood floor. The front door opened. The slam of doors, and the car took off down our driveway, its motor fading.

I flopped back on the sofa and stretched out my legs. I didn't feel sad or particularly angry or even resentful of him and Pam. Eric was right, of course. I'd checked out of our relationship, and our work schedules had provided the perfect excuse. Whenever we were together, a well of panic would rise inside me because I couldn't give him back all the things he expected of me.

In the very beginning, I had made a supreme effort, when things between us were new and fun and I'd convinced myself that it was for the best. A new adventure in a new world, a world I needed to lose myself in. But I was already lost in the dirty puddle Med had left behind, and lost foremost, in the love I had for Finger. I'd put those feelings high on a shelf, out of reach. But they only stared back at me from their lofty perch, towered over me, casting their shadow over everything.

The late morning rays streamed through the front bay window, and I enjoyed the warmth of the sun on my body. The vividly colored curtains I'd made last year created a warm glow of burnt orange, gold, and berry flowing through the small room. My life with Eric was colorless, and I didn't want to be his wife anymore. I couldn't pretend or make do any longer. He was frustrated and pissed, and he had every right to be. And Beck deserved better than growing up with parents who merely tolerated each other. I needed to clean up my mess.

I got up from the sofa and picked up the rest of my son's toys from the floor. My eyes went to the drawer where I'd tucked that divorce lawyer's business card a friend had given me last month.

I hadn't been able to make it work with Eric; it wasn't in me.

Would it ever be again?

40

FINGER

"WHAT'S YOUR NAME?" I ASKED him.

We stood outside the diner on Shepherd Street where I'd just had an early breakfast, and he'd bought himself a cup of coffee to go. I recognized him from the party at the club the other night. He'd been serving drinks. A new hanger-on. They mostly came and went, but a number of them hung on. Like him.

"Drew. Drew Reigert."

My gaze flicked over him. I knew that name. This kid definitely looked familiar, and it wasn't just from the party.

"Where you from?" I asked, already knowing the answer.

"Meager, South Dakota."

I hadn't seen or heard from Tania in years, and here was her baby brother offering himself up to me and the Flames. Drew was ten years her junior, and from what little she'd mentioned to me, he was a hell of a lot of trouble. They'd lost their dad when Drew was in kindergarten. The boy had never really known his father, was naturally hyper, and a crazy handful for his mother and two sisters who'd struggled to keep their family afloat.

His brown eyes beamed at me. I knew the signs. Boy wanted to prospect. Eager to sit on a huge burning piece of metal and wear leathers, colors that would make feeble humans sit up and take notice.

I adjusted my sunglasses on the bridge of my nose. "Yeah, I've heard of Meager."

His eyes widened under my silent scrutiny, his teeth scraped his bottom lip.

"Why should I trust you, Drew Reigert from Meager, South

299

Dakota, home of the One-Eyed Jacks?"

I'd become wary of the Jacks now that Jump was their President. And he certainly kept out of my way.

"You shouldn't trust me," Drew replied.

I cocked an eyebrow. Well, that was refreshing.

"Until you put me through the paces, that is. Do what you got to do. I get it. I'm good with it."

"Glad to hear it." I kept walking.

He strode alongside me. "I've been going from shit job to shit job. I came up here months ago to see if I could talk to you guys."

"What's the matter, tired of Mommy's cooking? Sounds like you get bored easy. That's real life, ever heard of it?"

"That's true, I do get bored easy. But that just tells me that I haven't been challenged properly yet."

Now I was listening. "That so?"

"Yep."

"I've seen you around here before," I said.

"I've come to a couple parties, and I've helped out here and there." He held my gaze. "I'm serious about wanting to prospect for the Flames. For you."

Not many hanger ons ever dared talk to me.

"You never prospected for the One-Eyed Jacks, hometown boy?"

"Nah, they aren't the Flames of Hell."

"Come by today and I'll have our housekeeper give you a toothbrush. You can get that grout between the bathroom and the kitchen tiles all white and sparkly. The way I imagine it used to be in the eighties."

"I could do that."

"Did you ever do it for your mother?"

He laughed. A full belly laugh. The kid was relaxed, sure of himself. I wasn't sure I liked it. I could spot bullshit a mile off, and as President of my club I had no time for it.

"I'll take that as a no. Shame. What do you got to offer me, though, other than potentially clean white grout and shiny tile?" I asked him.

He shook his hair out of his face. "Anything you want. Whatever you need. I'm a quick study."

He held my gaze, his brown eyes unwavering. All eagerness and sincerity. Maybe what he needed was the right direction for a change.

"Other than getting bored easy, you got any disabilities, quirks that would affect your work performance?"

"No quirks, not really, except for enthusiasm."

"Being a prospect, you're on call 24/7. Participation is mandatory at all functions, no exceptions. Club comes first before all things, even your dick, maybe even your mommy."

"Right, understood."

I gestured at the decked out Shovelhead chopper a few yards behind him. "That your bike?"

"Yeah. Got it last year."

"You got a trust fund maybe?"

"No, not me. I got a brain, and I use it to get what I want, and I wanted that bike. The previous owner placed it in a bet. Owed someone else a lot of money. I swooped in and won it fair and square."

"You come by in an hour. That toothbrush will be ready for you." I strode toward my bike, giving him a final look.

A grin broke across his face. "Yes!"

"I'M CALLING ABOUT YOUR BROTHER."

"Drew? What about Drew?" Tania's voice grew higher. "Is he okay? Is he in trouble?"

"He's been with me for a few months."

Silence. A sharp exhale of breath. "What does that mean exactly?" she asked.

"He came to me on his own. Wants to be a Flame."

"You're joking."

"Would I call you to joke?"

"No, you wouldn't."

"I don't know if he's told you, he doesn't talk about his family, but I wanted you to hear it from me that he's getting patched in. Didn't want you to think I set out and recruited him, targeted him on purpose."

"Okay. I don't know if I should say thank you or be careful."

I laughed.

"Look, he's been quite the anarchist since high school. My mom's real upset about his brushes with the law the past few years."

"He's proven himself a solid worker, capable. It's going up for a vote next week."

"Good luck to the both of you," Tania murmured.

"You mad?"

"I don't know. No. You might be just what he needs. You run a tight ship from the little I know. My mom and sister are going to freak, of course. Are you still vice-president?"

"No."

"Oh, sorr—"

"I'm president."

"Whoa. Oh boy. Congratulations, Finger."

"How are things with you, Tania?"

"I'm getting married."

"To that guy?"

"Yes. Kyle."

"So it's good?"

"Yeah, yeah, it's very good. We're happy."

She knew better than to ask my relationship status. I had none, anyway. Women frequently tried with me, but I was never interested enough. There was no point in exploring any "thing" with anyone.

"Stay that way, Tania."

She let out a dry laugh. "I'll try."

"YOU'RE DOING GOOD WORK, MAN. You caught the mistakes the accountant made last year, now you caught a prospect ratting out our business to a fucking cop. You keep catching shit for your club, well appreciated." I leaned back in my chair in my office, our German Shepherd, Leper, curled at my feet.

My office was no longer the mildewed former bedroom that Kwik's office had once been. We'd completely renovated the old farmhouse, as well as the detached barn out front, and the large shed at the other end. The old farm was an excellent location. Feds who constantly tried to do surveillance on us, and there were many, were easily spotted.

Even better, we'd finally stopped renting the property and bought it outright with the cash I'd insisted on putting to the side. There had been plenty of groaning among the men about the money crunch when I first presented the idea. I explained to them that you couldn't blow everything you had on partying or let it slip through your fingers on the usual expenses just because you happened to have some extra one month or two. Planning ahead was a good thing.

The memories of my dad always rushing to scrape cash together at the last minute not only for his old lady, their house, their kids, but even to pay his own club dues, had never left me. Misery. I detested it.

The cost of the farmhouse wasn't too bad as the family we got it from had sold off almost all of the property over the years in an attempt to keep up with expenses, taxes, their loans, and they were eager to sell. There was just enough land for us to have privacy for both our business and our good time. Now, my brothers were proud that we actually owned something. The "Farm," as we called it, was ours.

Over the past few years, Tania's little brother had proven his dedication, loyalty, and capabilities as a Flame. He'd settled in just fine with the bros, and now he even had an old lady, Jill. He had worked a lot of construction in his time, and spearheaded the final section that had to be done on our clubhouse and the adjoining garage we'd started building a few years back. He'd pitched in on security, too, setting up an improved alarm and camera system on our property. He'd then recruited a prospect, Den, who was a computer and electronics freak to maintain it. I'd been right about Tania's brother. He was all raw potential. He'd just needed the right opportunity and some guidance.

"Catch keeps catching." Drac ruffled Catch's hair, handing him a glass of whiskey. He filled my glass and his own, and hiked himself up on the edge of my desk.

"I still can't believe he did that, Prez," said Catch. "Mikey seemed like a good guy. He seemed all right. Always on time, positive attitude, never complained. He's insisting he just shot his mouth off when he shouldn't have. That cop was working undercover as a college kid. I mean, she was really hot, but—"

Drac cracked up laughing. "A female cop got his tongue flapping?"

Catch took a healthy gulp of his liquor. "Yeah."

"He did it, and you need to believe it," I said. "People seem to be a lot of things. You need to be ready for all those possibilities." I leaned back in my chair and enjoyed the sweet searing heat of the whiskey in my mouth.

"Really shouldn't be trusting the hot chick with her lips around your cock," said Drac, raising his glass to Catch.

I glanced up at Drac who shot me a grin. He was one of the very few people on this planet I did trust. I'd built my club up in the world of the Flames of Hell with him alongside me and Mishap in the shadows. We were now an island fortress in our piece of the USA.

"Yeah, trust is a very, very fine line," I said. "A fucking high wire."

Catch shifted in his seat. "So, uh, Mikey..."

"Tonight." Drac finished his drink and poured himself another. "Tonight he'll get what's coming to him."

Once the sun fell, the bonfire was fed and burned hungrily in the center pit of the compound. The flames crackled, darting and licking around each other. The heat rose in the crisp night air, lighting up everyone's faces. Glimmers and shadows. Anticipation and dread.

I motioned to my men and they brought out the informer: Mikey the prospect. His face was bruised and marked. His fingers broken. I had a thing for broken digits. Everyone needed a brand.

He stopped in front of me. "Please! Please, don't do this!"

"Beg." Drac shoved him forward.

Mikey's legs buckled underneath him and he dropped to the ground ten yards in front of me. The crowd quieted.

"She tricked me, man! I didn't know who she was! It was an honest mistake! I'm sorry."

Sorries, mistakes. I didn't have wiggle room for those notions.

"We don't talk to outsiders. We don't talk business to nobody."

My voice boomed over the buzz of the fire. "Fucking simple. You don't get it. You never will. Your weakness and your vanity put our club at risk."

"Please!"

"We are one percenters, boy, and that isn't some clever label. But it seems you didn't realize that on the other side of that coin, we are one-hundred percent in with all our blood, all our fire. We are the fire. That takes strength and character that you obviously don't have."

Drac handed me our old Marlin 1894. Murmurs rolled through the crowd at the appearance of the long rifle.

Mikey shuffled back on his feet, stumbling onto his back. "No! Please! I'll do anything! Anything you want! Please."

"There's no coming back from this shit. The damage is done. You're useless to me now. You're fucking scum."

I raised the Marlin and aimed at his face, my heart quieting; an odd quiet, a noiseless hush I relished. I took in a slight breath, and that satisfaction zipped through me, streamlining, focusing my every sense on my target, on the perfect weight of the firearm in my hands.

I snapped the lever down and pulled the trigger. The explosion silenced everything, the vibration shuddering through my shoulder, my arm, my chest. Mikey's body jerked back, quickly dropping in a pile. That split second of sweet ferocity possessed me, sating me.

There was a hush in the courtyard, except for the fire in the pit. Those flames roared and leapt to the drum of my heartbeat. I pitched the Marlin back at Drac who caught it with a lift of his chin.

I let out a whistle and Leper trotted to my side, head raised, eyes on me. "There's my boy." I rubbed his head, and his tail wagged back and forth.

Catch stood alone at a distance, his eyes on what was left of his prospect, a brooding expression on his face. Members took turns kicking and smacking at the lifeless body in the yard, until they lost interest.

The party took on a life of its own. The corpse was finally gotten rid of and forgotten.

41

LENORE

Bᴇᴄᴋ ʜᴀᴅ ᴄʜᴀɴɢᴇᴅ ᴇᴠᴇʀʏᴛʜɪɴɢ ꜰᴏʀ me.

He was my precious miracle, and I was a mama bear wanting to cuddle with her cub in a quiet cave all our own and experience the world again through him. Spending time with Beck was satisfying, and fulfilled a part of me that had been empty for so long. He was my center, my joy. I could let go of my many fragments of unhappiness by focusing on him and his happiness.

Eric and I separated, and he and Pam got married within months of the divorce. I can't say it didn't hurt, it did, but I was glad he was happy. Pam quit cheerleading, opened a children's dance studio in Brentwood and had a baby girl the following year. A part of me envied Eric and Pam's getting on with it and moving full steam ahead with their lives.

Although I enjoyed my work as a stylist and wardrobe designer, I decided I wanted something other than the LA rat race for me and my boy. All that celebrity crap and the constant shifting waves of what was trendy and what was not didn't intrigue me the way it had initially. Eric let me have the house in Rapid where I stayed and raised Beck. I'd grown to love the area. Rapid City was an odd combination of mountain city with desert sand. Beck and I enjoyed hiking and exploring in the Black Hills. The dense, sweet, earthy smell in the air from the variety of evergreens, the dirt actually shining and shimmering from the mica were magical to us. It was our special corner of the world.

At home, I designed and made my own clothing line, a few expensive pieces both formal and more funky casual, and sold them in LA via trunk shows and through stylist friends, especially Kelly who had gone on to great success. Whenever I was back in LA to bring Beck to see his dad for winter break or the summer, I'd stay for several weeks and network with Kelly's help.

From the beginning it was obvious that Beck was a born musician. Playing the guitar and the piano were instinctive for him. He had an ear for music, and he composed and played all the time even before he started taking formal lessons. His talent was something special, something beyond an ordinary aptitude. He wanted to follow in his dad's footsteps, and I knew deep in my gut he would surpass his dad's level of artistry, and hopefully, success.

Eric was doing well as a producer based in LA. Whenever Beck visited him, he went with his dad to work and met lots of people and saw how the industry operated. The music business became second nature to him.

After finishing junior high in Rapid, Beck auditioned for an arts high school in LA. He was over the moon when he got it, and Eric and I were so proud. Beck moved to his dad's in California, and I endured an empty nest much too early. I desperately missed my son, but I wouldn't deny him his dream. I would never do that. It was his time. It was also the way of parenthood, wasn't it?

I needed to focus on moving ahead with my own life and work.

I took the plunge and sold the house in Rapid and bought a much smaller one in Meager. Meager was small, quiet, an old pioneer settlement in the Black Hills that had seen better days when ranchers and farmers were more plentiful in these parts. There was a sense of comfort to me that this was Tania and Grace's hometown, even though neither of them lived here any longer. The town seemed sleepy and worn around the edges, yet there were signs of some renewal. We were a good fit.

With the extra money from the sale of the house, I opened my own store on the main street of town. My shop was one of the first new businesses to open up on Clay Street after decades of the traditional stores dying a slow quiet death. The pre-war general store had eventually become the five and dime and now, it too had been silenced. Only a post-war family-owned gas station and Peppers, the Western boot shop that had served generations of families, remained sturdy fixtures. A diner that still had tables and chairs from the fifties had closed recently and then quickly reopened as a trendy coffee house complete with freshly made baked goods. The locals loved it, and so did I.

Meager began to get noticed on visitors' tours through the Black Hills, especially during Sturgis Rally time. Younger families were moving in, and the town seemed to be on an upswing.

Opening a store was a risk I was willing to take. Hell, the rent was very low to begin with. My own boutique with my own designs was a dream come true. I started out with clothing for special nights out, hoping to attract a lot of the thirty-somethings who were looking for something different and had the money to spend. The bulk of my stock was loungewear—robes, sexy pajamas, slip dresses, a few unique accessories and the lingerie.

I'd kept working on corsets. I loved working on cut and silhouette and also the finer details, the fastenings, the decoration. Every time I was back in LA I'd find amazing new fabrics and forged relationships with the suppliers. My focus veered to creating lingerie—fantasies of delicacy and the sublime, intimacy come to life.

The first month I saw next to no business. One afternoon, as I lit a cinnamon incense stick on the small table I had in the center of the store, a tall, attractive, African American woman strode in. She was beautiful—long sleek black hair, no makeup except for deep red lipstick. I blinked. Naomi Campbell had nothing on her.

"Isn't this a novelty?" she said in a velvety voice full of genuine wonder as she explored the boutique, her gaze darting over every display.

"I suppose it is for Meager," I replied.

She admired a corset and matching robe on an antique mannequin torso dress form. "I've never seen anything like it." She eyed the colorful hanging gauzy material I had decorated the store with to create a sensual and out of the ordinary ambiance. "And I'm from Milwaukee, meaning a big city, not from around here."

"What brought you here?"

"Work. I manage the Tingle, the adult entertainment club in town."

I'd heard that the Tingle was owned by the One-Eyed Jacks.

"I hear it does very well," I said. "Good for you."

"Thank you, yes, business is good." She smiled again, her beautiful face beaming a genuine sincerity that warmed my insides. "I'm Cassandra, by the way."

"Good to meet you, Cassandra. I'm Lenore."

"You just opened, right? How's business so far?" Her fingers slid up and down a diaphanous purple robe.

"Like you said, I'm a novelty. They come in to gawk at my goodies and at me."

She turned, her light brown eyes finding mine. "When I first got here, I was a novelty too, but the people in this town are welcoming, maybe a bit reserved at first. In this store, you're offering something brand new, something they really want deep inside. Temptation on the edge of illicit." She let out a small, rich laugh.

"I like the way you think."

"I like your style."

I like this woman.

Cassandra tried on a variety of bras and nighties. She bought my most elegant push up bra and panty set made of burnt gold lace which looked incredible on her sleek cocoa skin. She took a handful of my business cards. "I'm going to pass these out to the girls at the club and a few friends."

"I custom make pieces too. I can go as demure or as kinky as a client likes."

"Always good." She took her shopping bag from me. "I enjoyed this. We should get together for a drink sometime."

"I'd love that." I walked her to the door.

The next day, a platinum blonde around my age, wearing huge black sunglasses and pale lip gloss strode in. She glittered. Standing in the center of my shop, she slid her glasses up over her head and scanned every piece in the boutique, every panty, every bra, every corset, robe, baby doll, every sex toy. I kept on trend. A consumer demand for erotica was blossoming for a variety of items that once could only be found in sleazy sex shops or catalogs.

"Hi there," I said.

She scanned me from the top of my blue and purple dyed hair, down my form fitting cropped top and low slung harem pants to my high-heeled sandals. "Tell me you're Lenore."

"I am."

"I'm Alicia."

"Welcome."

"I'm pinching myself here. I've been waiting for you to open."

"I've been open for about a month now."

"I've been out of town for a few weeks. My mom had cataract surgery. She lives in Texas."

"Oh. She okay?"

"She's fine." Alicia swished her long, straight, blonde hair as she moved by the table littered with colorful wisps of panties, the stands with bras dangling from them like overgrown blossoms. "Cassandra called me last night and told me how special your store is. I had to come see for myself."

"Are you looking for anything in particular? If you'd like to try anything on, please do."

She fingered a bustier, checked the label. "You made this?"

"I did. My design."

Her blue eyes lit up. "I want to try them all on."

She did.

Two hours and two cups of mint tea later, Alicia bought a bralette, a bustier, and a slip nightie. She paid in cash. "I'll be bringing my girlfriends here."

"Thank you."

"I like your tattoos, by the way. Did you get them done around here?"

"A couple of them, yes. I went to Ronny's in Deadwood. Do you know him?"

"Oh, did you?" She grinned, a well groomed eyebrow lifting. The Cheshire cat would have been proud. "Ronny is the best. He did mine. He does all of ours."

"Your family?"

"Yeah, the club."

"Ah."

Was Alicia a One-Eyed Jacks old lady? Meager was their home base. I'd seen them around town on occasion, of course, but I hadn't met any. They weren't a huge multinational institution like the Smoking Guns or the Flames of Hell. Only three chapters from what I'd heard, and not as over the edge outlaw either, although that was relative, of course. They were definitely less ostentatious, more low-key.

Their clubhouse was on the outskirts of town, tucked behind a small patch of woods and a rise of the Black Hills. I didn't feel antsy about being in the same area as a bike club anymore. Med was dead and gone. I'd read about it in a newspaper article a while back. His throat had been slit, his body found in a motel dumpster. Whoever had done it had wanted his corpse to be found and for the good news to be known far and wide. Had it been Finger? Had he been the Reaper, or had Med just pissed off the wrong person at long last, a person who would lash back? Whoever it was, the knowledge had me sleeping better at night.

Alicia snapped her oversized leather handbag shut. "I'm the president's old lady."

President's old lady. I gritted my teeth at the sound of that phrase. Alicia loved her position, her title. "Well, it was great to meet you, Alicia."

"You too, hon. I'll be back with the rest of the girls to show them what you've got."

I handed her the purple shopping bag with her purchases which I'd wrapped in lilac colored tissue paper. "Look forward to it."

Alicia was true to her word. She came back two days later with Mary Lynn, Dee, and Suzy, all One-Eyed Jack old ladies. They oo-hed and ahed, tried on plenty of items and purchased a number of them.

"I need these velvet cuffs in my life," Dee said, adding them to her bra and panty set by my cash register. "I love surprising Judge whenever possible."

"That's the way. Good for you," I said, ringing up her purchases.

Alicia and her friends became frequent visitors. They often came by the store for tea and a laugh. We went out frequently for ladies only get togethers at the local bar, Pete's Tavern, and for terrific meals and wine at the restaurant of the newly opened vineyard in nearby Hill City, which I always enjoyed.

Potential customers began to come into the store more regularly. At first they treated the shop like a museum, then I'd invite them to sit on my lemon yellow sofa and share a cup of tea with me and a chat. Soon enough, I noticed the change come over the ladies when they'd spot pieces they liked. The initial moments of denial would fade, and then there was—"Maybe I can be this." Then they'd try a piece on and that look of "oh wow, I feel good in this. I could rock this. Yes, yes, dammit, yes."

I enjoyed those moments myself, and I loved providing that speedy joy for others. Like beautiful frosting on a cupcake that you want to admire yet lick into at the very same time. A secret, often sinful treat that gave you a lift, that changed your perception of you. That beauty and joy all started on the inside, as far as I was concerned.

I wanted women to feel beautiful in their skin when they saw and felt their bodies being adorned by these webs of color and texture. Sleek or flowing, graceful or edgy, every piece came from my imagination. Like what the tattoos on my body did for me, I wanted to provide women with possibilities for their unique beauty and sensuality, and for them to revel in that glory. A glory they usually weren't in touch with, had little or no awareness of, or simply denied. The bulk of my inventory quickly became lingerie. "Lenore's Lace" had come into its own.

Cassandra encouraged me to advertise, and I came up with a marketing idea—another step in my liberation and transformation. I hired a photographer, who Ronny suggested, and had him take sexy shots of me wearing my pieces. We shot one day in my store, and another out in the woods with the autumn leaves as an amazing backdrop. It was freezing cold, but so worth it.

"I love them!" Mary Lynn said over coffee at the Meager Grand Cafe down the block. She shuffled through the proofs I'd brought with me to show everyone. "You are quite the wildcat—look at this one, you guys, prowling through the forest on all fours hunting down her man."

Cassandra laughed. "Damn, look at that. Roar, baby."

Alicia took off her reading glasses. "Why didn't you show that beautiful face of yours in any of these? It's a crime to keep your face hidden in every shot. My God, your eyes, woman! Your ass is certainly a holy gift, don't get me wrong, and your legs, your back, but—"

"Right? What workout do you do? I need to know," said Dee.

"I've been doing yoga for years." I jumped on Dee's question, avoiding Alicia's. "But I really like the Cardio Pump and Burn class Craig teaches at his studio down the street. Being a former stunt-man, he totally knows what he's doing."

"Ugh, I'm too chicken to take that class," said Dee.

"No thanks. Pilates and running for me," murmured Cassandra.

"We have a treadmill in the garage, but I keep forgetting to use it. Kicker loves reminding me that I was the one who insisted we spend the money on it." Mary Lynn rolled her eyes.

"Why don't you tag along with me and try Craig's class, Dee? You're going to feel on top of the world after, I promise," I said, sipping my double espresso with a hit of cream.

"Okay, you're on," said Dee.

"How can you not have a man, for Pete's sake?" asked Mary Lynn. "You must be fighting them off."

"We can introduce you to a few men," Dee said.

"That's all right. Really," I replied.

"You don't like bikers?" Dee laughed. "Golly, why?"

"I had a biker boyfriend once," I said. "First love. Didn't end well."

"Really? Which club?" asked Mary Lynn.

I ignored Mary Lynn's question. "I was sixteen, ran away from home with him, lots of fun, lots of trouble, then he took off with someone else."

"What a jerk, sorry," said Dee.

I shrugged. "Real life."

Alicia studied me, her fingers stroking the handle of her coffee mug. I averted my gaze and focused on Mary Lynn's lively chatter.

"Well, that's all right," Mary Lynn said. "We know tattoo artists, rodeo cowboys, bartenders, restaurant owners, a doctor, lawyers, a beer brewer, a landscape designer..." Her eyes danced. She was on a roll.

"I appreciate it, but don't worry about me. I'm not a nun or anything," I said.

"Oooo...Names," said Mary Lynn on a giggle.

"I've been out with Caleb from Ronny's shop a few times," I said.

Dee blinked. "Whoa, really?

"Caleb?" Cassandra said.

"Uh oh. Why?" I asked.

"Everyone tries to score with Caleb, and very few have achieved the dream," said Mary Lynn.

"I didn't realize," I said.

"Fuck," Alicia muttered. "He's so damn hot."

"He sure is," I said, winking at her.

Her lips parted, but she had no comeback.

"That hair...those biceps..." Mary Lynn murmured.

"That ass!" Dee laughed loudly.

"I think we need another round of coffee." Cassandra grinned.

"Lenore, you should come to the barbecue we're having at the club in a couple of weeks," said Dee.

"Yes, you should," said Alicia.

I swirled the last of my coffee in the mug. "I don't know."

"It'll just be our chapter, families only. Nothing too crazy," said Dee.

Mary Lynn rolled her eyes. "Yeah, never is."

I liked these women. I liked them a lot. I didn't have many friends here in town. A number of casual acquaintances, but not real friends. However, I didn't want to go to a club party, family style or no.

"That's real sweet of you guys."

I would come up with of some sort of plausible last minute excuse and not go.

That's what I did best.

OVER FOUR YEARS HAD PASSED, and I had settled into Meager very nicely. I enjoyed the quiet. I was designing and creating at my own pace, paying my bills, and had made good friends. Social media was beginning to explode, and I took advantage, bettering my business online.

One afternoon Alicia came to the store with a friend I hadn't met before. "Lenore, this is Grace." Alicia removed her sunglasses, gesturing at Grace who stood stiffly at her side. "She's an old friend from the club who's back in town. She needs a pick me up, and I'm treating her today."

Tania's best friend, the Grace I'd been hearing about for years and years, the woman whose heartbreak had been emotional signposts along my own path.

A slight smile passed over Grace's slim face. She was tired. Her clouded hazel eyes shifted around the store, taking in the swags of multicolored gossamer fabric that flowed down from the walls, the large piece of handmade stained glass hanging in the front window which filled the boutique with jewel-colored light.

"What a beautiful store," she murmured.

"Thank you."

I assessed her figure and quickly pulled pieces for her to try on, and she did so quietly. Alicia kept chattering though, more than usual. She pointed out a few kinkier pieces for Grace to try, but Grace refused. In fact, she didn't say much at all, but Alicia took no mind.

Something was off.

Grace decided on a few items, and Alicia paid for them. Grace thanked me, taking the shopping bag I handed her, and quickly exited the store. She went out to Alicia's car which was being commandeered by two One-Eyed Jacks.

"Grace came back to town recently. It's been sixteen years since she's been home," Alicia said, shoving her designer wallet back in her large handbag. "Her sister's been battling lung cancer, and she's real upset. We just came back from the hospital in Rapid, and I thought

I'd cheer her up by stopping here."

I glanced out the front window. Grace was talking on her cell phone, her body stiff.

"You're a good friend, Alicia," I said.

We moved to the doorway, Alicia telling me she wanted to organize a night out with me and Grace and the ladies, but movement on the sidewalk caught my attention. Bear, the heavy set biker in the front passenger seat, snapped out of Alicia's Cherokee, a hand on Grace's arm and guided her into the vehicle's backseat. He darted towards us, his bro in the driver's seat talking on his phone.

"Alicia, we gotta move. We got to get Grace and her nephew to the hospital right now. Shit looks bad."

"Oh dammit," murmured Alicia.

"Go, honey," I said. "Let me know."

Alicia waved absently at me as she rushed towards her car and got in. In the seat next to her, Grace only stared straight ahead. She was numb. More tragedy for this woman. Always more tragedy.

Grace's sister died the next day, and the club gathered for the funeral and burial at the town cemetery within the week. Alicia told me that Ruby had been a part of the club in the old days. She'd gotten over a drug addiction and went on to become a drug counselor, a wife and a mother to a young son. My heart ached for Ruby, for her boy who would grow up without her. So much inexplicable loss. Alicia mentioned Grace would stay in South Dakota now and help her brother-in-law raise him.

Within a few months, the gloom of this tragedy was unplugged by the good news that Grace was getting married. She was with Lock now, the Road Captain of the One-Eyed Jacks, an austerely handsome and quiet Native American. An unexpected second chance, a new bright future. What more could anyone want?

What more, indeed.

One cold winter afternoon, I walked a customer to the front door, when I saw Grace leaving Pepper's Boot Shop down the street with a huge shopping bag in her hand, a wide grin splitting her face. Her light brown waves shook over her thick leather coat as she moved quickly into the Meager Grand Cafe. The need to talk to her overwhelmed me. I flipped the "*Be right back*" sign on the front door and locked up my store.

I found her settling into a small table in front of the big bay window of the cafe, a steaming mug of frothy coffee in front of her.

"Grace, hi."

"Hey, Lenore, how are you?"

"Could I sit with you a sec?"

She sat up in the sofa. "Of course. Please."

"I heard about your engagement to Lock, and I wanted to say congratulations."

"Oh, thank you. We're really excited. It's happening fast, but when you know, you know."

My breath hitched suddenly, a coil of emotion taking me by surprise. "Absolutely."

Her head slanted a few degrees as she sipped her coffee. Had she heard the thickness in my voice?

I cleared my throat. "I don't know what you have planned for a dress and all, but I'd love to make you something special for your wedding."

"Lenore, that's so sweet of you. You don't have to—"

"Oh, I do. Please. I want to. I'd love to make your special day even more special." I took in a quick breath and steadied myself. "I love that you're getting your happily ever after. I really do." I struggled to maintain a grin, but my wobbly lips gave me away.

"Yeah, me too. Me too." She reached out and grabbed my hand. "Are you okay?"

"Yeah." I rolled my eyes, sniffing in air. "No. It doesn't matter."

"It does," she whispered, placing her other hand over mine. "It does to me."

A sense of calm came over me, looking in her eyes, feeling her strong grip on my hands. Grace Quillen was a good soul.

"I'm really happy for you, Grace. After everything you've been through, the little Alicia's told me. We don't even know each other really well, but I feel like we do."

"Maybe one day you'll tell me all about what you've been through. We think keeping it bottled up is a good thing in the beginning, that we're in control as we're picking ourselves up off the floor. But then one day you take a good hard look in the mirror, and you don't recognize the person staring back at you."

"No, you don't," I breathed. "But I'm used to her now."

Grace let go of my hand and sat back in her cushioned seat. "You know, my sister was a very wise woman. Just before she died she told me to let go of the ghosts and get on with joy. It seemed impossible to me at the time. But she was right."

"Hmm." I averted my gaze and rubbed my fingertips along the edge of a napkin that lay on the table. "If you have a minute or ten, come by my store before you head home so I can take your measurements and you can tell me about your wedding dress. Since I heard the news, I've been drawing a corset in my head for you."

She sat back and tugged her coat on once again. "Let's go. I can't wait to see what you have in mind. I'll get a cardboard cup for my coffee."

She wasn't going to push me. She knew the signs all too well.

I created a corset for Grace in a super sheer cream colored tulle decorated with intricate floral embroidery. The barely there bra was a padded silk quarter cup, and the bones and waistband of the piece were bound with smooth silk.

Three weeks later, as Grace came down the aisle of the church in Meager, holding on to her father, a slight wobble to her walk on her high heels, her figure looked divine in the elegant, strapless, pleated, off-white wedding dress she had chosen. I was thrilled to be at the wedding and witness her and Lock's happily ever after come true. Full circle.

I took in the high beamed ceiling of the old church. I didn't believe much in God. I'd never even been inside a church before this. There was never much talk about Him when I was growing up, or any reference except for the tiny gold cross my grandma wore around her neck and never took off. Sometimes I caught her murmuring to herself, hands clasped together and I'd watch her in these peculiar, intimate moments. I never asked, and she never shared, but I knew it was special to her, meaningful.

At the front of the church, Grace and Lock exchanged vows and rings under the guidance of a pastor. All their friends and family leaned forward, listening, participating in the ritual. Simple, beautiful. A stop in the daily grind of life to be thankful, and to mark that thanks forever with a blessing.

There was a strange harmony at work in the world to have gotten me here to this very place with these people.

I clasped my hands together like Grandma used to do. "Thank you," I whispered. I scanned the crowd. I had braced myself for seeing Tania at the wedding, but she wasn't here. I'd been looking forward to it, actually. I missed her. I missed Beck, I missed—

My gaze caught on a pair of velvety brown eyes that smiled at me.

Tricky.

I returned his smile.

Tricky was a One-Eyed Jack who worked with Lock at the club's car and bike repair shop. He had a thick mass of dark hair which usually fell in his brown eyes, giving him a sultry, but innocent look. I squirmed on the pew. He was maybe fifteen years my junior which put him in his late twenties. Whenever we saw each other, our exchanges usually segued into flirting.

After the ceremony, the celebration continued at Dead Ringer's Roadhouse, a historic and favorite biker haunt off the highway in between Rapid and Meager. Once she arrived, Grace immediately tossed her high-heeled sandals at me, Dee, and Alicia, and gleefully slid on her new western boots Dee had ready for her in a shopping bag. Grace jumped to her feet with a loud, exultant "Yes!" Lock came behind her and swept her up in his arms, kissing her hard as he took her over to the huge dance floor. We whistled, clapped and hooted as they took their first dance as husband and wife.

We drank, we danced, sang along to old and new hits. I met Grace's dad and her brother-in-law, Alex. I explained a couple of my tattoos along the insides of my fingers to her adorable nephew, Jake.

"Hey, Lenore."

I swiveled around in my seat. "Hey, Tricky."

Up close, Tricky inspired a little flutter in my tummy. Along with his toned body, he had a weary swagger to his step which gave his cute features a harder edge. He wiped his hair back as he settled into the chair next to mine. A white scar gleamed on his forehead, a scar from a knife fight when he was a prospect from what Mary Lynn had mentioned to me. Cute met sexy on a ledge.

"You having fun?" he asked.

"I'm having a great time. You?"

"Me too. You look fantastic, by the way." His gaze trailed down my body.

"Thank you." I crossed my legs, revealing them in the long split up my midnight blue dress that had a halter top along with a tiny silver shrug.

His finger traced over the skin of my shoulder, revealed by the thin cashmere shrug that had fallen back. I held his molten gaze.

"Aren't you warm?" he asked.

"Getting there."

"Oh yeah?"

I giggled. "Yeah."

He leaned in closer to me, his lips tipping up into a grin, inches from my own. "How about I help get you there?"

It had been a while since I'd kissed a man, been touched, had sex. I would indulge in the odd one night stand here or there, when the mood struck, when I'd meet someone I was attracted to. But that was that, and I preferred it that way. Uncomplicated. Live it, then keep moving on. Leave nothing behind.

After my divorce I was mentally exhausted, and I'd decided to not get emotionally involved again. I didn't have anything to give anyhow. Ask Eric. It was just as well. My heart was a particular bitch. I couldn't kid myself about that.

Tricky's coffee brown eyes gleamed at me, not in a predatory way, though. Eager. Anticipating.

"I bet you would," I replied, my fingertips tracing his jawline.

He kissed me, and I kissed him back. Tequila and beer flavored my tongue from the warm, slick slide of his. Arousal pitched inside me.

His hand went down my side, curving gently over my lower back, heating my flesh through the thin material of my dress. "Dance with me," he whispered against my ear, and a shiver shimmied over my skin.

I rose from my chair, and taking his hand in mine, led him to the dance floor. We stayed close for the rest of the evening. Hours later, he took me home, and like overheated teenagers, we made out in his Jeep the second he'd parked in my driveway.

I pulled back and opened the car door to the icy cold winter night. "Let's go inside."

"You sure?"

"I'm sure." I grinned, slamming the car door.

I unlocked my house, tossed the keys on the console table and released the straps of my dress letting it slide down my body to the floor.

He let out a low groan at the sight of me in my lacy silky underthings. "Holy fuck."

"Oh, I hope so."

"Oh, I'll make sure of it."

He lifted me up in his arms, kissing me as he held me, walking us over to my sofa. He laid me down, bending to kiss me.

I pushed at his chest with my knee and he stumbled back. "Take your clothes off."

His eyes flared, his body went rigid. He grinned and did as he was told.

"Uh-uh." I said. "Slowly." My hand slid between my legs and he let out a groan, the muscles of his torso contracting.

He went slower.

"Hmm. Like that." I enjoyed the revelation of his body as he took off his clothes, one piece at a time, his eyes intent on me.

Tricky was hot, and I was in need.

Naked, he hovered over me, pushing my legs apart.

I took in a breath. No qualms, no regrets. Good times.

Or so I thought.

42
FINGER

"WHAT THE HELL IS THAT?" My voice came out louder than I expected.

On the wall of the bar area where tens of other T&A shots beckoned, Drac tacked up an eighty by ten poster of a woman's curvy body, her hands clutching her breasts, torso twisted to the side, ass revealed in a sexy panty made up of a web of straps. The photo cut off right at her chin. Winding colored vines of thorns and flowers, tiny winged creatures, numbers, fancy writing were inked all over the woman's skin.

My chest tightened, the blood backwashed through my veins.

"Tell me you don't like it." Drac bit down on a piece of tape. *Rip.* "It's an ad for this underwear store in Meager. Krystal went there and she brought this back for me along with some mighty nice lace numbers. Smoking, huh?" His hand smoothed over the model's raised ass and down the back of her thighs. His hand lifted and the name of the store declared itself in gothic lettering.

I stared at the photo, staring at the vine down the back of her left thigh that was made of tiny linked letter J's and baby rosebuds. A vine I'd licked countless times a century ago. It was my vine. Mine.

"In Meager?" I asked.

Drac rolled the tape on his fingers, admiring his new acquisition. "Yeah, in Meager."

Last I'd heard she was in Rapid City.

Years ago, while setting up the WiFi and a new printer in my office, Den had logged on to some celebrity gossip site as he worked. He'd groaned about how the lead guitarist from Cruel Fate, a band he knew, was getting a divorce. Den often worked at local music festivals as his brother owned a security company. He'd worked with Cruel Fate at many gigs in the area.

"What an idiot," Den had said. "His wife is fucking hot. His bit on the side, not so much."

After Den had left the room, I'd gone online and typed the fuck's name in the search engine: E-R-I-C and Cruel Fate. The divorce came up right away. They'd filed in California, citing "irreconcilable differences." The article mentioned that Eric had a new girlfriend, complete with a photo of him and a smiley young blonde with lots of makeup boarding his tour bus together. The reporter noted that Eric's wife had been at home all along with their young son. A small inset photo of a woman with a hoodie over her green and blue hair wearing huge sunglasses, holding close to her chest a young boy who wore a baseball cap, a protective hand around the back of his small head, had lasered onto my brain. I'd recognize those long, bony fingers anywhere, the perfect oval of her face, the grim pull of her mouth, taut and resolute against all odds.

My Serena.

The wife was claiming their house in Rapid City as her own, and had left the rock star to his LA digs.

Lenore had put a lot of goddamn effort into sealing me out. Building walls, digging trenches, filling those trenches with boiling oil, lining the surrounding fields with mines, setting fires, exhaling thick black smoke. She'd abandoned the smoldering battlefield. And at some point, so had I. But her "normal" life had detonated and shattered. She was alone again and in Meager, not two hours away, closer than ever before. I took in a deep, long breath as if the quality of the air had changed suddenly, and I needed to take it in slowly, carefully, not sure how my body would respond.

"Hey, Prez." Slade was at my side. "Butler's waiting for you in your office."

My eyes traced every detail of that thigh, that round ass, that—

"Finger?" Drac looked at me funny.

Scowling, I headed for my office. Butler's icy blue eyes snagged on mine as I settled in my chair.

After Dig got murdered and I'd gotten out of jail, Butler had reached out to me, and we'd tried being cooperative the way Dig had once envisioned for our clubs—that "velvet network." But once Jump had taken over as President of the Jacks in South Dakota, he'd put a cold, hard stop to it.

Butler had risen to become President of the One-Eyed Jacks chapter in North Dakota, but almost a year ago, he'd resigned and taken off, tail between his legs, for being hopped up on coke and unable to lead like a President should, not to mention, making under the table deals with the Demon Seeds. He'd gone Nomad, doing freelance work for his club. He and I had kept in touch, and kept each other on top of shit in our region.

A hard grin tilted his lips. "Hey man, how are you?"

"I want to nail Creeper's ass to the wall and then blow his brains out," I replied.

Butler let out a gust of air. "I've been on his trail. He's as slippery as a—"

"I called you here to find him, Butler. He needs to die. He's been playing both sides of every fence between the Jacks, the Blades, and the Demon Seeds since he took off from your club. He was a useful rat in the beginning, but now he kidnapped one of my brother's kids, a baby, 'cause he didn't get what he wanted. Unacceptable. Insane."

Creeper had been pissed late last night that he hadn't gotten the payment he'd felt he'd deserved from Catch on a minor freelance job. Catch had called him on his shit, played hardball, and Creeper didn't like it. He'd made threats. This morning, Catch and Jill's daughter, Becca, had gone missing when one of the club girls had taken her into town for a ride in her stroller.

"I agree with you, completely on board." Butler ran a hand

through his newly shorn blond hair. "But Creeper is still a One-Eyed Jack, and I need to be the one to grab him and bring him in to my club first. That fucker is still wearing our colors, and I'm going to be the one to recover them."

"Damn straight. You want to score points with your Prez now. I get that." I picked up my Digi-Flex, a hand held exercise unit with separate buttons for each finger to individually compress. Working with it over the years had done wonders for developing isolated finger strength in my hands and maintaining my flexibility. Rubber stress balls were still a favorite, and I always had one handy, but this gizmo offered more intensity. Today was a very stressful day. A kidnapped child wasn't enough, my eyes were still burning from seeing Drac's fucking poster.

Butler's gaze darted to my hand working the Digi-Flex. "I know it isn't going to be easy with Jump." He shifted in his seat, twisting his lips.

He always looked uncomfortable when discussing Jump, the president of the Jacks. Butler wanted back into his club real bad, and Jump was going to make him "jump" through rings of fire to do it.

"You Jacks have had it rough for a while now. You had the Demon Seeds breathing down your necks, wanting to take you over, then the fucking Russians were salivating over all our territory."

Butler exhaled a thick stream of smoke. "Everyone wants a piece of the same pie."

"There are rules, or none of this works," I spit out. "These smaller links keep falling apart, it makes the heavy chain weak. We got the Mexicans watching us, dangling carrots in front of our usual clients. My contacts in South America are getting nervous. It's only a matter of time before all of us start losing money. I ain't having it for my club." I slammed the Digi-Flex down on my desk. "And now the Broken Blades just south of here, on my fucking backdoor, are all restless and full of attitude, disrespecting borders."

"Well, Notch thinks he can play mercenary and get away with it," Butler said, lighting another cigarette. "He's been making our life difficult in Colorado down through Texas. Shit's got to stop. The Blades aren't what they used to be. Business hasn't been going so good for them from what I've seen. Plus, they've gotten sloppy. Last month, a whole chapter of theirs in Montana got wiped out with arrests. They're grabbing at straws."

He eyed me as he inhaled deeply on his smoke.

"Their President refused every one of my demands for respect," I said. "He didn't like my proposal for them to patch in now that his numbers are way down and his reach isn't what it used to be."

"Notch is an arrogant asshole, but hey, he's protecting his club."

I held his icy blue gaze. "I want the Blades put down once and for all."

Butler took a deep drag and put out his cigarette as he gnawed on his lips. "You won't have any complaints from the Jacks on that score."

"I want Creeper gone."

"That fuck couldn't have gotten far with the kid. I've been checking in with your men every ten minutes. I'm going to get back out there."

My eyes darted to the main room where Jill, Catch's old lady, sat with Drac's old lady, drinking coffee and wiping tears from her red eyes. I had to hand it to Jill, she was keeping it together. I'd promised her I'd get Becca back, and I would. We were talking about a two year old baby here. This was beyond fucked up. Who the hell kidnaps a tiny little girl? A fucking sociopath. Catch's loud voice shouting in the courtyard seeped into my office.

His agony over his daughter hit home in a way I didn't want to admit. In a way that made my insides snap.

After Tania and I had stopped seeing each other, I'd hooked up with Rachel. She was good looking, put up with me in and out of bed, and we got along fine. We'd been together for a few months when she'd gotten pregnant and hinted that she wanted to get married. But I didn't want to get married; I wouldn't let myself go there again.

But the baby. Oh, the baby.

In her fourth month, Rachel had a miscarriage. Turns out she had some blood condition that didn't let her carry to full term. She hadn't known, and hadn't gone to a doctor soon enough. Afterwards, she'd gone off the deep end, and I didn't know how to help her. I couldn't respond. I felt helpless, numb.

Having a child was a secret hope I'd had with Serena and then it had failed, and I'd had to ignore it. Crush it. With Rachel's pregnancy, that hope had inflated again like a big red balloon. With the miscarriage, that balloon had popped loudly, its shredded remains littering the floor around us. If only I'd paid enough attention. If only…

If only a hell of a lot of shit.

Rachel had plummeted into a depression, started using. One night I tried to shake her out of her daze, literally shake her. She slapped me, shoved at my chest muttering all sorts of angry words. I'd grabbed her hand, stopping her, but then I asked myself, why are you stopping her? She's right. You're a concrete wall, that's what you are. I'd let go of her hand, and she punched and slapped me, kicking at me, yelling at me to leave her alone until she fell into a heap of tears on the bed. In the end her sister had come and taken her home, and I never saw or heard from her again.

I'd been kidding myself with Rachel, and she'd known it. I saw it in her eyes plenty of times, that wash of sadness, a submission to futility in the face of my barren landscape which, for her, would ultimately yield nothing.

Plenty of my bros had children. Many of them were devoted husbands and dads, and many weren't so devoted. Either way they had their own families. I'd once wanted that for myself.

Once.

Once it had been a dream, a goal, a burning desire. But all of that was wrapped up in Serena without any beginning or end, and even though there was no more Serena, there was no way to unravel it.

And I didn't want to. I was that stubborn. As stubborn as the prairie grasses that grew and grew, season in, season out.

Seeing Lenore pregnant with another man's kid in her belly was a sledgehammer slamming down on me. I'd chewed on shards of glass at the sight of her that day and then months later when I'd seen her in Rapid and she confirmed the boy wasn't mine. I'd tried to move on with other women, especially with Rachel. She'd been the last relationship. But after the miscarriage, I'd shoved the whole idea over the side of the table like some china platter, and it shattered into a thousand unrecognizable pieces. I would never be a father. I would never have my own family.

Catch had become a father, and it had made him stand up straighter. For all his swagger and personal crazy, he melted every time he saw Becca, and I liked that for him. I was glad for him.

I eyed Butler. "You get out there, find Creeper, bring him to me so I can have my fun with him, then do whatever the fuck you want and impress Jump with the leftovers."

A grin lit up his face. He relished the opportunity. "I'm going to get this done and get back to Ohio. Reich liked the job I did for him last month. Said he has other shit on the back burner he wants me to take care of."

"Oh, yeah?" I ground down on my teeth to control the charge of excitement that flickered through me.

I had sent Butler in Reich's path months ago and it was paying off.

Turo and I had continued to work together over the years. Our business alliance remained secret, the way we both preferred. It worked for us, and filled my chapter's vault with cash and maintained a firewall of protection from small fry interference throughout the Midwest stretching toward the East Coast.

He'd killed Med and sent me a photo of the fucker's mangled body. I'd celebrated by taking off and riding through the Sandhills of northwestern Nebraska to deal with the volatile emotions that had erupted through me at the sight of that picture. Riding the banked turns, the sweeping hills, the hidden descending curves on that road was a better high than any drug or booze. That's what made me feel alive, focused. At night the stars there can shine bright enough to cast a shadow over the grass covered ancient sand dunes. There I cleared my head, alone.

Turo also kept his eyes on Reich for me. Even sent a whore on his payroll to get close to him, and she did. She'd told Turo all about Reich's scarred dick, in fact. Although Reich had a wife, that hadn't stopped him from having plenty of action on the side, and Turo's Chandra became one of his favorite girlfriends. She reported back to Turo on his movements, his disappearances. Disappearances that

I'd tried to trace, but without much luck.

Finally, Reich took Chandra with him on a quick weekend getaway to Atlantic City that was really a business meeting with a local Jersey mobster. Chandra took photos. I made sure those connections went south for him with Turo's help—deliveries not made, promises broken, goods stolen, destroyed. Reich's reputation suffered. We let him have a few victories in between, and then tore him back down again. Eventually, Chandra let Reich's wife know about all the wild sex she was having with her old man, then Turo pulled her and Chandra disappeared from Reich's life. Reich looked over his shoulder all the time now, a permanent sneer on his mug.

"I got something for you," Turo had told me over the phone a couple of months ago. "There's a connection I can't place between Reich and a Tantucci." The Tantuccis were a rival crime family in Chicago.

"The Flames of Hell don't work with the Tantuccis. Never have," I said.

"I know. This Tantucci Reich talks to is connected to a state senator. Reich was spotted with this senator at a hotel in Michigan of all places. Brief. But it was a meeting. I'm digging, but you should dig too."

"Will do."

That was when I'd urged Butler toward Reich, and Butler had played it well, offering Reich his services under the radar of his club as well as mine. A nomad wasn't supposed to do a job for another club without permission from his own. Butler's reputation appealed to Reich though, so they both took the risk of bending the rules.

After his move to Ohio, Reich had set his sights on a position at the national level, and he'd succeeded. I wanted to slice him wide open, and I needed someone unattached to me and my club to do the dredging, and Butler was the perfect choice. Butler was no stranger to the subtle, the underhanded, the risky.

"Reich likes me," Butler said, his light blue eyes gleaming, that cocky grin of his tilting his lips. "As much as he can like anyone."

"Yeah, he pats you on the back with one hand, holds the knife over your head with the other."

Butler knocked his head back and laughed. "That's right."

"And don't you forget it."

He held my gaze. "I won't. As soon as I secure Creeper, and get back to Ohio and finalize a few details with Reich, I should have something for you. I'll be in touch. After that, I plan on heading back to Meager, to the Jacks."

"Good luck with that."

"Yeah, I'm working on it."

"You waiting on Jump to roll out the red carpet for you?"

"Well, some kind of carpet, yeah."

Butler was clever, a sneaky fuck in the past. Just cause he was sober now, could I be sure that he wouldn't stab me in the back with Reich somehow?

I stretched out my legs, crossing my arms. "You know, before the white man got to this area, the Native Americans used to burn large sections of land to divert the deer, elk, and the buffalo for easier hunting, driving the animals where they wanted them. A selective use of fire. Fire as destroyer, but fire as creator. Purposeful. That way they got rid of the brush and the tall trees, creating the wide stretches of prairie we got today."

"Huh. Didn't know. I like that," Butler said, packing his cigarettes and lighter back in his pocket.

"That's what I'm looking to accomplish here, Butler. That's my ultimate endgame. A stretch of prairie, animals who heed. Nobody's immune to flames. You get too close, you get burned."

Butler stilled, his jaw tightened. "I want the best for my club, Finger. I'm killing myself out there to make sure that happens, and you know it. I'm not interested in double crossing you in any way. This—what we have here, you and me—" he tapped two fingers on my desk. "—I'm respecting it, and it stays between us. Too much is at stake."

I picked up my Digi-Flex once more. "A hell of a lot is at stake. And you can either be a part of that purposeful fire or get destroyed by it yourself."

43

FINGER

LOUD VOICES AND RUSHING FOOTSTEPS echoed in the main room just beyond my office.

Slade leaned his head in, rapping his knuckles on my office door. "Prez, two women just showed up with Catch's kid."

I turned and scanned the security monitors at my side, Butler behind me.

"What the hell?" Butler muttered.

My pulse picked up. Tania stood in the center of the main room. She was with another woman in a baseball cap pulled down low, who held Catch's daughter. Jill flew over and took Becca from the woman's arms. Tania spoke with her brother as the main room filled up with Flames and their women relieved to see Becca safe.

Tania was here at my compound and under emergency circumstances. I hadn't seen her in over ten years or spoken to her since I'd called her about her brother prospecting. I'd checked in on her once, twice, and found out she'd gotten married and then left Chicago for Racine, Wisconsin.

She was older now, yet even more attractive than before. There was a sharp confidence in the way she held herself, but she seemed tired and strung out; she was coming down from an experience. Stern-faced, telling her little brother what for, pulling no punches. The two of them had been estranged for years from what little Catch had told me. I'd never let on I knew his sister.

That was over now.

I listened to their conversation. Tania and her friend had happened to cross paths with Creeper at some junkyard not too far from here. He'd held them hostage, but the women had managed to knock him out. My muscles tightened at her description of Creeper assaulting her and threatening them and little Becca.

Tania at the mercy of that fuck. All this time of keeping her on the sidelines, and now, years later, she got touched by Flames business.

Her friend was keeping quiet, body language pulled together. It was perfectly natural for a civilian woman to be anxious at our clubhouse. She and Tania shared a quick, knowing look. There was something familiar about her face.

She was no civilian.

It was Grace, Dig's widow. Catch knew her too from his childhood, but I was sure he hadn't seen her in years, and he was too emotional now with Becca safe to notice much else.

"Did you call the cops?" asked Catch, his eyes on Jill, who kissed and held their daughter, tears running down her face as she murmured to the baby.

"No," replied Tania. "We asked Creeper why he'd taken the baby, and your name came up. I would've called you, but my battery died, and I don't know your number by heart."

"Appreciate it, Tan," he said.

Tania intervening once again, getting the job done. She followed her instincts and reached out. That was a fucking gift.

I stepped further into the room. "Why don't you two take a load off and tell us where you found the kid and more about this guy, so we can catch up with that motherfucker?" I asked.

Tania took in a tight breath, her gaze landing on me. "Hey."

A slight smile curled my lips. "Tania. Been a long while."

Grace stiffened, her lips pursing.

"Yeah." Tania's voice was low, her eyes darting to my president's patch.

We stood there, taking each other in, maybe not knowing what to say, but hell, we didn't have to say anything. It was good to see her again. Real good.

Jill and the baby reemerged from a side hallway. Two bags were slung over Jill's shoulders, Becca in her arms.

"Where you going?" Catch hollered after her.

"Are you joking? I am out of here, once and for all. I am so done. Done!" Jill yelled.

"Babe, come on now. It's over," said Catch.

"Over? It's never over!" Jill let out a shrill laugh.

Catch shook his head. This was a well-rehearsed script between these two for months now. "You need time to settle down? Take it. Nothing's over, though."

"For God's sake, Catch! Let's be real for a change. This has been over since before Becca was born. But I stuck it out. You were supposed to be watching your daughter while I was at work. You! But no! Instead, you had one of your whores doing it while you were out. Unbelievable. I'm getting out of here, out of this shithole town, and—"

"And where you gonna go?" Catch dug his hands into his hips.

"I—"

"Yeah?" he prodded.

"Why don't you come home with me?" Tania's sharp voice demanded consideration. Jill spun around and faced Tania, her lips parted.

There she goes again, reaching out and helping someone she doesn't even know.

"Sounds like a plan," I said.

Catch's eyes hardened. "To Meager?"

"Why not?" Tania said to her brother. "There's plenty of room at Ma's house, and she could use the company once she gets out of the rehab center. She was just saying how she wanted to get to know her granddaughter. I'm living at the house now, too, helping her out, but someone needs to be with her full time." She turned to Jill. "If you're up for that sort of thing, that is."

Tania was living in Meager now?

Catch had mentioned that their mother had recently been diagnosed with Multiple Sclerosis. Suddenly, Meager was full of people I knew.

"Are you up for that sort of thing? Helping out with my mom and all?" Tania asked Jill.

"Yes, I am. Oh my God! Yes! Thank you." Jill practically jumped up and down.

Catch's face hardened. He didn't like the idea too much.

Jill and Catch hadn't been getting along for months now. She was unhappy, had accused him of cheating, and he had cheated on her. He didn't know which end was up and couldn't keep up. Their daughter was the only thing attaching them, but they'd become a worn out rubber band, loose and frayed, ragged, but still holding on. You stay together for the child, but you're still unhappy. Still bitching and miserable. Wasn't that going to stain your child? Make her miserable too? What the hell was the point of all that?

"Sounds like a fine plan," I said.

Catch glanced at me. He was worried, pissed off. He shot his girlfriend a harsh look. "How am I gonna keep you safe when you're not here?"

"Like you kept us safe before? Give me a break!" Jill said, wiping at her face.

I raised my chin at Catch. "Time to move this along, man."

Catch swallowed, his hard eyes glowering at his sister and then snapping back to his soon-to-be ex-girlfriend.

"Thank you, Tania," Jill said. "I really appreciate this. God, you don't even know me." She kissed the side of her daughter's face, her gaze hanging on Tania like she was grateful for the unexpected seat on the last lifeboat, the ship sinking fast underneath her feet.

"You're welcome," replied Tania.

Jill was a good girl from what I'd experienced of her around the club. She was friendly and helped out without having to be asked, without complaining, worked at the local laundromat to bring money in to her family.

Catch had to learn that to give up was not being less of a man or a failure, that there was strength in admitting the broken couldn't be fixed no more. But he was emotional. I'd checked that shit at the door years ago, hadn't I?

Catch jerked his chin toward the exit, and his girlfriend rolled her eyes. She brushed past Grace, and Becca reached out a chubby hand and nabbed Grace's sunglasses from her face. She nabbed them right back, sliding them on once more. Diamond bands were on the ring finger. She'd gotten married again.

Good for you.

"You okay?" I asked her.

"Me? Yes, thanks." She flashed a quick grin at me.

"Long day, Maddie?" asked Butler, an edge of irony in his tone. Of course he knew her. "Got a nice bruise there."

"It's not every day you get held at gunpoint and your life is threatened by a ratty-ass biker, is it?" Tania jumped in, shooting me a look.

I let out a laugh. I'd missed her.

"How 'bout you ladies give me the details on this piece of shit so I can head out after him?" Butler asked.

"Sure," Grace murmured, glancing at me. I held onto her gaze and didn't let go.

I'd started keeping track of Grace after I'd seen her in Colorado at that Harley Davidson store. She'd kept drifting all over the country, working at different HD stores, keeping pretty much to herself. I'd stopped after year two. Was she back with the One-Eyed Jacks now and that's why she was playing it incognito standing here in my clubhouse? Did Tania, Grace, and Butler think I wouldn't like a One-Eyed Jack woman on my property? I appreciated their caution. Now I wanted to see how they'd respond.

"You know these two?" I asked Butler. "Tania's from your parts."

"Yeah," Butler replied curtly. "We met years ago in Meager before I went up north."

My attention slid to Tania. She raised her chin and took in a long slow breath.

"Never seen this one before." Butler gestured at Grace.

Real smooth. What an actor. But Jacks loyalty came first for him, as it should.

Tania said, "Maddie came down with me from Racine last week to help me with my move."

So Tania was back in South Dakota, and it sounded like she was on her own.

Tania returned my heavy look with one of her own. *Don't ask me now. I'll tell you another time.*

I cocked an eyebrow. *I'll make sure there'll be another time.*

"Butler, find out what these two know, and bring me that motherfucker," I said.

"Let's go, ladies." Butler gestured towards the main door.

Tania glanced at me over her shoulder and smiled. A smile that raced through the dark tunnels and hallways of my soul, leaving a familiar trickle of warm light in its wake.

Good to see you too, baby.

BUTLER GOT THE JOB DONE. He caught Creeper that night and brought him into the safe house I'd designated for him earlier, about ten miles into the woods northwest of the clubhouse. Catch and I arrived within the hour. Catch jumped off his bike and tore into the shed. He wanted his revenge for his daughter, for losing his old lady.

I strode into the metal shed, an old seed warehouse we kept for storage between shipments and drop-offs. Plenty of shit lay buried in the ground here. Butler leaned against the far wall, his arms crossed, his hair damp with sweat. My men, eyes on me, had gathered around the prisoner. Creeper tugged on his chains, and my pulse beat hard at the sound.

I got in his face, two inches from his sweating, foul-smelling skin. "You fucking kidnapped a baby? One of mine?"

His red, glassy eyes flared as he twisted in his shackles. Moans and growls escaped his taped mouth.

"Such a fucking bad move, you shit. You're going to feel how bad, then Butler's going take you back to the One-Eyed Jacks. You don't betray your own club and other clubs over and over again and not pay the price. Am I right?"

"Yeah, that's right!" My men hooted their agreement.

I took in a breath, my chest lightening at the potency of communal anticipation, the fierce smell of blood in the air.

I removed my gloves and nodded at Catch. "Show him what you got."

Bᴜᴛʟᴇʀ ʜᴀᴅ ᴛᴀᴋᴇɴ ᴏꜰꜰ, ʟᴇᴀᴠɪɴɢ Creeper behind at our safe house. He'd let us know when he'd be back to take the prisoner to the Jacks. The man was designing his presentation for Jump.

"You good?" I asked Catch later that night in our lounge, pulling him from a potential threesome with two petite brunettes before he got his dick out. My men were thrilled that we'd taken down our target. The holy trinity of adrenaline, testosterone, and job satisfaction always demanded a celebration.

"For now, yeah." Catch drained his beer, leaning against a wall by my office door. "I have something for you. I found this on Creeper." He handed me a torn and blood-stained business card.

Alejandro Calderón
The Calderas Group
Denver, CO

"Found plenty of business cards and a bunch of crazy shit in his pockets and on his bike. From what Butler said, he started out as a petty thief, pickpocketing, breaking into cars. Old habits die hard."

I tapped the edge of the creased beige card. "I've heard of this guy. You get anything on him?"

"Me and Den did a little research after Butler left," said Catch. "This Calderas Group is Salvadoran mob parading around as a Latin American import-export business—coffee, wines. But back in the eighties, they were the Executioners—"

"The most powerful Salvadoran gang in Denver."

"You've heard of them?" Catch asked, wiping at his mouth.

"Yeah, the Executioners were big time back in the day."

"They got their shit organized in the nineties, transforming themselves into this "legitimate" commercial corporation. Word is they still have ties with a major player in Mexico."

"Which means, they're still heavy into crack, cocaine, weapons, like they used to be in the good old days."

"Yep."

"You asked Creeper about him?"

"I convinced him to share." Catch's eyes gleamed with a satisfying memory. "Seems this Calderón was at the Broken Blades. He's looking to spread his organization's wings outside of Colorado. New opportunities for all and all that corporate bullshit."

The ache at the base of my skull pounded. The Blades had been weakened over the years, and now Notch was flirting with a crime organization from Denver? An organization that was trying to control territory right next to mine? Push against mine?

Fuck no.

Catch gestured at one of the girls to bring him a fresh beer. "Calderón has got choice routes out of the old country through New Mexico to Colorado," he said. "And don't tell me he hasn't heard of the Blades's underground warehouse and meth factory which isn't too far away from us. Everyone's salivating over it. We're salivating over it. If the Blades hook up with them, that could be a real problem for us in the long run."

"Fucking Notch."

"You got to give him an A for effort," Catch said.

"He's going to be getting an F and in more ways than one."

"Looking forward to that," muttered Catch.

I clapped a hand on his shoulder. "Good work."

His back straightened. "Thanks, Prez."

One of the girls brought him a beer, and Catch slapped her ass, laughing as she strut away, heading back to the couch where he'd left her earlier. She sat in the other's girl's lap, spreading her legs for him. Catch chuckled. It was a dark sound. He was drowning himself tonight—in violence, in booze, in sex. But his eyes told me the raw sting remained, still burned.

"Go, enjoy your party."

"Yeah." Catch swallowed a mouthful of beer and strode off.

"Prez!" Den came up to me, his teeth scraping across his lip.

"Where've you been holed up? You deserve a break. What's with you?"

"I caught interference in the area today."

"Meaning?"

338

"I've been trying out this new detection equipment since this whole thing with Creeper started—"

"Yeah?"

"Someone was out there today. I picked up on them and then they disappeared. Been following up, trying to trace it, find it, but I can't."

"You're sure?"

"They were out there, Prez, and they were watching us."

44
FINGER

URGENT BEEPING IN THE DARK slammed into my rush, cutting in on my driving rhythm.

An emergency text from Drac. *Dammit.*

I pulled out of the girl and, reaching over her, grabbed my blinking cell phone on her nightstand. My dick groaned as she groaned underneath me, smashing her face in the crumpled sheets, her ass remaining in the air.

The One-Eyed Jacks had taken Catch and beaten him, but now he was back at the Farm.

What the fuck?

It'd been almost five months since Jill and Catch had broken up. Tonight, he'd gone to Meager to visit his daughter and his mother. How did he end up tangling with the Jacks?

My hand went to my straining, unsatisfied cock. Nothing like a case of blue balls at two in the morning. I yanked off the condom. Samantha sat up at the sound of the snapping rubber, a hand in her messy hair. She was a new hanger-on who'd caught my eye at our local bar last night.

"Gotta go." Getting out of the bed, I snatched up my clothes from the floor and got dressed again.

"You're leaving?" she asked, her voice unsteady.

"Yeah."

"Well, um, it's not that late." She pushed her long red hair away from her face, her full tits visible in the hazy candle light. "If you get done, you should come back tonight. You know, if you want."

I only let out a grunt as I slid my boots on.

My aching, unhappy cock twitched at the invite, but I knew damn well that getting some sleep in my own bed if I got the chance would be more important after this new headache with Catch.

I got on my bike and headed to the Farm where grim faces greeted me in the clubroom. Drac inspected a bloodied and bruised Catch who was stretched out on the sofa.

"Is he alive?" I asked.

"Oh, he's alive all right," replied Drac, his tone weary.

Led, a Flame from Reich's Ohio chapter, stood next to Catch, his arms crossed.

"What the hell are you doing here and why didn't I know about it?" I asked him.

Led shifted his weight. "I've been over at the One Eyed Jacks in South Dakota. Came down with Nina, Reich's sister-in-law. Nina's Butler's old lady now. Catch showed up at their clubhouse, there was trouble, and I brought him back here."

Butler hooked up with Reich's sister-in-law? What the hell?

Catch sat up, clutching his middle, his one good eye caught my hard gaze. "Prez—"

"What did you do?" I asked him, my tone sharp. "Why the hell were you at the Jacks'?"

"I was with Becca at my ma's house. Then Jill came home."

"And?"

"And I saw that she's fucking pregnant. I flipped out."

"You flipped out, huh?"

"Yeah."

"Then what?"

"I've been keeping an eye on her, and —"

"What the fuck for?"

"She's friends with Grace now, and Grace is a Jack."

"What are the Jacks going do to your ex, Catch? Poison her? Poison her against you?" My voice boomed and everyone winced.

"She's been hanging out with Boner, their SA," Catch spit out. "I saw her belly sticking out, and I figured she got knocked up with his kid. What the fuck, right? First me, then him? So, I took her over there and found him, and he tells me she's his old lady now. You believe that shit? She's Boner's old lady."

"That's bothering your ego, is it?"

His bruised and cut face reddened, his jaw jutting out. He was a ball of angry confusion. "Yeah, okay? It fucking is!"

I towered over him. "Not four, five months ago, Jill stood right here and told you, told all of us, loud and clear, that you two were over, then she walked the fuck out. What don't you get about that?"

Silence.

"When a woman tells you she doesn't want you no more, you believe her. When she walks out on you, you fucking believe her!" My harsh words seethed from the pit of my black soul and crackled through the room.

Catch averted his gaze to the floor, his jaw pulsing. The industrial light fixtures buzzed overhead.

"What you don't do is go chasing after her at her new man's clubhouse," I said. "A man who happens to be a respected officer of a club we are friendly with." The blood pounded in my head. "Back it up—define *took her over there.*"

"I, uh…"

I shot Led a look. "What did he do?"

"He dragged her over to the Jack's clubhouse on his bike," Led said. "Girl was barely dressed. Pulled her in by the hair like some cave man. Lock went up behind him, pulled a shotgun on him to get him down, and he let her go. Then Boner had his way with him."

"Good for Boner," I muttered.

Catch glared at me, wiping at his blood smeared nose. The hurt, misunderstood boy.

I slanted my head, returning his glare. "You expect me to applaud your fine example of manliness this evening?"

"I—"

"You put a pregnant woman in danger, the mother of your own child?"

Catch's head swung to the side. "Kid's not even his."

"What?" said Drac.

"Jill's new baby ain't Boner's. She's a surrogate mother for Grace. Grace can't have kids, and Jill offered to have her and Lock's baby."

Drac wiped a hand down his face. "Aw, shit."

"So, you were wrong," I said.

"I was wrong," said Catch.

"I'll bet Jill tried to explain, but you went off."

"Yeah. Yeah, I did," Catch said, his voice low. "In front of my mother, in front of Becca. In front of all the Jacks."

"Feel good?"

"No."

"You apologized?"

Catch let out a rough breath. "Every which way Boner and Lock wanted."

I clenched my teeth against the anger churning in my chest, boiling up my throat.

I glanced at the large clock hanging over the center of the room. 3:32 am. "First thing in the morning, you call your mother and apologize and talk to your daughter. Then you call Jill and apologize. This is called being a man. Owning up to when you're wrong. Making shit you fucked up right. Looking out for the people you love."

I squatted down next to him. "You got some growing up to do. That would be controlling yourself. You've got good instincts, but you can't go off the rails where women and children are concerned. You save up that fire for when your brothers need you, when you're called."

He nodded. "Yeah."

I rose to my feet. "Go ahead, throw him his pity party."

Slade clapped a hand on Catch's shoulder. Den handed Led and Slade a beer. Drac gave me a glass of bourbon, and I drained it in one shot, but it did nothing to alleviate the pounding ache over my skull. I was tempted to go back to that girl's bed and finish what we'd started. A good hard fuck, a good quick fix. But no matter how much my frustrated cock and high adrenaline level fed that urge, I didn't have the energy to get back on my bike. I was exhausted.

"Refill," I said, licking my lips. Drac poured me another. Leper crept into the room and sat at my feet.

I gestured at Led with my glass as I rubbed the dog's head. "Did he really say that Butler has a new old lady and she's related to Reich?"

"Yep, that's what the man said," Drac took a swig from the bourbon bottle.

I didn't like that. I didn't like that one bit. Butler "related" to Reich? "Related" to his club?

"I want to know about any business between the One-Eyed Jacks and Reich," I said. "Anything."

Drac glanced over at Led. "He's spending the night. I'll get something out of him."

Catch stretched out on the sofa next to Den, a beer bottle in his hand, a scowl etched on his busted face.

Catch wasn't going to let this drama die. Somehow I knew this wouldn't be the end of it.

And I was right.

45
LENORE

"WE DIDN'T MISS ALLEN'S FIRST set, did we?" asked Grace, hanging her fringed leather hobo bag from her chair. Settling into their seats at our table at Pete's Tavern, Grace and Lock glanced up at the small stage where a solo guitarist was jamming on B.B. King's "The Thrill is Gone."

"No, you didn't miss it," I replied.

Grace had invited me, Tricky, Boner, and Jill to come to Pete's tonight to listen to The Dwellers, a group of local musicians. Grace knew the bassist, Allen. Actually, it turned out Grace also knew Eric. Once upon a time, she had managed Pete's and helped promote many local bands, one of which was Cruel Fate who had gone on to big commercial success.

Grace and I spent more time together and had become friends. She'd had a crisis period recently when her first gestational surrogate had a miscarriage, and we'd all helped her through a bout of depression and self doubt. Then Jill had offered to carry her and Lock's baby.

Meanwhile, Boner and Jill had gotten together. I didn't know details, and I didn't feel the need to inquire. They seemed really connected and happy together, and that was a wonderful, beautiful thing.

I'd learned Tania was moving back to Meager full time. Whenever she'd been in town we kept missing each other between both our work and family commitments. From what Grace and Jill had told me, Tania was now back in Wisconsin packing up the last of her belongings then heading back here. She'd stayed longer in Wisconsin than expected though. Had she tried to patch things up with her husband? We'd find out soon enough.

I looked forward to seeing her again, even if I wasn't sure how she'd handle seeing me on her home turf after years of being out of touch. But I knew that Tania and I had one of those friendships that didn't waver over the passing of time, out of touch or not. We would pick up where we left off.

I sipped on my beer. "You two cut it close. Allen's up next. So, what happened?"

Lock's smug grin was our answer, and we all laughed.

Grace blushed. "Can I help it if I'm married to a demanding, bossy man?"

Lock let out a deep laugh. "I'm the demanding one?" Grace shoved at his chest.

The guitarist finished his set, and the applause broke out in the old bar. The lights lowered, and The Dwellers took the stage filling the bar with their moody jazz music.

Tricky slid an arm around my shoulders as we listened, planting a quick kiss on the side of my face. He'd become very affectionate in public lately. Very attentive. It was beginning to make me feel uncomfortable, as if something had suddenly shifted between us that I wasn't on board with. I'd made it very clear from the beginning that I didn't want any kind of commitment. Light and easy was good for me. It was enough, and he'd agreed.

I was certain Tricky enjoyed his fair share of women at bars and parties and other clubs whenever he roamed throughout the country on runs. Women always noticed him wherever we went, and he enjoyed the attention, and I didn't mind it at all. He didn't mind our age difference and I certainly didn't either. We didn't ask each other too many personal questions, and neither of us had a problem with booty calls. All good. I was at that time in my life when my lust hormones were in overdrive. Getting it from an attractive younger hardbody like Tricky whose one aim—aside from getting laid—was to please a woman who knew what she liked could not be missed.

Tonight, he'd wanted to come pick me up on his bike, but I told him I'd meet him at Pete's as I had to work late on inventory at the shop which was just around the corner. That was only partly true. I avoided riding on the back of men's bikes.

Being on a motorcycle only made me think of one person. Finger. Being with *him*, riding on *his* bike. The two of us breaking free, being free. A wedge of disappointment lodged in my heart and blocked my throat the one time I'd gotten on the back of Tricky's bike, and I'd never done it again. Anyway, it wasn't my place—I wasn't his official girlfriend, let alone his old lady.

But something was different this evening. Tricky was irritated, and I'd sensed it the minute he strode into Pete's and found me at the table Grace had reserved for us. He'd kissed me, taken my hand in his and hadn't let go, his thumb rubbing back and forth over the tiny F scar on the inside of my wrist.

Their set ended, and we applauded. The Dwellers signed off for a break.

"They're good," Lock said.

"Very good," I agreed.

Tricky leaned into me. "Hey, I've got next weekend off from the shop. There's nothing else going on with the club, so I thought maybe we could get away together."

"Get away?"

"I know this place in Wyoming—"

"I'm not up for camping, Trick. Never was a favorite of mine."

"No, babe, it's not camping. My cousin owns these cabins and he rents 'em out, and I thought..."

"Oh. I'm not sure."

"Yeah." He clenched his jaw together, his eyes hard. "You're never sure. You always have a meeting or a business thing or a whatever the hell it is thing. Just say you don't want to go. Just say it already."

My hand slid over his thigh. "Can you calm down?"

"No."

I took my hand back. "Then you should go."

"It's so easy for you, isn't it?" His voice seethed. "Keeping things between us on a leash."

"I like things the way they are. Whenever I don't want to change them, you get mad."

"I get mad because I don't get it, I don't get you."

"You don't need to get me," I said sharply.

Tricky pulled back as if I'd slapped him. He took in a tight breath and leaned in close to me, his eyes stabbing me with anger. "Any woman would be real excited to get away for the weekend with the man she's sleeping with. But you? It's like your skin starts crawling."

I crossed my legs, averting my gaze. I'd tried to convince myself that I could take things with Tricky a little extra further, like him staying over the whole weekend and not just one or two nights a week. But that asphyxiated feeling would come over me. Last week he'd insisted I attend a club function with him, and I'd refused. We'd argued.

"You're exaggerating. We discussed this from the beginning. I wasn't supposed to be your girlfriend or your old lady."

"Supposed to be, supposed to be. Why can't it just progress into whatever it could be? What the hell? You hit the brakes at every turn."

"Maybe you should be with someone who wants a full relationship. A woman who could give you a family one day."

"I don't give a shit about all that."

"You should. You say that now, but a little bit down the road that will probably change for you. You're at the age when you need to take into account your future. Not just think about what you want now."

"I see the bigger picture, and it has you in it. I don't care about kids and stuff," Tricky spit out. "Jesus, Lenore. Every time I take a few steps forward, you automatically pull back. It's pissing me off."

"That's a problem. I'm sorry, but I can't give what you want."

"Shit, woman! Why can't you just go with it?"

Done.

I pushed my chair back. "I'm leaving."

"No, stay." He gripped my arm.

I shoved him off me.

"I don't want to fight with you, Lenore. I really don't."

"You could've fooled me."

The waitress came over with another round for our table. Jill shot me a concerned look as Lock, Grace, and Boner talked with Allen who'd come to our table.

"Let's have another drink and relax," Tricky said, grabbing two bottles of beer, sliding them in front of us.

"Okay."

He let out a breath. "Okay."

But I didn't drink. I stared at the bottle. I stared beyond the bottle, across the table, and admired Grace and Jill's relaxed faces, their laughter. They deserved to be happy. Lock and Boner deserved to be happy. Tricky, definitely.

I'd had my taste of deep happiness a long time ago, but it was over, and I was okay with that. I was good with what I had now. Over the years, I'd trained myself to be content and it showed on the outside. Chained my hunger, caged the wildcat. But that wildcat was restless, unsatisfied. Starving. Hungry for the one thing she could never have again.

Provoke her, she'd bite.

46
FINGER

"PUT THE GUN DOWN," I said.

Catch lowered the Python revolver he aimed at Butler and Boner.

I stood in the doorway of our clubhouse great room at the side of the two Jacks. Both of them eased back slightly like wolves straining to launch at their prey, my presence, the sound of my stern voice the only things holding them back.

I'd just gotten in from a quick trip to southern Nebraska, and found Boner accusing Catch of stealing the Python from their clubhouse. Just as I suspected he would, Catch was taunting the One-Eyed Jacks in return for getting a beating, and as a follow up to his bitterness over Jill moving on with Boner. The gun Catch had stolen from them had belonged to Dig, a gun they considered to be a club treasure.

When was he going to learn?

I folded my arms across my chest. "I'm gone two days, and you managed to bust out your balls again, bro?"

"Did what needed to be done," muttered Catch.

"Not with that gun," I said. "I admire your play, but this? This isn't right." My eyes went to Boner, a lean, hardened man with long dark hair and gleaming eyes. He'd been Dig's best friend. "It's disrespect to a man I knew and admired."

Boner raised his chin.

Catch only raked a hand through his hair, considering, stalling.

"Catch," I warned.

Sulking, his dramatic tactic being cut short, he stuck out the revolver.

"Come give it to me," Boner said on a snarl, his distinctive green eyes shining.

Catch moved forward, got in his face, and dropped the revolver. Boner's hand snapped out and caught it just in time.

"Party's over," said Catch. "I'd invite y'all to stay, but I don't think that's a good idea."

"Ah, no thanks," Boner replied. "I've heard the beds around here suck."

"You motherfu—" Catch lunged at him. Two of my men dragged him back.

"How're we going to get past this shit now? You want to tell me?" Butler's voice thundered.

"I'm gonna need an apology," Boner said, eyes going from Catch to me. "Then the Jacks are gonna require a sweet form of payback for this heavy transgression. But first, I wanna know how you did it, Catch. Who'd you use to get it? Are you that much smarter than I took you for?"

"Your woman did it for me. Didn't take much to convince her either. Heart of flames, that one."

"Son of a bitch!" Boner exploded, his hands clamping around Catch's neck.

"Boner!" Butler yelled, pulled him off Catch.

"You lying piece of shit!" Boner said. "Jill would never—"

Catch choked and coughed, his face different shades of red, his hands shoving at Butler's chest. "Yeah, Jill would never a hell of a lot of things, but with me, she sure as fuck did. Goes to show you."

Shut the fuck up, boy.

Boner pounced on him, punching him in the face, and Catch fell back, grunting. Den lunged toward Boner, but I stopped him with a hand on his chest.

"Catch more than deserved that," I said.

A loud ping sliced the air. Butler untucked his phone from a pocket and glanced at it. "Fuck." He tapped the phone and put it to his ear. "What the hell's going on?" His eyes flicked up at Boner. "You and Jill did what?"

Boner grabbed the phone from Butler and listened to whomever was on the line. His face darkened at what he heard, and he shoved the phone back at Butler, and approached Catch. "You been watching me? You knew about my ex, Mindy, and you got her to do your dirty work, you slick scumbag?"

Catch let out a laugh. "Aw, you thought I was talking about Jill before, huh? Nah. This other girl, Mindy, she was more than willing. She wanted to stick it to you bad."

Boner's lips curled, nostrils flaring, his fierce, dark glare a thousand knives.

"Let's get out of here," Butler said to Boner and shot me a stony look. "Compensation needs to hit the table."

The Jacks left.

Everyone stared at Catch.

"You got balls, bro. I like that, always have," I said. "You took a stand, terrific. But not this. There's history with that gun that you don't get, and you need to respect it, respect them and not fuck with them anymore. The Jacks are important to me."

"I know."

"You know?" My voice got louder and Catch tensed. "Do you really?"

"Yes, yes, I know."

"Right. You made your point. But you're fucking with our plans now, plans you are aware of. That's what pisses me off. You're putting yourself and your sad ass ego before your club. You can't go running off into the night on a tear and especially not against the Jacks. We need them friendly, but now you've pissed them off. Tugged on their heartstrings."

"Yeah, I—"

"You hearing me?"

He scowled, his eyes darting everywhere, muscles fidgeting. He was the wild horse unwilling to take the saddle.

"Yes, I hear you," he bit out.

"You still sore that Jill doesn't want you no more? That she chose Boner?"

He winced at my words, skin reddening.

What a fucking soap opera. I took in a deep breath to keep my cool.

Catch wore his heart on his sleeve, and it twisted there and bled. He'd loved Jill, maybe he was only now realizing how much, or maybe his ego had snapped and filled the sudden void with all this bluster. Either way, he needed to see sense. And I had to show him the way.

He pressed his lips together into a firm line, his gaze glued to the floor, the muscle along his jaw ticking. The lit fuse hissed as it coiled and sparked. "I don't want my kid growing up around another club. Becca's my kid!"

"What else did you do? You threaten Jill?"

"I told her to give me full custody of Becca or I'd sic Mishap on Boner."

Mishap was Rhys. He'd never wanted to be an official part of the Flames of Hell, preferring to remain under the radar and on his own, which was just as well. We liked it that way, and it worked for both of us. I gave him plenty of assignments and, through me, so did Turo. No one knew who "Mishap" was or who he worked for. Over the years he'd become a legend: assassination for hire and done with precision and accuracy. Clean and smooth. The unholy Velvet Reaper.

My nerves exploded.

"Who the hell do you think you are using Mishap's name as a threat?" I yelled.

Catch jumped to his feet. "I'm Becca's father! Me! Not some One-Eyed Jack!" His voice was raw with emotion.

I got into his face, gripping his colors. His eyes widened, and he shook in my hold. "Then you be her father. You be there for her. She's only two hours away. Be responsible. Be consistent. Let her see that in you. Let her feel safe with you. Let her depend on you, and you deliver. And don't lie to her. Not ever. That's what she needs from you. Never forget that." My lungs burned at the words erupting from the charred remains of "Kid." I took in a deep breath to clear the fumes. "This bullshit high school behavior is not helping your case. With Jill or with me."

Catch nodded stiffly and dropped his head, his eyes closed.

I wrapped a hand around his neck, and a noise unfurled in his throat at the contact. "Dammit, Catch. We got a lot of work to do, and I need you. Shit's hitting the fan here."

"I'm sorry. Sorry. You got me," he whispered roughly. "You got me, Prez."

WITHIN THE WEEK, THAT SHIT hit the goddamn fan. And it was Jill who tipped us off.

She'd called Krystal, asking if she could see me.

"She sounded upset," said Krystal. "And real determined. She said it's life and death. I know that girl wouldn't ask if—"

"Tell her yes," I said.

Jill came racing down from South Dakota with her daughter. Krystal brought her to my office, and she told me Boner was missing. She suspected he'd gone to see Alejandro Calderón on his own. Turns out Boner used to be part of Calderón's Denver gang over twenty years ago, and Calderón was after him for some old vendetta.

"Maybe my coming here is wrong and against the rules," said Jill, her face flushed, "and I'll get punished for it by the Jacks and you, but I had to try. I had to. I love Boner, he's a good man. I know, from the years I spent with the Flames, that if anyone could do something to save him, it would be you."

Calderón was gunning for the Broken Blades, and now he was using Boner as some sort of sacrifice to his vengeful gods to get the winds of war blowing? Did he think that would make us all shudder in our boots as he marched into the Broken Blades's territory like some usurping fascist swallowing more and more territory?

Fuck no. Not on my watch.

It was time to blow this shit sky high and shut it down. Now with their brother in danger, the Jacks would appreciate any move I'd make, and that would tie them to me for a long time to come. I needed that. I wanted that.

Jill said that Butler and the Jacks were on the hunt for Boner. She also assured me she and Catch were over their crap and she'd taken his previous threats with a grain of salt.

"Finger, I brought my daughter here today to see her dad and her other family as a show of good faith. I want to believe that all the bullshit can be wiped clean. I want to believe that we can start fresh and be fair, for all our sakes and for the good of our clubs."

Sitting stiffly on the other side of my desk, she waited for my response. Any response. She was worried. She'd come all the way here on her own and taken a chance on me listening to her for the good of our clubs.

"I owe Boner one," I said.

Her eyes lit up, her back straightened. "You do?"

"That shit with the Python."

"Right." She licked her lips. "Well, maybe Mishap could be given a new target?"

Ah, Boner was a lucky man.

A hard knock and Catch stood in the doorway. "Finger, two of Calderón's men followed Jill here from Meager."

I would make my move in a memorable way. Blunt, definitive. But oblique.

Over the years, Turo had introduced me to a number of white collar men in high places—not only in his world, but in the finer stratospheres of politics and law and order. I didn't use these contacts often, only when absolutely appropriate and absolutely necessary. I would do it now for the preservation of my territory, my trade, and most importantly, the brotherhood.

I pressed my back into my thick leather chair. "I got calls to make."

Jill shot up from her seat, her knot of strawberry blonde hair bobbing on her head. "Thank you for seeing me." She darted out of my office.

I stared after her. The girl had taken a risk coming here, back to her hostile ex and his club in order to protect her new old man from a common enemy. She'd smelled danger and did something about it.

Holding Becca in one arm, Krystal put her other arm around Jill and led her into the clubroom, Catch at their side.

Loyalty. Family. Flames to the end.

The end had come for Calderón and Notch. I picked up my phone and dialed, my pulse buzzing.

Laying the fuses.

Setting my prairie on fire.

47
LENORE

BECK WAS EIGHTEEN GOING ON thirty, I loved to tease him. He was extremely passionate about music and extremely focused. Beck had done really well at his arts high school, and made a variety of contacts there and at the clubs he and his friends frequented, and of course through his dad. He made the most of the possibilities before him. He filled in for different bands and played at recording sessions as both a guitarist and a drummer. He wrote music with friends, and mentored to an award-winning songwriter who worked with country as well as a number of alternative rock musicians. He hung with a few kids of famous rock and rollers. Now Beck fronted his own band, Freefall, and was determined to do well. My boy was high on life, and I was high on that. So high.

This time, I'd stayed longer than expected in California. Freefall was playing a number of small venues and a couple of music festivals as well. Their release of two digital singles had been very popular. Their social media presence was proving to be a huge success, and they'd attracted a promoter who was barely twenty-one years old himself, a savvy publicist with plenty of crazy yet right on the money ideas. The music scene was a whole new ballgame from Eric's day.

Beck was making some money now, and his dad helped set him up in his own place which freaked me out a little, but also made me insanely proud. I stayed with him at his new small house for almost two months, helping him choose furniture, decorating, organizing, meeting his friends and bandmates. I kept busy. A very attractive record producer friend of Eric's asked me out, and we went out on a couple of drink and dinner dates. I took the time to meet up with a number of old clients and, with Kelly's help, got a few new ones for custom orders. Kelly and I hung out and brainstormed together on my makeup line idea.

Saying goodbye to my son at the crowded security checkpoint at LAX yet again was hell.

"I love you, honey." I kissed and hugged him, sniffing in the warm scent of his tanned skin and the mango coconut shampoo I'd created for him, which he loved and used religiously on his thick dark blond hair. I squeezed him harder. I didn't want to let go. Couldn't. Not yet. "Love you so much."

I took in a deep breath and finally released him. Released him out into the world.

My own blue green eyes smiled back at me. "Love you too, Ma." He held my hands. "I love what you did with my place. I love that we spent so much time together. That I got to take you out and show you off."

"Keep going," I said, swinging our hands, blinking back the wetness that gathered in my eyes.

"You're the best and the most beautiful and the hottest. And you need to get out more."

"Here we go again. I went out, didn't I? Just because I don't want a relationship doesn't mean that I don't—"

"I know, but hey, hey—TMI!" Laughing, he kissed my hand. "Text me when you get home, okay?"

"I will." I kissed his hand back. That was something I'd started between us when I'd walk him to elementary school, and before I'd let go, I'd always kiss the hand I was holding. It had remained our little thing. Now that hand was making music, creating a glorious present and a vivid future.

I let go of his hand. "You go kick ass, Beck Lanier."

"That's what you taught me, Lenore Lanier. And that's what I do."

I held his steady gaze, clear and crystalline in the stark light of the airport. He was confident, he had no ghosts hounding him, no bloody specters looming over him, no reasons to look over his shoulder.

I smiled. Grateful, knowing in my bones that I had done good.

"Love you, baby."

He passed me my carry-on suitcase. "I know," he said, his voice low. "Love you, too."

I stroked the side of his face one last time, and with my heart up my throat, got in line at security and took in a long, deep breath.

I GOT HOME TO MEAGER LATE that night and texted Beck right away that I'd arrived in one piece. I showered, changed into my favorite satiny slip nightgown and matching robe, and poured myself a glass of red wine. On my iPad, I hit the new playlist Beck had put together for me. Aretha's gorgeous "This Bitter Earth" swelled in the room, and I grinned, letting out a sigh.

My boy knew me well.

With a sip of wine warming my insides, I curled up on my sofa and went through my cell phone messages and email.

—*Hey, pretty lady. When you're back and conscious, give me a call*—

Tricky.

Tonight I was exhausted and a little sad and really didn't want company. I only wanted quiet to catch up with myself. I'd call him tomorrow.

I scrolled down and clicked on a text from my essential oils manufacturer about an upcoming delivery. I was now creating a line of perfumed oils along with shampoo, body wash, and candles, and I'd been waiting on this French lavender delivery for a while now.

I scrolled.

A text from Grace.

— *Welcome home! Tomorrow night is Ladies Night at Tingle and we're all going. You can't say no since you missed my baby shower! Last outing for Jill too! Mwah!* —

Ha. That Ladies Night at the club's strip joint had been in the works for a long while, and now it was finally happening. Jill's due date was coming up in a month, Grace's baby would finally be here. I smiled to myself as I tucked my feet under my legs on the sofa and texted back:

— Wouldn't miss it for the world! Let me know what time xoxo —

I was sure Tania would be there. Grace and I had shared a few phone calls while I was in California. She had told me about Tania finally leaving her husband and having moved back to Meager for good.

I shut off my phone and tossed it to the other end of my low sofa. I pulled out the pins from my hair, shaking it free as Otis Redding crooned. In LA, I'd gotten my hair dyed black with thick streaks of blue and mauve. I lit my fig candle on my Mexican carved wood coffee table, and zoned out on the sofa with my wine, a small bowl of almonds, and Otis, Al Green, Marvin Gaye, Nina Simone for company. Bliss.

The following night I walked into the Tingle on the outskirts of Meager just after ten o'clock. I spotted the Jacks' women the moment I'd stepped inside the nightclub. Mary Lynn, Suzi, Dee, Nina, and Alicia were there, as well as Grace and another woman with black hair. It was her. Those big and dark exotic eyes of Tania's were unforgettable.

My heart thudded in my chest as I snaked my way through the tables, the electro pop music thumping through the cavernous room.

"Lenore!" Grace hugged me.

"I finally made it. The traffic was really bad on the way over here," I said on a throaty laugh. "And there's a line outside."

"Lenore, this is Tania. And, Tania, this is Lenore, who has the lingerie store in town you love so much—Lenore's Lace. Finally, you two get to meet."

Tania was riveted to the spot. She raised her chin and made a great effort at an effortless smile. "Lenore?" she asked, a tentative quality to her voice.

"Yes."

She grinned wide. "Grace has told me so much about you. I love your store."

Tania, my protective soul sister. That hadn't changed. Grace's face was rosy, her eyes literally sparkling. She was thrilled that we were finally meeting.

"Oh, thanks," I replied. "It's good to meet you, Tania. Finally. Grace has told me a lot about you, too. Congrats on your art gallery slash antiques store. When are you opening?"

Tania's lips curved up.

We were smooth. Yes, we were.

"Next month, hopefully," Tania replied.

Tricky came up on my side, and slung an arm around my neck, planting a firm kiss on the side of my face. My eyes remained on Tania.

"You want a drink, hon?" Tricky asked me.

I squeezed his arm, shaking my head. We'd spoken earlier, and he'd told me he and the guys would be here to "check things out."

Grace laughed. "Geez, Tricky, it's ladies' night. We've got this covered! Stand off."

I flashed Tricky a smile and brushed my lips against his. He pressed against me, cradled my face with both of his hands and deepened the kiss into a tongue fuck, making my spine straighten. He'd missed me.

"After this pansy show, I'll be nailing you to the wall, giving you a performance you won't forget," he whispered in my ear, a hand sliding down my hip, squeezing. He sauntered back to the bar where all the One-Eyed Jacks were lined up, gripping beer bottles, scanning the club. This nightclub was their second home, yet now they looked more like squirrels trapped in a cage rather than tough dudes on a night out at their local strip club.

"Oh, look at them all." Mary Lynn let out a laugh.

A topless male waiter brought a tray of shots to our table, and Grace and Dee passed them around. Tania remained still, her gaze never leaving me.

I put my a hand on her elbow. "Nobody knows. Nobody here knows anything about who I really am," I said, my voice low. "Have you ever said anything to Grace?"

"No. I didn't even realize you were here, that you were...you. I've had a lot on my plate, and I never put two and two together. Over forty brain block."

"Right? I know that one well."

"I've never said a word to anyone. I'm sticking to that."

My eyes shifted around us. "Thank you."

"How are you? You look great."

"I'm good. Things are very good."

"You and Tricky?"

I shrugged. "We hang out off and on. It's fun."

"Good for you."

"Grace told me you're getting a divorce."

"Almost there," she said.

"I got myself one of those a while back, and I survived just fine."

Tania's lips twitched into a smirk and something inside me lightened. I'd missed that smirk. I'd missed her.

We fell into easy conversation, and Tania leaned in to me. "Have you seen...?" she asked in a whisper.

Finger.

"No." My voice came out more clipped than I would have liked.

"Oh, I have." Tania's face reddened, like she'd said something she shouldn't have.

My pulse skipped a beat. Grace had told me about their having gone to his clubhouse in Nebraska, about seeing him when Jill and Catch's daughter has been kidnapped by a biker from another club. I really didn't want to hear any more about it. Shit never changed. Ever. When you thought things were good, rolling, comfortable, Brutal Reality cut in for his turn with you around the dance floor.

Another validation for all I had done. Even now.

I glanced over at Jill. The girl seemed fine, but that shit changes you—your child at the mercy of a psycho, at the mercy of crazed men's twisted egos and dirty ambitions. She was lucky.

"You two getting to know each other?" Grace asked, an arm around Tania's waist.

I gulped down my cold beer, relishing its icy wash down my hot throat.

Tania's electric gaze met mine. "Lenore was just telling me about her divorce."

"I was." I shot her a grin and her eyebrows lifted, accepting my return volley. "Stay away from musicians, Tania, whatever you do. Fuck them, but don't marry them. Ever." I raised my drink at her.

Letting out a laugh, Tania clinked my glass with hers. "Ah, I'll keep that in mind," she said. "So, what kind of musician was your ex-husband?"

"He was the lead guitarist for this band called Cruel Fate."

"No way! They were huge for a while there. Aren't they from our parts?"

"They are. In fact, Grace here played a role in their success," I replied.

"Not really." Grace waved a hand. She explained to Tania how she'd helped the band in their early days by booking them at Pete's when she used to manage it almost twenty years ago. Tania had missed out.

Tania raised her glass at me again and smiled. A warm, honest smile, and I returned the gesture. It was good to be with her again, to talk, to laugh, to feel that special vibe we once shared. Very good. We were all home, either reinventing the home of our past like Grace and Tania or, like me and Jill, creating a new one.

We settled in our seats, Tania next to me.

"Sort of nuts we haven't met up sooner, considering," I said. "I've been out of town, but you avoid club events from what Grace has told me."

Tania raised an eyebrow. "So do you, from what Grace has told me."

"Too many memories of club parties, most of them not very good," I said. "Let's hear your excuse."

"Ah, it's nothing. No big deal."

"Tania, come on."

She licked her lips, and I followed her gaze across the room to the side of the stage where Cassandra stood with Butler, the blond Jacks manager of the Tingle. This man had amazing pale-blue eyes, and when he aimed his rakish grins your way, you felt them jag inside you.

Tania took in a sharp breath. "Let's just say, I have a history with a club member, and I made a wrong assumption about him recently, and feel embarrassed and awkward. And stupid."

"Butler?"

"Hmm."

"Butler who recently showed up surprising everyone with his new old lady?"

She batted her sooty eyelashes. "Yep. That's the one."

"Ah."

"Ahhhhhhhh," mouthed Tania, crossing her eyes, raising her drink to her lips.

"Details another time?"

"If you want the dirty, then you must ply me with much drink first."

"I can do that," I said, laughing. "I'll give you a call and we'll go out."

"Now you're talking." Tania clinked her glass with mine once again.

Cassandra got up on stage and spoke on the microphone, welcoming us to the Tingle. She was dressed like the goddess she was in a long, flowing, one shoulder, dark purple dress with a silver, ancient Roman style cuff around her bicep that I'd gotten her for her birthday last month. She introduced the male dancers and the evening officially began.

One of the dancers came toward our table, his eye on Mary Lynn. But we diverted his attention to Tania, shouting for her to go up on stage with him. She stood up. Dare accepted. She went with him, rolling her eyes, a huge smile on her face. The dancer sat her down on a chair and did his thing, and Tania gave as good as she got. From the stage, she caught my eye and gave me a thumbs up, laughing. A whistle from Butler ripped through the air.

I clapped and hooted for my girl onstage. Tania, Grace, and I were doing good, and we were here together. Enjoying ourselves, having fun, leading our lives. I sent whoops and cheers up in the air.

If only that blind euphoria could have lasted a little while longer.

48
FINGER

"I'M SORRY. I MUST BE bothering you or interrupting." Tania's shaky voice, her tight and shallow breaths set me on edge.

"Talk to me." Holding my phone, I charged out of the gas station store, pocketing my change for the energy drink I'd sucked down while waiting in line to pay for it.

She said, "I'm at the One-Eyed Jacks in Meager. You need to come here—quick."

"Tania, what's wrong?"

"I need you."

My chest tightened at those words, the pleading tone in her voice, the raw emotion seeping through. In all the years that we'd known each other, she'd never once called me for a favor, and now she was in emergency mode late at night at the One-Eyed Jacks?

"I'll be there in less than an hour. I'm not too far away."

"Hurry."

Christ.

I tried calling Catch, but he didn't answer his phone. Little shit. He was supposed to be with his daughter at his mother's house while Jill and Tania were out tonight at a Jacks party. This had to be Catch-related for Tania to call me and ask me to come to their clubhouse, for fuck's sake. What the hell did he do now?

Getting on my bike, I called Drac and Slade to drop everything and meet me in Meager. I lit out of the parking lot and made it there in record time. My bros waited for me at the turn off for the Jacks' property. We rode up to the gate together, and the lone prospect there froze at the sight of us.

Only one prospect at the gate?

"What's going on?" I demanded.

His mouth opened, but no sounds, no words came out.

"So we're clear," I said, shifting in my saddle. "I got a call from someone in there that I'm needed, and you aren't gonna stop us from going inside."

"Uh...there was a p-party," said the prospect.

"What fucking happened?" I said through gritted teeth.

"It's Catch," he spit out. "Catch showed up uninvited."

"Fuck, not again," muttered Drac behind me.

"Open up," I said, my fingers flexing around my handlebars.

The prospect opened the gate, and we followed the gravel path to the wide expansive driveway of what used to be an old go-kart factory. In the field in the middle of the racing track, white and silver balloons bobbed like a sea of moons over empty chairs. Two long tables were covered in platters of picked over food along with a mess of dishes and plastic cups and bottles, abandoned and forgotten. The tablecloths fluttered and snapped in the warm night breeze. An ominous welcome.

My mind ticked through the possibilities. I doubted Catch was here over his ex. That shit was done. Jill was an official Jack's old lady now, and he'd been good about visiting his kid without any incidents for the past few months. In fact, he'd been taking extra time off recently to come to Meager and spend more time with his daughter. But during that time, Catch had disappeared early at three different parties back in Nebraska, and I'd noticed he'd been ignoring the girls he usually favored. I figured it had to be a new woman, but one he didn't want to bring around to the club.

This smelled familiar.

My body pressing through the battering, icy wind, my pulse beating hot and wild at the sight of the *Welcome To Illinois The Land of Lincoln* sign.

Staring at her profile in a movie theater, her hand in the popcorn, mine between her legs.

Breathless kisses in musty hotel room beds, desperate poundings against bathroom tile.

Urgent whispers sweeping away nightmares.

Every chance I got I'd run off to Chicago to be with Serena. Had Catch found a woman here in Meager? If he was keeping her a secret from us, was it some woman connected to the Jacks?

Me, Drac, and Slade headed into the Jack's clubhouse. We passed through a dimly lit hallway and reached a noisy main room filled with men and women. All eyes turned to me, and the noise instantly died down. My appearance was obviously a total surprise and not a good one. Their shock, uneasiness, irritation was another rush of caffeine in my blood. I took in a breath, savoring the pulse.

"Where the fuck is Jump, and don't make me wait." My voice boomed through the space.

People scattered, others froze. Across the room, I zeroed in on Tania standing next to Grace, and I raised my chin at her. Tania's shoulders dropped a fraction, but her body visibly tensed. She was relieved to see me yet remained anxious as hell.

Jump moved toward me, a hard smirk on his face. The host of tonight's festivities was clearly enjoying himself.

I didn't give him a chance to open his mouth. I didn't want explanations just yet. I wanted to make sure my bro was okay.

"Where's Catch?" I said. A demand, not a question. The room cleared quickly.

"You don't teach your boys any manners?" One side of Jump's thick lips curled under that full beard and mustache. Still the arrogant prick.

Fuck, I hate this asshole.

Time hadn't erased the venom seeping through my blood at the sight of him, the sound of his voice, his inciting turns of phrase. For now though, I would be the diplomat.

"This is unfortunate," I said.

"Unfortunate?" Jump said on a growl, shooting Butler a smug you-hearing-this-shit-I-told-you-so look.

The party was over between those two.

I eyed Butler. "I need to see Catch. Take me to him."

I also wanted to get Butler alone to drill his ass about all this.

Jump let out a rumbly grunt at my dismissal of him. With a

sharp slant of his head, Butler led the way, taking me to a basement holding cell where Catch was being held. On the metal stairwell leading underground, Butler slowed his pace.

"How'd you know he was here? Who told you?" he asked.

"Tania."

He stopped on the bottom stair, his stark blue eyes round. "Tania?"

Ah, he didn't like that very much. "She was concerned about her brother's fate at your hands."

"He's been fucking my old lady."

"And I'm guessing, she's been fucking him right back. Your honeymoon phase is over already?"

Butler's jaw clenched, his face tightening. The big show was over, and he knew it. And now he had a problem on his hands—business, not personal.

I'd sent Butler Reich's way to do some digging for me, and he'd ended up doing a dangerous job for Reich and doing it well. Then Butler had told me Reich had warmed up to him and trusted him with another job, but he'd never gotten back to me on the details. I knew Butler was driven to get back in with his club as if the dogs of hell were biting at his ass cheeks, he'd told me so himself. So when I'd heard he'd hooked up formally with Reich's young sister-in-law and brought her to Meager, I'd had my doubts that true love was the reason.

Why go this far? Was he more ambitious than I'd given him credit for?

Butler had ended his exile and scored major points with his club when he'd given the Jacks their wanted criminal, Creeper. He'd scored more points by bringing a new money-making project to the Jacks, in the form of a job for me. Had Butler hooked up with Reich's sister-in-law to have access to more business opportunities through Reich? Had he been playing both sides to win big all along? He'd set his pretty Baked Alaska aflame. But with his "old lady" stepping out on him, he now had a melted soggy mess on his hands.

Tonight, the curtain had been pulled back on the blond wizard. Nina's adultery was going to attract Reich's attention—the girl wasn't happy and causing problems between brothers, and even worse, between two clubs. And once again, my boy had gotten himself in the thick of a clusterfuck.

Good times were ahead.

Butler said nothing at my honeymoon remark, only a muscle pulsed along his jaw.

No, he didn't seem torn up about his old lady getting it from someone else as much as he seemed inconvenienced. Yeah, that was the word for it. I'd seen plenty of men find out about being cheated on. They'd slam into and wreck everything in sight—objects, people, often their women, and especially the other men their women had played with.

And here was Butler being the responsible albeit tense host, showing me to his enemy's holding cell. Was he going to offer me a choice of flavored coffee next to make my visit as comfortable as possible?

Butler only took in a tense breath and continued down the metal stairs, headed down a short hallway, and finally unlocked a thick metal door, gesturing inside. I stepped into the room. Catch was slumped over, head in hands, a bottle at his side, blood and bruises marring his visible skin, jeans torn and bloodied. They'd had a field day with him. Probably every single Jack.

Butler closed the door behind me, leaving me alone with him.

I planted my feet in front of Catch. "You fucked up. Again."

A bruised and swollen eye slowly blinked up at me, a muffled groan rising from his torn lips. His one hand gripped the bottle as if he were steadying himself on it.

I crouched down in front of him. "What am I going to do with you, Catch? You're acting like some young pup, I can't—"

"I love her," slid from his lips along with a small stream of whisky, blood, and saliva.

I stilled.

I'd never heard such an effortless and candid confession out of Catch before. He usually hemmed and hawed, shifted his eyes, his body, tried every verbal angle to shimmy and shade and sway his way out of a definitive black and white reply.

He loved her. Rock hard truth.

I dragged my teeth across my bottom lip. "That's what you got for me? For fucking with an old lady from another club? Butler's old lady? He's a friend of mine, we work together. You know this."

"I know. I know how stupid it was to cross that thick red line."

"Glad to hear it."

His bloodshot eyes gleamed. "But I couldn't help myself. I love her. And knowing she's here, with him, but wanting me makes me fucking crazy."

The raw, haunted passion in his voice stabbed at my chest. I'd never allowed myself to wallow in feeling. I'd never given in to that particular throbbing torment or I'd have never gotten up on my feet again and faced another day.

But here was my boy, trying to make sense of it all.

"Are you sure it's you she wants and not just some adventure, some playtime?" I asked.

"I'm sure." He let out a ragged exhale. He was exhausted. "And before you say it, she isn't just another girl to me. From the beginning, I knew that it was wrong. I knew what was at stake, but I couldn't stay away from her. I can't." He brought the bottle to his chest and closed his eyes again, his head sinking back against the wall. "I'm sorry, Prez. I'm sorry you had to come save my ass, clean up my fucking mess, yet again. You don't deserve that. You've been nothing but good to me—" he coughed thickly, wiping at his mouth. "—and I've disappointed you."

Catch had disappointed me, but he'd also impressed me.

I stood up. "You're going to make this up to your club, and you're not going to like it."

"I know." He slumped over on the floor, the bottle wrapped up in his arms. "Whatever it takes. I'll do it."

A knock on the door and Butler opened up, lifting his chin at me. I followed him back upstairs, neither of us speaking. In the lounge, Jump and I made small talk. People around us relaxed again.

"Catch ruined your party?" I asked.

"We were having a family celebration," he replied, his voice a sneer.

"I was on the road, heading home when I found out. Came straight here," I said.

Butler shot Tania a look, and she shot one right back, her face streaked red. Why would he give a shit that Tania and I knew each other? That she'd called me? Because he gave a shit about Tania, that's why. And she seemed to give a shit what he thought.

"You and your men will stay," said Butler. "We've got plenty of food and drink and room for you all to spend the night."

My eyes darted at Jump who only shifted his weight, his lips pressed together. He still refused to be even a bit hospitable.

I was going to make this a memorable night. "Will do," I replied.

Butler motioned to one of the girls. "A bottle of Jack."

The old ladies hustled and brought out food for me, Drac, and Slade. I stuck to the liquor, my eyes sticking on Tania. She looked good. More than good. I wanted to test my theory about her and Butler. I also wanted to make sure that Tania, who'd called me in, the sister to the Flame who kept fucking up with the Jacks, was not going to be fucked with by them. Not ever.

Lock, Boner, and Kicker, their VP, came over for an official greeting and welcome. They explained that tonight had been the christening party for Lock and Grace's new baby boy.

"Ah, congratulations. Great news." I shook Lock's hand. "Could I congratulate your old lady?"

"Of course." Lock gestured at Grace, who stood with Tania, to come over.

"This here your old lady?" I asked, taking in Grace. Gone was the sad, hollow-eyed girl I'd seen in that Harley Davidson store in Colorado years ago. In her place was a very attractive and confident woman at ease in her own skin.

"Yes, this is Grace," said Lock, his hands on his wife's shoulders.

I offered her my hand. "We met once. Long time ago." Centuries ago, with Dig at a charity run in Iowa.

She shook my hand firmly. "Yes, we did."

We spoke for a bit, and I glanced at Tania who was suddenly keeping very quiet. "You and Tania are good friends?"

"Since forever," replied Grace, a wide grin warming her hazel eyes.

"She's a good friend to have." I rolled the liquor in my glass. "Congratulations on the baby." I raised my glass at Lock. "I apologize for Catch ruining your night."

"Thank you," murmured Grace, pressing into her old man's side.

Jump gestured at someone behind me, and two girls appeared and settled suggestively on either side of my chair.

"Anything you need, Finger, you let me know," Jump said.

I ignored him, I ignored the women. My eyes snagged on Tania's as I drank. I held the empty glass out to her. "Pour me another, would you, Tania?"

She shot up from her seat, bumping into Butler in the process. He stiffened, she got a bottle and poured the refill, and I grabbed her by the arm, pulling her to sit on my lap. The air suddenly got thick, a charge of electricity zapping around us as if the room were under threat of an impending thunderstorm. Everyone stilled, watching us, waiting for the black sky to break open. Butler's face hardened even more.

Jump rattled on and on about Catch, complaining, and I listened with one ear.

"Butler, your old lady is Reich's sister-in-law?" I asked, handing Tania my drink, and he and I both watched her take a long sip, her face reddening.

Butler cleared his throat. "That's right." His intent gaze darted to me then back to Tania.

Oh yeah.

"Reich is the VP of my club's national." I leaned back in the chair, my one hand moving down Tania's side. "If he asks me how this night went down, I'll be letting him know."

"So will I," replied Butler tightly, his eyes following my hand stroking Tania. "If he asks."

Were Butler and Reich close now? Or was Butler simply taking advantage of an opportunity as usual?

I shot Butler another look and he shot an equally fierce one right back. My tongue enjoyed the sweet heat of the liquor as my gaze flicked around the room. And again.

There he is. Tricky.

I had Lenore investigated after Drac had put her poster up on my club wall. She'd never gotten involved in another relationship after her divorce. She got laid here and there like the rest of us, but didn't linger very long over the pickings. Word was she and Tricky had been seeing each other a couple of months now. It hadn't stopped her from going out with other men, or him from seeing other women. Their thing was loose and easy, but busy.

Had she been here at the party tonight? There was no sign of her now. Jacket on, Tricky tagged fists with another Jack and headed out down that dimly lit hallway which led to the exit. He had somewhere he'd rather be.

I dug my fingertips into Tania's side.

"Close, but no cigar," my dad used to say.

"I've been riding all day," I said. "Could use a shower and that bed."

Tania slid quickly from my lap as I rose to my feet. She took the glass from my hand and set it on the table. She was eager to leave.

Not so fast, baby.

Gripping her arm, I kept her close. Butler winced at the move, and I wrapped my other hand around her neck. Yeah, he had a thing for Tania, meanwhile Tania was Catch's sister, and at this moment every Jack despised him.

"What are you doing?" Tania whispered, her hand clamping onto my wrist.

"I won't have them fucking with you, Tania. You hear? They need to know you're under my protection."

"Am I?"

"Always have been. From the very beginning." My thumb rubbed the back of her neck. "Now that you're back in Meager, I want Jump and the rest of them to respect you, not take any shit about your brother or me out on you after tonight. I won't have that fucker or any of them playing with you."

"But—"

"I'm glad you got Grace, but that ain't enough."

"I know them, Finger. It isn't like that."

"You're talking nostalgia. I'm talking here and now. Cold, hard reality."

Her teeth dragged across her lip. She was considering everything I'd said. Deciding. She slid an arm around my middle and pulled herself close against me.

She'd made the right decision.

Tania reached up and touched her lips to mine. My hand tightened around her neck and my tongue drove her lips apart, sliding against hers. Her fingertips dug into my arms as a noise escaped her throat.

I released her, a hand at the side of her face. "Good girl," I whispered, my lips brushing her forehead. My arm wound over her shoulders, and she leaned into me. We were going to play this for all it was worth.

Everyone stared at us, Butler glared at us, and that electrical charge buzzed in the air again. The storm had just been upgraded to a Category 4.

Jump had his old lady escort us to the guest suite at the One-Eyed Jacks resort.

"Is this really necessary?" Tania asked once we were alone in the small room.

I'd kissed Tania in front of the Jacks, and she'd kissed me back. We played it like we had a thing. History, which we did. And a present, which we did not.

What the hell.

I locked the bedroom door, locking out the bullshit grandstanding and everyone's startled faces. Especially Butler's. Bro had it bad.

I eyed her. "Come here."

Tania came over to me, letting out a breath. My hands slid around her neck, and I kissed her again. That familiar taste of booze, comfort, impulsiveness, gratification filled me.

"Finger..."

"You want to fuck?" I said against her warm lips, a small dark laugh under my words.

She laughed back. A nervous laugh, a relieved laugh. It was good to be alone with her after the parade of fools the past hour.

We relaxed on the bed together, kicking off our shoes.

"I guess I'm spending the night, huh?" she asked, letting out a sigh.

"You guessed right." I folded my arms under my head.

"I had to call you in. I was really worried about my brother and the new shitstorm he's brewed up," said Tania. "You were going to find out anyway, but I couldn't take the chance that they'd—"

"You did right. Better I handle this now, as it's happening, rather than later when shit blows up and gets out of control, according to every dumb fuck's perception of events."

I turned on my side, my hand roaming over her abdomen, sliding under her shirt. Her smooth skin was warm under my touch.

She let out a small gasp. "Well, after tonight, everyone will think differently of me."

"That was the point."

"I imagine the men will keep at least a five-mile distance from me from now on."

"You sound disappointed. Were you after Jack cock tonight?"

She laughed. "Well, that aspiration is shot to shit now, isn't it?" She pressed her lips together, her eyes on the ceiling.

She had it bad for Butler. But there was nothing to be done there.

My hand cupped a breast, and her breath caught as I stroked over the material of her bra. "Who's the lucky asshole?" I squeezed a nipple between my thumb and forefinger, and she whimpered at the sensation I'd provoked.

Her eyes met mine. "Forget it. I'm trying to."

You got that right.

I unzipped the side of her skirt.

"Finger," she whispered.

"Tania," I whispered back.

"You could've had one of those women in there, if not two or three, no problem, to service your needs. I cut into your action tonight."

"Yeah, what a fucking shame. Make it up to me."

I slid her silky top up her torso and pushing her bra out of the way, palmed a breast. Kneading it, I took a nipple in my mouth, and her body stiffened. I kept sucking, and she let out a groan, her back arching. She wanted this too, but she was fighting it.

"Have I ever said no to you before?" she said.

"Never." I glanced at her, unsure of where she was heading with this as I licked, sucked, stroked. "Have I ever forced you?"

"Never," she replied, squirming underneath me.

"After you got hitched and I didn't hear from you again, I didn't call you no more, did I?" I asked.

"I missed you," she murmured, "Missed this."

So had I.

My hand skimmed over her smooth panties, down between her legs. "You been faithful to your husband all these years?"

Her eyes held mine. "Yes."

"Still married?"

"Getting a divorce."

What a waste. "Fuck him."

My hand slid inside her panty, my fingers hitting wet flesh, dragging through her, and she cried out. Grunting, I ripped the panty off her body and got up from the bed, snapping off my dirty leathers.

"All these years later, Tania, and you still fucking do it for me."

A lazy grin curled her lips. "Hallelujah."

My clothes fell to the floor.

She sat up on her elbows, her mouth dry. "Finger—"

Tania always flew on instinct then immediately assessed the potential damages. Sometimes you just had to say fuck it all. Like right now.

My hand pumped my cock. "You want it?"

Her eyes went to my cock, her eyebrows lifting, her lips parting. No words.

I nudged her legs open with one of mine and leaned down and kissed her, our eyes still on each other, my hard length rubbing down her middle.

She gripped my arms. "We can't do this. Not now. Not anymore. We had our time, you and me, and I liked it. I fucking loved it. But we shouldn't go back there."

Can't? Shouldn't? Since when?

I lifted from the bed and sat up on the edge. She took my hands in hers, kissing one then the other just above where the middle fingers were missing.

"I don't want to go backward with you," she said. "I want you in my life—you are. You will always be in my life—but I need to keep moving forward. We both do."

Moving forward.

I pulled my hands from hers. I wanted this. I needed this now from Tania. She looked good, and I'd liked being with her tonight. I'd certainly enjoyed the show we'd given the Jacks a fuck of a lot. I'd missed enjoying a lot of things lately.

She tugged her bra back into place, pulling her shirt down. "You know she's here, don't you? I saw her. Talked to her. She's good friends with Grace now. She has a business here in town. She's—"

"I know."

Her dark eyes flared. "Of course you know."

"I've always known." Maybe not always, but long enough, long enough that it felt like forever. And now Tania and Lenore were buddies again? Let's all be fucking best friends. "Were you going to say anything?"

"I saw her for the first time a few weeks ago when Grace introduced us. Lenore, as she's called now, pulled me aside and asked me not to say anything to anybody." Tania sat up straighter on the bed. "Hell, I don't know what to say when it comes to you two. You had it all, and you both let it go."

"You call that having it all?"

"From where I'm standing today? Right now? You bet I do."

Loss, disappointment, disillusionment, regret. Fuck that.

"You called me to come here, knowing she was here?"

She shot to her feet. "I had to call you. My brother's life was on the line."

"You did good, babe."

Still fiddling with her bra, she let out a sigh, her shoulders dropping. "Everything's different now, Finger. Tell me it isn't."

Yeah, everything for her was different now—a divorce, a crush on Butler—but were things different for me? I'd made plenty of good and bad choices over the years and, for the most part, remained unrepentant. Those few regrets my stubbornness had kicked over my shoulder created a messy pile at my back that I'd only ignored. Could I change anything about that now?

Did I want to?

We stared at each other in silence, reality sinking in, cooling the temperature of our blood, easing the pace of our pulses. I'd gotten Tania into bed again, but we both knew it wasn't about her and me, not really, never had been, and that wasn't enough for her anymore.

Maybe it shouldn't be for me either.

I pulled the tie out of my hair, ripped off my bandana.

Tania wasn't someone who cowered or lit up in the shadow cast by my name, my title, my reputation, my scars. She was right, and I knew it the minute she'd hesitated.

I cupped her chin, brushing her lips with mine and planted a kiss on her forehead. I left her on the bed and headed into the small adjoining bathroom, stripped off and got into the shower. A cold shower.

Catch and Tania had shown me their true colors tonight. Catch flying off the handle, going full throttle on pure emotion, pure feeling. And Tania putting it all on the line and asking me to help her, knowing what that meant. Brother and sister did not hold back in the face of what they felt was right or just, and did it with an overwhelming passion.

The cool water streamed over my head, down my hair, my skin. I pushed my hands against the tile wall and took in a deep breath, letting it out slowly, and turned the water to full on hot. My skin reddened under the assault of the steaming, needling spray. I knew what I had to do. What I'd been wanting to do for years, but holding back. There was no reason to any longer. Here I was in the same general latitude and longitude as her.

Tomorrow morning, first thing, I would stop holding back.

Category 5.

49
LENORE

I SWIPED AT THE TICKLE GRAZING my nose. My mouth.

"Tricky, stop..."

Hold on.

My eyes snapped open, and I jerked up, clutching the sheet tightly around my naked body. It was too late to reach for my gun in the top drawer.

Two dark eyes bored into mine, a bandana wrapped around his head, his dark hair down past his jaw, peppered with hints of gray. His large body hovering over me filled my vision.

Finger said, "Good morning."

So casual, so warm, as if it were the most natural thing in the world for him to be in my bedroom after all these years. It wasn't natural. The world had turned upside down.

Madness.

My eyes darted to my alarm clock. Tricky had left maybe twenty minutes ago. He'd come over late after the brouhaha at the club with Catch and Nina, after he'd gotten his licks in.

Seeing that Flames patch last night on Catch's jacket had made my stomach flip over and knot, my head swim. I'd frozen up at the sight, then I'd gotten out of there as quickly as I could, taking Jill with me. I'd dropped her off, got myself home, and waited for Tricky in my bed.

When he'd finally shown up, he started telling me about beating up Catch, about Nina and Butler, but I didn't let him talk. He always wanted to talk, but I certainly didn't want to hear about what had happened to Catch and bike club rivalries. I'd climbed onto his naked body and then he finally shut up. I was good at focusing. I was disciplined. Years of physical pain and deprivation had made a great teacher.

I blinked hard, but Finger was no mirage. "What are you doing here?"

"I'll make the coffee," said that scratched, rough deep voice. "You take a shower and get that boy off your body."

"Finger—"

He took a wisp of my hair and held it between his thumb and forefinger. "I liked your red color."

"It hasn't been red for years," I replied. "It was green last month, in fact."

Something resembling a grin twitched a corner of his lips. "Ah, Lenore."

His scarred skin was more weathered than I last remembered. That voice, though. The way that scratchy, husky voice would coil around my name and jam like overloaded electronic circuitry in my chest. Oh, that was still there.

He rose from the side of the bed. "Get up." He stood in the doorway facing me, his hands over his head, planted against the lintel. He waited, his lips tightening as our eyes held onto each other's.

I got up from the bed, letting the sheet fall from me, the air rushing over my heated bare skin, and prowled toward him.

So many years, so long ago, and here he was now. How many times had I dreamed of this? Yearned for it? Then just as quickly tucked it away, hidden it, punched it, stuffed it back down as if it were a Jack-in-the-Box revealing a forbidding skeleton instead of a cute clown or a pretty fairy? Jammed it all the way in and locked it.

But I could never throw away the key.

I'd always fostered that tiny shard of deep dark hope.

I stopped before him, not two inches between his body and my naked one. "The coffee is in a yellow ceramic canister on the kitchen counter," I said. "The cream's in the fridge."

His eyes didn't shift from mine. Not one second. This stoic harshness of his sent a unique slow flutter right through me, a flutter that grew heavy, buckled and burned in my belly right up through my chest. A sensation I hadn't felt for such a long, long time.

Since him.

He remained still, his face severe. Goosebumps raced over my skin, my nipples hardening at his insistence. No hurry, no shame, no petty civilities.

Never between us.

Gone was the joyful man I once knew behind the scars; this man was ruthless and unyielding.

He dropped his arms, moving just a bit to the side, no longer blocking the doorway. I peeled myself from the magnetic force between our bodies and brushed past him, my bare breasts grazing uncomfortably against his leather. Closing the bathroom door behind me, I gripped the sink and took in a deep breath.

Under the burning waterfall of the shower, I shampooed and scrubbed with a jumbo loofah and plenty of almond and Shea butter soap. I did it all over again a second time with another shower gel, and a third.

I quickly towel-dried my hair and threw on a matching pair of my own bright green handmade undies, a billowy cornflower blue kaftan blouse, and my faded cropped jeans. Bright colors always centered me, like the ink all over my body. Barefoot, my thick hair long and damp down my back, I left my bedroom holding my breath, not sure of what I'd find.

Why was he here?

Pale sunlight filtered through my bank of kitchen windows. A fresh day, a new world, a different time.

My favorite pair of antique glazed earthenware coffee cups stood waiting on the kitchen table. Finger sat in a chair, his long legs spread open, his one heavily ringed hand on a bulky thigh, the other wrapped around the oversized golden yellow and stone colored cup. His missing middle fingers were an oddly comforting sight. Familiar, intimate even. A chill stole over my spine, and I released a breath to get rid of it. Three silver chains hung down his still defined chest sprinkled with coils of dark hair and covered in more ink than the last time I'd seen him.

Years had passed by, separating us further. A raging river of different experiences, people, sorrows, victories. We were different now.

Weren't we?

"Are you in Meager because of what Catch did last night?" I asked.

"I had to show my face and make sure things didn't get out of hand. Were you there?"

"Jump found him and Nina together, it got ugly, and I left right after," I said. "Everything under control now?"

"Yes."

"Good."

He nudged a chair out to the side for me, and I sat, bringing the full coffee mug to my lips and taking a sip. Perfect.

He only stared at me.

"Pretty stupid thing for both of them to do," I said.

"Very stupid. It's taken care of."

I met his gaze. "I have no doubt."

He stroked the thick, uneven handle of the mug. "You got a lot of these handmade mugs and dishes, flower pots too. You taking pottery classes or something? Hobby of yours?"

I drank more coffee. "No."

He scanned the three framed photos of Beck I had on the side-board.

"How's your boy?"

"Beck's good." I rubbed my fingers over the scalloping on the cup. "He's a professional musician."

"Guitarist?"

I smiled. "And a pianist, and a drummer. He lives in LA."

Finger crossed his long legs. "But you stayed on here?"

I swallowed more coffee, savoring its rich heat in my mouth. "I like the Black Hills, this is home for me."

He only nodded, his eyes flicking around my small kitchen. "You with Tricky? His property? His old lady?"

"I'm no one's anything. Tricky and I have a good time together off and on when it suits us."

His dark, probing eyes slid to mine once more. I was suddenly desperate to know if he had an old lady. He must have one. He'd been his club's president for a long time now. The chief of a dynasty, undoubtedly sought after by many a woman, and rightly so. Did he have kids? He must have had kids. He'd wanted children.

I didn't ask. I only clamped my jaw together. What was the point of asking? Life had pushed on, and we'd pushed on with it and against it.

"Tania's the one who called me, let me know about Catch at the club," he said. "He's her little brother."

"Yeah, she told me that her brother is a Flame. Ironic, huh? Small, crazy world."

"Isn't it?" His lips curved up in a slight grin. "I made sure the Jacks understood that she and I know each other, so they don't fuck with her now that Catch has pissed them off for the third time."

"Good, I'm glad. She's moved back home to be with her mom who's sick. She's getting a divorce and opening a business here too."

"I know."

"So, you showed up and defused any more fireworks over there, huh?"

"I only defuse when I want to."

Another shiver raced over my skin at his eerie tone.

He brought his mug of coffee to his lips and drank. "You good here then? Your business?"

"I am. It was tough getting started, but I've built a good reputation, and I have solid fans far and wide. I even get a number of tourists on their way to Mt. Rushmore or Sturgis. I'm thinking of expanding online, and I'm designing a makeup line now. I'm happy with my little success."

"You deserve it."

"Thank you."

"That's you in those ads."

My face heated, my tummy clenched tight. "You've seen them?"

"A few of the old ladies at my club have bought your stuff. One of my bros hung a poster of yours up on a wall at the clubhouse."

"Really?"

"Hmm." He drank, he drank me in. "Never a face, just a body."

A body he knew so well.

His gaze fell to my chest, studying my web of tattoos. He leaned forward slowly, and my pulse heated. He pulled my blouse to the side, out of his way. The rough pads of his fingertips seared my skin as they traced the spray of tiny stars, tear drops, birds, and flowers that exploded down my skin, over my left breast.

"This is beautiful," he said, a finger tracing the letter embedded in the flowers.

"Thank you. Work in progress."

My breath stalled as his knuckles brushed over the gold compass whose dial pointed north. His forehead wrinkled, and his heavy eyes lifted to mine once more.

"You still have my compass?" he asked.

"I—"

"No, don't tell me. Forget it," he breathed.

His careful stroke continued, and I wanted to wrap my fingers around his wrist, but not to stop him from touching me. No, to feel the sinewy strength in that arm, to kiss his hand. To encourage him. I suddenly wanted to run my hands up to his shoulders and let him crush me in his embrace. The crush of him. Fuck, how I missed that. I'd blocked it out.

His breathing deepened as his thumb caressed the top of my bare breast, setting off a spiraling ache inside me. It wasn't only the pulse of lust. This was fuller, richer, dizzying. All these years of living a half life when it came to men flared up in front of me, laughing at me, mocking me. Nothing but hollow, vacant…but his one simple touch, the weight of his stare.

I cleared my throat. "I'm proud of you for what you've accomplished." I clenched my jaw before I whispered something else, something more that I shouldn't.

His head dipped as his hand cupped my breast fully, an inarticulate sound escaping his lips. He was ignoring my superficial remarks, wanted more from me than just a friendly conversation.

So did I.

My hand reached out and brushed a scarred cheek. Years ago, I used to want to be able to magically heal those scars with a touch, a kiss. But now I liked the grooves, the jagged lines under my fingertips. They were him, us. A story. Our story. Pain and strength. Survival.

He groaned at the graze of my fingers, his eyes creasing as if he were carefully re-reading something familiar, taking it in. He bent his head and planted a gentle kiss over the compass just below the base of my neck, and I choked back a cry in my throat. The musk of old leather, metal, and the light, clean scent of shampoo rose between us. I held my breath, fought to remain still.

He slowly removed his hand from my flesh, and I sat up straighter in my chair, my pulse bucking uncontrollably. Neither of us said anything for a long while.

"You have a family now?" I started a conversation that would put distance between us once more. My chest tightened waiting for his answer.

"No."

"An old lady?"

"A couple have come and gone."

"Oh. I thought—"

"I was always yours," his voice rasped, his heavy eyes holding mine. "There's no one else but you. Never has been, never will be. No matter what pussy I've had in my bed, it's always been you on my cock, and in here." His long fingers landed on his chest.

Devastating, brutal honesty.

"Finger—"

"Not a fucking one," he breathed.

My heart twisted, my head swam. "What do you want from me?"

"You."

One word, and the house held its breath, the world stood still.

He said, "I want to be with you, Serena."

Serena.

My insides tumbled all over the dark wood floor. The first time he'd used my real name was in a gloomy, shadowy basement dungeon a million years ago. Hearing it then had touched me with a prick of sweetness, an unexpected rush of yearning for more, an inexplicable ache. It touched me now, but deep and thick and rough.

He'd come back for me once, twice, and he'd come for me today. The only one who ever had. No slinking away, no concealing. Finger kept his promises. His word was a vow.

My unrelenting steadfast soldier.

But Finger wasn't made of tin, like the fairy tale. He was made of volatile fire and fierce fury. That insistence of his, brewed on vengeance and laced with hope, had destroyed the iron chains that once held us bound and forged the gleaming metal of his hard faith that had set us free.

My heart beat wildly under his glare. "It's been years. We barely know each other anymore," I said.

A thick, dark eyebrow lifted. "Does that really matter?"

The room shifted around me.

"Do you think I'm just going to hop on the back of your bike, and we're going to ride off into the Nebraska sunset?" I raised my voice. "There's no point now. You've got your life, I've got mine—"

"No point? No point? Timing fucked us, but fuck time! From the first moment we met, we didn't have separate lives."

His raw urgency jolted through me, detonating everything in its path.

"What is it?" His scars tightened, his stern jaw jutted out. "You all up in this Jack?"

I smoothed my hands over the polished wood surface of my kitchen table. "This is about me. I finally have my life the way I want it. I'm financially independent, living off my own work, part of a good community, good friends, good people I trust. My son is grown up and following his own path. And all the ugly shit is over and in the deep past and it needs to stay that way."

"Seeing me brings the deep ugly all back, huh?" His eyes narrowed, his lips smashing together.

I touched his arm. "Seeing you makes me realize how far we've both come, and I'm glad. Glad you're doing well. Glad we can sit here and have a cup of coffee."

He threw his head back and laughed.

My scalp prickled.

"You think I came here for a cup of coffee with you?" he said, his eyes gleaming dark metal.

"Did you kill Med?"

"Turo took care of him. He did it for you. He told me himself."

Nausea swirled in my gut. "How do—"

"After he gave me your new name, I let him live, and that was the beginning of a beautiful friendship." He chuckled.

He was quoting Casablanca now?

"We ended up helping each other out," he continued. "For years now."

I choked back a slew of slimy images of Finger and Turo scheming together, killing together, consuming women together.

"To be clear, the Jacks are my friends. Are they your enemies now after all this crap with Catch?"

"No."

"But they could be?"

"You're so concerned about them, huh?" his voice snapped back, a shadow passing over his features. "You hang out with them now?"

"No, actually, I don't."

His eyes flared. "Just long enough to get laid?"

"Yeah, long enough to get laid. But, more importantly, to support my friends like Alicia and Grace who've been very good to me. Finger, everything's changed, we've changed—"

He swung his head to the side and pushed up from the table. The mugs shook, coffee spilled. We both stared at the puddles of dark liquid. In a flash of movement, he bent over me, a warm hand cuffing my neck. My pulse pounded under his grip.

"This hasn't changed for me, Sunshine. This hasn't changed, and we are not over," he said. A Mission Statement. Finger's Declaration of Us.

His raspy voice uttering his ridiculous nickname for me blazed through my veins; a whisper of an ancient intimacy sending a skitter of hot iron barbs around my throat, spiking my skin, burning deep.

"We've been over for years, Finger."

"All the reasons to be apart are done with—Med, your marriage. Why shouldn't we be together?"

I stiffened. There was one reason. One.

His grip eased, his fingers sliding down my throat. "We're alone, Lenore. We don't have to be."

"I'm not alone."

His lips quirked. "I wasn't alone last night either."

His words jammed in my chest like rotten garbage leaking toxins, infecting me. "I'm sure you weren't."

"None of that makes a damn bit of difference, both of us killing time. But I won't let time kill us any longer." His voice was firm, even. "You're a part of me, the very best part, and we belong together. If all it is with Tricky is getting laid, dump him. You got me now."

Finger released me and strode off, his heavy footfalls booming through my small house, the creaky wood floors groaning under his turbulent battering. The screen door whined, slammed, and I flinched. His bike's engine ripped the air and thundered away.

I sank back into my chair, wrapping my arms around myself. But it did no good.

The shaking wouldn't stop.

50
FINGER

"WHERE'S TANIA?" I ASKED BUTLER.

I'd made it back to the One-Eyed Jacks. I wanted to be gone within the hour.

Butler glared at me. "She's with her brother," he replied.

Before I'd left this morning to go see Lenore, I'd woken up Tania and told her to go check on her brother in his holding cell and make sure he was ready to ride home by the time I got back. I assured her I wouldn't be getting rid of Catch, but he had to learn to keep his dick in check. We both agreed that it seemed Catch had real feelings for Nina, that she wasn't just some joyride. Before we'd gotten to that conversation, though, she'd shot up in the bed when I told her I was going into town for a couple hours. She'd known where I was headed, that there was no way I wouldn't go see her.

She grabbed my arm as I shoved my boots on, stopping me. "Please, be kind to her."

"Tania, all I've ever wanted was the best for her."

"I know," she'd whispered.

I'd stayed up most of the night trying to figure out what I'd say, what I'd do. All I knew was I had to see her. Judge my reaction to her, judge hers. Feel it.

Oh, I'd felt all right. And I knew.

My blood knew. My skin knew. My heartbeat knew.

I wanted more.

I'd demanded to be with her. It was a force I couldn't control. A base instinct, a reflex that took hold of me sitting there in her beautiful house, watching her, breathing her in. Touching her. I was glad

I'd said what I had. Fuck timing, fuck all the reasons.

I wanted another chance with her. We were unfinished business. She was a river that still rushed through my veins, the source undiscovered.

I wanted her. I wanted her back, to try again. To have that life we always wanted together, or maybe to try something new.

Right now, I had to find out from Butler what the hell his intentions were by having Reich's sister-in-law as his old lady. Was it a ploy set up by Reich? Did the two of them have a secret deal between them and were pulling my chain? I wouldn't allow Reich access to my territory, no way in this hell or the other, and I'd freeze out the Jacks for good if Butler was double dealing me.

Butler glared at me, his pale blue eyes looking like chunks of glass in the sunlight out in the Jacks' courtyard.

"I want to talk to you," I told him. "Let's take a walk down by the track."

We walked down the side of the hill to the old go-kart track where two Jacks were testing a rat rod.

"I'll get straight to the point," I said.

"You always do."

"Why are you with that girl?"

"Excuse me?"

"Your old lady. Don't tell me you fell hard for her and dragged her all the way out here from Ohio 'cause you couldn't live without her."

Butler crossed his arms. "Something like that."

"That something ain't it."

He didn't say a word.

"It's me you're talking to, Butler, not Jump. You and me have always been able to put our cards on the table with each other."

"I went with my gut on this one."

Just like I thought, no heart involved. Only his strategic brain cells and maybe his dick, but not his heart.

"You went with your brain," I shot back. "Nina is connected to Reich's club—one of the strongest charters of my MC—which pushes product from the east into the south. He's been looking to find his own outlet through the Plains to the west, but that's my route, and so far, all these years, no one's fucked with me. Reich, your old lady's brother-in-law, has been dying to get some play out here. You hooked up with that girl and handed him access to the Jacks on a silver platter while you hooked up with me at the same time?"

"I haven't handed anybody anything, let alone on a silver platter. And I'm not interested in fucking with you, Finger. I worked for you whenever I was allowed to while I was nomad, even did it on the sly when I shouldn't have. I respect you, always have, for years now, and you know it."

"I do know. But don't tell me Jump let you back on board here at his club 'cause he missed your handsome face and witty personality."

He let out a dry laugh. "He definitely didn't miss me."

"You wanted back into your club. You had to bring something to the table, and you did. That's good. I understand that."

Butler explained his deep-seated guilt about having let down his club with his cocaine addiction and subsequent double dealing.

"That's a huge fuck-up," I said. "But you do something Reich doesn't like—let's say, kick his sister-in-law to the curb now that she cheated on you—he'll come after you. He's a possessive shit on all counts—business, family, women. He doesn't need much in the way of an excuse to drop everything and come calling." My neck straightened. "But you knew that already, didn't you?"

He returned my hard gaze with his own. "Yeah, I know a few things about Reich. A few things I shouldn't. I did a second job for his chapter last year, a job nobody else would touch. That gave me an in with him. An in I took advantage of."

I needed to know what Butler had found out. I'd been patiently waiting for years to hang Reich with a noose of his own making. To rally the Flames against him with solid proof. To ring that bell for all to hear—unmistakeable and clear. This was why I'd nudged Butler his way in the first place.

"And the frosting on that cake was hooking up with his old lady's sister to keep you and him on the same page?" I asked.

"Something like that."

"How long do you think this little deal you've got going with Reich is gonna last, bitch or no?" I let out a laugh. "Now that her and Catch have made a spectacle of themselves, you can be sure it's going to be common knowledge that there's a crack in your relationship, that she ain't happy. That you two are done. Someone's gonna try to exploit that rift. Exploit both our clubs."

"I won't let that happen. Nina fucked up, and she knows it. She knows what's at stake. She's keeping low for now."

"Damage is already done, Butler. Add to the mix the Broken Blades, who have had it raw for you and for me since we got rid of the Calderón group. Notch needed that alliance. Now he's like a hungry junkyard dog, desperate to keep whatever is left of his club together, desperate for a bone let alone a good meal. He's fucking rabid, and I like him that way."

Notch would never give in to me, and my mouth watered at the thought of his next move and my ultimate retaliation. It needed to be done right.

"And then you've got Jump on your back," I continued. "How long until your Prez pulls the rug out from under your sparkly ass? I bet he loved this shit last night, huh?"

Butler brushed his boot into the dirt. "Yeah, he enjoyed it."

"I don't want what we have going on to be fucked with," I said. "I'm trying to focus on patching in the Blades right now."

"And you don't think that's gonna stir up trouble?"

"It sure as hell is," I said. "But if I don't make a play now that they're down, someone else will, and soon. We can't have outsiders coming in so close to our territories. Jump thinks it's got nothing to do with him. He's living with blinders on."

"Jesus, you and Jump have never seen eye to eye," said Butler. "Two of you have been like oil and water for as far back as I can remember. Hell, Dig and I'd been this close to getting shit started with you, and then the minute Dig got killed, Jump made sure to break any ties with you. I never knew what the—"

"That's between me and Jump," I cut him off.

The rat rod roared past. That was Tricky driving, spinning around the track, fresh from Lenore's bed.

Fucker.

I spat on the ground. "Don't stay comfortable, Butler. After last night, shit's up in the air. You made a good play, but you'd better sprout eyes in the back of your head to stay above water."

"I had an opportunity with him, and I took it."

My eyes drilled into his. "You seem mighty confident to me. You've got something on Reich, don't you?"

Butler remained silent, his eyes following the car speeding around the track.

"And it's good, huh?" I folded my arms across my chest. "I can't get involved. You know I'll have to take his back over yours if it all comes crashing down on your head."

He eyed me. "I know, but you won't."

Yes. He had something I wanted.

"Things just got much more interesting then. Remember, you get Reich ticked at you, don't expect me to save you. He might just test us both." I raised my chin. "This ain't the eighties or the nineties no more. The landscape keeps changing, brother. Do not under-estimate the players on it. Wounded dogs do desperate things to stay alive. Be prepared. If Reich sniffs an opportunity to make you squirm, he's gonna take it."

Which way would Butler sway? Either way, I wasn't going to sit around and trust it would be my way. I wanted whatever he had on Reich.

Tricky raised a fist outside his open car window, a huge grin on his face as he gunned around the track again.

My jaw clenched. "I'm heading out."

Butler shifted his weight, his tongue toying with his bottom lip. "Hey, what's with you and Tania?"

Poor bastard, he had it bad for her. Did I seem freshly fucked after a night with Tania? I sure as hell hoped so. Butler needed to sweat. He needed to work for a good woman like her.

"What do you fucking think?" I asked, my tone perfectly pitched to the tune of irritation.

His eyes widened a few degrees. He was struggling to keep it in check. "I don't know what to think, but—"

"But what?" I eyed him, pushing down my amusement. "What's it to you?"

He shut the hell up and averted his gaze back to the track.

That's what I thought.

"You worry about Reich being pissed about his girl," I said. "You know you can't dump Nina's ass just yet, if that's what you want. Reich will use it as an excuse to come gunning for you and your club, and he'll try to rope me into the party. You got to sit tight, and you got to make her sit tight even if you gotta lock her down to do it. I don't want trouble for Catch or my club. And I don't want any blowback from your club on Tania because of her brother, you hear?"

"Loud and clear," Butler's voice clipped.

"Reich is a vengeful motherfucker. He's good at finding ways to make it burn, make it sting."

We trekked back toward the clubhouse.

"Shit changes fast out in the prairie, man," I said. "You've been away a while now. You've forgotten how the glare of the sun can create figments, illusions that just ain't there."

"I haven't forgotten a damn thing."

I tipped my head forward. "That's good, 'cause you can never be sure what's out there in the wild grasses, lying in wait, lurking."

51
FINGER

I RODE INTO SOUTH DAKOTA WITH Catch. Today was his daughter's birthday, and Jill was having a party for her at Catch's mother's house. After the party cleared out, Catch would have his daddy time with Becca. I dropped him off in Rapid to hang with a friend of his from high school until the birthday party was over. Nina would be at the party, being a friend of Jill's.

I eyed him one last time as I backed out of the friend's driveway.

"I'll be right here until Tania calls me giving me the all clear to come over," Catch said. "I swear."

"You call me."

"Will do."

I headed over to the Jacks in Meager to find Butler and discuss a few details he needed to be aware of for a meeting I'd set up for him with one of my transport connections in Idaho. He wanted business from me, he was going to get it. But he was also going to get me staying in his face keeping his feet hopping and him guessing. Once I was done with him, I planned on seeing Lenore.

Butler came out of "Eagle Wings," the club's former auto and bike repair center that had now been transformed, under Lock's direction and ownership, into a top tier refurb and custom design shop.

"Hey," Butler greeted me. "You came with Catch to make sure today is all about daddy and his little girl?"

I took off my heated gloves, flexing my fingers. "That's right."

He shot me a look. "You gonna go over and have some cake and juice, too?"

The man had it real bad for Tania.

"I've got other shit to do while he visits. Let's discuss this meeting. They've been wanting to meet you for a while now. Press is a brother from Idaho and I want him to work with you on a new route headed West using some of your tried and true and some of mine."

Nina showed up at the club in her small SUV and waved a plastic bag in the air at Butler. He gestured toward the clubhouse, and she nodded at him, heading inside. Within a few minutes, she came back out and joined us.

"Sorry to interrupt," she murmured, glancing at me then back at Butler.

"No problem," he said.

"I left the change of clothes you wanted for your trip in your room on the bed."

"Thanks."

"Sure. I'm off to the party."

"I'll walk you to your car." Butler threw an arm around his old lady's shoulders as they crossed the yard to her RAV4. They gave a show that they were a happy couple with a hug and a kiss, and she slid into the driver's seat.

He strode back toward me, pushing his blond hair behind his ears.

"She settled her ass down?" I asked.

"She's fine."

She was burning for Catch is what she was doing. I'd caught him texting with her the other day. I couldn't blame him. But I'd made it clear there was to be no physical contact until she and Butler had officially broken up.

A grin pushed at the edges of my mouth as I shoved my gloves back on. This was almost comical. "I'm off."

Jump pulled in the courtyard in an SUV, braking alongside Nina's car. Her head was bent over the steering wheel. She got out of her car, a scowl on her face, talking to Jump as she gestured at her RAV4.

"Looks like your woman's got car trouble. You gonna fly to her rescue?" I asked Butler.

Jump got down from his vehicle and got into the RAV4, settling in the driver's seat.

"Jump seems to be handling it," Butler said.

"Yeah." Jump was a regular hero.

Butler and I tagged fists, giving each other a nod. I swung a leg over my chopper, adjusting myself in my saddle. "Call me, let me know how the meet goes."

"Will do."

Suddenly, Jump propelled himself from the car, his long braid flying, shoving Nina back as he went.

Boom.

I launched off my bike, the ground shuddering underneath me. Nina's car burst into flames, shaking like a toy. Orange fireballs rolled and unfurled in the air. Nina's car had been bombed.

Butler was frozen to the spot. I grabbed hold of his arm, and we sprang behind a row of bikes, our hands flying over our heads. Charred debris soared in the air and rained down on us, crashing to the ground.

He shot up. "Nina!"

Women screamed, men shouted, alarms blared. Thick black billows of smoke blocked any trace of Nina or Jump.

Butler hurtled toward the burning car, me at his heels.

Nina lay facedown at the other end of the car, her one arm twisted awkwardly, blood splattered along the side of her face.

"Ambulance is on its way!" Boner's yell cut through the air.

Jump was sprawled on the ground in a heap on the other end within the black mushroom cloud of smoke. I crouched over his lifeless body. Was he dead? I hoped to fuck he was.

"I don't give a shit what you need. Can't help you." Jump's words from two decades ago were like a snake rattling its tail at me. *"Why should I take a risk for you? No fucking way,"* he'd sneered while me and Serena were on the run, bleeding, in pain.

I'd never forgotten it. That was the last time I'd ever asked anyone for a favor, ever begged or pleaded for anything.

Now that me and the Jacks were finding a rhythm between us,

Jump still hadn't dropped his pent up spite with me and my club. He'd bottled it up like old wine over the centuries, releasing the cork and setting off odorous fumes whenever he felt like it. I needed Butler to function in high gear, not be stuck in stop-start traffic. Once I finally dealt with the Broken Blades and their territory was all mine to restructure, I'd need the Jacks one hundred per cent cooperative, not defensive or wary.

I leaned over Jump sprawled on the ground, and a straggly wheezing filled my ear. My pulse picked up speed at his struggling to breathe. He was still alive; there was hope.

My father's words roared back to me: *"Patience, planning, and precise calculating. And many times you need to improvise at the last minute. You gotta be ready for anything at any time."*

Anything at any time.

I was ready.

I pressed one gloved hand onto Jump's chest, the other pinching his nostrils closed.

His wheezing intensified for a moment, his eyes jerking open, eyebrows flinching. He recognized me. Yes, he knew. He held my gaze for a split second, a choking sound erupting in his throat, and in that second the pressure I exerted on him sapped him of his shitty life. That feeling of a good, just kill never got old. Clean, bright, fucking enthralling.

Die, motherfucker.

"How's Jump?" Butler shouted out at me through the dense smoke.

I leveled my gaze at him, and Butler's mouth dropped open, eyes wide. He could see what I was doing. He froze.

I would crush him if he dared fuck with me.

"Butler!" Boner came up behind him. "How is she?"

Butler returned his focus to Nina. "She's out, but she's alive."

I rose from Jump's lifeless corpse and retreated. One-Eyed Jacks darted past me, wielding fire extinguishers. Shouts and foam flew over the smoldering vehicle. Kicker, their VP, pounded on Jump's chest, giving him CPR. Sirens wailed louder and louder in the distance, getting closer and closer.

"Jump's gone," Kicker hollered over the chaos. "He's gone!"

The burn of rubber, the singe of metal filled my lungs.

Fucking enthralling.

I WANTED TO GET OUT OF there, but I had to play along. We all followed the ambulance to the hospital in Rapid, and Tania arrived soon after with a bunch of the old ladies who'd been with her at the birthday party. She was relieved to see me, and we stood together waiting with everyone else to hear from the surgeon who was working on Nina. I'd called Catch and told him to stay put, not to dare show his face at the hospital, that I'd let him know how the girl was doing.

Butler was motionless, in a daze. He'd had a wife years back who'd gotten killed in a bike accident, and she'd died in his arms on the road. I don't think he'd ever forgiven himself for it, and it showed now.

The surgeon showed up and reported on Nina's condition and how she'd be okay. He adjusted the tablet in his grip. "And the baby is doing fine."

Tania froze at my side.

"Baby?" screeched one of the old ladies.

Tania slumped against me, and I wrapped a hand around her arm, steadying her. Her eyes were glued to Butler.

Oh, babe, I know that slice of hurt.

I let out a heavy breath, my lips twisting. There was no guarantee this baby was Butler's. It could be Catch's. This shit only got better and better.

Tania made a noise in the back of her throat and pushed back from me and went to him, talking to him in low tones. He took out a cell phone from a handbag. Nina's? He tapped on the screen and handed it to Tania who then tapped on it herself. She was looking for something, someone. Her face tightened, her lips parting. Her thumb swished once, twice, three, four times. She'd found something interesting. She took in a tiny breath and glanced around, catching my eye.

I slanted my head at her.

Tania only chewed on her lips and went back to the phone, finally holding it to the side of her face. She spoke briefly and handed the phone to Butler. She returned to my side, her mouth pinched, her large dark eyes cold. She was pissed.

"What's wrong?" I asked her.

"I just saw Catch and Nina's hot little love texts and selfies all over her phone—in full high resolution color. The phone Butler is using right now to talk to her sister."

I pressed my back against the wall. "Your brother's got it bad for her."

"Yeah, he told me, but newsflash, she's also been sexting with that Flame who brought her to Meager. Led, was it?"

I grit my teeth. Nina was cozy with Led, Reich's right hand man? This soap opera just got more interesting. Maybe Nina was really working for Reich undercover, setting up Butler and in turn, me?

"Good for Goldilocks," I said.

I had to blow this shit open. Now with Nina in the hospital, I was positive that Reich would get his ass down here any day, making accusations, and I had to be ready.

Tania shook her dark hair from her face. "Where does she find the time?"

"Keep your voice down."

"Oh please," Tania seethed.

Jesus, she had it bad too. She needed to be patient just a little while longer. I leaned in to her, my mouth at her ear. "Her relationship with Butler is as solid as the wind, Tania."

"What?"

"Butler and Nina—it's fake."

"No," she breathed.

"Yes. Pure business between clubs."

"What is this?" she said loudly. "The fucking eighteenth century?"

I clamped a hand around her upper arm and dragged her down the hallway away from the Jacks, who were already staring at us. I pulled her in close to me against a wall.

Her face was red. "Did you hear what the doctor just said? Butler's going to be a daddy."

"What makes you think that kid is Butler's? Could be Catch's."

Her mouth fell open. "Oh, shit." She glanced over at Butler still talking on the phone. She was worried about him.

Her hand tugged on the edge of my leather jacket. "We can't tell Catch about this baby until we're sure. Nina's family is going to be pissed about her getting hurt, aren't they? You think they'll come here and make trouble for the Jacks and for Butler? They'll blame him? Come after him?"

"Sounds right," I replied.

"Is there any way you can help him? Do you know who did this? Jump is dead. The president of a club has been murdered. All hell is going to break loose now, right?"

"You're worried?"

"Of course I'm worried. They're my friends. This is my hometown we're talking about."

"I meant, you're worried about Butler?" I asked.

She leveled her gaze at me. "Yes, I am. He's a good guy."

I'd help her make it happen, if that's what she wanted. If she really wanted him. I let out a huff of air. "Good, bad—it's all relative at the end of the day."

"It can't be," she said, her jaw tight. "Some things simply cannot be relative. For you, they probably are. But I don't live that way."

Some things were relative for me, yes, but the vein pulsing in my heart for Serena and the one for my club—they were absolute.

I pulled Tania in closer. "Shit's either real, or it isn't," I whispered, squeezing the back of her neck. I planted a kiss on her forehead. "Relax. I'm going to see what I can do. You make sure the pics on Nina's phone don't get erased."

"Okay," she murmured, taking in a breath.

I loved how Tania could rise above the mire immediately after feeling her shit out. Her loyalty, her concern for what was just—even in the face of the ultimate rejection—always compelled her forward.

My hand stroked the side of her jaw. "You go support your guy over there. He could use it."

She made a face at me. "He's not my guy."

I let out a laugh. I loved teasing her. "Baby, you haven't been able to tear your eyes away from him. You went to him in his hour of need, then jumped up and down in the man's defense like you just did? He's your guy."

52
FINGER

BUTLER WASN'T ANSWERING HIS PHONE. I tucked my cell back in my pocket.

Either he was annoyed with me about being close with Tania. Tough shit. Or he was keeping his distance because he'd seen me kill his Prez. A good reason.

Would he tell? I didn't think so, but I was sure it was eating him up. Even though Jump rode Butler's ass hard since he fucked up last year, and created roadblocks for almost every damned new idea Butler had, Jump was his Prez.

"What's up?" asked Drac getting off his bike that he'd parked alongside mine at the Broken Blades clubhouse.

We'd come to southern Nebraska to have a chat with Notch. Had the Broken Blades been the ones responsible for the bomb in Nina's car? That was the general consensus. They were pissed off at the Jacks and at the Flames not only for destroying their deal with the Calderas Group, but for a number of their members being arrested and a lot of their property seized (the underground warehouse was still safe, luckily).

I wasn't convinced they were the ones responsible for the car bomb. Why would they target Nina? Why not plant a bomb on a Jack's vehicle or bike or even at the clubhouse itself? Going after an old lady was just not done, unless she was some kind of traitor, and that was real old school. Then again, Nina had a Flame connection, Reich being her brother-in-law. Were the Blades taking care of two birds with one stone here to keep the Flames off their ass?

"I just heard that Reich and his old lady are in Rapid City to see

Nina in the hospital," I said.

"Terrific."

"Been trying to call Butler. I wanted to give him a heads up, but he isn't answering. Fuck it."

"We're going to have to pay Reich a visit at the hospital, huh? Give him the brotherly welcome," Drac said.

"Oh yeah. We should," I muttered under my breath. "Thank fuck I have you to remind me of my manners."

"You're welcome." Drac let out a snort.

"Let's get this shit done." I strode over to where Notch and three of his men waited for us.

Notch only scowled at me. He had pronounced eye sockets and a long nose, wrinkly, pasty-white skin, and long thin dark hair that stuck to his head. He was the Child Catcher from "Chitty Chitty Bang Bang," a movie I'd often watched at the neighbor's house when my mom would pull her disappearing acts. The Child Catcher had spooked me, made me actually shudder and hide under the covers at night. But boogey men in the dark and vile monsters didn't scare me no more. Notch only disgusted me. Instead of an English accent, he had a southern one, but he was just as snide, just as hostile, and as freaky as that movie villain of my memory.

"To what do I owe the pleasure of this visit?" he said, chewing tobacco, his lips twitching under the movement. "Although, you coming here is sullying my property."

"What's left of it. Ain't much."

"Whose fault is that?" He spat on the ground.

"Yours, for shitting on it for so many years," I replied. "Didn't appreciate what you had, didn't handle it right. Your problem. Now it's come to this. I'm here to offer you an out."

"Sweet. I ain't buying." He covered his balls with a hand, a smirk on his ugly, thin face. The tall, bulky guy at his side, Pick, remained grim.

Was Notch just being cocky or cock sure?

The sneer on his face stretched from self-satisfied smirk to all out taunt. "Keeping the Flames of Hell away from my club is high on my list of priorities."

"You don't want to give in to me. I get that. But this is your only way to survive. I'm not demanding total annihilation here. Patch in. You know you need to. You know it's the smart move. The strong one. You inviting outsiders into our territories is a huge mistake. You can't see that, you're an idiot."

"Fuck you."

Drac let out a heavy sigh, more like a grunt.

"You set the bomb in that old lady's car at the Jacks?" I said. "Because you know she's a Flame by family. Not to mention, Jump is dead because of it," I said.

Notch crossed his arms, his eyes narrowing. "Why the fuck would I do that?"

"You're pissed at them, pissed at us. Who the hell knows how your rancid brain works?"

He laughed, a lazy, wheezing sort of laugh, an I-got-nothing-more-to-lose-by-fucking-with-you laugh. "Oh, I like your compliments so early in the morning, I do." He ran his tongue across his yellow teeth. "Someone set off a fire in our junkyard last night. Fucking with our business. Today's Jump's funeral, and I'm thinking the Jacks' are playing games with us, but this ain't high school, and I ain't playing. Why don't you let them know for me, huh, seeing as to how you all sniff each other's panties now?"

My phone vibrated in my back pocket.

Catch. He'd called twice before, but I didn't want to interrupt the articulate poetry that was Notch. I'd left Catch holding down the fort while Drac and I were gone. In fact, I'd been giving him plenty of extra responsibilities lately, plenty of short term runs out of town in order to keep his head in the game. He was like a caged tiger, and I didn't want him going off again. Not now. He needed to feel the hum of work filling him, steering him. So far so good.

I lifted my chin at Notch. "You'll come crawling to me real soon. And it'll be too late."

"Yeah," he returned.

I aimed a look at Drac, and we both stalked off to our bikes where I dialed up Catch.

"Hey, Prez," said Catch. "I thought you should know that Reich called me earlier."

"And?"

"He's in town and wanted access to a safe house for tonight. And get this, he wanted one in South Dakota. Said he didn't want to cross state lines."

A sharp prickle razored up my spine. "Then he's up to no good in South Dakota."

"I sent Split to open up for him. I had too much shit to do around here, plus I have that call from Texas in about an hour."

"When's this happening?"

"Split's on his way now to Reich's motel in Deadwood to meet up with him and escort him to the cabin."

"All right. Drac and I are done with Notch, and we're on our way to Colorado now. Keep me posted."

I shut the phone down, and ground my jaw at the thought that Reich was on my territory using my property for fuck knows what. I wanted to head up there right now, but I couldn't blow off this funeral we were headed to in Colorado.

Drac and I took off toward Sydney, Nebraska where we'd shoot south on Route 80 to Colorado Springs.

All through the three hour ride, all through the funeral and then a meeting with our brothers over a new shipment of guns and assorted weapons, plus special top of the line surveillance equipment Den insisted we all had to get, the thought of Reich gnawed at me, clawing at one inch of intestine at a time, the sensation twisting through me. Couldn't shake it.

After business was taken care of, we spent the evening at our brothers' clubhouse in Denver. The barbecue pit fire had been cleared of the steak grill and was now roaring to keep us warm in the chilly night air as we shot the shit outside. I'd just finished my third beer when my phone buzzed, the screen lighting up with the time. Midnight. And Catch's name.

"Prez!" He was breathless, his voice stressed.

"What happened?"

"It's Reich."

"What about him?"

"He had Tania—"

"What the fuck are you talking about?" I shot up from my chair, knocking into a girl who was clearing the empties. I grabbed her arm, steadying her as I walked away from the table, my pulse speeding.

"Tania was over at Butler's house, and—" Catch could barely sputter the words out. "Reich showed up and took her as she was leaving his place. He brought her to his hotel and then to the safe house—our goddamn safe house!—and kept her there to push Butler's buttons or some shit. Butler called me, and I brought him and the Jacks up there and we took the fucker down and got Tania out."

My heart pounded in my chest, everything in my field of vision was seeped in red. *Tania.*

No.

I'd heard a lot of shit about Reich over the years since he'd left Missouri. He was rough with women, real rough. He also got his kicks on watching other men be rough with a woman, which was just for starters.

I ground my jaw. "How's Tania? Did he—"

"No, he didn't fucking touch her. Not like that."

"What the fuck does that mean?" I roared.

Drac and two other men stopped mid-conversation and stared at me.

"He had her tied up, and she was fucking bleeding." Catch's voice wavered. He took in a deep breath. "Shit…"

My insides dropped. "What did he do to her? Tell me."

"He—he was cutting her when we got there. I freaked. I grabbed Reich, got him down, and we brought him back. Butler took Tania with him to the Jacks. I just talked to him now and he confirmed they arrived and she's okay."

"I'm going up to Meager. Drac's coming to you to hold things down. You keep that fucker tied like a hog, I don't give a shit what he says, you hear?"

"Yeah, yeah, of course. Look—"

"What else?"

"There was a Smoking Gun there with Reich."

My heart jumped a beat, the blood surging in my veins. The enemy with Reich?

"Who? From where?"

"I don't know his name, but he was from Kansas. Tania got a knife in him, keeping him off of Butler. The Jacks got him down, but I let him take off because, well, I had to, right?"

That goddamn treaty.

"Shit was happening so fast," Catch muttered. "I was focused on getting my sister out of there in one piece and getting Reich in the van."

"I'm leaving Denver now. Keep him down. Drac's coming to you." I shut down the call.

Drac was in my face, eyes wide. "You all right? What the hell is going on?"

"We got to leave. You get to the Farm. Reich kidnapped Tania today. Catch and Butler got her free of him. I don't know what the fuck is going on, why he did this, but I've got to see her with my own eyes. I've got to see her, make sure she's all right."

"Okay—"

"I need to see her with my own eyes, make sure she's all right." My voice was loud, raw. I was repeating myself.

Drac gripped my arms. "Hey. Hey. Do what you gotta do. We'll keep him down 'till you get there. Let him stew until you get back."

"Slow cooker." Keeping him tied, isolated, in the dark.

"Right. Slow cooker." Drac's long teeth dragged along his bottom lip. "You good to ride?"

"I'm good, let's go." I thumped his chest with a hand. "Let's go!"

We said our goodbyes. Priest, the chapter president, gave me a quick hug.

"Sorry about cutting out," I said. "I appreciate the hospitality today. Need to get home."

Priest slapped me on the back. "Anytime. Always good to see you. You need back up, man? You got it."

"Nah, we're good, thanks. I just need to get there."

"Ride safe, Finger."

Priest tagged fists with Drac as I moved toward my bike.

We headed northeast for I-76 to take us out of Colorado. It would be seven hours to Meager.

I couldn't get there fast enough.

53
FINGER

I CHARGED THROUGH THE CLUBHOUSE OF the
One-Eyed Jacks just before seven in the morning. Alicia, Jump's
widow, gestured down the hall to the bedrooms, knowing what I
was after.

I pushed the door open and stopped short.

Grace sat on the edge of the bed, patting a piece of white gauze
over Tania's chest. They both turned abruptly, their faces haggard.

"Tania," staggered out of my mouth, a mix of relief and concern
sloshed with anger.

Tania's pale face was streaked with dirt, traces of mascara, remnants of fear and adrenaline. "I'm fine." She tugged at the big black
T-shirt she wore, adjusting it on herself, a hand at her chest.

"That's all she keeps saying," Grace said, her voice sharp. "I'm
fine. I'm fine."

"But I am, honey," Tania said, eyeing her.

"Sure you are." Grace pitched the gauze into a small plastic bag
at her side and shot up from the bed, wiping at her eyes. "Take a
look. See how fine she is. You'll appreciate it."

"Grace, don't." Tania's face reddened.

"I'll leave you two alone." Grace brushed past me and left the
room.

I approached the edge of the bed, my eyes darting to the red
marks around Tania's wrists to the cuts on her fingers. I yanked
down the loose V of her T-shirt. My pulse slammed to a halt and
hammered all at once.

An F sliced into the skin of her upper chest.

"Motherfuckers!"

"Finger—"

"That's about me, clear as day!" I bit out through my clenched jaw.

The vicious red F on her smooth white skin was a cheap imitation of the cuts on my face. She didn't deserve being held down and cut, she didn't deserve any of this shit.

My throat closed, my blood churned. "He used you to send me a message, to—"

"Please, please don't start some kind of war over this."

"War's already begun, baby."

Reich fraternizing with the enemy, laying out a red carpet for the Smoking Guns in my territory? I wasn't going to let that happen, no way, not ever, especially now with Lenore living here.

Tania pushed up in the bed. "They can't find her, can they?"

She was thinking what I was thinking.

"One of them was with Reich," Tania whispered. "And if you—"

"I'm going to take care of this."

"Oh, yeah?" Butler's voice came from behind me.

I spun around. "They took her from you, asshole. What was she doing with you anyhow?" The jerk had an old lady at the hospital, and the woman he really cared about had been taken out from under him.

"Finger, I was at Butler's place because I wanted to be." Tania raised her voice. "They took me when I left the building."

"I don't need you defending me, Tania." Butler's eyes flashed at her from the doorway where he stood.

"Both of you need to concentrate on getting things right between your clubs," she said. "That's how you can make this"—Tania pointed at her chest wound—"better."

Butler and I stood there glaring at each other. He blamed me, I blamed him. But hell, we needed each other now to clear the deck. Blades, Guns, Reich. All. Of. Them.

Tania touched my arm, and my thick gaze met hers. "I need you to do me a favor."

"Anything," I said.

Butler let out a huff.

"I need to see my brother."

"Of course."

"What are you up to, Tania?" Butler asked, his voice sharp.

"In this huge mess, I see an opportunity arising for everyone, something I don't think you see—a first step. I want to make it happen in an unequivocal way."

Butler's eyes narrowed. "Unequivocal?"

"That's right. Do you need me to define that word for you?" she asked.

Her sass was on track. A good sign.

Butler's lips pressed together. "No, I don't."

Her gaze darted back to me. "Finger?"

"I'll make it happen," I replied. "In a very unequivocal way." I shot Butler a pointed look, which he flung right back at me.

"Is Catch far away?" Tania asked.

"No," I said.

"Good. Get him up here fast. And you," she said to Butler, "let him come here to see me. Please. And I need to see Nina."

"Nina? What for?" asked Butler.

Tania was looking at the bigger picture to fix what could be fixed right here, right now. She was going to derail this circus train.

And if Butler would get his head out of his ass, he'd claim Tania for himself.

I lifted my chin at Tania. "You might not be my old lady, baby, but you sure are thinking like one, and I like it. A fuck of a lot."

Butler shot me an icy blue glare. *Ha.*

"There's something else I need to discuss with you. Alone. Sorry, Butler," Tania murmured.

"You two do what you want. I'm out of here." Butler pulled something small from his back pocket and threw it on the bed. A lipstick. "This is yours." He stalked from the room leaving Tania looking as dejected as a girl who didn't get asked to the prom.

"What did you want to tell me?" I asked, my voice lower, softer.

She picked up the lipstick, wrapping her fingers around it. "That Smoking Gun with Reich—"

"Yeah?"

"I recognized his club logo, just like her tattoo." Her voice shook.

The small tattoo of a gun wielding skeleton "Rena" had on her lower abs. The one she'd trashed by slicing an F over it in that motel bathroom a million years ago.

My eyelids jammed closed. "Tania," I cut off her trip down nightmare lane.

"Reich has set up the Smoking Guns with the Broken Blades," she said in a rush. "From what they were saying, it's been in the works for a while, but now, the Blades finally said yes to it."

So it was official. Reich had backstabbed his own club by engineering an alliance between two of our territorial enemies. Specifically, my primary enemies. This was the new deal Notch had been on a high about.

My eyes darted to the F carved into Tania's skin. "Who cut you, Tania? Who did it?"

"The Smoking Gun."

"What was his name?"

"Scrib," came the reply. The reply I didn't want to hear.

My breath hooked in my chest.

"He told me he's been watching your club since things got touchy with the Blades months ago," she said in a rush.

Scrib had been the one watching us.

"He recognized me from when I came to Nebraska with Grace," Tania said.

"Figured you and I were connected?"

She nodded. "Reich accused me of being Butler's mistress, and then after I opened my big fat mouth and said that I knew you, he accused me of being your and Butler's go between. He obviously doesn't like it that you two are allies."

Seething bile seeped through my veins polluting my blood.

Scrib was here on my soil, my territory, and Reich had brought him here, the two of them plotting. Together they had tortured an innocent woman for kicks to send me and Butler a message. To fuck with my head.

Fuck that.

Fuck both of them.

Fuck it all.

"I'd overheard them talking when Reich locked me in the bathroom at the cabin," Tania continued. "Scrib told him how Pick, this Broken Blade guy, was impressed with his offer this time around. Scrib said he was counting on this all to work out. That the Smoking Guns has been looking to stretch this way for a long time now."

I'll bet they were.

If I didn't do something about Reich now, if the Smoking Guns took over the Blades using them as a satellite for their own purposes and resources, it was only a matter of time before they pushed and shoved at my borders and chomped at my business, their ultimate goal and Reich's.

If they had cut Tania for kicks, what would they do if they found Lenore and realized who she was?

Scrib had been there that last night of my captivity. He'd gone down on Rena, he'd cut me. He'd taken part in the revelry that night, and on many, many other nights. She'd told me about his repeated assaults on her in hallways, while she'd be doing laundry, when he'd take her home after babysitting his own kid. If he found her, I had no doubt he'd be leading the rampage for her blood.

Reich had set this shit in motion, that motherfucker. This was Reich doing what he did best. Setting fires and keeping them blazing, all the while looking out for number one and hitting me where he knew it stung the most.

"You know how he got that name, Tania?" My voice was low, controlled.

"No."

"He scribbled on my face with his knife."

"Oh God."

"There was no God that day."

She put a hand on my arm, and I refocused on her big, emotion-filled eyes.

"Finger, Scrib boasted to me about when they'd taken you prisoner. That later you'd stolen from them and he'd wanted to go after you, but because of the truce between your clubs he hadn't. He said

'Maybe it's time that truce expired.'"

Screw that fucking truce.

Cold venom seeped through my chest. "Anything else I should know?"

"Yes, one more thing." She let out a heavy breath. "Reich admitted to me he was the one who set the bomb in Nina's car because Butler and Nina deserved it for fucking with him. That Butler took something of his, and he didn't mean Nina. That the two of them thought they were smarter than him, but he was going to put an end to it once and for all."

"Is he now?" I said under my breath.

Butler and Nina had taken something of Reich's that he was desperate to get back. So desperate that he'd even tried to kill his Goldilocks to get his point across and get it back. That explained Nina and Butler together—she'd helped him get some kind of hard core evidence, and he'd gotten her out from under Reich. He was protecting her. Why the hell hadn't he told me? And what the hell had they stolen from him?

Yeah, fuck it all.

I CALLED CATCH, AND HE ARRIVED at the One-Eyed Jacks in under two hours, and was brought to the room where Tania was resting.

"You told me a while back that you're in love with Nina," she said to her brother.

"Yeah."

"Still feel that way? Still want to be with her?"

He shifted his weight, his gaze darting at me then back to his sister. "Tania, what the hell?"

"I need to know," she said. "Because I'm going to go talk to her today at the hospital. And I want to be sure of what you're feeling."

"What I'm feeling?"

"Do you love her?" Tania raised her voice. "Do you want her for your old lady?"

"Hell yes."

"Good."

"You gonna to set us up?"

Tania's eyes met mine. Butler had told her that Nina's baby wasn't his, it was Catch's. Just as I thought, Tania was derailing the circus train and resetting it on the correct track.

"If you want to be together, you should be," said Tania. "Butler cuts her loose, you two get it together and show Reich and the world that you are the real deal, not fuck ups. She'll be under your protection and Finger's. Reich hates Butler, but you, you're a Flame, that changes his psycho game plan somewhat."

"You make it sound so easy, but it—"

"It is easy. You want something bad enough—" Her gaze shot to me. "—you make it happen."

I had lived my life by that principle. But I'd let Serena slip through my fingers, like a tiny pebble or a sleek ribbon that I couldn't quite grip in my maimed hands.

Make it happen.

Tania and Butler had something going on between them, but Tania was not about tossing the puzzle pieces in the air and seeing where they landed. No, she was making it happen by putting the puzzle pieces in their right place under a bright light.

Ten minutes later, a smile on her face, Tania got on the back of her brother's bike and with me alongside, we rode out off the Jack's property and headed to the hospital in Rapid. Tania went in to talk to Nina alone, while Catch hung with me in the hallway. He was jumpy, chewing on his lips. He was about to get what he wanted.

I planted a hand on his shoulder. "You ready for this?" In a few minutes Nina would tell him he was going to be a daddy again. His whole life was going to change.

He took in a breath. "The fuck of it is, I am."

Tania opened the door to Nina's room, beaming a smile at her brother. "Get in here."

He gave me a last look, a glimmer in his coffee-colored eyes, and he pushed Nina's door open wide.

54
FINGER

"**W**HY ARE YOU HERE?"

Lenore stood stock still in the center of her lingerie boutique as I entered the small, colorfully decorated shop. An exotic harem, a seductive woman's lair in a once upon a time cowboy and gold rush town.

I knew her question, in that deep, firm voice, so in control, wasn't meant to insult. She knew something was up.

"There's something you need to know, and I wanted you to hear it from me."

"What happened?" she asked.

"Reich showed up at Butler's yesterday. Tania was there, and he took her when she left his place."

Her eyebrows lifted. "Took her?"

"Held her hostage to piss Butler off and—"

"No." She put a hand to her mouth.

"Butler and Catch got her out. She's at the Jacks'. I saw Grace there earlier this morning, I thought maybe she would've called you."

"She did but I had my phone off. I just saw that she'd called as you walked in." She swallowed hard, her breaths coming faster. "What did he do to her?"

"It's what Scrib did to her."

Her brow knit, face went pale. "Scrib? What's Scrib got to do with anything?"

"Seems he and Reich are pals. Scrib wants to do business in our parts, and Reich brought him in."

Her eyes hung on mine. "What did he do to her?"

"Cut an F into her chest."

She stumbled back. I grabbed her, setting her down on the bright yellow couch. "Hey, hey. Look at me. Look at me, Lenore." I slid my arm around her pulling her close, her head falling on my chest.

"No, no, no. It can't be. Can't be..." she murmured against my skin.

I smoothed a hand down the side of her cool face. "They're eager and desperate."

"That's a lethal combination," she breathed.

"I'm not letting this stand. My boys got Reich tied up at my club. I'm heading over there now, but I had to see you first. I had to." I took her cold hand in mine and she didn't pull it away. I brought it to my lips and kissed it. "I had to."

She pressed deeper against me, curling into me, and my muscles tensed, my heart knocked in my chest.

This, once more. This.

"And Scrib?" Her lips moved against the base of my throat, the skin burning there.

"I'm going to take care of Scrib." My fingers sifted through her hair. So soft, the scent of flowers rising. Not sweet, but edged in green. Clean, fresh air bottled in a forest after the rain. I buried my face in the purply blue and black waves. "I'm going to keep him away from you. I won't let him get to you."

Her nails dug into my flesh. "So many years have gone by, but... oh shit. I still see his face sometimes. Hear that voice of his. Feel that—"

"I hear his laugh."

"That fucking laugh."

I kissed the top of her head, holding her tighter. "They're not getting away with this."

She looked up at me, our choppy breaths mingling, her eyes dark teal pools of swollen emotion.

My thumb grazed her quivering bottom lip. "Serena—"

"We gave up so much to stay safe from them, keep those around us safe, and yet even after all this time, it's as if everything we went through doesn't even matter."

I raised her chin with my hand. "Baby, I'm putting an end to this shit. And they're gonna pay."

"Okay."

"I'll keep you safe."

Her eyes glimmered, and she pushed off me, sitting up, sniffing in air. "Thank you for telling me. I mean it, Finger. Thank you."

The sudden lack of the press of her body, her warmth against me, was wrong. I was thirsty, withered, bone dry, and the gallon jug of cool water had been taken away from me too soon.

Lenore slid her hand from mine, and I released her. She swallowed hard, her face still pale. "I need to see Tania." Rising from the sofa, she moved toward the back of the store, through stands and racks draped with sexy lingerie.

I let out an exhale. Colorful bras, panties, scraps of fabric, erotic bands of ribbon mysteriously held together, begging to be stroked, begging to be filled with warm bodies. Her touch was on all of them. Her carefully planned out thoughts, her offbeat wishes. These were all personal items that people stashed in drawers or closets, keeping them hidden only to be revealed on special occasions and to a chosen few. Here in her store, Lenore had brought these fantasies out into the light to play and dazzle. It was another world, dreamy, sensual, seductive.

I brushed a hand across my mouth, where I wanted her lips to be right now. "Yeah, you should go see her. I just brought her to her house."

"Okay." She slung a huge black leather handbag studded with metal grommets over her shoulder, grabbing a set of keys by the register.

I stood up, taking her in. Her taking me in.

What radiated between us was an insistent bass that drilled deep. Adamant. Jarring even, like an emergency alert system that wasn't in your power to turn off. You had to listen to it, endure it. Pay heed to its warning.

I was paying heed.

I said, "I'm coming over tonight."

Her eyes flared. "You're what?"

"Tonight. Expect me."

THAT NIGHT AFTER VISITING REICH in his prison cell and making sure everything and everyone was locked down at my club, I got myself to Lenore's house around eleven o'clock. This time, I rang her bell.

She opened the door, her hair pinned up, no trace of makeup. Her cheeks reddened at the sight of me. "You're here."

"I'm here."

"Look, I'm okay, really. I was shaken up earlier, but you don't have to—"

"You going to let me in?"

She took in a breath and moved to the side, pushing her door open wider. I entered her house.

"Did I wake you up?" I asked, parking my helmet on a chair, taking off my jacket.

"No. I was working."

Sketches of small rectangular and round cases with her brand logo were all over the table.

"What's this?"

"I'm working on this makeup line idea. I'm picky about the packaging, I want to get it just right."

I sat on the edge of her sofa. "You saw Tania?"

"I did."

"Must have been real hard for you."

"Anything can happen at any time and usually does." She collected her sketchpad and colored pencils, piling them in a stack on the coffee table.

Suddenly, I didn't want to talk about any of that. I wanted to just be here, be with her. I handed her a charcoal pencil that had rolled away from her reach. "Your store's real nice. I like it."

She let out a laugh, taking the pencil from me. "Men usually do."

"I'll bet." I leaned back on the couch, stretching my legs. "I know a few of my men do. Their old ladies come up and shop once in a while. I heard you're a little pricey, though."

"It's all in the details—the materials, the workmanship."

I held her steady gaze, my pulse racing. We were talking about bras and panties and stringy things.

"I'm worth it," she added. "I mean, the pieces—they're unique."

"Yeah." *You are. You're worth everything.*

"Can I get you something to drink? Or eat?"

I untied the bandana from my neck. "Water would be good. Thanks."

Lenore left the room, and I finally let go of that pent up breath I'd been holding since I'd walked through the door. I toed off my boots and took in her living room. Full of color, pulsing with peacock blues, minty greens, soft pinks, pale golds. A variety of thick pillows on the floor and the long L-shaped sectional sofa, Persian-type rugs, long sweeping curtains. A vintage glass carafe in a burnt orange color sat on the coffee table before me, it's neck wrapped with a gold necklace with tiny red beads. Her furniture was a variety of natural woods and burnished metals. Her home was warm, comfortable, quirky. Refreshing. I'd never experienced anything like it.

I rubbed the back of my aching neck. Was this how she'd always lived? I'd never been able to go to any of her apartments in Chicago, and suddenly that bothered me. I'd never considered that before, that I was missing out. But I had missed out on a vital piece of her back then, a unique and intricate flavor of her.

She returned with a tall glass of water and a big bed pillow, a paisley quilt, and a folded sheet under her other arm. Handing me the water, she placed the bedding on the sofa.

"You look tired," she said as I drank. "My spare room is kind of a mess right now with boxes from the store and samples, but the sofa is comfortable."

I grinned, setting the now empty glass on the low table before me. "That's fine. Got an early start tomorrow. Don't want to disturb you in the morning."

"The bathroom's down the hall to the right. I left you a couple of towels in there."

"I could use a shower."

"Go ahead. I'll set up your bed."

I stood and brushed the side of her face with a kiss, my hands on her upper arms. "I didn't want you to be alone tonight. I needed to be here, make sure you're okay, that you're safe with everything going on, with Scrib out there."

"I know. I appreciate it." She moved to the other end of the sofa, busying herself with the bedding.

I didn't want appreciation. I wanted something else, something more, something I could hold and squeeze and grip and...

She smoothed the sage green sheet over the cushions, propped up the king sized royal blue pillow, unfolded the quilt.

The spring of tension that had coiled around the muscles of my chest and shoulders from the moment I'd walked into her house released. This was good, I'd take it. This was a beginning.

"You need anything, you just say the word." I removed my gun from its holster and set it on the low table by the carafe.

Her eyes darted to my gun. "Okay."

She was being all cool and collected now, but who knew what state her brain and emotions were in after seeing Tania today, knowing what she'd gone through, seeing the horrible evidence on her skin. Like the scars on her own skin and on mine.

The nightmares might come back tonight. Maybe they'd never left, or maybe she wouldn't be able to sleep. She didn't want to talk about it now, and frankly I didn't either. I was fried after all of the day's crazy, the back and forth, the riding.

"Hey." She touched my arm, her fingers warm on my skin. "You know, if you need me, I'm here for you, too."

My heart jolted.

She squeezed my bicep, sweeping past me down the hall.

And she took my heart straight out of my chest along with her.

55
FINGER

THE DOOR TO HER BEDROOM was open.

I stood there in the silent early morning darkness watching her, her face buried in a pillow, her chest rising and falling with every breath. There had been no nightmares, for her or me last night.

"I'll be back tonight, baby," I whispered.

Grabbing my gun, I left her house, heading for Nebraska. Last night Butler had called me, insisting we meet today. First I went home, changed clothes, switched bikes, checked in with my men, grabbed a cup of coffee, and then headed for the deserted gas stop Butler had told me about on Route 385 by the Dakota border.

He waited for me in the small back lot, leaning against his bike as I pulled in.

I knew what he wanted to talk about, what he needed to know. But I needed something from him too, and he'd been holding out on me, and I didn't like it one bit.

He stood up and moved toward me as I shut down my bike. We were alone except for a beat-up Dodge pickup, rusted steel drums, and plenty of garbage steaming in the midday sun.

"Finger—"

I raised a hand stopping him. "First, I need something from you."

"Like what?"

"What the hell did you and Nina get from Reich? That's why he tried to blow your old lady up. That's why he came here and ended up taking Tania, laying hands on her, to push you. What did you find in Ohio that you haven't told me about?"

His lips pressed together in a firm line. "Nina's been trying to get out from under him for years. He's been abusing her since she was a teenager, just after he married her sister. He's fucked up."

"Tell me something I don't know, Butler."

"When I was out in Ohio, she and I hooked up a couple of times, and she gave me some info on his movements. But then she asked me to take her out of there, and the only way he was going to let that happen was if she was my old lady. I agreed to it, figuring it was another way in. After a while of playing it together, I'd help her get lost in California or somewhere out west where he wouldn't find her. In return, I had her help me get to his pot of gold."

"Which was?"

"Info on his kinky trade."

"Kinky trade?"

"He's running a huge underground operation. By that I mean on his own, not with the Flames. No one knows anything about it," Butler said, bracing for a reaction from me. I gave him none. "What did the Flames used to do in the old days?" he continued. "Deal in sex slaves, snuff films, kids."

I crossed my arms. "Those were the way old, old days, and we put a stop to that a long time ago."

"I know. But Reich sniffed around, found a demand for it, and became a very successful and popular supplier."

"He found another niche along with the porn, the hookers, and the white supremacy crap," I muttered.

"Oh yeah. He's got a lot of clients, big names, big money. He controls all of it, takes care of purchases, money flow, product type and style, you name it. He stashes his money in some high brow investments too."

"You got proof of all this?"

"He kept all his info on a flash drive. Nina got a copy of that flash drive, and we got the hell out of Ohio and came here. He figured it out, though, and I promised him I'd keep my mouth shut if he'd unblock a deal I was trying to get off the ground with this weapons dealer I'd met in Virginia who he knows. Just one deal to raise some cash for my club. It took forever, he kept stalling, but he finally did me the favor. I needed to impress Jump by bringing some good cash in for my club. I needed back in. Then I was going to—"

"Then you were going to tell me?" My voice surged, drilling into him. "That's why I sent you his way in the first place, motherfucker."

"I always intended to give you any information I found, man. That was our original plan, wasn't it? My sharing with you was his biggest fear, so I used that and held it over his head. Wasn't supposed to be for long, but then Catch and Nina's love story fucked everything up the ass, and the end came sooner rather than later. Of course, I didn't expect him to blow Nina up and on my club's property."

"Mistake. I warned you," I said. "You expect me to trust you after all this?"

He held my gaze. "Yeah, you should. This is good shit. You want this."

"Don't you ever fuck with me again. Ever."

"I won't. You have my word."

"You need to hand that drive over to me tomorrow in front of him, in front of everyone there."

His face hardened. "And I need you to make sure he can't get to Nina, that he won't hurt her again."

The shit had a heart.

I leaned back against the wall of the abandoned building. "There's no question, now that she's Catch's woman, one of ours. You cool with Nina and Catch?"

He shrugged, an eyebrow lifted. "Of course I am. She's having his kid. They want to be together, they should be." He wasn't lying. He looked relieved.

"I've been holding Reich since we busted him at the cabin where he was holding Tania. Tomorrow, we're going to be putting on a little show for him, and you're going to have a starring role. You bring Nina and her stuff to my clubhouse at noon."

"Okay." Butler rubbed a hand down his face. "Now, I have a question for you, and it needs answering."

I knew good and well what was on his mind, I'd been waiting for it. Those baby blue eyes of his were smudged with dark circles, tired, heavy with strain. Was it guilt or anxiety?

"Tell me." His tone was dark, urgent, throttled with frustration and anticipating the worst.

"Tell you what?" I pushed back from the grimy wall.

"Why the fuck did you kill Jump?" he spit out.

"That keeping you up at night?"

His face tightened. "Yeah, it is." Butler had a conscience after all?

"An unpaid bill that had to be paid. In full."

His eyes narrowed. "I realized you liked being friendly with me because you knew Jump didn't like me much."

"Yeah. And you were way friendlier with me than I think Jump and your national president would have liked, nomad."

"I was. I took the risk, but that's between you and me," he said. "You liked that. I let you in, and I let you take advantage of that."

I hooked my hands on my waist. "And you got your in with me."

"And I got my in with you, and we pissed off Jump—"

"And Reich."

"—which benefited both of us," Butler added. "But Jump was my president, Finger. What did he do to you? You looking to step in, take over the One-Eyed Jacks like you're planning on doing with the Blades? Or maybe you're going to throw me a bone to distract me, shut me up, install me as your puppet and drain the Jacks dry until there's nothing left? 'Cause that is not going to fucking happen."

"I considered it, but that's not what I want. Not from your club. No, Jump and I were never about the Jacks," I said. "It was all about Jump."

"I need to know."

I held his unrelenting gaze. He needed to know the truth. He wanted to know how much of a monster I was.

"Once upon a long time ago, I was in trouble, needed help," I said. "I'd gone underground, and I was on the run from the Smoking Guns. My own brothers didn't even know. It was an impossible situation, and I'd put everything on the line, everything, but I had no choice."

Butler lit a cigarette, taking a long drag. "Was this before or after they held you prisoner?"

"After."

I told him about my rescuing "Rena," without telling him it was Lenore. About not being able to reach Dig when we were bleeding on the side of the road, about Jump being an asshole and refusing to help me. I didn't mention meeting Tania. That was up to her to share or not share with him.

"I managed. I survived, and got done what I had to get done." I ended the tale. "Jump...that fucker. I was never going to forget what he'd done to me."

"That was 'cause of me, you know—Dig getting married out of the blue. They'd kicked me out for flirting with his old lady, sent me to the chapter up north. He married her in a flash the next fucking week. Things were crazy for a while there."

I let out a laugh. "Well, don't expect a thank you from me. Things might have worked out differently, who the fuck knows. Doesn't matter now. I got safe. Here I am."

"You're a patient man."

I shot him a look. "I need to be if I want to get the job done right. Any job. Many times, a situation presents itself—like Reich's bomb at the Jacks' clubhouse, and I happened to be there. Purely random. That shit is real sweet when it works out, isn't it? I slipped right in and got done what I'd been wanting to do for years. No big fucking showdown, no fuss, no mess during, and especially after. The best part, Jump was conscious. Looked me straight in the eyes. He knew, and I saw his fear there."

Butler averted his gaze and tossed what was left of his cigarette to the ground, crushing it with his boot. Had I made him uncomfortable? Wasn't that a fucking shame.

"The next best part, I didn't have to get rid of the body. Your club got itself a new martyr and a fancy funeral, not a vanishing in the dark of the night."

"Oh, we should be grateful?"

"You should," I said. "Without Jump riding your ass, you got yourself a good chance to rise the ranks again, if that's what you want."

"I only wanted back in. That was enough for me. To be in good standing in my brothers' eyes, to bring something to the table. Not to take away again. Not that!"

"You accomplished what you wanted, Butler, and I got what I wanted."

Simple as that. Logical.

His eyes narrowed. "And the blame gets placed on Reich's dirty shoulders, just where you wanted it, am I right?"

"At the time, I didn't know he was the one who set that bomb, I thought it was the Blades. But yeah, it all works out real nice, doesn't it?"

Butler only chewed on his lip, a hand running through his blond hair.

"Patience, my friend, is an important virtue to cultivate," I said. "That taste of anticipation brews on the back of your tongue for years, and finally, finally, it transforms into a glorious amalgam of blood, satisfaction, and burning pleasure. It's lingering still."

Yeah, I could taste it, and I liked it. I made a sucking sound with my teeth as I shoved my gloves back on my hands.

Butler pulled back from me. Was he deliberating? The deed was done now. Jump was dead and buried, and a new light was dawning for all of us.

"And what about Reich?" he asked. "After what he's done to Tania? What he's trying to do to you and your club?"

New dawn for damned sure.

"What was that word Tania used?" I asked him.

"Unequivocal?"

"Yeah, that." *Fucking perfect.* "Looking forward to making that happen with Reich and his cohorts. You deliver the girl tomorrow. Tomorrow will be a very, very good day."

56
FINGER

"SHE'S ALL YOURS."

Butler had arrived with his pretend old lady, now his official ex. Fucking stellar acting skills. He played the pissed-off cheated-on boyfriend to the hilt.

Nina ran to Catch's arms, relieved, pouting. Butler had clued her in just right.

"What the hell is going on?" Reich eyed them from the sofa where he sat with Led and a couple of his men, his voice sharp. He was getting it now.

"What the hell is he doing here?" Butler gestured at Reich.

"Reich's been staying here since your little event," I replied.

"Event? Is that what you're calling it?" Butler yelled. "This is bullshit. We've been looking for him for days now. He's gotta answer for killing my prez."

"Butler, you need to leave now," said Catch, his arm firmly around Nina.

Reich's eyes bulged as he rose to his feet, his focus entirely on Nina. "I've been trying to call you, Neens. You haven't been answering your phone. What are you doin', sweetheart?"

Nina didn't answer him. She only wrapped herself up tighter in Catch.

"Nina's my old lady now, Reich," Catch said. "You got something to say to her, you say it to me. Otherwise, you're done."

"Watch how you talk, asshole!" shouted Led.

"Done? Done? What the fuck? Done?" Reich turned to me, his face red. "You gonna let your boy talk to me that way?"

"She caused a ruckus with my club and Butler's. But all the drama's over now." I shot Butler a look.

Butler raised his hands in the air. "I know I'm done."

"Neens, you need to come home with me and your sister and let us take care of you," Reich said. "You need to be with your family, with people you trust."

"I'm her family now," Catch said. "This is where she belongs. With me."

I pulled in a deep breath at the confident, firm tone in his voice.

"You told your sister about this?" Reich ignored Catch. "We thought you were coming home with us today. You'd said—"

"I'm staying here with my old man," Nina said.

"Your old man, huh? I've heard that shit before." Reich glanced at Butler who made a face. He didn't give any fucks.

"You need to hear it now," she said. "I'm with Catch, and I'm staying with him here in Nebraska. I love him, and I'm pregnant with his baby. I'm not going back to Ohio with you and Deanna. This is my home now."

"No." Reich shook his head, his teeth dragging against his lip. "No! Your sister's waiting for us back at the motel. She's waiting for you to meet her there, like you said you would. You lying, cheating little—"

"Yeah, she is a cheating skank. I hope you're proud of her," Butler muttered.

"You're such a cocksucker!" shouted Led.

"Shut the fuck up right now! All of you!" Catch said.

"This ain't right," said Reich through gritted teeth. He was a simmering iron cauldron of outrage, animosity, and desperation.

"You know what's not right?" Butler held up a flash drive. "This."

The color drained from Reich's face. "What the fuck are you doing?"

"The right thing, imagine that?" Butler's eyes flared.

"You're nothing but a two bit thief!" Reich's voice seethed.

"I am," said Butler on a dry laugh. "I wanted your cooperation on a deal for my club bad enough to force you. Bad enough to steal from you, blackmail you. I followed your invisible trails and found out your little secrets. You knew that if I told Finger what you've been doing, he'd wipe the floor of the Flames' national clubhouse with your ass. And you'd not only be out but shamed, backs turned on you. Power taken away. Money gone. And where would the great Reich be then? I don't think those VIP clients of yours would come to your rescue, do you?"

"Clients?" I asked.

"Yeah, politicians, big-business millionaires, crime lords, a few celebrities, too."

"What are you talking about? Drugs, weapons?" asked Catch.

Everyone was listening, eyes glued on Butler.

"Drugs were only the party favors here, the thank-you-for-your-business swag," Butler continued. "No, Reich catered to one of a kind personal tastes. Snuff films, kiddie porn, gay porn, sex slaves—male and female. All made to order according to clients' likes and dislikes. Reich here is a first rate entertainment mogul. Huge moneymaking business, and all of it going into a single pocket. His. I know the Flames have a history with a lot of that shit—legendary, in fact."

"We shut it down decades ago after too much heat with the FBI." I stated the obvious for my men, making my point clear.

"Well, news flash—Reich, your national VP, quietly resuscitated it all on his own. Only, this time, underground, way underground. And this here"—Butler waved the flash drive that he and Nina had stolen from Reich—"this little stick has the private information of every client on it. Not just names, dates, places, but also all their extra-special tastes and quirky preferences. You can imagine, if this shit got in the hands of, let's say TMZ, right? The backbone of this business is keeping the info-sharing down to the barest minimum. Reich is their only contact. No go-betweens, no secretaries. Just him. It's key for their confidentiality and his offshore bank account, of course. This shit gets out, he's gonna be burned to the stake in more ways than one."

"That's my business! Mine!" Reich shouted. "You've got no claim on it."

That wild prairie fire flamed in my veins, lapping hungrily at

Reich.

"You had that in your hands all this time?" My tone was harsh. "What were you gonna do, Butler? Use it to bait me, offer it to me like a fucking carrot, to make our tentative agreements go your way? Get thicker cuts out of us?"

"Why not?" Butler shot back.

I slammed a fist on the table at my side, and Butler's face tightened. A frozen silence gripped the room.

"Reich does have a point, though," Butler said.

Reich's head perked up at him.

"This is none of my business. Not anymore," Butler said. "It used to be a family issue for me. Nina was my old lady after all, and I got her out from under this animal. But she's not my old lady now. Now, this really isn't my business, is it?" Right on point, Butler brought out his legendary fuck-it swagger.

Reich's lips drew back in a snarl. "Give it to me."

His panic was fucking delicious.

Butler shot him that shit eating grin of his. "I'm giving it all right." He tossed the flash drive at me, and I caught it, my fingers curling over it tightly.

"You motherfucker!" Reich exploded.

"Yes, I am a motherfucker," Butler said, making a show of wiping his hands. "And now I'm done with you."

I gestured at two of my men, who immediately grabbed Reich by the arms. I held out the flash drive to Den who took it and hooked it up to his open laptop on the table.

I raised my chin at Butler. "Get out."

"You don't expect me to walk away now and leave Reich standing, do you?" Butler asked.

"You don't have a choice here, Butler," I replied. "You're one Jack among many Flames and on our property. Unless you've got a death wish, you need to leave now while I still give a shit. I got business to take care of here."

"You lied to me, Finger! He's ours!" Butler shouted.

Den raised his head from his laptop screen. "It's all here, Prez, just like Butler said. Plenty of fucked-up shit. Long list of names and info. Goes back for years."

Finally, I had Reich in a way that I'd only imagined years ago. Completely by the fucking balls. But I wasn't that kid screaming for vengeance and striking out in the only way I knew how, with my knife in the opiate dark of the night.

No.

Now Reich was sober and awake, eyes wide open, feeling the sharp rip of my blade through his flesh. Knowing it was me.

"Reich is mine," I said. "The second you leave, I'm going to blow his fucking head off myself." I turned to Slade. "Pick up the old lady and bring her here."

Slade lifted his chin and stalked off, his phone at his ear.

"What's going on?" Nina asked Catch, her voice thin. "Why is Deanna coming here? They're not going to hurt her, are they?"

"It's all right, baby." Catch rubbed her shoulder. "We just need to talk to your sister about what she knows."

I motioned to two of my men. "Get the Jack off my property."

They grabbed Butler.

"Fuck you!" he hollered, shoving back at them.

"Leave, Butler, or we're gonna have problems you haven't even dreamed of," I said on a hiss.

Led charged at Butler, his face red. "You're going to pay for this, you son of a bitch!"

Two more of my men stopped him in his tracks, yanking him back.

"Never trusted you! Never!" Led shouted, bucking in their hold.

"Oh, don't get me started with you, asshole!" Butler replied. "You always wanted a piece of my woman from the very beginning." He gestured at Nina. "You tried so hard, but she never wanted your crooked dick, did she?"

My hand itched. My heartbeat slowed, every sense loaded, primed.

"You!" Reich yelled. "You didn't deserve her, you son of a bitch!" He lunged toward Butler, a gun in his hand.

I slid my Smith & Wesson 1911 from the back of my jeans, released the safety, and fired. Reich's head knocked back, and he crumpled to the floor, the thud the only sound in a sudden, tremendous silence. Blood spouted from the raw opening my bullet had gouged in his forehead. Led fell to his side, a moan on his lips, his hands on Reich's lifeless chest.

For injustices of our past, our present. My future.

"You did good, Kid." My father's shadow passed through me.

That euphoria colored my vision, filling me with clarity, calm. Washing me with satisfaction.

Rena's eyes lit up at me from across that wild, rowdy smoke-filled room, through men's laughter and howls, through chains scraping and pulling, through the slice and chop of blades. Her growing smile lit me up, and I took in a slow, long breath on its blaze, my heartbeat steadying once more.

I shot Butler a look. "That good for you, Jack? Cause that's good for me."

"Yeah. Yeah, that's good for me," Butler muttered, shifting away from the carnage.

I pushed the safety back up and tucked my gun behind my back. "Get out of my club."

57
FINGER

"THAT'S EVERYTHING I KNOW," MUMBLED Reich's old lady, Deanna.

She'd been uptight and snappy when my men first brought her in from the hotel in Deadwood where she'd been holed up waiting for Reich and Nina. When she stepped into the clubroom, her eyes had followed the prospects who'd been scrubbing the floor with bleach and mopping it over with ammonia. She'd slowed down, but she'd kept moving. She knew. I'd bet she'd been prepared for years now.

After sitting in a hard wooden chair in my office with me, Catch, and Drac as we went over every detail of Reich's financials with her, she'd relented, bit by sour bit. Money stashed in dummy corporations, in her kitchen pantry in boxes where cookies, macaroni, and cereal ought to be. In winter comforter covers packed in her closets. In hollowed out speakers, stereo components, DVD players, fake books in her living room. In taped up packets in her attic walls, in an old rusted hot water heater, a broken vacuum cleaner in her basement

Catch got off his phone. "They're here."

I glanced at the bank of security monitors to my left. Each national officer of the Flames of Hell was on my property. President, Treasurer, Secretary, Sergeant at Arms. Their eyes flicked over the large room. Beers were put in their hands.

"They're here?" Deanna said, her voice thin.

"They came to see what your old man's been up to. It's time for them to face facts." I slanted my head at her. "We're done. You spend some time with your sister. Two of my men will be taking you home to Ohio and getting the cash from your house. I'll leave you with this amount." I slid a piece of paper towards her. Her eyebrows lifted. Was she pleased or disappointed?

"How's that look to you?"

She squirmed in her chair. "That's, uh, very fair."

"Fair? Pretty fucking generous is what that is. What do you say?" said Drac, his tone as sharp as his fanged teeth now showing.

A frown passed over her already pinched face. "Thank you."

"Yeah, that's more like it. Now move." Drac motioned for her to get up quickly.

"Get her out of here from the back," I said.

Catch led Deanna by the arm out of my office, and handed her off to another one of my men for safekeeping and transport to Catch's house, where Nina waited for her.

I headed into the meeting room, Catch and Drac at my sides. Four hardened faces looked up at me. They were on my turf now. The elite. The elders. The select elect. The higher ups of the Flames of Hell.

My captive audience.

"Welcome."

"What do you got?" Taz, my National President said. "This is serious shit, man, these allegations. You fucking killed him? Just mowed him down?"

"I stopped him from killing someone in my own house. And first of all, due to his obsession with his sister-in-law, he ended up killing the president of a friendly MC right next door to us. Set off a bomb on their property. That kind of crazy is not good for business or our reputation. But at the center of it all is this—"

I raised my chin at Den, and he went at his keyboard. Up on the television monitor streamed the evidence of Reich's great subterfuge. Accounting spreadsheets tallying up all his expenses, his profits. And what profits they were. At the end of the day, over seven figures.

Taz drummed a hand on the oak table, his concentration focused on the screen. Watts, the Treasurer was on the edge of his seat, his eyes jogging over each set of figures presented, his lips moving. Lenox, the Sergeant at Arms shook his head, gripping his beer bottle tighter, rapping it against the table in a steady rhythm.

"The documents go back to over twelve years ago," I said.

"How did you break this?" asked Watts, his attention fixed back on the figures marching down the screen.

"I've been keeping my eye on him since our big general convention in Atlanta, about ten years ago, back when the Mexicans started blockading and the Demon Seeds from the west were playing hardball. He didn't seem too uptight about cash flow like the rest of us were. He'd put on a good show of brainstorming colorful ideas, but none of them amounted to anything, he'd dropped every single ball. I smelled distraction. Set a course for getting hold of the evidence, and I got it.

"In front of my whole club yesterday, he admitted it, declared it was all his. He was actually annoyed with me for finding out and threatening to put a stop to it. But what Reich never got about me is that I don't threaten. I make shit happen. The question is, what are you all going to do about it?"

They stared at me, chewing on all my evidence like dogs with a single thick bone between them.

"I'm putting seventy-five per cent of these assets in National's coffers," I said.

Watts let out a gust of air, pressing his back into his chair. "Can't beat that."

"Twelve years is a damn long time," I said. "All those years, none of you—and you've all been in office that long, re-elected over and over again—never noticed a thing? It was just business as usual? Trust Reich with the reigns, with making decisions. Trust him with all our worldly goods and possessions."

Watts leaned his weight forward on the table, a ringed hand brushing over his long mustache. "He was always flush. Even when times were shit. I'd seen his wife driving around in a new car, taking trips. He always had a quick explanation for everything. Never a straight answer though, always a different story."

My pulse picked up at the row of stiff faces around me.

"How could you not know?" I asked Taz. "Did you look the other way? Or were you on the take too? Temptation just too great. Did you get a cut of the slaves and the snuff films?" I gestured at the screen. I fed the thick anxiety and dread at all the possible outcomes that hovered over our table like the heavy odor of frying grease. I was the one doing the frying.

"I looked for you on here," I continued. "Didn't find you though, but I did find a recurring monthly fee. And plenty of miscellaneous expenses. Maybe you were one of those, huh, Taz? That vacation to Cancun last year? Pretty fancy. But you didn't take your old lady or your kids or one of your local bitches. No. Maybe you had a girl chained to your side the whole time specially trained just for you?"

All eyes were on Taz.

Taz rolled his shoulders, twisting his neck, his mouth opened.

"Don't you fucking lie to me. This is selling out," I said. "A Flame does not sell out his brothers, does not undercut his brothers. Used to be a Flame was the finest there was. He stood for something. This? Crawling for pennies. It may be a mighty pile of pennies, but your allegiance, your loyalty went from the Flames of Hell to pennies? You've trashed what we stand for. Yeah, back in the day, that trade was good, easy money, but it ain't us no more."

"Listen, I—"

My fist slammed on the great wooden table. "What is this, huh? Right here, right now? You tell us."

Taz glared at me. "Flames of Hell."

"Yes. Who's the national president?"

Taz's eyes narrowed at me. "I am."

"Yes, you are. Shouldn't you have noticed what your own vice president was up to? You and Reich have been buds for years. Came up together. A well-oiled machine ruling the roost the past decade and a half."

"Ah shit, man," Lenox groaned.

Taz jolted in his chair. "You accusing me of—"

"Reich was always a resourceful thinker, an instigator. He produced all this fine tailor-made product by himself and maintained this network of contacts and delivery. Generated big bucks. He had

Led as his gopher, yeah, but he had to have used your Ohio money laundering machine to help with the extra. I imagine there was always lots of cream left on the sides of that big milkshake glass."

His back rigid, Taz planted his hands on the table. "Who the fuck do you think—"

I untucked my knife and thrust it into Taz's left hand. The blade stuck there, pinning his hand to the table. He howled like a wild bear caught in a trap, his body shuddering and twisting.

Flint shot up from his chair. "What the fuck, man?"

"Finger!" Lenox yelled.

I pointed at the screen. "Look."

"What is that?" Flint asked.

"Every investment that Reich made is signed over to either his old lady or Taz," Watts said, reading the projected documents on the screen. "Shit. Shit."

The men stared at Taz and looked away again. Taz only squirmed in his chair, blood streaming over his hand, on my table.

"Is that loyalty to your club? Is that the absolute heat of the Flame?" I asked.

Heads shook, hands running down grim faces. Flint kicked at his chair, grabbed it, and threw himself back in it.

"You need to sign this, Taz." I shoved a document my lawyer had drawn up this morning. "Signs over all your claims to this money to several of our corporations. Here's a pen."

"Do it!" Watts yelled at him.

Betrayal is a vile thing among brothers.

Taz's hands quaked as he signed the papers. Good thing he was a righty and not a lefty. Would've been messy.

"I'll tell you what this is—unforgivable." I sat back down in my chair. "It's not just the money. I've been here on my patch of ground for years and years, defending it tooth and nail from all manner of jerk off—corporate, law enforcement, mob, Mexican, Latin American, other clubs. I've got the One-Eyed Jacks of the Dakotas and Colorado playing friendly ball, and further west of us, the Demon Seeds have finally cooled their shit.

"But I've got the Broken Blades next door playing chicken with us, and now, they're aligning themselves with the Smoking Guns after I brought down their partnership with a crime organization from Denver. Do you think that's a coincidence? There was a matchmaker for that union: Reich. Our National VP sicced our enemy on me, his brother, giving that enemy a free fucking pass on a vital web of business within our organization. Took us long, hard years to get our shit tight, and we did it. That's one of the reasons the Flames are the envy of so many. We are tight. And Reich didn't just talk up any Gun to start a rupture, no. He brought Scrib in."

"Aw, fuck no," muttered Flint.

"I'm taking this personally, and you should too. Who knows how long those two had been meeting up? Did Reich think I would let that happen? Do you?"

"No, man. No way," said Lenox.

"Did he think that I would take that sitting down? Let it roll over me?" I asked.

"This ain't right," said Flint, shifting in his seat.

I eyed each and every one of them. "You know what you get with me. I don't make pretty noises to get your attention, that's Reich's way. That was the man ruling alongside this President."

Taz gaped at me.

I gestured at Catch. He came forward, his arms full. In the center of the table he made a pile of a Sig Sauer P320, a Ruger LC9, a Springfield XD, a Glock.

I liked variety on my menu.

"It's up to you now, the last remaining national officers of the Flames of Hell." I rubbed my hands together slowly. "Prove your loyalty to the Flame. To each other. I found the evidence, and I took care of Reich just as he was pulling his gun on us. He left debris behind him, though, and it needs to be cleaned up—it reeks. This club cannot be ruled by greedy lying bastards who will sell it out to line their own pockets. We've taken blood oaths to never allow that to happen. Our brotherhood comes first. I'm not going to be Reich's whore or Taz's whore. Are you?"

The men shook their heads, their faces long, eyes cold and weary.

"There are rules in place. Rules that had been set for a reason by those who came before us, rules that deserve our respect. These rules need to be followed, not broken or bent by any member on a kick, 'cause then we got bedlam. And that is not Flames of Hell. We are tight. We are clean in what we do and how we do it. By necessity, right, Taz? Adhering to that necessity is what keeps us whole and secure. That security has been put at risk because of Reich and Taz's greed. "

A rush of adrenaline washed through me. It was time for these fucks to prove their loyalty. Reich had dug a breach too wide and deep to be ignored or brushed over and had taken Taz with him.

Watts grabbed the handle of the Sig and stood up, his chair scraping along the floor, his right eye twitching as it did when he got anxious. "I'm ready."

"Watts, please. Not like this..."

"You should've thought of that while you were counting your dough," said Watts.

Lenox wrapped a hand around the Kimber, his chin raised, glaring at Taz. Flint leaned over and grabbed the Ruger. My pulse drummed in every vein, making my heart beat loudly, evenly. The clarity washed over me like cool rain on a sticky summer day.

I unstuck my knife from Taz's hand, and he groaned loudly, his side slumping against the table. Catch moved forward and led Taz outside the room.

I loved a ritual, especially one of my own creation. Rites were necessary, making the ordinary special and un-ordinary. Furthermore, a ritual invoked a visceral understanding. And that emotional connection in turn served the continuity of who we were, which was crucial to our survival.

Outside, past the metal sheds, past hulks of rusted cars and bikes Flames had embedded in the earth to leave their mark on the property, in the clearing of the brush, we stopped.

"It wasn't supposed to be like this," muttered Taz.

"It never is." I flicked a hand at his colors.

Taz removed his cut and handed it to me. I picked at the seams of the president's patch on the worn leather with my knife, ripping it off, handing it all to Catch.

The sweat beaded on Taz's forehead in the late afternoon sun, his grayed hair lifting in the hot breeze. I shoved him back, and he stumbled.

I raised my gun, Watts and Lenox and Flint aiming theirs.

Boom. Crack. Crack. Clip.

Taz flew back, collapsing to the ground.

Lenox lit a cigarette, his hand shaking. Watts muttered to himself. Motionless, Flint stared off into the distance. I said nothing. After a moment they turned back to me. The somberness was heavy in their eyes, because they knew and they understood. I had just leveled the playing field, and we were all standing on it together, fully present, passionate in our commitment, and potent in that unity. Informed and fueled in our new reality.

I'd always been steeped in that fuel, and was just as flammable.

After a quick glass of whiskey, Lenox, Flint, and Watts took off. I remained outside in the field. The wind had picked up and made Taz's shirt flutter on his still body on the flat ground. A heap of spent flesh in the dirt.

Four prospects huddled over him. One looked up at me, the others waiting behind him. I nodded, and they raised Taz's bullet-riddled corpse.

My pulse thudded in my neck. The Broken Blades would get what was coming to them. And so would Scrib.

The heat of the sun's glare burnished the dry brown brush with a coppery gold. I raised my face toward the sky, my skin warming. That huge open blue sky. Not one cloud visible today.

No, not today.

58

LENORE

A WISP OF COOL AIR CURLED over my skin, and I hugged the pillow closer.

Still cold.

No, exposed.

Something heavy was in the air, and that something was hanging over me. I opened my eyes, my body tightening around the pillow.

Cedar, a hint of tobacco. Metal and cinnamon gum.

That something was *him*.

A large figure loomed in the dark. The thud of his clothing hitting the floor had my pulse jumping rope double time.

"Finger? What are you doing?"

"Getting in your bed."

I sat up, pulling the sheet over my bare body. "You break into my house because you want a fuck?"

He chuckled softly, pulling back the sheet and climbing in next to me. The heat of his limbs, the wall of his torso pressing against me. His hair was wet. The fragrance of my shampoo tickled my nose.

"I repeat, you don't know how to ask?"

An arm wrapped around me pulling me close. "Sunshine," he whispered, the rough pad of his palm moving down my side to my hip. "Tonight I need to be here with you. You want to fuck, we'll fuck. But either way, I'm here in your bed." He was determined, but an underlying note of tenderness in that scratched husky voice of his made his words seem almost fragile.

My mouth dried, my pulse picked up. "Did something happen?

Something bad?"

"Only good things." His leg rubbed mine. "But it was a lot of different things all at once, and I'm waiting for the aftershock to hit."

My hands pushed against his chest. "Are you in danger? What the—"

"Not sure yet." His palm smoothed around my neck. "But it had to happen."

"What exactly?"

His hand dug in my hair at the back of my head. "Today I blew my horn and the wall fell down."

I swallowed hard at the purposeful tone in his voice, the tingles shooting over my scalp at his firm touch. "You're quoting the Old Testament?"

"Yeah. I always liked that Bible story of Joshua's destruction of Jericho. He blew his horn, the wall fell, and they burned the city with fire and 'all that was therein.'" He let out another soft chuckle. "Jericho, the Flames—harlots all."

"Joshua, Finger—whatever."

"Hmm." He took in a deep slow breath. "Everything's changing for the better. I'm making sure of it."

His erection rubbed against me. My skin heated, and I held my breath, suddenly unsure of what to do. Suddenly I wanted to run out the door. Suddenly I wanted to bury my face in his throat, wrap myself around him and hold on tight.

"You still deciding?" he asked.

"Yeah."

"Let me stay." His hand smoothed my hair down my back.

"That's really nice, you asking when you're already naked in my bed."

"Let me hold you tonight, Lenore. Sleep next to you. I'm wired, but I'm exhausted." His voice was low.

My hand opened over a pec, his heartbeat drumming under my palm. A simple gesture I'd done thousands of times in the past. Now it felt new, daring, exhilarating. My every sense was pinned on that touch. I stroked his firm flesh, and a low noise escaped his throat.

"You need me, is that it?" I asked.

His hand covered mine on his chest, keeping it still. "I've always needed you. Now more than ever."

The quiet sincerity and genuine yearning in his voice, despite his fatigue, clutched at my heart. But I wasn't going to let his blitzkrieg tactics get the best of me. I removed my hand and lifted myself away from his body. "You took a chance coming here. I might not have been alone. I still might not be. It's early yet."

His lips twitched. "Uh huh."

"Not concerned?"

"No." He inhaled deeply, a warm hand lazily sliding up my side brushing the curve of a breast. "Coconut and violet smells good on you. You still take a shower every night before bed?"

His memory was impressive. "Yes. Did you take a shower just now?"

"Yeah. I used the fig and vanilla, though."

"I made those shower gels, by the way."

"You're a talented woman."

"You're a man unafraid of fig and vanilla. I think I like you."

"Hmm." His eyes closed, his lips curling at the edges. His breathing deepened, his muscles relaxing underneath me.

Joshua slept.

I lay down once more, my body melding against his warm one. A heavy arm slid up my side.

I fell asleep, too.

I WOKE UP EARLY AS USUAL, but this time Finger was in my bed, and my lungs crushed together at the sight of him, at the feel of his massive body next to mine. His side of the sheet was twisted in between his long, powerful legs. His hair unfettered over my pillows. Those pronounced shoulder and upper arm muscles of his glaring at me.

He was beautiful. Scarred, battle weary, yet always battle ready. The biblical warrior.

I extracted myself from him and quietly got out of bed.

Instead of heading to Craig's early morning power cardio class as I did on an almost daily basis, I got dressed in a pair of yoga pants and a loose fitting top and headed for my living room to do a few yoga stretches. Otherwise both my brain and body would be cranky, and I didn't want to be cranky, especially with Finger in my house. I needed to be clearheaded and composed.

Good luck.

His big leather jacket with his patches was flung on the top of my sofa. I picked it up. The heavy weight was familiar, the smell of that worn leather and faded metal a perfume of my past. I hung the jacket on the back of a dining chair.

When I was done stretching, I put away my mat, and made a big pot of coffee and prepared two small bowls with my granola, sunflower seeds, cinnamon, blueberries, grated apple, and a drizzle of honey. I had no idea if he'd like it or make a face and call it rabbit food, but what the hell. Should I make him a huge eggs, bacon, and pancakes type of he-man breakfast? Maybe he didn't eat breakfast at all? *Gah.*

Movement from the bathroom made me blink. I took in a breath. "Will you relax?" I whispered to myself. Why did I feel like a girl on a first date with her longtime crush? I rolled my eyes at myself.

I waited for the shuffling of clothing, for footsteps. But there were only short quick breaths echoing down the hallway. I took my coffee mug in hand and made my way toward the sounds.

I stopped dead in my tracks.

Finger lifted himself up at the pull bar that was stretched across a doorway. He was focused on an imaginary point in the hallway, dipping down and swiftly pulling himself up in a smooth arc motion. His every muscle worked, body taut, skin flushed. Flex, pull. Flex, pull.

And he was naked.

Flex. Pull.

And he was magnificent.

And I'd had him next to me in my bed all night long. I took a

444

sip of coffee and burned my tongue.

His feet settled on the floor, his hands releasing the bar, his dark eyes hanging on mine. "Morning." He rubbed a hand over his sweaty chest, his morning wood, mighty wooden.

"Uh huh." I swallowed down more blazing coffee.

He smirked. "You use the bar?"

"Sometimes."

"Oh yeah?"

"Like twice a year. Maybe."

The smirk transformed into a full grin. "What do you have it for then?"

"Beck put it up. He uses it whenever he comes for a visit."

"Right." His face tensed for a second. "I haven't used a bar in a while. It's difficult for me to get a good grip with my hands."

"Oh, you were doing just fine."

That grin of his returned. "I stick to pushups."

That I'd like to see.

"Coffee?" I asked.

"Definitely." He went back to my bedroom and came out moments later wearing his jeans and a tight, long-sleeved T, a plaid flannel shirt unbuttoned over that, his boots in his hand.

I handed him his coffee and sat at my dining table.

"How's Joshua this morning?" I asked.

He laughed, taking a sip of coffee. "He's got to get back to Nebraska."

"What happened yesterday, Finger? Why were you so concerned?"

"Yesterday was the beginning and middle of the end. It was a long time coming."

"What did you do?"

"Punished the harlot."

"Which of the many harlots?" I asked.

"Reich for starters. My National President, who was coddling him. Clearing the land, baby. Outside and in." His dark metallic eyes stayed on mine as he drank his coffee.

I toyed with the edge of my beaded placemat. "You're concerned about blowback?"

He picked at the blueberries in the cereal, popping them in his mouth. "Not usually. But things are different now. Now I have you again, and I'm not letting go, for anyone or anything." He ate a spoonful of the granola.

"You have me?"

"Yes. And you have me." He chewed, those iron eyes on me again, making my stomach seize. "Tell me you made this granola yourself."

"I made this granola myself."

"It's real good. I've never liked cereal for breakfast. As a snack on the road, on hikes, yeah. But not for breakfast. Talented woman."

He sat on the chair next to me and shoved on his boots. Leaning in close, he brushed a hand across my jaw and up the side of my face, but he didn't go in for a kiss. In a tense, expectant silence, we stared at each other's lips, eyes, taking each other in, the differences, the similarities, applying brushstrokes of color to a pencil sketch, tasting the wine we had bottled ourselves a long, long time ago.

A giddy coil unwound inside me. He was still my Justin underneath the deeper lines, the thicker beard. That dark gleam in those savage eyes was still there, still unfurling me, still filling me. I glided, sails full on his wind.

His features remained intent and he pulled me in closer, planting a lingering kiss on my lips, his tongue taunting mine. My breath caught, my lips stung. I dug my nails into his formidable biceps. Was it possible to be infatuated, enthralled all over again all these years later?

He brushed a finger over the compass with the flaming blue N on my chest. "I like that tat." He planted a quick kiss on my cheek. "I'll see you tonight."

"Finger—"

He grabbed his colors from the chair and stalked out my front door. "Tonight, baby."

59
FINGER

I'D SPENT THE NIGHT WITH Lenore three times now. Slipping into her house, into her bed, holding her, pressing my body into hers. No words, only two or three soft kisses down her neck, and then sleep. A thick, full sleep with my arms full of her.

How had I done it all these years without her? Shut down, shut off. Would I ever feel satiated? I didn't think so.

At dawn, I'd leave and ride back to Nebraska and get back to work. Back to planning.

Tonight, Lenore was awake. Waiting. A small orange lamp glowed at the side of her bed, a glass of amber liquor in her hand. I took it from her and drank. Brandy. Its sweet heat spilled through me.

"I suppose it's not a coincidence that Tricky's been out of town all this week?" Her pointed question hung in the semi-darkness.

"Does that bother you?" I pulled off my long-sleeved shirt, tossing it to the side.

Her eyes darted over my bare chest. "No."

I unfastened my leathers, dropping them to the floor, but her eyes remained on mine.

The silence was skittish and fragile between us. A colt finding its legs, wanting to sprint, yet not sure how.

"Did you have dinner?" she asked. "I have barley soup I can warm up for you."

She'd changed the subject. *Good.*

"I'm fine," I replied.

"Okay." She chewed on her lip, studying me.

447

"You nervous with me?"

"A little, yeah." She licked her lips. "I'm not used to—"

Real intimacy? Raw vulnerability?

"Yeah. Me neither." I rubbed a thumb down her damp lips, and they parted for me.

She squirmed on the bed. It was a slow movement, an uncoiling of pent up anxiety, need, and desire. I bent over her and kissed her slowly, gently peeling away at that anxiety. Baring the need, unfurling the desire. I pulled a moan from her, and then another. Her hands went to my beard, my neck, and she opened her mouth fully, our lips enthralled in a search and discovery of taste and sensation. I gripped her jaw and nipped a trail down her throat and over to that spot below her ear that would always give her the chills. And there—she let out a cry, her flesh quivering—Yeah, there it was.

She grabbed at me, pulling us closer, her chest crashing into mine, her hips grinding slightly. I wiped her blue hair back from that beautiful face. I wanted to see her face. Her cheeks had reddened, liquid eyes heavy. Staring at each other, we caught our breaths. She released me, her one arm falling back over her head, the fingers of her other hand moving to her damp, swollen lips as she watched me, not saying a word. Watched and waited and wondered.

I wanted to give her plenty to wonder at.

I gave her the brandy and she finished it.

"What's this?" I gestured at four small labeled glass bottles on her night table.

"Perfumed oils from different botanicals. I've been creating scents for men and women to sell at the store. I was playing with different scent combinations tonight."

I opened a bottle. Sandalwood. Another. Cinnamon. Another was orange. The last, bergamot. A larger bottle was coconut. The base. I sat up and threw the thin sheet off her, she was naked like she was every night.

"Lie back."

She pushed up on the bed. "What are you—"

"Baby."

She gnawed on the edge of her lower lip again and laid back

down. I rubbed some coconut oil between my hands then dripped perfumed oil from the other bottles and rubbed again. I laid my warm hands between her breasts and stroked down her middle, and she let out a gasp. I rubbed in circles, small motions as I wedged my body between her legs, spreading them wide. My hands massaged up to her shoulders, down her arms, applying sure, slippery strokes. The concentrated scents filled the air, inviting the heat and energy to rise from her skin like holy fucking vapors.

She was my altar, and I was praying, making vows, uttering devotions.

Her flesh seemed to flow under my touch, her breath shortening, her muscles going limp. I stroked down to the inside of her thighs and back up again, around her breasts to her throat, around her neck, behind her ears.

"Finger…" Her voice floated.

She was in a trance, under my spell. And I was under hers.

"I want to see you like this in the light. Like that first time in the motel, remember? That was new for us, intense in a different way. I want to see you in the light now, Sunshine. Want to see it all."

Her lips parted, her eyes swirls of deep blue green. Her body melted under my hands, her desire rising like a cloud of perfume. I was touching her, opening her deeper, engaging her energy with mine.

The heat rose inside me, my hands gliding, moving, stroking over the inked delicate birds, suns and moons, many in different stages of eclipse, stars and waves. Goddesses dancing, fairies flying. Compasses. A lot of compasses all over her. Each one with numbers underneath.

I stroked around her full breasts, and they swayed with the movement of my hands. The tattooed blue N was in flames and visible in the purple and pink and red vines and flowers by one tit. The small silver balls of her nipple piercings gleamed in the muted light, and my mouth dried. I remembered when she'd first gotten them, and they'd been mine, all mine. I wanted those tits in my hands, in my mouth. I wanted her body under me, moving with mine. To fight me. Tease me. To beg me for more, demand more. I wanted inside her, taking from her every last drop of resistance and filling her with me.

But that could wait. My cock could wait. This, right now, was everything.

My thumbs rubbed up at the edges of her thighs then skimmed down on either side of her slit, and she let out a cry. I stroked over the top of her pussy, massaging in firm circles, applying pressure over the hood of her clit. She moaned, her mouth parting, her hips flexing up towards my sure strokes.

"Holy sh..." Her head swung to the side, her breathing uneven.

I kneaded her most intimate curves, massaging over her core, her flesh swelling under my touch. That's what I wanted for her, pleasure, heat. Her eyes found mine. Knowing, not knowing. I wanted to break down all the boundaries between us again. I searched for her. A serenade calling out to her. A tango challenging her, summoning her back. Every stroke brought her further, brought us closer.

I palmed her pussy and she lifted her hips, grinding into my hand.

"Yeah, baby, oh yeah," I said, my voice thick, sweat beading on my forehead. I swirled my thumb and index finger around her clit, never touching it directly, then down her opening, tugging at the sides of her slick lips.

Her gaze remained fixed on mine. Was she still anxious? Still disbelieving that this was happening? That it was me in her bed, making her come?

I'm gonna make you come, all right.

My other hand swept over a tit and settled on her upper chest. I needed to feel her heart pounding for me, connecting to mine. Her fingernails dug into my arm, her head shoving back into the pillow. Pinning her hands down into the mattress, I buried my face between her legs. Her back arched off the bed.

I had plunged into the ocean.

A thousand suns broke over the perfumed water, and I was blinded by the glare. I surged to the bottom, I flew to the surface. I breathed deep and took it all in, all of it, all of it was her.

Her breathy moans and cries got louder and more frequent.

They were beautiful, they were fragile, and I wanted more and more of them. Her body shuddered in my grip, her sharp taste filling my mouth, intoxicating me, feeding my hunger.

She stiffened, closing her legs, writhing away. "No!"

I slid up her body, lifting up on my arms, hovering over her. "What's wrong? What is it?"

She turned her face into the pillow, tears staining her cheek.

I pushed her hair back, my nose brushing the side of her jaw. "Serena, talk to me."

"Stop. I—I can't do this."

My erection pressed against her middle, a hand sliding through the slickness between her legs, and she relaxed. "Too real for you?"

Her eyes were a storm-pitched sea, turbulent, murky, the bottom no longer visible. I'd hit a nerve.

"Sunshine," I whispered. "Being with you again, so close, like this, is amazing. You feel it, don't you?"

"Yes." Her lips trembled. "Yes."

My index finger slowly made its way inside her pussy, pulsing there.

Her chin raised, her breath catching, making a strangling noise in her throat. She was mine. Always mine.

"Justin..."

"You're burning a hole right through me, baby," I breathed.

Her eyelids jammed shut. "Please stop." She hissed the word out long and slow. She was fighting it. She was uncomfortable.

I released her, removing my hand and gently brushed her lips with mine. "We'll take it slow. Spend time together with our clothes on. We need to—"

"No." With a heave, she sprang from the bed, grabbing her robe from the floor, charging from the room.

Dammit.

I followed her. "Why not? Don't run away from me. You're not doing that again."

She tried to catch her breath, pushing her wild hair behind her ears, her eyes darting over my cock, my legs, up my chest. She swallowed hard, a hand in the air. "I—just—"

"You're not in control and you don't like it, do you? You call all the shots with Tricky?" That stung the second it left my mouth. A low blow, but I couldn't fucking help it. I'd seen her with Tricky once in town, laughing, relaxed, a good time. No worries. But with me, now, she felt threatened, preferring to stay locked away in her Tower of Denial. "You tie him up and have your way with him, is that it? That your kink?"

"Fuck you!"

"No, fuck you," I replied, reigning it in, my voice low. Her eyes widened. She wasn't sure which way I was headed with this now. I was being honest, that was all that was left. "You once gave me something to believe in, but then you took it away. You threw me in a dark hole and abandoned us, letting us rot."

"I didn't."

"That's what it felt like. Especially when I was in jail. I needed you. I needed us, so goddamn bad. Everything hurt less, and everything made more sense when we had each other. For you too, I know it. Yeah, it was real difficult a lot of the time, but it was still good. It was real. I want us back. You need us back."

"Need?" Her eyes blazed, her jaw stiffened. "You have no idea."

"Tell me all about it."

"I want you to go."

"Do you want me, Serena? Do you?" My question, my voice came from the deepest and hollowest part of me. The part that used to be full of her, us.

"I said go."

She was hiding something. I could smell it, feel it in the slicing shiver up my spine. She stood there resolute. She was the guard dog at the gates, and I was pulling at the padlock, looking through the bars trying to figure out what lay beyond in the dark.

I grabbed a knife from the block on her kitchen counter.

She pivoted. "What the hell are you doing?"

I slashed a cut across the skin on my arm, holding it out to her. Red blood beaded up from the cut. "See?" I held out my arm to her, the knife still tight in my grip. "I bleed. Do you?"

"Finger—"

"We used to bleed for each other. Willingly, unwillingly." I grabbed her arm, and she jerked back in my hold. "I've been bleeding all these years, Lenore. Leaving a trail of blood everywhere I go. What about you? You left a trail?"

"I haven't stopped bleeding since Med took me. Haven't stopped!" she said through gritted teeth.

My heart squeezed in my chest at the familiar sound of that particular suffering. It was the most honest thing she'd said all night.

I wanted more.

I dragged the blade against her skin, and she took in a hiss of air, our eyes jumping to the blood rising on her arm. I held her hand in mine, crushing her fingers in my hold as I brought her arm to my mouth and sucked on the blood there, pressing my tongue against the superficial cut in her flesh like only a lover would.

She let out a husky gasp, a moan. She liked it. I pulled her in tighter against me, my grip firm, our lips a breath apart.

"Justin."

I took her in a deep, hungry kiss, the copper taste of her blood on our tongues. Yes. Our first kiss after all these years should be filled with blood.

Her robe shifted open, and the compass on her chest peeked up at me, sending an ice cold slice right through the heat we'd just generated.

"You still have my compass?" I kissed her again, nipping at her lips with my teeth. "Or did you lose it? Did you throw it away?"

Her shoulders fell, she took in a determined long breath, her lips pursing. Was she trying hard not to let any more emotion loose? "It broke."

"You were mad at me and you broke it?" I tossed the knife back on the kitchen counter.

"No." She wrapped her arms around herself as if she were suddenly cold, fighting shivers. "Motormouth broke it when he went through my stuff in Chicago. He broke it, and I realized right then that nothing could be held sacred anymore. Not you and me together, not my own life or yours, not our feelings, not our dreams. Nothing."

The colorless tone in her voice drained the vengeful lust-filled fervor in my blood.

"So, when I saw you in LA," she continued. "I let you walk out the door because no matter how much I wanted us back, how much I wanted to reverse time and change my choices, even if I could've, there was no point."

"No point? Being close to you, having that again, having you, then being sideswiped by your news of getting married. I found you, came to you so full of hope. Worst day."

"Worst day," she whispered hoarsely.

"I left you and tried not to look back," I said. "Tried real hard."

Her eyes gleamed. "You left, and then I followed your trail of blood all these years."

"What the hell does that mean?" I wiped the sweat and water from my eyes with a blood-smeared hand. "You got on with your life. You got married, had a kid!"

She only drew her robe tighter around her body.

"What does that mean?" I yelled.

She raised her hands. Surrender. Limit reached. "Go."

"I don't want to go!"

"There's nothing here but sadness. Now go!" Her hand went to her cut arm.

"Baby, I don't want to be sad, and I don't want you to be." I rubbed my hands down my face, my head spinning.

We stood there in the silence, amidst our wreckage.

"I'm going to clean us up." She left the room and came back with a box of sterile bandages and a small tube of antibiotic cream. She applied the cream on herself as I tore open a bandage. I wrapped it around her arm, then taped it. She applied the cream on my cut.

"I'm not leaving this time," I said. "I made that mistake once, twice. I should have fought for you, for us. This time, I'm going to do whatever it takes to hang onto you."

She taped the bandage on my arm without a word.

I flexed my hands. "My missing fingers and that phantom pain that comes and goes, have been a reminder all these years not only of that hell, but of you and me. Hell and heaven. Beautiful and horrible. We found each other first in the dark and then in the light and in all the shadows in between. No matter how I tried convincing myself that I should forget, the scars never allowed it."

She put the cap back on the tube of cream. "Go." Her voice was weary.

Weary like my soul.

I didn't want to fight with her, I only wanted her to see it like I did. From that moment on her bed, touching her, feeling her respond underneath my hands, my mouth, smelling her, listening to her sounds, tasting her. Through my hand I'd felt my own heartbeat joining hers, and for the first time in so, so long, I felt whole. I knew she felt it too. I knew she did, but she was scared.

My chest knotted. "Beautiful and horrible and beautiful again. That's us, baby."

"GO!" she screamed at the top of her lungs, her eyes wild. She launched away from me like an animal just freed from a trap. *Slam* went a drawer. She pivoted.

I froze.

A gun aimed at me. "Go."

I could command men to do my bidding with a look, a pitch in my voice, any number of almost unnoticeable gestures. But Lenore in pain? My body felt heavy, weighted down. My limbs locked.

I stood still under the watch of that Ruger. "What are you so afraid of, baby? After everything you've been through, you're operating on fear now? With me?"

"Fear brought me here, *baby*, safe and sound," she said, steadying the weapon in both hands. "I saw Tania's scar. That shouldn't have happened. Years ago, I stayed away from her and you to protect us all. And now we're here, together again and this happens. It shouldn't have happened. It was wrong. So wrong. Why should Tania suffer? Why?"

"No more suffering. That shit's done."

"Right." Her voice was laced with bitterness, irony.

"Lenore—"

"Go!" A plea. Desperate and despairing.

I pulled my hair back from my face. "All right, I'll go."

I got my clothes on and left. I started up my bike and glanced back at the open doorway. She still held the gun.

I LEFT BUT I WASN'T GOING to leave things like that. No. Something was wrong. Something had cracked wide open inside her, and she was desperate for me not to see and for her not to feel it.

I needed help.

I'd talked with Tania earlier that day, and she'd mentioned that tonight she would be going out with the One-Eyed Jacks for drinks over at Dead Ringer's Roadhouse.

I headed straight there and interrupted her and Butler getting it on in a back room. I didn't give a fuck, but he sure did. All the Jacks and their women shot me cold glares, but Tania was impervious to their protective shield. She strode straight through it and left with me, no hesitation.

"Are you going to tell me what's wrong?" She blinked up at me, wiping her mussed hair from her pink face, taking in a gulp of the warm humid night air in the parking lot. "What's going on?"

"Lenore's flipping out," I said. "She needs you. I made things worse. You need to talk to her, calm her down. Get through to her. Something's wrong. Something she doesn't want to talk about with me. But I think it's got everything to do with me."

"I've got my car here." Tania gestured at a blue GMC Yukon. "But I've had a few margaritas too many."

"Give me your keys."

She did, and I handed them over to Slade who'd come over to us. "Take her car and get it to Meager. I'll call you with the address."

"You got it." He got into Tania's Yukon and started her up.

"We'll take my bike. We'll get there quicker. I'll get you coffee."

"All righty."

On the road, I got us both caffeine, and we blew towards Meager, back to Lenore.

Less than an hour and a half later, I cut the engine in front of Lenore's small clapboard house. Tania got off my bike.

I grabbed her arm. "Hey. Thank you."

"Don't thank me yet."

She climbed up the small staircase of Lenore's house and knocked. "Lenore? Lenore, it's Tania. Open up, honey. Please. Lenore?"

The door opened a crack. Lenore glared at me through the darkness.

"Finger asked me to come see you," said Tania. "He's worried about you, and I want to make sure that you're okay. I need to make sure. Please. Just me. We'll stay up all night and drink and eat bad shit, like we used to."

Lenore's fierce eyes stayed on me.

"Lenore?" Tania moved closer to the front door.

"I don't eat bad shit anymore," Lenore replied.

"Okay, well, organic, sugar-free, gluten-free, whatever the hell you want—"

Lenore shook her head. "Stop."

"Come on honey, it's me," said Tania. "This is between us. I won't—"

"Go away. Both of you. Just leave me alone."

I got off my bike and stormed across her lawn. "Not leaving you alone!"

Tania shot me a glare, raising a hand. "Hey—"

"I'm not going anywhere until I know you two are talking and she's calmed down!" I said.

"Well, that's not going to happen unless you back the fuck off," Tania replied.

"I ain't backing off. Not ever."

"You need to calm down," Tania said to me.

I got in her face. "Don't tell me what I need to do."

"I wouldn't dare." Tania raised her voice.

"Stop it!" Lenore's searing gaze came back to me. "I put the gun away, so you don't have to worry I'm going to do something stupid. I wouldn't do that to my son."

"Gun? What gun?" Tania exploded. "What the hell is going on?"

"You think I would've dragged you here if it wasn't important?" I said.

"Go home. Both of you," said Lenore.

Tania moved toward her again. "Lenore, please, talk to me—"

"I don't want to talk! I don't!" Lenore shut the door, and the firm slide and click of two bolts resounded in the still night, flying bugs swirling in the glow of the porch light over Tania.

A haze of rain began. Tania descended the stairs and came to me. "Well, that went well. She pulled a gun on you?"

"I was mad, she was upset."

Tania tugged up the hood of her light jacket over her head. "Did we just make it worse?"

"I don't know."

"I'll check in on her later." She glanced at her watch. "I should get going."

"I'll take you home."

"No." She let out an exhale. "I have to go to Butler's."

"You got it bad, huh?"

"Yeah."

"So does he," I said.

"Well, I have explaining to do. And I have to do it tonight. Me leaving Dead Ringer's with you the way we did…"

"I hope it works it out for you and him," I said. "If that's what you really want. I hope—"

"God, don't you dare tell me to be happy. The last time you said that to me, things didn't end up too great."

"No, I'm not going to tell you that," I said.

"We should say, 'Be conscious,' 'Be aware.' 'Be mindful,' and definitely, 'Be good to yourself.'"

"I say, you fucking do what you want, but give it your best. Whatever you do, don't hold back. Lay it out there. All of it."

"That works for me. That I like."

Slade pulled up in Tania's car, a prospect behind him on a bike.

"You good to drive?" I asked.

"I'm fine. Butler's only a couple streets over." Tania leaned a hand on my shoulder and lifted up on her toes and kissed my cheek. "You take care of yourself."

"Yeah." I got on my bike. "Fuck you."

She let out a dry laugh that I drowned out with the roar of my throttle.

Slade and his prospect headed back to Dead Ringer's. I got the hell out of Meager and focused on the road home to Nebraska.

My body conformed to the vibrations and movements of my bike over the smooth highway. The familiar road signs with their arrows, route numbers, exit numbers shone starkly in the bright white lamps.

Numbers.

The numbers over Lenore's body flashed before my eyes. A series of numbers was inked under each compass.

"Nebraska...the good life" said the sign whipping past me as I crossed the border.

Seventeen minutes later, I passed the signpost for Elk with its small population tallied at the bottom.

My back stiffened, my heels pressed down.

Those weren't any random numbers on her body. They were the coordinates for my clubhouse here in Nebraska.

Why would Lenore have my club, my home base tattooed on her body all these years?

Her rough voice from earlier answered me, *"Trail of blood."*

60
LENORE

I DIDN'T WANT TO WAKE UP, but I did.

I didn't want to remember the feel of Finger's warm hands rubbing fragrant oils into my naked body under that harsh, possessive gaze of his that was like taking bullets to the chest, but I did.

I didn't want to feel fiercely aroused by that erotic memory, but I did.

I didn't want to use my vibrator pretending it was him pulsing inside me, but I did.

I didn't want to cry after coming, but I did.

I stayed in bed the whole day, and into the night.

The next morning I woke up at four thirty.

Time to deal.

I've always dealt, why should this be any different?

But it was different. The prospect of me and Finger together again loomed over me like the shadow of a two hundred story skyscraper. Stunning, breathtaking.

Ominous.

And he'd been right. I did like telling the men in my bed what to do. That had become my thing, my necessary thing after I'd left Finger and Chicago behind me. I liked the control. It was stabilizing, exciting. I kept my head above water that way. I'd never felt that need with Finger. With him sex had always been a kind of wild freedom, a raw intimacy, an intense passion. Giving in to him just that little bit the other night, submitting to his fiery attention, his extraordinary care was—

I ripped the sheets off my bed and shoved them in the washing

460

machine, took a shower, downed a greens drink, got dressed, and went to my store. I put everything out of my head and only concentrated on putting the finishing touches on the surprise I'd been making for Tania. I'd planned on giving it to her this week, but after the other night, after shutting her out, yelling at her, would she even speak to me?

I detested confrontations, especially with people I cared about. But emotions and denial made things muddy and ugly. Tania had always been there for me, always pitching in, offering solutions, a don't-worry-we-got-this hug. And now she was in the middle of my and Finger's tangle in more ways than one.

I had to make this right.

Once Mimi, my new assistant, showed up for work at the store, I went down the block to the Meager Grand and ordered a super large extra deluxe iced coffee that I knew Tania would enjoy. I headed back up the block to Tania's art gallery/antiques shop, the Rusted Heart. She'd opened up a couple of months ago, making her long time dream a reality, and right here in her home town.

I pushed open the front door of the Rusted Heart, a bell jangling overhead, and strode to the handmade wood slab front desk where she sat, glaring at her computer screen behind a pair of reading glasses. I set the Meager Grand cup on the desk and her eyes widened, tracking up the large iced coffee with a dollop of whipped cream. Good coffee was serious business.

She removed her glasses. "That looks insanely yummy."

"That's cold-brewed."

"Bless you, my child." She grabbed the coffee and took a greedy sip from the tall straw, groaning. She gestured to the rattan armchair next to her. "Sit."

I sat down, my muscles relaxing one by one. "I'm so sorry about the other night at my house."

"Are you okay?"

"Yeah. Better. I'm sorry I lost it. You came over because you care, because you were concerned. And I was a mess. I've been a burden to you. For years now."

"No, you haven't, Lenore." She eyed me. "Things are complicated. I get that. But maybe you could give an inch."

I traced over the fresh scab on my arm. "Finger was really angry."

"Being upset was at the heart of his anger. He's trying, Lenore. He's reaching out."

"He hates me."

Maybe he didn't, but he just might one day soon. Hiding behind denial was easier than having to chop its thick vines into little bits and burn the pieces, inhaling its bitter smoke, exposing the naked truth. Not easier, no. I'd just gotten used to it.

Finger hating me had always been a painful idea, but now it was no longer an idea, a "one day maybe" theory, but an imminent reality staring at me in the face with dark eyes that pierced my soul, their molten power melting everything inside me down to its essence. And that essence was us; if I was going to move forward with him, I'd have to be totally honest and fearless in that honesty.

"He doesn't hate you. He can't," Tania said. "I hate all these bad feelings flying between all of us."

He'd given her a hard time too, and she didn't deserve any of it. "That's my fault."

"I'm not trying to lay blame here." She put her coffee down and took in a breath. "I'm tired. I was up late last night with my mother."

"Is she okay?"

Tania explained how her mother hadn't been dealing very well with her MS this week. Two steps forward, one step back, over and over again.

"I'm so sorry your family's going through this. I have something that can cheer you up."

Tania shook the almost empty coffee cup, the ice rattling within. "Vanilla vodka over ice?"

I let out a laugh, and that cramping in the pit of my stomach finally released its evil pinch. "No, no. Too early for that. This is way better. I'll be right back."

I went to my store, and placed her gift in a small shopping bag, and went back to her gallery. I handed her the bag, a grin on my face. I knew she wasn't able to spend much time or money on herself with setting up her business and caring for her mother. She'd had a crush on Butler for a long time and now Butler was free, and her divorce was being finalized. If I could offer her a moment's pleasure, I damn well would. That I could do. Erase her stress for just a little while. To wipe away the smudges, dirt, and blurriness like efficient windshield wipers.

My grandmother had the right idea. The gift of hand-made pretty was like no other, and that's why I'd named my business for what she'd given me.

Tania's eyes widened at the sight of the purple Lenore's Lace bag. I drew out the piece I'd designed for her.

"Holy—"

"I know."

She stared at the dark red corset hanging from my hands. Tania speechless? The mark of success.

Her fingertips slid over the textures of silk bands and lace. "It's gorgeous. It's—"

"I made it for you. I'm almost finished with it. One piece. One size. Yours. Try it on."

Her eyes darted to mine. "Lenore—"

"Ah, Tania, trust me. I know these things. With your skin and hair..."

All she needed was encouragement, a last push up the mountain's peak to see the Promised Land beyond. The air got thin up there, you needed support. I knew the signs, and I knew how to encourage. But I wasn't only offering a dream here. Reality's beauty was reaching out to Tania. Her very own beauty.

She took in a deep breath, her gaze magnetized on the corset. She was envisioning herself in it. My pale skinned, black haired, dark eyed Cinderella and her scarlet ballgown. I made one hell of a fairy godmother. My heart swelled. If I could be Tania's fairy godmother, just this once.

"You can't take your eyes off it, can you?" I asked.

"Give it here."

I carefully laid it in her arms, the fabric gliding over our skin.

"Go," I ordered.

Kicking off her shoes, she went into her back room.

I gave her a few minutes. "Honey, you need help?" I stepped into the room and my heart thudded in my chest.

Hell yes, best Fairy Godmother ever.

"It's perfect. This color on you—it's even better than I hoped." I smoothed my hands down her back and across her waist. "Fantastic," I murmured to myself.

Her skin trembled under my touch, and my eyes went to hers in the mirror. "Hon, you okay?" I stood up again and put my arms around her, my chin on her shoulder. "Tania, what's wrong?"

"You're amazing," she said, her voice small. "This is a beautiful work of art. I feel beautiful."

"Babe, you are beautiful. Only you could carry this one off. The color on you is—"

"Stunning. Somewhere between blood and wine."

"Exactly. Your eyes really pop, and your skin is glowing, that dark, shiny hair."

She pressed a hand against her middle. "I don't even mind my tummy."

"Stop. Your body looks great. I think you've lost a few pounds lately. Stressed out much?"

"Just a tiny little bit."

"And don't say a word about that ass. It's glorious." My hand slid down the curve of her hip.

She let out a small breath, her eyes ungluing from her reflection.

"What is it, Tania? What's wrong?"

"I haven't felt this way in a long, long time."

"What way is that?"

"You know what I mean."

I squeezed her hip. "Say it out loud right now while you're feeling that shit."

She met my gaze in the mirror once more. "I feel like the me I want to be. The me I've always wanted to be, but was never usually on the outside—sexy, in charge of myself. Powerful. Bold."

I gripped her arms. "That's the Tania I know. This one right here. Very powerful. Very bold."

"That's the act I put on for everyone. Or when my back is up

464

against the wall."

"No."

"Yes. There's a part of me that's still a scared little girl. Scared of the dark, scared of twisty roller coasters, scared without her daddy, scared of bikers wielding knives."

My chin lifted. "That's not the Tania I know. No. This Tania is only scared of being alone, of not being enough."

She bit down on her wobbly lower lip, a tear slipping down her cheek. Her fresh scar visible on her chest.

I pressed into her. "I know. Don't I know?" My voice a hoarse whisper.

"You know."

I wiped the tear from her face. "Hadn't we said no more tears?"

"Tell me you've kept to that deal all these years."

I made a face. "Nope."

"Didn't think so. Me neither."

I sniffed in air. "It's all right. We're tough, you and me."

Tania covered my hand with hers. "I'm glad you're in my life again, whatever your name is."

I laughed.

This is what mattered. This.

Tania pressed the side of her face against mine. Her peppery flower scent rose between us, capturing the rush of emotion in my veins like a snapshot.

"I really, really am glad," she said.

I wouldn't have made it without you. "Me, too."

A small smile tugged on the edge of my mouth. "You're really falling for Butler?"

"Yes," she breathed, her lips pressing together.

"You're questioning it? Maybe it's too soon after your husband, and you need to be on your own for a while?"

"I've been on my own for years and years. That's not what I want."

Such conviction.

"Then, what is it?" I asked.

"I'm questioning myself. Maybe I don't have what it takes to go the distance."

"That's the fear talking."

"Says the expert."

"We're talking about you now," I shot back.

"I don't want to screw this up. He and I are both screwed up enough as it is. How many second chances do you get in life anyhow?" Tania's teeth snagged on her bottom lip.

Second chances. I'd felt there were no more "chances" to be had for me, that I'd used them all up. That fact was riveted deep after all this time, holding my tattered soul in place, otherwise it would jump out of my skin and leave a zombie behind.

I'd become a rocket blasting into the air, only to nosedive and crash back into the nameless field from which it came. No sprint through the stars, no landing on fresh, unchartered territory. Some nights, I still smelled the fumes over my ashes.

I refocused my attention on the gorgeousness that was Tania in the scarlet corset. Here I was urging her to grab her second chance by the balls. And what was I doing?

She smoothed a hand over the side of the fabric. "I want to be with Butler like I've never been with anyone before, ever. But now he knows that I'm keeping a secret from him. A secret involving Finger. I haven't told him all of it. Nothing about you."

Tania was having to keep secrets for me from her lover. This situation certainly wasn't fair. She needed to be unfettered. I was trying to do that for her with this corset, but she really needed something else from me, didn't she?

And so did I.

I turned her around and leaned her forehead against mine. "You're a good friend, Tania." I planted a gentle kiss on her lips.

Tania and I never got involved sexually again after the motel with Finger. The threesome had been my idea, and I'd made her feel safe and beautiful, and she'd given the same to me. She given all of herself to me and Finger, helping us get past the fresh sting of our hell. That intense, burning level of frankness between us had never diminished.

Tania cleared her throat. "I need to tell you something. Cards on the table. I can't keep it from you, and I don't ever want you to think that—"

"What is it?"

"After you left him, after you..."

"After I broke him, you mean?"

When he'd seen me with Eric, pregnant with Beck.

She shifted her weight. "Yeah. He and I, we bumped into each other after that and..."

Oh man.

They'd had a relationship? A thing?

An ache bloomed in my chest, gathering force, sweeping up my throat and down my limbs. An invading army marching across my tattered battlefield. But it wasn't jealousy that marched through me with every soldier's heavy footstep. No, it was an acute sense of sadness. Displacement. Guilt, even.

I held up a hand, shaking my head at her, stopping the booming tromp of words I didn't want to hear. I'd hurt him, I'd left them both behind, and they'd been there for each other.

"You don't have to explain, Tania. I'm glad that he had you in his corner. I'm glad he tried to forget."

She threw her head back. "Dear God, you are so wrong! He did it to remember."

My heart stopped.

Those soldiers lined up before me, and I backed up against a wall.

Ready.

Aim.

Tania's eyes pinned me to that wall. "His passion for you is some kind of fury. A fury whose fangs and claws have sunk deep. A fury that won't let go. A damn tidal wave of love, anger, pain, desolation. A tidal wave that won't quit. And he tortures himself with it."

My breath burned in my lungs. She'd just described my soul.

"He got on with his life," I said. "So did I."

"Yeah, he sure did. Just like you did." A flicker of derision crossed Tania's face. "Oh, there were the usual women. An old lady here, and another one there. They never lasted long though. Not one."

"Well, I'm glad he had you."

How long did it go on for? Did I want to know? It didn't matter. It really didn't. Why shouldn't he have tried for happiness with Tania?

"Oh Lenore, we were only two people grabbing at something we couldn't have."

I plucked the shopping bag off the floor. "It has nothing to do with me."

"That is such bullshit, and you know it! It was all about you!" Tania's voice snapped. "You have to let him in. You have to tell Finger. I won't ever. I made you that promise. But you have to tell him."

To tell him would upset and shock him, and he'd probably hate me. To not tell him held up the barrier between us, a barrier I couldn't pretend wasn't there and enter into a relationship with him, casual or otherwise. Hell, there was no casual between us. That wasn't us.

Either way, I'd lose him. Either way.

I folded the bag and placed it on a nearby box.

"Who's afraid now?" Tania asked. "Finger knows I know more than I've been letting on. Honey, the other night was crazy."

I'd pulled a gun on him, for fuck's sake.

"He was so angry," I said. "He got angry at you, too."

"Yes, he did. But that's because he felt powerless. He wants to help you, and he doesn't know how. He's desperate to reach you."

My stomach curled at the memory of his very real desperation to reach me that night, to be good to me, to make me feel safe, to make me feel the emotion he still carried for me. That we were still possible.

If only I would—

My hands went over my ears.

"You still love him." Tania pulled my hands from my head. "Can't you say it? Why can't you say it?"

Because the truth would slice deep. "Too much has happened."

"No. You have to be brave. You have to be brave enough to act on that love." Lacing our fingers together, Tania whispered, "How brave are you, Rena?"

I raised my head high. Since I'd met Finger, all I'd done was act bravely on that love. Everything I'd done was for that love.

Swords had hung over our heads, pendulums had swayed across our chests, we'd stood in line for our turn at La Guillotine. And yet, through all of that, all of it, we'd loved.

And now? Now that the way was clearer than ever before?

Still had to be brave. Still had to fight for it, risk for it.

I held Tania's eyes. "How brave are you?"

61
FINGER

Back in my office, I searched online for every Lenore's Lace ad. All of them were of her. Her face never in view, but she showed off her terrific body draped and wrapped in her sexy lingerie and her unique swirl of tats. So many tats. Over her body lay an epic composition in ink, woven with beautiful and menacing images. From behind vines and flowers and suns and moons and sparkling stars, lay savagery: a fanged beast with bloody claws ripping at a princess, a fairy angel dancing with a shrieking demon, a dragon rising over a hill of flames. A bleeding eye. Lenore had composed a restless, disturbing, oddly hopeful, gruesome baroque symphony.

I enlarged each photo, scrutinizing each compass on her torso, her ass, her upper back, her chest, the inside of a thigh. Each was paired with a series of numbers. Eight in all. I emailed them all to Den.

— *Find these locations* —

Within minutes, he sent me a list of locations. I ticked off each spot.

Missoula, Montana - *where she was born*
Emmet, Kansas - *Med's Smoking Guns chapter*
Chicago, Illinois - *her refuge with Tania*
Elk, Nebraska - *my Flames of Hell chapter*
Los Angeles, California - *where she got married and her son was born*

Rapid City, South Dakota - *where she raised her son*
Meager, South Dakota - *her business, her home*
Pine Needle, South Dakota -

Pine Needle?

Just past Meager, through wheat and sunflower farms, Pine Needle was a small town, much quieter, more rustic and worn than Meager. Although Meager had experienced something of a renewal the past couple of years, new businesses, younger families, Pine Needle remained sleepy, musty.

What the hell was in Pine Needle that warranted the honor of being tatted on her body?

My eyes shuffled over every compass on the photos, back and forth, back and forth. Every single coordinate tat had a compass above it, almost hidden, embedded in the leaves or the flowers or the birds surrounding it. Each compass had a different direction on it. But this compass in Pine Needle was the only one locked on True North. Only this one was on her chest. And the N for North on this compass was different from the others. This N was bolder, thicker, and in blue flames.

I headed for my bike.

It was late October and the sunflower and wheat and soy fields had been cleared, the air seeped with the aroma of resin and earth. The open land was shorn, gone was its former velvety fullness. The thick fabric of reeds no longer billowed in the winds, shuffling their mysterious music at me. This spartan starkness had its own special appeal. Bare essentials. Stubborn and uncompromising.

I parked my bike in front of Drake's Garden Center, the exact location of these coordinates on the northeastern edge of Pine Needle.

Potted trees, shrubs, fencing samples, oddball garden fountains littered the wide front yard. A small colonial house that was in dire need of a fresh paint job was also on the property and was probably where the owners lived. A truck was parked out front where a fit man with silvery blond hair tucked into a baseball cap, wearing sunglasses, struggled to unload a wheelbarrow from his pickup that was filled with them. Signs advertising roses and perennials and organic seeds stood on either side of the entrance to a large store with long greenhouses attached on the side and a long one in the back. A field of pumpkins was to the left, a wagon filled with hay stood alone before it.

"Hey there!" the man, who must have been in his mid to late sixties, stopped his attempt at unloading and checked me out. "Good morning."

"Good morning."

He wiped a jittery, shaky gloved hand across his sweaty forehead. "Anything I can help you with?"

"How about I help you with those wheelbarrows?" I asked him.

"Would you? That'd be great."

"No problem."

"Thanks. I appreciate it. I shouldn't be doing this on my own, got a bad back and lately my hands don't grip the way they used to."

"I know the feeling," I said.

"Damnedest thing, getting old."

"You don't look so old," I said.

"I certainly don't feel old, I can tell you." He let out a laugh. "The young man who helps me out won't be coming in until later this afternoon, but I need to unload 'em now." He held out a shaky hand. "I'm Steve. Steve Drake."

I shook it. "Hey Steve. I'm Finger."

He adjusted his baseball cap, his eyes going to my colors. "Good to meet you, Finger."

I hoisted myself up on the truck and maneuvered a wheelbarrow out, then another, and another while Steve rolled them inside his store.

He led me through to the interior of the Garden Center. "You looking for anything special today?"

"I am. Just not sure what that is."

He took off his sunglasses. "A gift?"

"Yeah, a gift."

"Lady friend?"

"That's right."

"I'll set you up. She like to garden?"

"Her garden is very neat and colorful, so yeah, she enjoys it."

He pointed at flowering plants, orchids, a flower box of oregano, mint, thyme, and chives. "That's good for a porch or big kitchen window. If she likes to cook, that's a good choice."

"Right."

The garden tools and fertilizer sacks, and bags of soil were all lined up in long rows.

And that's when I saw them, stacked in wobbly piles. Hand painted flower pots. Another pile of dishes for the pots, trimmed in stripes and zig zags and polka dots. These were the pots and matching dishes Lenore had all over her house and front porch.

My eyes lingered over them, urging them to tell me what they knew.

Steve came up next to me. "You like those, huh?"

"Uh, yeah. They've got a certain charm."

"My wife makes those. There are these over here too—" I followed his hand, gesturing to the left. A shelf of glazed earthenware dessert dishes and coffee mugs. Exactly like the coffee mugs Lenore used at her house.

"I like those. I think I'll get a set of two of the blue glazed ones."

"They're real nice. That blue doesn't come out that way very often. It's pretty unique. My wife is good at what she does. I'll pack them up for you."

"Thanks."

I followed Steve to the register by the front door. As he wrapped and packed each mug in butcher paper, I checked out his set up. A dollar bill was framed and hanging on the wall behind him. Next to it was a picture of a much younger Steve with darker long hair, his one hand on a shovel planted in the ground by a young tree, his other arm around a blonde who was holding a baby in her arms. The two of them smiling huge standing in front of their house which seemed fresher. Bright beginnings, big hopes. The all-American dream come true. There were other pictures of Steve and his wife at all different ages—riding horses, bundled up on a snow plow, drinking beers with friends at a bonfire, swimming at a reservoir in the summer.

He rang up the sale, and I handed him bills, picking up his business card from the neat pile at the side of the counter along with cards from other local businesses.

Steve gave me my change. "Hope she likes them."

"I know she will." I slid my chained wallet back in my jeans.

He led me outside and handed me a small bouquet of big dark pink flowers. "Take these for your lady friend. Dahlias are always a favorite."

"You don't have to do that."

"Please. I appreciate your help with those wheelbarrows. Have a good rest of your day."

"Thanks. You too."

There was nothing more to see. Unless, of course, Lenore had bodies buried out back in Steve's vegetable field or under his greenhouses. I'd have to come back at night and do my digging.

It wouldn't be wise to ask Steve if he knew Lenore. He might think I was after her for no good. He'd taken in my colors when I'd first approached him, that eye-widening thing happened for just a sec, but it happened. I expected it to happen, and I always liked it.

Twenty minutes later I arrived at Lenore's house. I left the bag with the mugs by her front door.

Years ago, she'd pulled a gun and a knife to protect me and had killed people who were threatening my life. The other night she pulled a gun on me. What the hell was she protecting now? What the hell was in Pine Needle?

I took out my pen and wrote, *Look what I found - F* on the garden center business card, and I tucked it into the dahlias, sliding the ends of the flowers into the bag with the mugs.

I'd set my fuse and looked forward to a spectacular explosion.

62
FINGER

SEAMLESS STILLNESS.

At one with the one. At one with the one.

"Let go of me, dammit!"

Her voice.

A ripple pushed through me, my pulse tripping over that voice. Meditation had never been better interrupted.

"It's all right, man. Let her through," said Catch.

Deep breath in. Breath out. One eye opened. The other. Dull light pressed in on me. The lines of my desk, the burgundy carpet beneath me.

"I need to see him now. Where is he?"

That voice, her voice, splitting everything in two, pulling the breath from me. A smile tugged at my mouth.

I uncrossed my legs and stood up. A single knock on my door, and my shoulders pulled back and released.

"Hey, Prez. Sorry. It's Lenore from Meager," came Catch's voice on the other side of my door. "She wants to see you."

Slowly rubbing my hands together, I focused on my door knob, re-familiarizing myself with the curves and angles of physical reality and unlocked the door. Flanked by Catch and a prospect, Lenore stood before me, her blue green eyes dark teal and icy. My gaze rode down her long, fitted black blouse, the studded seam of the low V revealing the delicious swells of her body and that mysterious ink. Tight black jeans and high leather boots completed the picture of perfection.

Oh, how I've been waiting for you, baby.

475

I stepped aside and she charged into my office, my world. Catch pulled the door closed.

"What are you doing?" came the voice, smooth as steel and just as hard.

I didn't answer. I took her in, her spicy sweet scent of flowers of the night settling over me, her jaw taut, those full lips that I could feel on my skin, the grace and adamance of her stance that only she could pull off.

She was here. Finally. She'd stormed into my club the way I'd always imagined. Taking prisoners, demanding. My skin heated. Shit, she turned me on.

"Finger?" The steel wavered.

"You liked the mugs, huh baby?" I asked, my voice low, calm.

Her throat moved as she swallowed hard.

She drilled herself into the floor. "Why? Why did you go there?"

"Why is that place inked on you?" My index finger brushed over that compass on her chest, lingering there. "Why, baby? Why there?" I whispered. "What's there other than pretty pots and mugs, flowers, watering cans, and great big bags of soil?"

Her breathing got rougher with every trace I made on her flesh. My hand wrapped around her neck, my thumb rubbing down her throat. "You going to tell me or do I got to dig deeper than just chatting with Steve and shopping at his store? He invited me back. Looking forward to meeting his wife."

Lenore's eyes widened. The ice was gone, molten swells of precious aquamarine simmered in their place.

Then she did something I never expected.

Her long fingers with the short mint green painted nails cradled my face, her eyes swimming in a turbulent emotion I couldn't name. She drew me close, her body pressing against mine, clinging to me, and kissed me. Lenore kissed me with a sweet ferocity, lips demanding, tongue searching. My arms whipped around her like chains pulling tight. She consumed us both with her mouth, my hunger blazing, her heat lighting me on fire.

She pulled back slightly, her thumb rubbing over my lips. Taking in a breath, she leveled her eyes with mine. She'd made a decision. "Come with me, and I'll tell you everything."

The hairs on the back of my neck lifted at the firm determination in her tone, yet there were sparks of vulnerability moving across her face.

"Lead the way," I said.

I unlocked my door but she stood still, studying me. Were we about to enter a new world and leave the old one for the final time? She strode through the door, me behind her. The small crowd of my brothers broke, and we passed through.

"Drac, take care of shit. This might take a while."

"You got it." Drac tipped his head at me.

On my bike, I followed Lenore in her vintage Mustang to the Garden Center in Pine Needle. She got out of her car and stood perfectly still, her eyes on the store.

"We shopping for fruit trees or pumpkins today?" I asked.

She shot me a hard look and without a word, turned and moved toward the entrance to the nursery. A blonde lady looking to be in her early sixties and wearing a parka vest waved, greeting her. Lenore's features instantly smoothed into an equally warm greeting. Steve wasn't here, neither was his truck. Was that his wife?

Leaving my gloves on, I followed Lenore into the cavernous store. She didn't look back at me. She kept moving slowly through the aisle of oversized pots, the aisle of weed killers, the aisle of fertilizer and plant food to the main greenhouse.

Loud music blared, a dance pop tune sung by some screechy young starlet who moaned in between verses. Pots of rosemary, basil, thyme, baby pine trees in small wood barrels, paver stones for patios and borders, the wheelbarrows. A short girl in glasses and a ponytail wearing a purple windbreaker danced at the end of the aisle. Her body moved and jerked off rhythm, like she was trying to keep up with it, but couldn't and didn't really care anyhow. She was smiling ear to ear, singing along loudly, her eyebrows wavering on her face as she moved with plenty of drama. She pivoted, swinging her arms up and around her head, as if she was copying moves she'd seen on a music video but also adding her personal twirl to it.

"Lenore!" She waved at Lenore as she did a hop and popped out a hip to the side in a big finish, her ponytail bouncing behind her.

"Hey, Zoë!" Lenore raised her hands in the air and the girl squealed and high-fived her. "Looking good, girl!"

Zoë wiped strands of her hair from her face. "Daddy's on a delivery and Mommy's busy up front, so I turned up the music." She giggled, tapping on her cell phone.

"You really like that song. You were playing it the last time I came," Lenore said.

Zoë's full face blushed. "It's my favorite." Her slanted, small eyes lifted and landed on me. She seemed Asian, sort of. "Hello." Her full smile grew wider, enlivening her face even more.

"Zoë, this is my friend Finger."

Zoë giggled and scrunched her eyes. "That's a funny name." She raised a hand and waved it at me even though we were two feet apart. "Hi, Mr. Finger."

"Finger, this is Zoë. Zoë's parents own the nursery."

"Hi. Nice to meet you, Zoë. I met your dad yesterday."

"Daddy's not here now."

"Finger bought me your blue mugs," said Lenore.

"You did?" Zoë giggled again.

"I brought Finger back to show him those clay tiles you made," said Lenore. "The ones you'd showed me the last time I came. Do you remember?"

Zoë's lips parted. "No." She shook her head. "Oh, oh—yes, yes, I remember. You liked them even though most of them came out c-c-crooked." She wrinkled her nose.

"That's why I like them, because they're made by hand. Your hands. Since Finger is so strong he's going to help me lift them and put them in my car and get them into my house."

"That's good. You shouldn't do everything all by yourself. Men help ladies. My mommy taught me that."

Zoë studied me, transfixed on my face. She pointed at me with her index finger. "Lenore—weird m-marks on his f-face." Her voice stuttered, the words stumbling thickly out of her mouth. She turned her head to the side dramatically.

"I know, honey," said Lenore. "It makes Finger look different, but he's just like you and me underneath. You know how that is."

"Yep, I know." Her heavily lidded eyes crinkled, her mouth pulling up into an immediate full smile, her shoulders lifting. She continued studying me with no sense of embarrassment or shyness, seemingly oblivious to a third wall of manners with strangers. "People look at me funny sometimes, but I'm used to it now."

"They look because you're so pretty." Lenore's voice had softened considerably, and I glanced at her.

"Pretty and born different," said Zoë.

"Born special," said Lenore, her tone breathy.

Of course, Zoë had Down Syndrome. The slanted eyes, the thick features. But she was a far stretch from what they used to call "retarded" when I was in school. I remember the disabled kids in special classrooms and on their own small school buses. Zoë wasn't like them from what little I remembered. She communicated clearly. She was a live wire.

Zoë snuck another look at me, pointing at my face. "Those scars are scary. Do they hurt?"

"No, no, they don't hurt," I replied. "They did once, but that was a long time ago. I don't remember it anymore."

Zoë let out a sigh. "Oh, that's good. I'm glad. I have scars like that on my heart."

"On your heart?" I asked.

"I had heart surgery when I was a baby, and I don't remember it either. Did you have surgery on your face?"

"Yeah, something like that," I said.

"They didn't do a good job," Zoë said.

"No, they didn't," I murmured.

"How's Mark?" Lenore asked, her voice slightly loud, almost off key.

Zoë's face beamed. "Mark is the best boyfriend in the whole world."

"You're so lucky," said Lenore. "Zoë has a birthday in a couple weeks, right, Zo?"

"Twenty-one!" A huge smile streaked across Zoë's face. "Mommy and Daddy got me an early present since I've been doing such a good job at school and here at the store. Look, it's a new cell phone. I play lots of games on it and play my music, take selfies. Mark and I Skype all the time. He sends me funny emojis. Here. Look."

Zoë showed Lenore her text messages with her boyfriend.

"Aw, Mark's so sweet," said Lenore.

They both peered at the cell phone screen as Zoë tapped at it.

"Which emoji is your favorite, Zoë?" I asked.

Both their heads turned up at me, and my breath caught, a chill ran up the back of my neck, like an icy whisper, a whisper telling me something important. And I couldn't avoid it, ignore it. I couldn't look away. It pierced my gut and twisted up my body, crushing my lungs, pounding in my chest.

In the sudden stream of sunlight hitting the two of them from the skylight above us, Lenore and Zoë's eyes shined at me. The same distinct eye color. That rich, unique blue green of Lenore's. Zoë had her eyes even if they were shaped differently, slanted differently.

Numbers, numbers ran through my head.

Zoë let out a soft laugh. "My favorite is the emoji face blowing kisses. That's my f-favorite. The k-k-kiss."

Zoë turning twenty-one. Subtraction, addition.

I'd gotten Lenore out twenty-five years ago. Lenore and I were together in Chicago for four years, then I got sent to prison, and Lenore had disappeared.

She'd disappeared.

Twenty-one.

Twenty-one. Twenty-one. Twenty-one.

The coordinates Lenore had tattooed under the compasses all over her body marking every event of her life and of mine. And yet the mystery one remained for this garden center. For this house.

The one tattoo over her heart. The big flaming N for North. Her North.

For Zoë.

Blue-green eyed Zoë. Zoë with hair the color of mine from when I was her age. That dark brown, not black, not chestnut brown. Dark coffee.

My pulse raced along with my thoughts that came faster and

faster, shuffling in front of my eyes, rearranging, scraping under my skin, scratching at my heart.

I'd gone to jail and Lenore had taken off. Left Chicago. Hidden from me. Mishap couldn't find her. A thousand electrodes went off in my veins, all of them short-circuiting, flaring. Lenore had set her own fuse.

Was Zoë our kid?

My heart brawled in my chest. I raised my right hand, reaching out for fuck knows what, somehow clasping Lenore's upper arm. She covered my hand with one of her own, gripping it tight, taking in a breath of air while she continued listening to whatever Zoë was saying.

Emojis, bitmojis, makeup apps, fashion apps, selfie sticks, YouTube videos.

I staggered, and Lenore pulled up next to me, sliding her arm firmly around my middle.

My heart spiraled.

I focused on Zoë's voice thudding over vowels, catching on consonants, those eyes of hers dancing under the glory of Lenore's full attention.

"Are you helping Lenore, Zoë honey?" asked the blonde woman we'd seen outside. She stepped up next to Zoë, hands firmly clasped together.

Lenore's back straightened. "Hey, Gail. I had to come back and get those pretty tiles Zoë had shown me last time I came. I haven't been able to stop thinking how perfect they'd be on my porch with the lavender and the hydrangeas."

Gail's gaze settled on me.

"Gail, this is Finger," Lenore said. "Finger, this is Zoë's mom, Gail. She owns the nursery with her husband, Steve."

Zoë's mom. Zoë's dad.

"Hey," I managed. "I met Steve yesterday."

"Ah, yes," Gail replied, her smile softening her face. "You helped him with the wheelbarrows, right?"

"Right, yeah," I said.

"Is Mr. Finger your boyfriend, Lenore?" asked Zoë, her forehead wrinkling. "You should have a boyfriend. I keep telling you that."

"Easy there, Zo." Gail laughed. "Let's get Lenore her tiles. How many you need, hon?"

"Fifty should be good to start with."

Gail guided her daughter towards a stack of colored small square tiles at the end of the aisle. Lenore and I stood in silence, our grip on each other deepening. Somehow we made it to the cash register, and Lenore paid for her tiles. I grabbed the box from the wagon Gail and Zoë had put it in, slamming it against my chest.

"Bye bye, Lenore." Zoë waved at us. "Bye, Mr. Finger."

I heaved in a breath, forcing my chin to raise a few degrees, forcing a hoarse "Bye" out of my dry mouth. My grip tightened on the box, the rest of me numb. I shoved one foot in front of the other.

I followed Lenore to her car, my vision blurred. She opened the trunk, and I set the box down. She shoved down the door, her eyes darting back to the nursery, to me.

I spit out, "What the fuck have you done?"

63
FINGER

SOMEHOW WE MADE IT TO Lenore's house. I don't remember how. I just functioned. Keeping clear of obstacles, passing trucks, watching for turns. Exits. Stop signs. Downshifting.

Parked.

We walked into her house and I stood there, an astronaut with no flight suit, a surgeon with no scalpel, a hawk with no wings.

A glass of liquor got shoved in my hand. I stared at the dark caramel liquid, the fumes prickling my numb senses. I drank.

She went to a small red velvet box decorated with aqua beads and tassels which sat under a funky candelabra on a console table, and pulled out a suede pouch. My grandfather's pouch for the compass. She took the drink from me and put the pouch in my hands. I opened it, and the broken pieces of my compass stared back at me.

"When Motormouth found me he ransacked my place, stole from me, broke your compass, tried to rape me. He was going to bring me back to Med and get a reward for it or kill me, because Med had gotten rid of his girlfriend and he was angry and upset. I was almost three months pregnant with Zoë at the time. I'd just found out that day, in fact. There was no way I was ever going back," she said. "Especially not with our baby inside me.

"When Motor found the pictures of us, he told me he and Scrib had always suspected you of getting me out but they'd never told Med. Now, he was going to tell him. I couldn't let that happen." Her eyes were that cool blue now, her tone even. She regretted nothing. "I had our baby inside me. Ours. And she deserved to live a beautiful life. And I would do whatever it took to protect our child and protect you. But if I'd contacted you in jail and told you the truth, you would've suffered there trying to get to us somehow, and they would've come after us and gotten to you. I couldn't take that chance."

She was right.

Motionless, I stared at her, listening, not listening, raging, burning, the compass pieces heavy in my hand.

"I couldn't wait to tell you about the baby on your next visit, but you got arrested. Sometime before that, Boner had shown up at Tania's apartment looking for Grace, screaming about Dig getting killed, Grace losing her baby and disappearing. I listened to him rant and yell and cry. He was devastated. Shit, I thought, that could be me and Finger, but not some random kill blowing us up like them, but Med and Scrib doing the honors, punishing us. I wasn't going to let that happen.

"I had to give our baby away. It was the only thing I could do. It was the last time I asked Tania for help. She arranged a place for me to stay in Pine Needle. She has a cousin there, Sarah, who's a nurse who helped me get some odd jobs and find an adoption agency. They found a couple right away. When the baby was born with Down Syndrome, I was in shock. The adoptive parents were in shock. They freaked out. I'd never had the amnio the doctor had wanted me to have after a sonogram showed a possible heart issue. All the other tests were perfect, and I was in my early twenties, I figured…but it turns out, age doesn't matter."

"How? Why?"

She shrugged. "I don't know of any DS in my family. The doctor told me that it could have been just a clash that happened when the egg and sperm got together." Her face clouded, she murmured, "A clash that made a mistake."

"Mistake." The word felt foul on my tongue.

"But she's not a mistake. Not to me. Not to Gail and Steve. Fuck the world that says she is. They told me to have the amnio to be prepared. Prepared for what? The worst? I should get rid of her because she'd be a burden? Because she's wouldn't be acceptable in normal society? Am I acceptable? Are you?"

"No," I breathed.

Lenore's eyes filled with water. "She just has an extra chromosome. Just one more."

Like I had one less finger on each hand.

She took in a breath of air. "But that couple didn't want her anymore. It got ugly, and I panicked. I thought that's it, everything's over, what was I going to do? I was so scared for the baby. How was I going to protect her now? But I'd come this far, I couldn't give up.

"Sarah knew this older couple in Pine Needle who'd never been able to have kids. They'd been through lots of miscarriages, lots of expensive fertility treatments they just couldn't afford. They also couldn't afford that disappointment anymore, and they'd given up. She asked them, and they said yes right away. They were thrilled."

"Gail and Steve."

"Yes, Gail and Steve." Her tone was flat. "I had two days alone with my baby. Two days in that bright and noisy Neonatal Intensive Care Unit, her in my arms while I held her feeding tube because she couldn't feed otherwise. I sang to her. Rocked her. Told her about you and me, about my grandma. Those were the best days."

"Lenore—"

"She ended up staying in that NICU for three weeks until she could use her mouth to suck on a bottle. Lots of Early Intervention therapies were mapped out for her, she saw a variety of specialists for a variety of tests. I didn't have health insurance or money for any of that. I had breast milk, though. I pumped every day so she could eat, handed it over, and left the hospital without seeing her. Every day."

She wiped at her wet eyes. "She needed a stable home, a steady income, and some kind of impenetrable cloak to hide her existence from Med and whoever the hell else was on my ass and yours for whatever reason. Even Turo. I couldn't trust that he wouldn't show up one day asking for something else."

She drained the liquor from the glass. "They named her Zoë," she whispered. "It's a Greek word. It means—"

"Life." My heavy eyes slid to hers.

"Yes. Life." Our gazes held tight, the silence around us vibrating

485

with a thorny joy, a murky sorrow.

"I took off for LA to keep a solid distance between me and Zoë and you. A fresh start. Clean slate," she said. "I met Eric, and when he told me he was originally from Rapid City, it was a sign to me, a good sign that maybe I would one day see our daughter in some way. Once he and I got married, we ended up splitting our time between Rapid and LA. After the divorce all I wanted was the house in Rapid. Eric thought I was crazy. Give up everything we had going on in LA for South Dakota?"

"It was your chance to be near her." I took in a breath, braced to say her name, for my lips to form the sounds, now, now that I knew. "Near Zoë."

"Yes. After the divorce, I wanted to be here."

"Did you tell Eric about her?"

"No, never. Then when Beck decided he wanted to be in LA for high school, I moved to a smaller house in Meager, figuring, that was as close as I could get, and anyway, Meager was familiar to me after hearing so much about it from Tania. Just knowing Zoë was nearby was so good. Knowing she was thriving, safe, doing so well, being loved the way she should. That was good. That was enough."

"Enough? She's our daughter."

"I couldn't have kept her, Finger. I could barely support myself. Always looking over my shoulder as it was. You were in jail, and I didn't know for how long. We always said leave no clues behind. The one time I did, I almost paid for it in the worst way. Don't you see? Our baby was a clue, just like those photos I'd hung onto and Motor found. Holding onto those was a mistake. Huge mistake. What if I'd kept the baby and they'd found me and taken me back and left her alone? Or killed her? Or taken her too, and fuck knows how she would've ended up. It was a good, clean thing to do. Like cutting off contact with Tania. I had to do it."

Lenore took in a deep gulp of air, eyes blazing. "Zoë needed heart surgery her first month, and she got it with Steve and Gail. Yes, you and I had love, so much love, but we didn't have stability and consistency, and those were the two things she needed that we would never have to offer her. And with you in jail for years, when would we ever be together to try and give her what she needed?

"What I did have then was determination to do the best for her. That's what I used to fuel a solution, I focused on that and made the decisions I had to make." She clenched her jaw. "It hurt. It burned. It was the hardest thing I've ever had to do. Harder than anything Med ever did to me. Worse than being separated from you, worse than having to let you go." Her voice caught, her head swayed to the side. "I had to let you go after giving her away. I couldn't be with you and lie. So I did it and tried to make peace with myself." She scoffed. "At least, I tried."

My eyes jammed shut. She'd closed the door on us to open a new door for our baby, our helpless, innocent child.

"The only thing I was sorry for was you thinking I'd turned my back on you," she said, her voice hoarse. "When I was pregnant with Beck and I saw you at that concert, the hate in your eyes—"

"But you didn't stay with your husband."

"I tried to love him, but I didn't have it in me. I wasn't good at being his wife. Giving up Zoë and turning my back on you were too difficult to get over. And when Beck was born, everything came back up again. You and Zoë twisted in my mangled heart as Beck filled it up." She took in a deep breath. "I figured you must have moved on and had a wife and your own kids. So I tried to get on with life, focus on my work, my son.

"Beck was a gift. But it was hard. Zoë was growing up far away, and every time Beck hit a milestone, I'd ask myself, when did Zoë start walking? What was her first word? What did her voice sound like? What was her favorite food? Her favorite bedtime story? What colors did she look good in? What did her first drawings look like?"

My throat constricted. "She's my only child. I want to know her. I want—" My heart veered like an eighteen wheel truck packed with heavy freight, out of control on an icy highway with a cliff up ahead. I had a child out in the world. A child who would never know that I was her father. My flesh and blood. My family.

Lenore had raised me up and destroyed me all in one go. My hand crushed the pieces of my compass as my eyes went to her tattoos. Tattoos of compasses and dreams. She had tracked the three of us and inscribed us forever on her flesh. She'd taken my broken compass and transformed it into a living, breathing thing, keeping her focused through all these years of wandering and doubt, stumbling and striking out, of forging ahead.

My knees buckled. I wrapped my arms around Lenore's legs, burying my face in her middle, into the soft flesh of the belly that had carried our baby. Humility before an unspeakable sacrifice.

All my years of unsatisfied wants, my roars in the dark night, my acrid frustrations—all were hollow and dry and crumbling in my hands, falling away like dirt and ash before her unshakeable belief in doing right, her bravery in the face of such choices.

My eyes were hot, my face burning against the thin material of her blouse. I breathed in her perfume, but the sweet fragrance only drove home the bitterness of my regret. Shame filled my blood, swelling like a drug shot directly in my veins, doing its best to cripple me, knock me out. I crumpled her blouse in my fists, raising it, gripping her hips, suffocating myself in the warm scent of her skin, in her soft touch that glided over my forehead. A touch I didn't deserve, but a touch I desperately wanted, ached and hungered for.

"She's alive, Finger. Alive and happy. Let that be enough. Letting go of her gave her a really good life. A full, healthy, safe one. No fear, no running." She ran a hand over my head. "Letting go of Zoë mended the broken hearts of two good people. Our girl made Gail and Steve's dream come true."

A horrible noise rumbled in my chest, up my throat. "I can't." My voice broke. "I can't be grateful. I hate them right now. I hate you."

Her hands dug into my hair, tugging, smoothing. "When I moved to Meager, I took the chance and asked Gail and Steve if I could visit at their store like a regular customer. Not often, just once in a while. They said once a month would be fine, and I assured them I wouldn't ever tell her I was her mother. I didn't want to anyway. The last thing I wanted was to confuse or upset Zoë. And I sure didn't want anyone figuring out a connection between us. I just wanted to see her. Maybe talk to her.

"Our baby was a real person with likes and dislikes and wants and favorites and opinions. She was Zoë, Zoë Drake. She was ours, but not ours. Mine, but not mine. I could see her from a distance, wave and say hello, be pleasant, ask questions, share a joke, but that was all. And I took it," she breathed. There was fire in those words, in her sharp, jagged tone. A primal roar, a growl that made the hairs on my arms stand at attention.

"And that's what you've been doing?" I asked.

"Yes. Gail and Steve are down to earth, gracious, simple people. I had to prove that I wouldn't be a problem. It was difficult at first, like falling off a bike when you're trying to learn how to ride. In the beginning, I could barely speak to Zoë. But I did it. Once a month. And it's been worth it. I don't stay very long. I shop. I chat. I leave. It was good, still is. Still special. I'm the friendly lady with the pretty tattoos and colorful hair who likes to garden, who decorates her house with colorful tiles and pots and dishes and mugs made by a little girl with a crazy creative streak a mile wide who's not so little anymore."

"She has your eyes."

"She does."

"She's beautiful," I said.

"She is. I used to wonder what she'd be like without the Down's, but then I realized she wouldn't be Zoë." A small smile broke over her lips. "I feel like I offered a little bit of good to this world."

Lenore lived her sacrifice every damned day and found the positive in it. She was the strongest person I'd ever known. Did I have such faith? I let go of her and stood up, my head swimming.

She took my drink and had a swallow. "She met Beck once. That almost killed me. Like today, introducing the two of you was the most beautiful thing. The most beautiful, terrible thing."

"Does Beck know?"

"No."

A strangled howl escaped my chest. "I should have known. I should've known!" I pulled on my hair. "When I was stuck in that fucking jail, I needed to know you were okay, I needed to know."

"I'm sorry."

"I don't want your fucking sorry! I don't want it! I just want my fucking daughter. I want the life we could've had together. All of us together."

Lenore said nothing. She only stood, watching me, letting me go. Now I understood her kiss back in my office, gentle then passionate. She knew once she told me everything would change. That kiss was *yes, I want you, yes, I miss you, yes, I love you, I'm so sorry, I know you'll hate me and never forgive me, goodbye.*

She said, "The other night in my bed, you kissed me, touched me, and…oh, how you touched me. I knew I couldn't be with you the way that touch demanded and deserved without telling you the truth. We can't be together if it's not completely real, completely honest between us. We can't. I can't."

"I can't either."

Tears streamed down her face. "I know."

A thick, heavy plunger rammed down my throat, jamming muck in my every vein. Everything we'd ever wanted had actually come true, but we'd had to deny it, close the door on it. We couldn't have it. Just out of reach, just out of reach. Like always.

"There's nothing but sadness here," she'd told me the night before.

She was so fucking right.

My pulse blew, my lungs crushed together. I couldn't breathe. For the first time in my life, I didn't know what to do, how to handle any of this. This sorrow, this disappointment didn't fit into a saddlebag on my bike along with all the rest of the crap I'd crumpled up and stuffed in there from day one. This…this…

I slammed out of her house, and she didn't try to stop me, reason with me, chase me. I took off, and headed for Tania's. I silenced my bike in her driveway and by the time I got to the front door, Butler had swung it open, Tania behind him.

Butler charged at me. "I don't know what's going on here, but you can't just come over here any damn time you want. Tania's my old lady, and I live here now." He pushed at my chest. "Her mom's not feeling good and is sleeping inside. What the hell is your deal?"

Tania stepped to his side, her hand on Butler's back. "She finally told you."

"Who told him what?" Butler snapped.

490

"That I have a daughter out there, practically next door," I said.

Butler's hand fell away from me. "You what?"

"She told you," Tania said.

"I forced her hand. Only after I did a little digging myself," I said.

"I'm glad."

"Are you?"

"Watch it," Butler's tone was sharp.

"I wanted her to tell you from the very beginning, but she refused. She said it was the only way to be sure everyone would be safe," said Tania.

"You helped her," I said.

"She was in shock with you in jail and her not being able to see you or talk to you," Tania said. "I knew it had to be more than a sad, lonely heart, but she wouldn't tell me. So, yes, I helped her. I got her a room at my great grandmother's house in Pine Needle which my mother had turned into a boarding house back then. She wouldn't let me visit, not once. She didn't want there to be any connection between us the moment she'd left Chicago.

"I did what I could for her, my cousin too, but she was on her own. And then she disappeared from Pine Needle, and I didn't hear from her again. But that was okay with me, because I knew that was what she needed to do. I respected her wishes and I supported her decision and kept her secret. I gave her that peace of mind, because that's what true friends do."

"Tania—"

Her huge black eyes flashed at me. "We protected that child's life. That's what all this was about, Finger. Not her, not you, not me. You once asked me to take care of your Serena, and I did. I did that. This was about protecting that child above all else and at any cost."

Something inside me cracked, the fissure spreading fast, cold shivers racing over my skin. A wave of emotion jolted through me, and my hands shook. Nausea surged up my throat and I choked it back down, but the acid boiled at my lips.

Tania touched my arm, and I recoiled. She said, "You were at the heart of every decision she made, every thought, every tear. There were so many tears, and you were in every single one."

I heaved for air, the sun had fallen and the sudden frigid air of the early night sliced through my insides.

"Man, come inside." Butler's voice floated over me. "Take a breath. A cup of coffee. Don't ride like this."

I slapped his words away, his outstretched hands, his invitation to Betty Crocker comforts. I staggered off, to where I didn't know. Away. Away from them, from all of it.

Tangled. I was tangled in a thick rope, clawing at it, no out, no escape. It only tightened and tightened around me. A savage snarl vaulted from my chest. I fell to the curb, my head in my hands.

"Baby, go inside," Butler said to Tania.

"But—"

"Go."

Footsteps behind me, a door closing in the distance.

"I had no idea," Butler said. "That's how loyal Tania is to you, to both of you. How faithful. You're real important to her, and you know it. I know it."

I knew that, and I didn't resent Tania. I didn't. I was glad Lenore had her to lean on in those terrible days. But nothing fit, nothing made sense, nothing. No words could help me, none came. The broken asphalt teetered between my legs through the blur as I struggled to catch my breath.

Butler propped himself on the curb alongside me. He leaned back on his hands, legs stretched out. The road lamp's buzzy hum a few yards away from us seemed loud. Tree branches shuffled in the cold breeze. A car stopped at the stop sign down the street and made a right, its red taillights disappearing. The world kept turning, the world was unaffected and didn't give a shit. Why should it?

Butler crossed his legs at his ankles. "Me and my first wife, we tried to have a kid, but it never happened, then she died. It's too late for me and Tania now, and I got to say, a part of me is disappointed. And yeah, it sucks that you didn't know you had a kid."

I grit my teeth at the stab of that uninspired, lifeless nickname of my childhood being used for my daughter.

"It sucks that you didn't get to raise her," Butler continued. "Or be a part of her life, that she doesn't know you're her dad. But bro, she exists. She's out there. You could get to know her, right? Maybe she can't ever know you're her real father, but you can still have her in your life in some way, a way that you'd both cherish. Me and Tania don't get to have that. You and Lenore do. And at the end of the day, that's a damn good place to be."

A place to be.

That's why Lenore had nestled herself here in the Black Hills, to be close to our daughter. To have a place. That's why Grace and Tania had come back home. Even Butler. To have a place.

I had the wind, the road, my bikes, my fortress, my little empire. But did I have such a place? A place in someone's life? In their heart? Where everything made sense, where you fit.

Next to me, Butler heaved a loud sigh. "Shit, I could really use a cigarette right now. Quitting sucks big time." He recrossed his legs, glancing at me. "I'm gonna shut up now. But I'm staying right here."

TWENTY MINUTES LATER, I TORE out of Meager, out of South Dakota. I rode hard.

Tania's words from months ago drilled in my brain as the wind pounded me. *You had it all, and you both let it go.*

I'd let it go. Me. All these years I'd thought Lenore had gotten irritated with the difficulty of being together, hadn't been able to cope in the long term, had let her fear ride her, and ultimately took the easy way out. My scorn at her wanting something normal had burned bright. Yet all this time, she'd remained true. She'd taken our broken compass and given it a new life on her body, stamping herself with the story of us, keeping us close to her always. A fairytale of dark and light. Evil and good. Ink woven memories, ink tears splattered on flesh. Her tears, blue green tears dripping down over us.

Love. All for love.

Had her love been stronger, truer than mine?

Mine was dark and mean and cruel. Bitterness had scorched my love, fueling me like a blowtorch that incinerated everything it touched.

Lenore had stayed the course of her True North. For a place. All for love, and the fruit that it had born.

My Harley plowed through the black night, the engine shuddering through me.

"Nebraska...the Good Life"

Why, why, why did we have to sacrifice love for love?

64
FINGER

I WAS HIGH ON RAGE.

Rage had never let me down. Rage always pointed me in the right direction, and this was the direction I'd been wanting to set my dogs free in for decades. Since the beginning of time.

Fuck treaties, fuck peace. Fuck all of it.

I contacted Mishap and gave him a new assignment. My plan was met with his usual silence. He calculated. I waited.

"You sure?" he finally said.

"You've never asked me that before. Not once."

"I know."

"I'm very sure."

"Good."

Within two weeks, Mishap brought me Scrib. We secured him in our specially-made soundproof barn, and I contacted Butler who was now Vice-President of the One-Eyed Jacks. I wanted total commitment up front or I'd crush the Jacks myself.

We met at that abandoned gas station again.

"We're with you on this," he said. "There's one thing, though."

"What's that?"

"There's a Blade I can vouch for."

"The one who saved your ass?"

Butler and Jump's teenage son, Wes, had been ambushed weeks ago on a stretch of road leading out of Deadwood, South Dakota. Led, Reich's right hand man, had wanted revenge on Butler for double crossing Reich. Luckily, Butler and Wes survived with the help of a Broken Blade who'd happened to be there.

"Yeah, him," he said. "His name is Pick."

"I'll keep an eye out."

Butler eyed me, chewing hard on his gum. "You okay? You seem on edge."

I scowled at him.

"You don't usually seem on edge, that's all," he said.

"This edge is a very special, once in a lifetime kind of edge. Trust me, I'm liking the view from up here."

He laughed, his face turning away.

"What's so fucking funny?"

"Nothing, man."

"Tell me."

He shook his blond hair from his face. "I just got this image in my head. You on that special edge up above, hands raised, parting the raging sea down below. Claiming what's yours. Tearing asunder all that deserve to be so torn."

He was not wrong.

Butler straightened, his arms folding across his chest. "This guy Pick could prove useful to you. He can see the forest for the trees, unlike Notch. I figure if he's shown some respect, he'll show it back."

I mounted my bike. "What are you telling me, Butler?"

He adjusted his fancy sunglasses, his lips turning up. "Maybe you don't have to massacre all of them."

"First I want to see how they deal with my shock and awe. That's always telling. That'll tell me who to massacre."

Butler gnawed on his growing smile.

I slanted my head at him. "Now what?"

His wide grin lit up his face. "I like that about you, you know. Every decision is precise and carefully calculated, every move has a purpose."

I hit my kickstand. "I know you like that."

"THIS IS HOW IT'S GOING to go down."

Notch, the Broken Blades president, struggled against his handcuffs, the thick metal chains strapped around his body. No use. He knew it too, but was giving us a good show of resistance. He had to. His men were looking on, their faces rippling with anxiety.

"You've pissed me off one too many times, Notch. You're unpredictable. Which keeps things interesting, but I've had to put up with your shit for a very, very long fucking time. You never listened to any suggestions I made over the years to be more—let's say, neighborly. You've got a mighty thick stick up your ass, and you didn't ever want to compromise, not one fucking bit."

"And you kept chipping away at us, bit by bit," Notch shot back on a sneer.

"I enjoyed that. Like I enjoyed destroying your little bonding session with the Calderas Group. Thought you were going to raise yourselves up from your little patch of mud that way? Make up for your numbers, your lack of funds?"

"Times are tough, amigo. I was watching out for my club. Gotta do what you gotta do."

"And I did what I had to do. But now you've been shaking hands with the Smoking Guns instead of dealing with me when I offered you the chance."

He chuckled, a stream of throaty laughter that dissolved into coughing. "I didn't think you'd like that."

"Oh, I like being dared, being provoked. Brings out the best in me."

His thin, drawn face creased like rumpled paper, his lips curling.

I scanned the faces of the Broken Blades on their knees in the room. "The rest of you get to choose. You'll be Flames or go down as Blades. Either way, your shit's over."

I caught Drac's gaze, and he motioned behind him. Catch and another bro brought in Scrib, tying him to a table next to Notch.

Notch's eyes bulged, his face shining with sweat. He writhed in his seat like someone had just planted itching powder in his ass. "What the fuck is this? What the hell are you doing?"

"Exactly what I want," I replied.

I took out my knife and ripped open Scrib's shirt, pierced his skin, slashing down his chest, his fat stomach. Scrib yelled and shuddered, his eyes following the movement of my blade. The blood slid forth. An "F." Huge. Glorious.

"You like my scribbles, huh? Fuck I'm having fun," I said. "Why aren't you laughing now? Come on, laugh!"

Scrib only shuddered. Notch was suddenly quiet and still, riveted on my knife.

I slashed at Scrib, cutting deep, my pulse beating a hammering rhythm in my head. "That looks good."

"Fucking beautiful is what that is," said Drac.

"Tattoos in the raw or some shit," said Catch. "Just like what he did to my sister."

Yes, what Scrib had done to Tania. What he'd done to me and Serena.

Blood and saliva dripped from Scrib's mouth. His dazed eyeballs hung on mine.

Massacre, Butler had said. Yes, I wanted to massacre them all, strike hot and blind and rid myself of them. I'd felt a sense of failure as a man and as a Flame when I'd listened to Lenore confess her truth. I had to make the world safer for my woman and my daughter. Even if they would never know it.

I held my blood smattered knife up high so Scrib could see it. "What's wrong is, I can't leave my signature behind, now can I, Scrib? If I do, your club will know it was me. But it wasn't me."

"Stop, you fucker!" Scrib wailed. "God, stop!"

I cut into his skin again drawing a deep line down his belly to his raping dick. He yowled and bawled through the pain.

"Fuck me," muttered Catch. "You're an artist is what you are."

"I owe that to Scrib." I cut him again and he yelped, his body twitching, his head hanging.

"What the hell you doing to him?" shouted Notch.

"I'm making all these F's into B's. Double B's for Broken Blades. So when they find his rotten corpse, they'll know it was you who double crossed a Smoking Gun. 'Cause you got balls, Notch, am I right?"

"Hey, that's a B word too, huh?" said Drac. "Balls."

"It sure is," I sliced at Scrib's dick, and his body writhed and shook on the table. "You remember raping Rena, don't you? You remember that? Open those eyes and look at me, motherfucker!"

Drac pulled on Scrib's head and Scrib's shocked, disturbed eyes sprang open, snagging on mine.

"Have you enjoyed having all your fingers all these years, Scrib? Did you appreciate them? Did you ever once think of mine all this time?" Scrib's arms and legs trembled, his eyes blinking open and closed. "But you know, it was your laugh that stayed with me all these years."

I turned to the Blades and my men in the room. "Any of you all noticed Scrib's really loud, snorting laugh, because it's fucking grating, especially when you're bleeding out, tied down, helpless like a fucking hog being chopped at." I turned back to my bleeding prisoner. "I remember everything about that day, Scrib. I remember your eyes burning as you cut me. I remember you practically coming as your Prez cut off my two fingers with those nippers."

"Oh man, oh man, come on now..." Notch twisted his head away, his fingers flexing, hands straining under his bindings.

"I don't feel like working hard for it today, though. I prefer convenience when appropriate." I glanced up at Drac, wiping at my face. He handed me the small axe.

"Holy fuck, holy mother of fuck!" Notch's voice was throttled by panic.

Scrib shuddered on the table, there were no moans and groans. Only a pathetic keening rising from his chest like helium escaping a balloon.

"This axe is sharp, so it'll be quicker, less painful. Lucky for you. But to make things fair—'cause I'm all about the justice of the thing, the balance—since you all only cut off two of my fingers, I'm going to have to take all your fingers with this axe. I'll leave the thumbs, though. Thumbs are useful. I've really appreciated mine. You'll see."

"No!" howled Notch. Grunts and shuffling rose up behind me.

I hacked at Scrib's hand, and his blood splattered on my colors, my face. I hacked. And hacked. The sweep of my axe, the slicing cleanly through flesh and hitting bone, the dig of the thick sharp blade in the table, my jerking it back—all of it a roar of victory screaming through me.

I'd never tasted champagne before, never celebrated anything with a drink of that pricey golden froth. But now, a cool, searing energy fizzed inside me. My mind raced on a sugar high, a crispness lashed over my tongue, sweet warmth flooding through me.

Yeah, champagne had to be like this.

"Bring me Pick."

"Cuffed or free bird?" asked Drac.

"No cuffs."

Drac returned with a tall bearded man about my age. He planted his booted feet firmly in the ground in front of me. His name was clearly patched on his colors and the letters for his club tattooed on each of his fingers.

"I hear you have a brain. And a heart."

His face stony, Pick didn't say a word.

"Butler, the VP of the One-Eyed Jacks, told me to keep an eye out for you."

He raised his shoulders, his head tilting at me.

"You want to prove to me why I should?" I asked him.

"You just came in and lay waste to my club. Correct me if I'm wrong?" he said, his voice deep and rumbly.

I took a step towards him, leaning in close. "I respect your loyalty to your club, I wouldn't be talking to you if you weren't that loyal brother. You have an opportunity here to not only stay alive, but build something new for your remaining men. I'm offering you membership to the Flames of Hell with all the resources and honor that signifies.

"I'm not interested in keeping slaves, Pick. I'm interested in leadership, responsible leadership. You know the lay of the land here. You have the trust of your brothers. This is an opportunity for you to create something new, something better."

Pick only eyed me, his thick arms taut at his sides, big hands curled into tight fists.

"Your national doesn't exist anymore, Pick. You have two other charters flailing on their own in two separate states. You got a kid and an ex-wife to support and a handful of men who look up to you." I rolled the bloody axe in my hand. "What's it going to be?"

WE GOT WORD TO THE Smoking Guns that their bro Scrib was being held by the Broken Blades. A crew of them arrived guns blazing to find Scrib dead on the table and an untied Notch with an axe in the Blades meeting room. Catch and Drac had overseen having the remaining Blades tied up and down on their knees in a row in the yard. Their bikes were splayed on the ground like fallen toy soldiers.

Dog surveyed the detritus. "Holy fuck, what the hell happened?"

"Notch happened. And I got here first and cleaned this shit up. Thought you'd want to claim your bro."

Dog glared at me.

"Notch hasn't been himself for a long while," said Pick, arms crossed, his face a mask.

Dog's eyes darted to Pick and back to Scrib and Notch's bloodied bodies.

"Look what he did to your bro." I gestured with my chin to Scrib's mutilated body.

"Holy fuck," Dog muttered.

"Scrib came to finalize shit between our clubs, but Notch wasn't too pleased by the money Scrib offered," Pick said. "He's been changing his mind a lot, was jittery with Reich out of the picture. Been mixing meds lately too. They argued. There was a lot of yelling and carrying on. The door was locked. I broke it down and found Scrib already dead. Notch was carving him up, laughing."

"You expect me to believe this?" Dog muttered, his brow a firm ridge, his small eyes piercing mine.

"I only expect you to take your corpse and get the fuck out," I said.

Dog wiped a hand across his mouth. "I wasn't around then, Finger, when Scrib done what he did to you. Those were bad times, that was another—"

"Yeah, it was another life, Dog. And we don't need to go there ever again."

Dog's shoulders shifted slowly, straining under a heavy, invisible weight.

"Now you need to get your garbage off my property and never come back," I said.

"Your property?" Dog's gaze went from me to Pick and back again.

"This chapter of the Blades is now Flames of Hell," Pick said.

Dog's eyes widened. "What?"

"I came in. I cleaned up," I said, my voice firm. Dog turned away from me, his jaw tight.

"This shit had to end. Couldn't go on much longer," said Pick. "Notch was playing games with Scrib, with Finger, the Jacks, with everybody. Only destroyed his own club in the end."

"Clear Scrib out and we're done here," I said.

Dog let out a breath, scrubbing a hand across his grizzly face. He knew what I meant. He needed to retreat and stay away. We were done, and we could all go back to abiding that treaty.

Dog muttered a directive at his men, and they removed Scrib's body from the room. Pick remained, standing over Notch's corpse.

"You get me the other Blade chapters on board," I told him.

"You'll have 'em." He grabbed hold of Notch's thin legs and dragged the body down the hall.

I stayed and took in the fading odor of blood and battle, soaked in the sting and echo of mayhem that lingered.

But another raging fire before me still blazed.

Still beckoned.

65
FINGER

I STOOD IN THE AISLE WITH the seed packets. Chives, onions, eggplants, bell peppers, tomatoes, parsley, dill.

The girl, the young woman who was my biological daughter, arranged red glazed dishes on a shelf next to mugs. The top half of her dark hair was pulled up in a small ponytail. She wore her earbuds, listening to music as she worked, picking up small dishes from a crate at her side. She sang to herself, her thoughts coming to life on her face.

I could've stood here for hours studying her. She was real, visible, tangible, but we were separated from her. A Christmas fantasy display in a department store window. We'd be glued to that pane of glass forever, our eyes and senses swallowing every detail with wonder, but unable to touch it, live it.

I moved toward her, not knowing what I'd say or do. Only that I had to do something. My hands were suddenly sweaty, my mouth dry. I was Frankenstein's monster, lumbering, awkward, intrigued. She was the innocent young girl picking flowers at the side of the lake.

"Oh, hello." Zoë's smile lit up her face.

"Hey. Zoë, right?"

Her lips twisted, her gaze darting away and back again. She was clearly pleased, and a bit flustered. "Mr. F-Finger, right?"

My breath tightened in my chest. "That's right."

She was the most beautiful flower, but I knew better than to throw her in the lake. I'd raise her above the world if I could.

I shifted my weight, my back stiff. "Those are real nice dishes.

503

Did you make those?"

"Yep. I love red. I made only red dishes yesterday. Everyone should have a red dessert plate. It would make dessert so much more fun."

I ground my heels in the floor, bracing myself under the spray of her diamond sparkles, the sheen of her fairy dust.

"Do you make cereal bowls?" I asked her.

"Sometimes."

"Could you make me two in that red?"

She giggled. "Sure! Hey, did you and Lenore put in the tiles?"

"Uhh. No. Not yet."

She scrunched her nose and pushed her glasses up. "Oh."

The bandana laying around my throat was a dead weight around my neck, and I tugged on it. "I want to help her with the tiles, but we forgot to buy glue for them, and I'm not sure what to get. Could you help me?"

"Not glue, silly." She let out a hearty laugh. "G-grout. Like cement. It's called grout."

"Oh, I didn't know. Could you show me which one I should buy for her?"

"Sure. This way."

I followed her over two aisles. A slight imbalance in the way she carried her weight gave her a shuffling step to her walk. She pointed to a bag. "This one. That's what I use." She picked up a small sack and handed it to me.

The sack thudded against my chest, and as I grabbed at it, our hands brushed. "Thanks, Zoë. I appreciate it."

"You're welcome. You must like her a lot, right? She's a very nice lady. She's been shopping with us for a long, long time."

My mouth dried. "I've known her for a long time too."

"You like her?"

"Yes."

"I mean, you like, like her, right?"

"How did you guess that?"

"I could tell. She was different around you. You both look nice together, especially with all the tattoos you both have. I want her to have a boyfriend."

"You want Lenore to be happy. Like you are with Mark?"

Her cheeks turned pink, and she let out a belly laugh, her blue green eyes darting around in a circle. "Yes!"

Something jolted through my chest. Dazzling.

"I want her to be happy, too," I said, clearing my throat. "Just like that. Like you and Mark."

"Yay. If you treat her right, she'll like you back."

"You're a smart girl, you know that?"

"You have that zingy thing."

"Zingy thing?"

"You know, that feeling between a boy and a girl. I could tell right away with you and Lenore. Mommy and Daddy have it too." She laughed, twisting her mouth again.

"Can I help you?" a young guy in his late teens came up behind Zoë. He wore a name tag—Tim—on his Pine Needle Garden Center Family Owned since 1936 T-shirt.

"I'm taking this." I handed Tim the sack of powder.

Tim blinked at my scarred hands. "Anything else you need today, sir?"

"That's it. For now."

"I'll ring it up for you at the front." Tim trudged up the aisle.

"Well." I shifted my weight. "Bye, Zoë. Thanks."

"Bye-bye. Say hi to Lenore for me."

"I will."

I paid Tim for the grout and left the nursery, holding the sack under my arm tightly. I clutched it like a football, and I was crossing the goal line with one second left on the clock. I closed my eyes, and burned her smiling blue green eyes into my heart. The soft giggly chirp of her voice. A spirit full of innocent positivity.

She had never known rejection, or life and death fear, or hunger, never been touched by anything sordid or miserable or degrading. There was only radiant sun and brilliant rainbows in that girl.

"Protecting that child. At any cost," Tania had said.

My and Serena's flesh and blood walked the earth and dreamed and danced and sang and laughed, setting the sky on fire.

Sunshine, our daughter is so beautiful.

A wave of light-headedness passed through me, and I gulped in air. Unbuckling a saddlebag, I shoved the small grout bag inside.

Then I tucked my experience of my daughter deep in my quaking soul.

66
LENORE

"Why didn't you come to the party?" Tricky strode through my front door, his glazed eyes ricocheting around the dark entryway, shoulders tense.

I stood stock still. "I didn't say I was coming to the party."

"Uh, yeah you did."

"No, I didn't. I rarely go to club parties, you know that. I said I might come."

"Oh, might. Right. She might come. She might like me today. She might spend the night tonight. She might go down on me tonight—"

"Get out of my house."

His eyes blazed, his stiff jaw jutted out. "So who is it? There's gotta be somebody else. Who is it?"

"Jesus. I'm busy working. Tania and Butler are getting married next week in California, and I'm making her a wedding dress as a surprise. You know this. I've been up late every night this week to finish it. Going to some club party is not high on my list of priorities."

"I know I'm definitely not one of your priorities. You wouldn't have just stopped us out of the blue, for no reason. I mean, shit, we're good together. That's a fact."

"Tricky, I told you from the beginning that this was a loose thing for me. You agreed. You said you felt the same way. Then you started getting mad at me and suddenly had all these expectations that weren't there before."

"None of this makes sense, Lenore! You been lying to me? You been sleeping with other guys all along, because for a while now, there's only been you for me. So, I want to know. I want to know who the fuck it is you're sleeping with now."

"Calm down, Tricky."

"Answer the question."

"We had fun. That's what this was. Fun."

"Was, was, was, huh?"

"That's right. The past."

"Well, now I want a real thing with you, not just fun," he said.

"I didn't know that. But I don't want anything else."

"Seriously?" his tone was snide.

"Tricky, you should leave. It's late."

He blinked, his head jerking back. "What the fuck—you're dismissing me like I'm the misbehaving boy and you're the teacher?"

"Tricky."

"You done with me now?"

"That's a shock to you?"

"Whoa." His hands flew in the air and he let out a tight laugh, the whites of his eyes flashing.

My stomach hardened at the sight, my muscles tensed.

"It is a shock, yeah." He moved toward me. "One day everything's good, the next, you're saying no more. You can't do this. You can't." He launched at me, taking me in his arms, squeezing me.

"Tricky, stop. Let me go!" My hands were stuck against his chest, and I pushed at him hard. "We'll talk tomorrow. You're drunk."

He buried his face in my hair. "Let me fuck you one more time. Let me show you how much you mean to me, baby, come on." His lips latched onto my neck and he sucked the skin there, a hand gripping my ass.

I squirmed against his hold, and his sucking turned into biting. "Stop it!" Adrenaline pumped through me.

"You love it when I do this shit. Just let me—"

Something reflected in the darkness, and I knew. I relaxed in Tricky's hold.

"Don't even breathe," came a harsh, low voice. A gloved hand went to the side of Tricky's neck and pressed deep. Tricky's eyes bulged, he gasped.

"Let her go or it gets worse."

Tricky's grip released me, and I quickly stepped away from him. A scuffle, thudding to the floor. I darted to the light switch, hitting it. Finger held a massive stainless steel gun to Tricky's head, his free hand pinning back his arms.

"You don't fucking breathe her way ever again, you hear me? Not one fucking breath," ordered Finger on a hiss.

Tricky buckled to the floor, his forehead planting onto the wood.

A heavy knock banged at the door, and my heart pounded up my throat.

"Open it," Finger said.

I opened the door and Butler stood there, my front porch light casting its yellow glow over him. "Hey, Lenore."

"Pick up your bro," said Finger, tucking his gun away.

"Finger called me when he saw Tricky's bike out front," Butler said to me as he helped his friend to his feet. "Let's go, Trick. You're done here."

Tricky glanced at me, but I offered no goodbye, no explanation. There was none to give.

"I'm sorry," he mouthed.

"Me too," I said as he brushed past me.

The door closed behind Butler and Tricky. Finger and I stared at each other in silence until a vehicle outside rumbled down the street and faded.

"You okay? He hurt you?" he asked.

"I'm fine." I turned off the foyer light and wrapped my arms around myself.

He went into my living room and eased back on my sofa as if he did it every night, his shoulders relaxed as he spread his one arm around the back of the couch. His dark eyes glimmered at me in the faint light. I held my breath at the sight of him relaxed, emitting pheromones of beast-like satisfaction, gratification.

His lips twitched, he was grinning. "I'd like a drink. Please."

"Would you?"

"I would. That Jameson would be perfect."

He'd inspected my house.

I raised an eyebrow. "The Gold Reserve or the—"

"The Gold." That grin got wider. Slightly sardonic, slightly devious, teasing.

A tickle rose in my throat, and I swallowed it back down. "Gold, it is. Straight?"

"Straight."

I poured the Irish whiskey for him into a crystal tumbler and one for me. I gave him his drink and sat down next to him, sipping mine. The kick of the liquor's sweet heat filled my mouth and subsided, soft vanilla blooming in its place.

He licked his bottom lip. "That is so good."

"It is."

He took my hand in his, warm and firm. His eyes remained on our hands which he'd brought to rest on his thigh. "I want to sit here with you if that's all right. Share the quiet in here. The colors. That sage candle burning. You." He raised his glass up, swirling the pale gold whiskey. "This beautiful delicate crystal glass with very fine whiskey that you poured for me. I want to sit here with you, like this, and drink it all in. That's what I want to do."

"Okay."

"Okay."

Had something else happened today? Probably. And all he needed right now was to sit with me and be close?

I wanted that too.

We sat without speaking for a long time. I couldn't say if it was minutes or moments or hours. A meditation filled with the sounds of quick breaths, tentative touches, whiskey wet lips, and warm hands lingering.

"I brought you something." He went to the front door, opening it, reaching down, then closing it. He propped a small paper sack on the floor.

"What's that?"

"Grout for those tiles you got the other day."

"You went to Steve and Gail's?"

"Yep. I realized you didn't get any grout when you bought the tiles, and I went and picked some up."

"I didn't buy any because I already have some."

"I didn't know that."

"You haven't been in my garage yet?"

"Not yet."

I finished my drink. "I have soil and mulch in there and some old pots and rakes and a shovel."

"You really like to garden, huh?"

"I like my surroundings to be inspiring and colorful, and if you put the time and effort into a garden, the results are pretty damned fantastic. Gail taught me that." I held up the bottle of whiskey. "More?"

"Please."

I filled his glass again. "Did you see Zoë?"

"I did. And she was real excited that I was going to help you tile up."

"She wants me to have a boyfriend."

"She told me. She couldn't stop giggling when she saw me. Said we were perfect for each other with all the tattoos we both got."

I let out a laugh. "Zoë doesn't have a filter."

"I realized. I like it."

I settled back onto the sofa, curling my legs under me. "Me too."

"She'd brought out some new mugs, red ones, and she told me how much she loved red."

"It was yellow last month. She made a whole line of dessert plates and ashtrays in every tone of yellow."

"Well, now it's the red. I asked her to make me two red bowls and I'd come back for them next time. Bowls for your cereal."

I let out a laugh, taking his hand in mine. "I like that there's a next time."

"I'll bet your whole life has been built on next times with her," he murmured.

I pressed my lips together, stifling the small moan that brewed there.

"Like me with you," he said, his voice low. "I always counted on there being a next time."

I put my glass down and straddled his lap, facing him. "Those nights we spent together, being with you like this. I like it. It makes me smile inside. Makes me feel lighter, positive in a deeper way than I've ever allowed myself for a long time. It makes me feel that there's good ahead, not just good enough."

His one hand rose up my back. "Good enough ain't enough anymore."

"There's hope for us? We're not only the rubble of what our explosions left behind?"

He rubbed my shoulder. "Ah baby, a little grout and elbow grease, and we can build us back up. As long as you don't mind it being a little crooked here and there, maybe chipped in places."

"No, I don't mind." I traced a line over his facial scars. "We could paint it red, paint it yellow."

"Blue green, too," his deep, scratchy voice caught as his hands moved up my middle, over my breasts to my neck, stroking me there. His index finger touched the tattoo of Zoë's compass on my chest. "Tell me why this N is different from the others, why it's on fire. A blue fire."

"It's not an N. It's a Z on its side, it just looks like a fat N. It's my secret little way to have Zoë's name on me."

"I don't get it."

"I didn't feel worthy of having her name or even her initial tatted on me. The Z on its side reminds me that I gave up having a place in her life, that I'm on the outside. I can't claim that Z."

"No, baby, no." He touched his lips to mine.

"Her letter is in a blue fire," I whispered. "A blue flame burns hotter than a red one, you know."

"I know." He kissed me slowly, the caramel flavor of the whiskey melding with the flavor of him across my tongue.

"Do you forgive me?" I whispered. "I need to know."

"You kept her safe." His thumb brushed at the side of my face. "Yeah, it's hard when it hits me, not going to lie. And it keeps hitting me, but those hits are not so rough and turning into positives, one at a time."

My fingers stroked the side of his face, his scars, his beard.

He pulled me in closer against him. "Baby, I don't hate you. I want to love you more, better than before. Those feelings didn't go away. Been burning deep. I stifled them, wrestled them down, chained them up, but I don't want to anymore. I can't. I just can't. There's no reason to."

His eyes studied me. Those harsh eyes that had once impressed me with their steadfastness in all the screaming insanity that had cavorted around us now gleamed at me. Expectant. Warm shimmers of light, gentle rays of possibility.

He slowly tasted my lips, his tongue nudging my mouth open to receive its blessings.

I opened, I received, I gave.

He cradled my face in his hands. "We got a clean slate now, baby. We can have that life we always wanted together with nothing and no one hanging over us. We can do this."

My fingertips dug into the back of his neck. "It's been such a long time."

"That doesn't matter. It doesn't," he whispered against my lips. "You and me matter. Us together. If you still want it."

"I still want it." The breath squeezed from my chest, and I kissed him.

His hips rose against mine, offering more friction. "I'm cutting it loose now, baby. Tell me that's a good thing. Tell me that's what you want. Tell me, I need to hear you say it."

"Cut it loose," I breathed, meeting his body, squeezing my thighs around him. "Cut it loose."

I kissed him. A hungry kiss, a kiss that discovered and demanded, invited and provoked, that insisted on healing. I soared in his taste, a taste that brought me back to the heady, lust-filled thrill of our first love and all its thousand, gentle and hard, intimacies. The clarity of believing, the spice of danger, the slices of risk. I reveled in the odd hum that rose in the back of his throat, the firm hand that held my head close to his own. My heart pounded out a strong, steady beat.

"I want you. I want you inside me," I murmured. I lifted and helped him pull down his zipper and tug down his pants until his erection was free.

"Oh shit," fell from my mouth at the sight of his hard length. That was mine. All fucking mine.

He tugged at my tunic dress, clawed at my panties. "I'm ripping."

"You're asking?"

"I figure your panties are pricey, one of a kind—"

"Rip it!"

He did, and a wild expression flared across his features at the sound, at the graze of his fingers against my wet slit. I took his cock in my hand and rubbed myself over it, getting it slick. His jaw tightened, his hands sliding over my ass, finding me. I let out a cry.

"There she is." His eyes were fierce. "I'm clean. Haven't gone bare in—"

"Me either."

"Do we need to—"

"Shh." My hips dipped against him, and I slid his cock inside me.

My heart stopped, my breath jammed in my chest at his groan, at him tight inside me once again, at the thick fullness of us. The world swung in another direction, and we clung to each other through the burning curve. For one delicious heavy moment, wishes and dreams collided with sorrow, ensnaring it, silencing its wail.

His forehead met mine. "Serena." He pulled apart the buttons on the top of my dress.

Ting, ting, ting.

I shivered as his lips landed on my chest. He filled his hands with my breasts, kissing them, his tongue flicking over my piercings as I moved over him, taking him in, taking him in deeper, mining that sweet, rich glory that lay buried between us.

His hands went to my ass, his hips meeting mine, urging me to move faster, driving inside me.

Taking my lower lip between his teeth, he whispered hoarsely, "Cut it loose, baby. Cut it loose."

67
FINGER

"You're sure about the border?"

"I'm sure about the border." Her voice had a snap to it.

"Easy, baby."

Lenore stayed focused on wiping down the blue tiles against the inner wall of her porch. "You asked me three times already."

"Just want to be sure."

"I'm sure." She bent closer to the line of tiles I'd help her set up and cement along the porch. Yeah, she was sure about a lot of things. She had an instinct about color and line, about the arc of a thing, the feeling of it, its sound. Her way of thinking must be like music. Mine was more numbers and graphs. I wasn't sure if it was a man/woman thing, or just a difference between me and Lenore. But it was a difference, and I liked it. I had to take my time with it.

Her cell phone came to life with a clip of a song with a driving guitar riff. She glanced at it and brought it to her ear.

"Hey, Mimi."

Her store.

"No, no, you let her decide herself. I know the coral isn't her best color, but that's what she wants. If you push too hard, she's going to have a spaz and cancel the order. She'll come around, she always does. Okay. Thanks for checking with me. I'll call you later." She put the phone back at her side.

I was surrounded by the Empire of Lenore, the many kingdoms. My girl had blossomed into a fine woman of distinct tastes and choice. All these years she hadn't hidden in the back seat. She'd gotten behind the wheel of her own car and steered through the dark, the fog, over broken bridges, steep climbs, twisty turns. And I was proud of her.

She sat back on her haunches, dropping the small microfiber cloth in her hand. "That looks good."

I slid back on her porch bench and took a final swallow of my iced coffee. "It does. You're right. Once we finish it up that strip of blue will liven up this view."

"It's soothing and stimulating all at once." She was pleased.

I let out a laugh.

She turned, her ponytail flicking over her shoulder. "What?"

"I could think of things to do that are way more soothing and stimulating than looking at tile."

She twisted her lips and joined me on the bench. "Head always in the gutter?"

"In your gutter, baby." I slid a hand high around her thigh, over her buttery soft leggings in the crazy green and yellow pattern, and squeezed, flicking my thumb at her core. "In you."

She took the coffee from me and sipped on the straw, placing a hand over mine on her leg. "That massage the other night was very soothing and very stimulating. Those hands of yours have major skills."

"There's a first time for everything."

An eyebrow skidded up her forehead. "Uh huh."

I wrapped an arm around her shoulders, pulling her close. "You naked in that light. Those oils, those scents." I nipped her earlobe. "Got inspired."

A small moan rose in the back of her throat, a slight tremble going through her.

"A good reminder," I said.

"Reminder? Of what?"

"That it's been a long, long time since you. My heart was pounding real fierce, like it was our first time being together. I liked it. I don't want to let another moment of another day go by and not feel that way. Even when it's just us talking, holding hands. You think what we have is common, just happens all the time? I don't. I know it doesn't."

"I know," she murmured in my throat.

She kissed the side of my jaw, and I closed my eyes, my heart thundering, my body charging with heat.

"You need to get back to your store?" I asked.

"Nope, Mimi's got everything under control."

"Nice ringtone, by the way."

"It's Beck." A smile lit up her face. "From one of his latest songs."

A twinge went off inside me. I couldn't help the surge of jealousy that came over me whenever his name was mentioned, or when I passed by his room here at his mother's house.

His mother.

She had another man in her life forever. And he was a part of her. The twenty plus years she was cut out of my life, she'd had him. I tried to ignore the tightness in my neck. These stupid, childish feelings kept creeping up, rolling through me like the blob in that old horror flick. It was asinine, I knew this. But those feelings were there like a fucking virus that wouldn't die and only balled up inside me injecting my organs with its poison. Jealousy of a life not lived, and at its core pulsed dreaded inadequacy.

I'd seen the photos of the two of them. There was one photo she had in a mother of pearl frame in her room of him as a toddler, her holding him from behind. She was young and tired. The two of them looked sort of sad, the same full expression in their eyes, her clutching him for dear life. Another of him as a ten year old playing the guitar and his mother, her eyes closed, a dreamy smile on her face, her head bent toward the guitar, listening, appreciating. In every pic of him through high school, becoming a young man, she was confident, glowing. Beaming. They had grown up together, they were close.

"He's on tour now. His band is one of the opening acts for The Heave," she said.

"Oh yeah? I've heard of The Heave."

"Beck did some major songwriting for this tour, not just the music, but lyrics too. He didn't think it was his thing, that he didn't have it in him, but he does, oh he does. I'm really disappointed that I'm not going to get a chance to go see him play on this tour, though. I have these meetings I can't cancel with the makeup man-ufacturer."

"That's happening?"

"Yes. Just a few pieces to begin with—a liquid lipstick, a face powder, an eyeliner. Ronny, a friend of mine who's a tattoo artist, had designed the Lenore's Lace logo, and we did the makeup pack-aging together. Now the company has the samples ready to show me."

Empire of Lenore, all the way.

"It's crap timing, but there's no getting around it." She chewed on her lip. "I've never missed a show before. We're both disappoint-ed."

"Have you told him about us?" I asked.

"I did. He's glad. He's been after me to be open to a new rela-tionship for a long time."

"You haven't been?"

"No. His dad got remarried and had another baby pretty quickly after the divorce."

"No kidding."

"He and Pam always had a thing going on. They're really good together. When you know, you know, and nothing else will do."

I kissed the side of her face. "No, nothing else."

She slid a hand up my chest. "Actually, Beck is coming out here next week." Her fingers curled in my shirt. "After the show in Den-ver, they have a two day break. He's going to come stay for a night, and I thought it would be nice if you two met." Her voice was quiet, her gaze soft. This was important to her. Of course it was.

"Great," I replied.

"Great."

"You think I'll pass inspection?"

"Oh please. He's a generous soul, you'll see."

My gaze went back to the tile border we'd made.

"Hey, it'll be fine." She sat up straighter, taking the glass from my hand and planting it on the table. "Are you nervous or something?"

"Nah, I'm just—"

"The great outlaw leader of the Flames of Hell is nervous to meet a boy?"

"He's no boy. He's a man. A man who's protective of his mother, and rightly so. A man who wants the best for her. I am the best for her, but I want him to see that and trust it."

She hugged me, planting a kiss on my mouth.

I stroked the side of her face. "Weren't you a little nervous or something just now, telling me about his visit?"

She let out a breath. "Yeah, a little."

"I don't want you to feel that. He's your son."

She frowned at the sudden harsh tone in my voice.

"Is that all it is?" She climbed into my lap, and something inside me shifted. It was her favorite spot when we talked about serious shit years ago, from the very beginning. She faced me, hands on my shoulders. "Is it something else?"

"Nah." I took in a breath, shaking my head.

"Just spit it out."

"He's a part of your life that I had no part of. Something that we'd wanted together but didn't get. Something I always wanted to be the one to give you. But it wasn't me. I couldn't give you that. I used to wonder what it would've been like, if only this or fucking that. I used to think it'd be great if I were able to turn back time, but that would erase Beck, and you wouldn't want that. Stupid."

"No, not stupid. Feelings are never stupid. They're never up for judgement."

"I had an old lady once who got pregnant. She had a miscarriage and freaked out after."

Her eyes widened. "Oh. Shit, I'm sorry."

My hands went around her waist, rubbing up and down her lower back. "I couldn't respond or react the way she needed me to, the way any normal man would've. I felt disconnected from it, and relieved. Having a baby was an experience I'd only wanted with you. All that time you were raising your son, enjoying him, living that, and a piece of me hated it while another piece was glad that you had that. I am glad. I am. Shit, I'm not—"

Her hand clasped the back of my neck. "You gave it to me. When you threw everything to the wind and came back to Kansas for me. And with no plans, no escape route in place. You just came onto your greatest enemy's territory. For me. The place where they made you suffer, tried to break you, kill you. When I looked up in that kitchen and saw you...totally blown away. Everything that I thought I knew about people, about life, my life, you blew it up in flames right there.

"Everything you see here—my house, my store, my son, my smile, my colors," she tugged on her hair "—all of it is because of your bravery and your love. Your desire, and I'm not talking about sexual desire. You are in all of this. No, it didn't work out for us back then, and I made sure of that, but you need to know something. Beck is the one who saved me, put me back together again, kept me sane. Not my work, not Eric. That boy. Through him, I got through having to let go of Zoë, of you. I stood up on my legs again and got stronger. I had to for him, and he made it easier and sweeter to face each day."

"Come here." I kissed her lips gently, gently, and she wrapped herself around me, squeezing me tighter. "Want to fuck you so bad right this second." My voice came out all creaky and hoarse.

"Baby."

"Just move an inch back, and I'll open up and slip it right in past those tiny panties you got on."

"Finger, no."

I shook with laughter. "Come on. You used to like doing it in public. This is your house for shit's sake."

"This is my porch, and this is a small town, and I have neighbors." She pushed back against my shoulders, but I held on tight.

"Yeah, but, you must have a naughty rep, what with the goodies you sell at your store." I tugged at the zipper of my jeans. "Show 'em what you're made of. You got any handcuffs around? A spreader bar?" I ripped my zipper down.

"Finger, you take that monster out, I'm going to get up and go in the house and lock the door behind me. And you'll be out here with your dick in the wind while Mrs. Morris next door is trimming her hedges like she's about to do now, every Saturday a.m. like clockwork. And across the street, Tom is prepping his lawn mower as we speak."

"Monster, huh?"

"Oh yeah," she breathed, the edges of her mouth curling upwards.

"Monster needs you, baby," I whispered against her lips, my hands curving under her ass, rocking her against my hips.

She let out a tiny moan. "I need him too." She kissed me again. "Let's go inside. But I want to finish the tiling after."

"Oh yeah, the tiling—" I let out a chuckle as I bit her throat.

"We have to."

"We will." I tucked her legs around my middle, sat up and got us through the front door into the house. She shut it closed behind me. I let her down, and she stumbled back a step as I toed off my boots, yanked off my shirt and my jeans, and then leaned against the front door, stroking my cock. Her head tilted, lips parted, her cheeks flushed pink. She could have whatever she wanted at the candy store.

"Get naked and suck on the monster 'cause he wants to fuck those tits," I said.

She tore off her thin sweatshirt. "Greedy monster." Her breasts bounced free of the material, and my skin heated at the sight, my cock pulsing in my grip.

Mrs. Morris's hedge trimmer rumbled to life, the lawn mower roared from across the street. Lenore laughed as she kicked off her shorts. "I'm going to make you groan real loud now."

"Gimme your best," I said on a grunt.

Her fingers went to her panty. A panty made of thin straps barely covering her.

"You keep that shit on," I said, my hand pulling on my cock. "I'm gonna bite it off you as soon as you're done with me."

Lenore only grinned, her nails dragging up my thighs, a hand going around the base of my cock. She got on her knees, and her tongue swept and slid its wet heat over my balls.

My heartbeat hammered against my ribs as she finally took me in her mouth, her eyes on me. I fisted my hands in her hair, heat exploding in my veins. "Yeah. Yeah. Ahh, fuck…"

Afterwards, I got down on the floor with her and bit off her panty, just like I promised. She moaned, begging for my mouth, but I teased her, taking it slow, one thin satiny strip of strap at a time, one small lick at a time. When I was done with it, that panty was nothing but shredded strips hanging from a band, like a little flogger.

I tore it off her and ran it up her thighs, down her slit. "What do you think I should do with this now, Sunshine?" I whispered roughly, snapping it over her clit.

She let out a gasp, her eyes fluttering, back arching. "Yes…"

I whipped her clit with it until she came again. Needing her in my mouth, I flipped her over on all fours, gripped her ass cheeks and licked at her. I felt every quiver, heard every moan wherever my mouth sucked and nibbled, my tongue lashed. To be in her again, taste her again was fantastic. She stretched a hand back and grabbed at my hair, keeping me close, tugging on me hard as I ate her. She yelled out as she came. I rose and pulled both her arms back behind her, holding them against her lower back, and thrust inside her. I fucked her right there on her entryway floor, hard and fast.

Greedy, greedy monsters.

68
FINGER

Beck arrived in South Dakota. He'd shaken my hand firmly, a grin on his face, not giving my scars a second look. He'd set the dining table like it was something he did regularly for her. Maybe he always had.

His wavy, dark blond hair hung in his face, barely touching his shoulders, and it shook with every full bodied laugh. He and his mother laughed together a lot. They both made the same scrunchy face right before the laugh ripped out of them. It was adorable. Was that in his DNA or had he picked that up from living with his mother?

She put a huge bowl of whipped mashed potatoes in front of him that she'd made herself with lots of butter, cream, sea salt, and a touch of garlic.

"Yes, yes, yes!" he said, taking the bowl in hand and spooning huge puffy mounds onto his dish.

She shot me a warm grin. "His favorite."

I brought the platter of braised lamb shanks to the center of the table, Lenore served an arugula salad with shaved parmesan and red seeds. The three of us sat down to eat.

They talked, exchanged stories about Lenore's store, the town characters, the type of songs Beck was working on.

I didn't have too much to say. I listened. I drank my beer. I ate the lamb, the potatoes, and they were damned good.

Beck poked at his salad. "Pomegranate seeds, huh?"

"Aren't they a good contrast to the peppery greens? What do you think?" Lenore asked, her eyebrows raised high.

"Mother, are you doing this to me on purpose?"

She let out a rich, satisfied laugh. "Of course I am."

"I haven't forgotten the dried goji berries and prunes you put in that roast pork in LA."

"You hated that."

"As if you've forgotten."

Lenore glanced at me. "We were at his father's house for this family meal which me and his stepmother made together. Beck turned the berries and prunes into projectiles during dinner."

"They landed in the swimming pool," said Beck.

"Except for the ones that landed on me and your sister."

"Then you two tossed them in the swimming pool too."

"Couldn't help it."

"Yeah, Dad and Pam weren't too happy with us."

She sighed dramatically. She was amused. "Oh well. The element of surprise is my favorite weapon. How else am I going to get you to expand your horizons, honey?"

I was lost. They had their own riff going between them. A riff of shared memories and experiences. Familiar likes and dislikes.

I pressed back in my chair. I didn't like feeling awkward. I didn't do awkward or insecure, for fuck's sake. Here I was on the outside looking in on an aspect of her life that was so important to her, her life with her son.

But her life was now my own. We were stirred together like a potent cocktail, each liquor's flavors discernible, but blended they created a unique flow of taste and color in the glass.

Beck wasn't my son, but he was the son of the human being I loved more than any other in this world. If I wanted to be a part of her life, and I did, I was, I had to find a way to be a part of Beck's life. This wasn't the family I'd foreseen for myself, but what the hell ever turns out perfect or the way we want it?

All my life I'd striven to create my own identity, to leave my own mark my way, and I'd achieved that. Now, here I was with Lenore, my Serena, in her house, eating at her table, sleeping in her bed, making love to her day and night, night and day.

I needed to try.

"I have to say," I began, and they both turned to me, eyebrows raised, forks stalled mid-action. "I'm not a fan of fruit in my food either."

"Voice of reason, there you go." Beck grinned as he resumed chewing. "Thanks, Finger."

Lenore rolled her eyes and shook her head at us.

"I speak the truth, babe." I raised my beer bottle.

Beck clinked my beer with his glass of water. "That's it, Ma. Fruit needs to be eaten on its own. My one exception is yoghurt in those fruit bowl creations. So please, no more underhanded undercover operations—no hiding in sauces or salad dressings or whatever else you come up with. Your men have spoken."

"I'll keep that in mind for future meals." Lenore smiled. A smile that told of hushed sunrises and vibrant sunsets, embraces that didn't need words, bare toes sinking in warm sand.

We finished the roast lamb, with Beck asking me questions about where I came from, where I lived. I gave him what I could of my story.

"Hey Mom, tell me about Pete's."

"Pete's Tavern?"

"That's the one."

"It's the old bar here in Meager, one of the oldest in the area. They sell a lot of local craft brews, basic eats, and they support local musicians. Why?"

"Dad mentioned it."

"Oh, of course. Cruel Fate played here when they first hit it big."

"I wanted to check it out." Beck arranged his fork and knife on his empty dish. "You guys up for going there for a drink or no?"

"Sure." Lenore glanced at me.

"Yeah, let's do it," I said.

"Great."

My gaze went to Beck. "I heard Cruel Fate play once."

His face lit up. "Oh yeah?"

"Yep." I folded my napkin and pressed over it. "At a rock fest in Colorado."

Lenore's eyes slid to mine.

Beck took my empty dish and stacked it on his. "What did you think?"

"They were good. Lot of fans, girls screaming, singing along," I said.

Lenore planted a kiss on the side of my face as she took the dishes from the table. My hand went to her lower back as she moved past me.

"Where you headed after Denver, Beck?" I asked.

"Albuquerque, then Dallas, then Houston." He told me about the last leg of his tour.

"Hey you two." Standing in the foyer, a thin shawl expertly wrapped over her shoulders, Lenore swiped dark red lipstick on her gorgeous mouth. "Let's get going to Pete's."

"WHO'S THAT?" BECK ASKED.

"Who?"

"That dude glaring at you." Beck drank from his longneck, his gaze on Tricky.

Tricky sat next to a wiry young brunette with sparkly makeup, dark lipstick, and big hoop earrings. She was talking to him, but Tricky's eyes were on me. At his table were Grace and Lock, Jill and Boner, and Butler and Tania, who Lenore had stayed to chat with after we'd gone over and said our hellos, introducing Beck to them.

"Ah, he's just some guy," I muttered, staring Tricky down.

He finally looked away, his arm going over the shoulders of the girl he was with, and she smiled huge as she drank her pink cocktail.

"Ah." Beck turned to me. "Some guy. Got it."

"Yeah."

"Small town, huh?"

"It is. Reality."

"My mom's always been popular, but she never gave it too much importance. When she told me about the two of you, I had to come see for myself."

"To check me out? See if I'm good enough for her?" I asked.

"No, the kind of man you are is up to her. She's no dummy. But when she told me about you two, about your history, I had to see her with you."

The noise and music playing in the bar faded as I focused on Beck's words. His concentrated, serious face.

"My mother is good at glossing over, making everything seem easy when it isn't at all. She did that with her work, with my dad, with guys she's dated. But I always knew there was a piece missing for her."

"You mean the right man?"

"It's more than that." He rubbed his thumb and forefinger together. "It's a core piece, the piece that lets her fly. It's different for everyone, of course, but I was never sure what that was for her." Beck set his bottle down on the bar with a clink. "It's that one verse in a song that turns everything around. That makes perfect sense and grips your heart and soul then sends it soaring. Without it the song goes nowhere. From what I've seen tonight, you're her verse, Finger."

This boy. I put my beer bottle down next to his and held his vibrant blue gaze. "She's always been my verse."

Beck's eyes glistened with water and he swallowed, looking away quickly, leaning back against the bar. "She always pushed me to go after my dreams, and it wasn't just mommy talk; she knew what that meant. I figured she had her own dream locked inside her. She inspired me with her focus and discipline and her sense of wonder. She literally bred that in me. She blended any fears I had with her excitement, and made me realize it was okay to go out on a limb, to risk, that it was actually good for me—I'd survive somehow, I'd make it. And when I did fall, I'd pick myself up and find another way. That was all part of the journey. And she was right." He faced me once more, his features back in control. "She's my rock and she's my waterfall."

My heart ached in the hollow of my chest at the frankness and passion in his voice, in those beautiful words. I knew exactly what he meant, and he knew I did.

"She told me your story," he continued. "I'm sure she's left plenty out, but that's okay. I know what I need to know. I'm real glad you two found your way back to each other and that she's happy.

Happy like this." We watched Lenore laughing at something Grace was telling her. "She finally got her dream."

"Ah, Beck." I took in a breath. "Your mother raised an extraordinary man."

He averted his gaze again. "She's the extraordinary one." His lips tipped up softly. He was pleased.

"Total agreement." My eyes went over his shoulder to the back wall of the bar where I knew there was a photograph. "I think that's your dad's band over there in that photo framed in red." I pointed to it.

He blinked. "Oh, man. Yeah, that's them."

I gestured to the bartender and, explaining who Beck was, asked him to bring the photo over.

"Sure thing." He took it off the wall and handed it to Beck.

"Look at that," murmured Beck.

I glanced at the image of Cruel Fate rocking in the late nineties in Pete's Tavern. Tables crowded, standing room only. His dad jammed on his guitar, sharing the mic with a bandmate, howls plastered on their young sweaty faces, long hair flying.

"You're headed in the same direction, Beck. Enjoy it."

He dragged his teeth across his lip, staring at the photograph.

I leaned my arms on the bar. "You going to play anything tonight?"

He looked up at me. "I just wanted to come here and see the place."

"Your mom mentioned she was disappointed she wouldn't be able to get out and see you perform on this tour."

"Yeah, me too."

"It's open mike tonight. Her best friends are here, and I know we'd all love to hear you play."

He scanned the bar. "I'm sure the sign up is probably closed by now."

I put a hand on his arm. "Hold that thought."

Butler was a guitarist and played here sometimes on open mike nights. If there was an in with management, the musical One-Eyed Jack would be it. I caught his eye, gesturing for him to come over. He did, and I asked him to talk to the manager to get Beck included in tonight's performers.

"Hell yes, you bet." Butler went across the bar to the front. He spoke with a heavy set man who stood by the entrance with the hostess and two security types. A few moments later he gave me a thumbs up and brought the man over to us.

Butler introduced Malcom, the owner of Pete's to me and Beck.

"Great to meet you, Beck," said Malcom. "I know your mom, and I was a big Cruel Fate fan back in the day. It'd be a real thrill to have you play here tonight."

Beck's face lit up. "Means a lot to me, thanks. I don't want to step on anyone's time though. One song only."

"It's actually a slow night tonight. You'd be doing me a favor. You can open the next set."

"Wow, great. Thank you, I really appreciate it."

"What do you need, Beck?" I asked. "A guitar, a piano?"

Beck rubbed his hands together, eyes wide, gears churning. "Yeah, I don't have my guitar with me—"

"No worries," said Malcom. "Johnny Z from my house band can hook you up no problem. Let me introduce you."

They left together. Butler clapped a hand on my shoulder, a thick blond eyebrow arched. "Come over and sit with us."

"I don't think that's a good idea, do you?"

"Ah, you're both big boys."

"Another time. Not just yet. Not tonight."

"Whatever you say. I'm looking forward to hearing Beck play."

"Me too."

Butler went back to the Jacks' table as Lenore returned to me at the bar.

"Did you want to sit with your girls over there?" I asked her.

"I want to sit with you. Right here's good." She slid her arm through mine and kissed me. "Where's Beck?"

"Ladies and gentlemen, tonight we've got a special guest with us," Malcolm's voice boomed over the mike. "Please welcome to Pete's, Beck Lanier. His mom lives right here in Meager. You many know his dad, Eric Lanier of Cruel Fate." The crowd applauded and cheered. "Beck's band Freefall is on tour right now with The Heave. And tonight, Beck's here and he's gonna play for us."

"Holy shit, did you know about this?" Lenore asked over the din of the applause. Butler let out a shrill whistle.

"Sort of happened this minute."

Her eyes were glued to her son adjusting the microphone and settling his hands around an acoustic guitar. The clapping died down.

Beck leaned into the mic. "This is for you, Mom."

Lenore pressed into me.

Beck played an intricate web of chords, making that wooden instrument in his hands sing.

"Your eye was full,
Full of the sea
A raging sea
You never hid the world from me
You thought I couldn't,
But I could see
Your waves crashed high
I heard the noise
That terrible, fantastic noise.
You, you are the storm,
Flourishing high,
Humming low,
Lifting me up.
Daring me.
Daring me.
You are the storm
And I want more
My hand in yours
I dance in your wind,
Sing in your roar
A roar that's mine…"

His voice was deep but also had this odd, breathy quality. It looped and dipped, scraped against his beautiful words, lifting them with this raw simplicity and a sense of intimacy that was staggering. The entire room spun in his notes, soared on those lyrics.

Beck was gifted.

My hand gripped Lenore's arm tight as she listened with everything she was. Beck nodded at his mother as he sang and she lifted her chin, moving to the steady rhythm of his music, hearing him on a whole other level from the rest of us mortals. I held her and her movement, her emotion rocking through me.

"...a roar that's mine." Beck's eyes closed, his hands stilled, his last note hanging in the air.

A second of sacred silence. Butler's sharp whistles tore through the room, slicing at the magic haze gripping us. Heavy applause thundered in the bar. Lenore jumped up and down at my side like a teen groupie, clapping wildly. Butler and Tania, Grace and Lock, Jill and Boner were all on their feet clapping and whooping. I gave Lenore a quick kiss, and she ran to Beck. He leaned down and hugged his mom, lifting her up on the small stage with him.

"I like being alive," she'd once said to me in a clear, sure voice in a dank, horrible darkness a long, long time ago. *"No matter what, I want to stay alive."*

She'd lived. Oh, how she'd lived. She hadn't allowed the brutal past to define or mar her. She'd become what she'd chosen, her own design. And she'd given that fierce passion to her son. And although I would've liked to have been alongside her for that, that's not the way it had worked out. I had played a part in it, though, and I was glad and proud of that for the first time in a very, very long time, and in a way that didn't hurt so bad, in a way that was humbling and just plain good.

I stood up and clapped loud and hard for my woman and her son.

69
LENORE

"REALLY? YOU'VE NEVER BEEN TO Nebraska before?" Finger asked me, adjusting his sunglasses.

"Except for going to your club that time," I said. "Otherwise, no. Never had a reason to go. Until now."

He grinned. He was planning something. "I want to take you somewhere special. Get on."

I snatched the helmet he held out to me and climbed on the back of his bike, settling into the saddle, my pulse racing. I pressed against him and a deep noise rumbled through his back. We took off and he punched up his speed, my arms tightening around his taut middle. He let the roaring bike hang loose underneath him on the smooth road, keeping our center of gravity easily at his core and in his control. I hadn't forgotten what this was like; I had kept it sacred in my shrine of shrines all these years. My limbs clung to man and machine, heat searing through me, heart pounding, flying through the wind, flying at the sun.

We left the Black Hills and the expansive farm fields of South Dakota behind, and passed into northern Nebraska. A sign for the Oglala National Grasslands shot by us. Vast sweeps of short grass prairie, waves of burnt yellow and pale green punctuated with small hills of towering dark evergreens swept by us. This used to be all prairie in the old days, but trees were encroaching everywhere now.

Two buffaloes slowly ranged up a hill. Another one hurtled across the golden grasses in the distance. My pulse twanged. Hell, they were huge and fast. Impressive and intimidating. Wild and free the way they had been for centuries in their natural habitat. Grace had been on plenty of bike trips through the region and once told me how buffalo group together in herds as the sun faded from the sky. That would be a sunset to witness.

A long wavy ridge of rock rose in the distance. Butte and peak formations that looked more like a mountain range of frozen layers of sand or a lost city of the stone age. This corner of Nebraska had its own Badlands, just like the Dakotas. Slopes of ground were shadowed from the occasional low lying cloud suspended in the wide open sky, making the greens of the hills sharper, the golden yellows of the dipping valleys deeper. Nature's pure drama.

He turned his head, gesturing at the sign. *"Toadstool Geological Park - Oglala National Grassland"*

We rode over a stretch of well kept dirt road, and in no time Finger parked his bike at the turn of the loop trail, and we got off. He immediately took my hand in his large one, keeping me close. Following the signs, we hiked on a dirt trail leading through the ancient riverbed that meandered and twisted. Tufts of grass and brush sprouted the occasional yellow wildflower. Rising before us were unusual rock formations and huge bluffs—an incredible strata of color and texture.

"This is thirty-million years worth of lava ash and sandstone," Finger said.

People milled around the great stones. A family with two teenagers talked excitedly about having seen animal fossil remains, and an elderly couple with walking poles and protective hats read from a guidebook admiring Nature's sculpture. And what stones they were—great mushroom-like formations, unlikely swirls and chunks of rock seemingly teetering on pillars at odd angles.

"Wow." I snapped photos with my phone. "Thus the toadstool."

"Yeah. A real walk back through time, huh?"

"It's amazing."

I took in the vista. A stark wilderness. Remote, desolate even.

He rubbed a hand across his chin. "I like coming here. Clears the mind."

I winked at him. "I can see the appeal for you. Do they know how these formations came to be? They're so unusual."

His lips tipped up. "This is all slow erosion. There are layers of soft clay which erodes away under layers of the hard sandstone, and that creates the strange shapes."

"It's strange all right. Even ugly. They look like the building blocks of a prehistoric monster."

He laughed. "I like that."

"That strangeness makes them beautiful, though. Wonder what they'll be like in another couple thousand years."

His long gaze clung to the big toadstool, unmoving.

I put away my phone. "You come here a lot, don't you?"

"I do. Here, I get away from the noise. There's something still yet not still about this place. The light's always changing, making you discover something new, different. Things get put into a better place when I come here. I sit on a bluff, take in the endless view. Sometimes a mountain sheep wanders by."

"Oh, what are they like?"

"They have these curled horns like rams. I've seen them once up on bluffs watching the sunset. You don't see them too often, but when you do, it's pretty cool. They're kind of majestic actually. Not your run of the mill sheep." An almost boyish, uncertain look swept over his features, and my heart swelled. There was something shy about him sharing his fondness for this land with me, for the simple private pleasures he treasured. A gift.

I took his hand. "Thank you for bringing me here."

He dug a boot in the dirt. "I thought you might like it."

"I do like it. I'd like to come back again with you and see a sunset."

"Can't beat the pink and purple sky out here." He squeezed my hand.

"We're definitely coming back soon."

The lines of his face tightened suddenly. "Babe, I realize we aren't the same people we used to be. We'll be learning new shit about each other and maybe we'll like it, maybe we won't, and it'll take some getting used to. It'll take patience. Respect." The sunlight gleamed off his sunglasses. "Right now, I need to know that from here on in, you and me in each other's arms is at the end of every one of my days."

My insides fluttered, and I stood up on my toes and kissed him. "I need that too."

"Want you with me, baby." He gently brushed my lips with his. "I don't care much for my apartment in Elk. It's not a home for us, and I don't want to bring you there. You've got your store and your house in Meager. We can make it our home too."

Our home.

My heart skipped a beat. He'd brought me here to his special place to declare himself, make a pledge.

He took me in his arms and held me. The sound of the breeze whipping around us, the crush of his body filled my senses. I kissed his scarred cheek. "I want that too."

He took in a sharp breath. "Let's go to the club."

"Let's go," I replied.

He slung an arm around my shoulders, and we headed back to his bike.

We got to Elk within the hour and drove through the gates of the Flames of Hell MC. He parked at the head of a long line of Harleys. My stomach tightened as he shut down the bike, and we snapped off our helmets. This was his territory, his realm.

And now it was mine.

We got off his bike, and my knees wobbled as I handed him my helmet. He pulled me close, throwing an arm over my shoulders. That familiar scent of metal, cedar, and sweat filled my nostrils, and the tension evaporated from my muscles. I slid an arm around his waist, his skin warm, taut muscles moving under my fingertips. Mumbled hellos and looks. Shouted greetings. He ushered me inside his clubhouse.

In the large common room I recognized a very pregnant Nina, Butler's ex and now Catch's old lady.

"Lenore!" She hugged me.

I pulled back and admired her swollen belly. "Look at you."

"Ready to pop," said Nina. "Get him out of me already."

"A boy?" I asked.

"Yeah, a boy." Catch whooped behind her, planting a kiss on the side of his old lady's face. "Hey, Lenore."

"Hey, Catch."

"So." Catch licked his lips, his eyes racing from me to Finger and back again. "You guys good?"

Nina snorted, elbowing her old man in the belly.

"We're good," I said. "Real good."

"Excellent." He beamed a look at his President. He cared about his mentor a great deal, and I liked that. Finger only raised his sunglasses over his head, giving Catch a lift of his chin.

"Holy shit. It's you?" came a strong female voice accompanied by the stomping of heavy boot heels.

A woman my age if not older with blond and brunette ombré hair and flashing eyes stood before me. I knew her. She was one of my very favorite customers. "Krystal?"

She grinned. "Lenore, Lenore, Lenore, Queen Bee of Undies and Naughty Goodness."

Krystal shopped at my store on her birthday every year, splurging on herself. Bright, opinionated, snarky, strong-willed, take-no-shit Krystal.

"I didn't know you were—"

"When in other club territory, I keep that shit to myself. Welcome to the Flames, babe." She pulled me in a big hug. "I'm that troll's old lady." She gestured at the Flame who stood with Finger, winking at him. He blew her a kiss. "Drac VP" was patched on his colors.

"Whoa, babe." Drac saluted me, his thick, dark eyebrows climbing his forehead, a grin splitting his pale face. "I'm one of your biggest fans."

Finger punched him in the chest with the side of his fist. "Easy."

Krystal put an arm through mine. "Thrilled to have you here, hon. Thrilled."

70
FINGER

LATER THAT DAY IN MY office, Drac and Slade and I reviewed the new additions to our club. All the remaining chapters of the Broken Blades had come under my control and been patched in as Flames of Hell. Pick had traveled to each one and made the case for joining me. They had no alternative really. They'd agreed, and the takeover was now done.

Butler had been right about Pick. I showed him trust and respect to get the job done with his brothers, and he got it done. No moaning, no games. I offered him the presidency of the new chapter of the Flames I'd set up in southern Nebraska, and he agreed.

My phone rang. Lenox, the national Sergeant at Arms in Ohio. "Yeah?"

"Finger, I got news," he said.

"What news?"

"We would've called you in, but things have been happening real fast—Cooper and Reich, you getting the Blades in. We need a national president."

"So elect one."

"We want you."

"Me?"

"Can't come as a surprise, bro."

But it did.

I hadn't been shooting for the throne all this time. I'd wanted justice served. I'd wanted my island kingdom to be prosperous and protected. That was my focus.

Full command.

I closed my eyes and took in a long, slow breath.

"Finger. You there?"

"Yeah."

"Unanimous, man. Get your ass up here."

I got my ass to Ohio, my old lady at my side, and after the "election," I was sworn in as National President of the Flames of Hell MC.

HAVING CHECKED IN AT THE airport for our flight back to Nebraska, we went through security and headed to our gate. I wasn't a fan of flying, but it was winter, and you couldn't ride in the Midwest through to the Great Plains this time of year. The snow and ice were incredible.

"I need a chai latte," said Lenore, tugging me toward an over-priced coffee bar chain.

"A what?"

"It's like a—"

"Hold on, I have a better idea." I tugged her hand in the opposite direction of the coffee joint. Past the doughnut chain, past the newspaper and magazine shop.

There it was. I'd spotted the place earlier.

Lenore squeezed my hand. "A photo booth?"

Two teenage girls giggled over their strip of photos by the side of the booth. I ushered Lenore inside and put her in my lap as she slid the curtain closed. We put in the money and I held her tight against me.

"You are too much," she said, kissing my cheek, smoothing the edge of my beard down with her hand.

"Kiss me," I breathed.

She stuck her tongue out at me instead, and I laughed, doing the same, our tongues touching as we cracked up. The camera clicked. We made faces at each other. *Click.* We made faces at the camera. *Click.* We kissed deep. *Click.* And we laughed harder.

The strip of pics dropped in the slot, and Lenore immediately picked it up. "Look at that. Oh, look at that." Her grin dropped, her bottom lip quivered, and she pressed her face in my chest, clinging to me, taking shuddery breaths.

I wrapped my arms around her, kissing the top of her head. "Yeah, that one we keep."

71
FINGER

"I WANT US TO GET MARRIED."

Her head turned toward me, her eyes blinked open. "Seriously?"

I sat up on our bed. Yeah, it was our bed now. I'd ordered a new mattress and had it delivered. She hadn't said a word. Then she went out and bought four new sets of sheets, new pillows, a quilt, and a down comforter.

"I want us to have the whole fucking package," I said. "I've always wanted it with you."

She stilled.

I waited.

Gently, I nudged her hip with my knee. "You going to say something?"

"By 'whole fucking package' do you mean a limo, a photographer, color coordinated flowers, a buffet reception?"

"Fuck no."

She let out a soft laugh.

"Babe, I'm still waiting for your answer."

"I've always wanted it with you too." She held my gaze. "Let's do it in the old church in Meager."

"A church?"

"It's a blessing thing. Grace and Lock got married there and baptized their baby there too. Trust me on this."

"Whatever you want, Sunshine."

"That's what I want. You know what else I want?"

"Name it."

"Your mouth all over me. Again."

"You're such a horn dog."

"Just like you."

I brushed my lips over an eclipsing sun tattoo on her back, raising myself up over her prone body on the bed, swiping away her hair. "Where to begin?"

"Surprise me." She wiggled her beautiful bare ass at me, her back muscles flexing. Her bare back. A woman's naked back was a sensual secret revealed. Long smooth curves, strong plains, my vulnerable, powerful woman.

Every moment. Cherish every moment.

I bent my head and licked a trail down her spine, zigzagging my tongue over the thorny vine on her hips and lower back. Goosebumps rose on her skin, and she let out a soft moan. My teeth sank over a plump cheek, and she gasped. I kneaded her cheeks and jerked up her hips, opening her legs wider, licking up the tatted chain of small J's up her thigh. Leaning over her, I pushed my thumb between her parted lips.

"Suck it."

She took my thumb in her, squirming in my tight hold as my cock stroked up and down her wet heat. Taking my thumb from her mouth, I slid it inside her cunt, thrusting and rolling as I gripped her ass.

Her head twisted in the pillow, her fingers digging in the sheets. "Ah, fuck."

I released her just as she was about to come. "Get up, grab the headboard," I muttered.

Groaning, she raised herself up and did as I said, one knee down, her other foot planted on the mattress. I slid underneath her and grabbed hold of her ass and pulled her over me, rubbing her pussy back and forth over my hungry mouth.

She cried out. "That fucking beard of yours is like nothing else."

I edged her. Three times. I knew all the signs her flesh gave. I knew.

"Finger...dammit!"

"Not letting you blow yet," I said in between long licks. "Breathe, babe." Her damp thighs finally relaxed.

Two more rounds later, a growl rising in my throat, I slapped an ass cheek, holding it firm and her eyes shot to mine, her moan filling the room. "Sixty-nine this bitch, and then you come all over me."

She turned quickly, her hair flying, and I guided her legs. She swallowed my throbbing cock in her eager mouth.

"Fuck!" I gritted out. Raising my head, I pressed the pad of my tongue over her clit and suckled it, and she ground over me wildly, shuddering, coming on my face. I held onto her, thrusting my cock deep, my own explosion fierce.

Every. Moment.

I GOT MYSELF NEW TATS. A huge flaming blue "Z" inked on the base of my neck, meeting the "S" that had been inscribed at the top of my spine years ago. I added the letters for the rest of her name. Now the full "Serena" was on me, meeting the Z over the red flames of my club that flared over my back.

"Oh, Justin," she breathed, a hand tracing up my spine.

"We deserve that upright Z, baby."

She wrapped her arms around my waist, her face pressed into my back.

THE WEDDING WAS ON.

Lenore got a date set with the pastor of that church in Meager. We would wait a month for Beck's tour and a couple other gigs he had in LA to be finished. Lenore immediately got to work on making her own dress. Her girlfriends threw her a bridal shower, a ladies night at the Tingle where her good friend Cassandra worked.

"You sure you don't mind, honey?" She batted thick false eyelashes at me as she headed out the door on super high heels with an equally glammed up Tania who'd arrived to pick her up.

"Knock yourselves out," I replied, giving her hand a kiss.

Butler, Boner, Drac, and Lock grumbled from the couches where we watched a not so exciting football game over too many pizzas. Four hours later, we picked up our women from the Tingle, and they were all sloshed. The minute I got her home, she pushed me into an armchair in the living room.

"Sit right there." She started to dance to the music playing in her mind. She was inspired, peeling off her clothes one slinky piece at a time.

"Oh, you hot woman, look at you…" I slid a hand around a thigh.

"No, no, no." She wagged a finger at me, licking her lips.

"No? What do have in mind, wild thing?"

She let out a throaty giggle. "You touch yourself. I wanna see."

I did as requested. Her dance moves began to slow down as my hand sped up.

Wearing only a corset, her beautiful full tits tumbling out, she teetered back to the sofa opposite me, and in a firm, sure voice which only made my cock harder, she said, "Get over here. Now."

I got over there, put my knees on the sofa and yanked her up against me, and she gasped loudly. Her back to my chest, my one hand cuffed her neck and my other held her arms, pinning them behind her. "This what you want, Sunshine? Huh?" I drove inside her. "This?"

She let out a series of harsh moans. "Yes, yes."

I thrust hard and fast, holding her tight against me. "I'll give it to you, baby. I'll give it to you."

And then she let out a long, rich laugh.

My favorite sound in the whole world.

72
FINGER

THE NEXT MORNING I GOT up early, Lenore still in a full, deep sleep beside me. I had an idea. My old lady wanted a church wedding, so I'd make it the best experience for her. Memorable. She needed beautiful souvenirs of our good times to keep forever, and I was going to do everything I could to make that happen for her. I headed to the Garden Center in Pine Needle.

Gail was at the front desk going over folders stuffed with orders, bills, and delivery slips. Steve and Tim were moving big planters into neat rows at the other end of the store.

I'd seen right through Gail's bright smile the second she'd looked up and laid eyes on me. It was a bit too forced; it was tired. Something was wrong.

"Hi, Finger. How are you? Getting ready for the big day?" She pushed the folders to the side. "Lenore and I went over the details for her bouquet and a few flower arrangements for the dinner party afterward."

"She mentioned that, sounds great. I'm here about something else."

"Oh, okay. Sure, go ahead."

I took in a breath, raking my teeth against my bottom lip. Shit, I was actually nervous. "I wanted to ask you if Zoë could be Lenore's flower girl. The wedding isn't going to be some big production. Just a few friends is all—no bridesmaids or limos or any of that. Having Zoë be Lenore's flower girl, to be there for the service, and you and Steve, of course, would be real special for her. So I was hoping you'd agree and—"

"No, no, Tim, not there! Just left of that." Steve's irritated voice rose from the other end of the room.

Gail's face tensed, and she took in a tight breath.

"Steve okay?" I asked.

"It's nothing."

"You sure? If I can help, I will. Believe me."

She let out a nervous laugh. "Oh, I do believe you." Her eyes darted to Steve and Tim working, her shoulders stiffening.

"Gail, what is it?"

"Steve used to do everything around here and at home, and that's the way he likes it, but he's just not strong enough anymore. And he's very frustrated."

"That sort of thing is hard on a man. Getting older isn't easy."

"It's more than that. We finally got a diagnosis this morning," she said, her voice low.

"A diagnosis?"

"He has Parkinson's. It turns out, he's had it for years, but he ignored the symptoms. Shaky hands, muscles that suddenly won't cooperate."

My mind went back to when I'd helped Steve unload the wheelbarrows from his truck. "I'm sorry to hear that."

"Everything's changing now," Gail murmured. "We always used to be so focused on Zoë and her progress, and we'd found a real good balance with that. She's done so well. She's in a good place. But now, this. Steve was always our rock."

"The business has suffered lately too," she continued. "The economy isn't what it used to be, and we haven't changed our way of doing things too much. We have a website, but it's terribly out of date. We were planning on…" Her hands smoothed over the folders. "Well. Anyway, Steve's had to slow down a lot, which upsets him. Asking for help upsets him. He has good days and bad days, and now there are lots of doctor and therapy appointments ahead of us, insurance forms to fill out."

"You need to be on call all the time for him. There aren't any breaks," I said.

Her tired gaze met mine, a spark of relief flitting over her face.

"No, there aren't. The other night, he fell getting out of bed. Luckily he didn't break a bone, but he bruised his arm. Zoë was very upset."

"I'll bet she was. Is there anything we can do for you?"

She blinked at me. "Oh no." She shook her head. "You don't… no."

"Gail, this must be real overwhelming for all of you."

"I need to take charge of Steve's care and make a lot of new decisions now."

"You have family who could pitch in?"

"There's just my older sister, but she can't really…" She shook her head, rearranging the pens on the counter.

"Do you need help with Zoë? You know Lenore would help you in a heartbeat. So would I."

Gail's face reddened. "Zoë likes Lenore very much and feels comfortable with her."

"That's great. Is there anything Lenore could do for you while you get settled with all this?"

"Oh no, really. Lenore has her own business. You're getting married—"

"What do you need to make your life easier right now? Gail?"

"I'm not sure what to do first." She pressed her lips together, swallowing hard. "He has to get more tests done. I have to find a physical therapist and get him settled with Steve, probably hire someone else to help out here at the store. Someone to do the accounting, too. I always used to do it, but now…"

"Okay."

She leveled her gaze with mine. She was proud, and this was difficult for her, asking for help from me on top of the shock of her family dynamics changing forever. "Maybe if Lenore could help with driving Zoë to her school related activities in Rapid and to her art class in Meager?"

"She could do that."

"If I know that Zoë is taken care of with someone she likes and knows, and someone I trust, I could better focus on everything else. Zoë's very independent and can take care of herself, but she still needs guidance. It's an imposition, I know, especially now. Just for a couple of months maybe, until things settle?"

My heart thudded in my chest. "It's no imposition. I want to help you and Steve, I really do."

She tilted her head, lips parted, eyes narrowing. "You know, don't you?"

My eyes flicked to the photo behind her on the wall that I'd noticed the first time I'd come here. A young Steve, a shovel in one hand and a young Gail at his side, who held a small baby, their Zoë, in her arms right here on their property. Their new, second chance start in life. Huge, happy smiles on their faces.

At the time that pic was taken, I was beating up douchebags in jail, making threats, getting knifed in my leg with a homemade shank, blackmailing, threatening, starting fights, making bets, cutting deals. And Lenore had been on the run out there, somewhere, alone.

"Gail, let us help you. I want to help you. It's the least I can do for you."

She stared at me, her neck stiffening at the intensity in my tone.

I took in a deep breath. "Years ago, Lenore and I were together. I'm Zoë's biological father."

"Oh." Her eyes widened. "Oh…I…"

"At the time, me and Lenore couldn't be together. Things were real difficult, and Zoë deserved more, she needed more." My throat thickened. "Zoë was born out of love, but she needed you and Steve. I want you to know that I'm real grateful that she has you, and I have no intention of ruining your family in any way. I don't want you to think that. You've been real kind to let Lenore have contact with Zoë. That's real generous of you. Thank you for that. It's meant the world to her."

"I know," she said quietly, her lips tipping up into a beautiful smile. "I'm real happy for you and Lenore, that you both found your way back to each other." Gail's face softened. "Zoë's never been a flower girl or a bridesmaid before."

"Oh yeah?"

"She loves surprises. She'll be over the moon when you ask her not only to be the flower girl but to be the surprise, too."

I only grinned. I had no words, and I didn't need any.

Gail cleared the pens from the counter between us. "She should be here in ten minutes. You can ask her yourself."

"Thank you, Gail."

Her head slanted. "You're very welcome."

"I'll have Lenore call you about pitching in."

Gail's pale hands clasped tightly together. "Thank you. It'll just be for a little while. On occasion, I might have to take Steve to a specialist out of town, and then—"

"Whenever you need help, we're here. That's a fact." I gave her a nod. "Now, I think I'll go see if Steve and Tim need anything else moved back there before a fight breaks out."

She let out a small laugh. "Yes, you do that."

FINALLY, LENORE AND I STOOD at the head of the small church in Meager, about to walk together up the aisle to where the pastor, Drac, and Tania waited for us. Beck and Krystal and Butler were in the front row. Catch and Nina alongside them. Grace and Lock. Boner and Jill. Cassandra and her man, Taye. Alicia and Ronny, the tattoo parlor owner from Deadwood.

Lenore, amazing in a curve-hugging, long silky purple dress she'd made herself, squeezed my arm. "Ready?"

"No, not yet," I said, holding her back.

Her eyes stiffened. "What? Why? Is something wrong?

I noticed movement from my right. Quick steps. A flash of blue.

"Psst!"

"Go on!" I said.

Zoë swished in front of us and swept down the aisle of the church.

"Oh my God," breathed Lenore.

"Happy Wedding Day, baby."

"Oh my God."

I quickly kissed the back her hand. "Look at her."

Zoë waved at us over her shoulder and kept moving, so pretty in a pale blue dress and matching short heels. She wore makeup, and her hair had been styled smooth, held in place with a rhinestone hairband. The princess crowned.

She threw fistfuls of red and purple flower petals in the air from a tiny white basket she held. The church was empty, but she didn't care. She performed her duties with style, with enthusiasm, her arm swinging high, those dark flower petals tumbling and cascading everywhere.

Gail, Steve, and Zoë's boyfriend, Mark, sat in the other front row, smiling huge. Once Zoë got to the front, Tania held out a hand and put her arm through hers, tucking her close to her side. They stood together, the two of them beaming at us. Drac raised his chin at me.

I whispered to Lenore, "I wanted us together on this day. Together."

Lenore's arm trembled in mine. "I love you. I love you so much."

But we both knew it was more than love; it was that bond that couldn't be broken and only made us stronger, fusing our pieces and us together. It was that *place*. Our place.

I put a steadying hand over her arm. "Let's do this."

We made it up the aisle. We pledged, we promised.

I do.

I will.

I am.

I love.

We are.

Lenore and I had dreams once upon a time, but the world had been cruel to us both, and I had returned that cruelty, ungrateful, vengeful. But there are such gifts in life, like Zoë. Like loyal friends. Like forgiveness. Like a true lover. Even in my numbness, I'd recognized them, because I'd hungered for them still.

I stood in that church, my wife at my side, our daughter before me, her flowers scattered over us under the eyes of that Higher Power that is called God. Split wide open, I prayed to be worthy of their gifts in this life and the next.

I kissed the scar I'd left years ago on the inside of my woman's wrist. I kissed her lips. We were one.

After the ceremony, we had dinner with our friends at the Meager Grand Cafe, the fancy coffee shop in town. The owner was a friend of Grace, Tania, and Lenore's. She'd shut down for the night just for us and catered the food, and created a real nice cake for us too. Grace and Tania had decorated the cafe with a ton of tiny twinkling lights stuffed in vintage bottles hanging from the ceiling, and small bunches of crimson flowers on the tables. It was unlike anything I'd ever seen before. A small magical paradise glowing in the dark of night just for us. Lenore loved it.

At my side, Lenore laughed at something Butler and Tania were heatedly debating. She laughed and her fingers curled over mine, our new thick silver rings engraved with a flame motif shone in the soft light from the candles on the table. I kissed that hand.

My old lady. My wife.

We went home.

Late that night, in our living room, the two of us holding each other as we danced to a blues tune she loved, her fingers dug in my shirt and she whispered roughly against my throat, "Make love to me."

I had to build around us. Build for us and the child who would never know us as parents. Maybe one day I could cope with that, but right now it was still a struggle. Right now all I knew was my Serena's kiss offering me peace, her body offering a devastating joy, flinging away the fragments of all that fucking sorrow, and soldering us together.

My blood heated as I raised her in my arms and she wrapped herself around me. I took her to our bed and laid her down.

Once, we were young and impulsive and breathed in each other day and night as if it were our last. That was still a part of us, but now there was an element of enjoying the finer points and savoring in a new way.

I unbuttoned, pulled, tugged, released.

"Yes, yes—"

I sank my mouth over her, tasting and nuzzling, teasing her.

"Baby. I love you, I love you..."

On my knees on our bed, I raised her one leg high, planted a hand on a breast and buried my cock inside her in one sure thrust. I moved inside her long and slow, kneading that tit. She was splayed wide open for me, taking me in, taking all of me, my victories, my failures, my anger, my commitment. I rolled my hips into hers, my heart heaving with fire. My love for her, molten iron.

"Justin, Justin. I love you."

Her gorgeous eyes held mine, our daughter's eyes; my stars leading me north, my steady signs of truth and real and faith were flaming blue green jewels, but they were all the colors.

Every single one.

73
FINGER

THE PAST MONTH, I HAD Den design a new website for Steve and Gail's business, and he'd gone over it with Gail along with setting up a new computer and printer and updated internet connection for the nursery. Den's brother set up a security system for their entire property as well. I sent a few of my prospects over to the shop on a steady basis to clean up, paint, renovate, fix. Lenore easily rearranged her schedule and took Zoë to her classes and activities.

Today, Zoë would spend the night with us as Steve and Gail had to go to Sioux Falls for more medical tests.

The girls spent the day together. Zoë wanted to shop at Lenore's store, so Lenore took her shopping at the mall. Zoë wanted a tattoo, so Lenore bought her new makeup and gave her a makeover with cat-eye eyeliner, sparkly eye shadow, and a dark pink lipstick. We went out for an Italian dinner in town, watched a movie at home, and then Lenore and I stayed up for hours listening to our daughter's soft snoring coming from Beck's room down the hall.

We'd all woken up late and had fruit and pancakes for brunch. Now it was past two in the afternoon, and Gail and Steve were coming to pick up Zoë in a couple of hours. Before she left, I was going to take her for a ride on my bike.

I pulled my Harley out to the curb. Standing with Lenore, Zoë watched me, her lips pressing together.

"Finger's been riding since he was a little boy." Lenore zipped up Zoë's windbreaker. "He knows everything there is to know about riding. His bike is like his best friend. It's a part of him. You couldn't ask for a better first ride."

"Okay." Zoë scrunched and unscrunched her eyes, twisting her lips. She was deliberating. She was gearing up.

Lenore swept Zoë's hair back from her shoulders. "Can I tell you a secret?"

Zoë's face lit up and she nodded, a slight giggle escaping her lips.

"Riding with Finger on his bike is one of my most favorite things in the world. From the very first time I did it."

"When was that?"

"A long, long time ago. Now it's even better."

Zoë glanced at me and took in a deep breath, her shoulders rising and falling. She went over to the bike and tried to swing her leg over it, but she couldn't quite reach. I grabbed her leg, steadying her as she hopped up and scooted in the saddle, Lenore at her side, a hand on her lower back.

"It's high," Zoë said.

"You want to get down?" I asked her. "You can get down."

"No. I want to ride with you."

Everything inside me melted like a chocolate bar in the summer heat.

"You look great." Lenore checked her helmet for the twentieth time. "You're all set. Let me take a picture with your phone." Lenore raised Zoë's phone and took several shots of us.

"Let's do a selfie with all of us," said Zoë.

Lenore moved next to Zoë and took a photo of all three of us. "Perfect," she said softly, her fingers tightening over the phone.

Small hands with fingernails painted a metallic blue clutched at the back of my jacket and let go as if she'd realized she'd made a mistake. Lenore put her hands over Zoë's, bringing them around my middle again, pressing them into my sides. I couldn't breathe, my heart pounded in my chest.

"Like that, okay, sweetie?" said Lenore.

"Won't I tickle him that way?" Zoë asked. "Won't that bother him?"

"No, it's okay. You hold on and don't let go." Lenore's voice wavered.

Zoë leaned against my back. The pressure of her weight minimal, the pressure of her overwhelming. "I won't let go."

My eyes slid to Lenore's.

Molten fire, drumming heartbeats. My woman and me and our daughter.

This may not have been a perfect outcome, not having Zoë all to ourselves, Zoë never learning the truth, but at this very moment that didn't add up to much but spilled milk. What mattered was us knowing our daughter, building a relationship.

All the kingdoms and empires in this ugly fucked up world could never add up to this sensation swelling in my veins, coursing through my heart, filling my ragged soul and binding all its thousand scars.

With precise movements I made my engine burst and rumble, and I braced.

"Eek!" Zoë's body jumped and she held me tighter.

My eyes squeezed shut.

"That's it. Like that." Lenore stroked her leg. "Remember, when you get back, there'll be brownies and ice cream."

"Yay! My favorite," replied Zoë.

"Mine too," said Lenore.

I leaned back. "Zoë, you ready to party?"

"Yes!" she shouted over the steady drone of the engine.

A smile took my lips hostage as Lenore's full eyes lifted to mine. Everything roaring inside me was written all over her face and resonated between us. Joy, sadness, elation, longing. Yet there was also a sense of achievement.

We got here, baby, through fire and blades, demons and curses, blood and plagues.

A fucking triumph.

I grinned. "We'll be right back."

"I'll be waiting." Lenore brushed my lips with hers and gave our daughter's leg a final squeeze. "Have fun!"

I kicked the toe stand and set my bike on fire. I took off, gaining speed at the end of the lane. My heart expanded, filling with the music of Zoë's squeals and the magnificent scream of my engine as we flew down the road.

And that fury erupted inside me.

But it wasn't that brutal rage that would rise like an inferno or that black sorrow that would slide all over me and harden into a spiked shell of desolation.

No.

It was my dad scooping me up off the floor, carrying me out of that house, and setting me on his bike,

it was me and my brothers riding in perfect formation down a long highway,

it was that bruised face looking up at me in that club kitchen, her realizing that I'd come back for her,

that glorious thunder of Beck's waterfall,

my woman's soft lips on my skin,

the heady whisper of her gaze,

a labyrinth of vivid ink,

a cartography of compasses,

my daughter's innocent pure laughter ringing in my ear.

I breathed it all in.

The heat of the bright, hard afternoon sun unfurled over us.

I shouted, "Hold on, Zoë."

Holding onto me tight, my daughter answered me, "I am."

THE END

BOOKS BY CAT PORTER

THE LOCK & KEY SERIES

Lock & Key

Random & Rare

Iron & Bone

Blood & Rust

Wolfsgate

Fury

ACKNOWLEDGEMENTS

The making of this book took a great many people whom I love and cherish. My deepest thanks go out to each and every one for their precious time, energy, and support.

Tina, working with you on this was sublime. Your instincts are incredible and you know of what you speak and it's from your heart. I couldn't have done this without your articulate precision, generosity, and belief. You always nudged me in the right direction, and I learned so much along the way. To many, many more.

Jenn, working with you again has been a gratifying joy. Thank you for your dedication and clarity, my dearest friend. I wouldn't be here without you.

Naj, for your beautiful visions time and time again. This one took a long while, and I appreciate your patience with every emotional detail.

Nada, working with you was a ray of light. Thank you for coming through so beautifully.

Memphis Cadeau for your enthusiasm, and your and Travis's fantastic artistry.

Needa Warrant for kicking my ass— exactly when and where I needed it—while holding my hand. Your generosity as a writer, friend, and sister knows no bounds. You are in my heart for life, woman.

Rachel, Alison, Needa, Lena for beta reading that raw early draft and giving me your time, precious insights, and vital signposts.

Jan, for Tania's Chicago and your proofreading skills and so much love and support along the way.

Mindy, for generously answering my questions about firearms.

Sherry, for your music suggestions for Lenore—perfect timing and utterly perfect, my friend.

My JoJill, for your friendship and incredible jewelry that always keeps me grounded and inspired throughout writing. Because #Dig-

Forever, baby.

Iza, for all the Finger enthusiasm and Instagram casting inspirations around the clock as I wrote. I love that we're in the same time zone!

Kandace, Cindy, Sammy, MJ, Soulla, Sue B for your constant enthusiasm and friendship which means the world to me.

Ryan for your rehab insights and occupational therapy suggestions.

Penny, I'm glad I asked and I'm so grateful that we did it! Love you, amiga.

Lori Jackson for your amazing teasers and designgasms. I love working with you, and I'm thrilled we finally are.

Linda R. Russell and everyone at Foreword PR for your tell-it-like-it-is savvy, for pushing me, and having my back. One day we will have our morning coffee together, for reals, woman!

Alison, the best transcontinental PA ever and my very dear friend.

Bloggers who make my book world go around—we writers could not do this without you. In particular, iScream Books, The Book Bellas, Book Babes Unite, Dirty Book Girls, EDGy Reviews, LABB, Perusing Princesses, Schmexy Book Girls, Kinky Girls Book Obsessions, Kindle Friends Forever, and so many more. My deepest thanks for the astounding work you do.

My Cat Callers who cheer me on and kept the adrenaline flowing as I chiseled away at Finger and Lenore and got them to where they needed to be. I loved sharing these two with you every step of the way.

To my author friendss who inspire, support, answer my silly questions, and share, share, share, I thank you from my very full heart.

To all my readers for sharing the book love, your messages, taking the time to leave reviews. Your enthusiasm and reader satisfaction mean everything to me. Thank you for loving my bruised characters and their difficult stories.

ABOUT THE AUTHOR

Cat Porter was born and raised in New York City, but also spent a few years in Texas and Europe along the way, which made her as wanderlusty as her parents. As an introverted, only child, she had very big, but very secret dreams for herself. She graduated from Vassar College, was a struggling actress, an art gallery girl, special events planner, freelance writer, restaurant hostess, and had all sorts of other crazy jobs all hours of the day and night to help make those dreams come true. She has two children's books traditionally published under her maiden name.

She now lives on a beach outside of Athens, Greece with her husband and three children, and freaks out regularly, still daydreams way too much, and now truly doesn't give AF. She is addicted to reading, cafes on the beach, Greek islands, Instagram, Pearl Jam, the History Channel, her husband's homemade red wine, dark chocolate, and reallllllly good coffee. Writing has always kept her somewhat sane, extremely happy, and a productive member of society.